THE NINE
WAVES

Books by Mihir Bose

History and Biography
The Indian Spy: The True Story of the Most Remarkable Secret Agent of World War II
From Midnight to Glorious Morning? India Since Independence
The Lost Hero: A Biography of Subhas Bose
Bollywood: A History
Lion and Lamb: A Portrait of British Moral Duality
False Messiah: The Life and Times of Terry Venables
Michael Grade: Screening the Image
The Aga Khans
The Memons

Business
How to Invest in a Bear Market
Fraud: The Growth Industry of the 1980s (co-author)
The Crash: The 1987–88 World Market Slump
Crash! A New Money Crisis: A Children's Guide to Money
Insurance: Are You Covered?
William Hill: The Man and the Business (co-author)

Cricket
A History of Indian Cricket (Winner of the 1990 Cricket Society Literary Award)
A Maidan View: The Magic of Indian Cricket
Cricket Voices
All in a Day: Great Moments in Cup Cricket
Keith Miller: A Cricketing Biography
Moeen (with Moeen Ali)

General Sports
The Spirit of the Game
Sports Babylon
Sporting Colours: Sport and Politics in South Africa
The Sporting Alien

Football
Manchester DisUnited: Trouble and Takeover at the World's Richest Football Club
Manchester Unlimited: The Money, Egos and Infighting Behind the World's Richest Soccer Club
The World Cup: All You Need to Know
Manchester Unlimited: The Rise and Rise of the World's Premier Football Club
Behind Closed Doors: Dreams and Nightmares at Spurs
The Game Changer

THE NINE WAVES

THE EXTRAORDINARY STORY OF
INDIAN CRICKET

MIHIR BOSE

ALEPH

ALEPH BOOK COMPANY
An independent publishing firm
promoted by *Rupa Publications India*

First published in India in 2019
by Aleph Book Company
7/16 Ansari Road, Daryaganj
New Delhi 110 002

ISBN: 978-93-88292-62-7

1 3 5 7 9 10 8 6 4 2

Printed and bound in India by Replika Press Pvt. Ltd.

In memory of Baba for first taking me to cricket and also to Naynesh, friend and counsellor, who I have played cricket with and spent long hours watching and talking about this great game.

CONTENTS

PREFACE

On 15 December 1951, I was taken by my parents to the flat of a close friend of my mother, Ella mashi, or aunty Ella, which overlooked Mumbai's Brabourne Stadium. It was the second day of the second Test match between India and England. As I recall, we were meant to watch Vijay Hazare grind England to dust. But, in trying to hook a short-pitched ball from the England fast bowler Fred Ridgway, he played it onto his forehead, cutting it badly. I was five years old and can still recall the surprise and anguish we all felt on the balcony as Hazare, soon after his injury, got out.

Since then I have been privileged to witness some of Indian cricket's great moments, from Subhash Gupte mesmerizing batsmen to Tiger Pataudi making us Indians believe that the game was thrilling. I have seen all India's seven Test triumphs in England starting with the historic one at the Oval in 1971.

My first journalistic assignment was the 1974 Indian tour of England and my first match, India vs Hampshire at Southampton. I was in the Lord's press box when Kapil Dev lifted the 1983 World Cup, also when he hit the winning run to seal India's first Test win at Lord's in 1986. But I also watched as India were bowled out for 42 in 1974. In 1979, I reported from the Oval on one of the most thrilling Tests ever seen and, in 1990, from Old Trafford when Sachin Tendulkar scored his first Test century. I was at Chennai in December 1983 when Sunil Gavaskar scored his thirtieth Test century, going past Donald Bradman's record of twenty-nine centuries and in Kolkata for Mohammad Azharuddin's magical debut in the 1984–85 series. And I was there for India's first ever tour of South Africa which was also the first non-white cricket tour of that country.

I have covered several World Cups including the 2003 World Cup in South Africa and the 2011 World Cup in India where M. S. Dhoni emulated Kapil Dev. Lalit Modi gave me the first and only interview he gave after he lost his baby, the IPL, and I have witnessed the impact Dhoni and Kohli have made. In 1991, I played a part in making sure Gavaskar met Nelson Mandela and I accompanied him to the great man's house in Soweto for a historic visit. Over the years, I have provided advice to Indian board members, including introducing them to Naynesh Desai, a London lawyer, who was very helpful in getting Jagmohan Dalmiya elected as the first Indian chairman of the International Cricket Council (ICC).

I have been chronicling Indian cricket and Indian society for nearly forty years. During that time, I have met many cricketers, both from India and other countries, as well as officials and fans. Indian cricket has also given me much journalistic satisfaction and my book, *A History of Indian Cricket*, published in 1990, was the first book on an Indian theme to win the Cricket Society Literary Award.

Indian cricket has given me much joy but also heartbreak. I went to school in Mumbai with Sunil Gavaskar and back in 1990 he saw India as a cricketing babe which was both a little parcel of joy but also despair. Now, as we approach the third decade of the twenty-first century, Indian cricket is a strapping man whose ability to generate money makes it the most powerful economic force in world cricket. Indian cricketers are finally beginning to punch their weight on the field of play. I am writing this, just days after India have won a series in Australia for the first time, having first toured the country just a few months after I was born in 1947. They are not yet supreme, but they can no longer be brushed aside as they were through much of my childhood.

As a child I would often come back to our flat at Flora Fountain in the centre of Mumbai having seen my heroes fail and I would practise in front of my father's wardrobe hoping I could avenge the defeats. I was never good enough to do so; I never even made it to my school team. But when I was watching a twelve-year-old Gavaskar practise batting at school, my teacher told me he would play for India one day. In the years since I first started writing on Indian cricket in the 1970s the literature on it has grown enormously with much made of how cricket was a religion in India. This book is a distillation of what has been a lifetime's obsession and is based on many hours of interviews and studies of material on what is now, along with Bollywood, also a great interest of mine, one of India's most potent weapons of soft power. I am writing just as India has completed a tour of England, providing some of the most compelling cricket ever seen. To have witnessed the fervour of Indian fans in the land of its former conquerors is to see how far Indian cricket has come in the last half century. Nobody on the balcony of Ella mashi's flat back in 1951 could have imagined that.

Mihir Bose
London
March 2019

Chapter 1

THE MIRACLE OF JOHANNESBURG

On 13 September 2007, a fifteen-man Indian team flew out to Johannesburg to take part in the first T20 World Cup. Their departure made few waves in India. For a start they flew out not from Mumbai but London. Nobody in India expected much from this team. Indeed, the Board of Control for Cricket in India (BCCI) had had to be bullied to even take part in the competition. Its very format, with each side restricted to twenty overs, had been mocked by board officials and meant little to the Indians. There had been one domestic T20 competition which attracted little attention, even the television rights for it had not been sold. This was one English idea the Indians were convinced they could do without. The English had invented the idea to attract more people to their game. The Indians saw no need to change.

INDIA DOES NOT NEED 20-OVERS CRICKET

They were sure they had got the format of their cricket right. India was in love with the 50-over game. Fifty-over one day matches played by Team India, as the national team was now called, attracted huge crowds and mouth-watering amounts of television and sponsorship income. This had completely revolutionized cricket's finances, making India the moneybags of the game. Such was India's financial power that the board earned $8 million in television rights for each One Day International (ODI) India played. A cricket match involving Team India also made money for countries India played against. For all the emotional hold of an Ashes series, the English board earned much more money when it played India at home. It could sell the television rights for vast sums to keep the Indian eyeballs, as Indian board members called Indians who watched cricket on television, happy.

So, when, in March 2006, the International Cricket Council (ICC) met to discuss whether to adopt T20 as an international event and hold a World Cup, the Indians dismissed the idea. Snorting in derision, Niranjan Shah, the then honorary secretary of the BCCI said, 'Twenty20. Why not ten-ten, or five-five or one-one?' He went on to make it clear that as Indian players had not played T20 they would be at a great disadvantage against other sides. Shah was considered such a fool by many in the ICC that Malcolm Gray, ICC president, had described his participation at ICC meetings 'as unnecessarily depriving a village of its idiot'. However, Shah's views could not be dismissed and with Pakistan joining India in opposing the World Cup the ICC knew it faced a problem. Its solution was to award the first T20 World Cup to South Africa but giving the countries the option of not taking part if they so desired. However, it then used the fact that India wanted to host the 2011 World Cup to put pressure on India to take part and India, reluctantly, agreed. But this did not change the Indian board's view that the T20 World Cup was an irrelevance.

This was evident in the players selected, the choice of the captain and even the way the announcement of the team was made. So, the team that flew out from London did not have any of the so-called Fab Four who had played such a huge part in Indian cricket in the previous decade, Rahul Dravid who had just led Sourav Ganguly, V. V. S. Laxman and the god of Indian cricket, Sachin Tendulkar, to its first Test series victory in England in twenty-one years. Zaheer Khan, whose bowling had made that victory possible was also not in the team. Tendulkar had given no thought to the T20, as his mind was focussed on the ODI 50-over series against Australia in the winter of 2007 followed by a full tour of Australia. Dravid, speaking for the greats, said, 'We thought it better if the younger guys played that tournament. Twenty20 is a game for youngsters. I think it was a proper decision and the way forward for Indian cricket.' The team with an average age of twenty-three was four years younger than the 1983 World Cup winning team and included one player, Piyush Chawla, who was only eighteen.

The selectors had chosen some seniors, Harbhajan Singh, Ajit Agarkar and, most interestingly, Virender Sehwag. However, he was not in England, not being part of the Indian touring team, and was the only member of the Indian team to fly to South Africa from India. It was as if this was a sop to him. He had some experience of T20, having skippered India to victory in the only T20 international India had played back in December 2006 in Johannesburg, also the venue for the final of the T20 World Cup. However, he was not selected as captain. Instead, Mahendra Singh Dhoni, a wicketkeeper batsman, who in that T20 match against South Africa had made a duck, was chosen to lead India's T20 World Cup team.

DHONI SEIZES HIS CHANCE

Dhoni's rise through the ranks of Indian cricket had had a touch of good fortune about it. In 2004, he was in the Indian team which went on an A tour of Zimbabwe and Kenya. Then, the first-choice wicketkeeper, Dinesh Karthik, was called to play for the senior side in England thus giving Dhoni his chance which he seized brilliantly. In the three years since his debut, although his wicketkeeping still made the purists wince, nobody could doubt his batting which at times could be explosive.

In April 2005, in an ODI match against Pakistan at Visakhapatnam, he made 148 from 123 balls hitting 12 fours and 4 sixes and powering India to 356 for 9, their highest against Pakistan and the third highest ever. One commentator described his batting as 'A Man Possessed'. Another felt Dhoni had violently changed the settled Indian batting order 'as if an explosion had gone off that would ring in the ears for long'. The next day eunuchs invaded Dhoni's parents' home, Ranchi and demanded ₹50,000 as they showered blessings and the police had to be called. Indian cricketing ears were ringing very loudly six months later when in Jaipur in October 2005 against Sri Lanka Dhoni made 183 not out, the highest score by a wicketkeeper, and, what made it sweeter, passing the record set by his hero the Australian wicketkeeper Adam Gilchrist. Dravid, captaining the side, was so enchanted he compared it to Tendulkar's 143 against Australia in Sharjah in 1998, widely seen as the greatest one-day century by an Indian. Lalit Modi, who then ran Rajasthan cricket and had unveiled a redesigned stadium, awarded him a ₹1 million cash prize and exulted that Dhoni had 'nerves of steel' and that 'it seemed he was gripped by some supernatural power'. The two innings showed how Dhoni could both set a score and chase runs. His score against Pakistan had been when India were batting first, against Sri Lanka it had come as India was chasing a Sri Lankan score of 298. In the Indian dressing room Yuvraj Singh, Sehwag and Harbhajan Singh danced the bhangra to the tune 'Maahi Ve' from Karan Johar's film, *Kal Ho Naa Ho*. Mahi was Dhoni's popular nickname used by friends and now the 50,000 people packed inside the Jaipur ground, sang 'That's the way—Mahi Ve'.

Nevertheless, none of this suggested that Dhoni would be a good captain. Yuvraj Singh, while a few months younger, had made his debut four years earlier and was just the all-rounder, with his left-arm bowling supplementing his batting, and looked the more likely prospect. But Dhoni had been tipped as a future captain by John Wright, the New Zealander who had been the first foreign coach of India on his very first tour in 2004. 'I would say he has all the potential to become a team leader. He understands the game well and understands his team mates.' Dhoni was also recommended by Tendulkar and Dravid to the chairman of the selectors, Dilip Vengsarkar, who 'liked his aggressive approach. He looked like someone who understood the game well and importantly was seen as a calm presence in the dressing room.'

Dhoni's calmness was certainly evident when he held his first press conference as captain. With India touring England then, Dhoni held it, not in his home town of Ranchi, capital of the state of Jharkhand, or the Indian board's headquarters in Mumbai, but in London. Never before had a man from Jharkhand, captained India. Dhoni, with the sort of shrewdness that would mark his captaincy, decided that, although London could never be Ranchi, he would use his first press conference to advertise his home state. Asked what it felt like to take over from the greats of Indian cricket Dhoni said, 'I am like the brand ambassador for the people of Jharkhand. It's a small state where the infrastructure isn't great for cricket. Five years ago nobody would have ever thought that someone from this state would play for India. Now, if I look back I'm excited for the job.'

A PENALTY SHOOT-OUT IN CRICKET

There was little for Dhoni to get excited about in the first match. It was against Scotland, a team India had beaten a few weeks previously, albeit in a 50-over match in Glasgow. But in Durban, rain meant not a ball was bowled. However, with Pakistan, who were also in India's group, beating Scotland, India faced elimination if they lost to Pakistan by a large margin. India knew they would have support for the match in Durban, a centre of South Africans of Indian origin and where Gandhi had set up his law practice more than a century earlier and created the satyagraha movement.

On the day of the match Dhoni had to convey a certain Gandhian calmness as news came in the morning that back in India Dravid had said he was quitting both the Test and one day captaincy. Instead of preparing for the match the players huddled in their hotel first to confirm and then digest the news. Dhoni could not have anticipated this but could take comfort from the fact that he had prepared the team for likely drama on the field. He had gone through the rules, discovered that in a tie the match would be decided by cricket's equivalent of a penalty shoot-out and prepared his players. Called a bowl out, it meant five bowlers from each side delivered one or two balls at an unguarded stump. Dhoni had divided his players into three teams and had 'fun practice sessions around who would hit the stumps and then chosen our first five bowlers in advance'. He had also chosen two batsmen, Sehwag and twenty-one-year old Robin Uthappa, who had not yet played a T20 international, as two of the bowlers. Pakistan did not bother practising the bowl out and this proved decisive. Not that as the match progressed a bowl out seemed necessary.

India through Dhoni and Uthappa who made 50, recovered from 36 for 4 to reach 141 for 9. They seemed to have the match won when Pakistan were reduced to 87 for 5 and needed 39 runs from fourteen balls. But then Misbah-ul-Haq took 17 from the penultimate over bowled by Agarkar and with two deliveries left, the scores were level. The situation was made for the young Indian side to lose their heads. Instead it was Misbah who did. He missed the fifth ball and was run out on the sixth. To the astonishment of the spectators, Dhoni in the bowl out tossed the ball to Sehwag and Uthappa, neither of whom had bowled in the match, and only after that to a bowler, Harbhajan. The Pakistanis went with three experienced bowlers, but it was the Indians who hit the stumps while all three Pakistanis, for all their experience of bowling and who had bowled in the match, missed. This proved the first of many Dhoni decisions which at the end of the tournament made *Wisden*, English cricket's bible, describe the Indian captain as providing 'inspired captaincy'.

The victory meant India had never lost to Pakistan in a World Cup match, be it 50-overs or 20-overs, although its real significance was how calmly Dhoni took the victory saying he did not like bowl outs to decide matches. 'It really amuses you. Winning a cricket match 3–0. It doesn't happen every time. But it is in the record books now. I can tell my friends when I was captain my team won 3–0.' Dhoni, who as a schoolboy preferred football and was a Manchester United supporter, knew his friends would get the joke.

DICING WITH DEFEAT

That bowl-out victory established the pattern of matches for India. They were never sure of victory until they won and in every match they faced elimination. Having lost to New Zealand by 10 runs in the first of the super eight matches, India needed to beat England. What happened could not have been scripted; it was like the classic schoolboy fairy tale end to an innings. India on winning the toss had made an excellent start but as Yuvraj joined Dhoni the pair knew they needed to accelerate if they wanted to post a really imposing total. Dhoni knew all about Yuvraj's powers of hitting, having played with and against him as he was making his mark through junior cricket. But not even he could anticipate what the Punjab player would produce under the floodlights on that September evening. And all thanks to some remarks made by the England all-rounder, Andrew Flintoff.

In the eighteenth over Yuvraj hit him for 2 fours. Flintoff said something; we do not know what but it so upset Yuvraj that Dhoni had to come down to the pitch to calm things down. That the less experienced international player was calming the more experienced one was interesting, but it seemed to work. Yuvraj nodded but he well remembered the humiliation England had inflicted on his bowling fourteen days earlier and he wanted revenge. Then, at the Oval, Dimitri Mascarenhas had clouted him for 5 sixes off the last five balls of the match. In Durban the nineteenth over was to be bowled by Stuart Broad, whose previous three overs had gone for 24 runs and, as the Englishman ran in, Yuvraj, decided to go one better than Mascarenhas, hitting every ball of the over for six. Whereas Mascarenhas had hit Yuvraj for sixes on the leg side between long-on and deep midwicket, Yuvraj used both sides of the wicket. The first over wide mid-on was the longest at 105 metres, the second sailed over fine-leg. Then he switched to the off and cleared long-off, the fourth a full toss was sent over backward point. The fifth, which saw him go down on one knee, was a mishit but cleared square-leg and the last saw him return to the midwicket fence. The sixes had taken him to a half-century in twelve balls, the quickest in international cricket and considered the fastest in representative cricket at the highest level.

Stuart Broad told me. 'I was aiming to bowl quite full. I was bowling into quite a strong wind. I knew he had to be aiming to hit with the wind because he had to just get up in the air and it would be going.'

Flintoff could not match Yuvraj and India won by 18 runs. However, while Yuvraj had lit up the tournament there seemed no prospect of India making progress. Their last match in the group was against South Africa and the hosts did not even need to win to make the semi-final. All they had to do was make 126. And Yuvraj could not play due to tendinitis in his left elbow. India batting first made a dreadful start, 33 for 3. But it was now that Dhoni gave the first glimpse of what would make him the great finisher. The general view was that in a 20-over match, as opposed to a 50-over one, you did not have time to build an innings. But Dhoni had worked out that twenty overs also allowed time to pace out an innings and partnering twenty-year old Rohit Sharma the pair put on 85 runs helping India reach 153 for 5 and a platform.

However, with South Africa requiring only 126 to win India had to do more than win. They had to keep taking wickets to slow the hosts down. In the two previous matches India had gone for 190 against New Zealand and 200 against England. But with the seventh ball of the innings R. P. Singh had Herschelle Gibbs lbw and so devastated the South African batting that they were 31 for 5 in the sixth over. South Africa were now caught in the classic position. Should they try and win or just crawl to 126? They managed neither and, despite Dhoni developing a back problem which made Dinesh Karthik move from slip where he had taken a great catch to don the gloves, India never loosened its hold on the match.

India played Australia in the semi-final. Dhoni was convinced that India should always bat first on winning the toss as it had successfully done against England and South Africa and he did so now. For almost half the match it seemed India would not be able to set Australia much of a target, managing only 41 for 2 after eight overs. But then a fully recovered Yuvraj came in and got off the mark with a six; Uthappa, clearly inspired, came down the wicket to hit a six. All this set Yuvraj off again and he now hit the longest six of the tournament: 119 metres; and what made it magical was that it was a flick off his legs that caused the white ball to soar over square-leg. But while 188 was a good score Australia looked like they had worked it all out. Matthew Hayden had a reputation for being a flat track bully but now he was the anchor while Andrew Symonds did most of the explosive shot-making.

What turned the match for India were three very shrewd bowling changes by Dhoni. In the fifteenth over he brought back Shanthakumaran Sreesanth to bowl his final over. Sreesanth would be fined 25 per cent of his match fee for excessive appealing, but there was no need for an appeal when he uprooted Hayden's off-stump. Yet it still seemed doable with 30 needed from eighteen balls. Now came Dhoni's second crucial bowling change. He brought back Harbhajan who hadn't taken a wicket and in his three overs had conceded 21 runs. He bowled Michael Clarke and gave away only 3 runs. R. P. Singh who bowled the nineteenth over was only slightly more expensive giving away 5 runs. Australia needed 22 from the last over and it proved too much. The Indian joy was a perhaps a touch frantic with Yuvraj waving his arms in the air like a dervish. But, given how often Australia had humiliated India in World Cups, it was only to be expected. Dhoni was calmer, gently reminding Ravi Shastri that he had read his column which had said Australia were favourites. 'I think we surprised you.'

On the same day at Cape Town, Pakistan had beaten New Zealand with great ease, winning by six wickets and so the two sides, whose boards had not even wanted to be in South Africa, travelled to Johannesburg for the final.

PREPARING FOR THE FINAL

The twenty-four hours before the final showed how Dhoni was maturing as captain. After the pre-final team meeting Dhoni had told his players that they should relax by watching a film. He himself liked watching movies in a multiplex. This was impossible in India as the cricketers would get mobbed but in Johannesburg they could behave like ordinary humans although Dhoni advised his players to ring up the multiplexes and say they were coming so as to get some privacy. However, Dhoni found none of his players wanted to go to a Johannesburg multiplex and went back to his room. There, perhaps his most temperamental player, Sreesanth, turned up to return the bat he had borrowed. Dhoni advised Sreesanth not to spray the ball around but concentrate on line and length. From Dhoni's window the pair could see the Wanderers ground and the World Cup trophy and pointing to the trophy Dhoni said, 'There's the trophy and loads of prestige at stake because it is a match with Pakistan.' This prompted Sreesanth to say, 'Who knows I would be involved in the final showdown of the finals.' It was meant as a joke but for Dhoni, aware of how the Kerala fast bowler could lose his head, said sternly, 'Then you should certainly not mess up anything.' Sreesanth was not best pleased but he was to play a crucial part in the final. During the tournament Dhoni had told his players he did not know why the Indian media devoted so much space to cricket. 'Perhaps they need every bit of a cricketer for their daily news updates.'

However, before the night was out, Dhoni discovered it was not just the media. He was woken up twice that night. First by a Bollywood mogul, Shah Rukh Khan, telling him, 'Sleep well, you will win tomorrow.' And then by Lalit Modi, the man who was about to become the great czar of Indian cricket, 'Still awake? Sleep now and play well tomorrow. This is a big match for us.' As we shall see it was to prove a huge match for Modi and Indian cricket as well.

DHONI'S MATCH-WINNING DECISIONS
Dhoni woke up aware he had to make a crucial decision. Sehwag had a groin strain. The coach Lalchand Rajput had left the decision to him, confident that Dhoni, who always seemed calm whatever the situation, would make the right decision. Dhoni waited until after breakfast and when it was confirmed Sehwag would not be fit he opted for Yusuf Pathan. He had never played for India before in any international and had been overshadowed by his younger brother, Irfan Pathan, who had played in all the matches, but Dhoni remembered his hundred-plus strike rate in domestic cricket for Baroda. Many an Indian captain would not have felt confident that Indian performances could be replicated overseas but Dhoni was and Yusuf Pathan, he decided, would open. Dhoni was determined not to lose having told friends that if a win was not possible he would prefer a tie and sharing the cup. As he led his team out for the match he told them,

'Jeetna hai, ab to Cup leke hi India waapas jayenge.' [We have to win, we will return to India with the Cup.]

Pathan, justifying the faith his skipper had in him, started brilliantly, with a six in his first over but then he overreached himself and was out for 15. It required Gautam Gambhir making 75 for India to reach 157 with Dhoni himself making just 6 and the last five overs producing 47. This looked well below par and Dhoni, observers felt, had looked tense as he led his side out. He had more reason to feel worried in the second over of the Pakistan innings which was bowled by Sreesanth. His bowling, as if he had not taken Dhoni's advice, was so wayward that he was hit by Imran Nazir for 21. He did follow this up with a maiden. Then there was a moment that had echoes of 1983 at Lord's when Kapil Dev caught Vivian Richards off a miscued shot off Madan Lal to turn the match around. Now, Uthappa showcased modern Indian fielding. In one almost balletic movement he picked up and threw, running out Nazir.

However, Pakistan recovered from 77 for 6 led by Misbah-ul-Haq. He had tied the match against India in the group match, steered his side to victory against Australia and now, while others fell, he remained, pacing his innings. He reserved his explosive Dhoni- or Yuvraj-style hitting for the seventeenth over when, with Pakistan needing 54 from four overs, he hit Harbhajan Singh for 19 runs, three of the balls going for sixes. It was now 35 from eighteen balls but with Sreesanth going for 15, although he took a wicket, it became a very gettable 20 from 12.

R. P. Singh restored Indian hopes with a tight nineteenth over which left a final over where Pakistan required 13 and India one wicket. In India everyone deserted the streets to cluster around the television sets and in Pakistan people, some even on the highway, prayed. Now came Dhoni's master stroke.

The obvious choice to bowl would have been Harbhajan—vastly experienced, the first Indian to take a hat-trick in Tests and a doughty fighter. But Dhoni judged the 19 runs he had conceded had damaged him and he brought back Joginder Sharma. Dhoni and Sharma had made their ODI debut together but then their paths had diverged. However, Dhoni had no doubts. 'I chose Joginder because Bhajji [Harbhajan's nickname] had gone for a fair number of runs in his last over. Besides, the opposition hadn't seen too much of Joginder, who had a good slower ball and change of pace which suited the occasion.' As he handed the ball to Joginder he told him to keep it simple and have the confidence that he could do it.

That confidence hardly seemed justified when Joginder's first ball was a wide, Misbah missed the second but hit the third, a full toss, for six.

Pakistan needed 6 runs from four balls. On the boundary edge Rajput could barely watch and kept chanting the Gayatri Mantra. Dhoni showed no reaction. He did not reprimand Joginder, merely told him to keep going. Misbah had it all planned out. He saw himself as a thinking cricketer, a big-match player, who had come into the final 'quite sure about how I wanted to score runs'. Aware a four would mean virtual victory, he had decided to scoop Joginder over square-leg. 'I had scored runs off it right through the tournament.' Instead, surprised by the bowler's lack of pace, he did not connect properly and 'was careless in not checking the fielders before that ball'. The fielder was Sreesanth at short fine-leg and he, with Dhoni's words ringing in his ear, made no mistake. The shot shattered Misbah, and would be endlessly replayed on Pakistan television, 'I regret it till today. It shattered my hopes of being a big-match player,' Misbah would lament.

India's joy was unconfined. In 1983, the victory at Lord's was a wonderful event in a foreign field with few Indians present in that very English setting. In Johannesburg the ground seemed full of Indians although Pakistan also had support. There were the Indians of South Africa who, as late as 1991, would have had to sit in cages, segregated from the whites while they watched the match. But there were also Indians who had benefited from the opening of the Indian economy, which had also taken place in 1991 and who would think nothing of flying in from India to watch their countrymen play. Nobody had deeper pockets than the Bollywood stars. Shah Rukh Khan had come with his family, so had actors Deepika Padukone, Priyanka Chopra, Juhi Chawla, Rani Mukherjee, Diya Mirza and Amisha Patel. During the match the sight of these stars, particularly Khan, would send the crowd into raptures of joy. Bollywood and all of India joined in acclaiming Dhoni and his team as the sporting heroes for which the country had so long craved.

Manmohan Singh, the then prime minister, issued a congratulatory statement within ten minutes. Dhoni was the one person who was calm. As he walked back to the dressing room, he heard a young boy shout out, 'Dhoni I need your shirt, can I have it?' Dhoni identified the boy, got the security officer to bring him to where he was, took off his shirt and gave it to the boy. Millions saw his bare torso rippling with muscles which together with his long hair suggested he represented the young vibrant India. The old India was represented by his mother in Ranchi. There Devaki Devi could not take her eyes off the statue of Lord Krishna telling her husband Pan Singh, 'Bete ne desh ko jitaya hai.' [Our son has led the nation to victory]. As crowds gathered outside their Ranchi home showering flowers not throwing bricks, as they had done after the 2007 World Cup debacle four months earlier, the pair held hands and wept. The 1983 victory at Lord's, as we shall see, changed Indian cricket. But this victory changed not only Indian but world cricket.

INDIA HELP DEFEAT A FRAUDSTER'S PLANS

The day before the final there had been a meeting in Johannesburg's plush Sandton Sun Hotel between the ICC and Allen Stanford, a Texan then claiming to be worth some $18 billion. Based in Antigua, his board included a West Indian Hall of Cricketing Fame: Everton Weekes, Michael Holding, Vivian Richards, Wes Hall, Lance Gibbs, Joel Garner, and Desmond Haynes. He was said to be paying each of his board members $8,000 a month.

Stanford had come to the meeting with Weekes, Hall, Holding, Gibbs, Richards, Garner and Haynes. He wanted the winner of the next day's final between India and Pakistan to go to Antigua and play his team, Stanford Superstars, for $5 million in a winner-take-all prize. He was sure it would attract an audience of a billion.

The ICC knew India was opposed to any such idea as it already earned $8 million in television rights for each 50-over match it played and was unlikely to travel to the Caribbean on the off chance of getting $5 million. The meeting ended with Stanford walking out and Haynes and Richards shouting at Malcolm Speed, then chief executive of the ICC, with Haynes calling Speed a racist and Richards thumping the table in anger.

That meeting confirmed how West Indian cricket had declined both on and off the field. This was further emphasized fifteen months later when Stanford was charged with fraud worth $8 billion. He is now serving a 110-year federal prison sentence although he continues to deny any wrongdoing and has vowed to clear his name.

THE FRUITS OF DHONI'S VICTORY

The ICC decision not to deal with Stanford—prompted by India—was to prove crucial. For even as their rookie cricketers were performing in South Africa, the heavyweights of Indian cricket officialdom were planning a different future for the game. The man at the centre of it was Lalit Modi. We shall hear much more of him but here let us sketch what he had done before the tournament began and during it. On 13 September, the very morning that Dhoni and his team flew to South Africa, Modi was in Mumbai at a five-star hotel. Flanked by the greats who did not go to South Africa, Tendulkar, Dravid, Ganguly, and foreign greats like Glenn McGrath and Stephen Fleming, he revealed that India would have a domestic T20

League. It borrowed from both England and America. The name—the Indian Premier League—had echoes of the English Premier League. But the concept of city-based franchise teams taking part in the competition was introducing an American concept into Indian sport. Two days earlier, Sharad Pawar, the man who had voted against the T20 World Cup, had given Modi .$25 million to prepare for the inaugural tournament.

Modi followed the Indian team to South Africa and, entering the Indian dressing room, promised any player who hit 6 sixes in an over whatever present they wanted. When some players suggested a Rolex watch, Modi announced, 'I will give away a brand-new Porsche if any player achieves the feat.' When Yuvraj hit his final six off Broad he rushed towards Modi who was waving the keys, seeing it (as he put it) as 'an answer to a prayer to God. Let someone do something that no one has done. And we got 6 sixes in an over! It simply lit up the screens in every home. Money can't buy that kind of thing, it just made Twenty20 cricket a must-watch.'

As soon as India had won, Modi rang Pawar in Mumbai to arrange for the team to be taken in a motorcade from Mumbai's international airport to the Wankhede Stadium. Pawar was not sure. Mumbai was still in its monsoon season and he feared the celebrations would be damp and fizzle out. But Modi insisted and took an earlier flight to Mumbai arriving at 4 a.m., two hours before Dhoni and his team. And although it rained, Pawar's fears proved unfounded. India, keen on sport but not a great sporting nation nor used to winning honours, now had a world champion in an inaugural competition and that after beating Pakistan. So many turned up to honour the team that the journey from Sahar to Wankhede took almost four hours instead of the usual one. What is more it was telecast live to the remotest parts of India. As Dhoni and his team accepted the adulation he realized for the first time what cricket meant for India. 'Till then we were just a group of young guys having a good time.'

Modi saw money and as he put it later, 'If I had any doubts left over the appeal of the new brand of Twenty20 cricket, the Mumbai road show settled it.' Modi was to use the win brilliantly and we shall have more to say about the IPL story and how it changed Indian and world cricket.

⌐

The nearly ninety-year history of Indian cricket, starting with the first Test in 1932, divides neatly into nine waves, with Virat Kohli riding the current ninth wave. Dhoni's victory marked the start of the eighth wave which has proved to be the most revolutionary in Indian cricket history. The previous seven waves had seen many dramatic moments. But these often proved to be one step forwards followed by a huge step backwards that wiped out all the gains.

This has not been the case with Dhoni's Johannesburg miracle. It provided an ideal launch pad for the IPL and that has revolutionized world cricket. April no longer marks the start of the English season but the start of the IPL and what happens in this great cricket tamasha means a lot more than what is going in often damp, chilly England. In 2013, James Astill, political editor of *The Economist*, even wrote a book on India seeing IPL as providing a window into India. No Englishman would have thought of doing that with the Ranji Trophy.

This revolution has been possible because the India of today is not remotely what the country was like during the previous waves of Indian cricket. Take India's first Test and series victory in England, exactly thirty-five years and a month before Dhoni's victory in Johannesburg, its first ever series win in the land of its former conquerors. In Mumbai, they were celebrating Ganesh Chaturthi. Rajdeep Sardesai, son of Dilip Sardesai, who helped India win at the Oval, was then six years old and recalls in his 2017 book, *Democracy's XI*, how as the idol of Ganesha, was immersed in the sea, he was lifted on the shoulders of his uncle.

Then Mumbai still had its old Portuguese name of Bombay. The airport was the old one at Santa Cruz and the board's headquarters were at the Cricket Club of India (CCI), a grand club that still reeked of the world the British Raj had left behind. Only two makes of car were produced in India, the Ambassador and Fiat, both of which had waiting lists of many years. In 1971, to showcase the triumphant team, the BCCI whisked them back in open-top pre-war American Buicks. Then they were seen as the most prized cars in India, driven by the affluent few. In 1971, I was a student in England and present both at Lord's where India came close to winning and also at the Oval. But Indians in India did not see a single ball of the epic Oval triumph as there was no television in India. They could only follow it on the radio and heard of Indian triumphs through English voices. The news came on the radio with an Englishman, Brian Johnston, announcing to the Indians that their team had won. Indians garlanded their radios.

The India that celebrated the victory of 24 September 2007 was a very different place, politically, socially and in the cricket sense. India was now being talked about as a great power rivalling China for world domination. Every ball was beamed live to millions of homes across the country and the commentators were famous Indian ex-cricketers. The fans felt they knew Dhoni and his cricketers intimately. And, unlike in 1971, Dhoni's men were rich. In 1971, the Indian captain Ajit Wadekar earned his living working for the State Bank of India, his colleagues worked for other commercial firms. The players' expectations were limited as the bank employed other cricketers. As Wadekar put it, 'The bank gave us respect and financial security. What more could we ask for as players?' The cricketers knew that just playing for India would not allow them to put food on the table for their families. Two years after the Oval triumph when Dilip Sardesai retired, he earned ₹2,500 for a Test match. In 2007, even before he had taken the side to South Africa, Dhoni had an agent representing him and had succeeded in building his own brand striking a deal with NDTV for exclusive interviews, views and special shows. On his return from Johannesburg with the media branding him 'Captain Cool' he would grow so rich that by 2009 *Forbes* named him the world's most expensive cricketer. And by the first decade of the twenty-first century cricket was a powerful Indian soft-power tool. India and its cricket had come a long way since the British brought the game to India.

I was made very aware of this when, on 31 March 2014, I was invited to a reception held at 10 Downing Street by then prime minister, David Cameron, to coincide with the twentieth anniversary of the genocide in Rwanda. The object was to promote a charity developing a cricket stadium in the country to help heal the wounds of that ravaged land. Among those present were the great and the good of English cricket, the West Indian batsman Brian Lara, whom some in cricket rate even higher than Sachin Tendulkar and also a rich Indian businessman.

The businessman knew Dhoni very well and had spoken to me admiringly about the Indian captain and how focussed he was on his cricket. As soon as Cameron arrived, the organizer approached the businessman: 'I have been looking for you. You must come with me to meet the Prime Minister.' The Indian businessman was whisked away for a very private tête-à-tête, while the rest of us sipped our drinks. I later discovered that the Indian had donated money to the charity, and the hope was that a few private minutes with Cameron would make him donate even more. On one of his visits to India, Cameron had played cricket with Kapil Dev, and now he wanted to harness India's love for cricket and the money power of rich Indians to heal the wounds of Rwanda. In the twenty-first century, the British see this as another wonderful example of using what they trumpet as the shared history of the two nations for the good of mankind. In no other wave of Indian cricket history would the British have turned to Indian cricket to help them.

Chapter 2

LEARNING THE CONQUEROR'S GAME

RELIGION, COLLABORATORS AND DEVELOPMENT OF THE INDIAN GAME

In his book *The Tao of Cricket*, Ashis Nandy says, 'Cricket is an Indian game, accidentally discovered by the English.' When in October 2018, Mike Brearley, launching his own book on cricket in London, read this out, the largely English audience fell about laughing, which would have delighted Nandy. The fact is the Indian love for cricket shows a culture which can, like a sponge, absorb and adapt to inventions and ideas from other lands. Such has been the Indian ability to take to cricket that even Indians who do not speak much English can say 'How's that?' in English.

However, despite cricketers being treated like gods in India, unlike the West Indians, Indians do not need cricket to define themselves. West Indian writers like C. L. R. James and V. S. Naipaul have said that for the West Indians, descendants of slaves, the game provided the one sure test of asserting who they were, judging their ability and worth where race, education and wealth did not matter. This explains why while there is no West Indian nation, there is a West Indian cricket team. These island nations are often at loggerheads, but the team defines all the people living in the Caribbean, represents their shared history. If Indians had seen cricket as the West Indians did, then there would be a combined India–Pakistan–Sri Lanka–Bangladesh team. There is much cultural affinity between these four nations, but they could never have a combined team to match the West Indies team.

The Indians, of course, have always had their own sports, in particular kabaddi and gilli–danda (a stick and ball game), but after the British brought cricket to India they soon realized that cricket was very different and also very superior to any game they possessed. I can recall when growing up that, after an Indian cricket disaster, people talked of going back to gilli–danda, but we never did, and I have never played the game. However, I did play kabaddi at my Jesuit school in Mumbai, also the school of Sunil Gavaskar and he, too, would have played this ancient Indian game. However, as a visit in 2018 to my school showed, things have changed, and this shows how, compared to our youth, cricket now dominates everything in sporting India.

On that visit I was surprised to find kabaddi was no longer played, while all the schoolboys knew who Dhoni and Kohli were. Yet, unlike our school days, when all of us spoke English, many of these boys struggled with the language and there were signs dotted around the school asking the boys to speak English, something we did not need to be told. What is more, while in my youth the *Times of India* would never have had a word of Hindi, and we looked down on people who could not speak English, it now often uses Hinglish, a mixture of Hindi and English. Call this the magic of cricket, which is further emphasized by the way the game continues to spread in India and parts of the country it has never reached before. Since I first started writing about cricket, places like Ranchi and Dharamshala have staged international matches, unthinkable in my youth. And cricket has provided a wonderful glue for modern India. In 1947, British experts were convinced India could not survive and Pakistan was the virile nation which would take on communism. Months after India's first ever Test victory in England, Pakistan split, creating Bangladesh. And now, such is the turmoil in the country that Pakistan can no longer even play international cricket at home, while no overseas cricketer can keep away from India.

It was, of course, all very different back in 1721 when Indians first saw cricket played by English sailors along the beachfront at the Gulf of Cambay. It is important to stress that at this time the British in India were traders and in 1721 they did not remotely look likely to become the rulers of India. The English had first arrived in 1583 from a poor, beleaguered country with a begging letter from Elizabeth I to Mughal Emperor Akbar pleading with the 'Invincible Emperor' to allow her subjects to trade. Things only changed in 1757, when with the help of Indian collaborators, the British converted themselves from traders into conquerors. And that first battle in Plassey in 1757, which set the wheels of conquest in motion, was something of a 'fixed' match. Robert Clive conspired with Bengal Nawab Siraj-ud-Daulah's general, Mir Jafar, to win the Battle of Plassey and launch British rule in India. More than 250 years later, Hansie Cronje, the South African captain, took bribes, but to fix cricket matches. Interestingly, both of them would face charges: Clive before the House of Commons, Cronje before the South African King Commission of Inquiry, to explain why and how they had taken money from the Indians.

It was thirty-five years after Clive's victory in Plassey that in 1792 the Calcutta Cricket Club came into existence, five years after the Marylebone Cricket Club (MCC) was set up in London. But while the English played cricket in India they did not want to play with the Indians. The British denied Indians admittance to where they lived; cities were segregated almost on the style of the deep south of America, with Indians excluded from the clubs even until 1964, as with the Breach Candy Club. Bombay Gymkhana, where the first matches and first ever Test in India were played, did not have Indian members until well after India got freedom in 1947.

KEEP THE BROWNS OUT

You get some idea of how the British saw the idea of playing with Indians from *Sporting Memories: My Life as a Gloucestershire County Cricketer, Rugby and Hockey Player and Member of Indian Police Service* by Major W. Troup. The book, exploring sport and society in India and Britain between the 1880s and the 1920s, is such a rare gem that when I came across it at the London Library in 2010, I had to sign a special agreement to borrow the book, that warned me not to put it in a bag with foodstuffs or leave it on the floor.

Published in 1924, it recalls Troup's life in sport, playing county cricket for Gloucestershire with W. G. Grace, a rugby reserve for England, and hockey and many other sports in India while serving in the Indian Police Service. He arrived in India in 1888 and worked there, with long breaks back in England when he played county cricket, until the opening decades of the twentieth century. While he loved his time in India, he had a very poor opinion of the 'natives'. As Troup put it, 'bribery amongst them is an inherited vice, and try as hard as he can, the European police official will never entirely stamp it out—it can't be done.'

In 1908, there arose the question of whether to allow Indians who held the King's Commission in the Indian Army to become members of the Agra Club. The British objected and Troup agreed with his fellow Brits. 'However decent a native may be, his ways and ideas and manners are not ours, they never can and never will blend, and to quote a hackneyed phrase, but none the less appropriate expression, "Familiarity breeds contempt".'

Troup did not even like the idea of watching a match sitting next to an Indian. He and a fellow Brit called Ropeland went to watch a police team play Ajmer in a hockey match:

> It was terrifically hot, and getting tired of standing, we wandered around to try and find a seat. All of those in our immediate vicinity were 'full up', and after a time we came across a native with a big form all to himself. Ropeland asked him to move up in Hindustani, whereupon the fellow insolently replied, 'When you speak to me in a language you understand—namely English—I will comply with your

request.' The seat was vacated alright, in about half a second. [Troup
and his friend using force to remove the Indian]

The viceroy, Lord Curzon, did encourage Indian princely rulers to 'learn
the English language and become sufficiently familiar with English customs,
literature, science, modes of thought, standards of truth and honour and...
with manly sports and games.' Curzon's sporting agenda was delivered to
princely and high-caste Indians in schools set up in India to imitate the
English public-school system. However, Curzon's agenda made no difference
to India's newly trained sportsmen *after* school. The British continued to
exclude Indians from their sporting clubs and they refused to yield any space
for Indians to play sport. The unintended consequence of Curzon's policy
was to create new classes of Indians who enjoyed playing British sports—or
wanted to play them as a mark of education and acceptance—but had no
opportunity to do so unless they formed their own clubs and organizations.
Indian hockey players, for example, were accidental beneficiaries of
exclusion from the crack British clubs. Forced to play on irregular baked-
mud surfaces instead of manicured fields, they learnt the stick techniques
and ability to control the ball which gave India years of ascendancy in the
sport: India were unbeaten in Olympic hockey between 1928 and 1960.
Indian cricketers also had to fight hard for space and recognition and their
early years were marked by hugely symbolic battles and dramatic victories
which fed self-esteem and nationalist feeling.

AUSTRALIANS FAMILY, INDIANS ALIENS

Indians taking to cricket was not like Australians falling in love with the
game. Australians were part of the British race. They saw themselves as John
Bull junior and when they played England they loved to beat the mother
country. Even the West Indians, although their team was largely black, saw
England as the mother country. India was alien and the British never failed
to remind Indians of that. As the British built their empire, millions of
British migrants settled in lands lived in by other races but which the British
considered virginal lands made for them to live in and enjoy. By 1914,
there were eight million in Canada, five million in Australia, more than a
million in New Zealand and upwards of 1.4 million in South Africa; all
these countries barring Canada are, of course Test playing nations. At the
height of the empire the total British population in India was 100,000 and
they had no intention of making India home. British politicians made it
clear that this white empire was not like their Indian empire. As the Liberal
MP Charles Dilke put it, 'England in the East is not the England we know,

flousy Britannia, with her anchor and ship, becomes a mysterious Oriental despotism.' J. R. Seeley, a Cambridge professor, in his book *The Expansion of England* pointed out that in India the British did not have a community of 'blood' or even of 'interest' while the white colonies were a 'normal extension of the English race into other lands'. That was written in 1883 but you get some indication of the appeal of the book in that it was still selling in 1956. And even in 1942, just five years before the British were forced to pack up and leave India, that Indians could never be seen as part of the wider British family was something fundamental to British rule. On 21 January 1942, Lord Linlithgow, the viceroy, wrote to the war cabinet:

> Cabinet will agree with me that India and Burma have no natural association with the Empire, from which they are alien by race, history and religion, and for which, as such, neither of them have any natural affection, and both are in the Empire because they are conquered countries which have been brought there by force, kept there by our controls, and which hitherto, it has suited to remain under our protection.

By then India had played seven Tests, all against England. Even as Linlithgow wrote, as we shall see, Vijay Merchant and Vijay Hazare were setting batting records which still feature in *Wisden*. It was against such a background of being an alien race that the Indians took to this very English game.

THE GOOD BRITISH

However, there were also some Britons who wanted to play with Indians and recent research provided to the MCC by Norman Down has a fascinating account of the British playing with the Bhil tribesmen. We get a brilliant description by an English adjutant of a cricket match more than a century ago between the Mewar Bhil Corps and the Malegaon Cricket Club in the Khandesh district of the Bombay Presidency. Adam Chadwick of the MCC, who provided me the material says, this 'must be one of the earliest records, if not the very earliest, of a contest between an Indian and a British side'.

The man at the centre of this match was James Down, a twenty-one-year-old Englishman. He was appointed to the police force in Khandesh, which also made him ex-officio adjutant to the Bhil Corps. In 1871 he found the Bhils keen on cricket and rather good at it:

> In the evening cricket was the order of the day and made a strong appeal to the Bheels. [They] turned up in numbers and we used to

pick sides daily, entering in a score book the names, runs made and other details in the approved manner. There was no slacking but all were on their toes, not content to wait for the ball in fielding but anticipating its direction and moving to meet it. I was not surprised at this for the Bheel is by nature keen, with splendid eyesight, agile as a cat and athletic in running, jumping and throwing... More remarkable, perhaps, than the fielding was their bowling, in particular that of havildar (sergeant) Khundoo and Sepoy Itoo. Both had acquired the knack of bowling with a break from the off to a remarkably consistent length so that most balls pitched practically on the same spot, just clear of the off stump, with a break back so as to take the leg stump. The spin was apparently imparted by a twist of the wrist rather than with the fingers. Both men took a very long run at speed before projecting the ball underarm at great pace, but their approach to the wicket varied widely. Khundoo held the ball behind his back until he reached the wicket, when he would swing his arm round and hurl the ball with great force and remarkable accuracy. Itoo on the other hand would keep up a series of swinging movements of his arm round his back and head so that it was not easy to see at what exact moment the ball left his hands.

Down decided to organize a match between the Bhils and an English team, the Malegaon Cricket Club. The Bhils were keen to take up the challenge and prepared hard for the match:

Immediately after breakfast the match began. Having won the toss, I decided to bat first feeling that the longer I could stay at the wicket the better I could control the impetuosity of my Bheels in this their first match. The total of 140 fully realised my most sanguine hopes as the Bheels batted with greater restraint than I had anticipated and at no time got over excited. So, when we went out to field I had every hope that we were in sight of a win. Nor was I disappointed; the bowling and fielding all-round was really excellent with the result that we got our opponents out for 120-odd and thus won our first match.

As Chadwick perceptively points out, 'This charming account is notable for its unusual depiction of cricket between European and Indian sides.' However, for the broader development of cricket in India, which helped make it a national game, we need to look at rather different groups of Indians who collaborated with the British.

RELIGIOUS CRICKET

India's Parsee community led the development of Indian cricket. Known as 'the boat people' they, unlike the British, had come not as traders but as refugees in the eighth century CE as their ancestral land, Persia, fell to the forces of Islam. British rule was to see the Parsees emerge as a strong, vibrant community and they were always proud to advertise their loyalty to the British crown. When I was growing up in Mumbai in the 1950s my friends and I would regularly go for evening walks along the sea front at Marine Drive and whenever we saw a Parsee sitting there looking out at the Arabian Sea we would say, 'They have come to the sea front to see whether the British ships are coming back.' Even our Parsee friends joined in the joke.

The early Parsee cricketers, having endured years of condescending remarks from British critics, went on to organize two ambitious tours of England, discovered the first great Indian cricketer, Mehellasha Pavri, and, most importantly, started beating English teams both in England and India. Parsees remained an important part of Indian cricket until well into the 1970s and I grew up watching Polly Umrigar, Nari Contractor, both captains of India, Farokh Engineer, a crucial member of the 1971 team that beat England in England for the first time, and Rusi Surti, whom we christened the 'poor man's Sobers'. Then Tata, the great Parsee firm, employed some of India's best cricketers, but now there are hardly any prominent Parsee cricketers in India.

The Parsee success at the end of the nineteenth and beginning of the twentieth century inspired the Hindus and the Muslims to get involved in cricket. From then on, Indian cricket was essentially in Indian hands: the British could use patronage to reward their favourites, but not to alter the game's basic patterns.

One important consequence of this was that Indian cricket developed through special matches which sound extraordinary and indeed deplorable in the second decade of the twenty-first century but were considered very normal in the first decade of the twentieth century in India: religious teams competing against each other. It suited both the Indians and the British. The British had always stressed that India was not a nation, Winston Churchill famously saying the Equator might as well be called a nation. To prove their assertion, they pointed to how the different religious groups, particularly the Hindus and Muslims, had fought each other. The Indian Army set up by the British was organized along religious and caste lines. Indian newspapers advertised their religious ties. So, the paper called *The Hindu* was set up. This, the leading newspaper of the south, still exists and is generally considered one of India's best newspapers. A paper called the

Mussulman was set up in Kolkata. And universities proudly displayed their religious affiliations: The Banaras Hindu University is still a great university of the country. There was the Hindu College in Kolkata, Delhi and also in Dhaka. For the British this helped emphasize that India was far too divided ever to be ruled by anyone other than a foreign power. The British, as one secretary of state for India put it, were the great composer bringing harmony to India's bitterly divided communities. So, on Mumbai's cricket fields, teams organized along religious lines played against each other very amicably in a tournament that helped the city become the centre of Indian cricket.

The tournament went through various name changes before assuming its final form—the Bombay Pentangular. Starting in 1877 as a match between the Bombay Gymkhana and the Parsees of the Zoroastrian Cricket Club, it developed over the years. But while the Indian teams represented the different religious communities of India, Parsee, Hindu, Muslim, there was no Christian team. The British in India called themselves Europeans. So, in their clubs and other places, notices barring Indians read not 'British only', but 'Europeans only'. Such signs have long gone, but even today if you enter one of these clubs, now wholly in Indian hands, you see plaques saying how the club was set up for the 'Europeans'. In this way the British stressed that they were a particular racial group, all the more important as their rule was based on European supremacy over all other races. This meant that Indian Christians and even people who were of mixed race could not play in this tournament and it was only in 1937, nearly half a century after such matches had first begun, that a 'Rest' team, composed of Indian Christians and other minorities like Jews, joined the tournament.

A star of this assorted team was India's leading Christian cricketer, Vijay Samuel Hazare, who led India to her first-ever Test victory against England in 1952. In his memoir, *A Long Innings*, Hazare describes his pleasure at beating the European variety of Christians in the 1940s. 'My side, the Rest, clashed against the Europeans. As if to punish them for keeping us out of the tournament so long, we thrashed them, totalling over 400. I scored my first century in the carnival when I made 182 against them, and but for dropped catches we could have won by an innings.'

Since the Indians were not allowed in British clubs, they set up their own with the help of the local government. Two miles from the European-only Bombay Gymkhana, along Bombay's waterfront, the Kennedy Sea Face, the government provided land, and here emerged gymkhanas catering to the different religious communities: Parsee, Hindu, Muslim, Catholic; the fifth one, curiously, is the Police Gymkhana. These still exist, an amazing testimony to India's remarkable religious-led discovery of cricket. In the

Mumbai of my youth whenever I wanted to watch top-class club cricket I would go there. It did not strike me, or my friends, as odd that these were clubs organized along religious lines. For me what mattered was that the cricket I was watching was of very high quality.

Within this religious cricket battle there was also scope for significant social change. One of the Hindu cricketers was Palwankar Baloo, not only a great spinner, but from the so-called 'untouchable' caste that higher-caste Hindus had, for centuries, treated as almost subhuman. Through cricket he could make a small dent in this caste iron curtain. And after he retired from cricket he took to politics and came close to defeating B. R. Ambedkar, like him, an untouchable. For many years the two men had formed a mutual admiration society: Baloo, the cricketer, breaking barriers, Ambedkar overcoming age-old prejudices to become a distinguished lawyer. But in 1937 they stood against each other for provincial elections held as part of a British plan to give Indians limited rights to rule themselves. Baloo lost. Ambedkar was to become the great leader of the community, and after India secured its freedom in 1947, he helped to write the Indian constitution. It was under Ambedkar's leadership that this oppressed community acquired a new name, Dalit, as they slowly began to make their way into the mainstream of Indian society.

It must be said that despite the progress Indian cricket has made, this remains a sore topic. Rajdeep Sardesai has argued that Indian cricket is a level playing field. Yet the life of one player in his book shows that it would be wrong to read too much into how far Indian cricket has come in changing Indian society. That player is Vinod Kambli, Tendulkar's partner in a record-breaking school stand in 1988, who had such a rapport with Tendulkar that they did not even need to call when going for a run. Most cricketers would love to have his record. In Tests he averaged 54.20 and in one-day internationals 32.59. But, unlike the Brahmin Tendulkar, Kambli is a Dalit and such was the burden caste-ridden Indian society placed on him that he has converted to Christianity.

The tournament also saw a cricketing innovation: the introduction of neutral umpires in the game for the first time. Initially, only Europeans umpired in the matches, as the British argued that Indians could not be trusted with such a delicate role, but soon there were Indian umpires. The Mumbai religious cricket model was exported to other parts of India including Lahore, Nagpur and Karachi, boosting the growth of the game. Questions about the religious nature of such cricket and the damage it might be doing to the community, given the growing religious strife in the country, began to be raised in the 1940s. Supporters said matches were played without any rancour despite all that was happening in the political world.

Gandhi wanted such matches to be stopped. He called on 'the sporting public of Bombay to revise their sporting code and to erase from it communal matches'. Indian cricket historians have since debated what exactly the Mahatma meant and whether this was more related to how India had been dragged into World War II, as Gandhi's declaration was made in December 1940. In the previous year, Britain had taken India to war against Germany. Not only had they not consulted Indians about this momentous decision, but they claimed they were fighting for Poland's freedom yet refused to give India freedom. In response Gandhi had launched yet another campaign to free India.

Even before his call, however, others had sought the end of such matches, not so much because they were religious, but because other more lucrative forms of cricket were developing. However, such was the hold of the religious tournament that it lasted another six years. The final tournament was played in 1946, a year before India won its freedom, was partitioned and the Muslim state of Pakistan created. But growing up in Mumbai long after communal cricket was a memory, I met many old residents of the city who looked back at these matches with great affection and told me how they produced great cricket and never caused any fights between rival supporters despite the fact that they were supporting different religious teams. For them it was proof that, on the cricket field, a team from one religion could play another in perfect harmony. The idea may seem absurd today, but its supporters remained convinced that, in Indian cricket at that time, it worked and benefited the game. This was a brilliant example that while the British brought cricket to India and talked of their civilizing mission there was no central plan for the export of British sport, and cricket in India developed largely due to the local conditions, with Indians showing a brilliant capacity to take to a foreign game.

CRICKET AND POLITICAL POWER
Along with the Parsees, the princes played a huge role in developing Indian cricket. With a third of India ruled by the princes, who enjoyed local autonomy with their own laws and many of them with their own railway systems, they were inspired to take up the game by the example set by Ranji. He was not born a prince but used his extraordinary cricketing skills, which he honed in Cambridge and Sussex, to become one. To many Indian princes the Ranji story suggested they could use Indian cricket to further their own political ambitions. Not many of the princely states sponsored cricket; the big ones like Hyderabad, which was bigger than France and had

a population in 1931 of 14.4 million, hardly did. Also, the overall period of active princely influence was short, no more than fourteen years. Cricket was important for the smaller princes, for with the 1920s seeing political changes they could not control, or understand, cricket provided a vehicle to curry favour with the British, the paramount power. So, Jammu and Kashmir with an area larger than many European countries, 85,884 square miles, and whose population in 1931 was 3.6 million, did not produce a single cricketer who played for India, although its eccentric maharaja played his own form of very peculiar princely cricket. Bika, 167 square miles and a population of 45,000, had in Yajuvindra Singh a Test cricketer. Pataudi, 53 square miles and a population of 18,873, produced two captains and most amazingly, Vizianagram, only 21 square miles, can also claim to have had a captain of India, albeit through princely chicanery.

The most significant princely patron was Bhupendra Singh, the maharaja of Patiala, who was a great promoter of Indian cricket in the 1920s and 1930s.

In the winter of 1926–27 Bhupendra Singh financed the MCC tour of India, which was a boost for Indian cricket. During the tour the team played a two-day match against the Hindus at the Bombay Gymkhana. The match was hugely significant. At this stage Indian batsmen had not fared well against the MCC team, none of them had made a hundred yet. Now, Cottari Kanakaiya Nayudu, known as C. K. Nayudu, not only scored a 100 but hit 153 runs in 116 minutes with 11 sixes and 14 fours. This was a world record for the number of sixes hit by a batsman in an innings which lasted until the 1962–63 New Zealand season.

The MCC captain, A. E. R. Gilligan, despite being a member of the British Union of Fascists, took to the Indians and encouraged them to set up a Board of Control for Cricket in India. This was done in December 1928. A year later India became a member of the Imperial Cricket Conference. Three years later, India made its Test debut at Lord's. It marked the start of the first wave of Indian cricket. Few then could have imagined that less than a century later India would be the dominant force in world cricket.

The First Wave

TESTS

Wave	Period	Mts	Won	Lost	Drawn	Tied	Win%	W/L
1st	1932–1952	34	3	16	15	0	8.82	0.19

TOP BATSMEN IN FIRST WAVE

	Mts	Runs	Hs	Avg	100	50
V. S. Hazare	25	1998	164★	55.50	7	8
M. H. Mankad	25	1196	184	29.90	3	4
D. G. Phadkar	18	940	123	37.60	2	7
L. Amarnath	24	878	118	24.38	1	4
V. M. Merchant	10	859	154	47.72	3	3
R. S. Modi	10	736	112	46.00	1	6
H. R. Adhikari	18	709	114★	30.82	1	3
S. Mushtaq Ali	11	612	112	32.21	2	3
P. R. Umrigar	15	574	130★	28.70	2	1
P. Roy	12	517	140	28.72	2	0

★Not Out

TOP BOWLERS IN FIRST WAVE

	Mts	Wkts	Best	Avg	5WI	10WM
M. H. Mankad	25	108	8/52	29.04	6	2
Ghulam Ahmed	13	45	5/70	28.13	2	0
L. Amarnath	24	45	5/96	32.91	2	0
D. G. Phadkar	18	39	7/159	32.94	2	0
L. Amar Singh	7	28	7/86	30.64	2	0
M. Nissar	6	25	5/90	28.28	3	0
V. S. Hazare	25	17	4/29	64.00	0	0
S. G. Shinde	7	12	6/91	59.75	1	0
R. V. Divecha	5	11	3/102	32.81	0	0
G. S. Ramchand	7	10	3/20	47.80	0	0

TOP WICKETKEEPERS IN FIRST WAVE

	Mts	Dismissals	Ct	St
P. K. Sen	14	31	20	11
P. G. Joshi	3	8	4	4
Dilawar Hussain	3	7	6	1
M. K. Mantri	3	7	6	1

Note: No One Day Internationals in this wave. These and all statistics in the book are by Rajneesh Gupta

Chapter 3

THE COLONEL AND HIS PROBLEMS

The first wave of Indian cricket was the longest and took place against the background of momentous changes in India and the world: Gandhi's civil disobedience campaign, World War II, India becoming independent. It was capped by Jawaharlal Nehru taking a controversial decision that ensured India remained a Test-playing nation. But the start was shaped by a decision Ranji took.

RANJI'S DREADFUL LEGACY

A captain in cricket has a responsibility that captains in other team sports, like football and rugby, do not have. The Australians have always followed the principle that they first select the best team and then choose from one of them to captain the side. Until 1952, England believed a captain should always be an amateur. It was only then that Len Hutton became the first professional to captain England, as it happened, during the 1952 series against India. Even then he never captained his native Yorkshire, which clung to its amateur status for another decade. With the princes ruling Indian cricket in the 1930s it was inevitable that a prince would captain the first Indian cricket team. The question was: which prince? The debate led to enormous problems and damaged Indian cricket even before it had made its international debut. All this could have been avoided had India's greatest cricketing prince, Ranji, taken charge of Indian cricket and allowed his nephew Duleep, then the best batsman in England, to captain India.

In the summer of 1932, despite playing only until mid-August and 21 of the 28 championship matches for Sussex, Duleep headed Sussex's batting with an average of 45.56 and scoring more runs than anybody else: 1139. Had he been able to carry on Sussex might well have recorded their first ever title. But Ranji not only did not help Indian cricket, he stopped Duleep playing for India. The Indians could still have had a cricketing prince play for them, the Nawab of Pataudi. In 1931, playing for Oxford, he had shown enormous potential as a batsman. His major scores were:

68 vs Yorkshire,
169 vs Gloucestershire,

183 not out vs The Army,
165 and 100 vs Surrey
138 vs Leveson-Gower's XI and
238 not out vs Cambridge University

In the lead-up to the selection of the 1932 team he had captained one of the trial sides, then withdrawn. The result was a sort of Indian farce with Pataudi in 1932 making his debut for Worcestershire against his fellow countrymen. And just to prove what India was missing, his 83 in the first innings was the second highest score in the match, 22 more than India's highest scorer, C. K. Nayudu.

Nayudu had captained in the match and led India to victory by three wickets, the first over a county side, and should have been captain on the tour. But he was a mere commoner, so the captain was the Maharaja of Porbandar, Natwarsinhji Bhavsinhji the ruler of Kathiawar, the princely state Gandhi came from. His brother-in-law, Prince Ghanshyamsinhji of Limbdi was the vice-captain. Initially, the Maharajkumar of Vizianagram (Vijay Ananda Gajapathi Raju also known as Vizzy), who was not a ruling prince, more of a rich landlord, was appointed deputy vice-captain. He did not tour and shall figure more prominently later in our story. Porbandar's cricketing abilities were quickly revealed. He played only in the first four matches, batting in five innings, making 0, 2, 0, 2, 2 and finished with a first-class average of 0.66. A popular joke was he was the only first-class cricketer in England to have more Rolls-Royces than runs. Limbdi could play, although he averaged 9.62, got injured and finally the Indians turned to Nayudu, who had spent the previous summer playing for the Indian Gymkhana at Osterley.

INDIAN CRICKET STRIKES A BLOW FOR RACIAL EQUALITY

The three-day Test began on Saturday, 25 June 1932. Twenty-four thousand people came to watch, almost filling Lord's to capacity in what was splendid cricket weather. Most of those gathered at the headquarters of the game were English. There were then very few Indians in England, but the ones that went to Lord's that day stood out in their colourful saris and turbans.

What those gathered that day at Lord's did not appreciate was that they were watching history being made which had a resonance that went far beyond cricket. For the first time a wholly non-white team would play a Test at the home of cricket. The Europeans then ruled the world as no one racial group had ever before done in history. Much of Asia was either ruled by Europeans or under their control. Nayudu going out to toss with Douglas Jardine meant a brown man was walking side by side in complete equality with a white man in one of the greatest clubs in the world. His fellow browns in India could not do that in the many clubs the British had in India. The British Indian Army, which had no Indian officers during World War I had, by 1932 acquired some, but they were still outnumbered by English officers and they could not discipline a British solider. Almost exactly a decade later, during World War II, Churchill, asked by Wavell, then commander-in-chief in India, to allow Indian officers to discipline British soldiers serving in the British Indian Army, responded furiously saying it was unacceptable for 'the poor, much harassed British soldier having to face the extra humiliation of being ordered about by a brown man'. Even at the end of the war, the highest-ranking Indian officer was a temporary colonel, K. C. Cariappa. Only after independence did he become the first Indian to command the Indian Army. And a year before Nayudu took the field at Lord's Churchill in a speech in Manchester had said that most Indians are 'primitive people'.

And at Lord's, for the first time there was an Indian nation, although it would be another fifteen years before India became a political nation. The team was called 'All-India', indicating that it was an alliance of British India and princely India, two very distinct entities. The hyphen only disappeared in 1947, when independent India emerged.

The match started with India springing a huge surprise on England. England's opening pair of Percy Holmes and Herbert Sutcliffe had the previous week scored 555 in a county match, then a world record for the first wicket. This time they managed only 8 and after twenty minutes England were 19 for 3, the damage being done by fast bowler Mohammad Nissar, and a run-out. Nissar was backed by Amar Singh and they proved such a deadly opening attack that the England innings lasted only four hours, during which they made 259, only two English batsmen making 50s. Nissar took India's first five-fer, 5 for 93, always the mark of bowling class, Amar Singh 2 for 75. Wally Hammond, England's greatest batsman, who was bowled by Amar Singh, was quite overawed by his bowling.

But while Nissar, Amar Singh and the other bowlers did well, Indian batsmen did not back them up and India lost by 158 runs. But this was no disgrace. Four years earlier at Lord's, on almost identical dates in June, the West Indies in their Test debut were beaten by an innings and 58 runs. Just over a year later, New Zealand playing its first Test, and that at home, had lost by eight wickets. Going back to 1888–89, South Africa, playing its first-ever Test, and that too at home, had lost by eight wickets. Apart from Australia, which won their first Test, England was in cricket the Victorian mother, ushering its children into the manhood of Test cricket with a rod in its hand. India had shown that it had a good attack, particularly quick bowlers; India's fast and fast-medium men, who included Jahangir Khan and Nayudu himself, took seventeen of the eighteen English wickets India claimed. India's quick bowlers would not have such dominance against England until the summer of 2018. It was Indian batting that had failed. Nayudu with 40 in the first innings had been the highest Indian scorer in the match and the contrast with his opposing number, Jardine, was evident. Mumbai-born Jardine, who in different circumstances might have captained India, made 79 and 85 not out, the highest scores in the match and crucial to England's victory. Not that Nayudu had reason to feel displeased by his overall tour performance as a batsman. Despite being thirty-seven, he had played in all twenty-six first-class matches scoring 1,618 runs at an average of 40.45 and heading the tour batting averages. *Wisden* made Nayudu one of its Five Cricketers of the Year, then considered the highest honour a cricketer could get. What made it so special was that in those days this honour was bestowed only once on a cricketer.

But Nayudu, far from being praised, began to be criticized by members of his own team who anonymously fed stories to the press about how useless he was as captain, that he had certain favourites and that Wazir Ali, a powerful right-hand bat and a more than useful medium-pace change bowler, would have been a better captain. By the end of the tour many members of the team were not on speaking terms with Nayudu. It was not, of course, easy to captain India. For many of the players the first time they met each other was just before a Test, and often their only common language was English, as each of the players spoke a different Indian language. Nayudu it must be said, was also a rather contradictory person. As his six-hitting shows, with the bat he could set a cricket ground ablaze; on the tour he hit 32 sixes. But off the field he could be authoritarian, almost behaving like a headmaster disciplining unruly boys. This did not go down well on the tour, particularly with players wanting to drink and have a good time off the field. There was much doubt whether Nayudu would captain India when Jardine brought his England team to India in the winter of 1933 for India's first home Test series and what was Jardine's farewell to Test cricket, Jardine had blotted his copybook by using bodyline tactics to thwart Donald Bradman and win back the Ashes in the winter of 1932. The repercussions of bodyline meant Harold Larwood, one of England's greatest fast bowlers, never again played for England and Jardine's team did not include many of England's best players: Hammond, Sutcliffe, Maurice Leyland, Eddie Paynter, Bob Wyatt, Gubby Allen and Les Ames, but it was still a strong side.

A BRIGHT NEW NORTHERN STAR

It was no surprise that the first Test in India was in Mumbai. Played from 15–18 December 1933 at Bombay Gymkhana, the one and only Test to be played at that ground, it drew a large crowd with 50,000 on the first day itself. The Test played over four days started on a Friday, which meant the second and third days were on the weekend and that remained the pattern for Tests for many decades in India. The British wanted to make it an advertisement for their great game and did that by granting a holiday on the first day and cutting working hours on the second, and there was a band ready to play 'God Save the King' whenever required.

There was much for the British to celebrate with India bowled out for 219 and England in reply making 438. On the third day with India at 21 for 2, it looked as if the match would not go into a fourth day. But then came the innings that surprised India and England. It was from Lala Amarnath, a twenty-one-year-old Lahore batsman making his Test debut. In the first innings batting at No. 3 he had been the highest scorer with 38. Now, helped by Nayudu, the pair put on 186 for the third wicket. Amarnath started at a breakneck speed and even though he slowed down his century came in 117 minutes. For a first Test century it was quite exceptional.

The crowd was ecstatic, and the newspapers the next day could not contain themselves. Amarnath's century was the front-page lead in the *Bombay Chronicle* whose four-decker headline read 'India's fine recovery after poor start, Amarnath saves India from disaster, flogs bowlers to all parts of field, 102 in superb style'. The story was considered so important that it was given much more prominence than Nehru's remarks that he disliked fascism. Yet there was a near tragedy when Amarnath got to his century. His son and biographer, Rajinder Amarnath, in his book, *Lala Amarnath*, quotes his father saying:

> When I completed the single to reach my century, C. K. Nayudu touched his bat at the crease and walked down the pitch to shake hands and congratulate me. Since the ball was still in play, the throw landed in the wicketkeeper's gloves with C.K. out of the crease. The wicketkeeper looked at his captain for his approval to run the Indian skipper out, but the English captain disapproved with a gesture. It was a wonderful display of true sporting spirit.

Amarnath was a 102 not out at the end of the day and when he returned to the pavilion discovered the impact he had made:

> I was unable to move an inch as hundreds of hands reached out to me

with gifts…ladies offered their precious ornaments to me, businessmen gave cash, and royalty, their Rolex watches and gold medals. The Maharaja of Chote Udaipur presented his gold cigarette case, and later took me on a lap of the ground where people showered me with gold and silver coins… When I reached the Taj Mahal hotel, a large crowd was waiting for me at the entrance. It took me almost 15 minutes to find my way into the lobby… On the bed lay a dozen-odd gold Rolex watches and other gifts…. There were so many functions arranged for me that at times I was literally dragged from one place to another to keep up with the appointments.

At the end of the match the young daughter of a Bombay jeweller, Dulan Mehta, came to his hotel room carrying, says Amarnath, 'a bag full of diamond jewellery and asked me if I would elope with her'. Amarnath told her to wait until the series was over but says that he knew he could never marry somebody like that and did not. The century meant the prediction of the pundit had come true. Soon after his birth a pundit, drawing up his horoscope, had predicted that the young boy would travel the world and rub shoulders with maharajas all his life. As it happened, within a couple of years rubbing shoulders with one maharaja brought Amarnath a lot of misery. He never again made a century and this established a trend which was not reversed until 1969 by Gundappa Viswanath, that an Indian batsman who scored a century in his first Test never scored one again.

Amarnath could not save India from defeat, and on the fourth day, after he was out for 118, India collapsed to 258, eight wickets falling for 51 and England emerged victorious by nine wickets. In Kolkata, India got its first draw, but in Chennai, despite some magnificent bowling by Amar Singh, taking 7 for 86 in the first innings, India lost by 202 runs. So, after four Tests, India had lost three, although by the standards of other countries this was not too bad. But what other countries did not have were club cricketers wanting to play Test cricket and even captain the national side. And one in particular caused Indian cricket much grief.

INDIAN CRICKET'S CHANAKYA

New Delhi's diplomatic enclave is named after Chanakya, the devilishly clever man who wrote the *Arthashastra*, giving advice to kings and rulers on how to plot, seize and maintain power. He predated Machiavelli by 1,700 years and the Italian probably copied many of his ideas. The Maharajakumar of Vizianagram, 'Vizzy', as the English nicknamed him, was to prove Indian cricket's Chanakya. No more than a club cricketer, he had sponsored cricket in the 1930s, bringing Jack Hobbs to India, but the prize he wanted was to captain India, and through a series of clever manoeuvres, including using the Nawab of Pataudi as a stalking horse to defeat Nayudu and cosying up to Lord Willingdon, the viceroy, he finally achieved his ambition in 1936 when India toured England again.

This must be the most extraordinary team any Test match-playing country has ever sent abroad. It was all about Vizzy who took to England thirty-six items of personal luggage and also two servants. There was no vice-captain, no selection committee. But he had a master in Captain R. J. Brittain-Jones, Willingdon's man in the Indian team, as he was the comptroller of the viceroy's household.

A cartoon in the *Worcester Evening News* when India played Worcester summed up Vizzy's team well.

India were seen as a joke team and were heading for a fall. They duly fell. They lost the first and third Test by nine wickets and only saved the second because of two cricketers who blossomed on the tour, one of whom would become one of India's greatest batsman. More about them later. Now we need to look at the event which overshadowed everything else on the tour and at the end of it led to a committee set up by the board to enquire into the affair, headed by Sir John Beaumont, Chief Justice of the Bombay High Court. At the centre of it was our northern star, Amarnath.

THE AMARNATH AFFAIR

Lala Amarnath had started the tour in great form, having scored 606 in twenty-one innings and taken thirty-two wickets at 21 runs per wicket. In a statement he later made to the Nawab of Bhopal, board president—which was provided to the Beaumont Committee—he would give fascinating details.Vizzy, he says, liked him and, 'I generally went in his [captain's] car to the field.' But in a match against Leicester in May there was an altercation:

> I was bowling from the pavilion end and asked the captain to remove the third man and place him between covers and point. Instead of acceding to my request, the captain said curtly, 'Don't waste time. Carry on.' ...After the match was finished, I was discussing the game and said that I had never saw [sic] a captain refusing to assist a bowler so curtly. When the captain was dressed, he called out to me and taking me aside asked me why I had shown my anger on the field. I said that I was not angry but was hurt to think that he refused to let me place a fielder so curtly. To this Vizzy said, that he was captain of the team and he could do whatever he liked.

This argument got quite heated and was resolved with the help of Captain Brittain-Jones, who asked Amarnath to say sorry to Vizzy and shake his hand, which he did. However, soon there were problems with the Englishman, who, according to Amarnath:

> ...accused me of running after women. I was startled by this new accusation. Ever since I arrived in England, I was always in bed by 10.30 pm on match days and by 11.30 pm on off days. I gave no occasion for anyone to reprimand me for late nights. I told the manager I had come to England to play cricket, which I like much more than women. Unable to pin me down, the manager then said he had seen me with women. To this I replied, that he could not have seen me misbehaving disgracefully or in a compromising way on any occasion. He was not in a position to make any such remarks. With all allegations refuted, Brittain-Jones said that he believed me and it ended this episode.

The flashpoint came when India played the Minor Counties at Lord's between 17 and 19 June. Amarnath got very upset that, having been told he would bat at No. 4 or 5, he was sent in at No. 7 and got only ten minutes batting against a side where he hoped to regain his form. To Bhopal he admitted he:

> ...came back to the pavilion rather excited. While undressing, I threw about my pads, gloves etc. near my bag in the corner. I felt quite disgusted and talked to several players in Punjabi. What I said was slang and it meant that I had not wasted four years uselessly but learned cricket. Similar slang has always been used without meaning any offence among Punjabi players. The captain asked me, 'Are you talking to me' I replied I was not talking to anyone...in the evening there was a conference in the captain's room.

Following this Amarnath was summoned by Brittain-Jones and told:

> 'All right, I am sending you back to India next week.' An hour later I was in Wazir Ali's room, the manager asked me to vacate the hotel by 10.30 the next day and leave by *Kaiser-I-Hind*. I was rather surprised at the attitude of the manager and realising he meant to keep his threat, I asked him for another chance to prove my sincerity to the team, but he replied that he could not alter his decision.

Although there were attempts at reconciliation Amarnath left for India on the *Kaiser-I-Hind* and a plan to send him back to England did not succeed. A picture of him climbing aboard the ship wearing a suit and trilby sums up his utter dejection. However, India had not seen the last of Amarnath and like Lazarus he kept coming back from the dead and would remain a part of Indian cricket as player until the 1950s and as selector a lot longer. Looked at broadly, the 1936 tour also marked the end of the first phase of Indian cricket with the departure of Nayudu from international cricket, although he went on playing domestic cricket until he was sixty-nine. In that sense he outdid W. G. Grace, the original grand old man of English cricket, whose last first-class match was at the age of sixty.

Nayudu's last Test innings came at that traditional England theatre for farewells, the Oval, in the third Test on 18 August 1936. Twelve years later, Bradman would leave cricket on the same stage, scoring a duck. That did not matter as Australia won by an innings. Nayudu had to make sure India did not suffer an innings defeat. Until that stage he had had a miserable Test series, failing thrice to get into double figures and a highest score of 34. Gubby Allen, the England captain and opening bowler, had been his nemesis.

Now, despite being hit on the chest by Allen, which was such a hard blow he struggled to breathe, he played his usual attacking game making 81, his highest Test score and which also meant he had scored 1,000 runs on the tour. With nobody else making even a 50 (Vizzy batting No. 9 made 1) he could not save India and England strolled to victory by nine wickets.

Nayudu would go on playing a huge part in Indian cricket as administrator and selector. Even Chandu Borde, who belongs to the second wave of Indian cricket that started in 1953, had first-hand experience of Nayudu playing cricket, playing against the great man in the 1952 Ranji Trophy semi-final for Maharashtra against Holkar. Maharashtra batted first and Nayudu, then fifty-eight, stood at silly mid-on and the Maharashtra batsman Marutirao Mathe's powerful drive hit him on the shin. The bowler looked concerned, but Nayudu told him to just carry on bowling. The match was played in extremely hot weather but during the drinks break he did not want players to consume water. While he was persuaded to let the Maharashtra players have drinks every forty-five minutes he still would not allow his team to quench their thirst. The previous year, when Mumbai's Dattu Phadkar had hit him in the mouth, dislodging two front teeth and bloodying his shirt, he asked Mumbai's captain to instruct his bowler to carry on bowling as fast as he wanted to. Borde also recalls how just before the Indian team was picked for the 1954–55 tour of Pakistan, Nayudu conducted the selection trials in Delhi. On this occasion he batted without pads and told the young fast bowlers, 'I want you all to bowl fast. Don't you want to be picked for India?' He middled every ball.

Nayudu's figures may not put him in the top bracket, a Test average of 25, but he only got to play seven matches. In first-class cricket, where he played 207 matches, his aggregate of 11,825 runs, with an average of 35.94, 26 hundreds and 58 half-centuries was more a reflection of his worth. And what cannot be denied is the enormous hold he had on the Indian cricket public as illustrated by this story that Sarojini Naidu, India's great poetess and a redoubtable freedom fighter, told. Once she signed an autograph for a young boy and when she asked him if he knew who she was, he said, 'You are C. K. Nayudu's wife!'

Chapter 4

INDIA'S FIRST FAB FOUR

The second phase of the first wave of Indian cricket saw the rise of the original Fab Four of Indian cricket: Vijay Merchant, Lala Amarnath, Vijay Hazare and Vinoo Mankad. If the twenty-first century Fab Four was Tendulkar-led, the original Fab Four was Merchant-led. To call Merchant, Amarnath, Hazare and Mankad Fab Four and even compare them to the twenty-first century Fab Four may seem absurd. They only ever played three Tests together but that reflected the fact that between 1936 and 1946 India did not play a single Test. Even afterwards there were many seasons when no Test team toured India and India had to be content with so-called Commonwealth teams, many of which were put together by George Duckworth, the former Lancashire and England wicketkeeper who had played against India in 1936. And while Tendulkar was a guru-like figure in his Fab Four, having made his debut almost a decade before the other three, Merchant did not quite tower over the others. Indeed, they came in pairs.

Merchant and Amarnath made their Test debut together in India's first-ever Test at home on 15 December 1933 where Amarnath, as we have seen, outshone Merchant. Hazare and Mankad made their Test debut together on 22 June 1946 at Lord's. Ganguly and Dravid, it must be said, did make their Test debut together and, like Hazare and Mankad, also at Lord's almost exactly fifty years later. And, unlike the Tendulkar Fab Four, the original Fab Four all had one mentor, Nayudu. Merchant as a fifteen-year-old was present at the Bombay Gymkhana on 1 December 1926 when Nayudu set his then world record of 11 sixes. He would always regard it as the greatest innings he had ever seen. As we have seen, Nayudu was batting with Amarnath when he made his century, Hazare considered Nayudu his mentor and Nayudu had a huge influence on Mankad's career, although not always beneficially. The Tendulkar-led Fab Four had no such figure from India's cricketing past.

There were other differences. Mankad was India's first great all-rounder and Amarnath, if not in his class, was also an all-rounder, a good bowler who often opened the bowling. Hazare, too, was a useful bowler in Tests and in first-class cricket took more wickets than Amarnath and a lot more than any of the Tendulkar-led Fab Four did. In first-class cricket even Merchant turned his arm. The only thing the Merchant-led Fab Four did not do was keep wicket, which Dravid did. And while the modern Fab Four all had coaches, Merchant never had a coach, although Duleep would say he would have been an even greater player had he been coached.

Both Merchant and Amarnath played key roles as selectors with Merchant taking, as we shall see, a crucial decision in 1971. As I write, the Tendulkar Fab Four are emerging as administrators, but that reflects the unprecedented role now played in Indian cricket by the Supreme Court of India.

One other interesting contrast between the original Merchant Fab Four and the Tendulkar Fab Four is that the first one was more cosmopolitan. Hazare was Christian and while Amarnath was a Hindu, as Peter Oborne revealed in *Wounded Tiger: A History of Cricket in Pakistan*, he was brought up in pre-partition Lahore by Tawakkal Majid, a Muslim. Jamil 'Jimmy' Rana, Majid's son, told Oborne:

> On the way home from a match my father passed some boys playing
> in the street. One of them unleashed a most sublime cover drive. He
> asked him to play it again and he did. He had a very good eye. The
> boy was Lala Amarnath. My father said, 'Take me to your family.' They
> turned out to be very poor people. He offered to take him into our
> house, and pay for him to learn to be a cricketer. They were delighted.
> As a result, Amaranth was brought up as member of our family.

Oborne spoke to Rajinder Amarnath and he told him he knew nothing of this as his father had never mentioned it. However, it is a fact that Lala Amarnath was very poor, as Fazal Mahmood who played a lot of club cricket in Lahore with Amarnath has recorded. Amarnath 'worked in the railways workshops in Lahore, on a salary of half a rupee a day'. In the era we are talking about, despite the growing political problems between Hindus and Muslims, the two communities lived amicably in Lahore and several other places in the Punjab that is now Pakistan and such Muslim generosity to a poor Hindu boy is very believable.

In contrast, the Tendulkar Fab Four are all Hindu Brahmins. It is a matter of speculation what the social and cultural impact might have been on Indian cricket had the subcontinent remained united after 1947. However, while the Merchant Fab Four, apart from Amarnath, all came from the west of India, the Tendulkar Fab Four can claim to represent all of India: from the west with Tendulkar through the south with Laxman, Dravid in many ways from the centre and Ganguly the east.

THE MERCHANT OF RUNS

Vijay Madhavji Merchant—that was not his real surname, but one given
to him by the principal of his Mumbai school, Bharda—was unlike the
previous generation of Indian cricketers. There was no princely influence in
his upbringing. He came from the Gujarati business community and is the
only cricketer to describe himself as an industrialist, his family being owners
of cotton mills. The family name, Merchant's real surname, was Thackersey
and Thackersey Mills were well known in Mumbai and were still there
when I was growing up in the city.

Merchant brought what was very much a businessman's touch to the
game, always carefully planning for every contingency. So, before the 1936
tour, he tried to recreate in Mumbai batting conditions he would find in
England, which meant trying to cope with swing and seam, something
batsmen do not have to worry about in India. In England's green and
often moist, misty conditions the ball can swing all day. In India, only a
shiny new ball swings. On the hot, dusty surfaces it soon loses its shine and
then it does nothing to surprise a batsman. This diligent study of English
conditions came in very handy during the 1936 tour. In cricket history
Merchant is the great opener. Before Gavaskar arrived, any all-time Indian
team would list Merchant as batting at No. 1. But he did not begin life as
an opener. When in 1933 he made his debut for India at the first Test in
Mumbai, he batted No. 6 and retained that position throughout the series.
On the 1936 tour in his first seven innings, scoring 366 runs, he batted
either at No. 3 or No. 5. A broken finger put him on the sidelines for
three weeks; after that, apart from one occasion, he opened. He scored 600
more runs than any other Indian batsman on the tour and of his total of
1,745 runs, 1,300 came when opening the innings. Opening the batting in
England has always been considered the most challenging task in cricket
because of the movement an opener has to cope with. It speaks volumes
for Merchant's character that he could make the transition so well and it
is a great contrast with the other Vijay, Hazare, who tried to become an
opener on India's next tour to England in 1946, made 0 and went back
to No. 4, the position he liked.

Merchant's other capacity to adapt was shown by how well he took
to playing six days a week during the tour. Indian cricketers were just not
used to it. Before Merchant came on the 1936 tour, he had had six seasons
of first-class cricket and played twenty-four first-class matches, and in one
season, 1930–31, none at all. In 1936, in five months he played twenty-three
first-class matches. He could do it because he had kept himself fit, running
long distances and skipping. Cricket meant so much to him that apart from

diet and sleeping regular hours, he did not drink or smoke and refused to be distracted. So, although the Indian film industry was developing, he did not go to films. Merchant would later say that he never had a plan when going out to bat, that he was never able to distinguish between the inswing and the outswing, the googly from the leg-break. The essence of his technique was to concentrate 100 per cent on the ball and get to the pitch of the ball and play it.

He had come to England with his career figures reading: twenty-four matches, 1,778 runs, average 52.59. On the 1936 tour he scored as many runs as he had scored during the previous six seasons. By the time he returned to India his career figures were: 3,523 runs, average 51.80. By the end of his career, his first-class figures were dwarfed by only one man: Bradman. The Don's first-class figures are legendary: 338 innings, 28,067 runs, average 95.14. Merchant played nearly a hundred fewer innings, 229, scored 13,248 runs and averaged 71.22. It is a pity that injury meant Merchant did not go on India's first tour of Australia in 1947–48, for the meeting on the cricket field of Bradman and Merchant would have been fascinating. India on that tour often batted on sticky-dog wickets affected by rain and there is no reason to doubt Merchant would have adjusted to these conditions and the series could have been a sort of 1940s version of Brian Lara and Sachin Tendulkar playing in the same match. Merchant had great respect for the Don. In 1948, the Australian ship carrying their cricketers home after their tour of England docked at Mumbai. Merchant, realizing Bradman was not planning to step ashore, went on to the ship to pay his respects to the greatest batsman in the world.

THE METHOD MAN AND HIS IMPROVISING PARTNER

It was in the second Test, at Old Trafford on 27 July 1936, that Merchant really announced himself to the world of cricket. He also showed how he could adjust to a partner who was not remotely like him. India that day looked doomed. In reply to India's 203, England made 571 for 8 declared, which meant India had to make 368 merely to make England bat again. Yet, until then India's highest score had been 258. Merchant, who had opened with Dattaram Hindlekar in the first Test, had a new partner, Mushtaq Ali. Merchant had got on the wrong side of Vizzy by suggesting he should step down as captain. Vizzy did not forget, and as Mushtaq got ready to walk out for the second innings he told him to run out Merchant. After all, in the first innings Mushtaq had been run out for 13, so it was now time to pay Merchant back. Mushtaq knew the first innings run-out was not Merchant's fault but a freak accident. A shot from Merchant hit Mushtaq's bat as he was backing up, bounced to Arthur Fagg, fielding at short mid-wicket, and he ran out Mushtaq. Mushtaq had no intention of following the captain's orders, and as the pair walked to the middle Mushtaq told Merchant what Vizzy had said. Merchant, laughingly said, 'Just you try,' Mushtaq joined in the laughter and a bond was formed between Mushtaq, perhaps the most unpredictable cricketer who has ever played for India, and Merchant, the ultimate method man. They did have one thing in common. Like Merchant, Mushtaq was not an opener, and on his Test debut, which had come only a Test after Merchant, he was in the side as a left-arm spinner and batted No. 7, although both in that Test in Kolkata and the next at Chennai injuries meant he opened in the second innings. Not until Sehwag emerged more than seventy years later, another middle order batsman promoted to open, did India have an opener like Mushtaq.

Merchant never wrote his autobiography. Mushtaq, along with Hazare, was one of the few cricketers of his generation to do so. But while Hazare, reflecting the man, called his memoir *A Long Innings*, Mushtaq, called his memoir *Cricket Delightful*, the title capturing how he felt about the game. In a foreword to Mushtaq's memoir, Keith Miller called him 'the Errol Flynn of cricket—dashing, flamboyant, swashbuckling and immensely popular whenever he played'. Miller described bowling to Mushtaq, batting in a pith helmet, against the Australian Services team in New Delhi in 1945. Miller bowled a good length delivery outside the off stump, Mushtaq hit it past square-leg 'with the speed and accuracy of a Robin Hood arrow in flight'. Miller soon discovered this was not a lucky shot but marked Mushtaq as 'a champion'.

At Old Trafford, while Mushtaq wore a conventional cap, the Mancunians saw Mushtaq fire many Robin Hood arrows in response to the English bowling. Mushtaq would later confess Indians batted like 'irresponsible kids confident of getting to the top [of Mount Everest]'. The Indian 50 came in three-quarters of an hour, Mushtaq's own 50 in eighty minutes. England bowled their first maiden over only after an hour of the innings had been played. As he would do with Miller in 1945, every time Gubby Allen bowled outside the off stump Mushtaq pulled it to leg for four. Merchant often came down the wicket to caution him and, as he got into the nineties, Hammond came up and asked him to steady on if he wanted his century. This he did before the end of the day's play, the first Indian to score a century abroad, and it ended with India 190 for no wicket, Mushtaq 106, Merchant 79. The then world record for the opening wicket was 323, held by two Englishmen, Jack Hobbs and Wilfred Rhodes. Merchant knew how wonderful it would be to claim this record and the next day reminded

Mushtaq that it was only 134 runs away. But such targets never meant anything to Mushtaq. The pair had got to 203 when Mushtaq was caught and bowled by Walter Robins for 112. Merchant and Mushtaq had batted together for a mere two and a half hours. The Merchant–Mushtaq opening stand remained a record by overseas batsmen in England until 1964 and an Indian first-wicket record against England in England until 1979, when it was broken by Sunil Gavaskar and Chetan Chauhan when they were trying to win a Test, not save it.

Merchant could have been out on 91 when Hammond at slip dropped a catch and showed his nerves when he got into the eighties, taking an hour to go from 88 to 100. Merchant and Mushtaq had ensured India would not be rolled over, and with the lower order responding, India got a draw. Merchant and Mushtaq would open on three other occasions in a Test, all in England, with the last at the Oval in 1946 seeing both batsmen run out, although this had nothing to do with Vizzy. By then, of course, the other two of the Fab Four, Hazare and Mankad, were well established.

OVERSEAS COACHES DISCOVER INDIAN GEMS

Hazare and Mankad could not have been more different in how they saw their cricket. Yet there was much in common in the way they were shaped to become the cricketers they did become. Both of them had enormous princely influence, both benefited from foreign coaches. Mankad's princely benefactor was Digvijaysinhji of Nawanagar, Ranji's nephew and successor as ruler. He had brought in Bert Wensley, the old Sussex professional, as captain to help construct a team that could win the Ranji Trophy, the national championships that had started in 1934, and he succeeded. The longer-term influence on Indian cricket was the one Wensley had on Mankad, who had been first spotted by Duleep. Mulvantrai Himatlal Mankad, Vinoo to his schoolmates, wanted to be another Amar Singh and Nissar and, until the age of nineteen, bowled medium pace, except he bowled left-handed but batted right-handed. Wensley quickly saw that Mankad was too short and stocky to become a fast bowler. But he had talent and could become a spinner, and he taught him the arts of spin: flight, variation of pace. Wensley also warned him not to bowl the off-break as this would mean he would lose control over his grip and action. Much better to bowl the leg-break, which is the natural break. The result was that when Mankad bowled to a right-hander, he nearly always bowled the leg-break, delivered with a slight round-arm action. He became so adept at varying his pace that it was said no two balls by him were the same. His deadly ball was a faster ball which went with the arm. In the years to come this was the ball that brought Mankad most of his wickets, with batsmen surprised by it. Wensley also converted Mankad into an opening bat, a process that was encouraged by Duleep. So, the man who became the first great Indian all-rounder—arguably India's greatest ever—was fashioned under Sussex tutelage.

Mankad really made himself known to India when, in the winter of 1937, a cobbled-together English side visited India, reflecting the fact that no one wanted to play Test cricket with India, West Indies and South Africa having turned down invitations. Lionel Tennyson, the captain, had last played for England in August 1921, captaining England to a 3–0 Ashes loss and retired as Hampshire captain in 1933. He had heard of the luxurious living of the British in India and wanted to shoot a panther: he did go on a shoot, but bagged a goat instead. When he played for England, the scorecard listed his name as Hon. L. H. Tennyson. The Indians called him 'My Lord, the Captain' and he went around the country repeating the same speech. While his players had all the comforts that Europeans then enjoyed, one of them, Alf Gover, who had opened the bowling in the 1936 Old Trafford Test, suffered from tummy problems which had dramatic consequences. He took some pills from an Indian doctor and, thinking he was fit, decided to play in a match and was about to open the bowling:

> I commenced my long run, but in my final stride to the bowling crease, just prior to delivering the ball, my faith in the local doctor quickly evaporated and, still clutching the ball, I tore up the wicket and past the batsman, who was backing away in some trepidation. The skipper called out to me as I passed and I tried to explain in one single word what happened only to receive the answer, 'That's ridiculous, you are fit to play.' Still at full speed I called out again, using the simple word that referred to dysentery, and carried on. [He is referring to the four letter word that starts with s]. I had almost reached the boundary in a time worthy of an Olympic sprinter when my long-leg fielder, Joe Hardstaff, called out, 'What's the matter, Alf?' I threw him the ball. 'I won't need this where I am going.' Tearing up the steps I met the twelfth man coming down. 'Out of my way!' I cried, shoving him to one side. But all to no avail, I lost by two yards.

As for the cricket that was played, Mankad, who had made an excellent debut in the Ranji Trophy, was top of the batting and the bowling averages of both teams—62.66 with the bat, 14.53 with the ball—and he was crucial in India's two victories in Kolkata and Chennai. Tennyson could not believe he was just twenty, and said that he would certainly be part of a 'mythical World XI' to play Mars or some other planet.

If Sussex fashioned India's first great spinner, then Clarrie Grimmett, a New Zealander who was a vital part of Australia's bowling attack between 1925 and 1936, transformed the other Vijay, whose batting rivalry with Merchant would be a feature of the first wave. He played against Tennyson, but as a medium-pace change bowler, and in the 'Test' in Lahore batted No. 9. As he records in his memoir, he was batting when an earthquake shook the ground and the crowds swarmed on to the pitch. One panic-stricken English fielder shouted that the end of the world had come. In fact, little damage was done. In the years to come it would be Hazare's batting that would worry fielders, and this was largely due to the tutoring he received from Grimmett.

Grimmett came into Hazare's life when Hazare was employed by the Maharaja of Dewas Senior as his aide-de-camp. The maharaja's brother-in-law, the Raja of Jath, hired Grimmett to teach him the googly. Grimmett also tutored Hazare. India did not have many leg-spinners, but Grimmett at once worked out he could not convert Hazare from a useful medium-pace bowler into a leg-spinner. However, his batting he could improve. And improve Hazare did, benefiting from Grimmett's shrewdness.

Many a coach might have changed Hazare's batting stance. As Hazare himself admits, it was not great to look at: 'hands too far apart on the handle of the bat to permit a free swing of the bat...bat firmly between the pads almost locked in'. Grimmett, using a tennis ball and bowling not from the full length of the pitch but a much shorter distance, instructed Hazare in how to play each delivery. They also played together in matches, after which Grimmett would analyse what Hazare had done. By then Hazare was twenty-two and it is a measure of the impact Grimmett had that Hazare regards him as his guru.

FROM PACE TO SPIN

Mankad's rise meant Indian cricket went from the fast-bowling era to the spin era. Before Mankad Indian teams had no problems finding fast bowlers; their batsmen played pace quite well, but it was spinners Indian cricket lacked. So, while Indian batsmen played pace well, they often had problems against spin, with leg-spin being a great mystery. In 1933–34, when England beat India by 202 runs at Chennai, Hedley Verity took 7 for 49 in the first innings, one of the best returns an overseas spinner has ever got in India.

Merchant was the highest scorer with 26 in a total of 145. And on the 1936 tour of England in the three Tests the English spinners took 31 of 55 Indian wickets that fell. In contrast India's bowling was carried by Nissar and Amar Singh. Over the decades, as India pined for fast bowlers, Nissar and Amar Singh were glorified. Loss tends to make what gems you have seem even more wonderful. They did not play enough Test cricket for us to claim they were among the best-ever fast bowlers. However, what can be recorded is their performance. Amar Singh played seven Tests, Nissar six and their Test figures read:

> Nissar: Balls: 1,211; Runs: 707; Wickets: 25; Average: 28.28
> Amar Singh: Balls: 2,182; Runs: 858; Wickets: 28; Average: 30.64.

All, of course, against England, whose batting line-up between 1932 and 1936 included Percy Holmes, Herbert Sutcliffe, Frank Woolley, Wally Hammond, Douglas Jardine, Harold Gimblett, Maurice Leyland, Bob Wyatt, Joe Hardstaff, as strong a line-up as any that has taken the field. So how well did Nissar and Amar Singh do? Nissar took five wickets in an innings three times in six Tests, and Amar Singh twice in seven Tests. What makes this all the more significant is that because of lack of depth in India's bowling, and true world-class spinners, they also had to bowl a lot of overs. So, in the first Test in 1932, of 195.1 overs the Indians bowled in the two England innings, Nissar and Amar Singh between them bowled 116.1, Amar Singh himself bowling 72 of them. As for the spinners, they bowled eighteen overs. Similar figures can be given for the other Tests India played in the 1930s.

Tennyson's tour was the last time this formidable pair bowled together. In 1940, Amar Singh was dead, seven months short of his thirtieth birthday, a victim of pneumonia. Nissar lived until 1963, by which time the idea that India had pace bowlers seemed like fantasy. Not producing another such pair meant Indian cricket developed a great 'hurt' about fast bowling which was deepened by the fact that Pakistan continued to produce fast bowlers in much the same quantity united India had in the 1920s and 1930s. This led to all sorts of extraordinary reasons given for India's failure, including that Hindus do not eat beef. And that Gandhi's ahimsa, non-violent philosophy meant spin not pace was seen as the true Indian weapon of choice.

RUNS GALORE IN AN OCCUPIED, HOSTILE LAND

World War II, the most devastating war in history, inevitably had an impact on cricket. It put a stop to first-class cricket in England and Australia. India did not see much fighting, except in Assam and Nagaland towards the end, but the conflict tore India apart. Millions of Indians supported the British with a million Indians joining the Indian armed forces, the largest volunteer army of the war. But Indians wanting freedom rebelled so massively that Gandhi's Quit India Movement launched in August 1942 (now called 'the August movement') saw the British use repressive measures, including whipping and machine-gunning from the air. On 20 March 1943, Major General Rob Lockhart, military secretary in the India Office, wrote in a secret note: 'For the duration of the War, and probably for some time after, India must be considered as an occupied and hostile country.' Lord Linlithgow reported to Churchill that it was 'by far the most serious rebellion since that of 1857, the gravity of which we have so far concealed from the world for reasons of military security'. In August 1944 the American consul wrote to his government that 'representatives of the United States government in India should bear in mind at all times that they are functioning in a police state.' And in 1944 in Bengal a famine caused by British indifference to the Indian plight and the incompetence of the local Indian administration saw four million Bengalis die, the worst famine in twentieth-century South Asian history.

So, what happened to Indian cricket between 1939 and 1945? It prospered like it had never done before. In the midst of war and destruction, Indian batsmen, led by the two Vijays, turned to runs.

The war saw the rise of Hazare as a great batsman. He was recruited to play for Maharashtra, the tournament's rabbits (before 1939 Maharashtra had not won a single match in the Ranji Trophy). In his second match he made 316 not out, becoming the first Indian to score a triple century; before that Amarnath had been the highest scorer with 241. The innings was classic Hazare. He batted for seven hours and accelerated towards the end with his last 151 coming at a run a minute. By the end of the season he had out-Merchanted Merchant, having scored 619 runs in five innings with an average of 154.75. For the next decade the two matched each other: if one made a huge score, the other—often in the very next match—responded and it became known as the battle of the two Vijays. Hazare, putting on his bowling hat, also sometimes took Merchant's wicket. And though Merchant did bowl in first-class cricket, he never took Hazare's wicket. The Indian media loved to highlight all sorts of contrasts between the two, but the one they never highlighted was that Merchant was Hindu and Hazare Christian. Not many Indians knew Hazare was Christian, just as in my generation not many of us knew Chandu Borde was Christian. The Hindu Gymkhana, that so zealously made sure every member was Hindu, unaware he was a Christian, even asked him to play for them. With newspapers never making reference to his middle name, Samuel, I only got to know he was a Christian in the 1980s when I first began to write books on Indian cricket.

The two played many great innings, but the Pentangular matches in the 1943–44 season are worth highlighting. In the Rest vs Muslims match, Hazare, batting for a time with his brother, Vivek, made 248 in a score of 395, breaking Merchant's record of 243 not out set in November 1941. The innings helped the Rest beat the Muslims, and in the final, a week later, they met the Hindus and Merchant came back with his answer. He scored 250 not out, having batted for five minutes short of seven hours and declared with the Hindu score 518 for 8. Hazare, who had bowled nearly fifty overs, was tired, and he scored only 59. The Rest, all out for 133, followed on. The match looked as good as over with the Rest 60 for 5. But now Hazare found a partner in his brother, Vivek, a moderate batsman but one who could hold his end up. And as Vivek did just that, Vijay made runs, first equalling Merchant's 250 and finally reaching 309. What is astonishing about this innings is that the entire side only made 387, which means Hazare made nearly 80 per cent of the score. Merchant showed no rancour, and what followed after the end of Hazare's innings showed the contrast in their personalities. Hazare had walked back to the pavilion, oblivious to the crowd wanting to acclaim his innings. Merchant, more receptive to the public mood and sensing that cricketers must acknowledge their fans, persuaded a reluctant Hazare to appear on the CCI balcony and say a few words. Hazare, never the best of speakers, did not know what to say and Merchant coached him, suggesting he should thank them and remind them they would in a week's time have a replay as Merchant's Mumbai would meet Hazare's Baroda in the Ranji Trophy.

But while Merchant was generous on this occasion the competitor in him wanted to answer Hazare when he next got to the crease. His chance came at the end of December 1943 when Mumbai played Maharashtra. Merchant, back in the middle order at No. 5, in an innings that stretched over two days, went past Hazare's 309 and he was 359 not out when Mumbai were all out for 735. Had Indian cricketers played as many first-class games as English cricketers did it would be fair to say Merchant and Hazare would have matched, even surpassed, the records of their contemporaries in England. The two Vijays' batting style was like the men they were: measured. Neither of them would ever bat like Nayudu did against Gilligan's team and hit sixes just for fun, although when Hazare went to his triple century in the match against the Hindus, he did it, Sehwag-style, with a six. But by then nine wickets were down and he knew he had to play a shot not normally associated with him. Merchant, who early in his career liked to hook, influenced by Bradman, decided not to play a shot which carries so much risk. The result of this was that by the mid-1940s Indian batsmen copying Merchant and Hazare rarely lifted the ball. This was so deeply ingrained in Indian cricket, particularly cricket in Mumbai, that, as Gavaskar recalls, when he was growing up in the 1960s he was told you 'do not hit the ball six inches above the ground'. And if he did not follow this instruction, then he was punished and would be asked by his coach to lift the bat above his head and with his pads still on run around the ground as a punishment. Now with IPL, batsmen are more likely to be punished if they do not lift the ball. It would be interesting to see what Merchant would have made of the deliberate lofting of the ball that is the essence of IPL batting.

The war also saw the two Vijays batting together in the 1944–45 season for CCI against an English Services XI. They put on 382 runs in the fourth-wicket partnership, Hazare 200 not out and Merchant retiring after reaching 201. And here both showed they could score runs quickly when they wanted. Merchant nearly hit a century before lunch, Hazare adding 113 runs between start of play and lunch to add to his overnight 50. But then, this was not a serious competitive match and both batsmen, normally so risk-averse, did not mind taking risks.

Around the great wartime run-making of the two Vijays, others also made runs with the 1944–45 season Ranji final between Mumbai and Holkar staged at the CCI producing a contest which was the only Indian domestic match selected by *Wisden* in its 100 matches of the twentieth century.

Mumbai batting first scored 462. Holkar responded with 360, Mushtaq Ali making 109. Merchant, who had made four in the first innings, made 278, and the double century meant he was the only player to score four double centuries in a season outside England in his home country. Mumbai ended up on 764, then the second highest second innings score (the highest being 770 by New South Wales against South Australia in 1920–21). Holkar would have to make 867 to win, otherwise Mumbai would win because of their first innings lead.

This looked extremely unlikely, but an amazing partnership between Mushtaq Ali and Denis Compton kept all of Mumbai on edge. After Mushtaq fell for 139, Compton carried on, making 249 not out. In the end, Holkar fell 377 runs short of their target, but no spectator could complain. They had seen a cricket match that provided them thirty-three hours of play, during which 2,078 runs were scored and 694.5 overs bowled.

In one of the great ironies of the war Indian cricket found the post-war world as disillusioning as the British rulers of India and the Congress. The

British emerged from the war confident it could retain its precious jewel without realizing the war had signalled the end of the British occupation of India. The Congress, which had played its war-time cards abysmally, paid no heed to the fact that Muhammad Ali Jinnah had been the victor of the war and planted the seeds of Partition. Indian cricket, basking in the copious run-making of Merchant, Hazare and others, contemplated world domination only to find the reality of international competition shattering.

Chapter 5

ALL-INDIA BOW OUT

GUPTA'S HAT AND THE BBC

The Indian tour of 1946 could be said to be Indian cricket's great gift to cricket broadcasting in Britain. The BBC had an Eastern Service whose biggest audience was in India with George Orwell broadcasting to India urging Indians to support the British war effort during the war. Now the world was different. A month before the team arrived in England a three-man British Cabinet mission arrived in India to look into transferring power to the Indians. This prompted the Nawab of Pataudi, the captain and a very good speaker, to joke before the Lord's Test, 'The task before my Prime Minister, Jawaharlal Nehru, is simpler than mine. For, I shall have to face eleven Englishmen tomorrow, whereas he will have to face only three.'

The BBC thought it would be a good idea to have a ten-minute report on India's first two matches at Worcester and Oxford and the three Tests. The BBC had an Indian commentator, Abdul Hamid Sheikh, who did live commentary in Hindi for five minutes from 3.23 p.m. to 3.28 p.m. Greenwich Mean Time, 8.53 p.m. to 8.58 p.m. Indian Standard Time. But, despite the fact the broadcasts were meant for India, the BBC felt his English was too Indian. So, five minutes of English commentary, from 4.10 p.m. to 4.15 p.m., 9.40 p.m. to 9.45 p.m., Indian time was by John Arlott, a former policeman, who had been hired as producer because of his ability as a poet. The English in India hated it saying 'the last thing they wanted to listen to is about Indians'. But the Indians loved it and the BBC soon extended it to cover the entire tour. Thus was launched the career of cricket's greatest commentator whose unique voice made ball by ball cricket commentary an essential part of the English summer. In the decades to come, Indians, including myself, wanting to be cricket commentators would try and imitate his unique style and make fools of ourselves. Arlott made it his mission to know the Indians and the first person he met was Pankaj Gupta, whose first love was hockey but who managed three cricket tours, England in 1946 and 1952 and Australia in 1947–48. In the 1936 Berlin Olympics he produced the tricolour in the Indian dressing room before the final which the Indian team saluted and went on to win the gold. Yet the British thought of him as a valuable collaborator and two years before he brought the cricket team to England he had been awarded the Order of the British Empire. Arlott recorded:

> I went to the team's hotel on the day after they were due to arrive. In the hall of the hotel was a small man (Gupta Sahib) wearing a blue trilby hat so soft as to change its shape and significance with each of the varied emotions that wracked him (in the entire four months this hat never attained a final shape). He had discovered that the telephone bore him a grudge, that airborne cricketers are forever announced but never arrive, and that, as T. S. Eliot had discovered before him, 'April is the cruellest month.' He had tickets for the Association Football cup final but no team to take to the match, limousines to command but no one to fill them, words to utter, but no ears to receive them. The rain peered greyly down from the sky and dully up from the sodden streets and I knew that cricket tours and English summers were mental mirages. Gradually in twos and threes the Indian team arrived, their heads ringing still with the noise of airplane engines, to wait in vain for their seaborne cricket gear, to skid through a mud-and-rain bound mockery of net-practice at Lord's and to leave, on the evening before the game for Worcester, in a coach that lost its way in the Midlands and deposited them at their hotel shortly before three o'clock on the morning of their first match.

In the match against Worcester, Indians on the field wore three sweaters, the top one long-sleeved and bulky which made them look shapeless. Never having met any Indian, let alone any of the cricketers, Arlott had to work hard to identify the fielders. His biographer, David Rayvern Allen, says he used his police training to work out who was who in the Indian side. The wicketkeeper was easy. Then he worked out the player given the ball to bowl. When Pataudi consulted with Merchant, the vice-captain, he worked out they must be captain and vice-captain. 'Bowed legs, head held at a certain angle, shirt sleeves showing below the sweater, distinguished three more, and very soon John was able to put a name to ten of the eleven and by elimination the eleventh as well—Shinde, the leg spinner.' Players not on the field, like Hazare, wore their overcoats in the dressing room 'and prepared to watch, through a firmly closed window'.

Arlott got to know the team well. Players shared secrets with him. Hazare was so shy that at social functions he would not speak until spoken to but revealed to Arlott that he went on tiger shoots. This was something he never spoke about publicly. Arlott brought some of the players, Mankad, Merchant, Hazare back to the basement studios of the BBC to record messages to their families and friends and then took them home to Crouch End in North London. However, he discovered that Merchant and Mankad were vegetarians, so had to feed them rice, potatoes and tea. The Indians travelled first class on trains. Arlott only got third class travel paying the difference himself but realized this was a chance of a lifetime to get to know international cricketers. The result was *Indian Summer* which has some of the most vivid pen portraits of the First Fab Four.

THE FELINE MERCHANT

Merchant was top of Test averages, with 245 runs in five innings averaging 49. He also headed the tour averages with 2,385 runs at an average of 74.53 and became the first Indian to score 2,000 runs on a tour. His tour was full of innings where, when all other Indian batsmen failed, Merchant made runs. He was the Indian batting rock and as Arlott put it, 'often he nursed the start of a big innings by Modi or Mankad or Hazare, each of whom batted better in his company'. It was on this tour that Merchant showed he had started a new school of Indian batting, not the Ranji, Duleep school reared in England, or even the older Indian school of Nayudu, but one where runs are scored slowly, carefully but remorselessly. Merchant, having made 148 against the MCC at Lord's could not reproduce this form in the first Test at the same venue, making 12 and 27, and India lost by ten wickets. But in the second, which was drawn—albeit with the last wicket holding out—he made 78. The night before the third Test at the Oval, Rusi Modi came to his room; Merchant told him he wanted to sleep early as he was keen to make a century the next day. When Modi expressed doubts saying that meant coping with Alec Bedser, who had made his debut that series and would become one of England's greatest bowlers, Merchant replied, 'So what?' Merchant made 128 in five and a quarter hours and he fell not to an English bowler but was run out when Compton at short mid-on not able to use his hand, stuck out his foot, and the ball hit the stumps. Arlott brought a poet's touch in evoking India's first great batsman:

> Merchant's physical quality is neither the massive might nor the whipcord leanness of other great batsmen. There is something softly feline about him...he moves pad-footed but the stroke, for all its control, is flash-fast... An innings by Merchant grows: it sprouts no exotic blooms but its construction is perfect to the last detail... Day after day, season-long I watched him, notching off each hour with

thirty runs and marking the meal intervals with his cap—when the peak is directly over his right ear it is time for lunch or tea or the close of play... Merchant's batting technique is never violent, he seems to have an unvarying system of ball-valuation which controls his batting reflexes. Bowl an over of balls two feet short of a length and he will hit you for six certain fours to midwicket on the leg-side: bowl a good-length over on the middle stump and he will play you back a maiden: and this holds good whether his score is 0 or 100.

AN UGLY DUCKLING WHO MAKES RUNS

Hazare was second in the batting averages but a long way behind: 1,344 runs at 49.77. And in the Tests his highest score was 44 at an average of 24.60. Of course, Hazare also bowled 604 overs on the tour and was second in the bowling averages with fifty-six wickets at 24.75. But he did make the highest score of the tour, 244 not out against Yorkshire, bettering Merchant's 242 not out.

Arlott wondered:

How on earth can a man with such a stance, the perfectly wrong stance, make runs? ...watch that awkward stance gradually melt as his square-cut finds the offside gap or his hook the leg-boundary, and see a batsman always difficult to dismiss, who seizes runs as they come: taking no risks... Few critics will become lyrical about his batting style... He captures runs and wickets, but not the imagination... Hazare has the qualities of truth and gentleness: I suspect that after waiting without stirring for three nights at the lure to shoot a tiger, he gives his dead victim an apologetic smile and explains that his is an exceptionally good gun.

THE GREATEST LEFT-ARMER IN THE WORLD

Merchant was known to the English, Hazare had been on a private tour in 1938, but Mankad was unknown and, in many ways, made the most impression achieving the double of 1,000 runs and 100 wickets. Only one other, the Englishman Dick Howorth of Worcestershire, did it that season and since Mankad no visiting cricketer has ever achieved this feat. Present touring schedules make such a feat impossible. Arlott was enchanted by the twenty-nine-year old:

His rebellious, straight black hair gleaming, laughter richly present in his deep-set eyes, he bustles powerfully through his short run and bowls with a thick left arm—the orthodox left-hander's spinner leaving the bat, or, when least expected and with no change of action, the ball that goes with the arm. And, the ball bowled, he is tense to scamper to mid-on or mid-off to stifle the single at conception. Given the ball, for he wants to bowl again, his over will last little more than a minute and he has so much to do. There is no time for expressions of regret or surprise or disappointment, there are many ways of dismissing a man and he will try them all... And Vinoo Mankad never allows a batsman to rest...by the end of the tour there is little doubt that he was the best slow left-arm bowler in the world.

Arlott also admired Mankad's batting but hoped he would not be made to open. However, as we shall see, it was as an opener that he set a world record.

THE ALL-ROUND ATHLETE

Amarnath at thirty-five was determined to make up for 1936 and do the double. He had told Arlott in early June, 'I'll tell you in July if I am going to get my 100 wickets.' By July, he knew he would not do the double. He could not have tried harder, bowling 782 overs, more than twice as many as the other bowlers in the side and opening the bowling. But for poor Indian close catching he would have taken 100 wickets. Arlott captured him beautifully:

Merely by seeing him walk you knew he was an athlete: he might have been a footballer or a boxer, moving with the rhythmic jaunty certainty that springs from the close mental and muscular sympathy of the born games player. He was jaunty with the jauntiness of certainty, not of cocksureness. He knew that he was a great cricketer, but he knew too that when the great cricketer is out of luck his figures will be no better than those of the ordinary player. He accepted this fact philosophically... It was as a bowler that Amar impressed most on the 1946 tour. There was no more accurate bowler in England, probably not in the world. More than once he bowled with a silly mid-on, two short legs, two slips, gully and silly mid-off while the wicketkeeper stood close to complete three parts of a circle round the batsman, Amarnath himself following through almost to close the ring—and only two men, mid-on and cover point, outside that tight circle. In the game at Taunton, Harold Gimlett, whom, through a long spell, Amarnath had tied down as few bowlers can do said, 'Don't you ever bowl a half volley?' 'Oh yes,' said Amar, 'I bowled one in 1940.' It was difficult to see that he ever bowled a bad ball. With a short, four-stride run-up, he delivered on a trip so that he appeared to bowl off his wrong foot... Something of his accuracy is reflected in his bowling figures which show that more than 36% of the overs he bowled were maidens and that an average of less than two runs per over were scored off him... A man of exceptional strength of character, it was impossible to remain indifferent to him; all who met him reacted violently. As a raconteur, explosive with gesture, laughter implicit in every part of his body, he was magnificent. Under all lay the cold thought and the strength.

This came out in the second Test at Old Trafford.

AMARNATH AND PATAUDI

Amarnath had picked up an injury but was determined to play. The problem was a swollen knee. His answer was traditional Indian remedies. He cut up a large grapefruit, applied turmeric and heated it in mustard oil. The grapefruit, now very hot, was tied to his knee. This self-cure worked. Amarnath opened the bowling in both innings, in the second he actually bowled the first over, and his figures for the match read:

First Innings: 51-17-96-5

Second Innings: 30-9-71-3

He had a fascinating duel with Hammond, England's captain and top scorer with 69. Amarnath often appealed for lbw against him and every time he did, Pataudi, who had batted with Hammond when he made his debut for England against Australia in 1932—both made hundreds—apologized. Finally, Amarnath went up to Pataudi and said in Urdu, 'Nawab sahib ab aap Hindustan ke liye khel rahe hai, thodi appeal me madad kijiye.' [You are now playing for India, please help with the appeal]. It showed Amarnath's character. He knew how he had got into trouble with Vizzy in 1936 but that did not deter him. In fact, Pataudi, a very different character to Vizzy, took a shine to him and he helped Pataudi out with what might have been a tricky situation with Pataudi's wife.

In the biography of his father *The Making of a Legend: Lala Amarnath, Life and Times*, his son Rajinder narrates a wonderful story about his father and the Nawab. Towards the end of the tour Pataudi asked Amarnath to be his aide-de-camp. He was entertaining English visitors in the team's London hotel and wanted to appear princely. Pataudi wanted Amarnath to wear his army uniform but Amarnath preferred a dinner jacket. The occasion took an unexpected turn when Pataudi's wife, the begum, suddenly arrived in London. The hotel, having been told guests must be escorted to Amarnath's room, did so. Amarnath did not know who she was, thought

she was 'a fan', asked her to wait in his room while he went and told the
nawab. As Amarnath described the lady the nawab quickly worked out it
was his wife and asked Amarnath to show her in straightaway. Rajinder
Amarnath says Amarnath then 'left them to sort out what might have been
unpleasant moments for the skipper'. The way Lala told his son the story
suggests the party was one where Pataudi, with his wife being away, was
entertaining lady guests. Pataudi would later tell Amarnath, 'Amu, marwa
diya tha.' [Amarnath, you almost got me in trouble]. This may explain why
Pataudi, having agreed to pay Amarnath £50, never paid. But Amarnath
did not hold a grudge. What really rankled was that Amarnath did not
realize his great dream of doing the double. This must have been all the
more galling as he had to watch the youngest of the Fab Four, Mankad,
achieve that feat, on his first tour and in a series which had seen him
make his Test debut.

WARNINGS OF A STORM AHEAD

The Indians had once again come to England and lost but more worrying
were the storm clouds gathering at home. Just on the eve of the Oval Test
came news of 'The Great Calcutta Killing' as a result of Muhammad Ali
Jinnah calling for a Direct Action day which saw Muslims slaughter Hindus,
followed by retaliatory killings of Muslims by Hindus. It was this that made
the partition of Bengal in 1947 inevitable. For Shute Banerjee of Bengal this
was very alarming. On 11 May, on the same ground against Surrey, he had
come in to bat at three minutes past four on the Saturday with India 205
for 9, joining Chandu Sarwate, India's No. 10. The groundsman walked out
with Banerjee to ask the Surrey captain what roller he would like, as it was
natural to assume Surrey would soon bat. The pair were only separated at
three minutes before half past twelve on Monday when Jack Parker bowled
Banerjee. The Indian total was 454, Banerjee 121, Sarwate 124 not out. They
had put on 249, the first time No. 10 and No. 11 had scored hundreds in the
same innings, and this remains a record. But now with the Test match going
on, the news from Kolkata must have chilled Banerjee. On 20 August, while
the sports pages of *The Times* led with Merchant's great 128, the news pages
were full of the gruesome killings in Kolkata. Banerjee was left wondering
what awaited him when he returned to his native city. During the tour the
Indian cricket team had kept at bay all that was going on in India, and here
Pataudi must be given credit. But they returned full of foreboding, although
none of them could have anticipated what would take place just a year
later as India won freedom amidst bloodshed and misery with a devastating
impact on Indian life, society and, inevitably, Indian cricket.

Chapter 6

AMARNATH AT THE HELM

WORLD RECORDS AMIDST REVOLUTION

The turmoil in the country in the winter of 1946 saw many Indians who had collaborated with the British rebelling against foreign rule and a mutiny by the Indian navy in Mumbai which virtually handed over the city for a few days to Indian revolutionaries. However, cricket went on as if everything was normal and a world record was set which was not broken for sixty years. This was in the Ranji Trophy final between Baroda and Holkar. On the matting wicket at Baroda, Hazare with 6 for 85 bowled out Holkar for just over 200. But the visitors struck back, and Baroda were 91 for 3 when Gul Mohammad joined Hazare. They batted for nearly two full days and put on 577 for the fourth wicket before Gul Mohammad fell for 319. It would have rounded things up had Hazare also made a triple century. But he fell twelve short. This remained the highest partnership for any wicket until 2006 and it still remains the highest fourth-wicket stand in first-class cricket. But a few months later, the events of 15 August 1947 meant that cricket was, once again, reduced to a game for boys played by grown men.

On that date India, after a great struggle, was at last free, but the country was partitioned and the new state of Pakistan was created. Hindus fled Pakistan, Muslims fled India in one of the greatest exchanges of population known in human history. Perhaps a million people never reached their sanctuary. Even now nobody knows how many were killed. This redrawing of the map of India had an immediate cricketing impact. Half of Punjab, the half that had produced some of the great bowlers like Nissar, was now gone. Fazal Mahmood, who should have gone to England, was selected for the Indian team which was to tour Australia in the winter of 1947. Fazal even went to the training camp at Pune with the team housed in the home of Shanta Apte, an actress who regaled them with her singing. But the turmoil of the country soon became evident when, as Fazal made his way back to Mumbai, Hindu mobs got on the train and wanted to kill him. It required Nayudu, who was also on the train, to fight them off with his bat. Fazal finally managed to make his way back to Lahore and decided he could not go on tour. He would later claim he was doing this to show his support for Pakistan, but Oborne has shown that Fazal was not motivated by nationalism but fear for his life.

Amarnath, the Lahore boy, was also well aware of the devastation going on, with the Hindus in Lahore, his home town, being slaughtered and the great Hindu quarters, where he was born and which had survived so many Muslim regimes, being razed to the ground. Amarnath on a railway journey from Patiala to Delhi via Ambala was lucky to escape. On the train he saw frenzied mobs butchering people. Amarnath does not say which religion they were from, but it seems they were Sikhs killing Muslims. He was saved because at Ambala station a policeman who recognized him gave him a kara, the steel bangle that Sikhs wear. The group approached him and, pointing to the kara, said, 'We were planning to kill you before Karnal, thinking you belonged to another community.' Even years later the incident would fill Amarnath with dread.

It was against this background that India left for a tour that marked many firsts for Indian cricket. It was India's first five-Test series, each Test lasting five days and, unlike the previous three tours which were all to England, India went to Australia. The man who should have captained the side was Merchant, but having finally been put in charge of an official tour—he had captained in unofficial series—he withdrew, reporting a mysterious groin strain and that there was something possibly wrong with his stomach. So Amarnath took over, but, just before the team left, he had to do without his vice-captain Mushtaq although this was more due to board bungling.

FACING THE GREATEST TEAM

Bradman's team has generally been considered the greatest side ever seen in the history of cricket and the gods favoured the Australians. Bradman won the toss in four of the five Tests and in two of the matches, Brisbane and Melbourne, India had the worst of the conditions, batting on an uncovered wicket where the ball did all manner of unexpected tricks. Hammond in *Cricket: My Destiny* would later describe the weather Amarnath had to put up with as 'a cruelty that amounted to personal persecution'. India lost three Tests by an innings and one by 233 runs.

Amarnath batted poorly in the Tests; his highest score was 46 and he averaged 14. But he was brilliant against the State sides: 1,162 runs on the tour at 58.10 and heading the averages. His greatest innings was 228 not out in six-and-a-half hours against Victoria, the Sheffield Shield holders and boasting a near Australian Test attack.

And Amarnath kept his sense of humour. When Amir Elahi dropped a catch off Bradman and, looking at the sky and slapping his forehead, exclaimed, 'Allah', Amarnath responded, 'Now Allah alone can get him out.' At the end of the tour Amarnath would take consolation from the fact that Bradman praised him in his *Farewell to Cricket*: 'Amarnath was a splendid ambassador. I look back on the season with him as my opposite number as one of my most pleasant cricket years.' He also took much pride in Hammond saying that India under Amarnath was at last breaking away from West Indies, New Zealand and South Africa and developing 'pitiless strategical leadership' and 'the spirit of aggression and domination'. He gave credit to Amarnath for that, saying that he was using his experience of the Lancashire League which, said Hammond, had made him 'analyse the play and the personality of each of his opponents just as a professional boxer has done'. But while this was music to Amarnath's ears, the fact is the Indians as a team laid very few blows on the Australians, and in the end the series boiled down to one Indian providing some consolation. And this was another of the Fab Four, Vijay Hazare.

HAZARE PROVIDES CONSOLING BALM

For a time Hazare's batting was like Amarnath's, only scoring outside the Tests. On the tour he was second to Amarnath with 1,056 runs at an average of 48. But until the fourth Test in Adelaide in six innings he had scored 84 runs with a highest score of 18. Perhaps he was not helped by Grimmett watching him play. Then, suddenly, he clicked in the fourth Test at Adelaide. It could not have been in more depressing circumstances. India looked doomed: in response to Australia's 674, the tourists were 69 for 3. From the start Hazare's bat made a different sound. The problem was nobody would stay with him. Gul Mohammad and Hazare, as we have seen, had a world record to their name, 577. Now they could only put on 9. Hazare finally found a partner in Dattu Phadkar. Hazare made 116, and Phadkar 123.

However, Hazare could not save the follow-on, and with India losing two wickets without a run on the board, Hazare was soon batting again. In this innings, Hazare was the last man to get out, making 145. The rest of the ten batsmen between them made 132.

Hazare had achieved Indian cricket's first truly international event joining a very exclusive club: batsmen who had made two centuries in a Test match. The club members were George Headley, Sutcliffe, Warren Bardsley, Hammond, Compton and Bradman. What made it special was it looked like Hazare had responded to what Bradman had done in the third Test in Melbourne. The difference was that Bradman's double saw Australia win by 233 runs whereas Hazare's was personal glory for India, who lost by an innings and 16 runs.

Hazare had shown that, like Merchant, he could also make runs abroad and, what's more, against the world's best attack, which had so often reduced opposing batsmen to rubble. However, the downside was that in the years to come, as India often came back from overseas tours badly beaten, they consoled themselves with one individual moment of glory. This meant Indians did not look into the causes of defeat, with the result that there was soon another overseas tour which again saw horrendous results. Interestingly, one man who followed Hazare and India's performance with great interest was the mathematician G. H. Hardy. He had discovered Srinivasa Ramanujan, was passionate about cricket and, as he lay dying, he got his sister to read out the scores from Australia.

MANKAD LEAVES A CURIOUS LEGACY

It would have been interesting to know what he made of a Mankad fielding action which has gone down in cricket history. Amarnath used Mankad as the bowling workhorse. The left-hander bowled 494.3 overs, 200 more than Amarnath, and took sixty-one wickets, twice as many as Amarnath, making him the leading wicket-taker and heading the tour bowling averages. With the bat he initially found Ray Lindwall an insurmountable problem, making in his first four Test innings 0, 7, 5, 5, out to Lindwall all four times, three times Lindwall hitting Mankad's timbers. But then Lindwall gave him a quick tutorial about how to play his yorker and Mankad proved a good pupil.

In the third Test in Melbourne he made 116, the first century by an Indian in Tests in Australia. And there was another century in the final Test—again at Melbourne. However, what Mankad will be remembered for is what Australians, playfully making a verb from his name, call 'Mankading'. On 13 December 1947, in the second Test at Sydney, Mankad ran out Bill Brown when, in the act of delivering the ball, he held on to it and removed the bails with Brown well out of his crease. This was the second time on the tour Mankad had dismissed Brown in this fashion. He was criticized, but Bradman defended him. In the years since, every now and again somebody does that: Kapil Dev did it in South Africa in 1992, and Mankading pops up again. That such a great all-rounder should be remembered for this may be cruel, but it was unusual while being within the laws, something the crafty Mankad was very aware of.

UNSPORTING WEST INDIANS DENY INDIANS A FIRST WIN

Amarnath might have lost the captaincy when the West Indies visited India in the winter of 1948, India's first home series as an independent nation, had Merchant been fit. But he was not, and Amarnath retained the captaincy.

The Tests saw West Indies making huge scores, over 600 in both the first and second Tests, with Everton Weekes making centuries in each of his first four innings. India did not have a Weekes but replied vigorously, more often in the second innings. But in the fourth Test in Chennai they batted worse in the second than the first and lost by an innings and 193 runs. Critics were quick to jump on Amarnath for starting a bouncer war, because, when the West Indians retaliated, Indian batsmen had been unable to cope.

However, all this would have been forgotten had Amarnath managed to secure India's first-ever Test victory in the final Test at the Brabourne Stadium. India finally bowled out the West Indians twice and were left to make 361 to win in 395 minutes.

This looked a daunting score in the final innings. Amarnath, who even kept wickets in the Mumbai Test after Probir Sen, the wicketkeeper, was injured, was confident and by the close of the fourth day India were 90 for 3, and Hazare and Rusi Modi, who had scored a century in the second Test, which had also been played at Mumbai, together.

By mid-afternoon Hazare and Modi were still batting and India had gone past 200. The desperate West Indians decided to use what Gerry Gomez, the vice-captain, confessed to me were 'negative tactics' but justified as 'it was within the laws'. What it meant was that to stop Hazare and Modi driving on the off-side, the West Indians bowled wide outside the leg stump and put most of the fielders on the leg-side. In modern cricket the umpires would not have allowed the West Indians to get away with it. However, even then India seemed set on victory, and while Hazare fell for 122, at tea India needed 72 to win with four wickets in hand.

More runs were scored, more wickets fell and the drama climaxed when Ghulam Ahmed, the off-spinner, and batting No. 10, joined Phadkar, the last recognized batsmen. Ahmed finished his Test career with a batting average of 8.92. But now all that was required was that he stay with Phadkar. And he did. India needed 21 runs in fifteen minutes. The West Indians now decided to waste time. They had a drinks break. Then Clyde Walcott, the wicketkeeper, wasted more time by slowly waddling down to the fine-leg boundary to retrieve a ball. Nevertheless, with two possible overs remaining, India required 11 runs to win. Five runs were scored from the first five balls. One ball of that over was left and with another to come, India needed 6 from seven balls. Joshi, the umpire, miscounted and called over. And then, despite the clock showing a minute and a half to go, he removed the bails and ended the Test. We cannot be sure India would have won, but the crowd were convinced that Joshi, an incompetent umpire, had helped West Indies thwart India. They booed and jeered the West Indians. It would take another twenty-two years for India to beat the West Indies. And in 1996, as we shall see, Clyde Walcott would try and stop an Indian from becoming president of the ICC but in this he failed.

The tour was also hard on the Indian players because the Indian board, giving in to complaints by West Indians, treated them much better than their own players. Amarnath complained, demanded more money and upset Anthony De Mello, the supremo of the Indian board. An incensed De Mello listed twenty-three allegations against Amarnath. These included claims for extra out-of-pocket expenses, not being a conscientious captain and, to top it all, that he had included Probir Sen of Bengal to play against the West Indies in return for a backhander of ₹5,000 from Bengal cricket officials. At an extraordinary meeting of the board on 10 April 1949, a resolution was passed suspending Amarnath from domestic and representative cricket in India 'for continuous misbehaviour and breach of discipline'. Amarnath responded with a 27,000-word statement and hired a lawyer, Niren De, who turned up at the board meeting of 31 July 1949 held at the CCI. Amarnath's supporters massed outside the clubhouse shouting their support for their man; inside Niren De flourished an envelope which he said was a defamation case of ₹1 lakh against De Mello. He also threatened to sue the board. After a nine-hour meeting the board accepted that the 10 April decision was ultra vires while Amarnath expressed 'his regret for allegations and conduct if any on his part against the Board or its President'. And the board withdrew all charges against Amarnath. However, this did mean Amarnath was no longer captain and Merchant was back as captain.

The problem for Merchant was both that he was struggling to be fit and that nobody wanted to play Test cricket with India. The MCC cancelled their proposed tour of India scheduled for the winter of 1949 and Merchant captained India against a Commonwealth side put together by George Duckworth both in the 1949–50 and the 1950–51 seasons. The two Commonwealth teams included good players, Frank Worrell in both, Jim Laker in the second, neither of whom played an official Test in India. There was good cricket and some bizarre moments. In Pune, Laker was about to run in and bowl when he found a rat, almost as large as a terrier, on the wicket: 'The rat had just reached the good-length spot when the drama reached its crisis. A big kite hawk swooped down, picked up the rat in its talons and took off again with its dinner.' Laker was so stunned that his next ball bounced twice, and the batsman hit it for a boundary. A unique case of a rat on the field resulting in a four. But while these matches meant the Indian public saw international cricket, they could never be classified as proper Tests, and even as they were being played, the real question was: would India even remain a Test-playing nation?

Chapter 7

NEHRU SAVES INDIAN CRICKET

Jawaharlal Nehru's role in Indian cricket has not received much attention from his various biographers but there is little doubt that it was a political decision he took that preserved India's Test status. Unlike Gandhi, who had no interest in sport (once, when requested to help the hockey team, he asked, 'Hockey, what is it?'), Nehru had played cricket at Harrow. He had not shown any great skill, but he clearly cared for the game. When the West Indies arrived he made sure the first Test was played in Delhi. It was the first representative match played in Delhi, and Nehru considered it important that free India's first home Test series should start in the capital. Nehru knew the power of sport and did much to promote the Asian Games, whose inaugural edition in 1951 was also held in Delhi. One of my most vivid memories when growing up was to see every year a picture in the *Times of India* of Nehru padded up, playing in the annual parliamentary match. However, what we need to consider is the impact one of his political decisions had on Indian cricket.

When India became independent in 1947 it became a self-governing dominion within the British Commonwealth, the first brown nation of the British empire to enjoy such a privilege. India accepted that the British monarch was still the king of India. The Indians saw dominion status in 1947 as a temporary measure until they could finalize their constitution, declare themselves a republic and leave the Commonwealth. A constituent assembly met in Delhi to frame the constitution.

But Winston Churchill and Clement Attlee began to pester the Indians to stay in the Commonwealth. Churchill suggested that even if India became a republic, in the style of republics in the Roman empire, India could remain a republic within the Commonwealth and still accept the king. The king seemed to like the idea and both he and Churchill thought of him becoming the president of India. Attlee, who wanted India's constitution to have a specific role for the British king, wondered if a republic was really in the traditions of India and suggested a title might be found for the king from India's heroic age. He talked about the royal family being of a universal nature, transcending creeds and races.

Nehru found such ideas 'juvenile' but, maybe because he liked being described as the last English prime minister of India, or, maybe because he was in love with Edwina Mountbatten, he decided to overturn established Congress party policy. Overriding fierce opposition, led by Sardar Vallabhbhai Patel, from within his own cabinet, he agreed to keep India in the Commonwealth. The Commonwealth was converted from its historic role as a white man's club into one where other races could all aspire to equality. India would become a truly independent country with its own president, but it would also remain part of a wider club whose permanent president was the British monarch. Neither the new Commonwealth nor the British monarch had any power in India.

For Indian cricket this decision was to have far-reaching significance. On 19 July 1948, when the debate about the Commonwealth was at its height with very secret letters flying between Delhi and London, the Imperial Cricket Conference (ICC) met at Lord's. At that conference, the first since India had become a self-governing dominion in 1947, the matter of India's changed status came up. It was decided that India could remain a member of the ICC but only on a provisional basis. The matter would be looked at again after two years. It is clear that the ICC, unsure whether India would remain part of the British Commonwealth, was waiting for the politicians to decide.

At this meeting in 1948 the future tour programmes, extending up to 1952, did not list any visits to or by India. Indeed, the winter of 1951–52 was left blank and it was agreed Australia would tour England in 1952, that year being the end of the traditional four-year gap for Australian visits to England.

On 26 January 1950, India finally became a republic, but remained part of this new British Commonwealth. The ICC met six months later, on 27 and 28 June 1950 at Lord's and, reassured by this, made India a permanent member of the ICC. Rule 5 of the ICC very specifically stated that membership of ICC shall cease should the country concerned cease to be part of the British Commonwealth. Had Nehru not agreed to keep India in the Commonwealth, then Indian cricket would have failed the basic test of ICC membership. In that case it is almost certain that at its 1950 meeting the Indian board's provisional status would not have been made permanent. India would have been cast out in the cricketing cold. The formal reason ICC gave for making India a permanent member was that the separation of Pakistan had not materially affected the standard of play in India. How it could have reached that decision is hard to see. There had been no cricket contact between England and India since 1946. Since

1947 India had been thrashed in Australia, lost at home to the West Indies and also lost to a side put together by a retired English wicketkeeper. This was the ICC using cricket talk to camouflage what was a naked political decision.

This is further borne out by the dramatic change to the tour programme that the ICC made in that June 1950 meeting. It was decided that the MCC would tour India, Pakistan and Sri Lanka in the winter of 1951–52 and India would visit England in 1952, in back-to-back Test series. The Australian visit was pushed to 1953, making the gap five years—the longest between Australian tours to the UK.

Nehru's decision could not have come at a more crucial time. In 1950, India qualified to play for the football World Cup for the first and only time. But there were many problems, including foreign exchange, transport—the tournament was held in Brazil—and also the Indian insistence that they play in bare feet. FIFA refused to sanction this and India, in a decision that was to haunt its football, withdrew.

At this point, it's interesting to do a thought experiment. Let's imagine that on 26 January 1950, India on becoming a republic, leaves the Commonwealth. Six months later the ICC meets and downgrades India from provisional member to non-member. However, even as the ICC comes to this decision, Indian footballers, playing with boots, are taking part in football's first World Cup since World War II—the ICC meeting took place in the middle of the World Cup in Brazil. And building on the impression they had created in the 1948 Olympic football tournament, they make a mark on the biggest world stage for team sports. Indian cricket, on the other hand, cut off from the world, withers.

We need to appreciate how fragile Indian cricket was throughout much of the 1950s and how much stronger Indian football was. In 1950, Indian cricket had achieved nothing on the world stage. It had yet to win a Test. Nor through the 1950s did India do much in cricket, and for most of the decade Indian cricket struggled to attract worthwhile opposition. For some seasons they had to make do with playing unofficial 'Tests' against so-called Commonwealth sides composed of players from many lands organized by George Duckworth. The decade ended with a series of mind-numbing defeats at home and abroad.

In football, on the other hand, India won the Asian Games gold in 1951, again in 1962, and came fourth in the Melbourne Olympics in 1956. Had football grabbed its chance, and Nehru followed settled Congress party policy and left the Commonwealth, who is to say that today football, rather than cricket, would not be the main sport of India?

Also, back in 1950, cricket was far from being the all-dominant Indian sport it has now become in terms of high-profile fixtures and public enthusiasm and attendance. Nothing had replaced the Pentangular, and Ranji Trophy matches attracted few spectators. In contrast, football was popular not only in Bengal and Goa but in much of the country. And to give you an example from personal experience, as a Bengali living in Mumbai I was taken to football more often than cricket, particularly when the Rovers Cup was on at Cooperage. The Western India Football Association (WIFA) was run by my father's friend, a fellow Bengali called Jagadish Maitra, and he always made us welcome. What is more, this was the only sporting occasion where I went to a match with both my father and mother. My parents come from what was East Bengal, now Bangladesh. My father was a fervent East Bengal supporter, but my mother, brought up in Kolkata, was a Mohun Bagan supporter. I was brought up on stories of the football rivalries of the two clubs and I recall how my mother was distressed when one year East Bengal beat Mohun Bagan, while I could not contain my joy.

Had India left the Commonwealth, hockey too could have got a boost. This was one sport where India was a superpower and had the sort of success it has never ever enjoyed in any other sport. In hockey India had made its international debut four years before cricket in 1928 in the Amsterdam Olympics and, while India lost in its first cricket international, in hockey India beat the world, winning gold. That this was no fluke was emphasized in the next forty years, India winning gold in the next five Olympics in 1932, 1936, 1948, 1952 and 1956. Indeed, India did not lose a single match at the Olympics until 1960, the greatest run by a field sports team. All these competitions were held abroad ranging from Los Angeles through Berlin, London, Helsinki and Melbourne. Yet during that period India did not win a single Test abroad or even come close and also had some disastrous results at home. It was only after India finally lost its gold to Pakistan in Rome in 1960 that the fortunes of the two sports were reversed. India did win two more golds in 1964 and 1980 but in the decades that followed it also had dismal results, almost matching the cricket defeats of the 1950s and did not even qualify for the 2008 Beijing Olympics. In contrast, in a remarkable reversal, India in cricket began to emerge as a power, although its rise took a lot longer than Indian hockey's dramatic world dominance since its golden moment in Amsterdam. Nehru did nothing to encourage hockey. It is only now that Indian hockey is recovering, but is nowhere near the world status it had or that Indian cricket now enjoys.

Also, by the time Nehru took his decision to keep India in the Commonwealth, India had produced the greatest player in the history of hockey, the hockey equivalent of Bradman, Dhyan Chand, among whose feats were thrashing the blonde German team in the 1936 Nazi Olympics while playing barefoot. Indian cricket would not produce its Bradman-like figure, Tendulkar, until half a century after Nehru's fateful decision to create the modern Commonwealth.

Rarely in international affairs has a political decision had such an impact on sport. How ironic that Nehru took the decision to stay in the Commonwealth, fearful that Pakistan would join and outflank India! Pakistan as a nation has failed, India has succeeded, and its cricket has taken over the game.

Chapter 8

HAZARE'S PRECARIOUS MOUNTAINTOP

BEATING ENGLAND'S CAST-OFFS

Vijay Hazare captained India fourteen times, and with only one victory his win ratio of 7.14 ranks him below Gulabrai Ramchand, Nari Contractor and Kapil Dev despite the fact that, like Kapil Dev, he made history— leading India to victory in Tests for the first time. But while statistics can be the worst kind of lies, these figures tell the story that Hazare's captaincy was a case of one moment of joy followed immediately by defeats that scarred Indian cricket for generations.

To be fair to Hazare, he was surprised to be appointed captain against the England team that came to India in the winter of 1951. Not being as flamboyant as Amarnath nor as shrewd and calculating as Merchant he wanted to be 'far away from the scene of undesirable and unwarranted controversy'. The decision was taken by the board on 5 August 1951, the same meeting which saw the demise of Amarnath's nemesis, De Mello. With Amarnath having gone AWOL, it was a straight battle between the Christian Vijay and the Hindu Vijay—not that religion came into it—which the Christian Vijay won 12–5. Hazare, playing League cricket in England, read about it in the papers and also learnt that the team England were preparing to send for their first tour of independent India was very much a second-rate side. England had five debutants in the first Test in Delhi including Nigel Howard, the captain, Donald Carr, the vice-captain, Fred Ridgway, the opening bowler, Don Kenyon, a batsman and Dick Spooner the wicketkeeper. Howard, captain of Lancashire, only played four Tests for England, all as captain, and was never beaten. In the second Test Eddie Leadbeater played for England before he was capped by his county. The greats of English cricket, Len Hutton, Denis Compton, Godfrey Evans, Alec Bedser, Jim Laker and Peter May, stayed at home and never ever played Test cricket in India.

The England team seemed ideal for India to finally win a Test, if not a series, with ease. But that euphoria only lasted until the third day of the first Test. England had been bowled out for 203; Hazare and Merchant, in one of their rare partnerships for India, put on 211, then a record Indian stand for any wicket against England. India ended with a lead of 215, but the Indians took a dreadfully long time to make the runs. Tom Graveney got the impression India was not a team pulling together and that Merchant and Hazare were, as in the war, having a personal competition. Merchant made 154, then the highest Test score by an Indian, but Hazare immediately claimed the record with 164 not out. In their second innings England dug in and a match India should have won was drawn. Merchant never again played for India, announcing after Delhi that he was retiring, content that 859 runs in ten Tests, all against England, gave him an average he could be proud of: 47.72.

Hazare made another century in the second Test in Mumbai, the first one I saw, but mishooked a Ridgway bouncer on to his head. After that he seemed to lose his batting confidence, making in the rest of the series 6, 2, a pair and 20. India also lost their way, drawing the second and third Test, and were beaten in the fourth in three days, not by English pace but the spin of Malcolm Hilton and Roy Tattersall, journeymen English spinners. India now needed a miracle worker to save the series and found one in Mankad. In the years to come, Indian spinners would take charge of Tests, but this, the first one by an Indian, is worth dwelling on.

MANKAD GOES FROM HERO TO ZERO

In the fifth Test in Chennai, Mankad came on to bowl with England, winning the toss on a wicket seemingly made for batting, well placed at 65 for 1. A few hours later, when Mankad delivered the fifth ball of his thirty-ninth over, England were all out for 266. His 8 for 55 included Graveney, Jack Robertson, Allan Watkins, Cyril Poole, Carr, Hilton, Brian Statham and Ridgway. This was indeed great left-arm bowling: Mankad teasing the batsmen by always varying his flight and, as Graveney put it, he gently drew him forward and had him politely stumped. Four Englishmen were dismissed this way.

India produced their most enterprising batting of the series. Mankad, bowling with a lead of 191, took 4 for 53, and, helped by Ghulam Ahmed taking 4 for 77, England were dismissed for 183. India had won its first Test ever most emphatically by an innings and 8 runs.

In sport it is a truism to say that the moment of victory is always the most dangerous, and India, having finally reached the summit after twenty-five Tests, showed they just could not cope. Within six months they would be coming back from England having suffered one of their worst overseas defeats, and such was their batting against English pace that Indians, who had played pace so well ever since their Test debut in 1932, were now labelled as scared of pace bowling, a slur on Indian batting which would scar an entire generation of Indian cricketers. There were many reasons for this amazing collapse: England had a new pace bowler in Fred Trueman, its first professional captain in Len Hutton and a much stronger side including May, Compton, Evans, Laker and Bedser, none of whom were in India. However, one of the main reasons was a self-inflicted wound that beggared belief. Despite Mankad winning the Chennai Test he was not included for the tour to England that followed. Not having received assurances that he would be selected to tour England he had accepted an offer from Haslingden in the Lancashire League to play club cricket during the English summer for £1,000, much more than he would earn with India—and he was no prince. The Indian board did not care. Nayudu, chairman of selectors, had dismissed Mankad as not all that special.

Imagine the situation. On Thursday, 5 June 1952, India, having beaten England just four months ago, take the field against England in the first Test at Headingley. At that precise moment Mankad, the man who won that Test, is staying with a family in Haslingden and turning on the radio to follow the cricket. And on Saturday, 7 June, as India begin their second innings against England, Mankad is playing for his club in the Lancashire League. The Indian innings had not long started when it became very evident that the self-inflicted wound would leave an indelible mark of shame on Indian cricket.

THE TERRIBLE HEADINGLEY LEGACY

That Saturday at Headingley, in front of a packed Yorkshire crowd, India began their second innings 41 behind. However, with England having to bat last this was not a losing position. Wickets in those days were uncovered, and a target in excess of 300 could have been challenging. And there seemed no reason why India should not make a decent second innings score. The first innings had seen the emergence of the third Vijay of Indian cricket, Vijay Manjrekar, which was immensely exciting. With India rocking at 42 for 3, he walked out to bat in the first innings, at twenty the baby of the team, unsure of his place in the side. Having made his Test debut only three Tests earlier in Kolkata, he had been dropped for the victory at Chennai. Hazare batting at the other end worried about how he would cope with English conditions, no sight screen and Trueman breathing fire. But Hazare need not have worried: Manjrekar was from that toughest of cricket's preparatory schools, Shivaji Park in Mumbai. Although he was born when India was still under British rule, he did not have a colonial complex. He could give as good as he got. A fair-skinned Indian, looking at his dark skin, had once mocked, 'So when where you born? Was it when the West Indians toured India?' He immediately shot back, 'And were you born when the Australians were here?'

Now showing no fear, and despite never having scored a first-class century, he scored 133, in an innings that proclaimed his class. In the years to come he would bat with such authority that his contemporaries were unanimous that between 1952 and 1964 he was the best Indian batsman of his generation. Frank Worrell, who was watching, was very impressed. Manjrekar's batting inspired Hazare, who had been going through a bad patch. He made 89 and the pair set a then Indian record of 222 for the fourth wicket.

The innings made a deep impression on the Yorkshire crowd, often the hardest to please, among whom was a young Vince Cable, who would become leader of the Liberal Democrats and a government minister. In 2017, at a reception in the Indian Gymkhana, he would vividly recall to me how he was taken by the way the Indian batsmen mastered the English bowlers.

However, on that Saturday at Headingley in the Indian second innings there was nothing masterly about the Indian batting. In fourteen balls India lost their first four wickets without a run being scored, Trueman taking three in eight balls, Bedser one. It was the worst start any side had ever made in Test cricket. It did not help that Hazare changed the batting order. Madhav Mantri, the wicketkeeper, who had batted No. 8 in the first innings, came in No. 3 and was bowled by a straight ball. Hazare, who batted No. 4, should have been the next man in but he sent out Manjrekar who in the first innings had batted No. 5. As Manjrekar walked in he told the departing Mantri in Marathi, 'Mala bakra banoola.' [I have been made a sacrificial goat.] Manjrekar was bowled. The scoreboard read 0 for four. Hazare, who had dropped down the order to nurse his injured thigh, faced Trueman on a hat-trick with his native Yorkshire crowd urging him on. Hazare denied Trueman the honour and on-drove the ball for four. Hazare made sure India did not make the lowest-ever Test score, which was then 30 by South Africa, putting on 105 with Phadkar, Hazare making 56, Phadkar 64. But India could not make enough to worry England, and the home side won by seven wickets. Worse still was the legacy that that Headingley afternoon left. It was that Indian batsmen were so afraid of fast bowling that instead of confronting it, they ran away from it. This generated many hurtful jokes. In fact, even at Headingley, this was not true. As Tom Graveney told me, Roy got out trying to pull a Trueman long hop and Manjrekar was out trying to cover drive which makes nonsense of trying to run away. In any case, as evidence over the years showed, he never ran away from any fast bowler in his life. Umrigar was different, for, as Hazare says, 'He looked most unhappy against pace and particularly against Trueman.' Against lesser bowling he could be devastating; against Trueman he was clueless. English fielders taunted him because he retreated as Trueman ran in to bowl and one joke that became famous was when the umpire asked Umrigar where he wanted the sight screen Umrigar replied, 'Between me and that mad devil Trueman.' I would have loved to hear Umrigar's side of the story, but he was one Indian cricketer who refused to help me.

PLEASE VINOO, SAVE US

After Headingley, India went back to Mankad with their tails between their legs and persuaded Haslingden to let him play for India for the rest of the series, with the board paying Haslingden the £300 fee they wanted to let their prize asset go. Mankad made history, going from Saturday club cricket in the Lancashire League to a Lord's Test. His impact on the Test was such that it has been dubbed 'Mankad's Test'. India actually lost by eight wickets early on the fifth day, but that takes nothing away from Mankad, who was almost continuously on the field either with bat or ball. Opening the batting on the first day, the match was barely half an hour old when he hit a 6 off Roly Jenkins, the leg-spinner. His presence gave Roy confidence, and now India did not lose their first wicket until the score was 106. Mankad went on to make 72. Then, after India had made 235, Mankad got hold of the ball and in an England innings of 537 did not stop turning his arm over: 73–24–196–5.

In the second innings he opened the batting again, nearly scored a century before lunch and, as Trueman realized, this was one Indian batsman who was not running away. In the process he set all sorts of records that lasted decades. His own score of 184 was the highest an Indian had scored in a Test. His partnership of 211 with Hazare equalled the Merchant–Hazare stand in Delhi against England for the third wicket. And then, in the England second innings, with England requiring only 77 to win, Mankad bowled another twenty-four overs. In the Test he had scored 256 runs, nearly half his team's runs, and bowled ninety-seven overs. Mankad had consoled India, and this was required for in the next two Tests with Mankad unable to provide such heroics, India did worse than at Headingley, making 58 and 82 at Old Trafford, the first team to be dismissed twice in a day and losing by an innings and 207 runs. At the Oval they made 98, losing their first five wickets for 6 runs. Only rain, which washed out two days' play, saved India from defeat.

AMARNATH'S LAST RESURRECTION

It was not a surprise that Hazare paid the price for the England debacle, although the captaincy merry-go-round that followed the tour was, even by the whimsical standards of Indian cricket, rather curious. Amarnath, having disappeared after the West Indian tour, had reappeared in the home series against England and played in the Chennai win but was not chosen for England. Now, in October 1952, as India faced Pakistan he was back as captain although Hazare remained in the side. Pakistan were making their Test debut, the first between two countries which only five years earlier had been one nation. For Amarnath the series had a poignant edge as he still saw Lahore as his home and his captaincy meant challenging Abdul Hafeez Kardar, a teammate on the 1946 India tour of England but now captain of Pakistan.

India made the best of starts, winning the first Test at Delhi by an innings and 70 runs with a day to spare, orchestrated by Mankad, who took 8 for 52 in the first innings and 5 for 79 in the second. However, in the second Test on the mat of Lucknow—the only Test to be played there—Fazal Mahmood with his medium pace took 12 for 94, and it was India's turn to lose by an innings and 43 runs. Amarnath was convinced that the Indian defeat was a case of backstabbing by three members of his own side. Hazare, Hemu Adhikari and Mankad had not played, which clearly weakened the side. These players, Amarnath alleged, did not 'understand the mental trauma that had affected the displaced players due to Partition. I could because it had affected me.' The Lucknow crowd did not take kindly to defeat. The Indian team bus was stoned and Amarnath had to wade into the crowd with a lathi to rescue his players. The result was that before the third Test in Mumbai he got the players to come to his room at the CCI and take an oath, holding the Indian tricolour, to pledge to play as one united team.

The Mumbai Test saw much debate about what India should do if Amarnath won the toss. Then captains nearly always batted first. However, in recent matches, the Mumbai wicket had given the impression that for a Test played in November, which this one was, as the sun dried the winter dew, batting could be a problem. The story told to me was that Amarnath asked Mankad what he should do and Mankad immediately replied, 'Arre Lala, saale log ko dal do' (Oh, Lala, put the bastards in.) Amarnath was worried that if he did, the press would criticize him.

There is, however, an Amarnath version of this story, which is that as he went out to toss with Kardar he fooled the Pakistan captain. He told him he would field if he won the toss and the distrustful Kardar thought

Amarnath was lying and that he really wanted to bat. So, when Kardar won the toss he batted and played into Amarnath's hands. Amarnath, who opened the bowling, took 4 for 40, Mankad 3 for 52, and Pakistan was bowled out for 186. Then, with the pitch dried out, Indian batsmen made hay, and when Pakistan batted again Mankad's 5 for 72 left India only 45 to make, and Mankad made the winning hit.

If what had happened at Mumbai was intriguing, what happened in the fourth Test in Chennai was baffling. After the Test was drawn the selectors decided they had enough of Amarnath and that he would not take the side to the West Indies, a series due to start just weeks after India played the final Test in Kolkata. The selectors hoped to keep the news secret until the Kolkata Test was over. But Amarnath was tipped off by a journalist and decided to outflank the selectors. He disclosed his own sacking at the post-match dinner following the Chennai Test and then sensationally offered to step down for the Kolkata Test and let Hazare take over. Hazare declined and did not even play in the Test. He says in his autobiography that when he was told he would captain the side in the Caribbean he decided to miss the Kolkata Test as he had 'to make preparations in a hurry for this trip'.

He does not specify what these 'preparations' were. It seems extraordinary that the selectors allowed their main batsman to drop out, given that a Pakistan victory would have meant India not winning the series. Is it possible the selectors thought that if without Hazare Amarnath lost it would be no bad thing, it would teach him a lesson? As it happened, in Kolkata Amarnath did not lose, turning down Kardar's bizarre offer to India of scoring 97 in fifteen minutes to win. It meant Amarnath, India's first century-maker, had also led India to their first-ever Test series win. But that final December evening in Kolkata marked the departure of Amarnath with figures which read poorly. In twenty-four Tests he averaged 24.38 with the bat and 32.91 with the ball. But this is a case of figures not telling the full story of this complex, tempestuous man, who could be brilliant but also drive people mad by his behaviour. Amarnath's departure marked the end of the first wave of Indian cricket. The second wave of Indian cricket was about to roll in and it was appropriate that it made its appearance in the New World, a region India knew little about but where, to their delight, they discovered an Indian diaspora waiting to acclaim the cricketers from their ancestral land.

The Second Wave

TESTS

Wave	Period	Matches	Won	Lost	Drawn	Tied	Win%	W/L
2nd	1953–1962	48	5	18	25	0	10.42	0.28

TOP BATSMEN IN SECOND WAVE

	Matches	Runs	HS	Avg	100	50
P. R. Umrigar	44	3057	223	46.31	10	13
V. L. Manjrekar	38	2388	189*	42.64	4	14
P. Roy	31	1925	173	33.77	3	9
N. J. Contractor	31	1611	108	31.58	1	11
C. G. Borde	28	1474	177*	33.50	2	8
G. S. Ramchand	26	1049	109	26.89	2	5
M. H. Mankad	19	913	231	33.81	2	2
M. L. Jaisimha	15	845	127	35.20	1	5
R. G. Nadkarni	21	794	78*	25.61	0	5
S. A. Durani	11	476	104	26.44	1	2

*Not out

TOP BOWLERS IN SECOND WAVE

	Matches	Wickets	Best	Avg	5WI	10WM
S. P. Gupte	33	144	9/102	29.25	12	1
R. B. Desai	21	55	5/89	40.36	1	0
M. H. Mankad	19	54	5/64	38.87	2	0
R. G. Nadkarni	21	41	6/105	33.43	1	0
C. G. Borde	28	41	4/21	46.85	0	0
S. A. Durani	11	40	6/105	30.77	2	1
P. R. Umrigar	44	35	6/74	39.51	2	0
G. S. Ramchand	26	31	6/49	45.83	1	0
J. M. Patel	7	29	9/69	21.96	2	1
Surendranath	11	26	5/75	40.50	2	0

TOP WICKETKEEPERS IN SECOND WAVE

	Matches	Dismissals	Ct	St
N. S. Tamhane	21	51	35	16
P. G. Joshi	9	19	14	5
B. K. Kunderan	8	18	14	4
F. M. Engineer	7	9	8	1

Note: No One Day Internationals in this wave

Chapter 9

THE NEW WORLD

UNEXPECTED HAPPINESS

The second wave was quite the most dismal of all the nine waves, two 5–0 thrashings in England and the West Indies and dreadful defeats at home. But this sporting performance must be judged against the wider situation India was in. This was the first decade of independent India, dismissed by the departing British as a state that could not survive—Pakistan was the virile Muslim state which Britain had helped create and the United States of America sponsored. India was short of food and relied on American surplus wheat, given essentially free, and known as PL–480 food (the numbers referred to a law passed by the US Congress). India was so short of foreign exchange that to travel abroad Indians required a Form P to be approved by the Reserve Bank of India before an airline could issue tickets. Before a Test series the board had to beg the Ministry of Finance for the release of foreign exchange. Dismissed as a poor, disease-ridden country whose cricket did not amount to much, not many Test nations came to India. No Tests were played in India in the winter of 1953–54, 1954–55 or 1957–58, despite the fact that 1953–54 marked the silver jubilee of the board. That winter Duckworth again stepped in. Set against this, the tour of the West Indies in the spring of 1953 was groundbreaking both on and off the field. And while India lost the five-Test series 1–0 and never came close to winning a Test match, the cricketers came back not fearful of what fans at home would say. Hazare's chapter in his autobiography describing the tour was entitled, 'The Happiest Tour':

> I had a most enjoyable time as we were a happy bunch of cricketers. There were no rifts in the party. We liked the sun, the beaches and atmosphere. As there are many people of Indian origin settled for long, we felt a home atmosphere with Indian food and customs still prevailing. I did not have to exert in the field. The others took over the load from me. It was a welcome relief.

What had happened was that Indian cricket had quite by chance discovered that there was an Indian diaspora for whom the visit of the Indian cricket team was a discovery of a world they had lost. I am writing this just as Virat Kohli's India has played in Australia with television cameras regularly panning to Indian supporters in various Australian grounds proudly advertising their Indian roots complete with banners and flags. Before Hazare's team arrived in the West Indies, this Indian diaspora was little noticed by both the blacks and the whites of the Caribbean. Now they found their voices on the cricket field.

It helped that the Indian cricket team was unrecognizable from the pathetic bunch that had left England in 1952. Indeed the Indians' individual performances showed the first tentative steps of cricket recovery. There were four draws and one defeat, a record which owed much to solid batting, superb fielding and sublime leg-break bowling by Subhash Gupte. Indeed, the only defeat came when they fell foul of a crumbling, low-bouncing final-day pitch in the Barbados Test.

Umrigar, who had run away from Trueman, making the most of lack of pace in the West Indian attack, was the most impressive batsman, making a century in the first Test and playing consistently through the rest of the series, scoring 560 runs at 62.22. There were also strong contributions from Pankaj Roy, all but runless when confronted by Trueman, and Madhav Apte, who on his first tour came second in the averages with 460 runs at 51.11, while the consistent but unspectacular Manjrekar confirmed he was the rock upon which Indian batting would be built. And despite the reputation that Indians were a poor fielding side, a reputation that would last until the IPL changed things in the second decade of the twenty-first century, the locals were particularly impressed by the Indian fielding—so much so that they would be rated as the best ever seen in the area.

The stars, Chandrasekhar Gadkari, Jayasingh Ghorpade, Dattajirao Gaekwad, Madhav Apte and Umrigar, were young, fit, fast over the ground and threw in hard, flat and accurately. Their fielding silenced the partisan crowd and the way eighteen-year-old Ivan Madray from British Guiana, who later played in two Tests for the West Indies, describes it, the fielding was out of the MCC coaching manual, the fielders moving at tremendous speed as the ball was bowled, picking it up and hurling it in one motion right above the bails. The enthusiasm of the fielders did however cause problems. In the second Test in Barbados Gaekwad and Hazare both went for a catch, collided, and Gaekwad dislocated his shoulder and did not play again, Hazare bruised his left arm and though he continued, his batting form dipped ever further. This was also the only Test India lost, with Gaekwad unable to bat in the second innings.

SPINNING AGAINST THE THREE WS

The quality fielding helped the bowlers grow in confidence, with the leg-spinner Subhashchandra Pandharinath Gupte one of the main beneficiaries. The selectors were initially worried that a leg-spinner who liked to flight the ball would be taken to the cleaners by the three Ws: Weekes, Walcott and Worrell, then the best batsmen in the world, on the Caribbean's fast bouncy wickets. But Gupte, with his flighted leg breaks and his top-spinner, confounded his critics. What set him apart from most leg-spinners of that era were his two extremely well-disguised googlies. Richie Benaud, one of the game's great leg-spinners, would say that Gupte's googly was one of the finest he had ever seen. The reason was it was very similar to Gupte's own leg break: both bowled from a great height, which caused both deliveries to bounce awkwardly. In a Mumbai club match Gupte would once deceive Merchant with a googly and should have had him lbw, but the umpire would not give the great man out and Merchant went on to make a double century. On sun-baked wickets, as in India and the West Indies, the light allowed batsmen to pick the ball as it left the bowler's hand. In England, in contrast, this is rarely possible, so batsmen have to wait till the ball lands. But even the three Ws, confident of distinguishing a leg break from a googly, could not always pick Gupte's googly. The three Ws made runs, Weekes being the most successful and Worrell the least successful, but then the trio made runs against all bowlers. Gupte made them think. Batsmen who had looked impregnable against the rest of the attack looked mortal when he bowled. The lesser West Indian batsmen had even greater problems. Gupte's tally at the end of the series was twenty-seven Test wickets at 29.22; and on the tour his fifty wickets were only seven less than the rest of the Indian bowlers combined. This included twelve wickets against Jamaica, India's only tour victory.

We get some idea of Gupte if we look at the first innings of the first Test in Port of Spain in Trinidad. With the Indians being concentrated mainly on that island, the Indian diaspora was out in force; the gates closed and 22,000 packed the Queen's Park Oval, something that had never happened before. India made 417 and the West Indies looked like they might double that, being 409 for 4, with Weekes on a double century. Now Gupte, who had Worrell's wicket, took over. West Indies lost their last six wickets for 27, got a lead of only 21 and Gupte finished with 7 for 162, including the wickets of Worrell and Weekes.

Leg-spinners do not mind getting hit, confident they can deceive a batsman. Gupte, who acquired the nickname 'Fergie' in England, while playing in the Lancashire League, was an exception. He did not buy his wickets. As Hazare would put it, 'The little leg-spinner with a jaunty walk and carefree outlook bowled extremely steadily and accurately for one of his type.' But while he knew he would be hit he never allowed this to depress him. In his demeanour he never gave the impression that he was worried by the fact that the batsman had just hit him for a four. He gave the impression of a scholar planning his next move to outfox a difficult pupil, and if the ball that had been hit was a leg break he could respond with a googly which the batsman could not read. Also, he often made sure no two balls in an over were exactly the same and kept the batsmen guessing. Leg-spinners are the ultimate rebels, as Shane Warne was to prove, and so was Gupte. But while Warne rebelled he returned to cricket. Gupte paid the price for rebellion and, as we shall see, his career had a sad, premature, ending which reflected no credit on Indian cricket administrators.

Gupte had arrived with Mankad the senior bowler, but by the end he was the senior spinner. It is interesting that from the very first Test Hazare brought Gupte on as his first change bowler, the moment he felt the medium-pace attack of Phadkar and Ramchand had taken the shine off. Mankad was the second-highest wicket-taker with fifteen wickets but proved expensive at a rate of 53.06 a wicket. However, the fact that this duo bowled together was historic, for it meant India had a great spinning pair, and soon India came to produce so many spinners that by the late 1960s they could field four world-class spinners. The question then became who to drop, although at times all four played. There were, of course, cricketing differences: Mankad, a left-hander, was an all-rounder; Gupte, a right-arm bowler, would never have claimed to be a batsman. But, beyond cricket, they reflected the wider changes in Indian society. No prince nurtured Gupte. He, like his great friend Manjrekar—they made their debut together—was from Shivaji Park, the maidan in the congested Maharashtrian heartland of central Mumbai. Over the years this would prove the great nursery of Indian cricket where, in the 1980s, Tendulkar honed his great cricketing skills.

The effect of the tour on the Indian diaspora is really a subject for a book on society not cricket, but here it must be emphasized that the Indian cricket team can claim credit for inspiring them to believe they were not worthless human beings. They were descendants of indentured labourers brought more than a century earlier to work the sugar plantations of the West Indies, Trinidad and Guyana. By the time the Indian cricket team arrived, indentured labour was history, but the Indians retained the customs of their ancestral land and even spoke Hindi. Watching the Indian cricketers play well made them feel India had more to offer than poverty. Gandhi was known in the West Indies but, reflecting white influence, he was seen as a

half-naked fakir. Also, by this time the Indian independence struggle had
begun to inspire the colonial world and the tour came as the West Indian
islands began to agitate for freedom. Suren Capildeo, an East Indian then
studying at Queen's Royal College, argues that the tour brought the Indian
community together for the first time. This would influence Gupte's life.
For one Trinidadian lady of Indian descent saw Gupte play. The lady in
question, whom I had the pleasure of meeting when I interviewed Gupte
in 1989, told me how enchanted she was watching Gupte. A few years later
they got married and Gupte eventually settled in Trinidad, which is where
I met his wife and him. The tour was also a boon for the West Indies
Board, who had initially not been keen on the series, but now discovered
that they could make money from West Indians of Indian descent. This was
a constituency they had known little about before the Indian cricketers
arrived in the islands. Indeed, the Indians had arrived by banana boat from
England accompanied by Worrell and when they docked in Barbados the
large crowd that had gathered had come to welcome Worrell back home.
He had to point to the Indians and ask the public to greet the visitors. By
the time Hazare and his men left, there were enough West Indians, albeit
of Indian origin, who knew who the stars were.

MANKAD IN LOVE, GUPTE IN WICKETS

The tour marked the departure from international cricket of the third
of the Fab Four, Hazare, although he continued to play domestic cricket,
taking Baroda to the Ranji title in 1957–59 and playing against the West
Indians when they toured India in 1958–59. There was even a campaign by
Merchant to have him return as captain. This he wisely rejected. This left the
last of the Fab Four, Mankad, who, as it happened, did play against the West
Indies in 1958 but in circumstances he would have liked to forget. His great
chance to prove he could captain India came when he took the team to
Pakistan in January 1955 but, to the surprise of everyone, his leadership was
dismal. A man who had always given good cricketing advice to captains he
had served now could not take decisions. Pankaj Roy, who was on the tour,
told me this was because he fell for a beautiful young Pakistani girl and did
not take any interest in the cricket.

　　Probably, Mankad was trying to make up for the fact that with Partition
casting a shadow there was much tension between the two teams and
the players did not mix. Maybe Mankad was bored, as the cricket was
dreadful: all five Tests were drawn, something that had never happened
before in nearly eighty years of Test cricket. The *Ambala Tribune* summed
it up brilliantly when its report of the fourth Test was headlined, 'Match

Saved But Cricket Killed'. There were also umpiring problems, with Indians feeling Pakistani umpires were being biased and turning down even clear run-out decisions. But in one hilarious case the Pakistani umpire in the Lahore Test gave Alimuddin, Pakistan's best batsman, not out when he was clearly caught by the wicketkeeper but gave him run-out when he was not. Alimuddin was not pleased.

Amarnath was manager and luxuriated in going back to Lahore, where he was treated like a king. But he fell out publicly with Kardar and the two men exchanged blows in a Lahore hotel. Oborne, in his 2014 history of Pakistan cricket, says he spoke to the Pakistani players and none of them remember such an incident. However, Kardar and Mankad nearly had a fight. Just months before Pakistan had come back from England covered in glory, winning the Oval Test and drawing the series. Kardar, never one to miss an opportunity to assert the superiority of Pakistan, and a man who had been close to Jinnah, in a speech contrasted how well Pakistan had played as opposed to India. Mankad furiously confronted him and according to Berry Sarbadhikary, the Indian journalist who was covering the tour, there was 'an angry exchange of words and almost on the point of a scuffle'.

The arrangements made for the team at Bahawalpur were so bad that Amarnath threatened to take the team home. Then, just before the last Test, Amarnath went to have tea with Kardar as a goodwill gesture and later claimed he had discovered a plot by the umpire, Idrees Baig. Baig had come into the room and, not realizing Amarnath was there, asked Kardar, 'Any instructions for tomorrow's game, skipper?' When Amarnath revealed himself, Baig fled and claimed it was a misunderstanding. Amarnath insisted the umpire be changed and Baig, who had officiated in all the previous four Tests, was replaced by Masood Salahuddin. However, on a forgettable tour, Gupte proved his performance in the West Indies was not a flash in the pan. On shirt-front batting wickets he took twenty-one wickets at 22.61 and would strike so devastatingly that the Pakistan batting would suddenly collapse. In the first Test Pakistan went from 122 for 2 to 158 all out with Gupte taking 5 for 18 in six overs. In the Lahore Test he took 5 for 133 in 73.5 overs, 32 of which were maidens; and in the fourth Test, at Peshawar, he caused another collapse, taking 5 for 63. But the batsmen did not back him. They had similar problems—not Pakistan spin, for Pakistan had nobody like Gupte—but the fast-medium bowling of Khan Mohammad and Fazal. It highlighted how, seven years after partition, the two cricketing nations were diverging. Pakistan's attack, like that of pre-partition India, was still pace-led, while India had become almost pure spin.

GUPTE'S BUNNIES

Gupte in these two overseas series had taken forty-eight wickets. In the winter of 1955–56 came his first home series. Gupte could not have asked for a team more suited to be devastated by his bowling. It was New Zealand on their first series with India. New Zealand is a rugby nation: many consider their All Blacks team the best ever, and cricket comes a long way second. At this stage, despite the fact that they had made their debut in January 1930, they had achieved little on the cricket field, not won a single Test, and were so little regarded by Australia that they had not even played a Test against their neighbours (they did not play Australia until January 1974) and were completely clueless against spin. They had arrived in India having lost a three-Test series in Pakistan 2–0, floored by the off-spin of Zulfiqar Ahmed. Leg spin was even more mysterious. Gupte quickly sensed that and struck like a vicious cobra. In the first Test in Hyderabad he took 7 for 128; only once, in the third Test at Delhi, did he fail to take five wickets in at least one innings. In the second and the fifth Tests, both of which India won by an innings, he demonstrated the wonder of leg-spin bowling. Neville Cardus had called leg-spinners the millionaires of cricket; Gupte was a miser, tormenting the New Zealand batsmen almost at will.

In Mumbai, after India made 421, New Zealand were bowled out for 258 and 136, Gupte taking 8 for 128. In the fifth, after India had made 537 for 3 declared on another easy-paced Chennai wicket, Gupte took 9 for 145, bowling New Zealand out for 209 and 219. Gupte finished the series with thirty-four wickets, two more than all the other Indian bowlers put together, at an average of 19.67. There is something magical about leg spin. And the New Zealand batsmen facing Gupte played him as if this was one Indian magic trick too far for them. They would play for a leg break, it would turn out to be a googly; they would play for a googly, it would turn out to be a top-spinner. Gupte had further developed his art, always willing to learn from more experienced players like Mankad. He would tweak his field placings depending on whether he was bowling on a turner or a flat wicket. Leg-spinners can sometimes find it difficult to bowl line and length, but Gupte never had any such problems. He had also worked out how to aim for the off-stump or just outside. On good batting wickets, flight, on turning wickets, where he knew the wicket would help him, a much flatter trajectory. He worked on a simple mathematical principle: when you bowl slow, you can spin more, if you bowl fast, you can spin less.

His domination of the Indian bowling since his first Test in the West Indies in January 1953 was extraordinary. He had played in three series. He had dominated the bowling, overshadowing Mankad, who for the last decade had been the leading Indian bowler, both in the number of wickets he took and his average. But now let us look at how Gupte had changed things:

Gupte vs West Indies: 329.3–87–789–27, average 29.22, Mankad, with 345 overs and fifteen wickets averaged 53.06.

Gupte vs Pakistan: 276.5–107–475–21, average 22.6, Mankad, with 263.3 overs and twelve wickets averaged 33.25.

Gupte vs New Zealand: 356.4-153-669-34, average 19.67, Mankad, with 167.1 overs and twelve wickets averaged 27.33.

This series also showed the growing interaction between player and crowd in a cricket match, which is now so common but back in 1955 was a novelty. Virat Kohli, India's captain, is the master of this, gesturing to the crowd to get behind the players as he did both in England in the summer of 2018 and in Australia a few months later. Back in December 1955, as Gupte bowled India to victory against New Zealand in the second Test in Mumbai he did not need to do that. The moment he ran in to bowl they erupted. Picture the scene. A baking hot afternoon in Mumbai. India have made 421. Sutcliffe, New Zealand's best batsman, is trying to offer some resistance. Gupte runs in to bowl and the crowds in the East Stand, swaying in rhythm with his run-up start chanting 'boh-oh-oh-ohwled'. Sutcliffe walks away, goes up to Umrigar, the captain, protests and Umrigar walks up to not far from where I am sitting in the East Stand, puts palms together and pleads for us to be quiet. We obey, although it makes no difference as, while Gupte did not get Sutcliffe's wicket, but caught him instead, he got most other wickets. For years I thought this was excitable behaviour, unique to India, until 2015, when I saw the crowd at Lord's also shout 'boh-oh-oh-ohwled' when Moeen Ali ran up to bowl. And, as it happened, this was also against New Zealand batsmen. In 1955 at Lord's this would have been unimaginable behaviour. In 2015, it was so welcome that the English captain did not plead with the crowd to keep quiet; the English players milked the chorus of support and England duly won.

Unlike in Pakistan, in this series, Indian batsmen made sure Gupte's bowling did not go to waste. Only once did India fail to make 400 runs, and batsmen competed to set new records. In the first Test, Umrigar became the first to score a double hundred in Tests. His 223 also meant he had passed Mankad's then Indian record of 184. But Mankad was dislodged only for one Test. In the second Test Mankad made 223.

What was required was a world record and this came in the fifth Test, played at a new ground in Chennai, the Corporation Stadium. India, batting on winning the toss, opened with Mankad and Roy and they did not get out until the afternoon of the second day. Mankad made 231, Roy made 173 and the pair put on 413 for the first wicket, setting a new first-wicket record that was not broken until 2008. Mankad's Indian record stood until Gavaskar surpassed it in the same city but not the same ground twenty-eight years later.

But what a pair to set such a world record. Mankad, as we have seen, was hardly a regular opener as he had batted in almost every position and Arlott had advised back in 1946 he should not be made to open. Roy was a middle-order batsman who became an opener to break into the Indian side. He started badly against New Zealand with a duck, was dropped, then quite accidentally discovered he was shortsighted. Equipped with glasses, he forced the selectors to look at him again and made a century in front of his home crowd in Kolkata, albeit batting No. 3. He would have loved to emulate Mankad and score a double century but told me he was misled by Umrigar, the captain, to hit out, telling him he was going to declare. He did not. Roy felt Umrigar, one of only two Indians who had made Test double centuries, could do nothing to stop Mankad joining the club but did not want Roy to become a member of such a select group. Roy, who never scored a double century, never forgave Umrigar. When Roy first told me the story, my publishers, worried what Umrigar might say, would not let me use the story. Now both are dead and Roy's anguish can be revealed.

The New Zealand series marked the high point of Gupte's remarkable raj. There would be other successes. But never again would he exercise such total dominance.

Chapter 10

SHAFTS OF LIGHT IN DARKEST GLOOM

THE WEST INDIAN-STYLE BODYLINE

India should have built on the success against New Zealand but failed to do so. The next three series until the end of the 1950s saw dreadful defeats both at home and abroad. What was even worse was that against two of India's opponents, Australia and West Indies, Pakistan at home were proving the masters, further boosting Kardar's ego.

In October 1956, Australia, on their way back from a drubbing in England, came to the subcontinent. They had lost their solitary Test in Pakistan by nine wickets and seemed to be there for the taking by India. Instead, India lost the three-Test series 2–0. Not once did the Indians top 300 and perhaps most galling of all, Gupte was overshadowed by Benaud, who took twenty-three wickets at 16.86. One of the best innings was played by Neil Harvey in Mumbai. I saw him score a magical 140 with Gupte scoring a hundred in the bowling column: 115 for 3.

The defeats at the hands of Australia were followed by even more dreadful thrashings at the hands of the West Indians in the winter of 1958–59, which brought back old memories of Indian batsmen being scared of pace and was quite the worst home series for India while I was growing up.

The West Indies, who arrived in November 1958, were still led by a white captain, Gerry Alexander, the wicketkeeper from Jamaica but with Sobers, Rohan Kanhai, Basil Butcher, Joseph Solomon and Collie Smith was bursting with black talent. Sobers had already made headlines, having broken Hutton's Test record with 365 not out against Pakistan earlier in the year. The first Test was in Mumbai and I was given a day off from school to see the first day. As Sobers came out to bat, I felt like Neville Cardus seeing his Australian hero, Victor Trumper, bat. He had prayed to let Trumper score a hundred and the Australians be bowled out for 103. I felt the same about Sobers. Sobers had got to 25 and, as was the tradition in India, the Mumbai crowd cheered. But then Ghulam Guard, the bald policeman who bowled gentle medium-pace, suddenly produced a bouncer. Sobers in trying to hook lost his bat, the ball looped up gently and Guard took the catch easily. After that, my hero Gupte took over, taking 4 for 86 and by the close of play the West Indies were all out for 227, which, batting first on a good wicket, was first strike to India. I went to school the next day in a happy mood.

What I and most of us did not know was that in Wesley Hall and Roy Gilchrist, the West Indies had two young fast bowlers who were ready to bowl the 1950s version of bodyline, bouncers around the wicket to a packed leg-side field, sometimes six bouncers an over. They and, in particular, Gilchrist seemed to aim at the batsmen, and even bowl the beamer. Gilchrist would sometimes deliver a beamer from 18 yards; he once charged a player with a stump in a Lancashire League match and almost a decade after we saw him play in India, on 2 June 1967, he got into an argument with his wife, Novlyn, grabbed her throat with his left hand, pushed her against a wall, and branded her face with a hot iron. The judge sentencing him at Manchester Crown Court said, 'I hate to think English sport has sunk so far that brutes will be tolerated because they are good at games.' My abiding memory is of seeing Gilchrist running up from the boundary edge of the Brabourne Stadium and bowling to a field where almost all the fielders were behind the bat but the batsmen could make nothing of as he did not give them a ball to drive, all of the deliveries being short and directed at the body. And this was an era when no one wore helmets or other protective gear. The best batsmen could do was wrap towels underneath their trousers. The only good thing was nobody was killed, although Hardikar must have come close when in the second Test a beamer grazed his temple and went for four. He never played Test cricket again.

Intimidation was the name of the game, and while India saved the first Test, they lost the next three, two of them by an innings. The series was so devastating that India went through four captains, Umrigar in the first, Ghulam Ahmed in the second and the third, Mankad in the fourth and Adhikari in the fifth. The choice for the fourth Test in Chennai was farcical. Umrigar had a row with the selectors about team selection and resigned the night before the match. The speed of the changes was matched only by the absurdity with which appointments were made. Mankad took over at the back of the toilets of Chennai's Corporation Stadium on the morning of the match. And Adhikari only got the job because the first choice, Ramchand, was uncontactable, as he had caught an earlier train from Mumbai to avoid the Republic Day crowds. The selectors decided that there was little point chasing after Ramchand and appointed Adhikari instead. Ramchand did not even make the team for the final Test in Delhi, nor the touring team to England in 1959 which was selected just afterwards. Ramchand is unique in Indian cricket history as the man who caught the Mumbai Mail on time but missed being captain of India.

GUPTE'S NEAR WORLD RECORD

Amid the depression of the 3–0 home defeat, Gupte did provide some cause for celebration when he came within one wicket of matching Jim Laker's then unique 1956 achievement of taking ten wickets in an innings.

Gupte's skill had tested even Sobers and Kanhai from the first day of the series and at Kanpur, where the jute matting had been laid on almost bare earth; he was all up unplayable.

Having won the toss and batted, the West Indies had slumped to 88 for 6, all falling to Gupte. He had taken three more when the last man, Gibbs, was dropped by Naren Tamhane, the wicketkeeper, a Mumbai man and a close friend of Gupte. He remains the only bowler to be deprived of such a unique honour because of a dropped catch.

With 9 for 102 he became the first Indian to take that number in a Test innings. One measure of the achievement is that India would have to wait forty-one years for Kumble to take all ten. Another, perhaps more significant, measure is the quality of his victims: Conrad Hunte, John Holt, Sobers, Kanhai, Collie Smith, Butcher, Solomon, Alexander, Hall; only Alexander made a 50. It is no disrespect to Laker or Kumble to say that neither faced such a formidable line-up. By then ball-by-ball commentary was being broadcast on the radio and one young boy listened to Gupte's magical spell. 'I was so inspired by that performance that I took up spin bowling. Gupte's feats really spurred me on.' That young boy was Bishan Singh Bedi, who in the years to come would weave his own magic.

DULL DOGS OF CRICKET

It was hard to imagine it could have got worse, but it did on the England tour that followed. The summer of 1959 was one of the hottest on record in England. The sun shone and India should have felt at home. Instead, captained by D. K. Gaekwad, who did not even expect to be in the team and was considering an offer to play in the Lancashire League, India did even worse than in 1952. England for the first time won a Test rubber in England by five matches to nil.

Before the tour Tom Graveney had identified Gupte as a match-winner in English conditions. Gupte did take seventeen Test wickets, but they were expensive at 34.64 runs each and he could do nothing to stop England. The Indian fielding and batting did not help. India passed 300 only once in ten innings, losing three Tests by an innings, one by eight wickets and the other by 171 runs. The final Test at the Oval ended before three o'clock on the fourth day, and so an exhibition match was played. Roy Swetman, who had kept wickets in the Test, took off his gloves and bowled; within a few minutes India were 13 for 4, Swetman taking three wickets. As John Arlott wrote in his *Cricket Journal*, 'thereafter it deteriorated into so poor an affair that the spectators could raise neither applause nor mirth and, apart from those who stayed to sun-bathe, began to drift away.'

The tour was so dismal English critics branded India 'the dull dogs of cricket'. It was no better when, in the winter of 1959, India lost the first Test against Australia in Delhi by an innings. The crowd threw bottles and jostled the umpires. India had lost nine out of their previous eleven Test matches and it was not surprising that some wags suggested that maybe Indians should abandon cricket for gilli-danda. At least in this India could not lose as no one else would know how to play it. But then, as so often happens, there was a new shaft of light.

THE ONE-TEST WONDER THAT SURPRISED AUSTRALIA

In the merry-go-round of the Indian captaincy, Ramchand, to his great surprise, found himself in the job for the series against Australia. A useful medium-pace bowler, and a hard-hitting lower-order batsman, he keenly felt the way the Indian board treated its own players, noting that their hotels and transport were often inferior to that offered to visiting teams. 'We were made to feel inferior in our own country,' he said.

This made him more determined than ever to win. This time the brilliance came from Jasu Patel, a shock choice for the fifteen-man squad, let alone the final eleven. He was not a classical off-spinner. A wrist injury had left him with a jerky action, which some thought suspect. He did not bowl spinners but cutters. His ideal bowling surface was matting but Kanpur had newly laid turf which was soft on top and Amarnath thought it might suit him.

The plan worked like a charm. In the first innings, Australia were 71 without loss replying to India's 152 when Patel persuaded Ramchand to let him switch ends so that he could bowl into Alan Davidson's footmarks. He did even better than Gupte and took 9 for 69, the best bowling analysis then by an Indian in a Test innings. Set 225 to win, Australia fell short by 119 runs, with Patel taking 5 for 55 to give him match figures of 14 for 124 runs.

This first Indian victory over Australia had come in an era when Australia could claim to be world champions. Patel's magical act had, with superb timing, come on Christmas Eve 1959. The victory was only the sixth time India had won a Test, but it was such a surprise after the previous four years that it made the front page of the *Times of India* with its cricket correspondent getting quite intoxicated as he hit the keyboard of his typewriter:

> Let the trumpets sound, the drums roll. Let the herald angels sing... Today was a day to remember, a day that will be inscribed for ever in our cricket annals; a day that will be enshrined for ever in the hearts and minds of the vast assemblage that had come to cheer an India victory... In years to come the story will be told how India, after years of wilderness found their place in the sun, how India despite all the ranting, raving critics, showed that there is still good cricket in their blood.

But Patel was never able to repeat the performance. In all he played only seven Tests, with fourteen of his twenty-nine Test wickets coming in that Kanpur match. He did not play in Mumbai where India fought back to draw. He returned for Chennai, where he got 2 for 84 in Australia's only innings, with the visitors clinching the series with an innings victory. His last appearance was in Kolkata where India ground out a draw and never played again.

THAT KISS

But if the *Times of India* had overegged the Kanpur victory, the tour of Australia had shown that Indian cricket was gaining a wider appeal. Test matches in India were now tamasha. During the Mumbai Test, Abbas Ali Baig was acknowledging his second 50 of the match, when a girl ran onto the pitch and kissed him on the cheek. The girl had come out from the respectable North Stand and was further proof that cricket was starting to appeal to women for the first time. My aunts would never have kissed anybody, not publicly, but they had begun to follow the game on the radio.

BOLLYWOOD AND CRICKET

Bollywood film stars, although that term was invented later, were also keen on the game. As Baig was saving India, Raj Kapoor, Dilip Kumar, Pran, and others were in the CCI pavilion trying to persuade Ramchand to declare. The crowd were baying for Ramchand to declare and pressured by Raj Kapoor, who actually walked into the Indian dressing room, Ramchand gave in. Many of these film stars themselves played weekend cricket although it would take another seventy years, the creation of IPL, and a new generation of stars led by Shah Rukh Khan for Bollywood stars to own cricket teams.

CRICKET FEVER

This Test also saw the first manifestation in Mumbai of what Indians would call 'cricket fever'. It was a transient mood, for the moment the match was over, cricket would almost vanish from the public consciousness—but even so it was of great significance. Such was the demand for Test match tickets that to see a match you had to buy a ticket for all five days, popularly called season tickets. Despite the demand, my father got me tickets for the first day of the Test, New Year's Day, 1960. The stands were so crowded that we could not move and there were no toilets—sadly my father fell ill and we left at lunchtime. However, I did carry a great cricket memory away: Davidson bowling Roy with an inswinger, Roy playing down the wrong line, and the wicket landing at the feet of wicketkeeper, Wally Grout. Great swing bowling from a great master of the art. Roadside paan and bidi stalls blared out the cricket commentary, with restaurants putting up noticeboards displaying the score. This was a very Indian show built around five days of Test cricket, rivalling Bollywood as entertainment and, what is more, not just cricket involving India. Visitors to India are taken by the fact that Indians take an interest in sport even when there is no Indian involvement, something unimaginable in the United Kingdom. But that is something that goes back to the 1950s. Then, with All India Radio (AIR) being puritanical and not broadcasting film music, a private radio station called Radio Ceylon started doing that, supplementing it with news from the BBC World Service and cricket commentary from Australia even when India was not playing Australia. The time difference meant Indians could get up early in the morning to listen to the commentary and then at lunchtime hear the close of play scores. Cricket was becoming more than just a game and urban India—it still had not penetrated rural India—was as keen as mustard. It helped that 1960 was also when hockey took a nosedive: India, Olympic champion since the 1928 Olympics, lost its gold medal to Pakistan. A sport that might have challenged cricket hit the buffers and its decline had come at the right time for cricket.

KUNDERAN DESTROYS DULL DOGS MYTH

During the Australia series, India also started to introduce players who brought a spontaneity missing for much of the dull, dreary 1950s. The most notable was Budhi Kunderan, a largely untutored wicketkeeper batsman whose natural talent became harnessed to the game through luck and chance.

A product of the maidans and Merchant's old school, Bharda, he scored a double hundred in his first school match, playing in borrowed whites and equipment. He was soon playing with Merchant and then, finding the Mumbai team difficult to break into, joined the Railways, where Amarnath, now coaching the team, quickly spotted his potential. He made a quiet debut against Australia in Mumbai, also his first-class debut, but at Chennai he came into his own. Going in first because the regular opener, Contractor, was ill, he started hitting the Australian bowlers, Alan Davidson and Ian Meckiff, around the ground.

He broke all the conventional rules about the need for opening batsmen to play solidly, prompting one Australian commentator to ask if he realized he was playing in a Test match or thought it was maidan cricket.

How ironic that nearly half a century later an Australian wicketkeeper, Adam Gilchrist, would achieve iconic status by attacking from the word go. Kunderan struck the first blow against the 1950s ethos that made it seem as if India always played for a draw and saw a draw as a substitute for a win. But it would require a prince to really lift Indian cricket.

Chapter 11

TRAGEDY AND ROMANCE

QUESTIONING MUSLIM LOYALTY

Nari Contractor's captaincy was marked by the emergence of a worrying attitude towards Muslims and sweet revenge on England, but ended with a personal tragedy for Contractor resulting in India's most romantic cricketer taking charge of the game and reshaping it.

Contractor's first series against Pakistan in 1960–61 resulted in five drawn Tests. As the two neighbours battled it out, in Australia, one of the most fantastic Test series ever was being played against a West Indian team led for the first time by a black captain, Frank Worrell. This saw the first tied Test and a gripping finish to the final Test. For me as a teenager it was a surreal experience. I would get up in the morning to listen to the commentary from Australia then follow the most turgid series in India, marked by both India and Pakistan being afraid to lose. India did make Pakistan follow on in the final Test but could not bowl them out in time to win.

It was what happened to Abbas Ali Baig that was very worrying. The series reduced Baig's cricketing world to dust. The Oxford man, around whom the next generation of Indian batting was supposed to be built, had a miserable series; in three matches he made 34 runs with a top score of 19. What was particularly distasteful was that his patriotism was questioned with some accusing him of sabotaging his own chances to ensure that Islam, in the form of the Pakistan cricket team, could triumph. He received a torrent of poison-pen letters, telephone calls and telegrams alleging he was a traitor. After the 1960 Pakistan tour he became the forgotten man of Indian cricket and played just two more Tests, seven years later.

I was made aware of this anti-Muslim feeling as a schoolboy on the first day of the first Test in Mumbai on 2 December 1960. I persuaded my parents to get me a ticket in the Brabourne Stadium's East Stand. The route to the ground passed Churchgate railway station. I was accompanied by one of my father's clerks. As we passed the station we saw a crowd of bearded men emerge from the station. My father's clerk, a devout Maharashtrian

Brahmin, quickly identified them as Muslims saying, 'No wonder these Miyabhais come crawling out now. It is their team that is playing. No prizes for guessing who they are supporting.' Until then I had never heard anyone say Muslims in India would always support Pakistan. In my Jesuit school, which as I have mentioned was also Gavaskar's, the top boys in our class were Muslim, my best friend was a Muslim, as was M. C. Chagla, later to become a renowned judge and probably the one Indian the whole country admired. I was shocked by my father's clerk's remarks. However, within a few years, as the Shiv Sena got control of Mumbai, this would be a very common sentiment.

GUPTE AND HIS ROOMMATE

This was the climate in which Ted Dexter brought an England side to India in November 1961. It was another England B team without Colin Cowdrey, Brian Statham or Fred Trueman. For India it was a bittersweet series, producing the first series victory over England but ending the career of Gupte, not because he could not perform on the field but because of what his roommate did off the field. Gupte, who had not played in the first Test in Mumbai—the Chennai leg spinner V. V. Kumar played and did not take a wicket—was recalled for the second Test in Kanpur.

After India made 467 for 8 declared, which showed what a good batting wicket it was, Gupte took 5 for 90—all first five batsmen—and India, having so often in England been asked to follow on, could now, for the first time, tell England to bat again. England, playing classic defensive cricket, got a draw, but for India the great news was the old Gupte was back. But in one of the most bizarre episodes in Indian cricket history, the next Test in Delhi ended Gupte's career due to something his roommate, Kripal Singh, did in the Imperial Hotel. Singh tried to make a date with a hotel receptionist and she complained to the Indian manager. The call was traced to their room, and even though Kripal admitted sole responsibility to the board president, Mr Chidambaram, they were both suspended, and the selectors were told not to pick Gupte for the tour to the West Indies that was to follow. In what is not unusual for India, the Indian board tried to conceal this and the story only emerged when journalists, intrigued that Gupte had been dropped, pestered Contractor and the Indian captain revealed the true story. Gupte's father wanted to sue Kripal but did not have the money. The story that went around later was that the lady in question was fancied by a powerful cricket administrator.

Gupte, understandably bitter about his treatment, never played again. He would have liked to end his career in the West Indian islands where he had first made his mark. Instead, having married the Trinidadian Indian girl he had met on the 1953 tour he decided to make Trinidad his home. He never forgot India and when I met him in 1989 regaled me with stories of his life in India and rated every leg-spinner who had played for the country since his sad departure.

So where does Gupte stand in the lexicon of leg-spinners?

In 2011, Amol Rajan, now Media Editor of the BBC, wrote *Twirlymen: The Unlikely History of Cricket's Greatest Spin Bowlers*. He bought me lunch and has quoted me at length, saying, 'Always excitable and loyal to the land of his birth, Mihir Bose contends that...Gupte was the finest leg-spinner that ever played... The evidence for Bose's view is not borne out by statistics or superficial appearances, but it does exist.' Actually, the statistics are not bad. Gupte's figures are thirty-six Tests, 149 wickets, average of 29.55. A comparison with other Indian spinners, some his contemporaries, others who came after, is also very interesting:

	Balls	Wickets	5 wickets in an innings
Mankad	14,686	162	8
Ghulam Ahmed	5,650	68	4
Bedi	21,364	266	14
Chandrasekhar	15,963	242	16
Prasanna	14,353	189	10
Venkataraghavan	14,877	156	3
Gupte	11,284	149	12

Only two of the great spinners of the 1960s and 1970s, Bedi and Chandra, had more five-wicket hauls, but both of them bowled many more balls—in Bedi's case, nearly twice as many.

Let us now compare Gupte with his international contemporaries:

	Balls	Wickets	5 wickets in an innings
Laker	12,027	193	9
Lock	13,147	174	9
Ramadhin	13,939	158	10
Valentine	12,953	139	8
Benaud	19,108	248	16

There is, of course, the question of calling Gupte the greatest ever when, since him, Australia has had Shane Warne and India has had Anil Kumble. Listen to Sobers. In his 1998 biography, which had a foreword by Bradman, Sobers wrote, 'In my opinion, Gupte was the best leg-spinner of my time in cricket—better than Richie Benaud or, from the modern time, Abdul Qadir.' In his 2003 autobiography, by which time Warne was already established as the great star, Sobers still said Gupte was the best. At Shivaji Park Gymkhana, where Gupte played so much of his cricket, there is a quote from Sobers, 'Warne is the latest but Fergie was the greatest'. Sobers also said that he could not read Gupte's googly. Kanhai, who Gupte often foxed, Graveney, Laker and Hanif all rated him the best.

Comparison across generations is impossible, all the more so as those that followed Gupte played a lot more Tests. However, Gupte versus the three great leg-spinners who came after him: Warne, Kumble, Qadir, makes interesting reading:

	Matches	Wickets	Best	Avg	SR	5WI	10WM
Gupte	36	149	9-102	29.55	75.73	12	1
Qadir	67	236	9-56	32.80	72.56	15	5
Kumble	132	619	10-74	29.65	65.99	35	8
Warne	145	708	8-71	25.41	57.49	37	10

And while there can be no denying Warne's status as one of the game's greatest-ever bowlers, it should be noted he played in an all-conquering Australian side and had bowlers like Glenn McGrath to support him while Gupte played in weak Indian teams and knew if he did not take wickets, no one else would.

Interestingly, in the Chennai Test which Gupte did not play in, an off-spinner from Bengaluru called Erapalli Prasanna made his debut. He took one wicket in the second innings, but he would prove to be the future. In the meantime, India's spinners were all genuine all-rounders: Chandu Borde a leg-spinner, and Salim Durani and Rameshchandra Gangaram Nadkarni both left-armers.

ALL-ROUNDERS LEAD THE ATTACK
Borde, a batsman and useful bowler, would himself admit he could not be compared to Gupte. He more often rolled the ball rather than produce the prodigious spin Gupte could. Nadkarni turned the ball so rarely that

Manjrekar, the great joker in the Indian team, once quipped, 'The only time Nadkarni turned the ball it was declared a national holiday.' His nickname was 'Bapu', a reference to his underwear rather than his bowling. He had copied Gandhi, discarding the western-style underwear for the langoti, a long, kite-shaped piece of cloth with a prominent V at the back draped around the body. No other Indian player wore the langoti and a feature of the Indian dressing room was for Indian players to gather around and watch Nadkarni as he put the langoti on.

Salim Durani was the true exception in this trio. Both Borde and Nadkarni could be dour cricketers, but Durani was exciting and a man who could captivate even his opponents. One story much retailed in the Mumbai cricket world was of Sobers, talking to an Indian cricket fan about Durani, saying, 'Give my regards from a good cricketer to a great cricketer.' His origins were exotic: he was the only Indian cricketer to be born in Kabul. In the fourth Test at Kolkata against Dexter's team, in Gupte's absence, he was used as the first-choice spinner and took eight wickets, helping India win by 187 runs. He had been coached by Mankad, and it could be said Mankad was repaying Durani for what his father had contributed to Mankad's development.

Durani's father, Abdul Aziz, a wicketkeeper, had been recruited by Digvijaysinhji, the ruler of Nawanagar, in the 1930s to help him build his side. As we have seen, Digvijaysinhji also brought in Wensley, who made Mankad a left-arm spinner. However, after partition Abdul Aziz left Salim behind in India and returned to Pakistan, where he ended up coaching the Mohammad brothers—Mushtaq, Hanif and Sadiq. Although Durani had made his debut against Australia in Mumbai, batting at No. 10 and making 18, and bowling just one over in the joke second innings, he did not play against Pakistan in the Test series of 1960–61 but did get a chance to bowl to Mushtaq in a state match. A Test encounter between the coach's son and the men he had coached would have been something else, in particular Durani bowling to Hanif in a Test.

The final Test against England in January 1962 saw the trio of Borde, Durani and Nadkarni really come into their own. They took eighteen wickets between them, Durani ten of them, and Nadkarni, batting No. 8, made a crucial 63. India won the Chennai Test convincingly by 128 runs, a second successive Test victory and the first series victory against England.

FELLED BY A CHUCKER

Alas, within a matter of weeks, this glory had turned to dust. Immediately the England series was over the Indians left for the Caribbean to meet one of the best ever all-round West Indian teams, wonderfully led by Frank Worrell. The first two Tests were quickly lost.

Then came the colony game against Barbados, who had in their ranks a bowler called Charlie Griffith. The Indians had been warned about him by Worrell and were worried that he had a doubtful action.

Contractor opened the innings as usual. He had faced ten balls and from the non-striker's end he heard his fellow Parsee, Rusi Surti, shout, 'Skipper, be careful, this man is chucking the ball.' Contractor brushed this aside, but as he faced the eleventh delivery someone from the pavilion end, from where Griffith was bowling, opened a window in a dark room. With the ground having no proper sight screen, the area behind the bowler's arm went black. Contractor did not see the ball and was hit on the head. He initially appeared all right but eventually had to leave the field. In the dressing room he suddenly started to scream, was taken to hospital and required an operation. The whole team attended the hospital as did a tearful Griffith. Worrell donated blood, with some joking he might have more alcohol than blood. All the Indian players and the journalists covering the tour also gave blood and when Nadkarni gave blood, Dickie Rutnagur, one of the journalists, quipped that *Lancet* ought to look into a 'skeleton donating blood'. It was a tense wait for everyone, but Contractor survived the operation. An iron plate was inserted in his skull and he even played cricket again, but not Test cricket.

The Contractor incident affected other Indian cricketers. The story Papu Sanzgiri, one of Mumbai's most famous journalists, narrated to me was, 'Sardesai, who was batting, told me that he pissed in his pants and that he was happy for me to broadcast this story. Manjrekar was hit on the nose and could not see for twenty minutes. Both Pataudi and Nadkarni could not see Griffith's ball.'

But while the cricket world is unanimous that Griffith was a chucker, off the field he was gentle, in contrast to Gilchrist. Brian Heywood's father played against Griffith and captained Gilchrist in the Lancashire League. Heywood told me, 'When Dad batted against Griffith he did not see the ball. He was certain Griffith threw his bouncer. But Dad said he was a gentle man. Gilchrist was nasty. Once upset that Tony Carrick, the umpire, had no-balled him he threatened to assault him after the match and Tony left the ground immediately the match was over and all the way back was fearful Gilchrist would catch up with him. Fortunately, he did not.'

In the second innings, Griffith was no-balled for throwing, while Manjrekar, in one of the bravest displays seen on a cricket field, scored 100 not out. The next three Tests were lost, making another 5–0 drubbing abroad, but India returned from the West Indies not as depressed as from England in 1959 and with hope that there were younger players, like Durani, who had made a century in the fourth Test, who could rise to the challenge.

And there was a prince who had taken over as captain after Contractor had been felled and who promised to bring something more than just princely intrigue to Indian cricket. A new wave of Indian cricket was about to start.

The Parsee team of 1866, the first Indian cricket team to tour England (MCC).

The history men, Jardine and Nayudu, during the first Test at Lord's, 1932 (Roger Mann).

First appearance of the All India team in a Test match, Lord's, 1932 (Ghaznavi).

Nayudu batting, Lord's Test, 1932, (Roger Mann).

The young Amarnath padded up during the First Test match at the Bombay Gymkhana, 1933 (Amarnath Collection).

Merchant showing his classic late cut, 2 May 1936 (WCCC).

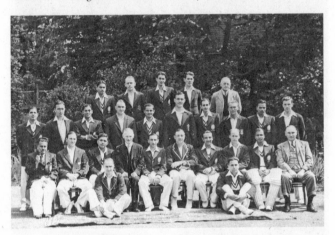

Final appearance of the All India team with the England team before the Oval Test, 1946 (Roger Mann).

Mankad cuts during his Test debut at Lord's in 1946 (Roger Mann).

Hazare shown hooking in the second Test in 1946.

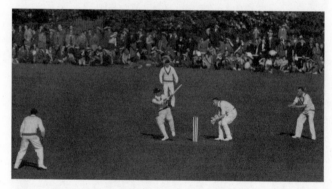

Ali playing one of his favourite shots but getting caught, Worcester 1946 (WCCC).

Gupte on his way to torment batsmen in the Lancashire League in the 1950s (Lancashire League).

Pataudi playing one of his classic innings, 148 in the first Test at Leeds, 1967 (Roger Mann).

Wadekar, the surprise successor to Pataudi, who took India to undreamt of heights (Roger Mann).

A young Gavaskar, seated centre, playing for Dadar Union (Mid-day Infomedia).

Gavaskar in his farewell match at Lord's in 1986 finally scoring a century (Bipin Patel).

Gavaskar and Bedi in Sydney during the Australian tour, 1977-78 (Mihir Bose).

Gavaskar, Viswanath and Kirmani, Karachi Test, 1978 (Mihir Bose).

An abiding image of Dev cover driving (Tim Jones Collection. Assoc. Sports Photography).

Dev, the first genuine Indian fast bowler for half a century (Lancashire League).

Dev holding the World Cup in a 2008 ceremony marking his 1983 triumph (Bipin Patel).

Dev celebrates the first Test victory at Lord's 1986. At far right is Prabhakar whose accusations of match-fixing against Dev would make him cry.

Greatness beckons. A young well-attired Tendulkar, with parents and Kambli (Prakash Parsekar).

Tendulkar acknowledging cheers after his first Test century, Old Trafford, August 1990 (Graham Morris).

Gavaskar with Mandela at his home in Soweto on 30 June 1991. I can be seen in the background (*The Hindu*).

The Third Wave

TESTS

Wave	Period	Matches	Won	Lost	Drawn	Tied	Win%	W/L
3rd	1963–1970	34	7	15	12	0	20.59	0.47

TOP BATSMEN IN THIRD WAVE

	Matches	Runs	HS	Avg	100	50
M. A. K. Pataudi	33	2216	203★	38.20	5	13
C. G. Borde	27	1587	125	37.78	3	10
A. L Wadekar	21	1364	143	34.10	1	10
F. M. Engineer	23	1362	109	30.26	1	6
M. L. Jaisimha	21	1168	129	30.73	2	7
D. N. Sardesai	17	1053	200★	36.31	2	6
R. F. Surti	19	942	99	29.43	0	7
B. K. Kunderan	10	803	192	42.26	2	2
Hanumant Singh	14	686	105	31.18	1	5
R. G. Nadkarni	20	620	122★	25.83	1	2

★Not Out

TOP BOWLERS IN THIRD WAVE

	Matches	Wickets	Best	Avg	5WI	10WM
E. A. S. Prasanna	20	109	6/74	26.56	8	1
B. S. Bedi	19	70	7/98	25.68	4	0
B. S. Chandrasekhar	16	62	7/157	31.32	2	1
S. Venkataraghavan	14	47	8/72	25.17	2	1
R. G. Nadkarni	20	47	6/43	25.27	3	1
R. F. Surti	19	38	5/74	38.13	1	0
S. A. Durani	12	31	6/73	38.90	1	0
S. Abid Ali	12	21	6/55	29.80	1	0
R. B. Desai	7	19	6/56	28.47	1	0
C. G. Borde	27	11	5/88	45.09	1	0

TOP WICKETKEEPERS IN THIRD WAVE

	Matches	Dismissals	Ct	St
F. M. Engineer	23	45	34	11
B. K. Kunderan	7	10	7	3
K. S. Indrajitsinhji	4	9	6	3

Note: There were no One Day Internationals in this wave.

Chapter 12

THE ADORABLE PRINCE

A ONE-EYED MAN TAKES ON THE WORLD

In 2007, as India arrived for their fifteenth tour of England, the *Daily Telegraph*, a paper I had recently left to take over as the BBC's first sports editor, asked me to name my best-ever Indian team. Most of the names were obvious. However, one name caused much controversy. For I selected Mansur Ali Khan, the Nawab of Pataudi, as captain. Bishan Bedi has argued that of his contemporary captains, a list that includes Frank Worrell, M. J. K. Smith, Garry Sobers, Bobby Simpson, Brian Close, Bill Lawry, Graham Dowling and Clive Lloyd, only Worrell ranked above Pataudi. Bedi rates three international captains highly, namely, Ian Chappell, Mike Brearley and Pataudi, and makes the point that Pataudi was a very shrewd, tactical leader working with extremely limited resources. However, on figures, Pataudi's record is hardly a great one.

They are:

Season	Venue	Opponent	Result
1962	West Indies	West Indies	India lost 5–0, Pataudi captain for the last three Tests
1963–64	India	England	All five Tests drawn
1964–65	India	Australia	1–1
1964–65	India	New Zealand	India won 1–0
1966–67	India	West Indies	India lost 2–0
1967	England	England	England won 3–0
1967–68	Australia	Australia	India lost 4–0
1967–68	New Zealand	New Zealand	India won 3–1
1969–70	India	New Zealand	1–1
1969–70	India	Australia	India lost 3–1
1974–75	India	West Indies	India lost 3–2

But for my generation, Pataudi could never be measured in figures. He had restored our faith in cricket and while he did not take us to the promised land, he, like Martin Luther King Jr., made us believe we would get to it if we believed in it fervently enough. What made him romantic was that he was a cricketer whose career seemed over when, at the age of twenty and just when he seemed on the verge of cricketing greatness, lost the sight in his right eye as a result of a car accident.

His comeback after the accident showed his remarkable determination. In November 1961, four months after his accident, he was batting again and scoring runs against Dexter's side. He could even joke about it. When asked when he realized he could play with one eye, he said, 'When I looked at the English bowling.' The previous winter Hazare, now chairman of the selectors, had seen Pataudi, then with two good eyes, batting in the nets and felt 'his judgement of a ball was astray'. However, now with one good eye, Hazare felt Pataudi was in excellent form and selected him to play against England, and in his third Test in Chennai he justified the faith shown in him by making 103. Then, Hazare and his fellow selectors, 'taking the long-term view', made Pataudi vice-captain for the tour to the West Indies:

> Many said a comparatively inexperienced, 21-year-old man, not familiar with his team mates, was rather an unwise choice for the important post of a deputy to the skipper. But we had taken the decision with due consideration to the latent ability and the future prospects of the person concerned.

Hazare's committee could not have anticipated that within five weeks of the Indian team arriving in the West Indies Contractor's injury would propel Pataudi to become captain, in the third Test in Barbados. Only twenty-one, he created a record by becoming the youngest-ever Test captain, a record that stood until 2004.

PATAUDI'S MOTHER AND NEHRU

But when the team returned from the West Indies it was far from certain that Pataudi would be confirmed as captain—it needed the casting vote of the chairman of the selectors to give him the job in the winter of 1963. And here a change in how Indians selected captains also played a part. Until the 1960–61 season, the captain was selected not by the selectors but by the board and, as we have seen, Hazare beat Merchant to the job. But in the winter of 1960, it was the selectors who made the decision. But did somebody even more powerful make sure Pataudi became captain?

Borde was much senior to Pataudi having made his debut in 1958–59.

Although he played under Pataudi in the West Indies after Pataudi took over
following the Contractor injury, it is significant that in the first two Tests
of that series with Contractor as captain, Pataudi did not make the team
whereas Borde was in the side, bowled well and in the second Test made 93.
Interestingly, once Pataudi took over, Borde's bowling form suffered because,
as Dickie Rutnagur covering the series for *Wisden* put it, 'Having learnt
and played most of his cricket in England, Pataudi seemed inexperienced
in the handling of leg-spinners.' Borde, talking to me from his home in
Pune on 19 March 2019, told me that for the Test series against England
in 1963–64 he was told he would be captain. 'I was told the previous day
[before the captain was to be named] by Colonel Adhikari, who was one
of the committee members of the selection committee. I celebrated that
occasion. We were in Delhi for the West Zone vs East Zone match at the
Feroz Shah Kotla ground. We used to get (a) very nominal amount for
playing the matches. It was something like 25 rupees. Just imagine. Then I
borrowed from my colleagues like Bapu [Nadkarni], Sardesai. I told them
I do not have that much money to celebrate. You give me your allowance
and then I will repay you. We went to a restaurant. I don't know why I
did not become captain.' I put it to Borde that the story that circulated
was that he was not made captain as Pataudi's mother wrote to Nehru
and said her son was from the minority community and hence he had
been denied the captaincy and Nehru intervened. Borde told me, 'I read
it in some paper, I think. I don't know that authentically. I have no idea.
Somebody told me this story but I don't know the authentic thing about
this.' When I asked him whether it was possible it happened, he said, 'I
don't know. I was surprised I was not captain.' Then with laughter gurgling
in his voice, he added, 'The previous day felicitated, the next day I was
not a captain. Frankly I never bothered.' When I quizzed him further he
said, 'There were rumours like this.' We will never know the truth of this.
Nehru, Pataudi and his mother are long dead. It is possible these are just
the sort of rumours that fly around to explain the fact that a decision was
suddenly changed and no explanation given. What makes it all the more
remarkable is that Borde was also from a minority community, a Christian.
So is it possible that Pataudi, being a Muslim, counted for more? Or that
Pataudi being like Nehru educated at an English public school and Oxbridge
India's first Prime Minister felt a bond with Pataudi. Rajdeep Sardesai has
suggested that Pataudi was 'a Nehruvian democrat in outlook'. Pataudi's
choice as captain also reflected the fact that Indians, despite claiming to be
the world's largest democracy, were still in love with princes. This was well
demonstrated when princes standing for election won by huge majorities.

Here, though, Pataudi was to prove the exception. In 1971, discarded by the selectors, he stood for election and lost heavily. Much as Indian cricket fans loved him to be in charge of Indian cricket, they could not see him running the country. Unlike Pakistan more than half a century later, Indians were not going to turn to a cricketer to provide political leadership.

There is, of course, no mention in Hazare's memoir about Nehru's intervention and it is possible it was done over his head. Although as a Christian he would not have liked such an anti-Christian attitude, Hazare, having benefited from princely largesse, may have felt that a prince, and a worthy one in terms of cricketing ability, unlike 'Vizzy', was the man to lead India out of a crisis. If all this was unusual, the name he was always called also reflected that Pataudi stood apart from his fellow cricketers. He was always known as 'Tiger', a nickname given to him by his mother because as a child he liked to crawl on all fours.

PATAUDI VS BORDE

Borde never gave up the dream of being captain, encouraged in his hopes by the fact that during his reign Pataudi gave the impression of always falling off the tantalizing tightrope Indian cricket captains have to walk. Indeed, he seemed to enjoy it. There was always talk of Pataudi resigning before being persuaded by the authorities to stay on. The most dramatic moment in this saga came just before the Indian team left for Australia on their 1967–68 tour. The Indians had returned from England in 1967 beaten 3–0 in the Tests and the manager, Keki Tarapore, had made critical references to Pataudi's captaincy. Then, cricketers were so badly treated that the daily allowance was £1; the board did not provide equipment, which obliged cricketers like Kunderan to try to save their allowance to buy a bat; flannels did not fit; and they had cotton sweaters, useless on a tour taking place in the early part of a cold England summer. Pataudi had made his views known and this did not go down well.

All this was, of course, going on behind closed doors. The public were made aware of the drama when, on the eve of a crucial Duleep Trophy final between the West Zone and the South Zone played at the Brabourne Stadium, Pataudi announced he was giving up the captaincy. It overshadowed all other news and I and my friends, watching the match, felt a deep sense of sadness that he was going. In Indian politics it was common for ministers to resign and then change their mind, and we hoped Pataudi would do the same. Throughout the match a remarkable pro-Pataudi sentiment built up and this was crowned by Pataudi himself scoring a double century for South Zone helped by Engineer early in his innings dropping a skier that he would normally have taken in his sleep. This enabled South Zone to take the first innings lead against West Zone and win the Duleep Trophy.

Raju Bharatan in *Indian Cricket: The Vital Phase* says Pataudi's announcement was meant to pre-empt the selection committee, who were due to discuss the manager's report on the England tour before deciding the captain for the Australia tour. Borde was in Mumbai captaining Maharashtra in the Ranji Trophy and, says Bharatan:

> I rushed to his sea front hotel room at 7.00 in the morning to get his 'spot' reaction to the Pat bombshell. 'You look at last like getting the honour that was always rightfully yours,' I said. 'Don't you believe it,' said Borde, 'What's the bet he'll be back on the scene at the "psychological moment"? Don't get me wrong, this kind of thing's happened to me before. I was then promised everything and got nothing, I now just don't hope for anything. Don't believe all that you read. It's ultimately going to be Pat, and Pat alone, as Captain of India to Australia.'

Borde was to be proved right. He went on the tour as Pataudi's vice-captain although he captained in the first Test when Pataudi was injured and in the third Test nearly conjured an unlikely win, India chasing 394 and losing by only 39 runs.

Despite this tussle over the captaincy on the cricket field Pataudi and Borde often batted together. In the third Test against England in Delhi in 1963–64, Pataudi made 203, the first Indian double century against England and put on an unbeaten 190 with Borde, then the highest Indian fifth-wicket stand against England. However, off the field, the stories that went around suggested Pataudi never forgot to remind Borde he came from a higher cricketing stock. One such story went that during a Test match Borde decided to wear his Maharashtra cap as he went out to field. As Borde left the dressing room Pataudi told Borde that he was playing for India, not Maharashtra, and should wear his India cap. Borde is supposed to have replied, 'But Tiger, you often wear your Sussex cap.' Tiger, looking down his long impressive nose, allegedly replied, 'Yes, Chandu, but Sussex is not Maharashtra.' There were different versions of this story with Tiger being credited with wearing the Winchester cap, or the Oxford cap, both teams he had captained. These stories may be apocryphal, but they were endlessly retold and, far from making Tiger sound arrogant, they burnished his image as a unique leader.

One reason for this affection for Tiger was that he was straightforward and did not suffer fools gladly. So, he himself disarmingly acknowledged that he was made captain because he was different. 'In fact, I was selected because culturally and regionally I was from nowhere in particular. I was the simplest way out for our faction-ridden Board. The Indian team is probably the hardest to captain anyway. First of all, you are invariably the weakest side and then you could have the problem of dealing with eleven culturally, ethnically and linguistically different people.'

Pataudi at a personal level himself crossed frontiers, his marriage to Sharmila Tagore being the classic example. An actress who was highly rated by Satyajit Ray, she was from the Tagore family and part of the Bengali Hindu bhadralok, who had always shunned such alliances with Muslims. Sharmila converted to Islam, Pataudi saying that was his mother's wish. Today in India such marriages are seen as 'jihadi marriages', Muslim men seeking out Hindu women. At that time they were not, and even my aunts in Kolkata, nursing memories of the Muslims of pre-partition East Bengal depriving them of the family wealth and hating such marriages, never said a word against the Pataudi–Sharmila marriage.

Even more significant was the attitude of Raj Singh Dungarpur, who would become one of the great administrators of Indian cricket. Dungarpur was immensely proud of his Rajput princely stock and would often tell me with great pride how his clans of Rajputs had never given their daughters in marriage to the Mughals in contrast to the Jaipur family. Yet he loved Tiger and would never hear a word said against him. It also helped that Dungarpur's cousin, Hanumant, the Rajput prince from Banswara, made his debut under Pataudi's captaincy, scoring a hundred in his first match. He often batted No. 5 and if Pataudi was batting No. 4, he always tried to emulate a shot that Tiger had played. Sometimes, as in the Mumbai Test against Simpson's Australia in 1964, this led to Hanumant getting out, but there was no denying the bond between the Rajput and Muslim prince. Dungarpur would tell me how mortified Pataudi was that the selectors did not pick Hanumant for the 1967–68 tour of Australia–New Zealand. Raj, reassured by Pataudi he would be in the side had, the previous winter on a visit to Australia, walked out on the Melbourne ground and told the groundsman that he would see the prince of Banswara use this wicket and then he would see batting he had never seen before.

THE ROYAL PRINCE VS FILMI PRINCE
The only cricketer to remotely threaten Tiger as a romantic hero, a personage off as well as on the field, was Durani. The Salim–Pataudi relationship was complex and interesting. In the early years of Tiger's captaincy, Durani's left-arm spin (Sobers found this particularly difficult and

Durani would crucially get him out when India won their first Test against the West Indies in Trinidad in 1971) and middle-order batting were quite crucial. By the mid-phases of Pataudi's captaincy it was clear that things were not working out well between them. Tiger's hold on the Indian public was derived from the nawabship, the ancestral royal blood that demanded loyalty from its subjects. He reminded Indians of the great Muslim inheritance of the country, and since this was still the Nehru era, when anti-Muslim prejudice had not become part of mainstream life, there was no problem in honouring him. It is interesting that in times of trouble Indians instinctively turned to Pataudi, as for instance during the Kolkata Test against the West Indies on 1 January 1967. Then, wretched ticket distribution by the Bengal Cricket Association, selling more tickets than the ground had capacity for, led to a riot and, as the crowd hunted for the officials, some of them, seeking shelter in the Indian team coach, turned to Pataudi begging him, 'Please, please don't let the crowds see us or we will be killed.' But his regal air also came out in the way he kept his distance from his cricketing colleagues. Even cricketers who adored him never became his buddies and in fact he only had two in this category, M. L. Jaisimha and Naresh Kumar, one of India's great tennis players.

Durani, in contrast, was everyone's yaar (friend), fans could make demands on him. They would shout 'chako maro, Salim' (hit a six), something they would never have dared with Tiger. Durani had all the Mumbai filmi charm: his slightly unkempt look—the long hair falling over the eyebrows and perpetually being brushed back—combined with his ability to convert lounging laziness into electric athleticism. He would after retirement take to films, although not as successfully.

I well remember the last occasion Durani played under Tiger's captaincy. It was the first Test of the 1966–67 series against the West Indies at Mumbai. India, after a bad beginning, had struggled to make a decent score, with Durani helping Borde in the rescue act. Durani made a lovely 55, including one huge straight six over Charlie Griffith's head into the CCI pavilion, much applauded because of what Griffith had done to Contractor. If this was classic Salim, so was his dismissal, head in the air, bat askew and bowled by Sobers all over the shop. For much of the match he fielded at third man, just in front of the North Stand, and throughout the innings I seem to recall him combing his hair, wearing a rather detached, vacant look. Once or twice his preoccupation with his hair led him to misfield, and one could almost feel the electricity passing between Pataudi and Durani. After India had lost the Test, with Sobers bringing the match to a close in good time to get to Mahalaxmi Race Course where one of the classics was being staged, Durani was one of the casualties. He was replaced by Bishan Singh Bedi. To most Indian cricket followers Bedi was unknown, and to some his inclusion was seen as yet another example of the daftness of Indian cricket selection. Little did we know the magic in Bedi's left arm. But even after we appreciated it, we continued to mourn Salim, though he did not make a comeback for almost five years. By then Pataudi had been replaced by Ajit Wadekar, and nothing could comfort Indian cricket for the lost years of Salim Durani.

TIGER POUNCES ON THE AUSTRALIANS

Pataudi really made his mark in his second series in October 1964 when the Australians, captained by Bobby Simpson, stopped in India for a three-match series on the way back from retaining the Ashes in England. Simpson's team lived up to their status as world champions by winning the first Test at Madras by 139 runs. But India was consoled by taking a first innings lead against Australia for the first time, led by Pataudi making 128 not out, in an Indian score of 276. Nobody else made a 50. October in Mumbai can be very hot and is rarely a time for Tests. But now the second Test started on 10 October and finished on 15 October. That was also Dussehra and provided one of the most enthralling days of Test cricket seen in India. Everything about this Test was unusual including an event which took place just after Simpson had won the toss. He returned to the CCI pavilion to discover that Norman O'Neill, one of his best batsmen, who batted No. 3, had symptoms suspiciously like polio. It was a false alarm (the Australians had had their injections) but O'Neill could not play which meant to bowl Australia out India needed to take only eighteen wickets in the match.

Australia had a new Indian bowler to face. Bhagwath Chandrasekhar, like Gupte, a leg-spinner, but a vastly different one. Whereas the Mumbai man was a classic leg-spinner, the nineteen-year-old from Bengaluru, who had made his debut against Mike Smith's team in Mumbai, was the great unpredictable of the Indian side. He could go from being unplayable to looking ragged almost in the same over. Like Pataudi the fact that he was playing cricket at all was a surprise. At the age of five he'd suffered polio, which left him with a withered right arm. He could bowl with the right, but it was not strong enough for him to use as his throwing arm when fielding. Unlike Gupte's classical, flighted leg-breaks, his basic ball was the googly and he took most of his wickets with a skiddy top-spinner. The explanation that had been offered was polio had made his right arm so thin, almost like a cord, that he could get extra bite from his top-spinner.

Until the afternoon of the fourth day, while Chandrasekhar made an impression on the Australian batsmen—only Peter Burge played him with confidence—the match seemed to be going the visitors' way. At that stage Australia were 246 for 3 in their second innings, which gave them an overall lead of 225 and on course to set India a score that they could not possibly make in the final innings. But then Pataudi paired Chandrasekhar with Nadkarni. In the biggest opposition collapse since the days of Gupte, Australia plunged from 246 for 3 to 274 all out. Chandrasekhar finished with 4 for 73, Nadkarni 4 for 33. India had to make 254 to win, and although India in thirty-two years of Test cricket had only ever won eight times, this did not look impossible.

However, with half an hour to go before lunch on the final day India looked down and out at 122 for 6. But here a Pataudi decision helped. Vijay Manjrekar, who normally batted at four, had been held back the previous evening by Pataudi. He now came in at No. 8 and Manjrekar and the captain made sure India did not lose any further wickets before lunch. Then after lunch they began to bat with conviction, blunting the Australian attack.

At tea, with both batsmen in command, victory seemed within touching distance. Bobby Simpson had one card to play, the new ball, but initially it did nothing to worry India. India were soon 215 for 6, and sitting in the North Stand I could hear the spectators around me taking bets on which of the two would make the winning hit.

But then Manjrekar fell, followed by Pataudi. India were 224 for 8, but who would get the remaining 26? It was immensely reassuring that Borde was at one end, but his partner was K. S. Indrajitsinhji, the wicketkeeper, who as a batsman was not in the Farokh Engineer or Budhi Kunderan class. The greater worry was if he got out, Chandrasekhar would come, and everyone knew he could not bat. At the end of his career, after fifty-eight Tests, he had made a total of 167 runs and averaged 4.07. In the end Chandrasekhar was not needed with Borde making the winning hit, thirty minutes before the match was due to end. At this stage the Indians did not know of the Pataudi–Borde rivalry for the captaincy. What mattered was Pataudi had produced a team that played as one, and there was his style of cricket, prepared to lift the ball when he batted, in such stark contrast to the Merchant school of batting. This promised excitement and now also victories. In terms of climbing Everest, Pataudi had taken the team to the South Col, and many felt it was only a matter of time before the summit was reached. But while the years that followed produced many moments to savour and some victories, the summit was not reached. Yet the Indian cricket public never fell out of love with Pataudi, and even years after his retirement the fact that he could bat with one eye would prove useful for advertisers.

THE BOY ON THE BURNING BRIDGE

Ten years after Pataudi had retired Air India, using him to promote the airline, ran a double-page spread in a magazine entitled 'Face to Face with a Tiger'. It said:

> If you've got a minute, try this experiment. Take a ball, close one eye, toss it up and try catching it. The chances are you will miss. Because with one eye, you will have what is known as a 'parallax' problem. Now imagine facing Jeff Thomson, John Snow, Fred Trueman, or even Lance Gibbs with one eye. Or imagine taking a hot, low catch. And imagine doing all that with style, power, and international class. Hard to imagine an ordinary human being doing that. But what about a Tiger? Or Mansur Ali Khan—the Nawab of Pataudi? Ah! Now that's possible isn't it!
>
> Within the first two minutes of meeting him, you'll know Tiger's no pussycat. He stalks into his lair, a brown, dark den loaded with books and a few photographs and fixes you with a steady, unblinking gaze. His agile mind ripples with tough opinions and he expresses them with tigerish conviction. Mansur Ali Khan is every inch his epithet—Tiger.

Pataudi as captain often played his great innings in a crisis, which meant that even if India lost, such was the emotion generated by a Pataudi innings that the love for Pataudi actually increased. Interestingly, Pataudi's great international innings always seemed to be played amidst tragedy. His memorable 148 in the first Test at Leeds on the 1967 tour of England was played while two of his colleagues, Surti and Bedi, nursed injuries and could take little or no part in the match. Helped by Wadekar, Engineer, and Hanumant, India, having made 164 in the first, following on made 510. They lost by six wickets but the individual glory belonged to Pataudi. This was all the more so as, in the England innings, Boycott, despite making 246 not out, had batted so slowly that he was dropped from the next Test. Pataudi's India could lose, but it could still set standards of play that the winning side could not.

In Melbourne a year later, he scored 75 and 85, with the first innings 75 considered a marvel. He had come in to bat with the score 25 for 5. He had not only one eye but batted effectively on one leg—he had a torn thigh muscle, which had made him miss the first Test. Dilip Sardesai, one of the batsmen who had been felled by the Australian attack, would later tell his son Rajdeep, 'Tiger didn't even have his own bat so he just picked up a bat that was lying around in the dressing room and with one leg and one eye hit the Australian bowlers all over the stadium.' In his second innings 85, he even hit Graham McKenzie, Australia's opening bowler, off the back foot over his head, one of the most difficult shots to play in cricket. But this is where the Pataudi story becomes unusual. As captain he had been responsible for India being in that position in Melbourne because he had chosen to bat first on a green wicket, despite being aware that Indian batsmen were not used to such conditions. But such was the effect of his batting that the story was not of captaincy blunder but Tiger once again coming to the rescue. And even the fact that India lost that Test by an innings and 4 runs did not diminish our love for him. There was something about the boy on the burning bridge about these innings, with Indians prepared to overlook the fact that the boy may have helped light the fire in the first place.

TIGER'S BOYS

Pataudi also had a band of players who worshipped him like no previous Indian cricket captain had ever been worshipped. More than thirty years later, as we shall see, Ganguly developed such a bond. They came to be known as 'Dada's boys', but the love for Pataudi was of a different order, and listening to Prasanna and Bedi, it seems more like the adoration subjects have for a king. Prasanna describes how, when Board Treasurer M. Chinnaswamy came to give the players their wages, which in the 1960s were ₹250 per Test match, Pataudi said, 'Please give the money to the cobbler who mends our shoes, he needs it more.' Prasanna adds, 'He said it without raising his voice, but the message was loud and clear.' And Bedi says that Tiger—without shouting—commanded obedience: 'You wouldn't hear him shout and scream ever on the field, but he knew what he wanted from his players and expected us to deliver.' Once, bothered by autograph hunters, he quietly said, 'Your parents should never have slept together.'

Both Prasanna and Bedi always remained devoted to Pataudi and felt, as did others, that he built the team which Ajit Wadekar took to glory; in effect, Wadekar usurped what rightly belonged to the prince. This included making Indian fielding sharp. He was the first Indian fielder to dive or slide to stop the ball; the first captain to prefer fielding in the covers rather than slips; and, being exceptionally fast, he could run the 100 metres faster than anyone else in his team. He gave the impression that in a race with a cricket ball he would win. In his era Colin Bland of South Africa set new fielding standards, but Bedi believes Tiger was better, not least because his throws to the wicketkeeper were more accurate. It was under his tutelage that Eknath Solkar emerged to become like a cat on the prowl at short leg or silly point, ready to pounce on any nick by the batsmen against the spinners. This was something sensationally new in Indian cricket as Mankad and Gupte never had such fielders who could take close catches in the way Solkar could. And above all, Pataudi built the greatest spin quartet that not only Indian cricket but world cricket has seen. This was Prasanna, Bedi, Chandrasekhar and Venkataraghavan.

It is interesting that three of them made their debut under Pataudi; only Prasanna made it when Contractor was captain, two Tests after Pataudi. Pataudi did suffer from the fact that during his reign India had no pace attack. Both he and Kunderan opened the bowling and it took some time for the spin quartet to emerge. Durani, Nadkarni and Borde were still important spinners for much of the Pataudi era. The first Test in which Pataudi's spinners made an impact was the third Test against the West Indies in Chennai in January 1967. It was a dead rubber, India having lost the first two Tests of the three-Test series, but came close to victory, Chandrasekhar, Prasanna and Bedi taking fourteen of the seventeen West Indian wickets to fall. His use of the four was interesting. Chandrasekhar, Prasanna and Venkataraghavan were the attack spinners while Bedi was used as a stock bowler.

Prasanna and Venkataraghavan made an interesting contrast. Prasanna had established himself in the team on the tour of the West Indies in 1961–62 with Frank Worrell saying he would be a star. But soon after his return, his father died and, reflecting the era when cricket could never be seen as an occupation, he had given up the game for five years to study engineering. By the time he returned, Srinivasaraghavan Venkataraghavan, who made his debut in the 1964–65 season, was established as the first choice off-spinner. Prasanna soon re-established himself and he was the first bowler Pataudi always turned to. But when Wadekar took over, he often preferred Venkataraghavan. Prasanna did not play in the win in England in 1971 and felt he suffered under Wadekar's captaincy. Bedi's problems with Wadekar were well publicized, with rows on the 1974 tour, and Bedi draws the contrast in the mindset between Pataudi and Wadekar. The Mumbai man, he says, was 'shy and introverted' and defensive. His first words to the team in his first Test as captain in Jamaica in February 1971 were, 'Boys, we are going to draw this Test.' The Test was drawn but, as Bedi points out, India made the West Indies follow on for the first time. It so spurred the team that India went on to win the series. Interestingly, the other two spinners, Venkataraghavan and Chandrasekhar, never displayed such adulation for Pataudi.

Pataudi's crowning moment as captain was undoubtedly becoming the first Indian captain to win a Test and a series abroad. This came after the Indians had lost all four Tests in Australia and went to New Zealand for the first time. Here they turned the tables so dramatically that they won three of the four Tests. India outplayed New Zealand in every department of the game and the home side just had no answer to Indian spin. Even as India were being crushed by Australia, Prasanna had shown his class, taking twenty-five wickets in Australia for 27.44 leading Ian Chappell to rate him as the best off-spinner in the world. Now he took twenty-four for 18.79. The victory was not entirely due to the spin quartet. Chandrasekhar because of injury had gone home and Venkataraghavan was not in the team, so it was old war-horse Nadkarni who, in his last series, took fourteen wickets at 17.92, heading the averages. Even the only defeat was due to Pataudi making a tactical error, putting New Zealand in to bat after winning the toss. This saw them make 502, easily their highest score of the series, and win by six wickets. However, such was the fervour produced by a first overseas victory that nobody raised the question why in Melbourne on a dodgy wicket he chose to bat and at Christchurch on a good wicket he decided to field. This decision was all the more inexplicable as he had no real pace attack, Rusi Surti and Syed Abid Ali, military medium at best, opened the attack, and Pataudi relied on spinners. Instead Indians readily accepted Pataudi's argument that the New Zealand victory showed India had taken time to show its true form. Had it been quicker, there might have been a different result in Australia. What Pataudi did not know was that he had actually sown the seeds of his own downfall. He had made Indians believe they could win and within a year was to pay the price for having changed the Indian cricketing mindset.

Chapter 13

MERCHANT BAGS HIS TIGER

A MILL DIRECTOR TAKES ON THE TIGER

Bishan Singh Bedi has described Pataudi's fall as a tiger being mauled by 'jackals and hyenas'. To describe Vijay Merchant, who shot the Tiger, in those terms is cruel. He, reflecting his day job, saw himself as a director of a mill whose production was declining. He had become the director of Indian cricket, or to give his proper title, chairman of selectors when, having taken no interest in cricket administration since his retirement in 1951, he was voted into that job on 30 September 1968. This was mainly because none of the factions in Indian cricket had been able to impose their choice. Through the winter of 1968 he tinkered with the team as India had a messy drawn series with New Zealand, which saw New Zealand win a Test in India for the first time. This was followed by defeat at the hands of Bill Lawry's Australia.

There seemed to be so much going for India against Australia. In Gundappa Viswanath they had discovered an immensely talented young batsman from Bengaluru. In the second Test in Kanpur he had scored 137 on his Test debut, earning India a draw. Though only 5 feet 4 inches, his lack of height did not affect his timing or stroke play. Unafraid of fast bowlers, he cut and drove them, producing strokes that oozed class. His approach and style suggested he would be more than a one-Test wonder. In the third Test in Delhi he helped Wadekar steer India to a seven-wicket victory and made the overall series score 1–1. But then India lost the next two Tests to lose the five Test series 3–1, and this is where the questions about Pataudi's captaincy began to be raised.

That series was to see epic bowling by Prasanna and Bedi. In the Delhi win they had combined so well that Australia were shot out for 107 in the second innings, Prasanna, 5 for 42, Bedi, 5 for 37. Along with Venkataraghavan, they bowled 725.9 overs of the 927.9 of India's overs in the series and the trio took fifty-nine of the sixty-nine wickets. The Australians never really mastered them, only scoring more than 300 runs three times, with a top score of 348.

But the final Test at Chennai exposed the lack of a 'Tiger' kill. On the third morning, Australia, with a lead of 85, were reduced to 24 for 6, Prasanna taking four wickets. But Australia were allowed to escape and set India 249 to win. Even this did not look impossible with India on 114 for 2 with Wadekar and Viswanath there. But then, as if worried by the idea of winning, India collapsed; the last eight wickets fell for 57 runs and Australia won by 77 runs. However, this was a poor Australian side as was soon evident. A month after their Indian tour they were in South Africa, where the white South African team thrashed them 4–0, one defeat by an innings, two by over 300 runs.

India's defeat against such an Australian side suggested to Merchant that Pataudi was a cricketing tiger who could wound an opponent but never make a kill. He had also not liked the way Pataudi ran what he thought was a cosy club. He was particularly upset that during the 1967–68 Australian tour, the injured Chandrasekhar was replaced by a batsman, Jaisimha, one of Pataudi's closest friends. Merchant then was not a selector and in a chat with me he did not mince his words about Pataudi's actions. The solution was simple: kill the tiger. The deed was done when the selectors met on 8 January 1971 to decide the captain for the tour to the West Indies. It narrowed down to Pataudi and, surprisingly, Wadekar, the Mumbai captain, who had rarely been talked of as a future captain. Wadekar did not expect to be anointed and was so unsure of being selected that he had canvassed Pataudi's support to make the team.

But Merchant, who had seen leadership qualities in Wadekar when he was still at college, duly proposed him. The selectors were split 2–2, and Merchant used his casting vote to instal Wadekar. It helped that a great Pataudi supporter, Dutta Ray, had been voted off the committee. Engineer has said that he failed to become captain because, although a 'senior Board member' sounded him out and even flew him out to India, Merchant told him he could not captain or even be in the team because he played for Lancashire.

Merchant certainly had strong likes and dislikes and did not forget those who had crossed his path. For example, Bhausaheb Nimbalkar, the Baroda skipper had upset him in a Ranji Trophy match in the 1945-46 season. This would rebound on him in December 1948, when Nimbalkar, playing for Maharashtra against Kathiawar, had scored 443 not out, just 19 short of Bradman's 452 not out, then the highest individual score in first-class cricket. By this time Maharashtra were 826 for 4 and the Kathiawar captain, unable to bear any more punishment, conceded the match. Nimbalkar would later say Merchant rang the captain to make sure the naughty Nimbalkar was denied his honour. We do not know if Merchant rang, but the idea that he never forgot is also something Bedi mentions, alleging that this shooting of Tiger was Merchant's revenge for Pataudi's father denying him the chance to captain India on the 1946 England tour.

The truth of this will never emerge, but what is not in doubt is that the Merchant-orchestrated change unleashed the fourth wave of Indian cricket, which would rock international cricket in a way Indian cricket had never done before.

The Fourth Wave

TESTS

Wave	Period	Matches	Won	Lost	Drawn	Tied	Win%	W/L
4th	1971–1983	94	20	28	46	0	21.28	0.71

TOP BATSMEN IN FOURTH WAVE

	Matches	Runs	Hs	Avg	100	50
S. M. Gavaskar	90	7625	221	52.22	27	33
G. R. Viswanath	87	5746	222	41.63	13	33
D. B. Vengsarkar	63	3484	157★	37.46	6	20
M. Amarnath	36	2632	120	45.37	7	16
Kapil Dev	53	2253	126★	32.65	3	12
S. M. H. Kirmani	69	2100	101★	24.70	1	10
C. P. S. Chauhan	37	1979	97	32.98	0	16
Yashpal Sharma	33	1550	140	36.90	2	9
A. D. Gaekwad	26	1289	102	29.97	1	7
S. M. Patil	20	1254	174	43.24	3	7

★Not out

TOP BOWLERS IN FOURTH WAVE

	Mts	Wkts	Best	Avg	5WI	10WM
Kapil Dev	53	206	8/85	29.52	15	1
B. S. Bedi	48	196	6/71	29.79	10	1
B. S. Chandrasekhar	42	180	8/79	29.20	14	1
D. R. Doshi	32	113	6/102	30.53	6	0
K. D. Ghavri	39	109	5/33	33.54	4	0
S. Venkataraghavan	41	108	5/95	40.25	1	0

TOP WICKETKEEPERS IN FOURTH WAVE

	Mts	Dismissals	Ct	St
S. M. H. Kirmani	69	160	128	32
F. M. Engineer	16	28	24	4
B. Reddy	4	11	9	2

ONE-DAY INTERNATIONALS

Wave	Period	Matches	Won	Lost	Drawn	Tied	Win%	W/L
4th	1971–1983	48	18	30	0	0	37.50	0.60

TOP BATSMEN IN FOURTH WAVE

	Mts	Runs	Hs	Avg	SR	100	50
D. B. Vengsarkar	36	921	88★	29.70	62.95	0	5
Kapil Dev	40	911	175★	26.79	108.19	1	4
S. M. Gavaskar	37	805	90	23.67	53.70	0	6
Yashpal Sharma	35	796	89	31.84	63.02	0	4
S. M. Patil	29	737	84	27.29	86.80	0	7
K. Srikkanth	17	518	95	30.47	82.88	0	3
M Amarnath	29	515	80	23.40	52.28	0	3
G. R. Viswanath	25	439	75	19.95	52.89	0	2
S. M. H. Kirmani	36	327	48★	19.23	59.02	0	0
R. M. H. Binny	23	306	35	16.10	54.83	0	0

★Not out

TOP BOWLERS IN FOURTH WAVE

	Mts	Wkts	Best	Avg	RPO	4W
Kapil Dev	40	46	5/43	28.39	3.58	1
S. Madan Lal	28	41	4/20	26.02	4.07	1
R. M. H. Binny	23	33	4/29	25.72	4.28	2
M. Amarnath	29	26	3/12	36.03	4.54	0
D. R. Doshi	15	22	4/30	23.81	3.96	2
S. M. Patil	29	15	2/28	39.26	4.09	0
K. D. Ghavri	19	15	3/40	47.20	4.11	0
B. S. Sandhu	14	12	2/26	44.83	4.10	0
RJ Shastri	15	10	3/26	45.70	4.75	0
S. Abid Ali	5	7	2/22	26.71	3.33	0
B. S. Bedi	10	7	2/44	48.57	3.45	0

TOP WICKETKEEPERS IN FOURTH WAVE

	Mts	Dismissals	Ct	St
S. M. H. Kirmani	36	25	20	5
F. M. Engineer	5	4	3	1
P. Krishnamurthy	1	2	1	1
B. Reddy	3	2	2	0
S. C. Khanna	3	1	1	0

Note: For the first time in a wave, one-day internationals are played

Chapter 14

SURPRISE!

THE UNKNOWN INDIAN DAZZLES

The Test cricket career of Uton Dowe, a Jamaican fast bowler, was unspectacular to say the least. He lasted only four games when he was in his early twenties, becoming more famous for bowling badly rather than well. Spectators in Trinidad made fun of him by adapting one of the Ten Commandments on a banner that read 'Dowe shalt not bowl'.

Dowe did, however, do something truly remarkable in the course of his brief Test career. He had Sunil Gavaskar caught for 1 run in the fourth Test of India's 1970–71 tour of the West Indies.

That was the first series Gavaskar ever played. He could hardly have made a bigger announcement of his talent. He missed the first Test with a finger injury, then from the second to the fifth Test his scores were 65 and an unbeaten 67; 116 and 64 not out; 1 and 117; 124 and 220. India won a Test in the Caribbean for the first time, which also led to it winning the five-Test series 1–0.

In eight innings he made 774 runs. One player alone had ever bettered his series average of 154.80—Don Bradman. Had Dowe not struck in Bridgetown, the numbers might have been even more mind-boggling. Gavaskar, who had just turned twenty-one, needed only 6 more runs to better Everton Weekes' 779 in 1948–49 the highest series score in a series between these teams.

But Weekes was an established batsman. Gavaskar had never played Test cricket before. No batsman had ever scored so highly in his debut series, and no Indian had ever scored anywhere near this level. Gavaskar was only the second player, after Doug Walters, to hit a century and double century in the same Test. Even the English press took note.

So, who was Sunil Manohar Gavaskar, who had played a mere twelve first-class games in five years before this remarkable introduction to Test cricket? I knew him better than most, for as I've mentioned I was at school with Gavaskar in St. Xavier's, in Mumbai.

I must have been fourteen, Sunil was probably twelve. I was two or three years away from the coveted matriculation and just about beginning to enjoy being a senior boy at school. We had graduated from shorts to trousers, Sunil was still in shorts. One evening a group of us senior boys were talking to Father Fritz, who took us in English and sport, while standing on one of the balconies that overlooked the St. Xavier's school ground. One end of the school playground housed garages for the school buses; as we leaned over the balcony, we saw a solitary little fellow in front of the red garage doors: Sunil Gavaskar. He looked comical. He was still wearing his school uniform of dirty beige shirt and shorts and tie, supplemented by full cricket gear. Pads, gloves, even a cap. The pads seemed to come to his chin, as he repeatedly and religiously played forward; every now and again we would catch a glimpse of the back of his shorts and his bare legs. We mocked and laughed, but Fritzy turned on us and said in his clipped English accent: 'You load of wash-outs. You think you can play cricket. You'll never be cricketers. That boy will be a great cricketer. He will play for India.' I do not know whether Sunil heard Fritzy's roar of disapproval, for it was certainly loud and very severe. And this remarkable Jesuit who also made me believe I could become a writer was proved right.

St. Xavier's, Mumbai, was not a school that won cricket trophies. If anything, it was stronger in football, which we also played, helped by the fact that many of the Catholic boys were of Goan ancestry where the beautiful game is stronger than cricket. During the time Sunil and I were there, which was over a decade, we only once won the Harris Shield, the competition for senior boys. This is the competition where, seventeen years after Gavaskar stunned the world, another little man, Sachin Tendulkar, announced himself by setting what was then a world batting record. In contrast, Gavaskar in his first match for St. Xavier's batted No. 10 and the *Times of India* reporting the score said, 'G. Sunil 30 not out.' Indeed, at school he was not even captain. He played under Milind Rege, who went on to play for Mumbai and might have had a more distinguished cricket career but suffered a heart attack when young. Rege has written that Gavaskar at St. Xavier's, unlike Tendulkar at school:

> ...was like every other cricketer. In fact, that was little or no encouragement for us at Xavier's. We played cricket on a mat which was half the length of a cricket pitch. Later we graduated to turf wickets—the turf being in the form of red mud spread evenly on a hard, bumpy outfield.

The only advice Fritz gave Gavaskar was, 'A good length ball you block and anything else, bang.' What there was was a lot of cricket, interclass matches, and Gavaskar would come to school even on holidays to play in these matches, batting with one leg-guard and no gloves but also bowling and taking quite a few wickets.

Concentration was Gavaskar's great weapon, something he learned as a young boy when he would play in a narrow corridor outside his flat in a building in Central Mumbai, unable ever to hit the ball more than 4 feet off the ground for fear of breaking neighbours' windows. While batting he would be in such a bubble of concentration that even if he was playing with friends, with whom he had played 'building matches' for years, he would not share a word with them.

Gavaskar was also a quick learner. In 1967, he was in the Mumbai reserves when, in the Ranji Trophy semi-final against Mysore (later Karnataka), Wadekar scored 323 driving Prasanna and Chandrasekhar through the covers. During the lunch and tea breaks Gavaskar took Wadekar's pads off and would later say he learnt to play spin bowling while watching Wadekar bat in that innings.

THE CLUB THAT MADE GAVASKAR

Another huge influence on him from the age of ten was Vasu Paranjape and Dadar Union, which plays its cricket on a maidan about a mile or so from Shivaji Park. It was Vasu who gave Sunil his nickname 'Sunny'. If Gavaskar had a mentor in cricket then it was undoubtedly Paranjape. For years they worked in the same Mumbai firm and he continued to act as a sort of father confessor.

Both Gavaskar's parents encouraged him to play, and Paranjape recalled the days when Gavaskar was ten or eleven, 'coming along with his father to watch Dadar Union play on Sundays, eagerly pressing for a knock before the start of the matches. I distinctly recall the obvious and conspicuous straightness of his bat. Even the seriousness during those knocks used to be beyond his years.'

It helped that his uncle Madhav Mantri, who was known as George, after George Headley, played for the club. In Gavaskar's youth Dadar Union was the greatest club in Mumbai and Gavaskar thought the world of it. He would return from foreign trips and if Dadar Union was playing he was ready to play for the club. He makes no secret that it was the club that made him, prepared him for how fortunes can change suddenly, and without the club he would not become the Gavaskar who rewrote cricket history.

Few outside Mumbai knew much of Gavaskar before that tour to the Caribbean—the first time he had been overseas in his life, apart from a visit to Sri Lanka, when it was still called Ceylon. Viswanath was reckoned to be the batting star for this tour. But he was injured before the first Test, as was Gavaskar, and the 'forgotten man', Sardesai, returning to the middle order, took his chance in style, taking India from 75 for 5 to 387 with a double century, the first of many fine innings on a tour in which he scored an impressive 642 runs. Sardesai, with a century, and Gavaskar with 65 were the top two scorers in the first innings in the all-important second Test in Port of Spain, in which Gavaskar hit an unbeaten 67 in the second innings to take India to victory.

The West Indies, a team in transition, were unable ever to devise a plan for Gavaskar, so surprised were they by his arrival and immediate success as a specialist opener. While he and Sardesai scored the runs, Abid Ali performed well as an opening bowler. But the top bowlers in Wadekar's side were the spinners Venkataraghavan, Prasanna and Bedi who between them took forty-eight of sixty-eight wickets. It was Sardesai who, just before the first Test, watching the West Indies fast bowlers in the nets, said in Marathi to Gavaskar, 'Yeh hai ganta bowling.' This bowling is rubbish. This, from a batsman who knew what the West Indian pace was like, was a great confidence booster for the Indians. India might have won the series 2–0 had they been more aggressive in the final Test, also in Port of Spain. The West Indies were eight men down and well short of their target at the close, with Uton Dowe one of the not-out batsmen. His two wickets in the match came at 77 runs apiece and, unlike Gavaskar, he never did anything remarkable in Test cricket again.

MAKING HISTORY IN THE HOME OF CRICKET

This was a momentous time for Indian cricket. The big question for their next series was: Could Wadekar's team follow up their first win in the Caribbean by registering their first series win in England, against a team that had just won the Ashes in Australia, and against whom they had never even won a match in England, never mind a series? The answer, remarkably, was yes. And there would be a third straight series win, this time at home against England, before India fell into their bad old ways again.

India took four spinners to England, the surprise inclusion being Chandrasekhar, who had not played a Test in more than three years, had not been considered for the West Indies tour and had become a forgotten man. Prasanna had bowled 160 overs in the Caribbean, taking eleven wickets, yet he would not bowl one in the three Tests in England as Chandrasekhar came to the fore, Merchant's calculated gamble of selecting him paying off handsomely. Venkataraghavan, Bedi and Chandrasekhar took thirty-seven wickets in three Tests, helped by the brilliant catching of Solkar. While

England had nine different wicket-takers India had just five—those three spinners plus Solkar and Abid Ali.

Gavaskar could not score at anywhere near the rate he achieved in the West Indies, hitting 144 runs at a meagre average of 24. And yet it was on this tour that he played, in his own opinion, the best innings of his career.

In their past two tours of England, in 1959 and 1967, India had played eight Tests and lost them all. So, a draw at Lord's in the first Test in late July was a good start, even if they were hanging on at the end with only two wickets in hand, 38 runs short of their target. That rain-affected match was most notable for an incident in which John Snow, the 6 foot 4 inch bowler, shoulder-charged Gavaskar as he went for a quick single, then tossed his bat at him. Snow was dropped for the next Test and told to apologize, while the Indians were happy as they seemed to have got under England's skin.

Next stop was Old Trafford, where the green-top wicket, cold weather, steady drizzle and England's first-innings total of 386 posed a formidable challenge to India. John Price, the Middlesex fast bowler, had dismissed Gavaskar for 4 in the first innings at Lord's—where Gavaskar made a valuable 53 in the second innings—and would get him again at Old Trafford, caught behind by Alan Knott for 57. But Gavaskar would say years later that, given the conditions—'the ball was skidding and coming a lot quicker'—it was his best innings, 'a turning point in my career'. Price, he said, bowled faster than anyone he faced until, later, he came up against Jeff Thomson and Michael Holding.

India were 174 runs behind after the first innings, with nobody bettering Gavaskar's 57, and England stretched that by 245 before declaring. Rain came to India's rescue and they went to the Oval for the third Test still level. What a match it would turn out to be.

Once more, England had a useful first-innings lead, thanks largely to wicketkeeper Knott's 90 batting at six. Gavaskar went for 6 and at 125 for 5, India looked in desperate trouble before Solkar and Engineer steadied the innings: they were all out for 284, a deficit of 71. Surely now England, who had not lost any of their past twenty-six Tests, would finish the series with another victory. After all, Wadekar had spoken of a draw being a good result, appearing not to consider the possibility of winning.

The man who made the difference was Chandrasekhar, first with a bit of good fortune, then with some quite brilliant bowling. Brian Luckhurst hit the second ball of Chandrasekhar's second over hard back at him. Chandrasekhar deflected it on to the stumps and John Jameson, backing up, was run out for the third time in four innings. That appeared to lift

Chandrasekhar, who bowled John Edrich with a faster ball, then had Keith Fletcher superbly caught by the outstanding close fielder, Solkar. Time for lunch, with Chandrasekhar on a hat-trick and England 24–3, having been 23–0 a few minutes earlier. Basil D'Oliveira missed Chandrasekhar's first ball after lunch, but his pads rescued him; he gave a difficult chance off the next delivery to Sardesai, who injured himself in his vain attempt to catch it.

Venkataraghavan chipped in with the wickets of D'Oliveira and Knott, who made only one before falling to a magnificent diving catch by Solkar. And here there was a little Solkar trick, what in Mumbai cricket is called khadus, which can translate into 'lout' but also means a street-wise cricketer. He had noticed that when Knott took guard he always marked the spot with a bail he lifted from the stumps. Solkar, brought up in the canny world of Mumbai cricket, now thought: if I hide the bails when he comes out to bat, will this disturb him, probably give us a chance? However, he was not sure if it was within the laws to remove the bails in this fashion and asked Wadekar's advice. Wadekar said that was not a problem provided he replaced them so play could restart.

So, as Knott came out to bat, Solkar quickly moved from his position at short leg and pocketed the bails. Knott, unable to find the bails, had to mark his guard with his bat as most batsmen do. Then, surreptitiously, Solkar replaced the bails. Whether this schoolboy prank unsettled Knott is difficult to say, but that Solkar catch, which he considered the best of his career, was the moment, too, when the reputation of Indian spinners and their preying fieldsmen at short leg was born. Captain Ray Illingworth was caught and bowled by Chandrasekhar, England were a mess: 65 for 5. By the time they were all out for 101, dismissed in two-and-a-half hours, Chandrasekhar had 6 for 38, the best performance by an Indian bowler in England. His team needed 173 to win.

Most of the crowd of 7,000 at the Oval on the final day, Tuesday, 24 August, were Indians. They, like so many millions back home, knew it would not be straightforward. They had had their hopes dashed too often before to be confident about victory.

Whatever confidence there was had taken a big dent when on the previous evening Gavaskar had been lbw to Snow for a duck. Mankad, his opening partner, made only 11. But Wadekar played a captain's innings and, despite being run out early on Tuesday, Sardesai and Viswanath carried on and by lunch India were 146 for 5. Not far to go now.

During lunch an elephant from nearby Chessington Zoo was paraded around the ground, as it had been before play started. This was India's day. Engineer and Abid Ali, who hit the winning runs, took them home for a famous victory. Wadekar, or 'Old Stone Face' as the English tabloids labelled him, at last felt able to smile.

I, then an accountancy student in London, had been privileged to watch history being made, standing rooted in one post on the final day as India made the runs. India struck a great blow for the so-called second division of Test-playing nations. The second division then was India, Pakistan, New Zealand, and the Oval triumph meant that for the first time a second division side had won a series in England. New Zealand did not do so until 1986, Pakistan a year later.

Yet, looking back from the perspective of 2019, it did not change the overall power structure of international cricket. The next England team to visit India was still a B side, led by Tony Lewis, who had not yet played for England. India did not figure in the plans of Australia, the other great power. There was no Australian visit to India for another eight years, which meant a gap of a decade after Lawry's demolition of Pataudi's team in 1969. And when in 2000 *Wisden* listed what it considered the hundred matches of the twentieth century, the Oval Test did not figure. This is despite the fact that it listed a match that was not a Test between England and the Rest of the World in 1970. It also recorded the victory by the white South African team against Australia in 1970. It noted that Graeme Pollock scored 274 and Barry Richards made 140 in that Test and commented with regret, 'A taste of what the world missed.' Yet no mention was made of the fact that the world *Wisden* was talking about was the white cricket world as white South Africa only played England, Australia and New Zealand who they considered part of the wider white family. Not only did they not play the non-white countries of India, Pakistan and the West Indies but they even made the white countries they played not select their non-white players. Pollock and Richards never felt strongly enough about such racism to stop playing for the white team. Indeed, Pollock's brother termed the anti-apartheid movement a communist conspiracy. It would be another thirty years before these racist power relations in world cricket changed and by then white South Africa was no more.

UNASSUMING STARS

In India the players were idolized. However, what distinguished these players from the present generation is that they did not behave like rock stars. They were the most unassuming of men, as I realized to my delight some years later. By then a journalist in the UK, I had my own journalists' cricket team, the Fleet Street XI. During one summer Chandrasekhar, on a visit to England, contacted me. I had a match against London Broadcasting

Corporation, the commercial radio station where I had started as a journalist. I asked if he would play. It was on a small council ground in south London, but he agreed, turned up in his sneakers, did not want to bat but bowled. I cannot describe the sensation of captaining the great Chandrasekhar, setting the field for him and deciding when and which end he would bowl from. For that brief moment, I was a captain of India.

Some years later, when I took my journalists' team to the United States, I met Abid Ali in San Francisco, where he had settled, and he too played for my team, and even coached some of my teammates' children. Neither Chandrasekhar nor Abid asked for money and treated me as an equal. Indian cricket has since reached new, undreamt of heights, but I could not expect a modern Indian cricketer to be so generous and down-to-earth. Chandrasekhar and Abid had made history but this had not made them arrogant. They had not forgotten their roots.

CONTRADICTORY RESPONSE TO GAVASKAR

It was not so clear-cut with Gavaskar. His efforts in the West Indies made him an instant celebrity—or VIP, as the Indians preferred it—and over the years he was seen as greedy because he became the first Indian to become a millionaire through cricket.

His darshan—'sight' or 'introduction'—was sought. If he went shopping in Mumbai, word would soon spread and suddenly, as if from nowhere, huge crowds would gather just to be near him, his magic. They did not want anything, not even an autograph. Film stars and politicians had always enjoyed such darshan, but Gavaskar was one of the first Indian cricketers to do so.

The adulation came with unease, disquiet and downright hostility. The English writer, Dudley Doust, misinterpreted the adulation as uncritical hero worship: it was more complicated than that, especially when it came to public perception (and myth) about Gavaskar's money. Pataudi, who, having been brought up in England often saw India more shrewdly than homegrown Indians, wrote that too many players felt that Gavaskar's focus was solely on himself, despite the fact that he fought for players rights against the board, which was reluctant to treat them fairly. Prize money for Indian cricketers started in 1969, shortly before Gavaskar's career took off. Players shared their earnings among themselves. Pataudi helped convince the tax authorities not to tax these earnings and Venkataraghavan was given the task of making sure everyone got their fair share. This was because, says Pataudi, not only was he honest 'but he had the knack of dividing thousands by any number and arriving at an even figure'. According to Pataudi:

But Gavaskar opened up entire new vistas of making money. He had noticed how quickly cricketers once out of the limelight were actually shunned by the same people who had fussed over them, fought for the pleasure of inviting them home and queued to have photographs taken with them. In Mumbai only money seemed to matter and there was more than one way to make it. Gavaskar found them all. Advertising, film producing (this may have been a lark), writing articles (on the same match but for different publications), taking a fee for organizing matches, writing instant books, appearance money, and contracts with sports equipment manufacturers.

Pataudi reckoned Gavaskar had become cricket's first millionaire, but in the India of the 1980s, when it was not considered good form to display wealth—that has changed in the new century—Indians, far from applauding his success, felt he was mercenary. This idea of Gavaskar being driven by money was also encouraged by a story he himself told that as a boy his father often motivated him by offering him rupees for centuries. By any international standards he was extremely poorly paid—he earned the equivalent of £35,000 a year, which was £5,000 less than Ian Botham got for his bat contract alone. It was a lot of money in India but very little compared to what global sports stars in Europe and the United States earned then. It is, of course, a measure of how Indian cricket has changed that M. S. Dhoni and Virat Kohli have earned money that now makes sports stars from other nations envious. But in the 1980s what Gavaskar did was something no Indian cricketer imagined was possible. And what made Gavaskar exceptional was that at the same time, like his hero Wadekar, and almost all other first-class cricketers, he was also employed by a firm for his cricketing ability and drew a regular income from that. That would change with the emergence of Tendulkar.

In fact, Gavaskar was always honest and meticulous about money. When he wrote a foreword to one of my books he negotiated a fee, as he was perfectly entitled to do, and not only wrote a beautiful foreword but agreed to come to signing ceremonies with me. His dedication was real, in everything he did.

One thing Pataudi did not mention was that Gavaskar was also honest about his writing. The books and articles he wrote were penned by himself, not ghosted by some journalist. This is important, for famous cricketers have often used ghosts but not admitted it. The classic was Keith Miller, whose autobiography *Cricket Crossfire* bore his name but was written by Basil Easterbrook, as I revealed in my biography of Keith Miller published in 1980. Easterbrook had described to me how difficult the job was and how he had to finish the book on his holiday. Lack of such honesty can deceive even renowned historians. So, in *Wisden India Almanack 2015* Ramchandra Guha could say, 'Among the first "adult" books I read was Keith Miller's autobiography *Cricket Crossfire*. Unlike present-day memoirs it was neither ghosted nor anodyne.' But while Guha got it wrong about Miller, Gavaskar, despite being very much a modern-day cricketer, did not spend a hasty few minutes talking to a journalist and have an article carrying his byline appear the next day, not a word of which he had written. His writing was his own creation, having been tutored in the English language, as I was, by Father Fritz.

SUCCESS COMES WITH A WARNING

India had a long wait of sixteen months, after that famous victory in England, before they would play Test cricket again. Because of the brief war with Pakistan in December 1971, England cancelled a planned tour to India. They did, however, play the 1972–73 series, though Ray Illingworth, John Snow and Geoff Boycott all declined to tour. Tony Lewis was the new captain and like Nigel Howard had never played for England before. In the first Test in Delhi, Chandrasekhar was the star performer for India again claiming 8 for 79 in England's first innings. But wretched batting by India in both innings, and an unbeaten 70 by Tony Greig as England chased a winning target of 207, sent India to a shattering six-wicket defeat. That performance led to changes: for the next Test in Kolkata, Sardesai was dropped, and Durani and Prasanna were brought back. Sardesai reacted by retiring.

The changes worked. Durani hit the top score of 53 in the second innings and, with Bedi taking five wickets, India won by 28 runs. Chandrasekhar was again the bowler England could not cope with, 5 for 65 in the first innings, 4 for 42 in the second. Bedi also took five wickets. By the third Test in Chennai Pataudi was back, this time as a batsman. Pataudi, under his new name, Mansur Ali Khan Pataudi or M. A. K. Pataudi, had covered the first two Tests from the press box. He scored a fine century for South Zone against MCC to convince the selectors he should play in Chennai; his willingness to play under the man who had usurped him as captain was applauded, and his refusal to play in the West Indies tour was forgotten.

All the while, Chandrasekhar was in marvellous form. He took another six England wickets in their first innings, for 90 runs, as the visitors were dismissed for 242. Pataudi came in to bat with India having lost three wickets for 89. The crowds welcomed him as if he was the old king come to reclaim his throne. Pataudi responded with a wonderful range of strokes, passed his 50 with a six, and made 73. How important this innings was can be judged by the fact that in the previous four innings India had made: 173, 233, 210,155. Now they made 316. The one-eyed man might no longer be leading India, but he could still bat.

A lead of 74 was too much for England, who made only the 159 the second time around. Chandrasekhar took his hundredth wicket but this time the key bowler was Prasanna whose second innings figures read: 10–5-16–4. India required just 86, and after a wobble at 51 for 4, Pataudi, who had actually bowled an over in the second innings, now with the bat made sure India won by four wickets. After Chennai, with India 2–1 ahead, Wadekar became more defensive. The last two Tests were drawn, and India had come from behind for a third series win in a row. Chandrasekhar had taken thirty-five wickets at 18.91, Bedi had twenty-five, Prasanna ten and Venkataraghavan, who had been the main wicket-taker in the Caribbean, one. India had not just the best spin attack in the world at that time, but one of the best in cricket history. Spinners had taken a total of 156 of the 193 wickets India took in those three series, with Bedi leading the way with fifty-one wickets.

Those three straight victories meant Wadekar, who had never lost a series, was India's most successful captain, beaten only once in thirteen Tests. He took advantage of his popularity by publishing his autobiography, in the foreword of which Merchant predicted a long and even more successful future for him. He was wrong. Wadekar did not know it at the time, but he had reached the pinnacle of his career. The only way was down.

Chapter 15

WADEKAR STOPS SMILING

THE DREADFUL SUMMER OF '42

Quit when you are at the top is an old maxim in public life. But politicians rarely get it right and neither do sportsmen, and the England tour in 1974 would prove how dreadfully Wadekar misjudged things. The summer of 1974 was my first as a journalist, having secured the job of cricket correspondent of the recently set up London Broadcasting Corporation. I had hyped the series up to my editor as India coming as world champions, but almost from the first day of the first Test I was broadcasting miserable news about Indian cricket, capitulating in the manner of the 1950s and 1960s.

At least the first Test was a contest until the final day, when England set a not impossible 296 for India to get in three sessions. Sitting in the old press box high up in the gods at Old Trafford, which you approached through what looked like a fire escape stairway, I was much taken by what veteran journalist Basil Easterbrook did. He had a habit of collecting soap. He would collect them from the toilet next to the press box and line them up on his desk. Now, as Gavaskar and Solkar, forced to open as the regular openers had failed, came out he put a big clock on his desk to see how India progressed. Then there was no stipulation that the bowling side had to bowl a certain number of overs, so time mattered. Gavaskar, who had scored a wonderful century in the first innings, his first in England, started as if he might take India to victory, and while he was batting Easterbrook gave regular updates on how India was keeping up. But as Gavaskar got out for 58, Easterbrook put the clock away and went back to his soaps. Viswanath did make a wonderful half century, but the others gave up and India lost by 113 runs.

I assured my sports editor that the conditions, wintry and rainy, had not suited the Indians. Let the sun shine. It did at Lord's, and England made 629—their highest score in more than thirty years. Chandrasekhar injured a finger and barely bowled. Bedi took six wickets but at the cost of 226 runs, while Prasanna conceded 166. England no longer feared the spinners.

Gavaskar once more batted well in India's respectable first innings of 302, but when they followed on their batting was embarrassing, an all-time low. On that Monday morning before lunch they were bowled out for 42 in seventeen overs. The third Test at Edgbaston saw a second straight innings defeat in which they took only two English wickets in the entire match. David Lloyd, who in his Test career scored 552 runs, made 214 not out in this one innings alone. Bedi took one wicket for 152 runs, Prasanna one wicket for 101 runs.

The defeat was marked by disagreements off the field between Wadekar and Bedi. Despite the huge crowds for the home series wins against England, the players had received little reward. The daily allowance, on top of match fees, for the 1974 tour was a measly £2; the hotels were anything but top-class.

Bedi refused to sign his contract for the board and asked Wadekar to seek more money for the team. Wadekar, who knew Bedi was Pataudi's man, saw it as a threat to his captaincy and refused. There were also differences between the two about how Bedi should bowl. When England were on the rampage Wadekar wanted Bedi to stop trying to tempt batsmen with flight, which, far from deceiving them, often led to a four. Bedi, ever a millionaire as a bowler, refused.

To worsen matters, there was an incident which many Indians felt was shameful. The opening batsman, Sudhir Naik, was accused of shoplifting at Marks & Spencer. He bought twenty pairs of socks for teammates and was said to have stolen two more pairs. He denied it but was persuaded to confess, although this so depressed him that he felt suicidal. However, he recovered, and his 77 was the highest Indian score in the dismal third Test. Delays in resolving the dispute made the team late for a meeting with the high commissioner in West London. The high commissioner was not pleased and the Indian press, which before the tour could not praise Wadekar highly enough, now pilloried him.

They paid little attention to the fact that Wadekar had not been well served by the players who had brought success. Gavaskar, after his record-breaking heroics in his debut series, had averaged only 24 in those two subsequent winning series against England. Sardesai was gone. Viswanath was inconsistent. Here it must be emphasized that this was a rare blip for Gavaskar during this wave. As the figures for the 1971–1983 wave show, he averaged 52.22 with a remarkable conversion rate: 33 fifties, 27 hundreds (see figures at the beginning of Chapter 14). Viswanath, in contrast, over the same period averaged 41.63, converting 13 of his 33 fifties into hundreds. And spinners were hampered by being required to bowl to a new law which meant they could only have five fielders on the onside. This particularly affected Prasanna. Also, they operated in the less spinner-friendly climate of the early part of the English summer. The 1971 tour had been in the second half of the summer.

As India lost at Edgbaston I told Easterbrook that the Indians' fans, having found their heroes had feet of clay, would react ferociously. He could not believe it. But so it proved. Angry crowds stoned Wadekar's home in Mumbai. He was a dead man walking, yet the selectors chose to humiliate him by sacking him as captain not just of India but of the West Zone. He was dropped from the team for good measure and announced his retirement.

THE KING IS BACK

It was inevitable that Pataudi, despite turning down Wadekar's invitation to tour England—his great admirer Rajan Bala told me this showed his shrewdness—came back for the visit by the West Indies. For the first Test against the West Indies Pataudi was without Bedi, who was dropped for refusing to explain his actions, which included giving a live television interview on the England tour, to a committee of enquiry into that debacle. The players were cleared of any misdemeanours, but Bedi paid for not going along with the charade. Only after a huge public outcry did he return for the four remaining Tests—by which time India were already 1–0 down.

The Test, the first in Bengaluru, was also the first for Gordon Greenidge and Vivian Richards. Greenidge enjoyed himself, scoring 93 and 107. Just as the West Indies in their previous series, back in 1958–59, had used the Indian tour to blood a young team that would dazzle the world, so this series marked the new post-Sobers-and-Kanhai West Indians, led by Clive Lloyd. So dominant were the men from the Caribbean that the West Indies won by 267 runs.

While the West Indies played winning cricket India squabbled. Pataudi had injured himself in the first Test, Gavaskar, his deputy—although for some reason this was kept a secret—injured himself during a Ranji Trophy match before the second Test in Delhi. When the players arrived in Delhi they did not know who their captain was. The 2017 authorized autobiography of Farokh Engineer provides a fascinating story of what happened moments before the Test was due to begin. Engineer thought he would be captain, and the players even congratulated him. He was ready to go out to toss with his Lancashire teammate, Clive Lloyd, when, says Engineer, Raj Singh told him, 'Something sinister is going to happen behind our backs.' Then Venkataraghavan arrived and 'presented a note from the hierarchy—Gopinath [chairman of selectors] and his chum M. A. Chidambaram, the board

president, who [was], also, surprise, surprise from Chennai—saying that he
was to captain India.' Engineer thinks, 'It was a deceitful masterstroke.' It
certainly showed that, like the Bourbons, Indian cricket administrators had
learnt nothing and forgotten nothing.

Chandrasekhar, who had taken six wickets in the first Test, Richards
falling to Chandrasekhar in both innings for 4 and 3, was dropped to make
way for Venkataraghavan. Richards scored 192 not out with 6 sixes and 20
fours. India lost the Test by an innings, the match finishing after an hour's
play on the fourth day. India had lost only one Test in more than three
years before they went to England in the summer of 1974: now they had
lost five in a row in seven months. As if to emphasize how ridiculous the
subterfuge over Venkataraghavan was, he was dropped for the third Test in
Kolkata and did not play again in the series.

This is when, 2–0 down, Pataudi performed what his admirers fervently
believe to this day was his last great act for Indian cricket. While he was
no longer the batsman he had been (his highest score in the series was
36), he could still inspire and lead.

Viswanath, since his century in his first Test, had scored only one
other century, but at least this had lifted the curse that an Indian who
scored a century in his first Test never scored another, a curse which had
started with the first centurion, Amarnath. In Kolkata, Viswanath scored
139. Andy Roberts had been devastating, having taken fifteen wickets in
five innings with a 5 for 50 in the first innings. But Viswanath tamed him.
The result was that in Kolkata India was very much in the match, setting
the West Indians 309 to win the series. Pataudi was confident about India's
chances, even after the tourists made a good start. Late at night, on the
eve of the final day, he went to see Prasanna. 'The wicket is turning,' he
said. He was not worried about conceding runs—he wanted Prasanna and
Chandrasekhar to skittle the West Indies. As if the spinners had waited for
the king to come back, they responded: four wickets for Bedi, three for
Chandrasekhar—West Indies bowled out for 224. India were still alive at
2–1 down with two to play. Pataudi had worked his magic: India's run of
defeats was over.

Viswanath carried on in the fourth Test in Chennai. Batsmen at the
other end had no answer for Roberts, who took 7 for 64, but Viswanath
played one of the great Test innings, scoring an unbeaten 97 in a total of
190. Prasanna always performed better for Pataudi than for other captains,
and he shone with the ball. In a thirty-one-ball spell he dismissed Lloyd,
Richards and three more batsmen. India batted more like a team second time
around and set West Indies 255, but they got nowhere near and suddenly it

was 2–2. History beckoned: only Bradman's Australia had come back from 2–0 down to win a series, against England in the 1930s.

The decider was in the new Wankhede Stadium in Mumbai and for Pataudi there was something delicious in that. For it meant that the CCI run by Merchant, his old nemesis, had lost out to the new Maharashtrian powers, keen to advertise their control of Mumbai cricket. What a story it would have been if Pataudi had led India to victory—once he lost the toss, though, their chances were all but dead. The West Indies, on a good batting wicket, made 604 to put an end to India's hopes, with Lloyd making an unbeaten double century. Solkar scored a century, with Gavaskar, who had not played since the first Test, making 86 and Viswanath 95 in an impressive reply of 406, but India eventually lost by 201 runs.

Although Pataudi had averaged a measly 13 in the series, and despite India's defeat, he was still seen as a hero for making such a good contest of what had seemed a hopeless cause. It was just what his public expected: brave, audacious, even romantic. Pataudi had played in forty-six Tests—all but six of them as captain. Nine wins, nineteen losses. Win ratios over different periods are difficult to compare but this puts him below Umrigar, Wadekar, Bedi and Azharuddin, let alone most of the captains who came in the twenty-first century, when Indian cricket took a new, decisive turn. But even if we discount the sort of praise for him that was to be expected from Raj Singh and Prasanna, there can be no doubt that in his final series as leader he had made Indians believe again in their cricket, just as he had done in his first stint as captain when, as Viswanath says, 'When you think of Indian cricket in the 1960s you only think of Tiger.' So much so that there would only ever be one Tiger in Indian cricket. His aura would remain, and Yajuvindra Singh would tell the story of travelling on a train with Pataudi which has a touch of how the old Raj officials were treated. The great man drank whisky, oblivious to crowds wanting his darshan; as his servant went to the kitchen to heat up his food, the stationmaster held the train up. All the while Pataudi sang a ghazal.

However, the Indian team he had left behind in the mid-1970s often sang rather an uncertain tune.

Chapter 16

BEDI'S HEAVEN AND HELL

ONE BRILLIANT MOMENT

It was by no means obvious that Pataudi would be succeeded as captain by Bishan Singh Bedi. The choice was largely driven by the elimination of the other three candidates.

Gavaskar had been formally censured for his display against England during the inaugural World Cup in 1975. Gavaskar opened in India's reply to 334 in sixty overs. That was a massive total by the standards of the time, but not unreachable. Inexplicably, he used all of India's sixty overs for batting practice, scoring 36 not out in a total of 132 for three. Venkataraghavan had captained India in that World Cup but won few admirers as India failed to reach the semi-finals. Prasanna was always an unlikely choice, an ageing genius with an in-out Test career.

Jim Laker, one of the game's greatest spinners, once said, 'Heaven is seeing Lindwall bowl at one end and Bedi at the other.' I can well understand what Laker meant, having been privileged to see Lindwall bowl against India in Mumbai twice: in October 1956 and January 1960. And in my journalistic career I reported often on Bedi's quite magical bowling. Yet, Bedi the captain did not take India to heaven. Indeed, there were many moments when his leadership made Indians feel they were peering at hell.

His one moment of heaven as captain came in March 1976 in Trinidad when India broke a record that had been held for twenty-eight years by the team widely considered the greatest in cricket history. At this stage, under Bedi's leadership India had drawn a series in New Zealand—winning the first Test when, with Bedi injured, Gavaskar captained—and losing the third by an innings after a fit-again Bedi had taken over. This loss was by an innings and 33 runs. India flew from Wellington to Barbados and lost again even more heavily, by an innings and 97 runs.

It was after having the best of a draw in the second at Trinidad, where, on his favourite ground, Gavaskar made 156, and Bedi, proving heavenly with the ball, and helped by Chandrasekhar, nearly conjured a win, that India enjoyed what proved to be a stroke of luck. Rain in Guyana forced the West Indies to switch the Third Test back to Trinidad—with dramatic results. By lunch on the fourth day a confident Lloyd declared the West Indies second innings, setting India 403 to win. Only one team had ever successfully chased 400—Bradman's invincible Australians in 1948.

And this is where India's batsmen showed a determination and class nobody thought they possessed—certainly not away from home and against such formidable opposition. Gavaskar, who had thought only of saving the match, made his customary hundred in Port of Spain, his fourth in five innings there. Mohinder Amarnath, Lala's second son, whose powers of concentration had been doubted by his critics, confounded them in a mature display, making 85, and after Gavaskar was out Viswanath took over. The omens suggested failure: Viswanath rarely made big runs in the same innings as Gavaskar. What is more, he had never scored a century abroad. But just as he had proved that there was nothing in the Indian belief that an Indian who made a century in his first Test never made another, now he demolished this myth as well. He made 112, and by the time he was third out India needed just 67 more from twenty-two overs.

Such was the self-belief inspired by Gavaskar and Viswanath that Brijesh Patel, who in his Test career against England and the West Indies had shown every sign of being out of his depth, now played like a batsman who truly belonged in Test cricket. The Indian dressing room relaxed. Chandrasekhar had a massage, Viswanath with a towel wrapped around his midriff, had a beer and, reassured by Gavaskar that 'Tabu' (Patel's nickname) was doing well, began to perform a jig, singing, 'Oh, that's the way, uh-huh, uh-huh, I like it...' Meanwhile, Bedi, who loved writing letters and had complained that Indian batting collapses did not give him a chance to get beyond 'My dear...', now looked up from his writing to say 'Good, Lads'. He had time to write several more by the time Patel's late cut for four gave India victory by six wickets with six overs to spare. With 406 they had overtaken the Australians' winning score of 404 in 1948.

The victory was Bedi's zenith. He would win only five more of his next seventeen Tests and lose nine. West Indies gave up on spin and used a pace battery for the final Test on the much quicker pitch in Jamaica to batter the Indians, with Bedi declaring the second innings at 97 for five, just 11 ahead because he had no fit batsmen left. West Indies duly won by ten wickets and began a long era of success built on a rota of intimidating fast bowlers.

India returned as martyrs, but the series renewed doubts about Bedi's captaincy. They were powerfully reinforced when Tony Greig led England in India in the winter of 1976.

BEDI MADE TO FEEL A FOREIGNER IN HIS OWN LAND

It was the first full-strength England touring party to India under a reigning captain. They outperformed any previous tourists from any country by winning the first three Tests. India won the fourth, but Bedi could not do a Pataudi and make the score line 3–2, which might have put a gloss on a dreadful series.

There were individual successes. Gavaskar became the first Indian to complete 1,000 Test runs in a calendar year, but his series average was (for him) a disappointing 39, while Viswanath's was only 19. The other batsmen could not compensate. Bedi and Chandrasekhar took twenty-five and nineteen respectively in the series, but only at Bengaluru, in a dead rubber, could they force victory.

The third Test was marked by a sour episode. England's surprisingly successful opening bowler, John Lever, was found to be using a strip of bandage smeared with Vaseline. Bedi angrily accused him of using this on the ball to make it swing. Lever and the MCC denied it, and nothing was done. Bedi may have been right, but the timing of his complaint (when India were about to lose) made him look like a squealer.

It was a public relations debacle made worse by the inspired crowd-pleasing efforts of Tony Greig. The blonde, white South African proved far more popular than the home captain. Bedi chafed as Greig's football-derived antics amused the fans but distracted the Indian batsmen.

Bedi made things worse for himself. He regularly took the field ten or fifteen minutes after lunch or tea, prompting lavatorial jokes about his reason for absence. Both captains inspired poetry, Bedi's mocking, Greig's adulatory, all of it terrible.

In the first Test in Delhi, Greig changed the match with a standard ploy in English county cricket. Bedi had played in England for several years, so he should have been alert to it. England had bowled eleven overs off which India had scored an easy 43 without loss. Then Greig persuaded the umpires that the ball was out of shape and they changed it. The replacement swung prodigiously, and India lost four wickets for 6 runs. It set a pattern for the series, in which Greig seemed to master the local environment and Bedi looked like a baffled stranger. I covered the series for the London Broadcasting Corporation and the at end of it called Greig, the Clive of cricket, the man who had come with nothing and walked away with the loot, while Bedi looked like one of the forlorn Indian princes hoodwinked by Clive.

Chapter 17

THE BEST OF TIMES, THE WORST OF TIMES

A PAWN IN AN AUSTRALIAN GAME

In the four years between 1977 and 1981 India won some victories worth celebrating, fought out an astonishing Test match and produced its first genuine pace bowler since the far-off era of Mohammad Nissar and Amar Singh. However, it also showed India had not yet won its seat at the top table of world cricket and that Pakistan ranked much higher.

The most dramatic illustration of this came in the winter of 1977, when India went on their first tour of Australia since the days of Pataudi, a decade earlier. Australian, and indeed world cricket, had been rocked by the Australian TV magnate, Kerry Packer. Balked of the right to televise Australia Test matches, he had created World Series Cricket (WSC) in direct competition to them, recruiting top players from England, Australia, Pakistan, and the West Indies.

However, Packer recruited no Indian players. But the Australian cricket authorities consoled the Indians by saying their team would be coming to Australia not just to play a Test series but to save Test cricket from the Packer barbarians. Indian players, administrators and, in particular, the fans bought this argument, delighted to be seen as the moral guardians of the established game. Far from being cricket's saviours, however, they were in reality pawns in a game between Packer and the Australian board. This was underlined when the Australian board came to a settlement with Packer.

At the height of the fight between the board and Packer, India had agreed to the board's request to return to Australia in the winter of 1979–80. India knew how the Australian board had previously shunned them, having had only three visits to Australia since 1947, the gap between the first and the second being twenty years, that between the second and the third, ten years. Even in times of trouble Australia would not entertain India. In 1971, after protests made it impossible for Australia to carry on cricket relations with their white friends in South Africa, India offered to step in. They proposed an interesting twin tour: Australia would visit India in the first half of the winter of 1971, then India would visit Australia. The Australian board rejected it saying quite bluntly that this would 'interfere' with selecting the team for the 1972 Ashes tour of England, a tour that meant more than any other. But now, menaced by Packer, they had turned to India and India were overjoyed. However, on 30 May 1979, when Bob Parish, chairman of the board, revealed that a deal had been done with Packer, it was quite clear India were no longer required. 'The Board has agreed to ask the Indian board to defer their visit until next season 1980–81 and will invite the West Indian board to send an official team to participate in the 1979–80 programme.' That Australian summer would see a tour by England followed by the West Indies.

In a curious way, the 1977–78 series had turned history upside down. In 1935–36, unable to get a board to send a team to India, the Maharaja of Patiala had imported a team of retired Australian Test players. Now the Australian board was keen to play India but Australia's best players had defected to Packer. So, to captain the side, Australia went back to a player who had last played Test cricket against Pataudi's team and had not played first-class cricket for ten years, namely, Bobby Simpson. He was forty-one years old, five years younger than Jack Ryder, the captain of the old crocks Australian team that Patiala had brought to India in 1935.

There was one genuine player of class, ultra-fast bowler Jeff Thomson, but otherwise this was such a second-string team of greenhorns that the first Test in Brisbane in December 1977 saw six Australians make their debut. In the entire series of five Tests, twelve Australians wore the baggy green cap for the first time. In contrast, India in the series had no debutants and should have won their first series in Australia but failed.

The reason was that Simpson rediscovered his appetite for Indian bowling, and while Bedi often bowled brilliantly, Simpson's imaginative captaincy was superior to that of Bedi's and he handled his inexperienced team much better. The first two Tests illustrated that graphically. Australia squeezed out victories by 16 runs in Brisbane and by two wickets in Perth. In the second Test, India allowed a nightwatchman, Tony Mann, to score a century. India then recorded two emphatic wins, the third by 222 runs (the first Indian victory in Australia) and the fourth by an innings. Chandrasekhar took eighteen wickets in these victories, which was a sort of delayed consolation for being sent home injured in the last series. Led by Gavaskar, with three centuries, the Indians had batted resiliently. In the final Test, despite a rare failure by him, they made an epic attempt to score 493 for victory, finally succumbing at 445—making it the highest fourth innings to lose a Test. A melancholy record now held by New Zealand's 451 against England at Christchurch in 2002.

India won many plaudits—but their full-strength team had still lost the series against almost unknown Australians. And over twenty-five days of Test cricket the total attendance of 256,594 was just a few more than the crowd that had been attracted to a solitary Test, the Centenary Test between the full-strength Australian and England team in Melbourne, in March 1977, just before the Packer storm broke. Fourteen of the twenty-five days of the Australia–India series had seen crowds of less than 10,000. As India failed to beat Australia, in the rival Packer series the cream of Pakistan cricketers displayed their talent: Asif Iqbal, Imran Khan, Javed Miandad, Majid Khan, Mushtaq Mohammad, Sarfraz Nawaz and Zaheer Abbas. India was soon to realize the huge gulf between Indian and Pakistani cricket.

PAKISTAN ENDS THE GREAT AGE OF INDIAN SPIN

Two wars had kept India and Pakistan apart on the cricket field since 1961 but by the winter of 1978 relations had thawed enough for Bedi to take his team to Pakistan.

The Pakistanis had nearly all their best players under contract to Kerry Packer. The remainder had performed indifferently in home and away series against England, so Pakistan hastily broke ranks with the countries banning Packer players from their national teams and recalled their stars to face their biggest rival. The result was a massacre. After a comfortable draw in the first Test, Pakistan won the second by eight wickets and General Zia's new-minted dictatorship ordered a national holiday. They won the third by the same margin. Their batsmen plundered the ageing Indian spinners. Mushtaq Mohammad averaged 75, Javed Miandad 119 and Zaheer Abbas a mighty 194. Chandra took eight wickets at 48 apiece, Bedi six at 74.83 and Prasanna only two, while conceding a total of 251 runs.

Only one Indian batsman matched the Pakistanis—predictably, Gavaskar, who averaged over 89, with two hundreds in the third Test. However, the real consolation was the discovery of a teenaged fast-bowling all-rounder from the northern state of Haryana.

INDIA FINDS A FAST BOWLER

The debut series of Kapil Dev Nikhanj (the last name soon disappeared) looks inauspicious: seven wickets at 60.85, and 159 runs at 31.80. But he more than hinted at the future.

His best series score of 59 was made from forty-eight balls at No. 9 after Imran Khan and Sarfraz Nawaz had reduced India to 253 for seven.

Better still, Kapil opened the bowling with real pace based on a beautiful action. A daredevil boy who enjoyed all sports, especially freeing police horses and riding them bareback, he disciplined himself to become a fast bowler after an incident reminiscent of Oliver Twist when he was fifteen at a coaching camp. He was served a tiny helping of lunch. He protested that as a fast bowler he needed more. An Indian board official, Keki Tarapore, (a former left-arm spinner who had been an obsequious manager of India's 1967 tour of England) scorned the request, saying 'There are no fast bowlers in India.' Kapil was stung into proving him wrong—Tarapore's biggest, if accidental, service to Indian cricket.

But to his great credit Kapil has not nursed grudges. In 2014, he told me with a yogi-style calmness, 'There was a time when England, Australia, West Indies used to come to India and charge extra money. The Indian board did not have the money, so I don't blame them. Our coaching system was different. We were struggling. We were trying to come up.'

LITTLE MASTER TAKES CHARGE

Defeat in Pakistan finished Bedi as captain and player. Gavaskar, inevitably, succeeded as captain for a home series against the West Indies. India were now indirectly rewarded by Kerry Packer. He had removed the top West Indian players and their new captain, Alvin Kallicharran, led an inexperienced side in which Malcolm Marshall made a barely noticed Test debut.

However, India won just one Test out of six, a fighting three-wicket victory in a bumper war in Chennai. India could at last retaliate with Kapil in their attack and a hitherto unremarkable left-arm seamer, Karsan Ghavri. He blossomed with twenty-seven wickets in the series, Kapil took nineteen, and the spinners had only a minor role.

The other Tests were drawn. Kapil also served India as a thrilling batsman. Unlike most Indian batsmen, who ducked and defended against pace, he hooked bouncers fiercely. His 329 runs in the series included an undefeated 126 not out in Delhi off 124 balls, his first Test century, completed with a six.

However, Gavaskar continued to dominate the Indian batting, undiminished by the cares of captaincy. His nine innings produced 732 runs at an average of 91.50, setting a series of records which matched Hutton and Bradman. Still less than thirty years old, he seemed poised for a long reign. But then suddenly the spectre of Packer loomed over Indian cricket.

PACKER DISRUPTS INDIAN CRICKET

Packer had made approaches to Gavaskar and Bedi during the winter tour of Australia in 1977. Then, on the Pakistan tour, Packer's right-hand man, Lynton Taylor, offered contracts to Gavaskar and the wicketkeeper, Syed Kirmani. Gavaskar confirmed this to me in 2018. He said that Taylor was then thinking of offers to other Indians but did not mention Bedi. Taylor also promised Gavaskar that he and Kirmani could continue to play international cricket for India but not domestic cricket (the arrangement he had just made for Pakistan's stars). Gavaskar cleared this with the Indian manager in Pakistan, Fatehsinghrao Gaekwad (the former Maharaja of Baroda), but in the end neither he nor Kirmani signed. As to Bedi, according to Rajdeep Sardesai in his 2017 book, *Democracy's XI*, he furiously rejected three offers from Packer, the last accompanied by an open cheque book.

However, when the story broke back in 1979, both Gavaskar and Kirmani were punished. Gavaskar was dropped as captain for the forthcoming tour of England: Venkataraghavan replaced him, with Viswanath as vice-captain. Kirmani was dropped altogether, in favour of Reddy, his inferior behind the stumps and in front of them.

GAVASKAR HELPS INDIANS DREAM

For long periods in the summer of 1979 it seemed this would be another England tour to forget. India had a dire performance in the World Cup, confirming that they had yet to master one-day cricket. They lost to the West Indies, New Zealand and even Sri Lanka, not yet a Test team. Gallingly, their rivals, Pakistan, reached the semi-finals.

In the first Test, at Edgbaston, India lost by an innings and 83 runs in four days. It was a Test finale for Chandrasekhar, but a sad, unmagical one: nought for 113 in an England innings of 633 for 5 declared.

At Lord's, India were bowled out for 96 in the first innings, in which Gavaskar made 42, but drew, thanks to Viswanath once again proving his class with a century and Dilip Vengsarkar, of whom little was known in England, scoring a hundred in a third-wicket stand of 210. The contrast between the diminutive Viswanath and the upright Vengsarkar with his military bearing could not be greater and Vengsarkar would so take to Lord's that in two subsequent visits he would also score centuries, something no overseas batsman, not even the great Don, had managed at the Mecca of cricket.

What made the tour memorable for the Indians was the final day and a half at the Oval when England, having dominated the match, left India 500 minutes to make 438: bookmakers offered 500–1 against. On 27 August 1979, just before the Test, Mountbatten had been assassinated and the Indian team had held a minute's silence, a gesture to the last British viceroy which had a touch of colonial India about it. However, on the cricket field the new India emerged, led by Gavaskar.

Thus far Gavaskar had done little by his standards in Tests and seemed to be using county matches for relaxation. The one major exception to this had been 166 against Hampshire, but, as he recalled to me in the summer of 2018, he was not expecting to play and had arrived at the ground without his whites. But Venkataraghavan told him that he wanted him to play to disprove allegations being made by Rajan Bala in *The Hindu* that Venkataraghavan was not in charge of the team and also that Gavaskar was fearful of Malcolm Marshall, the great West Indian fast bowler who played for Hampshire. Gavaskar batted in such an un-Gavaskar style that his last 60 was scored at breakneck speed. As he returned to the pavilion, Venkataraghavan came down the steps, congratulated Gavaskar and then gestured to Bala as if to say 'This shows you I am in charge.'

At the Oval, Gavaskar needed no persuading to play one of the most masterful innings in Test history. It helped that he had found in Chetan Chauhan the reliable opening partner he had long sought. After a long in-out career, Chauhan had finally established himself in the role in Australia in 1977. Before that, Gavaskar had had a dozen opening partners in six years. (In total, Gavaskar opened with twenty-three different partners, a record no one is likely to beat. Alastair Cook had only fifteen, despite England's capricious selectors.) The fourth day ended with the pair still together.

It was on the final day that England finally saw Gavaskar bat in the way that crowds elsewhere in the world were so familiar with. The day had begun with Ian Botham looking at the Oval scoreboard and having a premonition that Gavaskar would score a double century. He was to be proved right. As batsmen came and went at the other end, Chauhan made 80, Vengsarkar 52, Gavaskar defied everything devised by Mike Brearley, arguably England's most astute captain, as he marched to his double century. Brearley had only one ploy left: slowing the over rate. Under the rules then applying, he could do this until the last hour, when twenty overs were mandatory. In the half hour before that time, England bowled just six overs.

With eight overs India needed 49. Brearley now tried two more ploys. One was to bring Botham (hitherto very ordinary) into the attack. The other was to call for drinks. The second ploy worked. Gavaskar lost his concentration: after nearly eight hours at the crease, he holed out at mid-on to Botham, having made 221, the highest score he would ever make in England. India should still have won, but Venkataraghavan made a tactical error in promoting Kapil Dev and Yashpal Sharma ahead of Viswanath, who batted No. 6 instead of No. 4. He also got a poor umpiring decision. India reached the last over needing 15 with two wickets left. All the results were now possible, a win for either side, a tie or a draw. England's all-rounder Peter Willey delivered his off-spin. India made 6 off it without losing another wicket. The most thrilling Test since England at Lord's against Frank Worrell's 1963 West Indians had been drawn.

English observers, led by Len Hutton, recognized Gavaskar's greatness. *Wisden* named him as one of its Cricketers of the Year—only the fourth Indian after C. K. Nayudu, Vijay Merchant and Bhagwath Chandrasekhar. But some Indians, notably his bête noire Bala, persistently disparaged him. We were sitting next to each other in the Oval press box and as Viswanath came in Bala told me that, while Gavaskar only played well against second-string attacks (halfway through the day's play England's best bowler, Mike Hendrick, retired hurt), Viswanath was god.

The Indian board disagreed. Poor Venkataraghavan was sacked while still on the return flight to India, and Gavaskar replaced him.

His first task was a home six-Test series against a still Packerless Australia. India won 2–0. Gavaskar's twenty-second Test century, scored appropriately in Mumbai, caught him up with Wally Hammond and Colin Cowdrey: only Sobers (26) and Bradman (29) then lay ahead. A great Australian, Allan Border, came into view with 162 in the first Test. He and Gavaskar now give their name to the Test trophy between India and Australia.

SETTLING SCORES WITH PAKISTAN

Gavaskar's team then faced Pakistan at home. They had a new captain, Asif Iqbal, but were otherwise much the same team that had crushed Bedi's.

Indian gloom lifted in the second Test at Delhi. They did not win, but Kapil Dev took nine wickets and Pakistan's massive batting line-up was twice bowled out.

Gavaskar did his first job by winning the toss in the third Test at Mumbai. India made 334, which gave them control of the match as the pitch deteriorated. Pakistan struggled against pace and spin, even the unsung medium pace of Roger Binny, India's first Anglo-Indian Test cricketer. (So far, the only one, although his son Stuart has played for India in ODIs.) India set a fourth-innings target of 321 in plenty of time: the Pakistanis never looked like achieving it and lost by 131 runs with a day to spare.

Pakistan, already restive and unhappy under Asif's leadership, now seemed to implode. They accused Indian umpires of bias (a charge bitterly repeated in graffiti in some Indian Muslim districts) and the Indian authorities of preparing a substandard pitch at Mumbai. In reality, as Imran Khan acknowledged later in his memoirs, Pakistan were simply unprepared mentally for the intense atmosphere created by the massive partisan crowds and the weight of expectations on them from their own media and supporters.

Zaheer Abbas, the destroyer in Pakistan, could scarcely buy a run, and averaged less than 20 in the series. The normally resilient Asif lost weight and took tranquillizers. In the fifth Test at Chennai, Pakistan's players were so nervous that they could not watch each other bat. Now Kapil Dev showed himself a world-beating all-rounder. On a perfect batting strip, his four wickets for 90 helped dismiss Pakistan for 272. In reply Gavaskar batted for all but ten hours to make 166. No one else made 50 until Kapil at No. 8 smashed 84 in ninety-eight balls. India earned a lead of 168.

Kapil then hustled out three demoralized batsmen as Pakistan fell to 58 for five. They eventually staggered into the last day, but Gavaskar was fittingly at the crease, making 29 not out as India made 78 to record a ten-wicket victory. It was India's first series win over Pakistan since the far-off inaugural series in 1952–53. Kapil was a national icon after barely a year in the side. He had won the all-rounder's duel with Imran Khan, who returned with the other Pakistan players to a jeering chorus of fake news from their media.

But Imran would soon avenge himself on Gavaskar.

Chapter 18

ADMIRED BUT NOT LOVED

Gavaskar's status as one of India's greatest cricketers, admired but unloved, was confirmed in 1981, an especially extraordinary year in Indian cricket history.

THE GREAT ESCAPE

It began with a tour of Australia and New Zealand in the winter of 1980. For three months the Indians were generally outplayed by an Australian side to which their Packer players had returned.

Australia won the first Test by an innings and 4 runs in just three days. India managed 201 in each innings; Greg Chappell managed 204 in 296 balls. Australia posted 528 in the second Test. India in reply were faltering at 130 for four. Then Sandeep Patil made himself into a legend. In the first Test he had been felled by a bouncer which left him with an agonizing earache and doubtful about batting on the tour—or ever again. He practised in one of the new helmets which were becoming common. It gave him the confidence to play an innings of 174, combining grace and power, in just 240 balls. It earned India a draw. Seventeen months later, in June 1982, in Manchester, Patil would earn India another draw during which he tucked into the first over with the new ball by Bob Willis (then one of the fastest bowlers in the world), savagely driven for 24. Nine balls took him from 73 to 104 and earned him a celebration drink from the watching Viv Richards (who did not like Willis).

Patil had learnt his cricket in Shivaji Park, in Mumbai, which had also been the nursery of Vijay Manjrekar, Gavaskar and his rival and friend Vengsarkar. But he was a different kind of player, with a style reminiscent of discos and Bollywood movies. Salim Durani was his predecessor, many since have carried the same slightly louche glamour.

But to return to Australia in February 1981 and what is known as 'The Great Escape' at Melbourne. For four days, India were outplayed again. They began their second innings 182 behind. Gavaskar was having one of his leanest spells with just 48 in five completed innings. Now he summoned up his greatest powers of concentration. With the faithful

Chauhan, he put on 165. Then Dennis Lillee won an lbw appeal against him. He was convinced that he had edged the ball. It was long before reviews were allowed, and the decision had to stand. He lost his composure and reverted to boyhood tantrums by walking off and opting to forfeit the match, dragging an unhappy Chauhan with him.

Fortunately, the Indian manager, Wing Commander S. K. Durrani, took charge of the situation, meeting the pair at the gate and ordering Chauhan to return and resume the match. India eventually left Australia 143 to win. It looked simple enough, especially as the Indian spinners, Dilip Doshi and Shivlal Yadav, were injured, and Kapil Dev was in such pain from a pulled thigh muscle that he could not bowl for the rest of the day. Nonetheless, India took three wickets, including Greg Chappell, first ball, bowled by a rank long hop from Karsan Ghavri.

The next day Kapil Dev, after a series of pain-killing injections, bowled unchanged for over two hours. He took five wickets for 28, Doshi also fought through his pain barrier, and Australia were all out for 83, losing by 59. The pitch was poor, but India in adversity had discovered a new will to defy fate.

As often happens, after this great effort India faltered against lesser opposition in the shape of New Zealand. Poor batting saw them all out for 190 in the first Test after being set 253. The other two Tests were drawn. A teenaged slow left-armer from Mumbai, Ravi Shastri, was plucked from a Ranji Trophy match to cover for the injured Doshi and thrown into a Test match in alien conditions after a twenty-hour flight. He responded superbly, taking fifteen wickets in the three-Test series at an average of 18, besides batting well.

Instead of being praised for their talent-spotting, Gavaskar and the tour manager, Bapu Nadkarni, both from Mumbai, were accused of Mumbai bias for choosing Shastri ahead of an established Ranji Trophy wicket-taker, Rajinder Goel.

This was a new strand in the attacks on Gavaskar, and it would recur through the 1980s. But few could challenge his record as captain as England arrived in the winter of 1981 for a five-Test tour: twenty-four Tests, six wins, two defeats, three series wins at home, a drawn series against Australia abroad.

MADAM SAVES TOUR, GAVASKAR UPSETS ENGLAND

This 1981 tour had nearly been cancelled, because two of the England party, Geoff Boycott and Geoff Cook, had played in South Africa, contrary to the Gleneagles Agreement, which, in the wake of the D'Oliveira affair, had called for a total Commonwealth sporting boycott of the apartheid regime. This led to hectic diplomacy starting at the high commission in London, where, helped by Robin Marlar, a columnist for *The Hindu*, the high commissioner spoke to Boycott, then in Hong Kong. At the end of the call the high commissioner said, 'I can tell by that telephone call that he's a very awkward character. We can't allow an awkward character to wreck the tour.' The final decision was taken in the unlikely cricket setting of Mexico City, where 'Madam' Indira Gandhi, the prime minister, was at a conference. She saved the (lucrative) tour by discovering a passage in Boycott's recent book of his loathing of apartheid. In fact, he had been secretly organizing a rebel cricket tour of South Africa and spent much of the tour recruiting English players in a way which was so secretive that cricket and South Africa were not even mentioned. Instead, it was called 'Operation Chessmate'. The prize catch was clearly Ian Botham. He was offered £45,000, more than six times his then yearly earnings and, as Botham says in his autobiography, 'I was prepared to have a look at the deal—after all, who in his right mind wouldn't be?' This led to remarkable cloak-and-dagger scenes, particularly during the second Test in Bengaluru, where Alan Herd, Botham's lawyer and Reg Hayter, his agent flew out to discuss the deal. They managed to fool us journalists. Hayter, who during the 1950s was often the lone English journalist covering England's tours to India, suddenly flew in, telling us, 'I have come to see my old friend Lala.' He was referring to Amarnath, who was in fact not in Bengaluru. Herd and Hayter told Botham he would be worse off financially and banned by England. Botham also did not want to be seen to be supporting apartheid and turned it down, to Boycott's fury. Boycott himself did not complete the tour, leaving after the Kolkata Test, having fallen out both with his teammates and the tour management. Such was his relationship with his fellow players that, as Botham says, when Boycott said he would quit, 'That was the signal for 15 teammates to grab hold of the nearest piece of paper they could find and get him to sign a resignation note before he had time to change his mind.' Kolkata marked Boycott's last Test. Raman Subba Row, the England manager, has always maintained, 'I didn't send him home. I had every reason to do so, but I didn't.' Boycott had not taken to Raman, whose father was Indian, and told him during the tour that the problem with Raman was he was 'one of them', meaning Indian. Raman took it in his stride, although Chris Tavaré, the Kent batsman, was most upset. Just a month after the series finished it emerged that Geoff Boycott, Graham Gooch, John Emburey and Derek Underwood, who had all toured, had arrived in South Africa for a rebel tour.

By this time Gavaskar had every reason to celebrate India's having won the series, their first victory over England—home or away—since

1973. It was not stirring stuff, a solitary Test win in Mumbai, followed by mind-numbing draws in the remaining four with Gavaskar at Bengaluru scoring 172 in 708 minutes (ten long hours and forty-eight minutes). But whereas Bedi had been outwitted by Greig in 1976, Gavaskar made the England captain, Keith Fletcher, look petulant and Fletcher was forced to apologize when he hit his stumps after he was given out, caught at the wicket in the Bengaluru Test. His reaction in the dressing room was more violent, he hurled his bat in a fury against the wall.

Gavaskar showed a mastery both with bat and words that few Indian captains had in the past. Boycott (before leaving) overtook Garry Sobers's record number of runs in Tests: 8,032. Gavaskar watched my interview with Boycott and told him sarcastically to enjoy the record before he took it from him, as he eventually did. The tour had seen English criticism of Indian umpiring—Raman had tried unsuccessfully to have the umpires changed after the Mumbai Test—and the conditions and the food. Before the Tests began, when I mentioned to Gavaskar that England were considered the favourites, he had reacted angrily, 'Who told you that?' Now his response to English criticism was thunderous:

> And yes, the food. That is one common cause for complaint. But what is not taken into account is the fact that when Indians go to England they also find food a problem. The vegetarians in the side struggle because it's hardly spicy, it's insipid, cold most of the time and many times we just find an odd leaf taken from a plant somewhere in the garden and dressed up and called a 'salad'. But the Indians don't complain about that, do they?

What Gavaskar did not know that soon Indians would have cause to complain about his own captaincy and he would suffer the same fate his predecessors had. He had routed the British Raj. He would himself be routed soon.

The tour showed India was changing. I kept a diary of the tour and my entry for 22 November 1981, made as I arrived in Mumbai for the first Test, read:

> Bombay has a new international airport complete with bays which allow you to walk straight from the aircraft into the arrival lounge. So, for the first time ever I miss that strange assault on my nostrils—a combination of heat and the smell of sewers—that in the past 'greeted' visitors. But, as ever, cricket is a magic word and I waltz through customs ahead of the long goods-laden line of expatriates returning

with their spoils from the rich Arab lands. The customs officer seems so impressed with my journalistic credentials that he does not even issue a 'chitty' for my tape-recorder. Later, a friend points out that this means I could make a hefty profit by selling it on the black market in Bombay. Cricket, I suspect, would sell just about anything in Bombay. As we journey towards the centre of town, past the biggest slum in Asia, I see numerous advertising hoardings using cricket to push their products. A local butter manufacturer has its mascot struggling to tie the laces of his cricket boots underneath a slogan reading: 'If you Dilley-dalley [sic], butter will melt'—a reference to the boot problems that Graham Dilley has had on the tour.

Chapter 19

GAVASKAR'S DECLINE AND FALL

THE FIRST NAIL IN GAVASKAR'S COFFIN

Gavaskar figured high in England's thoughts as the Indians landed in the UK in May 1982. Derek Pringle made his debut in the first Test at Lord's in June and recalls that after a team dinner the question would be, 'Sunil Gavaskar, what do we think about him?' The conclusion would be, as he cuts and pulls and is strong off his legs, England should bowl outside his off stump to a good length. Botham disagreed, and pointing to Gavaskar's height of 5 feet 2 inches suggested the bouncer was the weapon. Actually, if the England players had seen the figures, they would have realized Gavaskar never much enjoyed playing in England as this table shows:

Season	Mts	Inns	NO	Runs	Hs	Avg	100s	50s	0s
1971	3	6	0	144	57	24.00	0	2	1
1974	3	6	0	217	101	36.16	1	1	1
1979	4	7	0	542	221	77.42	1	4	0
1982	3	3	0	74	48	24.66	0	0	0
1986	3	6	0	175	54	29.16	0	1	0

Only in 1979, when he made that great 221 at the Oval, did he show the English that his reputation for huge scores was not fake. However, he could not have anticipated that the first notes in the dossier compiled against his captaincy would be made on that tour.

It started at Lord's, which India lost easily, and much was made of the fact that his opening partner was another Mumbai player, Ghulam Parkar, who only played the one Test, scoring 6 and 1. India drew the second, but there was another Mumbai debutant, Suru Nayak, who did slightly better and played in the third at the Oval as well. The third saw Gavaskar hobble off after a Botham hit struck him on the shin. Botham made 208; Gavaskar took no further part in the match. Back home, India played Sri Lanka for the first time, and while Gavaskar made 155, India did not win.

Gavaskar had gone nine Tests without a win, and complaints against him multiplied, especially from the 'northern' players and their supporters, who accused him of bias towards Mumbai.

Gavaskar's captaincy was therefore under challenge when he took his team to Pakistan in the winter of 1982–83. There it was destroyed.

IMRAN HUMILIATES INDIA

The six-Test series opened at the Gaddafi Stadium in Lahore. (It still bears the name of the Libyan dictator who helped to fund it for his friend, Zulfikar Ali Bhutto, in the early 1970s. The Pakistanis cannot agree on a replacement for him.) India performed well enough in a drawn match. They then lost the next three in a row, two by an innings, the other by ten wickets. Draws in the fifth and sixth gave Pakistan a clean sweep.

India's bowlers were mauled as Pakistan made 485, 452, 652, and 581 for 3 declared in the first four Tests. Then they had to face the best fast bowling of all time on Asian pitches: Imran Khan took forty wickets for below 14 apiece. Only Gavaskar (434 runs, average 48) and Mohinder Amarnath resisted him consistently. Others produced occasional defiance, but Viswanath could manage only 134 runs in the series from eight completed innings.

Amarnath had endured a fits-and-starts Test career for over a decade. Now he earned Imran's tribute as the best player of fast bowling in the world. Although hit on the head (by Imran), he hooked fearlessly and scored three hundreds in his 584 runs, average 73.

As I wrote in a *Sunday Times* article in 1983, this series subjected Gavaskar's captaincy to a litany of complaints: he was defensive, defeatist, biased. There was even a crazy rumour that he listened to his wife Pamie in picking the team. A bizarre row with Bedi, now a selector, over the travel arrangements for the team's return sealed his fate. Bedi was a northerner, who blamed Gavaskar for his own sacking as captain and player. He had his revenge when Gavaskar was sacked and replaced by the northerner, Kapil Dev.

Kapil and Bedi, the northern axis, were eager to launch a new wave of Indian cricket.

So, they did, and it gave India a ride the like of which it had never had before.

Tendulkar playing at English club Lashings, 2006 (Bipin Patel).

Pataudi presenting the trophy named after him to England, August 2011, a month before his death (Bipin Patel).

Tendulkar at the Oval, 2011, trying to score his hundredth Test century (Bipin Patel).

Tendulkar dressed as a Yorkshireman in 1992 (John Rogers).

Tendulkar relishing captaining MCC in the bicentenary match, 5 July 2014, a year after retirement (Bipin Patel).

Tendulkar, Kambli, with their late coach, Achrekar (Prakash Parsekar).

Chandrasekhar, hair flying, bowling his remarkable leg-spin (Mid-day Infomedia).

Prasanna and Venkataraghavan, two great and contrasting off-spinners (Mid-day Infomedia).

The millennial Fab Four, L to R, Dravid, Ganguly, Lakshman, Tendulkar (Bipin Patel).

Cricket on the Kolkata Maidan, 1984 (Mihir Bose).

A historic Ganguly moment, celebrating with Kaif after a
dramatic victory over England at Lord's in the NatWest trophy
2002. Flintoff is not amused (Bipin Patel).

Ganguly getting ready, 2002; a summer which saw a great Indian victory at Leeds (Bipin Patel).

Laxman batting in the 2011 Test series against England (Graham Morris).

Dravid proving wrong those who considered he could not play the one day game, Wanderers, March 2011 (Bipin Patel).

Sehwag during his double century against Sri Lanka, 3 December 2009 (Mid-day Infomedia).

Kumble having scored his first Test century in India's winning 2007 series as a happy Tendulkar looks on (Bipin Patel).

Khan pointing to the jelly beans at Nottingham, a turning point in the 2007 series (Bipin Patel).

A picture that captures a historic moment as India celebrate winning the 2007 series in England. Present are all the Fab Four: Tendulkar, Dravid, Ganguly, Laxman (Bipin Patel).

The shot that made history, Dhoni's 2011 World Cup winning hit (Mid-day Infomedia).

Dhoni on his toes in an explosive innings of 77 at Edgbaston in 2011 (Bipin Patel).

Dhoni scatters pigeons in a one-day match at the Oval, 2011 (Bipin Patel).

THE FIFTH WAVE

TESTS

Wave	Period	Mts	Won	Lost	Drawn	Tied	Win%	W/L
5th	1983-1989	47	8	12	26	1	17.02	0.67

TOP BATSMEN IN FIFTH WAVE

	Mts	Runs	Hs	Avg	100	50
D. B. Vengsarkar	42	3014	166	56.86	11	12
S. M. Gavaskar	35	2497	236★	48.01	7	12
R. J. Shastri	46	2203	142	35.53	6	8
M. Azharuddin	30	1912	199	46.63	6	7
Kapil Dev	46	1834	163	29.58	3	9
M. Amarnath	32	1730	138	39.31	4	8
K. Srikkanth	29	1683	123	37.40	2	11
A. D. Gaekwad	14	696	201	30.26	1	3
S. M. H. Kirmani	19	659	102	38.76	1	2
R. M. H. Binny	18	632	83★	27.47	0	5

★Not Out

TOP BOWLERS IN FIFTH WAVE

	Mts	Wkts	Best	Avg	5WI	10WM
Kapil Dev	46	141	9/83	28.29	6	1
R. J. Shastri	46	97	5/75	38.40	1	0
Maninder Singh	23	74	7/27	30.29	3	2
N. S. Yadav	20	61	5/76	34.93	3	0
C. Sharma	23	61	6/58	35.45	4	1
N. D. Hirwani	7	42	8/61	20.71	3	1
Arshad Ayub	11	41	5/50	27.75	3	0
R. M. H. Binny	18	32	6/56	28.18	2	0
L. Sivaramakrishnan	8	26	6/64	40.38	3	1
G. Sharma	4	9	4/88	39.22	0	0

TOP WICKETKEEPERS IN FIFTH WAVE

	Mts	Dismissals	Ct	St
K. S. More	24	59	44	15
S. M. H. Kirmani	19	38	32	6
S. Viswanath	3	11	11	0

ONE-DAY INTERNATIONALS

Wave	Period	Mts	Won	Lost	NR	Tied	Win%	W/L
5th	1983–1989	107	49	53	5	0	45.79	0.92

TOP BATSMEN IN FIFTH WAVE

	Mts	Runs	Hs	Avg	SR	100	50
K. Srikkanth	94	2628	123	28.87	71.43	4	16
D. B. Vengsarkar	80	2367	105	40.11	70.55	1	17
S. M. Gavaskar	71	2287	103*	42.35	65.96	1	21
R. J. Shastri	95	2099	102	32.29	67.08	2	14
M. Azharuddin	86	2081	108*	33.03	68.43	2	7
Kapil Dev	99	1897	87	27.49	100.31	0	10
M. Amarnath	47	1151	102*	34.87	58.60	2	9
N. S. Sidhu	23	826	88	41.30	70.00	0	10
R. Lamba	22	517	102	25.85	69.11	1	3
R. M. H. Binny	49	323	57	16.15	66.18	0	1

TOP BOWLERS IN FIFTH WAVE

	Mts	Wkts	Best	Avg	RPO	4W
Kapil Dev	99	115	4/30	26.14	3.75	1
R. J. Shastri	95	93	4/38	33.80	4.08	2
Maninder Singh	52	61	4/22	29.63	3.80	1
C. Sharma	53	60	3/22	32.41	4.85	0
R. M. H. Binny	49	44	4/35	32.06	4.78	1
S. Madan Lal	39	32	4/37	33.43	4.02	1
K. Srikkanth	94	24	5/27	15.20	4.88	2
Arshad Ayub	19	17	5/21	41.47	4.02	1
M. Amarnath	47	17	2/19	50.00	4.14	0

TOP WICKETKEEPERS IN FIFTH WAVE

	Mts	Dismissals	Ct	St
K. S. More	37	35	20	15
C. S. Pandit	31	25	13	12
S. Viswanath	22	24	17	7
S. M. H. Kirmani	13	11	7	4
S. C. Khanna	7	7	3	4

Chapter 20

KAPIL, THE CRICKET REVOLUTIONARY

When Kapil Dev and Madan Lal had a brief conversation on the pitch at Lord's on 25 June 1983, during the World Cup final, little did they know that the result of their deliberations would have a profound effect not just on Indian cricket but on the game globally. Over the next few overs these two men, and their teammates, would help to send cricket into a new era.

India had surprised everybody, except perhaps themselves, by reaching the final of the third World Cup, a tournament which, like its two predecessors, was hosted by England. The West Indies had won the 1975 and 1979 World Cups and, having bowled out India for a meagre 183 with more than six overs to spare, were strong favourites to lift the trophy again.

The Caribbean bands had been in a celebratory mood since early in the day, and there was no let-up from them as the imperious Viv Richards, with 7 fours in his 33 runs, helped his team past the 50 mark for the loss of only one wicket. As Richards feasted on the Indian bowling, Sandeep Patil shouted out to Gavaskar in Marathi, 'At least we will have time to go shopping.' Kapil's wife, Romi, did indeed leave to do just that.

Madan Lal, like the other Indian bowlers, had taken punishment, but he felt the champions, and Richards in particular, had become overconfident. He had already had Desmond Haynes caught and, although he had been made to look as if he was giving Richards batting practice, he sensed a chance for India to change the course of what had so far been a one-sided final.

Kapil, India's captain, recounted that pivotal moment at a promotional event in Mumbai in 2017. He wanted to change his bowling attack, but he relented when Madan stated his case:

> Before that particular over, 2 or 3 fours were hit off Madan. So, I went to Madan, asked him to take a break and come back after a few overs. To which Madan said 'You give me the ball. I have earlier dismissed Vivian Richards, I can do it once more.'
>
> When a player is so confident, even though I was not too keen, I thought, let him bowl another over. They say, some things just happen for you and this happened with us.

Madan felt Richards was vulnerable and he was right. He delivered a ball with more bounce; an overconfident Richards mistimed his shot and hooked it. Kapil ran backwards. Sitting in the press box, surrounded by English and Australian journalists who had written off India, I held my breath. But while I, and all of India fretted, Kapil was calm. In 2014, talking to me at Lord's, while India played England in a Test, he recalled, 'I thought nothing when I took the catch. If I had been thinking I would not have taken the catch. Reflexes take over.' I could not contain my joy as Kapil took the catch over his shoulder with breathtaking ease. This was the turning point of the match. Madan soon struck again, removing Larry Gomes. Lloyd came and went; from 50 for 1 the West Indies had slid to 76 for 6. The steel bands fell silent.

Jeff Dujon and Malcolm Marshall attempted to stem the tide, but Amarnath got them both, and when Kapil trapped Andy Roberts lbw it was 126 for 9. Joel Garner and Michael Holding held out, adding 14, but West Indies were 43 runs short when Amarnath had Holding lbw. India, the team nobody had predicted would do anything in the World Cup, 66–1 no-hopers, had won it. The Indians had gone where Australia and England could not, both of them having been beaten by the West Indies in the two previous finals.

The Indians, not expecting to win, had no champagne with which to celebrate. The West Indians were well stocked, and Kapil, having gone to their dressing room to commiserate, saw the bottles stacked and asked Lloyd to give him some so he could toast the victory. It provided a wonderful final touch: beat the opponent and then drink his champagne.

The West Indies may have been overconfident, but this was a well-drilled Indian team which had worked out its plans. It preferred to bat first, make a score, and then use it to pressure the chasing team. Also, there was remarkable cohesion in the team, the leading players being all from the north. Apart from Roger Binny in the second match against Australia, in every successful match the Indian 'Man of the Match' award went to a northern cricketer: Yashpal Sharma, Madan Lal, Kapil himself and, in the semi-final and final, Amarnath. The re-emergence of the north was finally being reflected in the national side.

In the next day's *Sunday Times* my colleague Robin Marlar's piece was headlined, 'Kapil's men turn the world upside down'. Mine was headlined 'Tigers find their claws' and I wrote it is 'the Northern mafia who have made this astounding World Cup series possible'. Kapil, I said, was a 'yaar', a friend, who had a bond with his team more than other Indian captains had ever managed to create:

It is this relationship between a great player and a strongly motivated group of individuals wanting to prove themselves that explains much of the Indian revival... Some credit for this resurgence must also go to the fact that Indians in England no longer feel alien... The Deputy High Commissioner and the Political Officer have travelled with the team, and the players have struck up much the same rapport with the Indian section of the crowd as they do in India.

Before the final, young Indians had gathered outside Lord's holding up the Indian flag and a hand-written placard that read 'Patel bookies, India 11/10, Windies 8/1'. It was meant to mock the real odds, which made the West Indies hot favourites. After the final, they swarmed around Kapil's team as a previous generation had done around Wadekar's but in even larger numbers. So delirious were they that it took three hours for the Indian team to make their way to their hotel, which was just over the road. Back in India millions of Indians watched on television. Among them were four kids who would become the second 'Fab Four': Rahul Dravid, Sachin Tendulkar, Sourav Ganguly and V. V. S. Laxman. For Dravid, then ten, it was the first match he had watched on television and, as he told me, 'Cricketers of my generation, Sourav, Sachin, Laxman, and Anil, we all grew up with that memory.'

Just as the Oval, 1971, had been a new dawn for my generation, so was Lord's, 1983, for these young kids. Winning international competitions was no longer a fantasy.

As Kapil would say years later, 'Once we started winning matches, everyone was more motivated and played like leaders. We had a team.' And for this team, winning matches had started not just in England in June but in the Caribbean in March. On an otherwise difficult tour—beaten in the Test and one-day series—India achieved a remarkable, and significant, one-day victory over the West Indies in Berbice, Guyana, on 29 March 1983.

It was like a home game for them, where the Indo-Guyanese were the dominant population.

The West Indies put India in. West Indies' great pace attack of Holding, Roberts, Davis and Marshall had no reason to suspect Indian batsmen would do much. But Gavaskar was lifted by those thousands of supporters and he played a superb innings, scoring at almost 5 runs an over. Gavaskar made 90 before being run out, while Kapil hit 3 sixes and 7 fours in his whirlwind 38-ball 72. India's score of 282 for 5 in 47 overs was not only their highest in a one-day match, it was the best score by any team against the West Indies in this format. Kapil Dev, Balwinder Sandhu, Madan Lal then all bowled well against a home team whose confidence seemed to wilt. The spinners kept it tight and the majority of the 15,000 crowd celebrated an Indian victory by 27 runs, their first in what is now called white-ball cricket—then the red ball was still used for limited-overs—against the West Indies.

But while India lost the five-Test series 2–0 and the one-day series 2–1, they proved that the victory at Berbice was no fluke when on 9–10 June 1983 they played the West Indies in their opening World Cup game at Old Trafford. The West Indies had never been beaten in a World Cup match; India's solitary win had been against East Africa in 1975. But as at Berbice, the West Indies were surprised. India made 262 for 8 in sixty overs—more than they had ever made in a World Cup match. They then bowled the West Indies out for 228.

In their next game against Zimbabwe at Leicester on 11 June they struggled, despite registering a five-wicket win. The match was notable for the large number of Indians in the crowd, and for the first time on an English ground, announcements were made in Hindi and Gujarati. The Indian diaspora in England was emerging. That victory was followed by two heavy defeats within three days, first against Australia, who scored 320, then the return against the West Indies.

After those two defeats India knew only wins would be enough to take them to the semi-finals ahead of Australia. Next was the second encounter with Zimbabwe. Kapil decided India would bat first, thinking this was the best way to have a better run rate than Australia. But on a difficult Tunbridge Wells wicket Gavaskar made a duck and India were reduced to 6 for 3. Kapil, not expecting to bat so soon, was still in the shower after his morning workout and had his towel wrapped around him. He rushed to pad up, and 3 runs later, as the fourth wicket fell, strode out to join Yashpal Sharma, only to see him get out and reduce India to 17 for 5. Kapil made sure no further wicket was lost until lunch and then decided to attack Kevin Curran, Zimbabwe's most potent bowler. Making the most of the small ground, he hit Curran for sixes into the hospitality tent or clean out of the ground. Kirmani and Kapil put on 126, a World Cup record for the ninth wicket. Kapil's unbeaten 175 was also a World Cup record individual score, and the total of 266 was enough to defeat Zimbabwe, who batted well but fell 31 runs short.

If this was the great match of the tournament, then beating Australia to get to the semi-finals and there beating England were also major upsets. The look on the faces of the Australian and English journalists told the story. India beat Australia by 118 runs with Binny taking 4 for 29, and Madan Lal, 4 for 20. England, bowled out for 213, were beaten by six wickets.

Kapil was now a great hero. A popular advertisement for bikes featuring him showed him on his way to the airport in a ramshackle taxi. It breaks down and he seems destined to miss the flight and the Test. Then a pretty woman cycles by. She lends Kapil her bike, he reaches the airport in time and in the Test devastates the opposition. Then, just as he goes on national television to receive his 'Man of the Match' Award, he winks to acknowledge the help of the woman and her trusty bicycle.

Looking back in 2014 to that victory Kapil told me, 'My proudest moment was winning the 1983 World Cup. Because when the country enjoys with you that has to be the most important thing. It was just not me. It was my entire team and every person in India was happy.'

However, the World Cup victory did not go to his head. Karan Thapar, then an associate producer at London Weekend Television, recalls how on the morning after the victory he went to the Indian team hotel to find a pack of journalists following Kapil Dev asking for an interview. To all of them he said yes, including Thapar. But Thapar, not sure he meant it, wanted to make sure and after endless telephone calls finally spoke to Kapil Dev. Although it was well past midnight he very politely said, 'Haan yaar, it's tomorrow morning at 9, but why don't you let me get some sleep before that!' Kapil kept his word and also brought along his vice-captain, Mohinder Amarnath, which emphasized how well his team had bonded together.

But for all the guts they had shown on the field these World Cup winners were also very much part of an Indian cricket world which believed in fairness and decency. So Kirti Azad flew back to India with the team but twenty-four hours later flew back to England to fulfil his commitment to the Lancashire League club he was contracted to play for, scoring a century and helping them win a match. Madan Lal never allowed getting Richards' wicket go to his head. Soon after, playing in a Lancashire League match, he beat Brian Heywood and while he did not appeal the slip and wicketkeeper did and Heywood was given out caught. Heywood told me, 'After the match Madan Lal asked me, "Did you hit the ball?" When I said no he said, "I wanted you to know I didn't appeal." That to me reflects how the Indians played the game.'

To the great credit of the World Cup-winning team, they resisted the lure of white South African gold. Immediately after the win the white South Africans had approached the Indians hoping to entice them into a rebel tour. Gavaskar told me, 'The proposition was put to us after we won the World Cup, but to the great credit of the players they turned it down without another thought. It was just out of the question.'

India did not treat this victory to mean that India had arrived as a nation as the West Indies had in the past treated their cricket victories. India had any number of national symbols. For Indians the triumph meant that a dreadfully underperforming sporting nation, which had not won any world competition since the demise of Indian hockey almost two decades earlier, could still take on the best in the world in a sport and beat them.

THE ONE-DAY WAVE SWAMPS TEST CRICKET

The famous victory of Kapil's team changed Indian and world cricket. Although at this stage there had been three World Cups, they were essentially English World Cups, all held in England and sponsored by an insurance company, Prudential, little known outside Britain. The next one would be held in India and the World Cup would become truly global. And with India not having long summer days like England, the 60-over game was shortened to 50 overs. Since then, all one-day internationals have been 50 overs—and the West Indies have never been in another final.

The impact on Indian cricket was even more dramatic. India had played its first international one-day match at home when England had visited India in 1981 and lost. On the 1982 tour of England, India had again performed badly in the one-day matches, but Raj Singh, the Indian manager, had reassured me that such defeats did not matter, what mattered was Test cricket. Yet by the time England came to India in the winter of 1984 they could not believe that Test cricket was being played in stadiums very far from full, the only exception being Kolkata.

Indians took to one-day cricket at the first opportunity they got following the miracle at Lord's. In the winter of 1983–84, India played two one-day internationals against Pakistan, and a day-night match under floodlights in Delhi (the first time lights were used in a cricket match in India). The matches attracted huge crowds, but in the three Tests the stadiums were far from full, although it was not helped by all three Tests ending in dull draws, the third rubber between these two teams in which every Test was drawn. However, as events were soon to show, the World Cup had begun to fundamentally change Indian cricket. One-day cricket had taken over from Test cricket as the format Indians flocked to watch.

But if this was wholly new and unexpected, the other major development was a familiar Indian story: rivalry between two great stars, in this case Kapil Dev and Sunil Gavaskar. Kapil versus Gavaskar would become an even bigger story than Merchant versus Hazare or Hazare versus Amarnath or Pataudi versus Borde. This personality factor would overshadow Indian cricket, dominating it for the next three years, and almost ruin its international chances.

Chapter 21

GAVASKAR VS KAPIL DEV

GAVASKAR BETTERS BRADMAN, FALLS OUT WITH KAPIL

In the period between India's two great triumphs at Lord's, the World Cup final in June 1983 and their first Test victory there in the same month in 1986, there was more failure than success. Two of their four Test series in that period were lost, the other two drawn. They batted well enough but their bowling was substandard. They fared better in the one-day game, following up their World Cup triumph with other trophies in Sharjah and Australia, but suffered many defeats too. Consistency was not their strong point. There were changes of captain, from Kapil Dev to Gavaskar and back to Kapil Dev. There was an embarrassing episode when Kapil was dropped for playing a reckless shot that contributed to a Test defeat at home to England. All the while in those three years there was an undercurrent of disharmony in the team because of the rift between Kapil and Gavaskar. Newspapers and cricket magazines repeatedly stoked the controversy, and the single biggest feature of Indian cricket in the years after the nation's most glorious victory seemed to be the relationship between its two highest-profile individuals. Kapil vs Gavaskar made more headlines than India vs anybody.

This battle was like a three-act play and, what is more, both prologue and the last act were played in England, while, to add the right spice to the drama, the last act of reconciliation took place in an obscure car park in the middle of England. The prologue came in the middle of the World Cup. Gavaskar had been unfit for the group match against Australia and then been dropped for the second group match against the West Indies, the only time he was dropped. India lost both matches heavily. Kapil spoke to Gavaskar and basically told him to pull himself together. Gavaskar, who had not been spoken to like this since his sensational debut back in 1971, saw it as Kapil questioning his commitment to the team and told the manager that if that was the feeling, the management could drop him. It was Kapil's turn to take umbrage, and his explanation was that as English was not his first language, Gavaskar had misunderstood what was meant to be encouragement as accusing the great man of not being a team player. Gavaskar returned to the team for what turned out to be Kapil's match against Zimbabwe, made a duck, and his contribution to the World Cup victory was minimal. His scores in the competition were 19, 4, 0, 9, 25, 2. The celebration after the victory at Lord's was all about Kapil Dev, and the man who was then India's, and one of the world's, greatest batsman seemed a forgotten figure.

But Gavaskar had not lost his ability to bat, not in Test cricket. He demonstrated this in India's first Test after their World Cup triumph. Against Pakistan in September 1983 in Bengaluru, Gavaskar scored his twenty-eighth Test century albeit in bizarre circumstances. With the match heading for a draw, Pakistan did not want to waste time fielding, but the umpires insisted. Gavaskar's unbeaten 103 put him one short of Bradman's record: it seemed appropriate he should get his twenty-ninth in the next series against the West Indies, given his record against them.

He never came close in the first Test in Kanpur, which the West Indies won by an innings and 83 runs. Gavaskar was out to Marshall in both innings for 0 and 7, and was spooked by his second dismissal, when a throat ball got him: he tried to play it, was never in control, the bat flew from his hand and he gave Winston Davis an easy catch. He would tell Vasu Paranjape, 'I just didn't see that ball.' There had been talk of retirement after his failure in the World Cup; now it resurfaced, and at that moment Gavaskar considered it. Paranjape used the example of Stan McCabe coming to terms with Harold Larwood in the 1932 Bodyline series, not by defending against the demon bowler but attacking him. The fiery Maharashtrian sounded like one of Shivaji's warriors facing the Mughal army. Gavaskar took heed. What followed in Delhi was a Gavaskar innings few had seen, and no one had anticipated. He did not duck to Marshall but hooked him. His 50 came in thirty-seven balls, he took ninety-four balls for his century. It was then one of the fastest in Test history. Given that he knew a century would mean equalling Bradman's record set in 1948 it showed he had lost neither his ability nor his nerve.

Now buoyed up, he went into the third Test in Ahmedabad and batted more like Gordon Greenidge or Virender Sehwag would do later, rather than with the legendary patience he was known for. In the first nine overs of the match India scored 50 and Gavaskar's contribution was 40. He had reached 90 and seemed destined to give Ahmedabad, hosting its first Test, something memorable to mark the occasion. But then Holding bowled a ball that might have defeated even the Don, and Gavaskar was caught by Lloyd. But he had during the innings become the highest run scorer in

174

THE NINE WAVES

Tests, having gone past Boycott's record of 8,114 runs. So, when would he go past Bradman? Mumbai, the venue for the next Test, would have been ideal, but he made 12 and 3.

Kolkata, which then did not have any great cricketers of its own (Sourav Ganguly was an eleven-year-old boy), had always been fond of Gavaskar. What better place than Eden Gardens to score his thirtieth century? I was one of the crowd and was eager to see my school friend make history. But Marshall got him out with the first ball of the match. If this was bad, what followed in the second innings was worse. Gavaskar came out to open the second innings with India 136 runs behind. This was the fifth Test of the six-Test series. India were 2–0 down and needed a win to keep the series alive. Gavaskar batted as if this were a one-day match, making a frenzied 20 before poor shot selection let him down. India collapsed to 90 and were beaten by an innings and 46 runs in four days.

India's performance in the match had done little to humour the crowd. India in the first innings had recovered through Kapil Dev, who made 69, to make 241 and reduced the West Indies to 88 for 5, all the great batsmen including Richards having gone and only Lloyd being left with the tail. But then India allowed Lloyd to stage such a recovery that he and Andy Roberts, batting No. 10, added 161, a record for the eighth wicket, giving the West Indies a decisive advantage. Gavaskar could hardly be blamed for that, but the crowd took it out on him. He was jeered by the crowd and police had to escort him from the ground after close of play. Rumours spread that a disaffected Gavaskar, having lost the captaincy to Kapil, was trying to do down his successor, a familiar story in Indian cricket.

Kapil, meanwhile, gave an interview in which he suggested some players were more interested in money than the game. He had a point, but his timing merely brought the rift with Gavaskar back to the fore. In reality, there was little money. World Cup cricketers got no prize money for winning and only ₹20,000 from the board plus their daily allowance. It required a music concert which featured Lata Mangeshkar, a great friend of Raj Singh and a cricket buff, to enable the cricketers to get ₹1 lakh each. Gavaskar was seen as the only player who knew how to make money and promote himself. For evidence, his critics pointed out that on the rest day of the Kolkata Test he had signed copies of his recently published book.

Gavaskar's response was to ring Narendra Kumar Salve, board president and a fellow Maharashtrian. The question Gavaskar posed was, if Kapil felt he was not a team player, perhaps he should not play in the last Test in Chennai? Salve, Kapil and Gavaskar met in Delhi and there was a classic Indian fudge. Gavaskar would play but not open. Kapil blamed the press for misquoting him, but Gavaskar was now so unhappy that he thought of not playing in Chennai. Madhav Mantri, Gavaskar's uncle, advised him to pretend to be injured, but Gavaskar rejected this advice and eventually decided to play. It turned out to be a momentous decision.

This was the first Test that I covered at Chennai. I had heard that it had the best facilities and most knowledgeable crowd. But on the third day, after Davis was hit by a missile thrown from the crowd, Lloyd led his players off. The West Indians only returned half an hour after receiving reassurances from the state governor, Sundar Lal Khurana. By then Gavaskar had laid the foundations for what was to prove a history-making innings. After the West Indies made 313, he had returned to the pavilion and for the first time in his cricket career when India began their innings he did not have to pad up but could put his feet up. But in the third over, Marshall got two legs of a hat-trick and Gavaskar walked out with India yet to make a run. He denied Marshall his hat-trick, but it only prompted Richards to have some fun. Richards, between overs, said, 'Sunny, man, wherever you bat the score is always 0.' Richards was laughing then, but not at the end of the innings. By the end of the day India's position was still precarious, 69 for 5. But Gavaskar was 36 not out and, having nearly not played in Chennai, he had got his old, very typical, Gavaskar sunshine back.

I got a glimpse of how his mindset had changed when that evening I attended a felicitation party hosted by the Tamil Nadu Sports Journalists' Association for the Indian team. Gavaskar made a speech which pressed all the right diplomatic buttons and had a touch of humour. So, there was a joke at Kapil's expense, saying that Kapil had asked him to reply on behalf of the team, 'Kapil always gets me to do the dirty work.' There was extravagant praise for his teammates and, as Kirmani looked on sardonically, Gavaskar said that his twenty-seventh Test century in Guyana in March 1983 was only possible because of the midwicket tutorial on patience that Yashpal Sharma had given him. That Sharma could give the master of patience any lesson showed that, even after a season of turmoil, Gavaskar still retained his legendary sense of humour. Then, towards the end of the speech he whispered that, while the series had been a debacle for India, perhaps the next day the journalists would have something happier to report. With that he smiled as if to say, 'Well, boys, I know we have had a rotten series, but tomorrow I shall do something to remove the wretched taste.'

He proceeded to do just that on the fourth day. Nothing disturbed him. The West Indies went into a sulk when he was given not out to a catch they claimed off Marshall. Wickets fell at the other end, and it was 92 for 5 before he found a reliable partner in Shastri. The two put on a then sixth-wicket record against the West Indies of 170. He passed Bradman's twenty-nine centuries with a single. The West Indies did not applaud, but 40,000 spectators gave their hero the cheers he deserved. Gavaskar did not rate this century as highly as he did the Delhi one. Chennai was more of a bread-and-butter innings, full of nudges backward of square on the on-side and just past point on the off, profitable, but hardly any of his great driving through the covers or straight past the bowler. There was a streaky patch in the 90s, but then Gavaskar, talking to himself incessantly, got back on course. At the end of the fourth day he was still there, 149 not out. And despite the fact that the West Indians had not cheered, he, as promised, gave his bat to Jeff Dujon, the West Indian wicketkeeper.

There was nothing left in the match on day five. The West Indies, still unhappy about the Gavaskar not out decision, showed little interest; they had, after all, won the series, and Roberts looked as if he found even hobbling difficult, while Holding did not seem to be in the best of humour. The way Gavaskar was batting this would have been an ideal occasion to fill in an amazing blank in Indian cricket, namely, for an Indian batsman to score 300 in a Test innings. At that point eleven batsmen had achieved this feat, including Hanif Mohammad of Pakistan. He had done it only six years after Pakistan made their Test debut, but no Indian had managed it even after half a century. And this from a country that had produced Merchant, Hazare, Mankad and Viswanath was staggering. Gavaskar had a splendid chance to set it right on that fifth afternoon in Chennai.

But here Gavaskar vs Kapil became an issue again. At tea Kapil told Gavaskar that once he went past Mankad's 231, then the highest score by an Indian in a Test innings, he would declare. This made no sense to Gavaskar, for with less than two hours to play there was nothing in the match. However, Kapil was keen to win his own battle with Marshall for best bowler of the series. They were level on points and if Marshall took another wicket he would win the prize. Gavaskar had noticed Marshall was wearing sneakers and was sure he would not bowl. But Kapil was captain, so, after Gavaskar passed Mankad's record, he declared and beat Marshall to the bowling prize. It would be another three decades before Sehwag, finally, became the first Indian to score 300 in an innings.

Kapil Dev may have taken Indian cricket to heights it had never reached, but winning the World Cup did not give him the captaincy for life. This wave of Indian cricket was like the others. One triumph, however great, did not excuse subsequent failures. That would change dramatically in the eighth wave when Dhoni emulated Kapil Dev and won the World Cup. In 1984, the embarrassment of losing that series 3–0, and all six one-day games, was too much to bear. Kapil was sacked as captain for the three-Test series in Pakistan in October 1984, and for the home'series against England that followed, Gavaskar was back in charge.

It was no surprise, for it was noticeable in Chennai how, even on the field, Gavaskar, far from being an aloof non-team player, had gone up to Maninder Singh, the left-arm spinner, encouraging him to keep a good line and length almost as if he were captain. And when he was batting he protested to Umpire Swaroop Kishen about Marshall's little rests in the pavilion every time he had finished a spell, presumably to change his shirt. All this suggested Gavaskar was preparing to come back.

SUNNY'S MISERABLE RETURN

The series with Pakistan, however, gave little joy to Gavaskar or, for that matter, the cricket world. Gavaskar was angered by biased umpiring, and the series was brought to a sudden end when halfway through it Indira Gandhi was assassinated.

The big question was, would England's tour of India go ahead? The England team had flown into Delhi just hours before the assassination. Within weeks the British diplomat Percy Norris was murdered just hours after he had hosted a party for the England team. The players were encouraged by the press to go home, but the Foreign Office did not share that view. Margaret Thatcher had rushed to India on hearing of Mrs Gandhi's death saying she had come to honour 'Indira'. The two women, despite their very different political philosophies, had struck up a friendship and for cricketers to go home would send the wrong signal. What the Foreign Office, or nobody else, could have anticipated was that the stage was being set for another act in the Gavaskar vs Kapil Dev cricketing drama.

It began with one shot played by Kapil Dev on the final afternoon of the second Test in Delhi. India had come to Delhi having won the first Test in Mumbai by eight wickets with Laxman Sivaramakrishnan showing signs that he could inherit the mantle of Gupte and Chandrasekhar by taking 12 for 181. In Delhi, India, with a small lead and wickets in hand, were heading for a draw. As Kapil Dev went out to bat, Gavaskar said, 'The match is not safe.' But Kapil clearly thought otherwise. He hit a six off Pat Pocock, England's off-spinner, tried to repeat the shot and was caught. India collapsed to 235, leaving England 127 runs to win, and, presented with such a gift, England did not fail.

The Indian reaction was inevitable. Kapil was dropped for the third Test in Kolkata. What followed was an action replay of the drama of the previous winter against the West Indies except that Gavaskar and Kapil had switched positions. Once again Salve, now a minister, summoned both men, this time to his Nagpur home. Gavaskar now appeared to favour reinstating a repentant Kapil, but the selectors decided unanimously against recalling him. Kolkata was a boring draw. Kapil returned for the fourth Test at Chennai, where England won by nine wickets, and with the fifth at Kanpur a draw, England became the first touring side in India to come from behind to win a series.

INDIA DISCOVER A BATTING JEWEL

There was only one thing Indians took from the series, and this was a batting jewel that would adorn their cricket for many a decade. Kolkata saw the debut of twenty-one-year-old Mohammad Azharuddin. He scored a 110 and followed it up with a 105 in Chennai and 122 in Kanpur. He still remains the only batsman to score a century in each of his first three Tests. At the end of the series, he headed the batting averages at an astonishing 109.75 with a total of 439 runs in five Test innings.

His rise was a very unusual Indian story. He was only forty days old when his maternal grandfather, Vajehuddin, requested his son-in-law to allow Azharuddin to come and live with them. Normally in India parents of daughters do not have as much privilege as do parents of the son, but Azharuddin's father agreed. Azharuddin was thus much influenced by a man who was seen by fellow Muslims in the lower middle-class area of Hyderabad's Musheerabad as something like a Sufi saint. It is from him Azharuddin acquired his devotion to Islam. And while Vajehuddin had no interest in cricket—he wanted his grandson to concentrate on mathematics— his son, Abid Zainulabidin, played cricket on Hyderabad's maidans and, encouraged by him, Azharuddin took to the game. In the cosmopolitan world that is India this devout Muslim went to a Jesuit school, and there Brother Joseph became his cricket coach and, something rare for Indian cricketers of that era, gave him lots of catching practice. He had to take a hundred catches every day, which made him one of the most natural fielders India has ever produced. My abiding memory is of India's 1992–93 tour of South Africa where I saw Azharuddin in the Indian team hotel catching the balls with such natural grace that it seemed he was tied to them. The Azharuddin story would take many turns and twists, but India had discovered a batsman who could fill the hole left by the departure of Viswanath, although their batting styles could not have been more different.

Gavaskar, in contrast, averaged 17.5—his worst in a Test series. He knew what the problems were, feet and arms in the wrong position and a poor grip, but was unable to correct them. He had had enough of the captaincy and, although he agreed to lead the side to the one-day Benson & Hedges World Championship in Australia, he announced that the tournament would be the last time he would skipper India. The media predicted there would be an Australia–England final. Instead, as if determined to make his farewell memorable, Gavaskar's team won the trophy and that in a manner so resounding that nobody could question their right to be champions. They started with an emphatic six-wicket win against Pakistan, then saw off England by 86 runs and Australia by eight wickets to reach the semi-finals, where they easily beat New Zealand. The one-sided final against Pakistan ended in another resounding Indian victory, by eight wickets. His players were in awe of Gavaskar as they gathered around him, showering him with champagne as he lifted the trophy.

Gavaskar did not use the victory to try and stay on as captain, but he willingly agreed to be a player again under Kapil Dev.

KAPIL'S SEARCH FOR THE KILLER INSTINCT

Kapil's second coming lasted from 1985 to 1987, longer than the second comings of most Indian captains, including Hazare, Gavaskar, Tendulkar and Azharuddin, and had a certain symmetry. If his first stint was marked by the great World Cup win, then his second was marked by a World Cup defeat. In that period Kapil's win in one-day matches, in particular his first tournament back, where he beat Pakistan and Australia in a one-day tournament in Sharjah, made him claim India had acquired a 'killer instinct'. That proved a false dawn, and in this period Kapil, still to win a Test, struggled to become a winning captain. He lost a three-Test series in Sri Lanka in August 1985, 1–0 and then drew all the three Tests in Australia in the winter of 1985. This against a weak Allan Border team, which in the summer of 1985 had lost the Ashes in England 3–1, two of the Tests by an innings. The series gave no indication that Indians could kill off their opponents.

This was made worse in the five-nation Austral–Asia Cup between Pakistan, Australia, New Zealand, Sri Lanka and India held in Sharjah in April 1986. It was decided by a shot from Javed Miandad that Oborne describes as 'the most famous shot in cricket history'. It came in the final. India had made 246 and with the last over to be bowled, Pakistan needed 11 to win. Chetan Sharma bowled this final over. The over saw more runs and a run-out, and with the last ball about to be bowled, Miandad, who had scored a hundred, faced Sharma and needed to hit a four to win. Sharma decided he would bowl yorker, but Miandad, clearly anticipating this, had walked out as Sharma ran in and hit it for six. It was Pakistan's first major one-day trophy and to get it at the expense of India, the world champions, was particularly special. A billion people were estimated to have watched the match, many billions more have since seen the replay on YouTube.

The match generated all sorts of stories, one being that the shot may have saved Dawood Ibrahim, an underworld don, a great deal of money. In October 2013, the Press Trust of India would quote Dilip Vengsarkar saying that a day before the match Dawood walked into the Indian dressing room and promised each player a Toyota car, should India beat Pakistan and win the trophy. Dawood at that time was a frequent visitor to Sharjah and had a special enclosure in the VIP lounge, from where he would wave the Indian flag. After the Mumbai bombings in 1993 he became a fugitive and is now wanted by the Indian government and believed to be living in Pakistan. Miandad's son married Dawood's daughter. Indian cricket would be haunted by memories of Miandad's six for decades.

PEACE DECLARED IN THE NORTHAMPTON CAR PARK
It was with Miandad's six echoing in their ears that Kapil brought his team for India's eleventh tour of England. Few would have predicted the success India enjoyed in that memorable series, or that the captain paying the price for failure would be David Gower, not Kapil Dev.

The turning point, and what proved the final act in the Kapil vs Gavaskar drama took place on a dreary, wet Saturday afternoon in the car park of the Northampton county ground. The Indian press was full of the rift between Kapil and Gavaskar having reopened. On Saturday, 31 May, with heavy rain falling, journalists in the Northampton press box were called out to the team coach for an impromptu conference. I was covering the match for the *Sunday Times* and was surprised when I received the invitation from Raj Singh, the manager. Kapil Dev and Gavaskar both joined us on the coach. They declared an end to the so-called feud that had made so many headlines in the Indian newspapers, publicly putting an end to their differences.

This had a galvanizing effect on the Indian team. While they did not beat Northants when play finally got going on the Sunday, Kapil demonstrated that India's opening bowlers were no longer there to take the shine off the ball. Northants, one of county cricket's strongest batting sides, were bowled out for 118 and Kapil did not call on his spinners. So, while the tour was in the early part of the summer when, in the past, Indian spinners could do little, India now had swing and seam bowlers who could test England.

They put that knowledge to good use at Lord's, where Kapil put England in and watched Chetan Sharma, putting his Miandad nightmare behind him, taking 5 for 64 as England were all out for 294, nine wickets falling to pacemen. There was more good news to follow, when Vengsarkar's superb century made him the first overseas batsman to score 3 hundreds in Tests at Lord's, a remarkable feat given this was only his third Test at the home of cricket. A draw looked the likely result as the fourth day began, but Kapil turned the game around with a devastating nineteen-ball spell in which he dismissed Graham Gooch, Tim Robinson and David Gower for 1 run. England could not recover, and when they were all out for 180, India had all the time they needed to score 134 for victory. Kapil hit Phil Edmonds for 18 off the last over, pulling a six into the Grandstand to confirm India's first win at Lord's, and his own first Test victory as captain at the twenty-first attempt. With bat and ball, Kapil did it in style.

While India could enjoy the moment, England reacted by sacking Gower as captain—though he was unfit anyway for the second Test at Headingley—and giving the job to Mike Gatting. Botham was also absent, suspended for the whole series for smoking cannabis. India, too, lost key men to injury, Amarnath and Chetan Sharma, who had played such an important part in the Lord's win. Kapil made a wise decision when he turned to his old friend, Madan Lal, who was playing Lancashire League cricket for Ashton. Kapil made an even better decision when he won the toss and, surprisingly, opted to bat. India made 272 and then, on a ground where in the past England's pace attack had tormented India, it was Madan Lal and then Roger Binny's turn to give England a taste of the same medicine. Madan Lal took 3 for 18, Binny 5 for 40. Binny numbered Gatting among his four victims in thirty-seven balls for 17 runs. England were all out for 102. That day, talking to people in the hospitality boxes, I was struck by how shocked the English spectators were by this new cricketing face of India.

In India's second innings, Vengsarkar on his own made as many runs as England had made, an imperious 102 not out. Vengsarkar was so far ahead of all other batsmen in this Test that while he had scored 61 in the first innings, the next highest score in the entire match by a batsman from either team was Kiran More's 36. Vengsarkar's match aggregate of 163 was more than the entire England team had made in either the first or the second innings. And this on a wicket that was considered so unsuitable for cricket that immediately after the match it was dug up. England, chasing an impossible 408, were bowled out for 128, India winning by 279 runs. India did have chances of winning the third as well, but rain intervened, making it drawn.

Even today, thirty-three years later, it remains India's most successful tour of England, two Test victories and no defeat in any first-class match. Looking back in 2014, Kapil highlighted a main reason, 'The only way you can win is if you can break the opposition captain. They had a change of captaincy every Test match. If you create uncertainty in their team then nobody knows what to do. In 1986 England were totally gone. It had happened to India during a series.' And England, 'gave us the pitches where our bowlers [could] take advantage of seam bowling and we did better than their seam bowlers.' Kapil Dev's captaincy was widely praised. The rift between Kapil and Gavaskar was history. But, as Kapil soon realized, leading India was never easy.

Chapter 22

INDIA PAY THE PRICE FOR COMPLACENCY

That famous victory in England made India, in the view of the outgoing chairman of selectors, Chandu Borde, the second-best team in Test cricket—behind the West Indies—as well as one-day world champions. The next three years showed how complacent he was and that Indian cricket, far from advancing, would go backwards.

NOTHING TO SHOW FOR A GREAT TEST

The 1986–87 season was India's busiest in Test cricket, with Australia, Sri Lanka and Pakistan all touring. India went into the series against Australia in a buoyant mood, and with an historic tie in the first Test there was plenty of early excitement, but it finished all square largely because India were unable to bowl out Australia. The second and third Tests were drawn.

With Australia still at a low ebb in the game, India were clear favourites to win the series. In the first game, though, they were heading for defeat when they avoided the follow-on by a whisker. On the final day they had turned around their fortunes to such an extent they looked likely winners, only to fail at the death and finish with only the second tie in Test history.

India were chasing 348 at the outset and needed 118, with twenty overs to play and seven wickets in hand, thanks largely to a superb innings by Gavaskar. India wobbled when Gavaskar was out, but Shastri stood firm and led India to a very strong position: 18 needed off five overs with four wickets left. More wickets fell, and both sides sensed victory when it came to the final over. Australia needed one wicket, India needed 4 runs, with Shastri still there. When Shastri scored 3 off two balls it fell to Maninder Singh to complete the victory—but he was lbw to the penultimate delivery and for the second time in 1,052 Test matches, there was a tie.

The subsequent two draws meant that for the second straight series India were held when they had been expected to beat Australia. At least they saw off Sri Lanka, winning two of their three Tests by an innings and drawing the other. This series was very significant for Kapil, who took his 300th Test wicket to join Botham on the Test 'double' of 300 wickets and

3,000 runs. The third and final task would prove to be the toughest: five Tests against Imran Khan's Pakistan.

IMRAN GETS HIS REVENGE

The first four Tests were all drawn. There were rows off the field, the cricket was boring, and despite their competent batting India never once looked like getting twenty Pakistani wickets to win a Test.

It all changed in the fifth and final Test in Bengaluru, on a wicket that took spin from day one. Maninder, with 7 for 27, led the way as Pakistan were bowled out for their lowest score against India, 116. Things could not have looked better for India when they passed the 100 mark for the loss of only three wickets, but they collapsed to 145 all out, a score that looked even worse when Pakistan made 249 in their second innings to set India 221.

Step forward Gavaskar, whose innings of 66 in the fourth Test had made him the first batsman to score 10,000 runs in Tests. This would be his last Test innings and it was a masterpiece. He batted for almost five and a half hours, keeping the strike cleverly and often as wickets fell. But the behaviour of the Pakistani players and the Bengaluru crowd's reaction broke his hitherto rock-solid concentration. When Pakistan had an appeal turned down, the team complained so vehemently they were showered with missiles by spectators. Play was held up for ten minutes and soon after it resumed Gavaskar was caught in the slips, 4 runs short of his century. Javed Miandad, who always called Gavaskar, 'Sunny bhai', in his autobiography *Cutting Edge* called it 'one of the finest Test batting performances I've seen from anyone. He was using his feet beautifully and negotiating turn in both directions with equal command.' He describes how against Iqbal Qasim, 'despite the fact that he was moving the ball at sharp angles, Gavaskar played the on-drive. For any other batsman playing an on-drive on that wicket to a ball spinning away from the outside edge would have been suicide; for Gavaskar, it meant getting boundaries. It showed the great depth and range of his skill.'

India were 16 runs short when their last wicket fell: Imran celebrated Pakistan's first series victory in India. Pakistan had also won the one-day internationals 5–1, and since Miandad hit that famous six in Sharjah in 1986 they clearly had the upper hand against India, who would not beat them in a Test series until the twenty-first century.

INDIA CHANGE THE WORLD CUP BUT STILL LOSE

For all the problems between the two countries, India and Pakistan successfully co-hosted the 1987 World Cup. There were group games and semi-finals in both countries, and the co-hosts were expected to meet in the final at Eden Gardens. But they both lost 'home' semi-finals, India against England and Pakistan against the eventual champions, Australia.

The choice of venues for the tournament was unpopular in England, not least because of the travelling distances from city to city. The tabloid press complained and the BBC ignored the matches, televising only the final. The hosts proved their detractors wrong, however, by hosting the most successful and colourful World Cup to date.

India began with a thriller, which they lost by 1 run to Australia. It did not knock their confidence, and they won all their remaining group games to finish top and earn a 'home' semi-final against England in Mumbai. Indians were buoyant for had they finished second in the group, they would have had to play Pakistan in Lahore.

In 1983, India had never lost when batting first, but Kapil preferred to chase and, after winning the toss, he put England in. It did not work. Kapil's guess that the ball would swing was wrong, and England performed well against the spinners to total 254. When India batted they soon lost Gavaskar, and news of Pakistan's struggles in Lahore seemed to spook rather than inspire them. Kapil and others batted recklessly, perhaps responding too readily to the crowd's urging for big hitting, and India fell 19 runs short of England's total.

It was a highly successful tournament in terms of viewing numbers and global appeal, regardless of the BBC's indifference. India had helped to change the World Cup, and the 1987 tournament would be a harbinger for even more dramatic changes to world cricket initiated by India. But at the time that was not obvious: and being a trailblazer in cricket compared to losing the Cup was, for Indians, scant consolation. For Kapil Dev, it was even worse.

THE COLONEL WHO FAILED TO LEAD HIS MEN

Kapil, like many revolutionaries, paid the price of being devoured by his own revolution and was removed as captain. He was now India's Botham; an all-rounder who was an integral part of the team. But he was not an Imran, who was both an all-rounder and a leader.

Shastri, who frequently appeared in gossip columns and had the same popular appeal as Imran, was favourite to succeed Kapil and had the backing of both the deposed captain and Gavaskar. But for the next series, at home to West Indies starting in December 1987, the new man in charge was Vengsarkar.

It was a curious choice by the selectors. Vengsarkar was an outstanding batsman, called 'colonel' because he was seen to have some of the traits of Nayudu as a batsman. But in terms of character, leadership material and popularity with the public, he was no match for Kapil. He did not last long. Having started with a defeat in the first Test against the West Indies he could claim a respectable 1–1 draw by the end of the four-match series, but India's victory in the final Test came when he was injured and the side was led by Shastri.

Vengsarkar was banned for six months for breach of contract with the board—he continued to write a newspaper column against the rules. His persistent arguing with the umpires in a minor match led to his team being disqualified. But he retained the captaincy in 1988–89 and led India to a 2–1 home series win against New Zealand. The series against England was cancelled because several England players had played on a rebel tour in South Africa and were not granted visas. So, with no international cricket for almost four months, India set off in March 1989 to face the West Indies, then the greatest team in the world. That India lost was not surprising; what was dispiriting was the spineless display, miserably losing all five one-day internationals and three of the four Tests, the one draw coming in the first in Guyana because of a washout after the first two days.

The tour management was sloppy; the manager was also part-time coach, but as Sanjay Manjrekar, the one batting success, found, he was often asleep when the Indians were batting. Manjrekar learnt he was playing in the Guyana Test just before the toss and through Desmond Haynes, the West Indian opener. Vengsarkar, the best batsman in the world when the tour began, according to the new Deloitte rankings, averaged only 18.33. The bowling was an even bigger problem. Much had been expected from the leg-spinner Narendra Hirwani in the Caribbean. I met my hero, Subhash Gupte, on this tour, and he was very critical of Hirwani: of the way he bowled; how he set his field; of his not knowing whether to aim for the off side or the leg side, all so different from how Gupte had performed. Thousands of East Indians in Trinidad felt the same way about the team and many of them asked me why the country which had the second largest population in the world had such a poor team.

The dreadful West Indies defeat led Pataudi to claim that Vengsarkar had put Indian cricket back ten years. Another captain was sacked. But there was an uplift on the way. Waiting in the wings was a sixteen-year old who was very upset that he had not been selected to tour the West Indies. The sixth wave of Indian cricket was about to hit the shores, led by a cricketer the like of whom Indians had never seen before.

The Sixth Wave

TESTS

Wave	Period	Mts	Won	Lost	Drawn	Tied	Win%	W/L
6th	1989–2000	77	19	23	35	0	24.68	0.83

TOP BATSMEN IN SIXTH WAVE

	Mts	Runs	Hs	Avg	100	50
S. R. Tendulkar	77	6054	217	55.03	22	24
M. Azharuddin	69	4303	192	44.36	16	14
R. Dravid	38	2890	190	47.37	6	16
N. S. Sidhu	42	2786	201	44.22	7	15
S. C. Ganguly	36	2589	173	46.23	7	13
S. V. Manjrekar	32	1828	218	38.08	3	9
M. Prabhakar	37	1514	120	32.91	1	9
N. R. Mongia	42	1382	152	24.24	1	6
A. Kumble	61	1192	88	18.06	0	3
Kapil Dev	32	1161	129	30.55	2	6

TOP BOWLERS IN SIXTH WAVE

	Mts	Wkts	Best	Avg	5WI	10WM
A. Kumble	61	276	10/74	28.00	16	3
J. Srinath	47	171	8/86	30.33	6	1
M. Prabhakar	37	95	6/132	36.62	3	0
S. L. V. Raju	27	92	6/12	29.79	5	1
Kapil Dev	32	87	5/97	32.13	2	0
B. K. V. Prasad	29	85	6/33	34.70	6	1
R. K. Chauhan	21	47	4/48	39.51	0	0
S. B. Joshi	13	35	5/142	30.40	1	0
A. Kuruvilla	10	25	5/68	35.68	1	0
N. D. Hirwani	10	24	6/59	46.54	1	0

TOP WICKETKEEPERS IN SIXTH WAVE

	Mts	Dismissals	Ct	St
N. R. Mongia	42	101	94	7
K. S. More	25	71	66	5
M. S. K. Prasad	6	15	15	0
C. S. Pandit	2	11	10	1

ONE-DAY INTERNATIONALS

Wave	Period	Mts	Won	Lost	NR	Tied	Win%	W/L
6th	1989–2000	299	137	146	13	3	45.82	0.94

TOP BATSMEN IN SIXTH WAVE

	Mts	Runs	Hs	Avg	SR	100	50
S. R. Tendulkar	258	9612	186★	41.97	86.18	26	49
M. Azharuddin	248	7297	153★	38.20	75.78	5	51
S. C. Ganguly	154	6020	183	44.26	73.50	15	34
A. Jadeja	196	5359	119	37.47	69.80	6	30
R. Dravid	134	4343	153	37.43	67.88	7	28
N. S. Sidhu	113	3587	134★	36.23	69.66	6	23
V. G. Kambli	104	2477	106	32.59	71.94	2	14
R. R. Singh	133	2307	100	26.21	74.58	1	9
S. V. Manjrekar	70	1909	105	32.91	63.73	1	14
M. Prabhakar	108	1661	102★	24.07	60.59	1	11

TOP BOWLERS IN SIXTH WAVE

	Mts	Wkts	Best	Avg	RPO	4W
A. Kumble	208	274	6/12	28.56	4.20	9
J. Srinath	187	252	5/23	28.66	4.43	7
B. K. V. Prasad	154	186	5/27	32.46	4.65	4
M. Prabhakar	108	143	5/33	27.61	4.36	5
A. B. Agarkar	65	97	4/35	30.82	5.18	3
S. R. Tendulkar	258	95	5/32	46.86	4.91	4
Kapil Dev	86	92	4/31	28.60	3.74	2
R. R. Singh	133	69	5/22	42.62	4.78	2
S. B. Joshi	65	66	5/6	35.21	4.39	2
S. L. V. Raju	53	63	4/46	31.96	4.36	2

TOP WICKETKEEPERS IN SIXTH WAVE

	Mts	Dismissals	Ct	St
N. R. Mongia	140	154	110	44
K. S. More	57	55	43	12
S. S. Karim	34	30	27	3
M. S. K. Prasad	17	21	14	7
V. Yadav	19	19	12	7

Chapter 23

GOD IS REBORN AS A CRICKETER

ONE VERY SPECIAL SCHOOL MATCH

The sixteen-year-old was Sachin Ramesh Tendulkar. Just over a year earlier, failure in the 1997 on the afternoon of 23 February 1988, he had walked out to bat at the Sassanian Sports Club ground in Azad Maidan in the semi-final of the Harris Shield, playing for Shardashram Vidyamandir (English) against St. Xavier's, Gavaskar's and my old school. The score was 84 for 2. He joined his best friend, Vinod Kambli.

By lunch the following day the two were still batting and the score was 748 for 2—Kambli was 349, Tendulkar 326. As they hit the ball high and wide and the Xavier's fielders ran to the far ends of the Azad Maidan, the two boys sang. The Xavier's boys were in tears, saying they did not want to bowl any more. They could have got more, except at lunchtime Tendulkar was ordered by his school coach, Ramakant Achrekar, a disciplinarian, to declare. Had he not, Kambli was convinced they would each have made 500 and put on 1,000 runs. Even then their partnership of 664 runs for the third wicket was a world record broken only in 2006–07, also by two Indian schoolboys from Hyderabad's St. Peter's High School who put on 721 runs. This was also for the third wicket. And not having had enough, Tendulkar went from the Harris Shield match to the other end of the maidan, and, in the Giles Shield, scored 178 not out.

Soon everyone who mattered in Mumbai cricket was convinced that Tendulkar was a very special talent and they displayed a tenderness for him that showed what an amazing and close-knit cricket community this capital of Indian cricket was. Back in 1980, Gavaskar then at the height of his fame, had waited outside a tent pitched at Mumbai's Cross Maidan to present a bat to Sanjay Manjrekar, because his father, Vijay, had asked him to, and he had brought it back from England after a season with Somerset. Now, when young Tendulkar had a rare failure in not winning the best junior cricketer award, Gavaskar wrote him a letter consoling him. And when India played an ODI, Vengsarkar teased Kapil that 'there's another ghoda [horse] coming from Mumbai, Sachin Tendulkar. You know, he's just 13 or

14, but what a superb player he is. So, watch out.' Soon after, Vengsarkar arranged a net for Tendulkar at the CCI, where Kapil bowled to him. He made his debut for Mumbai at the age of fifteen years, seven months and sixteen days on 10 December 1988, going on to score a hundred in the match, what Maharashtrians called 'Shambhar'. Tendulkar is still the youngest debutant centurion in the Indian first-class game although Dhruva Pandove is the youngest Indian to score a hundred, but that was not on debut.

Tendulkar might have been out lbw in the first over but after that gave every indication he would score a hundred. It was his confidence that amazed everyone. When his partner Alan Sippy, thinking the fifteen-year-old might be nervous, suggested he relax, Tendulkar's response was to use the Marathi word bindaas which means fearless, to indicate he had no worries. There were not many people who witnessed the innings, but the greats of Mumbai were there, led by Gavaskar, who instantly realized that now that he had retired India had found a successor. Rajdeep Sardesai covered the match for the *Times of India* and it made the front page under the headline, 'A New Dawn in Indian Cricket'. This proved to be no newspaper hype.

By March 1989, as Vengsarkar led the Indians to the West Indies, Tendulkar, in his own mind, was ready to face the best team in the world. As he told me later, he had no fears about facing what is widely considered one of the greatest pace attacks in the world: he was in this Tendulkar cocoon, just thinking of making runs. The Indian selectors did consider selecting him but then decided it was too much of a gamble. Even in the winter of 1989 they were not sure.

In October 1989, the Nehru Cup was held to celebrate the centenary of Nehru's birth. England, led by Graham Gooch, played a warm-up match in Delhi against an Air India XI. Both Tendulkar and Kambli played, making 50. Afterwards one of the Indian selectors asked Gooch whether Tendulkar was ready to face a Pakistan attack of Imran Khan, Wasim Akram and Waqar Younis. Gooch responded, 'I wouldn't if I was you.' Derek Pringle, who was in the England team, narrating the story in his 2018 book, *Pushing the Boundaries,* says, Gooch felt 'young talent like that could be set back if traumatised by fast bowlers'. But the Indian selectors, and in particular the chairman of selectors at that time, Raj Singh, had an assurance from the Mumbai man, Naren Tamhane, that Tendulkar never failed. Raj Singh, an Anglophile, valued English opinion but on this occasion decided they should not listen to English caution. So, on 15 November 1989, in the National Stadium in Karachi, Tendulkar took the first step to what would be a glorious road to making cricket history.

THE CONTRAST WITH KAMBLI

But before we go ahead with the Tendulkar story, consider the contrast with Kambli, his partner in that record-breaking innings, a dispiriting story both of Indian cricket and society. He did play Test and one-day cricket but does not make the top Test batsmen list of the sixth wave, and while he does make the top one-day international cricketers list, he is way down in the table, both of which are headed by his old teammate (see figures at the beginning of this chapter). Several factors played a part. There was caste. Unlike the Brahmin Tendulkar, he was the outsider by caste, being a Dalit. He is well aware that being dark is a liability in India and greets visitors singing, 'Hum kaale hain to kya hua dilwale hain!' [We may be dark-skinned, but we are large-hearted!] Unlike Tendulkar, who has had a famously successful marriage, Kambli's first marriage ended in divorce. He also had health problems, a heart condition that required hospital treatment. Long after retirement he rejected Hinduism, the religion that had made his community pariah, but while the great leader of the Dalits Ambedkar converted to Buddhism, Kambli became a Christian. Tendulkar, in contrast, is a devout Hindu. Just before he scored his first century, aged thirteen, against Don Bosco, another well-known Mumbai Catholic school, he went and prayed to Ganesha at a temple and after that would do so before every series. And while they both shared the same coach, Achrekar, Kambli did not have the extraordinary family support system.

Tendulkar had a devoted brother, Ajit, educated parents, and his father was a professor, ready to allow him to live with his uncle several miles from home during the week to further his career. Kambli also left home as a teenager to play cricket, but in his case he fought his father and lived with a friend in a chawl, in Mumbai. He would later tell Sardesai, 'I have taken the stairs to success while Sachin took the elevator.' However, Kambli fell off the stairs. Although nicknamed 'Dessee' by his colleagues in the Indian team, a reference to Desmond Haynes, he had nowhere near the consistency of the West Indian and was always making comebacks. Then, when he seemed to have cemented his place in the side after some wonderful innings against England and Sri Lanka in 1993–94, failure in the 1996 World Cup banished him from cricket with charges of partying and drinking. He would become something of a jester, a role perfectly illustrated when, in 1992, Tendulkar came to play for Yorkshire. When Tendulkar took the field for Yorkshire, Kambli, standing at the boundary edge, made a motion as if he was holding a Kalashnikov ready to mow down everybody in sight. Then, when I was interviewing Tendulkar, he poked his head around the corner and made a face which made Tendulkar smile. Over the years the two drifted apart, and in the speech he made when he took leave of cricket in 2013, Tendulkar, very significantly, did not mention Kambli. Nor was he invited to the gala party Tendulkar had after retirement where everybody who mattered, both in cricket and public life in Mumbai, was there. But since then the two have been reconciled. Kambli has declared his love for Tendulkar. And on Kambli's birthday, on 18 January 2019, Tendulkar tweeted a photo showing him with his arm around his shoulder with the tweet saying 'May you always be in the "Pink" of health my friend.'

TENDULKAR, THE HISTORY MAN

In the three decades that followed, Tendulkar made history in such a remarkable way that almost everything in Indian cricket appeared to reflect what he had done. If Tendulkar was at the crease India were capable of doing something. And as the 1990s turned into the new millennium, it was not merely Tendulkar with the bat who could swing a match India's way but also Tendulkar with the ball, particularly in one-day matches.

What has made Tendulkar exceptional was having no peer with whom he could be compared. Merchant had Hazare, Gavaskar had Viswanath, but Tendulkar was on his own. There would be many Tendulkar clones, but no one came close to matching his mastery of the art of batsmanship. In that sense he was like Bradman. But while Bradman did not leave a successor, and Australian cricket for years agonized over who might take over and never found one, in Virat Kohli Tendulkar appears to have done just this. Tendulkar is like the head of an old-fashioned Indian joint family. He occupies the top floor of the Indian cricket mansion, there are siblings like Ganguly, Dravid, and Laxman, and then children like Dhoni and Kohli. And in Prithvi Shaw he has a grandchild. He spotted him at the age of eight and advised him not to change his grip or stance: 'If anyone asks you to do so, tell them to come and talk to me.' In October 2018, Shaw aged eighteen, made a century playing his first Test. We'll come back to Shaw later, but he illustrates the Tendulkar joint family of cricket.

What sets Tendulkar apart is that his arrival coincided with India rejecting the socialism that had marked the first forty years of independence in favour of a less state-controlled society. That change came two years after Tendulkar had made his Test debut and it is interesting to look at figures for economic growth just before and just after he emerged. The socialist era saw the so-called Hindu rate of growth of only 1.5 per cent. Between 1985, three years before that Harris Shield innings by Tendulkar and 2010, per capita income quadrupled. Having been well down the list in the GDP rankings of countries based on purchasing power parity, by 2014, a year after Tendulkar retired, India was third. Economists have estimated that by 2022 India will have a middle class of around 650 million. When Gavaskar and I were growing up, the two rich Indians were the Tatas and the Birlas and we used to mock those who displayed their wealth by saying, 'Who do you think you are? A Tata or a Birla?' But they had no world ranking. By 2010, Forbes ranked Mukesh Ambani and Lakshmi Mittal among the five richest men in the world. And Tendulkar, of course, played for Mumbai Indians, owned by Mukesh Ambani, who in 2019 was ranked the world's richest sports team owner, displacing Microsoft CEO Steve Ballmer, who owns the Los Angeles Clippers. It is against the backdrop of this new India that Tendulkar played his cricket, and it is no surprise that compared to what cricketers in the first four waves earned those in the sixth wave did much better.

At the beginning of the 1990s, a Test cricketer could earn ₹10,000 a day, a one-day cricketer ₹6,500. By the time Tendulkar retired in 2013 it was the eighth wave and Test cricketers then earned ₹7 lakh, and one-day cricketers ₹4 lakh. Tendulkar earned a lot more because the Indian board, just two years after Tendulkar's international debut, discovered that it could sell television rights for a profit. It brought money and helped cricketers become India's rock stars, aided by the fact that the very social fabric of the country had changed.

Tendulkar was also helped by one of the greatest transformations the media world has seen anywhere in the world. When I left India in 1969 to come to England, two years before Gavaskar surprised the world, I had seen two minutes of television on a visit to Delhi, where there was an experimental channel. Television did not really take off in India until just about the time Tendulkar appeared. Now India has nearly 900 TV channels, many of them in regional Indian languages, and while this has dwarfed the print media, that also has grown: my home-town paper, the *Times of India*, is able to claim it is the world's most read English newspaper. In the five cricket waves that preceded Tendulkar, Indians saw very few of their cricketers on television; since Tendulkar, it is difficult to avoid cricket on television. Towards the end of his career Tendulkar also profited from the rise of the internet and social media. Three years before he retired in April 2010 he joined Twitter and now has 27.8 million followers (Narendra Modi the Indian prime minister has 44.9 million). Even Tendulkar's daughter, Sara, has a Twitter account with 5,500 followers. All this has meant Tendulkar has had a presence in Indian homes that no cricketer before him has ever enjoyed. The very opening up of the Indian economy means Tendulkar could aspire to goods and luxuries that no cricketer before him could have dreamt of having. And here again there is a great contrast with Gavaskar. In 1983, when Gavaskar passed Bradman's twenty-nine centuries he got a Maruti and in the middle of his fight with Kapil was often portrayed as money-obsessed. When Tendulkar passed Bradman's figure and Fiat gifted him a Ferrari, nobody suggested he thought only about money. In this case he did get into a bit of bother when he tried to have the import duty waived. But that was a rare blot on his career.

Tendulkar's status has been such that the only figure in India who has matched him has come not from cricket but from Bollywood, Amitabh Bachchan. Shyam Benegal, one of India's great film directors, told me that Bachchan, or 'Big B' as he is called, is a greater figure, but many would argue that Tendulkar ranks higher.

Such has been Tendulkar's impact that his story has encouraged Indian novelists to use cricket to develop their themes as in Aravind Adiga's 2016 novel, *Selection Day*, where a father markets the cricketing ability of his sons to make vast amounts of money. He got the idea for the plotline when he had lunch in Mumbai with a businessman who went to the slums to find young, aspiring cricketers who—he would sponsor so that if their careers took off, he could share in their wealth. Adiga wanted to develop the theme that cricket and Bollywood are the two religions of India and that an English game which was 'an aristocratic backlash against emergent capitalism—that game has become the spearhead of the new Indian capitalism, in the sense cricket is used to sell everything here from mobile phones to consumer products like shampoo and soap.' As we have seen, back in 1981, trying to market butter by using the problems Dilley was having with his boot laces was a novelty. Now, visitors arriving in India are met by billboards with the faces of some of India's greatest cricketers advertising products, and Tendulkar was the pioneer of this marketing drive using cricketers.

TENDULKAR ABROAD

Here, though, attention must be drawn to the fact that while from the beginning Tendulkar was creating waves in India like no Indian cricketer has ever done, that was not the case abroad. The best illustration of this came when in 2000 *Wisden* published its choice of the five cricketers of the twentieth century. An electorate of hundred from around the cricketing world was selected. I was one of the ten from India—there were three other Indian journalists, and six cricketers, led by Gavaskar. Not surprisingly the electorate of twenty-eight from England and Australia's twenty outnumbered the Indians, but there would not have been much dispute that Bradman and Sobers had to be on the list. Bradman got 100 votes, Sobers 90. Jack Hobbs made the list with 30, Vivian Richards with 25, and the real surprise was that Shane Warne was one of the five with 27. Tendulkar got 6 votes and was equal seventeenth with Harold Larwood and Ray Lindwall. He was ahead of Kapil, who got 5 votes and was twentieth. Gavaskar got twice as many as Tendulkar, which made him twelfth. Imran was tenth with 13 votes. In his notes the editor, Matthew Engel, discussed the many who had missed but did not mention Tendulkar, although he thought, 'though one suspects an Asian or three will be up there for the twenty-first century.' Such choices are, of course, highly individual. By the time the voting was done, Tendulkar had had a decade in international cricket, which is essentially the sixth wave of this book. It could be argued his figures were impressive but not exceptional (see the figures for the sixth wave at the beginning of the chapter).

But move forward a few years into the twenty-first century and it is clear that the world at large began to see Tendulkar very differently. I was made acutely aware of Tendulkar's unique status by two incidents in Britain. On 17 October 2008, when playing a Test in Mohali against Australia, he became the first batsman to score 12,000 runs, thereby overtaking Brian Lara's then record. The editor of the BBC's *Ten O'clock News,* Craig Oliver, did not like sports news on his programme, which is the most-watched nightly news bulletin in Britain. Yet, he asked me to do a piece on Tendulkar as I was then the BBC's sports editor. I went to Old Trafford, where, back in 1990, Tendulkar had scored his first hundred and, against the background of the pavilion, I did a piece on Tendulkar's achievement that was seen by millions in Britain.

The second incident occurred in 2014. When Tendulkar came to Britain to publicize his autobiography I was invited to a seminar to discuss the book with him. On the train taking me there I mentioned Tendulkar's name to an Englishwoman. She immediately recognized it although she had no interest in the game. No other Indian, in any field, has ever attained such a status in Britain.

THE TWO LITTLE MASTERS

Tendulkar during his career was often compared with Gavaskar. In batting styles and their approach to the game they could not have been more different. Milind Rege has no doubt that while Tendulkar was a child prodigy, Gavaskar made himself a great player by working at his batting just as Father Fritz had told us he would. In terms of pure talent, Kapil has no doubt that Tendulkar ranks higher, but Gavaskar's sheer determination to succeed meant it was never easy to get him out, while Tendulkar's more attacking style always gave the bowlers a chance. Kapil in his chat with me also made the shrewd point that when Tendulkar emerged, 'There was only one benchmark, Sunil Gavaskar. It was very difficult for Sachin to motivate himself because what target should he set for the rest of the world?' Tendulkar's era has meant, 'Now in one breath they have four, five cricketers who got 6,000, 7,000, 8,000, 13,000, 15,000 runs: Dravid, Ganguly, Laxman and Tendulkar. Your motivation is much better.' Both had to cope with one very important political development in their home city of Mumbai: the rise of the Shiv Sena.

In Gavaskar's and my youth the Shiv Sena started as a movement to get rid of south Indians from the city. By the time Tendulkar emerged, it had become a pro-Hindu, Hindutva party and won political power not only in Mumbai but across the state of Maharashtra. Now such is the influence of the Shiv Sena that the press box at the Wankhede Stadium is even named after their leader, Bal Thackeray. While Thackeray had deep interest in cricket and knew a great many Mumbai cricketers, normally only cricketers with exceptional achievement have stands or boxes named after them. Cricket being so much part of Indian life, particularly urban Indian life, Thackeray never hesitated to express his views on the game, declaring that Muslims could only prove their loyalty by applauding Indian victories over Pakistan. Both Gavaskar and Tendulkar had to tread carefully, which they did. On one occasion Tendulkar did upset Thackeray but came out triumphant. In its issue of 29 March 2010 *India Today* reported:

> Shiv Sena supremo Balasaheb Thackeray is making a last ditch attempt to save the party from total ignominy. Taking on the mantle of responsibility to keep his flailing Sena in public memory, Thackeray is using an old formula to attack anything, or anyone, who he thinks comes in his way. This time though he picked on a national hero whose Maharashtrian origin is as accepted as his batting is celebrated. Lashing out at Sachin Tendulkar's harmless comment about Mumbai belonging to all of India, Thackeray found no one in agreement. Dismissing it as an act bordering on 'desperation' politicians from most parties in and outside Maharashtra were not amused. Nor was the BCCI. Says Madhav Bhandari, Maharashtra spokesperson for BJP, 'We have distanced ourselves from Balasaheb's comments. Sachin is a respected citizen and has every right to convey his sentiments.' Even Thackeray's beloved nephew Raj, the erstwhile torchbearer of all things Marathi, maintained a stoic silence. A senior BJP official from Maharashtra says, 'Raj is very smart. His silence speaks for itself. Not

only is he good friends with Sachin, he realises this is a non-issue.' As in most other matches, in this verbal one too, looks like Tendulkar has hit a six.

However, where Tendulkar has differed from Gavaskar is that, even outside politics, he has always avoided controversy. Gavaskar has never been afraid to voice his opinion on cricketing matters. When in 1976 West Indian pace terrorized Indian batsmen in the Jamaica Test he wrote, 'All this proved beyond a shadow of doubt that these people belonged to the jungle and forests, instead of a civilised country.' And, as we shall see, during Tendulkar's first tour of England, in 1990, Gavaskar refused MCC honorary membership, thus provoking Bedi's wrath. Tendulkar would never have done that, and it is fascinating that in his 2014 autobiography he carefully sidesteps any explosive issue almost as if he were India's supreme diplomat. As we shall see, the only exception to this was regarding Greg Chappell. In 2007, Tendulkar gave an interview to Rajdeep Sardesai and was frank in his criticism about the damage he felt Chappell had done to Indian cricket but then asked Sardesai 'to edit out some of the more explosive parts'. He has been awarded the Bharat Ratna and been appointed to the Rajya Sabha, but it took him three years to ask his first question, not having attended many sessions. It is as if to be seen as prominent in such a political forum would mean upsetting somebody. But that is no surprise, for this diplomatic skill was evident even when he was a teenager.

At the age of fifteen he told a television interviewer that his best friend was his bat. Some years later, when I asked him why he did not mention Kambli, without batting an eyelid he told me to name an individual could upset others, but there was no such danger in naming a bat. That ability to always skirt any problems has been the hallmark of Tendulkar's career.

It was this teenager already thinking like an adult who journeyed with the Indian team to Pakistan in November 1989.

JOURNEY TO PAKISTAN

Much has been written about Tendulkar's first series in Pakistan. There was his baptism as a Test batsman in the first Test in Karachi on 16 November 1989, aged sixteen, facing three great fast bowlers in the shape of Wasim Akram, Waqar Younis and an ageing Imran Khan, as well as the world's best leg-spinner at the time in the person of Abdul Qadir. And this in a Test match in which on the first day Tendulkar was so scared that he was getting ready to run back to the pavilion. The reason for his fear was that a bearded Pakistani in a salwar-kameez ran onto the pitch shouting about

Kashmir and other anti-Indian slogans and, after insulting Kapil Dev and Manoj Prabhakar, assaulted the Indian captain, Kris Srikkanth. As Srikkanth defended himself, he lost the buttons on his shirt, there was a general fight involving all the Indian players, led by the combative wicketkeeper Kiran More, who despite having pads on tried to kick the assailant. Tendulkar, fielding at cover, feared he might be assaulted and does not say whether he joined in the fight. One must presume he did not. The next day the Pakistani papers indulged in bit of fake news and presented the man as having come on to the field to congratulate Kapil, who was playing his hundredth Test Match.

Against this background it would have been understandable if Tendulkar, while batting, had shown nerves. But he did not, and the series contained two great defining moments of Tendulkar's batting.

The first was in the second innings of the fourth Test at Sialkot, where Waqar, who had also made his debut in the Karachi Test and was only two years older than Tendulkar, hit Tendulkar on the nose. Tendulkar was not wearing a grille and blood started to flow. While Imran showed fatherly concern, Miandad, always quick to get under the skin of the opposition, said, 'Arre tujhe to abhi hospital jana padega; teri naak tut gayi hai.' [You will have to go to the hospital. Your nose is broken.] The crowd held up a banner which read, 'Bachhe ghar jaa ke dudh pi ke aa.' [Child go home, and drink milk.] Tendulkar told the Indian doctor he would continue, took up his stance and settled down to face Waqar. Waqar bowled one on Tendulkar's legs and, in what would become his trademark shot, he flicked it to the boundary. Tendulkar went on to bat for over three hours and his stand of 101 with Navjot Sidhu helped India get a draw.

But the match that is most talked about was an exhibition match in Peshawar on 16 December. It was meant to be the first one-day international, but with rain making it impossible it was decided to have a knock-about game of twenty overs. Tendulkar was determined to take it seriously. When he came in to bat the asking rate was 11 an over and he rejected Srikkanth's advice that he concentrate on getting some batting practice. That as a sixteen-year-old in his first series he could disagree with his captain showed his confidence. He told Srikkanth India could still win and hit Mushtaq Ahmed for a couple of sixes in his first over. Mushtaq was then trying to establish himself in the Pakistan side, and Abdul Qadir sauntered down and taunted Tendulkar: 'Bachhe ko kyun maar rahe ho; dum hai to mujhe maar ke dikhao?' [Why are you hitting a youngster? If you really have strength hit me and show what you can do.] Tendulkar very respectfully answered that Qadir, being a great bowler, would not allow Tendulkar to hit his bowling.

When Qadir bowled, Tendulkar hit 28 off him in an over: 4 sixes, three in succession and Qadir, speaking in Urdu, acknowledged that his batting was great. By the time the innings came to a close Tendulkar was still batting, having scored a 53 in eighteen balls which included 5 sixes. What was also noteworthy was that right from the beginning he seemed to have few problems playing Wasim, then one of the best bowlers in the world.

Tendulkar's debut had come in a series which did nothing to solve India's fundamental cricket problems. Srikkanth, India's sixth change of captaincy in the 1980s, managed to draw the series, a feat which had proved beyond Bedi and Gavaskar. But he could hardly lay bat on ball, achieving a highest score of 36, and like Bedi and Gavaskar he was sacked on his return, proving that the stakes in an India–Pakistan series were always higher than in any other. His replacement was a man nobody could have predicted would captain India, for he had required a large slice of luck even to play in the Test series.

AZHARUDDIN GETS LUCKY

The Pakistan tour marked a turning point in Azharuddin's career. He was no longer the magician with the bat as he had been when David Gower's Englishmen came to India in 1984. After the West Indies trip, where his scores had been 61, 14, 25, 13, the general view in Indian cricket was that his wristy play was a delight to watch, but that he was technically deficient, which was masked in India but exposed abroad.

He was not supposed to play in the first Test in Karachi, but Raman Lamba broke a toe and he got a chance. (Lamba never played again for India.) Given this reprieve, Azharuddin made the most of it. In Karachi, he made 35 in both innings, but here all the catching practice Brother Joseph had given him came in handy. He took five catches, some of them slip catches, never an Indian strong point, and what is more not Azharuddin's normal position. He had equalled the world record for catches other than by a wicketkeeper. Azharuddin had been seeking advice on batting and Zaheer Abbas proved a good tutor, telling him to wrap his right hand further around the handle so he could stroke the ball with greater control and assurance. The results were immediate. In Faisalabad, where the second Test was played, he scored 109—his first century abroad—there was a 77 in the third and a 52 in the fourth. He ended the series having scored 312 runs, averaging 44.57.

But what happened when he returned to India was even more amazing. He was captaining South Zone in the Duleep Trophy when Raj Singh approached him. 'Miyan,' said Raj Singh, 'captain banoge?' [Will you become captain?] Azharuddin, not realizing he was being asked to lead the national side, replied that he was already captain of South Zone. Then Raj Singh explained he was being offered the captaincy of India and Azharuddin could not believe it. Raj Singh had thought of appointing Sanjay Manjrekar, who had been the one outstanding batting success of the Pakistan tour, but he had just come into Test cricket and Raj Singh felt he did not have enough experience to take over. He also did not want to go back to Vengsarkar. Azharuddin seemed the way forward. The incident shows the relationship between Raj Singh and Azharuddin. For Azharuddin he had the sort of affection an indulgent father has for a son who may not always make the most of his gifts. Azharuddin called him 'Raj bhai', Raj called him 'Azhar'. Indian cricket history has no comparable love affair, wholly platonic, between an administrator and a cricketer.

Azharuddin's first foray as captain was in New Zealand in early 1990, and the team display seemed to be modelled on his batting style. The Indians played some of the most entertaining cricket seen there for years but were also reckless in their batting, losing the first Test and with it the three-Test series 1–0. In the second Test Tendulkar could have become the youngest-ever century maker in Test history had he been just a little bit more patient. Having rescued India and got to 88 with 2 fours off Danny Morrison, he went for a third and was caught at wide mid-off. A few months later Tendulkar and India were in England and by the time the second Test was played at Old Trafford, Tendulkar showed that even at the highest level he could, when necessary, bat patiently.

Before he left for England Tendulkar had one mission to perform. The word in Mumbai cricket was if you had a meal at Sanzgiri's house, you would score a hundred. Sanzgiri told me, 'Sachin came to my house. He did not have time for lunch or dinner, he and his brother Ajit came for breakfast. I made them some poha. I then got him a taxi.' The world had to wait for a few weeks to find out if Tendulkar had acquired enough good luck from the breakfast to score his first Test century.

TENDULKAR WOWS ENGLAND

We have seen how Graham Gooch advised the Indian selectors that Tendulkar was too young to face Pakistan. So now that he was part of India's team it generated a great deal of English interest. The very structure of English cricket meant that such teenagers could never get anywhere near the Test team. That summer, John Morris played his first Test for England, and he was twenty-eight years old. Bishan Bedi, the Indian cricket manager, revelled in the interest shown in Tendulkar, and told English journalists that

Englishwomen 'wanted to seduce Sachin', which was a godsend for the tabloids.

Tendulkar had come to England in 1988 on the private tour Kailash Gattani organized and had got a feel playing on English wickets, where the ball swung and seamed. England had to wait until the final day of the second Test at Old Trafford to see Tendulkar the batsman, use the knowledge that Gattani's tour had given him.. Then, with India facing defeat, he showed he might be a teenager but already had a very mature cricket brain and could indeed shape the course of a match.

India had lost the first Test at Lord's heavily whereas England had made a massive 653 for 4, with Gooch making a monumental 333. However, while that innings made the summer of 1990 Gooch's summer, many at Lord's drooled over Azharuddin's magnificent 121, one of the most beautiful innings seen in a Test match. And then there was Kapil Dev. He had not done much with the ball, prompting Alec Bedser to make the astonishing comment that he had a bad action. But as he showed on the fourth day, there was nothing wrong with his bat. He was at the crease when Narendra Hirwani, the No. 11 batsman walked out. India still required 24 to make sure England could not enforce the follow-on. Kapil Dev knew Hirwani was no batsman, so in an over bowled by Eddie Hemmings, he hit the third, fourth and fifth ball for sixes. After Kapil had hit his third six, Hemmings turned to Gooch and said, 'I suppose he will hit this for six as well.' And Kapil duly did, saving the follow-on. He knew he needed to. The very first ball of the next over Hirwani was out. All this was wonderful entertainment but could not prevent India being beaten.

India looked doomed to defeat in the second Test at Old Trafford as well. Azharuddin had batted even better than at Lord's by making 179, but the Indian bowlers, with Anil Kumble making his debut, had taken such punishment that England could ask India to make 408 in the fourth innings confident India would not get to such a score. The England plan seemed to be working very well when India were 183 for 6. Tendulkar had held firm at one end—in the first innings he had made his first half century in England—and now he had at the other end the last recognized batsman in Manoj Prabhakar. Nobody gave them any chance of saving the Test. But save it they did. By the end of the Test the pair were still together having put on 160, and Tendulkar had made his first Test hundred, 119 not out.

But the boy in Tendulkar remained. He wanted to skip the post-match press conference and had to be persuaded to attend. Also, being under eighteen and not able to drink, he did not open the bottle of champagne he had won as Man of the Match until eight years later, on his daughter

Sara's first birthday.

India, drawing strength from what Tendulkar did, made 606 for 9 declared, their highest score in England, at the final Test at the Oval. They even made England follow on for the first time in England, but there was never enough fire power in their bowling to win the Test. India had lost the series 1–0, but for the Indians, Tendulkar's century was widely seen as a sign of the good times to come. However, while the non-Indian world took notice, it is interesting that at the very ground where Tendulkar scored his century, one single ball bowled by an Australian three years later made a much greater impression on English and world cricket. That was the leg break bowled by Shane Warne to Mike Gatting in the 1993 Ashes series. It so surprised Gatting that he was bowled, and that leg break was immediately dubbed 'the ball of the century', superior to anything that had been bowled in the previous ninety-three years. Warne went on to take many other scalps and was part of an awesome Australian side, but that ball played a part in Warne becoming one of *Wisden's* five cricketers of the twentieth century whereas Tendulkar, as we have seen, did not.

A FURIOUS SARDAR

Apart from Tendulkar, the other major talking point of the tour was Bishan Bedi's management style. While India battled England at Lord's, news leaked that Gavaskar had turned down the honour of becoming a member of the MCC. It was said he was unhappy about the way he had been treated by the officious Lord's gatemen. Bedi came to the Lord's press box and gave the journalist a letter he had written to Sunil Gavaskar. [Picture on p. 204]

How Bedi could speak for Indians in Britain was not clear. His comments that he felt ashamed to have played with Gavaskar hurt Gavaskar so much that, as he told me in the summer of 2018, during India's tour, he vowed to have nothing to do with Bedi again.

I would soon be made aware of how volatile Bedi could be. This series was the first in England where both teams had cricket managers. The *Sunday Times* asked me to do a piece comparing Fletcher, the England manager, with Bedi. Bedi had taken charge during the New Zealand tour and, as Sanjay Manjrekar has since revealed, in his first stint, unhappy about how M. Venkataramana, the off-spinner from Tamil Nadu, had bowled, he demanded an explanation. When he did not get it he shouted, 'Cat got your tongue? Speak up.' Interestingly, Manjrekar while narrating the story in his 2017 book *Imperfect* does not name the coach and there is no mention of Bedi in the book. During the 1990 tour Bedi made comments about Azharuddin's captaincy, making it clear he did not agree with his decision to field first at Lord's which was widely reported. During the Old Trafford Test, I spent an evening with Bedi. He was outspoken, and I was fascinated to hear that he was appalled that Kumble was bowling to field with a sweeper on the deep cover boundary. For Bedi, who bowled to attacking fields, this was anathema. This was remarkable criticism by a manager of his captain's field settings and I wrote a piece contrasting Bedi with the taciturn Fletcher but with great affection. I returned to London for the Oval Test to find Bedi was incensed by the article. During the Old Trafford Test he had come to the press box looking for me and told journalists he wanted to find the Bengali as he wanted to shove an umbrella up his arse.

31 July 1990

OPEN LETTER TO THE LITTLE MASTER

Dear Sunil,

Following the recent publicity concerning the M.C.C., I felt I must write to show how shocked and ashamed I am at your decision.

In September 1989 you were offered an Honorary Membership of the M.C.C., to which you did not reply.

In November 1989 you were sent a reminder by the M.C.C., to which you replied that for "personal reasons" you did not wish to be a member of the M.C.C.

As the greatest run-getter of all time in Test Cricket you have undone all your deeds at one stroke by ridiculing the greatest institution of cricket in the world. You have proven that only the mighty can be petty.

I feel personally quite disgusted and ashamed I ever played cricket with you and like so many cricketers I have met in the last few days, I wonder what kind of a person you are. Not only have you let yourself down but you have let down the Indian Cricket Team, World Cricket and more importantly, the Indian people in Britain.

Bishan Bedi

Bishan Bedi
(Indian Cricket Team Manager)

That season I had published my *History of Indian Cricket* which had a foreword by Sunil Gavaskar. I had presented it to Bedi, inscribing on the title page, 'Bishan, with fond memories of his great cricketing deeds.' At the Oval he came to the press box and chucked the book at me. He did not want it. I opened it at the title page to see he had crossed out my thanks and instead scrawled this handwritten message just above my name:

> You gutter journalist, shove it up your filthy bum & enjoy being the worst historian [this was underlined] ever. 'You are a cunt of the highest order'—nay, 'odour'!! Try carrying this quote you swine.

When I showed it to Gavaskar he asked if he could borrow the book to show his fellow commentators. They were amused but also incredulous that a manager of an international team could write this. I discovered later that Bedi felt his remarks to me in Manchester were off the record although he had not said so, and I had therefore felt free to report.

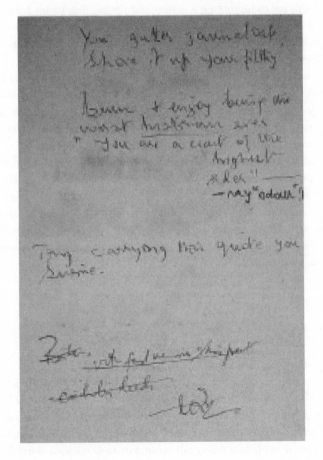

TENDULKAR PROVIDES SOLACE

Tendulkar also stood out when the Indians returned home for the 1990–91 season, which saw little international cricket, and domestic cricket ruined by court battles between the board and Punjab and shocking behaviour by players. The exceptional Tendulkar, not just technically but also temperamentally, emerged in the Duleep Trophy final in Jamshedpur between North and West Zone. It was a match marked by player behaviour that was shameful. Players publicly disagreed with umpiring decisions, and one captain, not content with expressing his views on the field of play, even entered the umpires' room and carried on the argument. Then Rashid Patel of West Zone bowled a beamer at North Zone's Raman Lamba. He followed this up by uprooting a stump and threatening to hit Lamba with it. Lamba defended himself with his bat and both players used obscene language. The match also saw a crowd riot, with several objects in the ground being burnt. Not surprisingly, the match was abandoned.

Any other teenager might have been tempted to copy Patel and Lamba. Not Tendulkar. When, having made a mere 25, he was caught at short leg by Ajay Jadeja off Kirti Azad, he walked off without any dissent. It made a deep impression on the discerning Indian cricket public. The wider public was also taking notice of Tendulkar.

When he had returned from Pakistan in 1989 Tendulkar, going out onto Chowpatty, the famous Mumbai beach, to have bhelpuri, the great Mumbai snack, was stopped and asked, 'Are you Sachin Tendulkar?' Soon he would not be able to go out without being mobbed, and in the years to come, as he came out to bat, the crowds would shout, 'Sachin, Sachin' not just in Mumbai but all over India, as they continued to do until he played his final innings in 2013.

Chapter 24

MANDELA, GAVASKAR AND THE CRICKET MISSIONARY

COFFEE WITH GAVASKAR AND MANDELA

Early on Sunday morning, 30 June 1991, I was in a convoy of cars whose passengers included Sunil Gavaskar, going to Nelson Mandela's home in Soweto. The previous day had seen the birth of a unified cricket board for South Africa. For the first time since South Africa made its Test debut in 1889, it had a cricket body that could truly claim to represent all the races of the country.

I had played a part in bringing Gavaskar to Johannesburg. In the previous eighteen months I had got to know Ali Bacher, the captain of the last white team to play Test cricket, who was now leading the unified cricket body. When Bacher drew up the list of those to be invited for the unification ceremony, he had no problems with cricketers from England, Australia or even Garry Sobers, who Bacher knew. But he knew nobody from India.

India then had no relations with the white South Africa government. The Indian government treated the African National Congress (ANC) as the government of South Africa, having granted its mission in the Indian capital diplomatic status. The wife of Anand Sharma, then spokesman of the ruling Congress party, was a South African Indian with very strong views on apartheid. There were no direct flights between the two countries and it was hard to even talk on the telephone.

Bacher turned to me for help, and one day I received a call from him in my London home asking for the names of Indians to invite to the black-tie dinner to be held in Sandton in Johannesburg to celebrate the formation of the unified body. I immediately suggested Gavaskar. He was the obvious choice and we were in regular touch as he had just written a foreword to my book. I gave Bacher Gavaskar's telephone number in Mumbai. I also suggested to Bacher names of some prominent Indian cricket journalists including R. Mohan, Ayaz Memon and Kishore Bhimani.

The celebratory dinner on Saturday, 29 June, was in the ballroom of the Sandton Sun. In this symbol of white South African prosperity, where not long before the only blacks would have been servants, that evening they were the honoured guests, wearing elegant tuxedos as they mingled with whites. There were also South Africans of Indian descent. One of the South African Indians told me with a smile they never had had any problems with the white females. It was the white males that caused all the problems. For me, it was touching to see Gavaskar and the Indians from India in their Nehru jackets being warmly received in a land which had so long treated them as second-class citizens. As they were introduced to the South Africans of Indian descent, it filled me with pride that I had played a part in these two distant cousins, long cut off by apartheid, rediscovering each other.

During the visit, Bacher had taken both Sobers and Gavaskar to the black township where he was trying to introduce blacks, whose sport is football, to cricket. As Gavaskar and Sobers stepped on to a cricket field, I suggested to Bacher he should get Garry to bowl to Sunil. The picture of these two greats playing cricket made the headlines in the South African media the next day. Our visit to Mandela had also been prompted by me. Mandela had received Garry Sobers. I mentioned to Imtiaz Patel, Bacher's right-hand man, that surely Mandela should also receive Gavaskar. Imtiaz could not agree more. For Imtiaz, a South African proud of his Indian origins, it was a point of principle that Mandela, having received a great West Indian, should also receive a great Indian cricketer.

At the dinner Imtiaz came up to me and whispered that early the next morning we would go to see Mandela. So it was that a whole host of cricket journalists, all of Indian origin and all, barring myself, from India, were tagging along with Gavaskar to Mandela's home.

As we left Sandton that Sunday morning, for several miles there were no cars on the highway except our convoy. Then, just as we turned off the main highway to Soweto and neared Mandela's home, a Ford Cortina suddenly zoomed ahead of us as if it had been waiting. It now escorted us to the great man's home.

'That is Mandela's security car,' said the man who was driving us, 'they watch every car that approaches his house.' Sure enough, as we turned into the driveway of Mandela's home, the car so positioned itself that we had to stop. The electric gates opened to let the Cortina in, two men got out, our credentials were checked and then the gates opened to let us in to the palatial home that Winnie Mandela had built while Nelson Mandela was in prison. It would have looked impressive anywhere. In Soweto it looked incongruous—hidden behind high walls, it looked like a house from the white suburbs of Johannesburg transplanted to the township.

But then everything about this meeting with Mandela was strange. This was one of the most momentous weeks in his life. The ban on the ANC had been lifted and it was about to hold its first open session in South Africa in thirty years. That session was to confirm Mandela as president. The previous week the media had reported that Mandela had his hands full trying to cope with the bitter divisions between the old guard, so long in exile, and the young activists who had been carrying on the struggle against apartheid within the country. When some of us had asked whether we might see Mandela at the cricket celebrations, we were told he was far too busy preparing for the historic Congress to see anybody, certainly not a cricketer, accompanied by some cricket journalists.

But through his contacts Imtiaz had opened the door, and now we were led up a small flight of stairs to a room dominated by a huge oil painting of Robert Mugabe on one wall. In the middle was a long V-shaped table filled with the presents and gifts Mandela had acquired from his various foreign travels since his release.

It looked like the office of a company chief executive, although when Mandela arrived, dressed in a tie and a jumper, it became more of a throne room. His associates, who had been milling around in the room, withdrew to a distance, whispering softly 'Madiba', father, the term invariably used to refer to him. As he began talking it became obvious that he quite liked using the royal we, reflecting his own royal roots.

We had been told before the meeting that Mandela would not talk about politics and that we should not ask him political questions. But once the pleasantries were over and coffee was served, it was clear Mandela was more than happy to talk about sporting politics and how politicians can use sports. Without much prompting he said:

> De Klerk [President of the apartheid regime] has made it clear in our conversations, 'Look if you would make it possible for All-Blacks [New Zealand's great rugby team] to come here, then we can smash the system.'

Mandela was all too aware of the part sport had played in the boycott of South Africa and saw the ANC successfully using sports to its own advantage. In the 1970s, the ANC had pioneered the boycott of South African sports to spotlight apartheid, but now, with the cricket bodies united, Mandela made it clear he wanted the world to start readmitting integrated sports bodies back into the international sports community:

> We have never been against cricketers coming to South Africa to coach our children. What we object to is anything that has

interrelationship with the regime. We want to use it to isolate the regime.

Mandela himself had never played cricket—boxing being his sport—but he told the story of watching the Australians paying a Test match in Durban in 1950. When I asked him about the experience, he said:

> Yes, we watched it from the segregated stands and, of course, we cheered the Australians. The South Africans had made a big score. We were cheering [Neil] Harvey, who was playing very well for the Australians, but we were both nervous and excited. As he took Australia to the South African score we were very scared. What if he gets bowled out? Then Harvey came to our segregated stand and spoke to us. But I didn't speak to him. They would have kicked us out if we had tried to approach him.

Since his release, cricket had figured in his travels. Bob Hawke, the Australian premier, mentioned it in Australia, and so did John Major, the then British Prime Minister. 'You know,' said Mandela, 'Mr Major seemed more interested in cricket than the issues.' As he recounted the story he was overcome with laughter. 'I have instructed Steve Tshwete to visit London and meet Major.' Tshwete was the ANC executive member in charge of sports and had played a crucial role in helping the cricket bodies to unite.

Mandela knew that he could not move too far ahead of the young radicals in the ANC on the sporting front:

> On our side we have people who are extremists who want not only that sport must be normalised. They argue that there can be no normal sport in a racial society. That is true. But at the same time sport is sport and quite different from politics. If sportsmen of this country take steps to remove the colour bar, then we must take that into account.

As we were being ushered out, Gavaskar suddenly piped up, 'Sir, can I have a memento of this visit?' Most of the journalists there reeled back in shock, fearing Gavaskar had committed a dreadful faux pas. I immediately thought of Father Fritz and the confidence our school had given him to even make such a request. Mandela just nodded, went out of the room and, leaning on the stairs, called to Winnie to give him a key. He re-emerged with a key and went to a locked door behind the huge conference table. 'That', whispered one of his associates, 'is where he keeps all the presents he has received on his travels.' He quickly re-emerged, saying, 'I thought I might give you the belt Joe Frazier has given me. But I would like to keep it.' Mandela, a keen boxer in his youth, could clearly not part with such a gift. But he did present Gavaskar with a book to which he added a gracious inscription. Then the electric gates opened, and we were back in the heat and dust of Soweto.

The conversation with Mandela lasted no more than half an hour, but it revealed how the man who was to lead his nation out of apartheid saw sport. Before that meeting the common assumption was the sports boycott of South Africa would not be lifted until South Africa became a normal society and had one person, one vote. Now it was clear Mandela was going to use sport to make South Africa normal, to achieve his great dream of a rainbow country.

A month after the cricket bodies united, the ICC held its annual meeting. Bacher, not wanting to waste time, targeted the meeting to return to the international fold. He shrewdly worked out that for that he needed India and in April 1991 he had contacted Jagmohan Dalmiya, the then secretary of the Indian board.

BACHER AND DALMIYA

At first Dalmiya could not believe he was getting a call from South Africa. Like almost everybody in India he did not think there was a telephone link between the two countries. But soon the pair were having regular chats. Dalmiya was persuaded to be the proposer of the motion at the ICC conference to be held in London in July calling for South Africa's readmission. However, when Bacher met Dalmiya in London in July, days before the ICC meeting, Dalmiya told him there was a problem. Dalmiya's decision had met with opposition in India and now Bacher had to persuade Madhavrao Scindia, the board president, who had not come to the meeting and was in India. Bacher may have worked his charm with Dalmiya, but he knew that to convince Scindia, a man deeply involved in Indian politics, he would require a politician. The obvious one was Tshwete. Tshwete after a fifteen-minute conversation persuaded Scindia that India should propose that the ICC readmit South Africa. Australia, which had always yearned to resume ties with its white friends, happily seconded and South Africa was back. After more meetings behind closed doors it was agreed South Africa would also take part in the 1992 World Cup to be held in Australia. This ICC vote took place in Sharjah. And this is where Bacher first met Scindia.

INDIA OVERWHELM SOUTH AFRICA

Both Dalmiya and Scindia had major roles to play in what was now turning out to be a fascinating cricket drama between India and South Africa. The

speed with which it developed was quite astonishing. In April 1991 nobody
in the Indian board knew who Bacher was. By the last week of October
the Indian board wanted South Africa to play three one-day internationals
in India between 10 and 14 November 1991. This urgent request was
made when Bacher, accompanied by Geoffrey Dakin, Krish Mackerdhuj,
and Percy Sonn came to India from Sharjah. They were also visiting Sri
Lanka, Pakistan and Kenya, countries with which white South Africa had no
relations but which the united South African Cricket Board now wanted to
get to know. The visit itself showed how delicate it was. The trip to Pakistan
looked most difficult. Pakistan, unlike India, had not been keen on voting
for South Africa's return. To make sure Pakistan was happy Bacher suggested
they have a Muslim in his party, so Sonn was added. But with Bacher being
Jewish, he was described as 'a Turkish gynaecologist'.

Bacher, of course, had never visited India and he wanted to express
his appreciation in particular to Dalmiya who, as he would later put it,
'was the driving force in 1991 to get South Africa back into international
cricket'. Bacher and his team flew into Mumbai and found the Indians
wanted a favour. The scheduled tour by Pakistan had been cancelled due
to security issues and when he met Dalmiya in Kolkata he asked Bacher
to fill in. Bacher asked, 'When?' Dalmiya replied, 'Well, next week actually.'
And to strengthen his case he took Bacher and his team to meet Jyoti
Basu, then the chief minister of the CPM government of West Bengal. He
virtually ordered Bacher to be back in a week's time with his team to play
an international match in Kolkata. Scindia was also keen, having made sure
that the ANC representatives in Delhi were happy with the tour. In Delhi,
Bacher got a feel of Indian cricket politics with one Indian cricket official
telling Bacher not to make too much of Dalmiya in Delhi, as Dalmiya and
Scindia led opposing factions on the Indian board. Bacher and his team
returned to Johannesburg on 2 November.

At this stage it was by no means certain the tour would take place. The
whites were not sure, but Tshwete, working on the agenda Mandela had
set to use sports to break apartheid, said the South Africans had to go to
India. On 7 November, the South African cricket team flew to Kolkata for
their first visit to India. The journey made aviation history being the first
direct flight from South Africa to India and the white South African pilot,
for all his experience of flying, had never before seen a flight plan for this
route. The Boeing 707 had seen better days and it had no markings and as
Chris Gibbons, a reporter on the flight, recalled, 'the seats were decrepit',
but there was a great deal of beer to make everyone jolly.

The flight was making history and in many ways the passengers on board being the first rainbow team of cricket officials, South African whites, Indians and blacks, were also making history. The apartheid regime still existed; blacks and browns were herded into areas far from the gleaming city centres and posh suburbs where whites lived. Racial division went so deep that the South African *Sunday Times*, its greatest English language paper, had special supplements for Indians and blacks which were added to the main edition distributed only in the white areas. On my first visit, just months before Mandela was released, a black paperboy, seeing I was Indian, offered me the Indian edition of the *Sunday Times*, saying, 'Indian, Indian.' I would later compare it with the mainstream white edition that Bacher read, and found the differences were interesting. While all the stories in the paper distributed to the whites were in the Indian edition, none of the stories concerning Indians were in the white edition. And at that stage with Mandela in prison his picture was banned and could not be printed. Bacher's wife did not know what he looked like because she had never seen a picture of him. The plane flew into Kolkata's Dum Dum, where the first match was to be played. One prominent South African white on the plane was board official Ewie Cronje and his wife from Orange Free State. Indians were banned from living in the state. If they had to travel through this supposedly free country they had to get a pass and complete the journey in twenty-four hours. Ewie Cronje did not know any Indians, did not know what to expect and was overwhelmed by the welcome Kolkata gave. Thousands lined the route from the airport to the Grand Hotel, where the team was staying, carrying banners which read 'South Africa-India friendship long live', which given the apartheid regime still reigned was amazing. At the Grand there was a banner welcoming 'the Springboks', the Indians not being aware of how hated the word was for the blacks and the Indians as under apartheid that was a term exclusively reserved for white sport. The South Africans persuaded the Indians to take it down.

However, the South African Indians were both conflicted and afraid. South African Indian officials like Hoosein Ayob, whose cricket career and life had been blighted by apartheid, were fearful their fellow whites would humiliate the Indians. While they wanted South Africa to win they also hoped the Indians would put up a good fight. S. K. Reddy, in the days when cricket was racially split, had taken steps to make sure a rebel Indian tour to bolster white cricket did not take place. Having heard Bacher was in secret negotiations with some Indian players, The introduction sets how the scene he had sought and received a guarantee from Azharuddin that the Indians would not be seduced and Azharuddin had kept his word. He was now convenor of the selectors that had selected this South African team and wanted it to win. However, Reddy's wife, like all South African Indians who were not officials, wanted India to beat South Africa. That would mean at least on a cricket field they were the equal of the whites.

And the Indians did win, beating South Africa in the first two internationals in Kolkata and Gwalior before losing the final one in Delhi, the only day-night match of the series. This, despite the fact that batting first they made 287 for 4. But South Africa responded with 288 for 2. The surprise result led South African Indians to wonder if the match was fixed, but there was no evidence to back such allegations and it was more a reflection of the hurt these South African Indians felt that their white oppressors had beaten their fellow Indians. However, there was one allegation made by the South African players that very nearly brought the tour to an abrupt halt. In Kolkata, India restricted South Africa to 177 for 8, the Indian bowlers got a lot of reverse swing. In this, one side of the ball is kept shiny using sweat and spit and the ball swings in the opposite direction to the one it normally does. This was by now the norm in international cricket, but the South Africans appeared to be surprised by it. Mike Proctor brought the ball to the attention of Bacher and the result was what was termed 'an informal protest' about the condition of the ball. Bacher insists that 'at no stage did I ever suggest or even imply that the Indian team was cheating'. That is not how the Indians saw Bacher's protest, and they were incensed. Scindia, who had lavishly entertained the South Africans, told Dakin, 'Your manager has made a statement and accused us of being dishonest. Unless you and your Board rescind the statement, there is no point in continuing with this tour.' Dakin then called his board together, a meeting Scindia attended but Bacher did not, and then held a press conference where he said:

> It would appear that certain unfortunate remarks have been made. My executive was never approached in respect of this matter. To me there is no controversy, the matter is a storm in a teacup, and we find the statement most embarrassing. As President of the United Cricket Board and on behalf of the executive, I wish to say that we totally dissociate ourselves from the statement allegedly made by Dr Bacher. I apologise to Mr Scindia and the Board of Control for Cricket in India.

Bacher was not pleased as he felt he had been hung out to dry, but the tour was saved.

The tour saw two developments which would have wider repercussions later. The South Africans had originally selected an all-white team. Scindia rang Bacher to say that would be a problem for the Indians. The South

Africans added four development cricketers, two black, two white. They would not play but get experience of the subcontinent. One of them was Hansie Cronje, and his experiences of the subcontinent would, nine years later, lead to the greatest match-fixing story in world cricket, a story that is still rumbling on two decades later.

The other impact was on Indian cricket finances.

INDIAN CRICKET DISCOVERS TELEVISION RIGHTS

Bacher told me:

> Before we left for India because of the huge interest in South Africa, it was unbelievable, I spoke to one of the local sponsors, Panasonic. I said, 'Look, to show the series in South Africa it is going to cost us a lot of money, a quarter of million rand, can you support us?' There were two people I was talking to outside my house on the street. They said, 'Ali, you are on.' When I got to Kolkata, I asked Dalmiya, 'Who is televising the matches?' He said Doordarshan, the national broadcaster. I said, 'You will be financially well compensated for this match.' He said, 'Ali, it does not work like that. They televise all the matches and no money changes hands.' I said, 'What are you talking about? In South Africa there is extraordinary interest, our public want to see the three matches on television. I have contacted Panasonic. They will give me a quarter of million rand. Here you are. We want it to be televised back in South Africa.' His eyes opened up. He couldn't believe it.

Dalmiya's response was to contact Amrit Mathur, who worked closely with Scindia, and the first question Mathur had to get an answer to was did the Indian board own the rights. He found the board did. Then the question was, how much should they charge the South Africans? The Indians had no idea and Dalmiya, plucking a figure from the sky, said $10,000. Mathur thought about it and decided he would ask for $20,000. There were two South African channels bidding: a state-owned one and the cable channel, M-Net. Mathur first spoke to the South African state channel, and even before Mathur could say what his figure was they said they were willing to pay $200,000. Mathur could not believe what he was hearing. In fact, M-Net was willing to offer more, but as most people watching it were whites, and Bacher wanted this first non-racial tour to go to all the races of the rainbow nation that was being constructed, he advised Mathur to take the lower figure from the state channel. Mathur has no doubt that this was the first time the Indian board realized they owned the rights to the cricket matches they staged and that it could earn them a lot of money.

This was, of course, the board doing a one-off overseas deal. To get the rights for good, the board would have to fight many court battles with Doordarshan before they secured them, and then they began to exploit them so well that they became the richest cricket board in the world. But there can be no doubt it was the South African series, and Mathur and Bacher, that had started the process.

Chapter 25

HISTORY-MAKING OFF THE FIELD, MISERY ON IT

ANOTHER DRUBBING IN AUSTRALIA

The South African visit to India in November 1991 was great theatre and good cricket politics, but it did little for Indian cricket. Nine days after the day-night match in Delhi, the Indians were in Lismore playing their opening match of the Australian tour against New South Wales. There was little preparation, and this showed in the Test series: the Indians had not even been a month in Australia and had lost the first two Tests. They drew the third but lost the last two, the same 4–0 defeat as in the first tour in 1948. As on that tour, there were moments of individual glory with the Australian batsmen discovering that the Indian bowling was not as weak as everyone had said it was. Kapil Dev took twenty-five wickets in his best series abroad, and with that he had got more than 400 Test wickets. In the fourth Test at Adelaide, with Azharuddin using his wrists to make his bat look like a conductor's baton and making an effortless 106, India offered hope they might make the 372 they needed to win before they fell, 38 runs short. And there was the batting of Tendulkar and his first duel with Shane Warne, which he won easily.

Tendulkar, having been subjected to Australian sledging by Steve Waugh in the first three-day match, made 148 in the third Test at Sydney, the youngest man to score a Test century in Australia. Warne, on his debut, took 1 for 150 in forty-five overs, although Tendulkar was impressed with his talent. Shastri made 206 and India 483, their highest score of the series. But rain and bad light meant 49.1 overs were lost, and while Warne may have done nothing with the ball, coming in at No. 10 he batted the last seven minutes, helping Border draw the match. At the end of the match, Australia were 173 for 8 in their second innings, just three ahead of India's first innings score.

Then, in the final Test at Perth, after Australia had made 346, Tendulkar, coming in with the score on 69 for 2, took India to 240, his 114 coming from 161 balls. This was when Tendulkar showed how he could hold an innings together. At the other end wickets fell and, as he batted with the tail, he scored more quickly, taking only fifty-five balls for his second 50. He was ninth out. The Australians won by 300 runs but had to acknowledge Tendulkar was special. Tendulkar himself felt this was one of his best hundreds.

Any Indian hopes that the World Cup hosted by Australia and New Zealand, which started three weeks after the Perth Test, would see a dramatic Indian revival were quickly dashed. This was the first World Cup played with a white ball and where players wore coloured clothing, with India in blue. But these Indian cricketing colours did not shine. The opening match against England was close, a defeat by 9 runs. But after rain allowed only two balls to be bowled in the match against Sri Lanka, they lost to Australia by 1 run. India had just three points after four matches, and all hopes of making the semi-finals were gone. The only consolation was that they beat Pakistan by 43 runs. However, Pakistan, who had also started dreadfully, recovered, with Imran making his famous declaration, 'We must fight like cornered tigers.' They did, and went on to win the trophy.

There was some glory for Tendulkar, who, still batting in the middle order, won the only two Man of the Match awards India was awarded in the World Cup. However, much more significant than this was that it was in Australia that Tendulkar learnt he could make cricket history by becoming the first overseas-born-player and also the first non-white to ever play for Yorkshire. The way Tendulkar describes it in his autobiography makes it sound very simple. He is in his Mumbai home playing tennis ball cricket, his brother Ajit comes down and says, 'Yorkshire are on the phone, they want you,' and he immediately accepts. 'I did not bother asking about the contract and other details.' The real story is more complicated.

TENDULKAR BREAKS ENGLAND'S OLDEST CRICKET BARRIER
It begins with Craig McDermott, the Australian fast bowler Tendulkar thought about a great deal during the Australian series. On the night before his Sydney innings Tendulkar had got up in the middle of the night and started to practise his shots, much to the astonishment of his roommate, Sourav Ganguly. When Ganguly asked, he told him he was practising facing McDermott. As we have seen, in the Sydney Test, the midnight practice session paid off. In the summer of 1992, Yorkshire decided to have an overseas player for the first time and chose McDermott. But when McDermott could not come due to injury, Solly (his real name is Suleiman) Adam, an Indian who lives in Dewsbury, decided that this was a splendid opportunity to break the last colour bar in cricket. By 1992, for almost half a century, immigrants from India, Pakistan and Bangladesh had been making Yorkshire their home. They played cricket but, often denied opportunities

in clubs which regularly produced players for the white rose county, had set up their own clubs. Subcontinental immigration had changed the make-up of several Yorkshire towns, making many whites feel they now lived in a foreign land, but there was no Asian in the Yorkshire team. The Asians in the county deeply resented this discrimination as I had learnt when I wrote an article about Asian cricket in Yorkshire.

Adam told me:

> I spoke to Lawrence Byford, who was the chairman and president of the club. Byford called me to a meeting where Brian Close and the full committee was there. I said, if an Australian can come to Yorkshire and he is not coming because he is injured, then why not an Asian from India, Pakistan? I did not mention Tendulkar. I was thinking any Asian. At that time cricket in Yorkshire was segregated with Asians having their own league. Only one or two were in favour, a lot of people in Yorkshire were against, especially Fred Trueman. He was not keen on any Asian. I had an argument with the members of the committee. I said, 'Listen, these people have never shared a dressing room with a coloured bloke for 128 years. It is my dream to get an Asian to play for Yorkshire. We have got a chance. I don't want to lose it.' Byford said, 'Give me a name,' and I said, 'What about Tendulkar? Tendulkar is a young lad and I am sure he will change the whole system because everybody thinks you are prejudiced. You have to take that crown off your head. If you sign an Asian, people will appreciate you are not prejudiced.' Byford said, 'Okay, but can you get hold of him?' I said, 'Of course I can get hold of him. I know him personally.' Next day, when I went to Headingley, Trueman called me and he said, 'Solly, this is bloody stupid.' He was very, very cross. I don't know if it was racism. I spoke to Sachin in Australia. He was there with Vinod Kambli. He said, 'Solly, I am too tired. No, no, no. It will be too long.' I said, 'You can stay with me and my family. Home atmosphere. It is not just cricket. I want to change Yorkshire. They never ever had an Asian in their team.' He said, 'Let me think about it.' I then phoned Sunil because Sunil is my family friend. I said, 'Sunil, you talk to him. See if you can persuade him.' Between me and Sunil we both managed to persuade him.

But Tendulkar's salary had to be negotiated. Yorkshire had agreed to pay McDermott £30,000, but Tendulkar £20,000. Adam says: 'Yorkshire said we were looking for a bowler. Tendulkar is coming first time. He is not experienced. I said no. You are having an overseas player. He should get the same as McDermott gets. They agreed with me.'

Yorkshire, having earlier been reluctant to hire Tendulkar, now decided they would broadcast this breaking of the county's last glass ceiling. They presented Tendulkar not as an unknown overseas cricketer arriving to little notice, 'jockstrap in back pocket, will play anywhere', but as a superstar. His welcome was choreographed like a celebrity media event: 10 a.m. arrival at Heathrow after an eleven-hour flight from Mumbai on 28 April 1992; 5 p.m. press conference at the banqueting suite at the Oval, where Yorkshire was playing Surrey; 7.30 p.m., another press conference at the hotel in Bayswater where the Yorkshire team was staying; next day, photo session with Tendulkar, where more gathered to see him bat at the nets than watch Yorkshire's match with Surrey, followed by another press conference; then a drive to Yorkshire, where he was interviewed in Leeds for Yorkshire Television. The following day he was ceremoniously welcomed to Headingley by Boycott. I got exclusive media access to write a piece on Tendulkar for the *Mail on Sunday* magazine where he would be dressed up as a Yorkshireman wearing a flat cap and tweeds. The piece that I wrote was entitled 'Will this Lad be Better than Boycott?' The introduction sets out how the scene looked as Tendulkar made history at Headingley:

> It was as incongruous as the Pope going backstage at the Folies-Bergère, or Cliff Richards topping the bill at a heavy metal thrash. To certain supporters of Yorkshire County Cricket Club it was worse than that—it was akin to the end of civilisation as tha knows it, lad. Here is Geoffrey Boycott giving Sachin Tendulkar a guided tour of Yorkshire's hallowed dressing room, taking him to the very corner which, for so many years, the uncrowned king of Yorkshire had made his own. Less than 100 yards away is the Tarique Chinese restaurant. A 20-minute drive away is Bradford, where angry Muslims made a bonfire of Salman Rushdie's *Satanic Verses,* convinced that the book had blasphemed their religion. But, until now, no Asian has ever set foot in this exclusive territory. Even worse, Tendulkar, a 19-year old cricketing prodigy from India, is not here merely to look. He is here to take part. He is here to stake his claim as Yorkshire's first overseas player. All round you can almost sense the presence of past cricketing greats; in the far corner Fred Trueman kept his pipe; on the table Brian Close, endlessly smoking, spread his racing paper; but this corner of the dressing room, giving a lovely view of the ground, is forever Boycott. He gazes at it a bit like Daddy Bear on discovering that Goldilocks has eaten his porridge. 'Who's taken over this corner? Oh, it's Jarvis (then

a current player) isn't it? He moved in as soon as I'd gone. Couldn't wait.' He waves his hand over the wooden bench which runs along the wall, saying, 'That's where I spread myself.' And then miming the placing of the bat against the wall, he says, 'That's where I placed my bat. Everyone knew this was my area.' Next, he turns to Tendulkar and says, 'Always get your corner. Make sure of it first. It lets everyone know where you are.' Then, beckoning him to the corner, he places his arm round Tendulkar and looks out on the ground: the true son of Yorkshire welcoming its first adopted cricket son.

Boycott also presented Tendulkar with his Yorkshire blazer and tried to make a joke of it: 'It will put a little colour on you.' Unlike Trueman, Boycott had for over twenty years been saying Yorkshire should hire an overseas player, and as he showed Tendulkar around, said, 'It is 20 years later than it should have been, but better later than never.' He also suggested to Tendulkar that there were some female secretarial staff in the Yorkshire office who might be susceptible to a curry and worth chatting up. What none of us watching the scene knew was that Tendulkar had already met his sweetheart, Anjali, whom he would marry three years later. In front of Boycott and the media Tendulkar kept Anjali hidden, smiled, and behaved in a manner so exemplary that all of Yorkshire, including those who had opposed his recruitment, was charmed. He had also mugged up on Yorkshire county cricket history, and the only fault the obsessive Yorkshire writers could find with him was that he had not heard about York City, a famous Yorkshire football club. He was endlessly photographed wearing a cloth cap and holding a pint of Tetley beer, despite the fact that at that stage he had not started drinking. This would produce a slight misunderstanding when he met his Yorkshire colleagues for the first time. As he walked into the bar his teammates were holding pints of various kinds of beer. He was asked by Byford what he would like to drink. He answered 'Anything soft.' Byford was one of the most prominent police officers in England and used to dealing with any situation. But he had not catered for this and, very confused, said 'Pardon?' thinking Tendulkar was asking for some special kind of beer. It took him a few minutes to realize that Tendulkar wanted a bitter lemon. However, as I discovered, while he was still to take to hard liquor, even at nineteen Tendulkar knew that cricketers had to market themselves. We were at the nets at Headingley and Tendulkar had delved into his cricket bag to find some pads. But as my photographer started taking pictures of some of his pieces of equipment he moved them aside, saying he did not want pictures taken of them as he was no longer involved with the sponsors whose names were on them. Yet during the course of my interview he could not have been more helpful and put up with all the demands I and my photographer made.

I also discovered that Tendulkar could quickly switch from public mode to private. I had spoken to Tendulkar in one of Solly Adam's houses; a dinner was laid on in another. As Tendulkar went next door he abandoned the interview mode he had assumed with me, and, surrounded by the Adam clan, some 250 of whom live around Dewsbury, he became like their young brother who happened to be famous. Then, as Chris Hassell, chief executive of Yorkshire County Cricket, joined them for dinner, he became the expert guide on Indian food, briefing him about the various delicacies. Adam says:

> Tendulkar came and stayed with us. Tendulkar made a big difference. He changed the whole thing. They loved him. He changed the thinking of the supporters and the Asian community. Trueman could not say anything.

Evidence for this came even as Boycott was showing him around the ground: an Asian doctor from Sheffield wrote to the club saying that not only was he joining but so were six of his patients. Tendulkar's time in Yorkshire must be judged not on what he did on the field. That was good but not outstanding: 1,070 runs, average 46.52, one century. However, he had a tremendous impact by becoming the first Asian to be part of the Yorkshire family. This may not seem much in 2019. Back in the summer of 1992, Tendulkar had broken barriers of race that had disfigured Yorkshire for so long. Integration would take time, and it was a decade later that Adil Rashid, who was four years old when Tendulkar arrived in Yorkshire, broke through to play for both Yorkshire and England. Tendulkar was the trailblazer. A few months after the end of the English season the entire Indian team was breaking racial barriers in South Africa that had existed even longer.

INDIA CREATE HISTORY IN SOUTH AFRICA

India's tour of South Africa in the winter of 1992–93 was epoch-making. This was the first time a non-white team had toured there. It shone a spotlight on the reaction of different races to this historic cricket tour. It also revealed how Indians were still struggling to come to terms with the caste system and it introduced technology to the game. This came in the first Test in Durban, where, for the first time in Test history, a third umpire sitting in the stands could, after watching replays, signal with either a green light or a red light whether a batsman was out in the case of run-outs, stumpings and hit wickets. Kepler Wessels, the South African captain, had not been keen, but Bacher had insisted on this innovation. Tendulkar was the first victim. He had made 11 when he changed his mind about a run but could not beat a Jonty Rhodes throw from point. Cyril Mitchley, the square-leg umpire, referred it to Karl Liebenberg sitting in the pavilion, using his fingers to shape out a television. For a few seconds we all paused, and then the red light came on to say Tendulkar was out. That moment showed that in such tight situations umpires needed the help of television. Something we take for granted now, but then a tremendous innovation. However, this was at Tendulkar's expense, and may, perhaps, explain why in the years to come he would be opposed to extending technology to judge other cricketing decisions, particularly lbws, arguing that the camera in this case could lie.

India's problems with caste and failure to advertise the welcome changes in Indian society was also highlighted in the first Test. Pravin Amre, like Tendulkar, a Mumbai boy coached by Achrekar, had been knocking on the Test door for years, having made his first-class debut five years earlier. In Durban he finally made his Test debut and, coming out to bat with the score 38 for 4, rescued India with a century. As he came out to bat, an Indian colleague in the press box told me Amre was a Dalit. But I was told I should not mention it. In contrast, at that very moment South Africa was telling the world how they were breaking racial barriers. The first Test in Durban saw Omar Henry become the first 'coloured' South African to play for his country, at the age of forty years and 295 days. Nelson Mandela came to watch on the Saturday of the second Test in Johannesburg and for the first time saw a Test, not from a cage reserved for blacks but as an honoured guest with the VIPs. South Africa could not wait to proclaim such changes. The Indian team were not keen to advertise the caste barriers Indian cricket was helping break.

The relationship between South African whites and South African Indians was highlighted during the second one-day international in Port Elizabeth, and the man who triggered it was Kapil Dev. In the previous one-day match at Newlands, as Peter Kirsten had strayed out of his crease and as Kapil ran in, had removed the bails but not appealed. Now Kirsten strayed again, and Kapil removed the bails and appealed. When the umpire asked Kapil, 'Do you want me to give him out?' Kapil said, 'Tell him to ****.' The umpire had no choice. As Kirsten remonstrated, Kapil replied, 'I warned you three times! Three times!' While back in 1948 Bradman had found nothing wrong with Mankad doing the same, now Kepler Wessels, who was batting with Kirsten, was furious. A few balls later he ran a single off Kapil's bowling, then, as he turned for the second run, swung his bat in an arc and the side of the bat hit Kapil's shins. Did he hit Kapil deliberately?

Kapil was asked this question both by the umpire, Cyril Mitchley, and the match referee, Clive Lloyd, and on both occasions he answered, 'I'm not sure.' Lloyd decided Wessels was not guilty, but he was fined 1,000 rand for 'remonstrating and using offensive language'. There was a hint of what might have happened had Lloyd found him guilty when he added, 'If the conduct alleged did take place it would be reprehensible and would warrant extreme censure.'

South African Indians I spoke to had no doubt Wessels had deliberately hit Kapil. What they wanted to know was whether this had been accompanied by Wessels, or Kirsten, calling Kapil 'coolie', the derogatory term whites had always used when referring to Indians. Amrit Mathur, the Indian tour manager, assured me that race was not involved. In comparison to this, the cricket was tame, often sleep-inducing, and the Tests revolved around Tendulkar and his battle with Allan Donald, with cameos from Amre and Kapil Dev.

Tendulkar's best moment came in the second Test in Johannesburg, where he played an outstanding innings, 111 out of 227. During the innings Tendulkar also reached a thousand runs in Tests; he was nineteen years and 217 days old, which made him the youngest to reach this landmark. And who had held the record? Kapil Dev, who got to a thousand aged twenty-one years and twenty-seven days. As Tendulkar broke his record, Kapil made 25, the second highest scorer in the Indian innings. One of Tendulkar's most sensational shots was upper-cutting Donald, who was bowling at 150 kph. The other very impressive feature was how, resuming on 75 on the third day, and with Donald at his best, he played only one cover drive before lunch and did not get to his century until after lunch, having faced 270 balls. This was a forerunner of the determination he would show many years later when, to regain his form in Australia, he decided not to play the cover drive and went on to score a double century. In Johannesburg it ensured India had a toehold in the match and could not be beaten.

Donald got his revenge in the third Test at Port Elizabeth, where he took 12 for 139, and South Africa won, a victory which gave them the four-Test series by 1–0. By now it was evident that South Africans saw Tendulkar as the main batsman: 'Get him and you get India', and their joy when he failed at 6 and 0 was uncontained. However, the superlative innings of the series was played in this Test by Kapil Dev. He walked out in the second innings with India 27 for 5, 36 runs adrift and facing what looked like an inevitable three-day defeat. What followed was a repeat of his innings against Zimbabwe in the 1983 World Cup. India added 188 runs, of which Kapil made 129 in 180 balls. The figures of his colleagues show how incredible his batting was that day: the first six failing to reach double figures, 17 was the next highest score. But more than the figures were the grace and beauty with which he played; at times in his innings there were shots he played that made him look like a cricketing Nataraja. Unlike his innings against Zimbabwe, he could not save India, but the match went into a fourth day before South Africa won.

What the series also showed was that Kapil was still the greatest star in the Indian cricketing firmament. While the whites knew little about India or its cricket, and did not show much interest, the South African Indians could not get enough of the Indian cricketers. Kapil was the man most in demand and got the gift of a car. Tendulkar was still a young man with a future and had to live in Kapil's shadow. In some ways he received even less publicity on this tour than Manoj Prabhakar, who put everything into his bowling when backing Kapil Dev, was much liked by the South African Indians and even had an article about him which described him as something of a sex symbol, accompanied by the sort of photographs Bollywood male stars like. It created quite a stir. But this was in the Indian edition of a paper and, given this was not distributed in white areas, only the Indians read about it. I had to lend my Indian edition to an English journalist so he could understand what the fuss was about.

Kapil's success inevitably raised questions about Azharuddin's future. Since Azharuddin had taken over in 1990 India had lost a four-Test series, scraped a draw against debutant Zimbabwe, and won one Test at home against Sri Lanka. In the final Test in Cape Town, the media was unanimous in thinking Kapil Dev would return to take charge. They seemed spot on when, after the team arrived in Mumbai, Kapil Dev was taken away and given what was described as an important message from the selectors.

But Azharuddin was not sacked. However, he was on probation, only appointed for the first Test and two one-day internationals. And England, who had arrived in India as India was playing in Cape Town, were confident Azharuddin's team held no threat. This was based on the report given by Keith Fletcher, who had checked out the Indians during the Test in Johannesburg. Boycott also had been scathing about the Indian team.

Chapter 26

CANNOT STOP WINNING

AZHARUDDIN MAGIC

Fletcher's optimism lasted until mid-afternoon on 29 January 1993. Azharuddin had come in to bat in the first Test in Kolkata with India 93 for 3. Azharuddin had always liked the English bowling and by then had scored five centuries against them in three series, two of them in England. Now, on the ground where he had first announced himself to world cricket, he played an innings that showed that, whatever his shortcomings as a captain, with a bat he could still be a magician. Gooch, the England captain, knew that Azharuddin could time the ball beautifully and had a very precise hitting area. If the bowler bowled outside the off stump but pitched it even a fraction short, Azharuddin would smash it through the covers, West Indian style, on the up. And a ball bowled outside the off stump but of a fuller length would see his marvellous wrists come into play, and it would whizz through mid-wicket or square-leg for four. But, despite knowing this, his bowlers could not stop Azharuddin scoring 182, nearly half the Indian total of 371. It is not hard to imagine where India would have been without Azharuddin, for the rest of the Indian batting did not do much, apart from Tendulkar, who made a half-century. And, just as Azharuddin had helped Gooch at Lord's in 1990 by deciding to field, Gooch helped the Indian captain in Kolkata by choosing on a wicket made for spin four quick bowlers. In contrast, India's three spinners provided the right variety: leg-spin with Kumble, left-arm with Venkatapathy Raju, and off-spin with Rajesh Chauhan, playing his first Test. These three took seventeen wickets of England's twenty wickets and, having followed on, England lost by eight wickets.

The match showed how one Test can change everything. Now all talk of Kapil Dev coming back vanished and never revived. The series and the victories that followed ensured Azharuddin would remain captain until India met England in 1996. Azharuddin won both the other two Tests by innings—an innings and 22 runs in Chennai, an innings and 15 runs in Mumbai. Batsmen queued up to make runs. In Chennai on the first day

Sidhu scored 100; on the second day Tendulkar went on to make 165. In Mumbai Tendulkar missed out on a century, making 78, but Kambli made 224 and the two put on 194 for the third wicket. Achrekar Sir, as Tendulkar and Kambli called him, watched, recreating memories of days when he had watched the pair demolishing Mumbai school attacks. Now, however, there was no question of him ordering Azharuddin to declare to spare England's pain as Achrekar had spared St. Xavier's.

The Test series also saw the second coming of Anil Kumble. After his debut against England in 1990, Kumble seemed destined to join the now growing list of lost Indian leg-spinners, bowlers like Sivaramakrishnan and Hirwani, who often promised to be the next Gupte and Chandrasekhar but proved one-Test wonders. While those two had made startling impacts early in their careers, Sivaramakrishnan in his second Test, Hirwani in his first, Kumble, in contrast, had had a dispiriting debut season in England in 1990: three wickets, each costing 56.66. He was nineteen, wore glasses and looked more like the engineering student he was than a potential match-winning leg-spinner. A year later he did not even make the team to Australia and thought he had no future in cricket. By the time he returned to the Indian side, having done enough in the Indian cricketing nursery that is the Ranji Trophy to impress the selectors, he had discarded his glasses. On the South Africa tour he took eighteen wickets in the series for a very respectable average of 25.94, better any other Indian bowler. This included a 6 for 53 in the Johannesburg Test. Fletcher, watching him, claimed he had not seen him bowl a ball which turned from leg to off and had written him off as carrying no danger to the England batsmen. Now Kumble finished with a series haul of twenty-one wickets, costing 19.80 each. His bowling, backed by the batting, meant India had done something they had never achieved before, namely, win every Test in a series. So, a tour that began with Azharuddin's captaincy in peril ended with Gooch, the master of the 1990 series in England, now talking, rather emotionally, of giving up Test cricket. He actually went home after Mumbai, leaving Alec Stewart to take over for the Sri Lanka leg of the tour. This was preplanned, but Gooch admits the defeats in India meant 'all my hopes had turned to dust'. And, having announced before the tour began that he was separating from his wife, Brenda, cricket 'was the last thing on my mind'. England were so shattered that on the team's return, the English supporters wondered whether the defeats in India were not due to the fact that players, in particular Gooch, wore designer stubble; in other words, they had facial hair in the form of a short, tight-cropped beard. Ted Dexter, chairman of the selectors, even announced, 'There is a modern fashion for designer stubble, and some people believe it to be attractive. But it is aggravating to others and we will be looking into the whole question of facial hair on our cricketers.' Gooch, of course, had had the same designer stubble when he had made 333 against India. But that is what sporting defeat does.

Azharuddin, the victor, could do no wrong and could not stop winning. Following on from their demolition of England, India beat Zimbabwe in Delhi by an innings and 13 runs, which saw India make 536 in the first innings, the third time in successive Tests that India had made more than 500 in the first innings. Kambli scored 227. India also won all three one-day internationals. Then, on 1 August 1993, the Sinhalese Sports Club ground in Colombo saw India win their first Test overseas since Leeds in June 1986. Compared to the huge totals at home this was a low-scoring match, but the Indian victory by 235 runs was nevertheless quite emphatic. With the other two Tests drawn, India won the series 1–0.

India were back in their England crushing form when in January 1994 Sri Lanka came to India. India had to bat only once in each of the three Tests. These were the sort of win margins that if engraved on a plate would make a wonderful wall mounting:

First Test in Lucknow, an innings and 119 runs;

Second Test in Bengaluru, an innings and 95 runs;

Third Test in Ahmedabad, an innings and 17 runs.

The number of runs India had made from February 1993 onwards was truly staggering. Chennai 560 for 6 declared; Mumbai 591 (against England); Delhi 536 for 7 declared (against Zimbabwe); Lucknow 511 and Bengaluru 541 for 6 declared (against Sri Lanka).

There was also a great personal landmark for Kapil to celebrate. This came in Ahmedabad. In the previous Test in Bengaluru he had joined Richard Hadlee at the top of the bowler's table for the highest number of Test wickets: 431. But could he claim the top spot on his own? He did so on the morning of 8 February 1994 when Manjrekar, fielding at short leg, caught Hashan Tillakaratne. True, Kapil had taken forty-four more Tests than Hadlee to do it, but he was a fast bowler mostly bowling on Indian pitches which did not help pace and swing, unlike those in Hadlee's native New Zealand.

TENDULKAR'S ONE-DAY ROLES

India were again playing New Zealand in New Zealand by the second last week of March, four one-day matches and a Test. The Test was drawn, but in the second one-day international in Auckland, Tendulkar opened for the first time at the international level. He showed he could easily take to this position, hitting 15 fours and 2 sixes, scoring 82 from forty-nine balls. Tendulkar had already shown that he could also be a very useful bowler in one-day internationals, even a match-winner. In the semi-final of the Hero Cup held in November 1993 against South Africa, India, batting first, had played poorly, making only 195. The match seemed South Africa's when the last over began. They had three wickets and needed just 6 runs to win. In a team huddle, Azharuddin was advised to bring on Tendulkar. He did. And although Tendulkar had not bowled in the match, he took two wickets, restricted South Africa to 3 runs and India had won by 2 runs. Tendulkar also took a wicket in the final against the West Indies, bowling Brian Lara after taking his brother Ajit's advice to bowl stump to stump. Compared to the South Africa match this was a stroll: victory by 102 runs with Kumble unplayable. In twenty-six balls the West Indies scored only 4 runs off his bowling and lost six wickets to give Kumble match figures of 6 for 12.

I had watched Tendulkar's Hero Cup success against South Africa on a television screen at the Long Room of the Oval and actually broadcast on the England series again based in London. The reason was that the Indian board had discovered how to make money from televising rights. It marked a momentous development in Indian cricket where an Englishman had played quite a significant role.

Chapter 27

EYEBALLS NOT CRICKET BALLS

INDIA PROFIT FROM THE PERFECT STORM

My commentary stint was with Farokh Engineer for Sky television. We were based in West London, not far from the Indian Gymkhana and, to be frank, deceiving the viewers. In a little studio we were watching pictures beamed back from India, and while the commentators based in India were speaking in English, we were talking in Hindi. Viewers could press a red button to switch to our Hindi commentary. I had first seen this done during my first year in journalism in 1974 by London Broadcasting Corporation. They neither had the rights, nor could they afford to send a team to the World Cup in West Germany, so Theo Foley, a former Arsenal assistant manager, sat in a studio off Fleet Street and commented on the play based on pictures beamed back from West Germany. He did the same for the 1978 World Cup from Argentina. Sky had the rights and no lack of funds, but this was meant to cater to Indians living in England. For me, due to the time difference with India, it meant getting up at four in the morning to get to Sky's studios, but to commentate with Engineer and speak Hindi again, albeit Bambaiya Hindi, was fun. However, the very fact that this series was being televised was because an Englishman had convinced the Indian board that there was money to be made from television. It was the start of the era when Indian board officials more often talked of eyeballs, the people who watched cricket on television rather than cricket balls.

That Englishman was Andrew Wildblood of International Management Group (IMG), a sports marketing group which had pioneered the marketing of sports and was prominent in tennis and golf. Wildblood, having televised cricket from the West Indies, decided he would tap the Indian market. He has now retired, but talking to me in November 2018 from his home he recalled:

> England were touring India in 1993. So, I took myself off to India, in
> the company of Henry Blofeld, who was to help me open the doors
> of the Indian board. The Indian board were meeting in Pune. So,

Henry and I found ourselves boarding a train at Mumbai's VT station to go to Pune. I remember very clearly sitting in a coffee shop in the Blue Diamond Hotel in Pune. I. S. Bindra and Jagmohan Dalmiya, two guys that turned out to be the main men on the Board, were on one side of the table, and me and Henry on the other side of the table. We wanted to know how we could acquire the rights to produce the coverage of the 1993 England Tour and then distribute it. Dalmiya and Bindra wanted $200,000 [a significant figure as this was what South African television had paid two years earlier], I wanted to pay them $175,000. We were squabbling over $25,000, which gives you some context of the value. I lost the argument, we paid them $200,000. The $200,000 we paid in 1993 wouldn't buy you an over today. The Indian Cricket Board earns billions from its television rights. We were both the production and the distribution company. In return for giving the Board a guarantee of $200,000 we were taking the risk that we could sell the rights to broadcasters, the winner being whoever was willing to pay the highest price.

Dalmiya and Bindra asked Wildblood whether his company could produce the coverage:

I said yes, having no idea what I was talking about. We had to put the entire production together, source and import all of the kit, cameras, sound desk, everything. We had to build camera platforms at every cricket ground because they didn't have any camera platforms in India in those days. We had to put together an entire engineering and technical crew, commentary team. Then we had to get all the kit there. We hired three Russian Ilyushin airplanes and flew all of the kit and the crew to India in the same airplane. I can remember very well when I visited India, we'd be strapped in the back of the plane on benches that ran down the side of the fuselage, and the front of the plane was all of the kit. I thought that by applying first-world television production standards you would produce a picture that you could sell to a broadcaster back in the UK, i.e. Sky.

Indian cricket had timed its arrival on the world television scene at the right moment. As Wildblood recalls:

There was kind of a perfect storm, and we took advantage of that perfect storm in 1993. This was the very early stages of sports-dedicated channels. Sky needed content because if you're going to broadcast sport twenty-four hours a day, the value is in live sport, and cricket was perfect. It takes a long time, and it's competitive, and interesting. In the early '90s satellite technology had developed to a point where you could with reasonable confidence get a signal back from anywhere in the world to anywhere else in the world. If you produced quality coverage in India and you had an appropriate uplink station—we used to take our own satellite uplink with us— you could then fire a signal up onto a satellite that could then be down-linked into the broadcasting nation. You had an ability to put together a quality of coverage that was acceptable to consumers in more advanced television countries. This was important because you couldn't just broadcast what was then available in India. It was of such poor quality. I had seen a picture of the 1987 World Cup final when Gatting played his reverse sweep; it looked like it was snowing in Kolkata. Viewers in the UK would not have put up with it. And in 1993 you had a market to sell it to, which was Sky which you didn't have in 1987.

However, the Indian board had one huge problem:

Doordarshan had up until that point taken the rights as if they were a birthright. On the basis that they were the national broadcaster. Dalmiya and Bindra alerted me to the Doordarshan problem, and I said precedents all over the world suggest that sports rights are owned by the governing bodies. The Indian Cricket Board wanted to make some money, which it had never done before. It wanted to establish itself as the owner of the rights rather than Doordarshan. That all played out in the Supreme Court of India. I can remember doing the Hero Cup in '93 when there were parallel coverages running. This was before the Supreme Court had reached its final conclusion in favour of BCCI, and Doordarshan were in the ground covering the match at the same time as we were. There were two television crews, two rigs producing in parallel because Doordarshan wouldn't concede, and nor would the BCCI. Once the Supreme Court ruled in favour of the BCCI, there was only one coverage, which was our coverage on behalf of the BCCI. That was what was then broadcast in India.

In 1996, Wildblood also organized cricket outside India:

I said to the Indian and Pakistan Boards, 'Look, you can't play each other at home in either of your countries. Perhaps you could get away with playing each other offshore where neither of you is the host.' We guaranteed each Board a million dollars net. Today that sounds like small potatoes. Then I went off to see the USA Cricket Association. But they're so fractionalised, they can't make a decision about anything. So, I went to see the Canadians, who were extremely helpful and obliging. Toronto was where the matches were held. The Sahara Cup ran from '96 to '99. The Sahara Cup was notable because Sourav Ganguly was often Man of the Series. He was head and shoulders above everybody else. He took very well to Canadian conditions. Things changed in 1999. It became clear that the Indian board were not going to send a team to play Pakistan. This was because the Kashmir problem had become very prominent again. The political difficulty was even greater than had previously been the case. We had to produce something, and we had India playing West Indies for three games and then Pakistan playing West Indies for three games. After that, the Sahara Cup stopped.

GOLD IN THE BOARDROOM

But while they could not play each other, the Indian and Pakistan cricket officials also formed a very effective alliance to ambush England. In a sense, India–Pakistan cricket relations had become a triangle: there were the cricketers on the field of play; the fans on either side, with Muslims in India often accused of being disloyal; and the administrators. At this stage the administrators got on very well, although that relationship has now changed, particularly after the start of the IPL and problems with what India sees as Pakistan-inspired terrorism. Roping in Sri Lanka in an Asian alliance, and cleverly offering more money to associate countries than England, they snatched the 1996 World Cup from England's grasp. However, Wildblood's IMG in turn were beaten for the television rights to the World Cup by a man who was then virtually unknown, Mark Mascarenhas, a native of Bengaluru who had settled in the US. Looking back in 2018 to what happened to him, Wildblood says:

> Mark was a ballsy guy who was a one-man band and bet the farm on the 1996 World Cup television deal. He was a punter basically. He went and took a risk. If it had gone wrong with me, all that would have happened was that I probably would have been fired, but with him, he would have lost everything he had.

Mascarenhas guaranteed the Pakistan–India–Sri Lanka Organising Committee (PILCOM) $14 million. This was unheard-of money for cricket then, and many in the television industry in the UK predicted that Mascarenhas would indeed lose the farm. But he made money selling the rights worldwide for sums that back in the early 1990s no broadcaster had so far paid for televising cricket. Wildblood says, 'I have a great admiration for Mark. He tried to get me to go and work for him once, but I chose not to.'

However, Mascarenhas hired Gary Francis, the head of IMG's cricket production company, the technical production expert:

> Mark would obviously not have been able to produce the coverage, but he knew a man who could. He just went to Gary, who was our key guy, made him an offer he couldn't refuse, and because the nature of television production is basically freelance, he would have ended up with pretty much the same crew of people as we would have used. Gary was very determined to do the World Cup in Pakistan, India and Sri Lanka.

The event was heavily sponsored and earned more money than any previous World Cup, although one of the sponsors, as Wildblood points out, lost out to its great rival:

> Coke became the official soft drink provider for the ICC Cricket World Cup of 1996, and Pepsi lost out on that process. There are only two countries in the world, one of which is India, where Pepsi are dominant over Coke. Pepsi were defending their turf. They very cleverly came up with a campaign the strapline of which was 'Nothing official about it'. They positioned that towards their target market, which was the youth. Youth don't like official, they like unofficial, and Pepsi played on that very cleverly and completely destroyed Coke's positioning as the official drink.

In Pakistan, says Wildblood 'they had an official horse-worming tablet, something you use to deworm horses'.

Interestingly, the one Indian cricketer who did not have a bat sponsor was Tendulkar. The others carried the Four Square cigarettes logo, but Tendulkar had promised his father he would never promote liquor or tobacco. Tendulkar could afford to be moral. That year Mascarenhas, who had met Tendulkar in 1995 and become his agent, offered him a five-year management contract worth ₹25 crore, making him the first Indian cricketer to be a crorepati.

Dalmiya, now secretary of the Indian board, was the convenor of PILCOM and formed a very effective partnership with Bindra, who was the president. Just before the start of the World Cup Dalmiya also got the idea that he should stand for the presidency of the ICC, the idea came to him after Anna Puchi Hewa, president of Sri Lankan cricket, suggested to him that it was time an Asian finally took over the chair of the organization running international cricket.

ASHES ON THE FIELD OF PLAY

But while the World Cup brought gold to the Indian board on the field of play, Indian cricketers failed to win the Cup. Yet everything suggested that this time Azharuddin would emulate Kapil Dev. India got to the semi-final after beating Pakistan. There they faced Sri Lanka. India had met them in the group match and lost. In the World Cup, Sri Lankans had revolutionized the batting strategy for one-day cricket. Then in one-day cricket the batting side began slowly, making sure they did not lose too many wickets so that they could hit out in the middle and closing overs. But borrowing a term from baseball, the Sri Lankans opened their batting with a 'pinch-hitter', whose task was to strike out from the first ball. In the team meeting before the semi-final match India decided to put Sri Lanka in if they won the toss. Sri Lanka batting first made 251 for 8. India seemed on course to win at 98 for 1 with Tendulkar and Manjrekar having a 90-run partnership, but then India lost seven wickets while scoring 22 runs. Much was made of the India misreading the pitch and there were accusations of match-fixing, but Manjrekar in his 2017 book, *Imperfect,* which devotes a chapter to the World Cup, dismisses them and has provided the best picture of what went on behind the scenes in the Indian dressing room. This included Wadekar, the Indian coach, tearing into his players after they had won a match for behaving as if they had won the World Cup. The seeds of the defeat against Sri Lanka may have been sown after the victory against Pakistan because the Indian players reacted as if they had already won the Cup. Manjrekar argues that the pitch in the semi-final did not change when India batted, and in any case, unlike in Tests, the nature of a pitch has little bearing on a one-day match. The pitch, he points out, looked fine when he and Tendulkar were batting.

The Indian dressing room after the match was a picture of desolation. Kambli, who was not out, cried, the only Indian player to do so. It upset Jadeja. But, says Manjrekar, Kambli's tears were due to the shameful end of the match. There was a violent reaction by the Kolkata crowd to the Indian collapse and the match could not be completed. The match referee, Clive Lloyd, declared Sri Lanka winners. Manjrekar, who had both been showered with praise for his batting and then twenty-four hours later abused by the same Kolkata fans, writes, 'I consider Bengali food one of the best cuisines in the world. I love Kolkata, the city. I just wish the cricket fans there had a better understanding of the game than just following it passionately.' Sri Lanka went on to win the final.

But while Azharuddin, like Kapil Dev, may have lost a World Cup semi-final at home, he did not suffer the same fate as Kapil Dev. Although there were many calling for Tendulkar to take over, Azharuddin followed in the footsteps of Wadekar and captained a second tour to England in the first half of the summer of 1996. Azharuddin needed some new faces, yet as the team left for England it looked unlikely that there were any promising surprises left in the Indian locker. But there were, and one of them was a man from Dalmiya's city and one he knew well.

Chapter 28

NEW INDIAN FACES AT LORD'S

22 June 1996 was a day all of England was glued to the television. It was a Saturday, the third day of the Lord's Test, always the high point of an English cricket summer. Yet the interest of the nation was not focused at Lord's, where England were playing India in the second of the three Test series, but at Wembley where England faced Spain in the quarter-final of the UEFA Euro 1996. The country that invented the sport has only ever won the World Cup once, when the competition was held at home in 1966. It has never again even been in the final. In 1996 the hope was that, with England again the hosts, they would repeat the feat of 1966 and win the Euros, the second most important world tournament. But English fans knew Spain was tough and would not be easy to beat.

Four hours before England's footballers took the field at Wembley their cricketers had walked out at Lord's as India resumed their first innings at 83 for 2 in reply to England's 344. Tendulkar was still 16 not out and England's view was that if they could get Tendulkar out early the rest of the Indian batting would provide no resistance. The morning began with a piece of luck for India. Tendulkar was dropped by Graeme Hick off the bowling of Chris Lewis. Recalling the match in the summer of 2018 Lewis told me:

> I thought that was pretty much our chance gone. He is going to score a hundred. Right throughout my career when you played India you had to get Tendulkar out because nobody else could hold us up. Sachin was the prize wicket. Now I felt that hope had gone. But I was physically fit, in my prime, I would later have a hip problem. I bowled fast and took a great deal of pride in hitting the stumps of the batsmen. So, despite being disappointed by the Hick drop, I ran in fast.

Tendulkar, who emulated Gavaskar by never scoring a Test century at Lord's, had always had problems with the Lord's slope. He could not work out the effect of the slope that runs across the ground. On this occasion with Lewis bowling from the Pavilion End and aware that Lewis bowled in-swingers, Tendulkar felt the ball would come into him even more. So, he decided to play inside the line. The ball pitched just short of length and forced

Tendulkar on the back foot, but instead of coming in, it went the other way, missed his bat and hit the off stump. The ball that Lewis bowled was widely judged to be the ball of the match. Tendulkar had made 31, India were 123 for 3. The crowd at Lord's relaxed and felt that come 3 p.m. England would be in such command of the match that they could forget all about cricket and turn their attention to the much more important match at Wembley.

THE UNLIKELY INDIAN SAVIOUR

But what neither anyone in the England team nor in the crowd had taken note of was the batsman at the other end. He was a total unknown as far as England was concerned and not much known in India. His name was Sourav Ganguly, a twenty-two-year-old left-hander from Kolkata, only the second Bengali after Roy to play in a Lord's Test. The previous evening he had come out to bat for the first time in a Test match and by the close had made 26 not out.

Ironically, on a day that England concentrated on its football team, Ganguly had grown up in Kolkata more interested in football than cricket. His older brother, Snehasish, was the cricketer, Snehasish would go on to play for Bengal making six first-class centuries and Sourav looked up to him. Snehasish was known as Raja, a common nickname for a well-off young Bengali boy. Sourav's pet name was Maharaja. Sourav was thirteen when, pushed by his sports-mad father, he took to cricket. Four years later at the age of eighteen he had been selected for the Indian tour of Australia, having scored just one first-class century. The tour proved a flop and Ganguly returned feeling he would be branded a one-tour wonder, like Bengali cricketers before him. He had hardly played at all in Australia and worse still had come back with a reputation that made him seem even more of an outcaste. Brought up in a well-off Bengali Brahmin family, the story told was that when he was asked as twelfth man to carry out drinks he retorted that such duties were for servants not a high-caste Brahmin like him. Ganguly disputes this story and says that incident in Sydney took place because he had got too engrossed watching the television and did not realize that a wicket had fallen. In any case in Australia he found himself in a side with well-established batsmen and could not break through. The tour gives a fascinating insight into Indian cricket in the last decade of the twentieth century. The team flew economy class in Air India. Ganguly was roomed with Dilip Vengsarkar and he was so in awe of him, he hardly said a word. In any case Vengsarkar spent most of his time speaking in Marathi to Chandrakant Pandit. Ganguly took shelter in Tendulkar's room. His roommate was a fellow Bengali, Subroto Banerjee, and Ganguly spent his time speaking to him in Bengali.

Ganguly was so little known in England that the brochure produced for the Lord's match had misspelled his name and in any case his name provoked mirth among the English for it was very similar to a funny rhyme sung by English boy and girl scouts that went 'ging gang gooly, gooly watcha.' The English team knew nothing about Ganguly. As Lewis recalls, 'I knew several of the Indian players and had played against them, but I had not heard of Ganguly. I had never come across him. Nor had anybody else in our team.' Even in India Ganguly's selection was widely seen as further proof of that well-known Indian 'pull', influence in high quarters, without which you cannot get anywhere. Sambaran Banerjee, the selector from the East, had been Ganguly's captain when he made his first-class debut in 1989–90. But the feeling was the greatest 'pull' came from Dalmiya, the classic case of the administrator from Bengal helping the cricketer from Bengal. That a player from Bengal would be picked for the tour was not a surprise. In the quota system of selection that has always applied in India, there had to be a cricketer from the east zone. But if form was the criterion, then in the 1995–96 domestic Indian season, which had concluded just before the team left for England, two Bengal players had made the batting averages based on players who had made 500 runs. They were Saba Karim and Devang Gandhi. Ganguly failed to make the list. His selection was such a surprise that when Arun Lal, now living in Kolkata, suggested before the team was announced that Ganguly deserved to be selected, his fellow panellists hooted with laughter.

Ganguly had, before the Lord's Test, played in the third one-day international at Old Trafford, scoring 46. But while this improved India's batting, India managing to get past 200, they were still beaten and the whole match was overshadowed by what had happened on the morning of the match, just after the toss and before the first ball was bowled. This involved Ganguly's roommate on the tour, Navjot Singh Sidhu. Sidhu had come on the tour as a senior, established batsman of the team.

In the first two one-day internationals Sidhu had made 3 and 20. Azharuddin and Sandeep Patil, the cricket manager, decided the Punjab batsman should be dropped. But neither spoke to him. However, as the team sheet fixed on to the notice board in the dressing room did not carry Sidhu's name, his teammates knew he was dropped. Sidhu settled down in the Old Trafford dressing room, having not read the team sheet, and never thinking for a moment he might get the chop. His only concern was whether the Indian skipper would win the toss and bat. If he did then he would pad up as he would be batting No. 3. Sidhu along with the rest of the Indian team watched Azharuddin go out to toss with Michael Atherton. Azharuddin won the toss and Sidhu began to prepare to bat. This provoked laughter from a few of his teammates and one or two even uttered the familiar taunt of 'Sardar ka bara baj gaya' [It is gone twelve o'clock]. Sidhu, senior to many of the players in that dressing room, felt humiliated. He decided he would not take it lying down and that if he was so little regarded in the team he could no longer be part of it. Sidhu hinted he might play under another captain and the board banned him from international cricket until 14 October and confiscated half his tour fee.

When news of this story emerged, I was very intrigued. I found out where the Indian team were staying and rang their hotel and asked to be put through to Sidhu. The phone was answered not by Sidhu but by Ganguly who identified himself as Sidhu's roommate but very politely refused to say anything. I certainly had no reason to think he was in anyway arrogant and I must say that in the years since I have got to know him he has always addressed me as Mihirda. Ganguly had developed quite a bond with the Sikh, a relationship strengthened as a result of a very scary moment while travelling on the London tube. A few young Brits started making gestures at the pair and then threw a beer can at Sidhu who confronted them. The situation got so ugly, there was a fight which only stopped when the train reached the next station and the English hooligans got off. However, one of them then came back and started waving a gun at Sidhu. Ganguly dropped to the ground, covered his face, pleaded with the boys and managed to drag Sidhu away, avoiding confrontation. An English cricketer, having such an experience in India, might have made much of it but Ganguly and Sidhu did not.

I soon learnt what had happened in the Old Trafford dressing room from a very good source who had excellent contacts inside the Indian dressing room. I wrote about it in my column 'Inside Sport' in the London *Daily Telegraph*. It appeared just as the Indians were due to play Leicestershire in a county game. Azharuddin knew he was under pressure. Sidhu's decision to quit had prompted the burning of effigies of Azharuddin in India and he had to respond to my article. He turned to Naynesh Desai, a lawyer who would soon have a more prominent role to play in Indian cricket, to draft a statement denying my story which he read out at a press conference at Grace Road where India were playing Leicestershire. Both Azharuddin and Patil insisted that they had informed Sidhu the night before the one-day international and had also told him he was dropped because of his poor running, Sidhu having been run out in the previous international.

But, although Ganguly had taken Sidhu's place in the Old Trafford international, he was not chosen for the first Test which followed the internationals. This, given India went in with four debutants, was a surprise. Only one of the debutants, Venkatesh Prasad, justified his selection and Sidhu's absence was clearly felt when on a sporting wicket at Edgbaston, India were bowled out on the first day for 214 with Javagal Srinath, batting No. 9 and coming in at 127 for 7, the highest scorer with 52. There was another batting collapse in the Indian second innings. Tendulkar who made 122 out of India's second innings score of 219—no other Indian batsman made more than 18—ensured the match went into the fourth day but could not prevent a defeat by eight wickets. Boycott acidly commented that Tendulkar should bat at No. 1, 2, 3, 4, 5 and 6.

Before the next Test at Lord's India played a match against Derbyshire and, although India were humiliated, losing by ten wickets, in the second innings Ganguly made 64; no other Indian batsman made more than 29. And this after Tendulkar, not playing himself, had worried Ganguly by saying that Devon Malcolm, Derbyshire's ferocious fast bowler, was being vetted by the England selectors which implied he would go flat out.

Azharuddin and Patil clearly decided that there was little harm in giving Ganguly his debut. So, there was Ganguly on that Saturday morning in the Lord's Test with India's cricketing god out and everyone thinking he stood no chance. Let Lewis take up the story:

> Bowling to Ganguly I did not really get close to getting him out. I remember I dropped one short to Ganguly and it disappeared over mid-wicket. He played me quite easily. Alan Mullally a left-hander asked a few more questions. But we did not trouble him.

THE RESERVE WICKETKEEPER BECOMES A BATTING STAR

But while Ganguly effortlessly drove the English bowlers through the off side, his problem was he kept losing partners. With the score on 202 Azharuddin was out and in walked the second debutant, Rahul Dravid. While the English did not know Ganguly, and many Indians felt he should not be there, Dravid had been knocking at the gates of Indian cricket for some time and the English, and Lewis in particular, knew all about him. On the England tour of India in 1992–93 Dravid had played for the India Under-25 XI against England at Cuttack. Lewis had reason to remember him as he had bowled Dravid out for 15.

There was an interesting contrast in the upbringing of Dravid and Ganguly. Ganguly was very much a product of Kolkata and Bengali society. Dravid represented how Indians since independence were also becoming

cosmopolitan. He was a Maharashtrian Brahmin born in Indore, but grew up
in Bengaluru where his father was a food scientist at Kissan, famous for its
jams, which gave Dravid the nickname 'Jammy'. Growing up in Bengaluru
meant he was in an outpost of cricket. At school he played more hockey
and badminton than cricket, and the cricket he played was on matting
wickets, the only turf wicket being at the M. Chinnaswamy Stadium. When
he met young cricketers from Mumbai he was made aware, as he puts
it, that he 'was simply a big fish in a small pond called Bengaluru'. But
from an early age he showed an appetite for making big scores and had
a father who was very interested in cricket. He was born the day before
India started playing England in Chennai in a Test, and the story goes
his father kept his mother, an artist, informed about the score. His father
also took him to Test matches at Bengaluru where Dravid saw his hero
Gavaskar score a hundred. Later, on a visit to London, Dravid's father had
a picture of him taken in front of Lord's which he then gave to his son.
Dravid had played for the Under-15 and Under-19 teams, displaying both
persistence and patience in waiting for his call. In both the 1994–95 and
1995–96 season he made runs in domestic cricket which were remarkable.
He impressed Sandeep Patil, who thought Dravid showed maturity. He
always knew his mind and Gundappa Viswanath was sure he would be
part of the national team.

Yet, he was not chosen for the 1996 World Cup and his choice for
the England tour seemed an afterthought. It seemed that like Ganguly he
was, as a previous generation of Indian cricketers had put it, expected to
be part of the sight-screen team, players who had to wait patiently at the
boundary edge, hoping to play. He had come as a reserve batsman who
could also be useful as a wicketkeeper batsman, important as India had
only one regular wicketkeeper, Nayan Mongia, on the tour. Dravid had
little reason to believe he would get many chances except when Mongia
needed a rest and had played as a wicketkeeper in the second and third
matches of the tour, against Gloucestershire and Sussex, while batting No. 7.

Dravid had only been told ten minutes before the toss for the Lord's
Test that he was playing as Manjrekar, injured in the first Test, had not
recovered. Venkatesh Prasad, now a one-Test veteran and a colleague from
Karnataka, wished him luck and Dravid, pointing to the boards in the dressing
room that record a century by a batsman or five wickets by a bowler, said,
'You put your name on the bowlers' board and I will put my name on
the batsmen's board.' Now, as he went out to bat Tendulkar advised him,
'It's all right to be nervous. Even I was nervous when I started. Just stay
there for 15 minutes and things will improve'. Dravid would later recall

that as he walked down the famous Lord's steps he felt a tingle in his spine. Dravid's nerves were calmed by the fact that although he and Ganguly had made their way into the Test team in different ways they were part of the same Tendulkar generation of cricketers. Both he and Ganguly, who was six months older, knew each other and had batted together, having played in the same team from their Under-19 days. For Dravid to see Ganguly batting so elegantly but also showing a steely determination which made the English bowling look easy was an extra bonus.

Ganguly continued to reassure Dravid, getting to his century with a cover drive which was also his seventeenth boundary. But while the small group of Indian supporters applauded, the great mass of people at Lord's who were English was by then glued to England playing Spain at Wembley. As I walked around Lord's that afternoon I could see that most of the television sets were showing football. The match with Spain went to penalties and as England, who often lost such penalty shoot-outs, won, such was the cheering by the Lord's crowd that the cricket was halted. But Ganguly, and increasingly Dravid who had begun cautiously, refused to be unnerved and began to master the English bowling, putting on 94 before Ganguly was eventually out for 131, having batted for seven hours and hit 20 fours. Dravid ended the day 56 not out. On the fourth day with only the tail to support him he went on to 95 and then did something hardly anyone does in modern cricket. When the English appealed for a catch he walked even before the umpire raised his finger and said afterwards that everybody at the ground had heard the nick. That response in his very first innings established the distinctive character of Dravid and one which would always mark his career. Ganguly and Dravid had ensured India got a lead and held out hope that they might even win. But with England's tail proving obdurate in the second innings the Test ended in a draw.

India needed to win at Trent Bridge and, batting first, Tendulkar scored his second century of the series, Ganguly again scored a hundred. Four other batsmen: Alvin Kallicharran, Lawrence Rowe, Yasir Hameed and Rohit Sharma are also in this exclusive club. Dravid looked like he would score a century in India's first innings but was out for 84 as India made 521. When England batted, Indians rued Dravid's failure to hold on to a catch Atherton, who had not yet scored, offered off Srinath. Srinath and Prasad had one of those days when they kept going past Atherton's bat but he did not get an edge and made 160. Atherton admits that he was woefully out of form and that his innings 'was damned ugly to watch'. Kumble congratulated him but could not help adding, 'That's the worst hundred I have seen.' However, Atherton could not help jab back saying, 'Yeah, but at

least it keeps coming off the middle of the bat when you're bowling.' As
he puts it, 'It was a terrible hundred but Kumble only ever spun the ball
on a dustbowl and he did provide some light relief from India's opening
bowlers, Javagal Srinath and Venkatesh Prasad.' Atherton was being a little
harsh. Kumble had played for Northants the previous season and been a
great success, taking 105 first-class wickets for an average of just over 20,
the first to reach a hundred wickets since 1991 and voted Player of the
Year by Northants. On the tour he had failed, in the three Test series he
had five wickets for 334 runs. Atherton's innings meant India could not
make up for the defeat at Edgbaston losing the series 1–0.

India could look to Prasad, who proved himself the opening bowling
partner for Srinath that India had long been seeking. The pair was rated by
English critics as superior to the English bowlers. They would have done
much better had Indians held their catches and the umpiring been better.

INDIA REMAIN THE BACKWATER OF CRICKET

However, this could not hide the other problems the tour revealed. Just
before the Lord's test I wrote in an article for *Outlook* that the tour showed
the short-sightedness of the board:

> The Indian Cricket Board is now one of the richest sports bodies
> in the world. The profits from the World Cup were staggering, yet
> India are touring England as if they are still poor country cousins. The
> team was initially housed in pokey, cheap hotels, often with no gym
> facilities. Indian cricketers had to beg and borrow training facilities
> from friends and sponsors. Hotel facilities have been improved but no
> self-respecting cricket team should be put through such an ordeal.

Then there was the question of how Azharuddin's girlfriend was handled.
He was, I observed, given:

> Special permission to come on tour and the entire tour—mind
> you, not for a couple weeks, which would have been fine—with
> his companion. She sits in front of the team coach alongside the
> captain, in the very front row. When an Indian cricket team is on
> tour, it represents the nation. It is not a holiday jaunt. It is on official
> business. Nothing can be more damaging for the moral and team
> spirit, particularly for a young team than to find that the front row of
> the coach is occupied by the captain's girlfriend.

Azharuddin, who had left his wife, would later marry the girlfriend,
Sangeeta Bijlani, but what upset many of his teammates was that she also

attended official receptions for the Indians. And Azharuddin being a devout Muslim did not drink and did not like the smell of drink. On coach trips he would not allow Tendulkar and others if they were drinking to sit near him.

India in 1996 was still a backwater of cricket. During the tour, with much of the British press concentrating on the Euros, the Indians hardly featured in the English press. And when the press turned up it was not because they were interested in the Indian team. I was made very aware of this when I drove down to Worcester for the traditional start of the tour. There were very few spectators there but the car park spaces for journalists were all taken. The Worcester car park attendant told me, 'We have 15 media places, but they've all gone. Never seen anything like this.' The English journalists were there not to see the Indians but because David Lloyd was being unveiled as the new England coach. My abiding memory is of the English journalists in the Worcester press box clustering around Ramaswami Mohan, then the cricket correspondent of *The Hindu*, asking him how to spell the name of Vikram Rathore. The next day most newspapers carefully pointed out his name was pronounced 'Rathod'.

But while for the English press India was not a cricketing power to take much note of, the cricket administrators of England had their hands full. Even as the Lord's Test was underway, India, led by Dalmiya, were trying to prove that England and Australia could no longer claim to run world cricket. The Lord's Test was then the traditional time for the ICC annual meeting. Dalmiya wanted to be ICC Chairman and he came to Lord's having prepared a well thought-out plan to make him chairman of the ICC.

INDIA WIN IN THE BOARDROOM

This boardroom Test match took place just as the one in the middle had finished in the committee rooms of the MCC. The ICC needed a new chairman to replace Sir Clyde Walcott. There had never been an election to decide who should head the ICC. It had always been decided by the old boys led by England and Australia. But Dalmiya, egged on by Sri Lanka and having the support of Pakistan, was determined to take over. The key to the vote were the associates but the Indians had to make sure they were actually present at Lord's. With their cricket bodies poorly funded, they did not have the money to make the trip to London and often had an Englishman represent them. The Indians knew these representatives often did what England wanted them to do even if the board they represented had a different view. In May 1996, the working committee of the Indian board meeting in Shimla decided that the board would pay for the travel, hotel and even the cost of their travel in London so that the officials of the associates were physically present for the ICC meeting. There would be a dinner for them. The Reserve Bank of India was asked for £30,000 in foreign exchange which was also meant to meet any legal expenses that might be incurred.

Opposing Dalmiya was Malcolm Gray from Australia and Krish Mackerdhuj of South Africa. Dalmiya won the first round, getting sixteen votes, the three Asian Test nations and thirteen associates. Gray had fifteen with England, Australia, New Zealand and the West Indies supporting him and Mackerdhuj had nine.

Walcott as a player had helped prevent India win its first ever Test against the West Indies in 1948. Now as chairman, keen to carry on, he decided to stop Dalmiya. He ruled that to be elected chairman a simple majority would not do, it had to be a two-thirds majority of the Test-playing countries: six of the nine. This led to a second round between Dalmiya and Gray, with Mackerdhuj dropping out. Before the vote was held Australia wooed South Africa and, given its historic ties with South Africa, albeit the old white South Africa, hoped they could persuade South Africa and Zimbabwe to switch to Gray. That would give Gray six of the nine Test playing countries and make him chairman. But to Australia's dismay South Africa refused. The two southern nations formed an interesting strategy, South Africa would abstain, Zimbabwe would support Dalmiya. In the second round Dalmiya comfortably beat Gray. But as he had only four Test-playing countries not six supporting him, Walcott ruled he had not won the chairmanship.

But did the ICC rules allow Walcott to make such a decision? Bindra, who I had got to know, approached me and asked me if I could put them in touch with a lawyer. I introduced him to Naynesh Desai, whom I had come to know well when he had acted for Devon Malcolm in a successful libel action the cricketer had brought against *Wisden Cricket Monthly*. He advised them and also arranged a meeting with Sir Michael Beloff, a noted Queen's Counsel (QC) who deals with sport, and the advice was unanimous: Walcott was not right. All you needed was a simple majority. But the old powers England and Australia refused to accept this and there developed a bitter power struggle, basically a brown versus white (with the black West Indians backing their former white masters) battle. The participants in this cricketing boardroom war would carry wounds that took years to heal. For the Asian countries, that despite Dalmiya twice winning the vote, England and Australia would not accept the result, it meant that the old colonial racial attitude towards browns still existed. England, Australia, New Zealand clearly felt the Asians were uppity. There was also a personal factor with regard to Dalmiya.

I had first met Dalmiya during the Kolkata Test in 1984 and he had come across as a man who was keen to advertise that he was different to other Indian cricket administrators. He told me firmly that while Test cricket may be declining elsewhere in India he would always sell out Eden Gardens. The Indian cricket officials the English were familiar with were of a certain kind. Like Raj Singh Dungarpur, a prince, or the Apte brothers who had played for India and had a flat opposite Lord's. Both Raj Singh and the Aptes were friendly with Raman Subba Row and other English cricket officials. For the English, Dalmiya a Marwari businessman was a strange kind of Indian. They had never met an Indian like Dalmiya. They could not pronounce his name, calling him Dalmaya, and were often flummoxed by Indians calling him by his nickname, Juggu. England and Australia were prepared to accept another Indian and made it clear that it would be a very different story if Bindra, a high-powered civil servant, stood for the ICC chairmanship. Bindra stayed loyal to Dalmiya, although they would later fall out. Asians had their eyes on the prize and had no intention of giving up. The issue was resolved with the chairmanship made rotational and a reorganization of the ICC. Dalmiya still had to fight to get a three-year term and he took over in June 1997, determined to change cricket.

At Lord's Dalmiya had unveiled one of his radical ideas, quite shocking the English: a tournament to celebrate fifty years of Indian independence but held in the month of May. In my youth such an idea would have been considered absurd. Dalmiya argued that with many grounds having lights this would mean matches starting at five o'clock in the evening. By then the temperatures would cool down and cricket would be very possible. With government help late night transport for the fans would be no problem. When he mentioned this to the English they dismissed him as a crank and a further reason to keep him away from the top job in cricket. But in this case Dalmiya was the innovator and today IPL matches played in May seem so natural that nobody considers them at all odd.

On the field the tour also marked a change for Indian cricket. Azharuddin was replaced by Tendulkar. This filled Indian cricket with great hope that the master batsman would prove the master captain. The tour also showed that Ganguly and Dravid were radical thinkers about the game. As Dravid told me, 'I remember on my first tour of England in 1996 the players discussing that we did not do too well away from home. It became a goal for some of us to start winning Test matches and series abroad. Over the years I have sensed this even more in the young guys. They were a bit sick and tired that we lost a lot when playing abroad. So, you'd see guys preparing specifically for those tours, recognizing the skills required to do well abroad and setting out to achieve it.'

It would take time but the performance by these two at Lord's may be said to mark the starting point of how this generation of Indian cricketers was thinking. While these two cricketers would never have dreamt of questioning Tendulkar's status as the greatest cricketer of India, they were not just chelas, pupils, following a master, but people who reflected on the game, bringing radical new thinking and they would play an important role in fashioning the cricketing India which emerged as the twenty-first century dawned, bringing with it a new and very different wave.

Chapter 29

THE PERILS OF CAPTAINCY

THE TENDULKAR INNOVATIONS

Tendulkar had two stints as captain, with Azharuddin coming back for a brief period, and by the time he finally stepped down in 2000, never to return, Tendulkar in twenty-five Tests as captain had won four, lost nine and drawn twelve. In ODIs he had captained in seventy-three matches, he had won twenty-three, lost forty-three, tied one with no result in six. This was very much in the second division of Indian captaincy records, far less than anything Ganguly, Azharuddin, Dravid, Dhoni or Kohli would achieve. This was also the period when allegations of match-fixing emerged, with one Test when Tendulkar was captain coming under the spotlight. Although he was questioned by the K. Madhavan enquiry, there was never any suggestion that he was involved in match-fixing.

All this was way in the future when Tendulkar went out to toss for the first time as captain on 10 October 1996 at Feroz Shah Kotla against Australia. Even as a player Tendulkar had disliked the short Test series which he felt were so unsatisfactory that, as he put it, 'You blink four times and a two-Test series is over.' This time Australia were only playing just one Test in India but the fact that Australia were happy to fly all the way for a solitary Test showed how world cricket relations were changing. Australia wanted to cultivate this new economic power. India saw Australia as a powerful cricketing country with whom they could develop a relationship to correct the traditional English-centric nature of the sport. Kotla also marked the inauguration of the Border–Gavaskar Trophy.

Kotla provided a wicket made for spin, ideal conditions for Kumble to put his English nightmare behind him. The Australians also did not know Kumble and he introduced himself to them by taking nine wickets in the match. With Mongia, who had opened in England, carrying on in his new role and making 152, India's winning margin was seven wickets.

The Australian visit was followed by the Titan Cup one-day tournament between India, Australia and South Africa. India beat both teams on their way to the final, where they met South Africa. The final had special significance for Tendulkar being in Mumbai as this would be the first time his home crowd would see him captain India. However, with India scoring only 220, and Tendulkar making 67, the match looked lost. This is when Tendulkar came up with a strategy of which he felt very proud. Robin Singh, the all-rounder, was being used as the fifth bowler and Tendulkar decided to make radical changes to the field Singh had set. Although medium-pacers in an ODI match generally do not bowl to a field where they have only four fielders on the off side, that is what he got Singh to do. So, no deep point but a third man, short-point, cover and long-off. Singh was told he must bowl stump to stump and never bowl outside the off stump. Tendulkar felt the South Africans would be caught unprepared and their run scoring would be restricted. He was proved right. India won by 35 runs.

Tendulkar was even more pleased with his captaincy in the three-Test series with South Africa that followed. In a low-scoring first Test at Ahmedabad, South Africa were left only 170 to get in just under two days. India had three spinners, Kumble and Hirwani providing leg-spin, and Sunil Joshi left-arm spin. Aware the South Africans would expect the ball to be tossed to the spinners, he decided to use Srinath, confident that even on a wearing pitch he could reverse swing the ball and make life difficult. At the other end he had Joshi, who was asked to bowl in the rough and prevent the South Africans scoring. The strategy worked like a treat. South Africa were bowled out for 105 in thirty-nine overs. To Tendulkar's delight Cronje confessed the South Africans had not anticipated this and Tendulkar sees it as the high point of his captaincy.

The other innovation Tendulkar claims credit for is that he moved Ganguly, who had made such an impact in England batting at No. 3, to No. 5 and Dravid to No. 3. In fact during this series Ganguly often batted No. 3 and Dravid at various positions, opening, No. 3 and also at No. 5 and No. 7. But in essence Tendulkar did initiate a change which became part of Indian cricket and served it well. The Indians lost the second Test in Kolkata badly but with Azharuddin scoring a magnificent 163 in Kanpur in the third Test, India won by 280 runs and the series 2–1.

SOUTH AFRICAN BLUES

The Indians followed Cronje and his band back to South Africa for a series of back-to-back Tests and one-day internationals. With Bob Woolmer, the South African cricket manager, determined to teach the Indians a lesson the South Africans repaid the Indians for their spinning wickets with seaming ones. It might have helped had the Indians played some practice matches, but they were immediately pitched into an almost unplayable seamers' wicket in the first Test at Durban. In Allan Donald, the South Africans had a bowler who was, probably, the fastest bowler in the world, and Donald's partner, Shaun Pollock, while not quite as fast as Donald, was able to swing the ball both ways. Donald took nine wickets in the match. India made a total of 166 runs: a first innings hundred, followed by a second innings 66 and batted for just seventy-three overs and two balls. The only consolation for the Indians was that Srinath and Prasad's bowling showed India was no longer the land that could only produce spinners. The pair took fifteen wickets between them, Prasad taking five-fers in both innings and South Africa made 235 and 259. Had Indian batting been anywhere near even average Test standard, Tendulkar's first overseas Test as captain might have been a contest.

India also lost the second Test in Cape Town but in a losing cause Indian batting sparkled. It came when India were 58 for 5, in reply to South Africa's 529 for 7 declared. Tendulkar and Azharuddin, in a mere forty overs, put on 222 runs. The crowd at Newlands had seen nothing like this. Azharuddin's 115 came from 110 balls and he fell not to a South African bowler but was run out. Tendulkar scored 169, his highest Test score against South Africa. A change in Tendulkar's technique was key to this. In order to cope with Donald's pace, Tendulkar decided that he would shuffle back and across. He normally stood just outside the leg stump, now he stood a good few inches outside to give him room to shuffle. What is also interesting is he worked out this change while practising against throw-ins on the morning of the day's play. It showed both the astuteness of his thinking and the speed with which he could adapt to changing conditions.

There was a moment of humour in the battle with Donald which also showed the complexity of Indian society. Tendulkar for a time batted with Dodda Ganesh, a medium-fast bowler. For Donald, the duel with Tendulkar was what he expected, but for Ganesh to hold him up irritated him immensely and he started foul-mouthing him. At the end of one over when Ganesh had played and missed several times, Donald confronted him and told him off in no uncertain terms. Ganesh did not react. An angry Donald strode back to the umpire to take his cap and Tendulkar, standing at the non-striker's end, decided to intervene. He told Donald that Ganesh only knew Kannada, that Tendulkar, himself, could not converse with Ganesh, perhaps Donald should speak to Ganesh in Kannada. This should have echoed with Donald as South Africa is as much a mosaic of various cultures and languages as India, but it did not and he just stalked out. South Africa did not enforce the follow-on but then defeat was inevitable, a loss by 282 runs.

But it said something of the new spirit then emerging that unlike previous Indian teams this one did not just lie down and accept defeat. In the third Test in Johannesburg, Dravid, batting No. 3, finally made a hundred in the series, 148 in an Indian score of 410; he also made 81 in the second innings. With Srinath taking 5 for 104 India led by 89 and could set South Africa a fourth innings score that was challenging: 356. On the fifth day South Africa had lost five wickets for 76 but then weather, a thunderstorm, bad light, combined with resistance from Lance Klusener and Daryll Cullinan denied India its first Test win in South Africa. At this stage, great as Tendulkar was as a batsman, as captain he was not very different to most Indian captains, able to win at home but not abroad.

NO CHAMPAGNE FOR TENDULKAR

All this should have changed on Monday, 31 March 1997. It should have been a red-letter day to match the deeds of Wadekar's team back in 1971. Instead it was a day of misery and one from which Tendulkar's captaincy never recovered. On that day at Bridgetown, Barbados, once the impregnable heart of West Indian cricket, India required a mere 120 to win. The night before, Tendulkar had been so confident of victory that when, over dinner, a West Indian waiter predicted a West Indian victory telling Tendulkar that Curtly Ambrose would bounce India out, Tendulkar told him that if Ambrose bowled a bouncer he would hook it so hard it would land in Antigua. Tendulkar reminded the waiter that in the first innings he had pulled a bouncer bowled by Franklyn Rose for six. Then gesturing towards the fridge, Tendulkar told the waiter to chill a bottle of champagne as he would return the next evening to celebrate the victory. Recall that in 1990, after getting a bottle of champagne at Old Trafford, he did not know what to do with it. Now he looked forward to drinking it. But the next day this proved to be empty dinner-table banter. Tendulkar was out for 4, caught in two minds, and the other Indian batsmen failed to live up to their boasts. In a Test series where in no completed innings had the Indians failed to pass 300, and where they had made 319 in the first innings, they now made only 81, losing by 38 runs. The defeat shattered Tendulkar. He confessed 'I can't believe it' and wondered when India might get another such chance. He locked himself in his room for two days and says in his autobiography, written in 2014, 'I still feel the pangs of that defeat when I look back at the series.' Madan Lal, the victor over the West Indies at Lord's in 1983, and now cricket manager was left speechless.

    In Tendulkar's defence, it must be said he was not helped by the Indian selectors. Before the tour began, Srinath withdrew because of a shoulder injury. Tendulkar, who by now had to put up with selectors not giving him the tools he needed, wanted three quality bowlers but only had two. Then there was the umpiring in the Barbados Test. The Indians had come in to this third Test in good heart having secured draws in the first two. The dreadful umpiring came in the first innings. India were 212 for 2 and Tendulkar on 92. India seemed on course for a huge score and a big lead. Just then, facing Ian Bishop, Tendulkar was given caught off a no-ball and a very clear no-ball that the umpire Lloyd Barker did not see. Barker was later replaced by a stand-in umpire and Tendulkar was told he had been taken to hospital with a serious headache because he could not focus. India did go on to make 319, but this was only a slender lead and not the one India might have got had Tendulkar not been wrongly given out. India also displayed their old failing of not being good finishers by allowing the West Indians, who had been reduced to 107 for 9, to make 140. True, the wicket still had some pace, but even then, 120 should have been within reach.

We can only speculate what might have happened had India won. It is not unreasonable to say that the Tendulkar captaincy story would have had a different, happier ending. As if the Barbados failure were not enough there were some quite bewildering losses in one-day matches from what seemed sure winning positions. In St. Vincent, victory seemed in sight, India requiring 250 were 201 for 3. But they added only another 30 and lost by 18 runs. After the match Tendulkar would for the first time berate his colleagues, telling them that to lose a match not because the opposition played well but the Indians themselves did not perform suggested there was something seriously wrong. He had, though, no solutions and this depressed him. On his return to India he told his wife he felt he could not do anything to get it right and even contemplated walking away from cricket. The St. Vincent collapse would have another, very far-reaching effect. For it was after this match that rumours of match-fixing began to circulate, of which more later.

August 1997 brought another foreign tour, to Sri Lanka. Both Tests were drawn, Tendulkar was among the runs, but Sri Lankan batsmen treated Indian bowlers with such contempt that they set up records that lasted decades. Take the first Test. India made what seemed a winning score: 537 for 8 declared. Sri Lanka came back with 952 for 6 declared. Sanath Jayasuriya, 340, Roshan Mahanama, 225. This second wicket having come together on the third day, batted the whole of the third and fourth.

Their partnership of 576 was the highest for any wicket in Tests and only just short of what was then Vijay Hazare and Gul Mohammad's all-time first-class record. The two Sri Lankans still have the first-class record for the second wicket although a decade later the Test record for any wicket was broken by their fellow Sri Lankans, Kumar Sangakkara and Mahela Jayawardene. India drew the match but lost the one-day matches.

TENDULKAR AT HOME, THE EXPECTANT FATHER

It was shortly after this that I interviewed Tendulkar in Mumbai. The editor of the British magazine who had sent me back to my hometown had been impressed by the stories he had heard about Tendulkar. How, when he celebrated his eighteenth birthday, the *Times of India* had relegated an Indian political crisis to an inside page while Tendulkar cutting his birthday cake was on the front page. Or how at the age of seventeen he had had to give up thoughts of getting a degree because he kept getting mobbed by his classmates: 'I could not move around at all.' It was now six years since I had interviewed Tendulkar when he had come to play for Yorkshire and I was keen to know what this demigod was like at home.

Yet when I met him in Mumbai at his father-in-law's home, the only sign that there was anything unusual about Tendulkar was the house where we met: a sprawling nineteenth-century colonial home set in a sea of Manhattan-style skyscrapers and looking like a relic of the vanished past of a city that had for centuries borne the Portuguese given name of Bombay as opposed to the more recent Maharashtrian name of Mumbai.

Inside, as the old retainer led the way to Tendulkar, the scene could not have been more typical of everyday Indian domesticity; Indian rugs on the floors, Indian pictures on the wall and in the corner a Singer sewing machine. Tendulkar was sitting on the wicker chair looking like almost any plumpish twenty-four-year-old young Mumbaikar, albeit with more tousled, curly hair than most, and an earring in one ear, a man's bracelet on his wrist and opposite him his wife, who was then expecting their first child. This picture of domesticity was completed by the presence of his father-in-law and, on a small table, a pot of tea kept warm with its tea cosy.

The shuttered windows kept out much of the strong afternoon light but not the noise that is so much part of Indian street life: the honking of the cars, the cries of the hawkers, the odd completely unintelligible shout and the occasional sound of hammering as yet another skyscraper went up. As I tried to balance my tape recorder with the cup of tea that Tendulkar's wife had poured, Tendulkar with almost paternal concern said, 'You can actually finish the tea before we start.'

Demigods are not expected to behave like that, but then, as Tendulkar explained to me, 'At home I am Sachin Tendulkar, not Sachin Tendulkar, the cricketer. That is where my family really help; far from my head being in the clouds, they don't allow my feet to leave the ground.' Thus, for all his fame and fortune, an income of $5 million a year which made him the highest-paid cricketer in the world, he told me, 'Circumstances at home haven't changed.'

Tendulkar could point to the fact that he still lived in the home he had grown up in and learnt his cricket in, a rather dingy collection of nine buildings in Bandra, except now Tendulkar lived in his own flat above his parents and was still able to see the trees whose trunks formed his first wicket as he learnt to play the game.

The trees, he explained, had shaped how he played:

In our colony, the moment the ball touched the tree you were not out, even if somebody took a catch after the ball had hit the tree. That is the reason I developed the habit of hitting the ball in the air, I knew I would be not out if it touched the tree or even a leaf.

But he went on to say with just a hint of a sigh, 'Now it is a different ball game, there are no leaves to protect a ball I hit in the air.'

We were meeting when newspapers were full of bile directed at certain Indian cricketers, although not at Tendulkar himself. He said, 'It is a human tendency, if you win today and lose tomorrow people only remember you have lost. There are very few people who remember you have also won the game before. The expectations are very high.'

He also seemed to have worked out how to cope with what Gavaskar has called the pressure-cooker atmosphere that Indian cricketers face when they play at home.

Yes, I feel there is a lot of pressure; if you fail people are very disappointed. In India you get so many phone calls in the evening at home before the match asking you to bat better, then after the match there are calls asking: why did you get out early? Every time you take guard you are expected to get a hundred, maybe more than that.

Yet unlike superstars of many other countries, Tendulkar refused to blame the Indian supporters. Instead, in a very Indian way, he made it sound as if he was uniquely blessed to play for India:

Every time I go out to bat I keep telling myself that so many people are supporting me and wishing well for me it is very hard for me to fail every time. With their blessings and their good wishes, I am definitely going to be successful.

What was interesting was when talk turned to other cricketers. 'When I was about 11 or 12,' said Tendulkar, 'I really admired Vivian Richards and Gavaskar. Because I was always fond of hitting the ball hard, Vivian Richards played the same way and, of course, I admired Gavaskar's concentration and consistency.' And it was interesting how he responded when I asked whether he wanted to beat Brian Lara's Test record: 'I have never told anyone what I want to achieve.' As for Lara himself, all Tendulkar would say was:

> He must never have dreamt he was going to score 375 runs. You do not get up in the morning and say, 'Today I will score 375 runs.' It just happens, when all things come together: determination, form, the ball rolling for you, pitch and luck.

So, who are the world's batsmen he considers as rivals? Tendulkar's answer was:

> If I don't win matches and I score runs, what is the point of scoring runs? You want to score runs so that your country wins. If your country does not win and you score 100s or 50s, that does not have much value.

Such reticence about his batting rivals was in contrast to the bowlers. Then he was quite eloquent about several of them. His attitude to his batting rivals seemed to be: they do not concern me, I do my job, let them do theirs. His interest in bowlers was dictated by the fact that he knew they could make or break him.

I was aware that Tendulkar, for all his demigod status, had an Indianness that had surprised the English when he came to play for Yorkshire. He always called Gavaskar Sir, and he softly told me, 'That is my upbringing. I have always called him Sir, never called him Sunny. He is my senior, that would not be right.'

A similar picture of the properly brought-up Indian boy was evident as I finished and prepared to leave. His wife brought me a plate of local Mumbai delicacies, and as Tendulkar joined me in eating he once again became just another young man in Mumbai looking forward to becoming a father for the first time. Should he step outside onto the seafront, he would be mobbed. There, tucking into the titbits, he was just Sachin.

But despite the stoicism with which he had taken the press criticism, the tone of the press was going to get worse when the Sri Lankans returned to India in November 1997. All three Tests were drawn, with India unable to kill off the Sri Lankans when well placed in the first and third Tests. For all the calmness with which he had answered me, Tendulkar was under strain. This became evident—not to the public but his nearest and dearest—during the third Test at Mumbai. At the end of the first day's play when he was not out and should have rested, he was so restless that he asked a friend to accompany him first to the Shivaji Park temple, then to the Siddhi Vinayak temple and finally to have a milkshake outside Haji Ali, that famous Mumbai shrine to a revered Muslim pir. The following day Tendulkar made 148, but India dropped a crucial catch, there was drizzle and despite India getting seven Sri Lankan wickets in the second innings, it was yet another draw. There followed an unsatisfactory four-nation tournament in Sharjah, where Tendulkar's captaincy was criticized as India lost all three matches and failed to reach the final. This was followed by a home one-day series against Sri Lanka where India took the lead but lost the last match and drew the series. By the end of 1997 Tendulkar's record as captain was: seventeen Tests played, three victories, none of them abroad. Fifty-four one-day games captained of which seventeen were wins. The god was not working a cricketing miracle. Without any warning or even a call from the BCCI Tendulkar was sacked and replaced with Azharuddin. Tendulkar heard the news from the media.

Chapter 30

THE MIYA RETURNS

Azharuddin on his return struck gold immediately. A week after his appointment, he won a limited-overs tournament against Pakistan and Bangladesh in Dhaka. In the deciding final match in Dhaka, India, set 314, made 316 for 7 to win in splendid style. Tendulkar was miffed when he watched how the press treated Azharuddin in contrast to him. In the final Azharuddin had promoted Robin Singh to No. 3 and his 82 was crucial in the run chase. Yet Tendulkar had also promoted Singh, albeit to No. 4, against Pakistan in Sharjah months earlier when Singh had made a duck and India was beaten. Then the press had been on Tendulkar's back for promoting Singh; now they hailed Azharuddin's move.

TENDULKAR TAKES ON WARNE

Azharuddin's big Test was a home series against Australia. This series provided a classic cricketing duel of Tendulkar versus Shane Warne. During my interview with Tendulkar he had told me, 'He is the complete bowler. He is a genuine leg-spinner who can turn the ball, who can flight the ball, who can bowl a googly, flipper. He has proved it all over the world.'

Tendulkar spent hours studying Warne's bowling and concluded that what made the Australian special was the drift he managed to get. The only way to counter this was to have less of a side-on and more of an open stance and stand outside the leg stump. He should also not waltz out of the crease to meet Warne's deliveries but play from the crease and as late as possible. So, when Warne tried to take advantage of the rough outside the leg stump, Tendulkar was ideally suited to hit him through midwicket but also have options to pay him on the off side. A month before Australia arrived Tendulkar practised against the best leg-spinners Mumbai had, getting them to bowl on rough crater-like surfaces outside the leg stump. One of the leg-spinners was his Mumbai colleague Sairaj Bahutule, who had been one of the St. Xavier's High school bowlers reduced to tears when the fourteen-year-old Tendulkar had ravished the Xavier attack. Now, Tendulkar hoped that Bahutule would help him, not reduce Warne to tears, but diminish his potency so that he could not power Australia to victory.

This being a proper series rather than the 'wink and it is over', the Australians had a practice game. And as if to give a flavour of the old days, this Australian tour-opener against Mumbai was played at the old CCI ground. Tendulkar leading Mumbai had told his batsmen to attack Warne and not worry about getting out. Tendulkar hit Warne for a six in his first over and scored 204 not out, his first first-class double century. It had taken 192 balls. Just as crucially, Warne in sixteen overs conceded 111 runs. Mumbai won by ten wickets. Visiting teams did not normally lose such practice games, for the Australians to do so was sensational. Warne had not tried to bowl round the wicket into the rough outside the leg stump in the match although Tendulkar was convinced he would when the Test series started.

However, in the first innings of the first Test in Chennai, when India batted after winning the toss, Tendulkar made only four. With Australia getting a lead of 71 India had to bat well in the second to win. Venkataraghavan, who knew the Chennai wicket, felt India did not have enough time to win, but Tendulkar was confident India could still conquer. Before the Indian second innings began he did a mini-Churchillian speech, telling his fellow batsmen that they had to each try and score 75 runs. Sidhu fell just a little short, making 64, Tendulkar came in with the score at 115 for 2, India only 44 ahead, and began watchfully. But as soon as Warne bowled round the wicket Tendulkar attacked and provided as rich a feast as anything Chennai had ever seen. Tendulkar made 155 not out, the third time he had scored a Test century against Australia, Warne's figures were 1 for 122. India declared at 418 for 4, setting Australia 348, and with three spinners at their disposal India won by 179 runs.

Tendulkar did not score a century in Kolkata, he was out for 79, but with everyone in the top order making runs, led by Azharuddin's 163 not out, India set all sorts of records. Their 633 for 5 declared, was their highest score against Australia, their highest ever at Eden Gardens. Warne conceded 147 runs and did not get a wicket. For Australia, having made 233 in the first innings, the question was whether they could survive on a wicket with variable bounce where India had both a paceman in Srinath and a spinner in Kumble to take advantage. The two Karnataka boys worked well in tandem: Kumble had a five-fer and India won by an innings and 219 runs. India seemed all set for a series whitewash when Tendulkar scored 177 in the third Test at Bengaluru and while Australia batted well, India started their second innings with a lead of 24. But a second innings collapse, to the pace of Michael Kasprowicz, left Australia 194 to win and they won by eight wickets, although Tendulkar did take one of those wickets. Australia won the one-day series which also involved Zimbabwe but this paled in comparison with Tendulkar's Test achievement: 446 runs, average 111.50. His strike rate per hundred balls was 80.65. It was this series that would make Warne rate Tendulkar as the best batsman of his era, higher than Brian Lara, in contrast to Ricky Ponting who rates Lara higher because he says he could win more matches than Tendulkar.

Interestingly, a player who was making his debut as an off-spinner in Bengaluru and did not take a wicket in the Australian second innings would prove one of the most remarkable cricketers ever to play for India. His relationship with Australian cricketers would, a few years later, nearly lead to an Indian tour of Australia being abandoned. Tendulkar himself would form quite a relationship with him. This was a teenager off-spinner called Harbhajan Singh. Harbhajan, known by his nickname of Bhajji, not only brought cricketing skills but a certain personality which would be very evident when, a few weeks later, the Indians flew to Sharjah for the Coca-Cola Cup, a tri-nation tournament which also featured Australia and New Zealand. On the flight to Dubai, Bhajji was sitting next to another Sikh, the medium-pacer Harvinder Singh, who had also played in the Bengaluru Test. Unlike Bhajji, he was not very fluent in English. When the flight attendant asked him if he wanted soup, he thought he was being served coffee and added sugar-free sweetener to it. Bhajji instead of telling him what he was drinking kept asking him if he was enjoying his food. Tendulkar and the whole team were very amused, and it established that Bhajji was a man of fun although opponents did not always find his antics very funny.

In Sharjah, Tendulkar, almost single-handedly, won India the tournament. He rated it as one of his best ever one-day series, pulling India through to the final against Australia and scoring 80 and 143 in the round-robin matches. The 143 was in a match affected by a sandstorm the like of which none of the players had experienced and Tendulkar used Adam Gilchrist as a human shield and lay down behind him. Although India lost the match, they made it to the final. The night before the final, Tendulkar was told by his then agent, Mark Mascarenhas, that Coca-Cola had been so impressed by his 143 they wanted to give him a £25,000 award, and Tendulkar decided he would share it with the rest of the team. The final saw Australia make 272 for 9 in their fifty overs. Tendulkar was so masterly in his 134 that India passed it with only four wickets down. It was a wonderful way to celebrate his twenty-fifth birthday. In five innings in Sharjah he had scored 435 runs at an average of 87.00.

INZAMAM AND A POTATO

On 14 September 1997, in the second one-day match played at the Toronto Cricket Skating and Curling Club, there was one of the most bizarre incidents seen in cricket that almost matched the infamous moment in an English Premier League match between Crystal Palace and Manchester United. Then Manchester United's Eric Cantona, incensed by what a Palace supporter had said, waded into the crowd and launched a kung-fu kick at the spectator which resulted in his being sentenced by a British court to 120 hours of community service. Now, Inzamam-ul-Haq, whom Imran Khan had once compared to Tendulkar, had a Cantona moment of madness in reaction to what a spectator in Toronto was saying to him.

India were chasing a modest Pakistan total of 116. Inzamam has always been bulky, his physique and lack of movement more like the subcontinental cricketers of the 1950s and 1960s. One spectator, clearly part of the Indian diaspora in Toronto, using a microphone started shouting 'aloo', potato, at him, mocking his weight. The spectator knew calling a man aloo was a dreadful insult in the subcontinent. Inzamam was so furious he decided to retaliate. Even though Pakistan were fielding he asked the Pakistani dressing room to send him out a bat. The Indians sitting in their dressing room watching their batsmen at the crease were astounded to see a Pakistani player carry a bat out to Inzamam. This is not what fielding sides do and they thought Inzamam would autograph it and present it to one of the Pakistani supporters. Inzamam had no such thoughts. He took the bat and charged the man with the microphone.

Wildblood recalls:

> I was sitting in the pavilion with David Richards, chief executive of the ICC. Suddenly one of my crew came running in and said, 'Andrew, there's an incident going on.' So, I went out onto the ground and I saw Inzy by now was halfway up the stands. He was waving the bat and was about to sort this fellow who had been calling him a potato. I went up and said to Inzy, 'I don't know if this is a great idea.' He realised that his intended course of action wasn't the smartest thing and he came away. I don't think he would ever have hit the guy.

The match was stopped for thirty-five minutes and Inzamam was banned for two matches. Nothing like this had ever been seen on a cricket field. The Indians had to be careful that no such incident happened when Pakistan arrived in India in January 1999 for the first visit by Pakistan to India in twelve years. But even before this they had to make sure the tour did not fall prey to political forces determined to stop India–Pakistan matches. There certainly was such an attempt.

The pitch at Kotla was dug up. The board offices were ransacked and board officials manhandled. Supporters and opponents of the tour held marches in various towns. But after a political intervention by Prime Minister Atal Bihari Vajpayee, the tour went ahead. However, the tour saw unprecedented security. Commandos and plain-clothes policemen shadowed the Pakistani players, and the Indian board even hired snake charmers as there were rumours that Indian extremists might release snakes in the crowds or on to the pitch.

The damage to Kotla moved the first Test to Chennai. Pakistan had not been to India since 1986. Having made his debut in Pakistan, Tendulkar had never played against Pakistan in a home series and neither had the players who formed the spine of the team now: Ganguly, Dravid, Kumble, Srinath. In Chennai, in a match in which fortunes swayed, Pakistan set India a target of 271. It looked all over at 82 for 5, but among the unbeaten five was Tendulkar and with Mongia he now began what looked like a match-winning partnership.

To destabilize Tendulkar the Pakistanis had begun to indulge in their own form of sledging; Waqar Younis, after bowling one ball to Tendulkar, asked him in Urdu, 'Ball nazar aayi?' [Did you see the ball?] Tendulkar, as always, did not respond but thought to himself, 'You are not bowling that quick, my friend.' He now prayed before each ball, and when Mongia was batting he also played the stroke Mongia was playing. The pair had taken India to 218 when Mongia, trying to slog Wasim Akram, top-edged it. Despite being in severe pain because of a bad back, Tendulkar struggled on, but on 136 he tried to hit Saqlain Mushtaq out of the ground and was out. India still had three wickets remaining and required only 17 runs for victory, but they failed by 12. Tendulkar, watching from the dressing room, dissolved in tears and was so distraught that he refused to come out to receive the Man of the Match Award.

APPLE CRUMBLE CRUMBLES PAKISTAN

Tendulkar, probably, should not have played in the second Test at Kotla. He certainly did nothing, made 6 and 29, and neither caught anyone or turned his arm over, but India won thanks to a quite unique performance by Kumble, and Tendulkar could claim that he brought Kumble good luck. India had set Pakistan a target of 420. Such a fourth innings total is always daunting, but Pakistan got to 90 for no loss at lunch on the fourth day. After lunch, with Kotla now quite chilly, Kumble changed ends, from the Football

Stand End to the Pavilion End. At 12.47 he had Afridi caught behind. Kumble recalls:

When I got my first wicket Sachin Tendulkar told me 'let me change your luck' and took my sweater and cap and gave it to the Umpire. I got another wicket. So, after every couple of overs when we felt we should get a wicket Sachin used to take my sweater, cap and give it to the Umpire.

After getting Afridi's wicket, Kumble took charge of the match and in another nineteen overs and two balls went where the great Subhash Gupte had not against the West Indies back in 1958, taking all ten wickets. In the dressing room before the Pakistani innings began, Andrew Kokinos, the team physio, had put a small tape on Kumble's foot. As he did so he asked whether he could have the tape signed if Kumble took five wickets. After Kumble had taken four, the physio, who happened to be around fine leg providing a bottle of water, told Kumble, 'One more to go, you will have to sign the tape.' Kumble shot back, 'Six more to go for the team.' It was when he took his sixth wicket, Saeed Anwar caught off bat and pad at short-leg by Laxman, that he began to feel 'all ten could be mine'. At that stage he had taken six for 15 in forty-four balls.

As Kumble neared ten, Azharuddin, realizing he might get the holy grail, told Srinath, who was bowling at the other end, 'Bowl anywhere but on the stumps.' Srinath, one of Kumble's closest friends, needed no encouragement. After Kumble had got his ninth wicket, that of Saqlain Mushtaq, he thought, 'If I am destined to get ten wickets, I will. If I'm not, I won't.' Saqlain's wicket meant Kumble had got two legs of a hat-trick but that was the end of the over. Srinath, following Azharuddin's advice, faithfully sprayed the ball around. Kumble had originally thought his best hope for a tenth would be to target Waqar, but when he began the over it was Wasim facing him. He had batted for an hour-and-a-half. Kumble did not get the hat-trick but two balls later Wasim top-edged Kumble and Laxman at short-leg took the catch. It was the third ball of his twenty-seventh over and his figures read: 26.3–9–74–10. This was only the second time in history that a bowler had taken all ten wickets in an innings, the first being Jim Laker against Australia in 1956, when he took 10 for 53. Laker had taken nine in the first innings. Kumble, having taken four in the first innings, could not match that, his overall match figures were fourteen for 149, but his dominance was proved by the fact that he had got all ten after lunch, bowling nineteen overs and three balls. Pakistan, having been 101 for no loss, had been bowled out for 207 in 10.3 overs after tea. India's win margin was 212 runs.

After the match, mopping the sweat off his eyebrows, Kumble spoke of how:

> This is a dream. I just can't get over the fact that I've taken all 10 wickets. Tomorrow, when I get up, probably I may still not realise that I have 10 wickets. When I read the newspapers, it may go into my mind. Probably every bowler dreams of getting all 10.

He also revealed that, 'Whenever I am leaving for a match my mum says, "Get a hat-trick". Probably next time she will say, "Get ten wickets".'

Although this marked the end of the two Test series, India and Pakistan did play a third Test in Kolkata, as part of the Asian Test championship. It proved to be one of Indian cricket's darkest moments. India failed to kill off Pakistan on the first day, allowing Pakistan to recover from 26 for 6 and make 185. This made a match of it and India in the final innings were set 279 to win. What followed was the Kolkata crowd allowing their passion to blur their judgement. Tendulkar, who had made 9, hit a ball to the boundary, ran two, which meant he had now scored over 5,000 runs in Test cricket and began to jog for what looked like an easy third run. But then he collided with Shoaib Akhtar, fielding at mid-off. The result was as the throw from the boundary directly hit the stumps, Tendulkar's bat was in the air and he was run out. The Pakistanis appealed, and the crowd were certain that the collision with Akhtar was not an accident but something Akhtar had deliberately done to try and impede Tendulkar. The crowd reaction meant the match could not carry on. Dalmiya came to the dressing room to ask Tendulkar's help to pacify the crowd and Tendulkar, despite feeling he had been a victim of the Pakistanis, joined Dalmiya in metaphorically putting their hands together and pleading with the crowd to allow play to resume.

Play did resume that evening, but it was unsettling for the Indian batsmen, and Dravid, who was then batting with Tendulkar, was soon out. The crowd remained on edge but were restrained by the thought that their great hero, Ganguly, might still rescue things. But he did not. On the final morning, as Ganguly fell and with India 231 for 9 and doomed to defeat, there was another riot. The match restarted, but in an empty stadium, barring the players, officials and the media, and Pakistan beat India by 46 runs.

Tendulkar in his autobiography, published in 2014, does not condemn the crowd but merely says, 'Perhaps it could have all been avoided if Shoaib had not stood in my way or if Wasim had withdrawn the appeal.' For all his killer instincts as a cricketer, the diplomat in Tendulkar can never be critical of the Indian cricketing public.

NO REPEAT OF 1983

In May 1999, India arrived in England for the World Cup, the first time the competition was being held in England since Kapil Dev's victory in 1983 and the Indian cricketing public began to hope Tendulkar's generation would do what Kapil's had done. Indian sponsors could not wait to sponsor anything remotely connected with 1983 and even ended up endorsing members of the 1983 winning side. Indians were boosted by the return of Tendulkar, who had missed one-day internationals played before the World Cup. Yet Tendulkar was not fully fit, and in the second match of the tournament he was struck by tragedy.

India, despite losing to South Africa, came to Leicester for their second match against Zimbabwe in great heart. This was like playing at home. Indian fans streamed into the Grace Road ground happily singing 'Jeetega, bhai, jeetega' [We shall win, brother]. Leicester by 1999 had become a city testifying to the growing power of the Indian diaspora in England. They were prosperous and eager to use the Indian cricket team to assert their identity. Victory over Zimbabwe, they felt, would be easy and kick-start India's tournament. But they arrived to hear shocking news.

The previous night, well past midnight, Tendulkar heard a knock at his room in the team's hotel in Leicester to find his wife, Anjali, along with two of his teammates, Robin Singh and Ajay Jadeja, standing there. She had received a call from Ajit saying Tendulkar's father had died. She had hurried down from London, where she was staying during the tournament, had asked the hotel manager not to transfer any calls to Tendulkar's room and had rung up Singh and Jadeja to be outside the room when she knocked on her husband's door. Tendulkar could not believe what she was saying and flew back home.

The players were told when they woke up the next morning. I can still recall the shock I felt when I arrived at the press box to learn the news. My fellow journalists were also numb, both sad for Tendulkar and also worried about how it would affect the team. It clearly had an impact. On the field during the entire match the Indians just could not get their heads around to playing cricket. In a Zimbabwe total of 252, they conceded fifty-one extras, twenty-one wides, sixteen no-balls, fourteen leg-byes. Worse still, they bowled so slowly they were deducted four overs when their turn to bat came. Then, when they batted, there seemed no method or any strategy in Azharuddin's captaincy. Nevertheless, India should still have won the match as they required only nine from the last two overs with three wickets in hand. Singh and Srinath were batting well. I certainly expected an Indian win and, facing a deadline to file for the *Daily Telegraph*, began to finish my article on that assumption. But Henry Olongo, who had conceded seventeen in three overs, now had Singh caught at cover off the second ball, Srinath yorked with his fifth and Prasad lbw with his last. India lost by three runs.

Tendulkar, having decided that his father would want him to carry on playing, returned and scored a century against Kenya, who India beat easily, but his back still troubled him and the mental strain of losing his father meant he always wore dark glasses during practice sessions to hide the fact that he was crying.

India also beat England. This set up what for both Indians and Pakistanis was the match of the tournament, the two neighbours meeting in the land that had once ruled over them. It was to prove the most high-profile match of the tournament.

A MATCH THAT WENT BEYOND CRICKET

Given the passion India–Pakistan aroused, the general feeling was that this match could see football-style violence. The World Cup had begun with pitch invasions in the match between Australia and Pakistan which had made Steve Waugh, the Australian captain, express his fears that if something was not done a player could get hurt. The World Cup organizers had a meeting to review security and tried to persuade the Home Office that legislation directed against football pitch invasions could also be applied to cricket pitch invasions. The British media, expecting crowd trouble, sent news correspondents in addition to cricket correspondents to cover the match. In the *Daily Telegraph*, I contributed to a front-page article, headlined 'Security Fear over World Cup Tie', which drew attention to the fact that India would meet Pakistan with the countries on the verge of war over Kashmir. At Edgbaston, after England's defeat, Indian fans had started singing, 'Stand up if you hate Pakistan'. There had also been cries in Hindi accusing the Pakistanis of being cheats. In the days leading up to the match suggestions that alcohol should be banned at the ground were discussed. Michael Browning, the tournament organizer, was confident: 'There is no question of the match not going ahead, the tournament will run its course.' Certainly, diplomats from both sides worked hard to ensure that. When the Indian high commissioner, Lalit Mansingh, held a party for members of the Indian team, the Pakistani high commissioner, Riaz Samee, attended. Before the start of the tournament, Mansingh had attended a party at the Pakistani high commission where he had chatted with leading Pakistani players. Asian businessmen also sought to diffuse talk of violence, predicting an exciting game and emphasizing that any trouble would be the work of a few hotheads.

The players were evidently tense and Azharuddin gave the impression he was very uptight at a press conference before the match at the Oval. So much so that I got under Azharuddin's skin. Thinking of how India had not often fared well against Pakistan at Sharjah and that, as Gavaskar had told me, Pakistan always seemed more motivated when playing India, I asked whether he felt India went into such matches feeling they were not quite as good as their neighbours. Azharuddin reacted sharply and said India had won more matches than Pakistan in one-day head-to-heads. The actual statistics did not bear this out as they were, matches 77, India 26, Pakistan 47, no result 4.

I was aware that, for all their differences, the players from the two teams shared a common cultural tradition and, on the day of the match I wrote in the *Daily Telegraph* about the extraordinary nature of an India–Pakistan encounter. The piece was titled 'Neighbours who would rather stay apart':

The match can best be understood in terms of one of those steamy Hindi movies Bombay specialises in, built around a family quarrel between two branches of a family violently separated 50 years ago and still unable to come to terms with it. And like a family, the links between the players are astonishing. If the match is a duel between Sachin Tendulkar and Shoaib Akhtar, then they also share the same agent, Mark Mascarenhas. Mohammad Azharuddin and Wasim Akram have the same lawyer, Naynesh Desai. It was Desai who arranged for the two teams to be sponsored by the same phonecard company. Desai's client supports Pakistan but Desai, a classic British Asian, persuaded him to sponsor India as well. The links extend to the supporters. Both sets of fans will closely follow every word of encouragement and rebuke in Urdu that Moin Khan, an incessant chatterer, will utter. They will also share a common tongue where the word yaar, meaning 'dear', will be freely used. At some stage chants like 'Kiss my chuddies' (underwear) and how big is his danda ('stick', although this has a sexual connotation) will feature. And while the Indian desire to win is keen, it is Pakistan, like the younger brother, that brings to these matches an intensity and a desire for victory that the Indians can rarely match. The results bear this out. Pakistan have won 47 to India's 26 in one-day internationals, including nine of the last ten. Privately, Pakistani cricketers believe that when it comes to pressure they are better able to cope with it than the Indians and they use an expression 'Uski gaand phat gayi hai.' Literally it means 'His arse has cracked' and is the subcontinent's equivalent of 'He has lost his bottle'.

The players in both dressing rooms read my article and had a laugh about my reference to 'gaand'.

Old Trafford was a sea of Indian and Pakistani faces, and on one occasion as I walked around the ground I felt the much-anticipated violence between fans might break out. Two youths squared up to each other, but then a middle-aged lady came up and told them to behave, and they parted saying 'Sorry, aunty' thereby showing the power of a strong maternal hand in the subcontinent. I had spent the day talking to the Indian and Pakistani supporters and in the next day's *Daily Telegraph* wrote:

> Halfway through the Pakistan innings Sachin Tendulkar caught Moin Khan on the boundary. An Indian who had driven up from London turned to me and said: 'It's all you media guys who hyped up this match as a Third World War.' Then he paused, dropped his voice and said: 'But I don't know what will happen if Pakistan lose. They can be fanatical, you know.' The Indian runs an electronics firm in Tottenham Court Road and employs more than a dozen who support Pakistan. They are, he says, as good as gold. And if the crowd at Old Trafford yesterday were not quite as good as gold—at the end, there were a few minor scuffles, some bottle throwing, and police had to prevent an Indian flag being burned—the pre-match concerns about violence proved largely unfounded. What is more, the spectators demonstrated how British Asians can produce the tumultuous noise, colour and glamour involved in a cricket match in the subcontinent. The immense culture shock that this represented for the many English in the crowd can best be illustrated by the reaction of the man who sat in the top tier of Old Trafford's pavilion. He could have been the archetypal English cricket watcher: Panama on his head and a novel by Joanna Trollope in his bag. Just before the match began, he brought the book out, no doubt hoping to read it while Shoaib Akhtar walked back to his mark. But the moment Shoaib began his run-up, the decibel count rose to such a crescendo that the Englishman quietly closed the book and never brought it out again. This was not a day to peruse novels by authors beloved of middle England, but for the whistles, flags and chants of the subcontinent mixed with some English football culture. So, when Tendulkar got out, the Pakistanis taunted the Indians with: 'You're not singing anymore.' When I asked a Pakistani supporter why he combined his Pakistani hat with a Celtic shirt, he said: 'Man, they're both green', which is probably the first time that a Muslim–Catholic alliance has been argued based on a colour code.

The match bore out Azharuddin's confidence. India's total of 227 for 6 did not look enough but Pakistan were reduced to 78 for 5 and, with Prasad taking a five-fer and Srinath three, they never really recovered and lost by 47 runs. India had met Pakistan three times in the World Cup and won on all three occasions.

Yet in the complex and totally absurd way the World Cup was organized, despite this win India required other results to go in their favour to make the final. They did not, and it was Pakistan who made the final where they lost to Australia.

DRAVID EMERGES FROM GANGULY'S SHADOW

The one encouragement the Indians could take from the World Cup was that it had established Dravid as a one-day player. Dravid's place in the Test side had not been in doubt since Lord's in 1996, but he had not been considered for the one-dayers, the theory being his innings contained too many dot balls. However, his scores in New Zealand in 1998–99 could not be ignored. In the four one-dayers, which were shared 2–2, he made 123 not out, 38, 68 and 51, and his one-day place was secure. When the coach, Anshuman Gaekwad, asked the selectors why they had ignored Dravid for the one-dayers, he was told 'Rahul had changed'. He first caught everyone's attention in the World Cup when batting with Ganguly in the match against Sri Lanka at Taunton. India lost their first wicket at 6, but then Ganguly, 183 in 158 balls with 17 fours and 7 sixes, and Dravid, run out for 145, took India to 324. They eventually made 373. By the end of the World Cup, Dravid headed the run-scorers with 461 runs and Ganguly was third with 379.

Having long ago proved he was a class Test player, the 1999 World Cup showed Dravid as the complete batsman in both formats of the game and established him in English eyes. Editors wanted to hear from Dravid and I interviewed him for a piece which was headlined, 'Dravid relishes driving on the right side of Indian selectors'.

He told me, 'for a long time a lot of people said I could not play one-day cricket. There were so many theories about what was wrong with my one-day game—I did not rotate the strike, I always hit the ball to fielders, I should bowl more off-spin to become a true one-day player—that I even stopped reading newspapers.' He went on to say he did not like being labelled unsuitable for one-day cricket and that made him go back to the nets to seek further improvement, particularly shot selection on the off side.

Dravid also told me an anecdote about facing Donald in a one-day match against South Africa. Dravid hit Donald for six back over his head and the South African fast bowler came down the wicket and, using four-letter words, warned the upstart that cricket was not that easy. 'Donald was not happy but I did not react. I find if you do that it detracts from your game.'

I was struck by the fact that until fairly recently Dravid had combined playing Test cricket with trying to get a Master's degree in Business Administration to add to his Bachelor's degree in Commerce, and how, when the Indians went to Toronto to play in the Sahara Cup, he took time off to go to the theatre. During the World Cup he had been catching up on his cricket history, reading about Neil Harvey along with an enthralling study of Michael Jordan by David Halberstam.

Dravid came over, in marked contrast to the god-like Tendulkar, or the brawny Bollywood film hero Ajay Jadeja, as a level-headed guy who took everything in his stride. I concluded my piece by reminding readers that he had led cricket teams ever since he started playing for St. Joseph's School in Bengaluru and his name might well be written in as the future India captain. I was not wrong in my forecast except he was not going to be the successor to Mohammad Azharuddin.

Talk about who might succeed Azharuddin began in the last match India played in the competition against New Zealand at Trent Bridge, which meant little. India lost, and with Trent Bridge virtually a home match for the Indians—not only did they fill the stands but also most of the executive boxes—for much of the day there was a continuous seminar on what the Indians should do next after the disappointment of this World Cup.

I listened to Raj Singh, now president of the board, and Gavaskar discuss alternatives, with Gavaskar calling for a public enquiry into the circumstances in which India had lost to Zimbabwe. A predecessor of Raj Singh went even further and called for wholesale changes—including the departure of Raj Singh, Azharuddin and the coach, Anshuman Gaekwad. On the Saturday night, after the defeat against New Zealand, Azharuddin had said that he had no plans to resign. Yet, I soon learnt that he had discussed with close friends the option of standing down. On his recent form he would struggle to get into the team if he was not captain.

One man mentioned as a possible successor was Ajay Jadeja. He was seen as a stopgap appointment to see India through the many one-day matches they faced over the next few months.

The talk about Jadeja got some attention because Tendulkar, the most obvious choice, was not interested in making a comeback. He was wracked by back pain and had by now deep doubts whether he could really captain India well. When 'Wadekar Sir', as Tendulkar calls him, visited him at home Tendulkar told him he was 'reluctant'. Wadekar appears to have read 'reluctance' not as a no, but that Tendulkar would be willing to accept the job if he was asked to do so. Certainly, that seems to have been his advice to the board, for the next thing Tendulkar learnt was that he had been appointed captain. And once the selectors announced he was captain Tendulkar felt he could not now say he could not captain India. But this time he had Kapil Dev as coach and this suggested a strong partnership which could revive Indian cricket.

Chapter 31

SACHIN'S SECOND COMING

Tendulkar began his return to the captaincy by winning the home series against New Zealand. But the Indians had to fight hard to win. This did not fill many Indians with hope as Tendulkar led the side to Australia at the end of 1999. India lost all three Tests: 285 runs, 180 runs and an innings and 141 runs. Tendulkar averaged 46, scoring a century but that was what was expected from him. To see the Australians celebrate at Sydney when they got him out showed how highly they rated his wicket. But there was a century by another Indian that was, in many ways, more significant. This was by V. V. S. Laxman, in the final Test at Sydney, who suddenly came good with 167. The innings gave notice of how much he liked Australian bowling although it would be another year before India would reap the benefits of that.

NOT IN THE SMALL ONE'S DESTINY

Tendulkar returned from Australia and decided that he could no longer captain the side. He could not control everything and plans he made were not implemented by his teammates. In one one-day match against Pakistan, having told his fast bowlers not to bowl a slower ball without telling him, the bowler did, the batsman hit a four and Tendulkar felt helpless. In a sense this bore out what Azharuddin had said towards the end of Tendulkar's first stint as captain: 'Nahi jeetega! Chote ki naseeb mein jeet nahin hai!' [He won't win! It's not in the small one's destiny!].

On his return to India Tendulkar told A. C. Muthiah, the BCCI president, that he no longer wanted to captain the side. He also suggested that the person best suited to succeed him was Ganguly. Tendulkar felt Ganguly was a leader, and in Australia when Tendulkar got injured or left the field he would ask him to take over. While this was accepted by the selectors and the board, it was felt that it would be unwise to pitch Ganguly into the job so suddenly. So, it was agreed Tendulkar would continue to captain the side for the two Tests against South Africa but then step aside for Ganguly to take over for the five one-day matches that would follow.

Tendulkar was doing what had never before been done in Indian cricket. He was giving up the captaincy and taking on a guru-like role in the Indian team, the man who would still be the most important member of the team without whose approval no crucial decision could be taken, as was shown in the long Indian opposition to the Decision Review System (DRS). The result was Tendulkar remained in the team for thirteen years as a player, not captain, playing under five different captains: Ganguly, Dravid, Kumble, Sehwag and finally Dhoni, without any of the acrimony such an arrangement might have provoked and which had in the past split the Indian team. As Tendulkar puts it, he got on with all of them and when:

> I felt it was necessary I would give them my opinion and then leave it to them to take the final call. As a senior player in the side I felt it was my job to give the captain options, as he had way too much on his plate and it was sometimes easy to miss things. I loved being involved and they all seemed to welcome my contributions. The final decision was always the captain's but it was important for me to tell them what I thought was best for the team.

So why did Tendulkar opt for Ganguly and not anybody else? We had to wait for his autobiography, published fourteen years later, to find out. Here he assesses four captains. Although at the time of the decision in 2000 Dhoni was not in the picture, Dravid and Kumble were possibilities. Ganguly, says Tendulkar, was 'an excellent strategist and had a very good understanding of the game...an aggressive captain and wasn't afraid to experiment in difficult situations.' Kumble was 'an excellent communicator and clearly explained to the players what he wanted from each of them. He was aggressive and trusted his instincts. Sourav and Anil were both great players and equally capable leaders.'

Tendulkar's assessment of Dravid is somewhat different. The two men knew each other well. In contrast to Ganguly, with whom Tendulkar spoke in English as Tendulkar does not know Bengali and Ganguly does not speak Marathi, Dravid and Tendulkar would often during their stands speak to each other in Marathi. However, Tendulkar said of Dravid's captaincy that Dravid

> ...was more conventional. He was more methodical and his mental toughness was an added strength. He was committed to the job but stayed away from experimenting too much. Dhoni, in contrast was impulsive and loved to back his instincts. He has a really good grasp of the game and is not afraid to try something different. He is never flustered and handles pressure well.

It is interesting that, of the international captains Tendulkar played against,

Nasser Hussain gets the top billing. Among the Australians, Tendulkar's vote goes to Michael Clarke. And for South Africa, Tendulkar opts for Graeme Smith.

As for his own captaincy, Tendulkar feels, as he mentions in *Playing it My Way: My Autobiography*:

> ...I could have achieved better results during my first stint as captain had there been more cooperation. I never felt totally comfortable with the relationship with the selectors. This was reflected in the teams I was given, which were not always the ones I would have chosen. In my first stint as captain, it seemed that each series was a personal test and losing one series badly meant my position was immediately in question...it was as if I was constantly being evaluated...at times they [the opposition] simply played better cricket than we did. That was the case in Australia in December 1999.

Over the years, Tendulkar was asked to come back several times. He does not detail all the occasions and there was one during the disastrous Greg Chappell era. The two occasions he talks about were in 2007 after Dravid, and then again in late 2008 after Kumble stood down. But this second time, Tendulkar, having recommended Dhoni and seen how successful he had proven in the Twenty20 World Cup and in the ODIs, had no doubts who should take over the Test captaincy as well. Tendulkar, having fielded next to Dhoni in the slip cordon, had observed how he 'read' the game at critical times. Dhoni's youth was also a factor: he was young enough to be leader for a long time.

AN INEPT HANDOVER OF CHARGE

On 20 February 2000, four days before the first Test against South Africa in Mumbai began, Tendulkar announced that he was going to quit as captain as soon as the Test series was over. However, his successor was not announced, fuelling speculation he was quitting because Azharuddin and Mongia, who had been out of the side since Tendulkar had come back as captain, were now back in the side. Commentators observed what one veteran observer called an 'unpleasant atmosphere'. India had tried hard to make things difficult for South Africa. The visitors had only one practice match at the old CCI ground before the first Test. India prepared spinning wickets; so much so that in the second Test at Bengaluru India played three spinners in the shape of Anil Kumble, Nikhil Chopra and Murali Kartik, with Kumble opening the bowling. India also won the toss in both Tests and batted first. But they lost both matches. In the first Test at Mumbai where South Africa won by four wickets, the match lasted only three days. In the second, they were beaten by an innings and 71 runs. India's batting was so poor that only twice did an Indian batsman make 50 in the series. The selection showed the sort of panic associated with Indian cricket in the 1950s. Laxman, having failed as an opener in the first Test, was dropped and Dravid opened in the second. Tendulkar did make 97 in Mumbai but his other three scores were 8, 21, 20. In contrast, Azharuddin, who had missed the first Test through injury, returned for the second and made the only century in the series by any batsman, the highest South African score in the series being 97. Azharuddin's innings stood out all the more as his 102 came in an Indian innings when no other batsmen made more than 28, and it helped post India's highest score of the series: 250. It was also Azharuddin's ninety-ninth Test and it seemed the man whose batting was so enchanting would not only go on to play in a hundred Tests but many more. Having been omitted from the Australian tour, his position now seemed secure. But, as we shall see, this story would turn out very differently.

India had not lost a home series since losing to Pakistan in March 1987. And having lost 3–0 in Australia, India had now lost five consecutive Tests. Ganguly did win the one-day series 3–2 but clearly India had to reorganize. However, before any such plans could be made, telephone conversations between a cricketer and a bookie during the one-day series, which a Delhi policeman had heard quite by chance, were to rock the world of cricket as never before. India found itself at the centre of cricket's greatest corruption crisis.

Chapter 32

THE NEVER-ENDING SAGA

Westminster Registrars' Court is not normally a place you go for Indian cricket stories. However, that was the place to be on Monday, 7 January 2019 when District Judge Rebecca Crane recommended to the British Home Secretary, Sajid Javed, that Sanjeev Chawla, born in Delhi but resident in Britain since 1996, whose passport had been revoked by the Indian government in 2000, could be extradited to India.

Back in October 2017 the same judge had considered the Indian government request and in her judgement given on 16 October she had said:

> 24. I am satisfied that there is a prima facie case, based on the evidence provided by the JA, in 4 bundles labelled Requests 1-4 with annexures A-W2. The affidavit of Bhisham Singh, the Deputy Commissioner of Police, dated 18.05.15, also contains a very detailed summary of the evidence.
>
> a) Evidence of the RP [Requested Person] shadowing Hansie Cronje, the South African cricket captain, during South Africa's cricket tour [of India in 2000], by staying in the same hotels.
>
> b) Telephone evidence of multiple conversations between the RP and Hansie Cronje in which match fixing discussions are taking place.
>
> c) Telephone evidence demonstrating the RP's frequent phone contact with other identified conspirators/co-accused, particularly around match times.
>
> d) The testimony of other co-conspirators; Rajesh Kalra, Krishan Kumar and Sunil Dara, which names the RP and details his involvement in match fixing.
>
> e) Evidence from Shiri Arun Gonbare who worked at the Taj Mahal Hotel in Mumbai, where both the South African cricket team and the RP were staying. He observed Hansie Cronje going into the RP's room empty handed and leaving the room with a bag.
>
> f) Other evidence of the South African investigation into the match-fixing allegations provided in Annex T, demonstrating the RP's involvement in the match fixing.

25. There is clear evidence sufficient to make a case requiring an answer that the RP acted with others to fix the outcome of cricket matches by provided [sic] money to members of the South African cricket team.

Crane had dismissed Chawla's contention that he should not be sent back to India because of the 'passage of time', since the alleged crime took place in India in 2000 and also his 'right to family life'. However, Crane ruled against the extradition of Chawla as she felt conditions in Tihar Jail in Delhi, where he would be housed if returned to India, would be a risk to his human rights.

But on 16 November 2018 the High Court overturned Crane's ruling deciding that conditions in Tihar Jail did not pose any 'real risk' to Chawla's human rights. That is how the case had come back to Crane and now she agreed with the High Court. On 14 March 2019, a Home Office spokesperson said to me, 'On 27 February 2019, the Secretary of State, having carefully considered all relevant matters, signed the order for Sanjeev Chawla's extradition to India. Sanjeev Chawla is accused in India of match fixing in international cricket.' Mr Chawla has sought leave to appeal against the decision of the District Judge. Should the Chawla case go to trial in India it could provide the final act of the most extraordinary match-fixing drama in cricket history which has been a sort of legal timeless Test. Back in 2000 this rocked not just Indian but also world cricket and forced the ICC to combat cricket corruption by setting up the Anti-Corruption Unit. In recent years, the work of the unit has increased and includes trying both to educate and warn players of match-fixing. And what makes the drama truly interesting is that the whole thing was the result of a man walking into the crime branch of Delhi police with a complaint that had nothing to do with cricket.

THE ACCIDENTAL DISCOVERY

The man was Ramakant Gupta, a businessman from Delhi's Karol Bagh, and he went to the offices of K. K. Paul, then Commissioner of Police, on 13 November 1999 to complain that he was getting extortion calls for money from someone in Dubai. Paul, who went on to occupy many high-powered posts including being governor of several states, has now retired. In November 2018 he spoke to me from his home in Delhi about the events that had taken place almost twenty years earlier and provided me with an article he had written recently giving details of what had happened. In it he recalled that at that time Delhi Police had to deal with a large number of such extortion rackets. An anti-extortion cell had been set up headed by

Inspector Ishwar Singh. But initial surveillance produced nothing and after a time it seemed the threat to Gupta had disappeared. However, Paul kept on extending the right to monitor telephones as he had a 'sixth sense' that something would turn up:

> Suddenly in March [2000] the Dubai contact became active. Inspector Singh told me the chatter had started but it was not about extortion, but about cricket. Having played cricket in my younger days and being a follower of the game, I had a hunch and extended the monitoring. The conversation, of a highly abusive nature, was about a dispute in payments. There was, however, no clarity as to the nature of the dispute. The second tape I heard was a stunner, as the stakes and the bets placed on the first ODI of the Pepsi series played at Kochi between India and South Africa were being discussed very explicitly. The punters had backed the Indian team and had placed heavy bets on the team to win. The match was played at Kochi on 9 March 2000 and as South Africa scored 301, which was a high score in those days, chances of India winning receded. So, the money put in stakes on India started to get withdrawn. To the utter surprise of everyone and thanks to some lofty hitting by Ajay Jadeja (92) India won the game by scoring 302. Those who had backed India did win, but most of the money had gone, as SA scored 301, so the profits were much less. The dispute was out in the open with one party claiming that after all you wanted India to win and they had won (with 2 balls to spare) so full payments be made, and so it went on and on. After listening to the tapes, one was left in no doubt that there was heavy betting taking place on the PEPSI series ODI, and this betting syndicate appeared to be the key. At that stage Sanjeev Chawla, who was based in London and had also travelled to South Africa, appeared to be emerging as their frontman.

The way the operation worked Singh, sitting in a small airless, first-floor room at the telecommunications hub of Delhi's crime branch, first listened to the calls before passing them to his boss, Paul. Five days after that first tapped call, came the call that shook Singh, Paul and the whole cricket world. The first voice, allegedly that of Chawla, said, 'Hello, Hansie, I'm waiting in the lobby.' The response came, 'Hello, Sanjay. Come up to my room, I'm in 346.' Hansie was Hansie Cronje. Paul says, 'Hearing the voice of Hansie Cronje on tape in such an explicit and a self-incriminating manner was beyond all expectations.'

The call lasted barely a minute and Singh was struck by the intimacy in Cronje's voice. Unable to believe his ears, he played the tape back several times. Knowing South African cricketers were staying at the Taj Palace Hotel in Delhi, a ten-minute drive from his office, he hurried there. Although his vigil that night yielded nothing, over the next few days his examination of the tapes produced much detailed and valuable evidence of match-fixing. And here, says Paul, his team had a stroke of luck as a result of a decision Cronje took:

> Fortunately, Hansie did not play in the Faridabad ODI and instead went into the Doordarshan commentary box. His voice tape was discretely obtained and informally we compared it with the intercepted tape. Thereafter began the debate on registration of the case and its legality. After some very hush-hush negotiations it was decided to lodge a FIR.

Singh himself went on the morning of 6 April to lodge the FIR at the Chanakyapuri police station and Paul held a press conference at Delhi Police headquarters:

> It was one of my most crowded press conferences and when I named Hansie Cronje, there was an initial hush, but then a storm broke out. I made it a point to read the incriminating extracts from the transcripts of the monitored tapes which were a part of the FIR. The most incriminating part that was made public was the taped conversation in Afrikaans between Hamid Cassim Banjo [Hamid 'Banjo' Cassim] and Cronje. While allegations of fabrication were being made about the tapes which were in English, this one was beyond challenge as none in Delhi could speak so fluently in Afrikaans.

The actual tapes have never been released but if Chawla is extradited and the case comes to court it may be heard.

DENIAL AND SCEPTICISM

I was then chief sports news reporter of the London *Daily Telegraph*. The initial reaction of the sports desk was that the story was a fake. The South Africans certainly made great efforts to debunk the Delhi Police claims. Bob Woolmer, who had been the South African team's coach, went on the BBC rubbishing them. I was also being interviewed by the same programme, and as Woolmer and I waited to go on, he turned to me and said, 'The Indians have put this story out because they lost the series. They are trying to find some excuse to explain why they lost at home.' In 2005, Woolmer visiting India as the coach of the Pakistan team visited Paul at his home and once

THE NINE WAVES

again tried to convince him that he had got the story wrong. Four days after Paul's initial announcement, Cronje was exposed as a cheat and a liar, making the first of his many confessions.

I had told my sports desk not to instantly rubbish the Delhi Police story. The reason was that I knew gambling was in the Indian DNA and, talking to Vinod Mehta, editor of *Outlook*, and my Indian contacts, I was well aware that for years magazines like *Outlook* had been writing stories which suggested that illegal betting was going on in matches involving India. *Outlook* in May 1997 had quoted Manoj Prabhakar alleging that in Sri Lanka in 1994 he had been offered ₹25 lakhs to play below his usual standard in a match against Pakistan. But he did not name the player who made the offer. The writer Aniruddha Bahal, named a few officials of BCCI as well as journalists who were allegedly aware of and or involved in the 'betting' racket. Bahal's damming conclusion was, 'There is betting in cricket. And India loses matches.' I used to write for *Outlook* from London and Vinod Mehta, who had a keen interest in cricket, would often express suspicions that India had lost a match due to players being in hock to bookies.

On 28 April 2000, Sukhdev Singh Dhindsa, the then union minister of youth affairs and sports, asked the Central Bureau of Investigation (CBI) to look into match-fixing and whether any Indian cricketer or administrator was involved.

KAPIL'S TEARS

The first consequence of the CBI enquiry was the revelation of the name of the Indian player who Prabhakar alleged had offered him a bribe. It was Kapil Dev. Soon after this news broke Karan Thapar approached Kapil for an interview. Kapil agreed and, as Thapar has recorded in his 2018 book, *Devil's Advocate: The Untold Story*:

> From start to finish, the interview was about the allegations he faced. For the first ten minutes he took my questions squarely on the chin. He seemed unruffled and undisturbed. But when I asked if he was worried about the fact that history might remember him not just as the captain of India's World Cup-winning cricket team or the highest wicket-taker, but also as someone accused of accepting money to throw a match, a dam inside seemed to burst and his emotions poured out in a flood of tears. It happened so suddenly, it took me aback. Tears rolled down his cheeks, his voice began to quiver and then actually broke. His nose started to run. In fact, he was crying like a baby.

Thapar has no doubts, 'that the tears were genuine and the emotion real.

I interpret them as the cry of an anguished soul, expressing both pain and helplessness. If I were in his position, it's possible I would behave similarly too. But were they also tears of remorse? I don't think so, but of course, they could have been.'

The CBI, which questioned Kapil Dev, would say, 'In conclusion, it can be said that there is no credible evidence to prove Prabhakar's allegations against Kapil Dev and further, of Kapil Dev's linkages with the betting syndicate during his playing career or after retirement.'

THE CRONJE DRAMA
The rainbow nation had to respond and decided to hold a judicial hearing headed by retired judge Edwin King. I arrived in Cape Town to find the commission hearings were in a place called the Centre for the Book. It had a sign outside describing it as an Internet cafe. The room where King held the enquiry looked like a library, having walls lined with books and a raised platform, along one side of which South African members of parliament could sit and look down on Judge King as he heard the evidence. King was assisted by Shamila Batohi, deputy director of public prosecutions. Although it was Cronje's confession that had prompted this enquiry, it was by no means certain that Cronje himself would appear. He had a formidable legal team headed by Clem Druker, former president of the Western Province Cricket Union. In my experience as a journalist I have always found lawyers and accountants the best sources for news and I decided to cultivate Shamila Batohi. She agreed to have dinner, and over the meal in one of Cape Town's swish restaurants she told me that Cronje had been offered immunity from criminal prosecution by the South African government provided he came clean on match-fixing. The immunity would apply only once he had told the truth to the King Commission and the commission were satisfied that it was indeed the whole truth. Should they find that Cronje had not told them the whole truth, he could be prosecuted under the Corruption Act, which allows South African citizens to be charged with offences committed outside the country.

I heard every word of the commission's hearing, but it meant that I began to associate very different things with cities like Nagpur and Kanpur. As a child travelling on the old BNR train from Mumbai to Kolkata, we often stopped in Nagpur, where a good friend of my father lived, and my Mama, my mother's brother, lived in Kanpur. In Cape Town, I was hearing stories of how in these cities visiting South African cricketers had taken money from Indian bookies to cheat Indian cricket fans.

Cronje as a batsman was stodgy. Now in a testimony that lasted four days he revealed various aspects of his personality. Unlike the other witnesses, he was allowed to read his prepared statement and read it like an undertaker. Then, when gently questioned by his lawyers, he was alternatively pensive, and stern. His witty jokes at the expense of his wife and other cricketers during cross-examination had the packed room in stitches. Cronje said that he considered the payments from bookmakers as 'money for jam', but that he was so tight-fisted he rarely bought his teammates a drink and due to the generosity of South African restaurant owners, he could save nearly all his meal allowance. But at times he was fierce, even rebuking Judge King.

In the end, he was a pathetic sight. Marlon Aronstam, a Johannesburg bookie who had paid Cronje 53,000 rand and a leather jacket for his wife to make a match of the rain-ruined Centurion Test against England in January 2000, was due to be cross-examined after Cronje. But watching the former South African captain he fled to the lavatory in tears, wailing, 'Look how they're treating Hansie. I can't bear it.' Cronje himself had shed tears when giving evidence, and at the end his testimony would produce the sort of drama more appropriate to the Royal Shakespeare Company. As he stood up, this once-revered figure broke down. His legs seemed to give way and his brother, sitting behind throughout his testimony, rushed to his side and half-carried him from the room. Tears flowed down Cronje's cheeks.

At the end of the hearing I came to the conclusion that Cronje was more calculating, artful and clever than he was given credit for. My impression was that despite the fact King was holding a commission of enquiry, not presiding over a criminal trial, Cronje had treated it as if this were a criminal trial and he cricket's O. J. Simpson. Cronje had a huge legal team, with two senior counsel and two other attorneys. He also had a psychiatrist, a security team and a private auditor, and it was estimated the hearings had cost him £60,000. What is more, his legal team had intervened every time they felt the cross-examination was venturing into areas they did not want.

A Cape Town psychiatrist, Dr Ian Lewis, took the stand and revealed that Cronje had been on psychiatric medication since May, when he consulted a psychiatrist in Bloemfontein. On 13 June, two days before he made his statement, he consulted Dr Lewis in Cape Town, who diagnosed that he suffered from clinical depression. Dr Lewis explained that while he was capable of giving evidence, he had difficulty concentrating, might not cope with complex questions and suffered from lapses of memory. According to Dr Lewis, this meant that while Cronje could remember his cricketing performances, including details of his batting record, he might not remember whether two days ago he had worn trousers or a tracksuit. He suggested that during cross-examination lawyers should not be too aggressive with his client or ask too many complex questions. Cronje gave the impression that he was on a damage limitation exercise, and it was hard to disagree with Shamila Batohi's argument that he was tailoring his evidence to fit whatever facts had emerged. Despite having confessed to his 'unfortunate love' for money and that he was like an alcoholic who could abstain for some time but eventually returned to drink [money], he did not at first admit that he cheated on the players who he asked to fix matches. And, of course, he persistently maintained that he had never thrown a match and was only playing with the bookies. In this Cronje was like athletes who are caught doping but refuse to admit they took drugs, always saying they were victims. By not admitting that he had taken money to fix matches, Cronje would do immense damage to South African cricket. South African cricket followers, unable to accept that the man in whom they had such trust could possibly have betrayed them, believed he did not cheat the game, let alone his country. When the country staged the 2003 World Cup, many fans dedicated it to Cronje, seeing him as a saint and not the crook he undoubtedly was.

CRONJE AND AZHARUDDIN

The Cronje testimony that had the greatest impact on India involved Azharuddin. In a statement made by Cronje in Cape Town on 15 June 2000, he told the commission:

> On the evening of the third day of the third test against India at Kanpur [in 1996] I received a call from Mohammad Azharuddin, who was friendly with a number of South African players. He called me to a room in the hotel and introduced me to Mukesh Gupta ('MK'). Azzaurddien (sic) then departed and left us alone in the room. MK asked if we would give wickets away on the last day of that test to ensure that we lost. He asked me to speak to other players and gave me approximately US$30,000 in cash to do so. I led him to believe that I would.

Cronje then went on to say that he did nothing, just took the money, and South Africa lost in any case thanks to a brilliant 163 from Azharuddin.

Azharuddin visited the CBI offices in Delhi as Cronje was giving evidence in Cape Town, and the CBI enquiry remains the most comprehensive ever undertaken into match-fixing in cricket.

It described how betting worked, named eight bookies headed by Gupta also known as MK or John, and nine punters, providing addresses of both the bookies and the punters, and then warned that, 'It is only a matter of time before major organized gangs take direct control of this racket, a phenomenon that would have implications not only for cricket but for national security as a whole.'

The picture the CBI painted was devastating. Gupta had come a long way since he had taken to cricket after India's victory in the 1983 World Cup. Over the next decade Gupta had travelled the world following cricket, meeting some of the best players of their generation. As I've reported in the *Daily Telegraph* in November 2000, the CBI estimated that 'during his association with Azhar, MK must have paid him ₹90 lakhs.' However, Gupta, finding that some of Azhar's 'predictions proved incorrect', asked for his money back and was repaid ₹30 lakhs, in instalments from Azharuddin's locker at the Taj Palace.

The CBI claimed that Azharuddin in his testimony:

> ...has specifically recalled that he 'did' the match between India and Pakistan at Jaipur for the Guptas during the Pepsi Cup Match, 1999, after which he received around ₹10 lakhs from an 'unknown' person, on behalf of Guptas. However, in view of the large amount of money Azhar has received from Guptas and the 'hospitality' he has enjoyed through them it is very difficult to believe that he 'did' only one match for them.

CBI's conclusion of one of India's most successful cricket captains was:

> It is clear that Azharuddin contributed substantially towards the expanding bookie/player nexus in Indian cricket. The enquiry has disclosed that he received large sums of money from the betting syndicates to 'fix' matches. There is also evidence which discloses that he roped in other players also to fix matches, which resulted in this malaise making further inroads into Indian cricket.

However, the CBI, having consulted the Solicitor General of India, concluded that no criminal charges could be filed and that Azharuddin had committed no offence under the provisions of the Indian Penal Code or the Gambling Act.

AZHARUDDIN DEFENDS HIMSELF

The BCCI could not brush this aside and asked K. Madhavan, a former joint director of the CBI, to examine the CBI report and recommend action to be taken. He decided to question Azharuddin and the other players mentioned in the CBI report. Despite the fact that he had been told Azharuddin was 'an introvert and lone ranger, I found him pleasant mannered and externally calm during my interaction'. The real surprise for Madhavan was Azharuddin's response to the CBI report:

> I never said as above before the CBI. I have never known any person called Mukesh Kumar Gupta alias MK. I have never known him as John also. I never introduced him to anyone. In particular, I did not introduce him to Hansie Cronje at Kanpur in 1996 or at any other time. As I did not know Mukesh Kumar Gupta at all, my knowing him only as a jeweller does not arise.

He also told Madhavan, 'I do not now know why Hansie Cronje has deposed like that.' But he made it clear he had no enmity with Cronje.

Azharuddin then provided Madhavan with details of his receipts as shown in his Income Tax returns going back to 1989–90. And that, 'I have also paid approximately ₹2 lakhs in 1992 to Kapil Dev for some land at Gurgaon. However, I have not acquired this plot so far since it is under some litigation.'

Azharuddin's overall rebuttal about fixing matches was robust:

> I would like to state that I was never a party for receiving anything from any person and I never contacted any person for any match-fixing. I have done my best for my country and broken many records. As a captain I have won the maximum number of matches for India. This applies to Tests as well as for One-dayers. In the game of cricket, while skill is required, luck also plays a major part. A player makes a double century in the first innings but can be dismissed for 0 in the 2nd innings. If such failures can be taken as indication of his under-performance in a match, no player can escape such allegations. This applies to bowlers also. For example, Anil Kumble who holds world record for taking 10 wickets, can totally fail in another match.

Madhavan refused to accept that the CBI could have fabricated evidence:

> ...in the past five decades, to the best of my knowledge, not a single Court has ever held that a statement recorded by the CBI was falsely recorded or a case was falsely prosecuted. I do not therefore, believe that Azhar has spoken the truth before me when he totally denied before me all the facts that he had set out before the CBI.

Madhavan's verdict on Azharuddin was:

(i)   He had close contacts and nexus with bookies/punters like M. K.
       Gupta, Ajay Gupta, Gyan Gupta and Ameesh Gupta etc. and was
       involved in match-fixing.

(ii)   He is guilty of unbecoming conduct and misconduct as a national
       level player in maintaining such frequent contacts with bookies/
       punters.

(iii) In his case, the misconduct is aggravated, as he was the Captain
       of the Indian team for long and let down the country and the
       cricket loving public in a despicable manner.

It is on the basis of the Madhavan report that in December 2000 the
BCCI banned Azharuddin for life. But had Madhavan allowed Azharuddin
a fair trial? Madhavan had made it clear that his investigation was like a
departmental enquiry and the level of proof was lower than that required
in criminal cases. But he had not allowed Azharuddin to cross-examine
witnesses, something that even Cronje had been allowed at the King
enquiry. Nor was he supplied with the allegedly incriminating documents.

Azharuddin, strenuously maintained his innocence but despite the best
efforts of Raj Singh, who was convinced of his innocence, Azharuddin never
played another Test and remained marooned on 99. However, in 2010 he
was elected as Member of Parliament for Moradabad in Uttar Pradesh on
a Congress ticket. Two years after his election, on 8 November 2012, the
Andhra High Court absolved Azharuddin of match-fixing and revoked his
life ban. After the verdict he told Rajdeep Sardesai, 'The High Court has
exonerated me, no evidence has been found against me. Please look at my
performance and tell me how I could fix a match.'

The BCCI held a special general meeting in Kolkata on 29 November
2000 and defended itself saying that Indians had 'developed their own
style of the game, mesmerising the world'. Just over a decade later another
match-fixing scandal would force the BCCI to its knees. It was to prove
the final revenge of Cronje on Indian cricket. The match-fixing saga marked
a sad end to the sixth wave.

The Seventh Wave

TESTS

Wave	Period	Mts	Won	Lost	Drawn	Tied	Win%	W/L
7th	2000-2007	74	29	19	26	0	39.19	1.53

TOP BATSMEN IN SEVENTH WAVE

	Mts	Runs	Hs	Avg	100	50
R. Dravid	73	6579	270	62.65	18	32
S. R. Tendulkar	63	5096	248*	54.79	15	21
V.V. S. Laxman	65	4267	281	47.94	9	24
V. Sehwag	51	4072	309	49.65	12	11
S. C. Ganguly	60	3223	144	37.91	6	16
W. Jaffer	20	1345	212	37.36	4	8
S. S. Das	22	1275	110	34.45	2	9
A. Kumble	57	1020	110*	18.21	1	1
M. S. Dhoni	20	1019	148	36.39	1	6
Harbhajan Singh	49	954	66	17.03	0	2

TOP BOWLERS IN SEVENTH WAVE

	Mts	Wkts	Best	Avg	5WI	10WM
A. Kumble	57	290	8/141	29.42	17	5
Harbhajan Singh	49	217	8/84	29.02	19	4
Z. Khan	49	157	5/29	33.53	5	0
I. K. Pathan	25	91	7/59	30.79	7	2
J. Srinath	20	65	6/76	30.90	4	0
S. Sreesanth	11	46	5/40	28.23	1	0
A. Nehra	16	43	4/72	41.20	0	0
A. B. Agarkar	20	41	6/41	53.17	1	0
R. P. Singh	7	27	5/59	30.44	1	0
L. Balaji	8	27	5/76	37.18	1	0

TOP WICKETKEEPERS IN SEVENTH WAVE

	Mts	Dismissals	Ct	St
M. S. Dhoni	20	63	53	10
P. A. Patel	19	46	39	7
K. D. Karthik	11	38	34	4

S. S. Dighe	6	14	12	2
A. Ratra	6	13	11	2
D. Dasgupta	8	13	13	0

ONE-DAY INTERNATIONALS

Wave	Period	Mts	Won	Lost	NR	Tied	Win%	W/L
7th	2000-2007	206	109	88	9	0	52.91	1.24

TOP BATSMEN IN SEVENTH WAVE

	Mts	Runs	Hs	Avg	SR	100	50
R. Dravid	189	6070	109*	42.15	73.79	5	52
S. R. Tendulkar	137	5813	152	48.84	84.73	15	34
S. C. Ganguly	145	4985	144	38.34	73.79	7	36
V. Sehwag	164	4874	130	32.06	96.89	8	24
Yuvraj Singh	171	4819	139	36.78	86.54	7	29
M. Kaif	125	2753	111*	32.01	72.03	2	17
M. S. Dhoni	81	2303	183*	42.64	94.61	2	14
V.V. S. Laxman	73	2252	131	34.64	74.49	6	10
D. Mongia	57	1230	159*	27.95	71.47	1	4
I. K. Pathan	73	1006	83	25.15	80.09	0	5

TOP BOWLERS IN SEVENTH WAVE

	Mts	Wkts	Best	Avg	RPO	4W
A. B. Agarkar	126	191	6/42	26.34	5.01	9
Z. Khan	118	160	5/42	29.87	4.89	6
Harbhajan Singh	136	152	5/31	33.07	4.12	4
I. K. Pathan	73	115	5/27	25.91	5.02	4
A. Nehra	69	90	6/23	30.85	4.81	4
V. Sehwag	164	74	3/25	39.31	5.17	0
J. Srinath	42	63	4/23	25.77	4.51	3
A. Kumble	61	60	4/32	41.21	4.62	1
S. R. Tendulkar	137	57	5/50	38.47	5.43	2
S. C. Ganguly	145	47	5/34	38.44	4.97	1

TOP WICKETKEEPERS IN SEVENTH WAVE

	Mts	Dismissals	Ct	St
M. S. Dhoni	81	97	79	18
R. Dravid	66	76	63	13
A. Ratra	12	16	11	5
P. A. Patel	14	15	12	3
V. Dahiya	10	13	11	2

TWENTY20 INTERNATIONALS

Wave	Period	Mts	Won	Lost	NR	Win%	W/L
7th	2000–2007	1	1	0	0	100.00	–

Chapter 33

A REMARKABLE INDIA-NEW ZEALAND PARTNERSHIP

Just over a month after he had clinched victory in the one-day series in Nagpur, Ganguly was in a totally different world, playing for Lancashire against Kent in Canterbury, England, for whom Dravid was making his debut. Because of rain only sixty-six soggy overs were bowled and the two Indians must then have pined for the blue skies of the Orange City of India. What was truly significant about this encounter between two of India's leading cricketers, playing against each other in England, was the competition they were involved in. Through much of the 1950s, Gupte, Mankad, Umrigar, Hazare, Manjrekar, Phadkar had played against each other in England, but in the Lancashire League, not county cricket. That Ganguly and Dravid now played in the county championship, the oldest cricket tournament in the world and the template for many other sports tournaments, reflected how English cricket had changed and also how English cricket now viewed Indian cricketers. This match between Kent and Lancashire is also important because it set in train one of the most dramatic developments in Indian cricket: the appointment of the first foreign coach. More of that later: here, let us dwell on Ganguly and Dravid's contrasting experiences in county cricket.

THE GENTLEMAN CHARMER AND THE ALOOF OUTSIDER

Dravid was a wow in Kent, both with the bat and as a person. He was the only Kent player to score more than a thousand runs in the county championship, 1,039 runs at an average of 49.47. The next highest run-getter for the county, who played two more innings, made only half that: 558 runs and averaged 22.32. And Dravid's personality charmed players. Ed Smith, who that season batted No. 4, and is now chairman of the England selectors, would later write:

> When Rahul Dravid walked into the dressing room of the St. Lawrence ground in Canterbury on a cold spring morning, you could tell he was different from all the others. He did not swagger with cockiness or bristle with macho competitiveness. He went quietly

round the room, shaking the hand of every Kent player—greeting everyone the same, from the captain to the most junior. It was not the mannered behaviour of a seasoned overseas professional; it was the natural courtesy of a real gentleman. We met a special human being first, an international cricketer second.

The contrast with Ganguly could not be greater. His championship batting did not match that of Dravid (644 runs averaging 33.89) although he made up for this with his one-day performances, where he made three centuries. Colin Evans of the *Manchester Evening News*, who also covered cricket for *Wisden* and ghosted Farokh Engineer's book, told me:

> There was some surprise when we heard Ganguly was coming because we always had a bowler. To go for a batter when we had a lot of good batsmen still there seemed a bit strange. As for salary, overseas players got a premium and Ganguly was treated pretty well. We had had Wasim Akram, who was popular, gave 100 per cent and won important matches. After his last match at Old Trafford he stood on the players' balcony while fans gathered below chanting his name. He had tears in his eyes. In Ganguly's year Lancs finished runners-up in the championship but never looked genuine title contenders and Ganguly's contribution in the championship was below par for the overseas player. If he had done better on the pitch, maybe the personal difficulties would have been brushed over. He did a lot better in the one-day game, but Lancs lost the B&H and NatWest semis both to Gloucester at Bristol and were relegated in the National League only 12 months after winning it. Ganguly did score a century against the Minor Counties in the NatWest Trophy in the early rounds. Ganguly was very proud of this. The rest of the lads said, 'That's what he should be doing. An Indian Test player. A flat pitch against the Minor Counties.' Overall, Lancs needed everyone in the team to be on the same page. They felt Ganguly wasn't even in the same book. I understood their feelings.
>
> When Ganguly first arrived at Old Trafford I asked for a one-to-one interview and, while he seemed reluctant, he sat down with me in the Indoor School. I was very disappointed with his attitude. He seemed distrustful, extremely wary—and perhaps that was understandable. But I also felt he looked askance at me (even though for once I wasn't wearing jeans!). As the season progressed I heard dressing-room mutterings about his reluctance to get involved with traditional dressing-room banter, refusing to have a drink after play etc. One player told me: 'He's always the first out of the ground.' Then

came the floodlit game at Old Trafford when he got a half-century but ran out Flintoff on the way. When he reached 50 and waved his bat towards the dressing-room there was no one on the balcony. No one came out on to the balcony to acknowledge it. He obviously realized that, as did the crowd. Others, particularly in the media centre, saw it as a protest against his lack of team spirit. I know fully well Ganguly just didn't go down well at Old Trafford. One senior player in the team took Ganguly to one side at one point and told him about the importance of the team ethic. This was because they believed Ganguly was too independent. Not necessarily on the pitch, but he didn't get involved in what was called the dressing room 'crack', which was very important to Lancashire. People like Neil Fairbrother and Atherton and one or two others almost insisted that everyone join in after the day's play in the dressing room over a beer or a soft drink or whatever to have a chat about things. Fairbrother, particularly, was very much into this. It was mentioned to me by one or two players that they were resentful about Ganguly's conceit or arrogance. Ganguly was so upset by this rift between him and the dressing room that he asked me to meet him after a day's play at Grace Road during a championship match. We wondered what he wanted to say. So, we went and interviewed him in the pavilion stand. He opened his heart. He said he realized that there were issues. He felt it was because of different cultures, the English culture and the Indian culture. He claimed that the English culture was to go for a beer after a day's play. And that wasn't part of his culture. He didn't see anything wrong after a day's play in saying, 'Goodnight, I am leaving' and going away while the rest of the lads were still there. He was then going out with the woman he married. She often came to the match and after the day's play he did not mix with the lads just went away with her. I think he was actually bewildered by the players' reactions and what was going on. I was sympathetic to his claim that there was a clash of cultures. But while the problem was based on the cultural background, it was also a clash of personalities. He would have been used to an Indian dressing room where his personality was a primary factor. No one at Lancashire that I know was sorry to see him leave, which was a great shame.

Years later Andrew Flintoff in his book *Being Freddie: My Story So Far* wrote:

He turned up as if he was royalty—it was like having Prince Charles on your side... He wasn't interested in the other players and it became a situation where it was ten players and Ganguly in the team.

A HERO IN HIS OWN COUNTRY

However, all this had no impact on Ganguly's Indian leadership. Few in India even knew of Ganguly's Lancashire reputation, and within weeks of playing his last match for Lancashire Ganguly was leading India in the 2000 ICC Knock Out tournament in Nairobi. The chain of events caused by the Delhi Police unmasking Cronje had claimed Kapil Dev and India needed a new coach. The Indians brought back Anshuman Gaekwad, but this was a stopgap appointment. India began in style, evicting Kenya from their own party, but everyone knew the real test would be Australia and South Africa, the favourites. India were given little chance, but this is where a team led by Ganguly showed for the first time that India were no longer pussycats when playing abroad. In a classic quarter-final against Australia, India prevailed by 20 runs. What made the match really significant was the emergence of two cricketers who would become Ganguly's men. Against Kenya, eighteen-year-old Yuvraj Singh and twenty-two-year-old Zaheer Khan had made their debut. Now against Australia Yuvraj made an explosive 84 from eighty balls; no other batsman made more than 38, and that was Tendulkar. Zaheer took two wickets, having Gilchrist caught by Ganguly and then bowling Waugh with a full delivery. Australia were bowled out for 245 in 46.4 overs. This was followed by victory over South Africa in the semi-final: Ganguly made 141 not out, while Yuvraj with 41 and Zaheer with two crucial wickets contributed to a more emphatic 95-run victory. But having proved winners as underdogs, and then having been installed as favourites against New Zealand in the final, they failed. Nevertheless, this was the first final of a one-day tournament of all the Test-playing countries India had reached for fifteen years since Gavaskar's epic triumph in Australia in 1985.

However, as if made giddy by this, India soon came crashing down. The Indians flew from Nairobi to Sharjah and there, in the final of the Coca-Cola Champions Trophy, after Sri Lanka scored 299 for 5, India were bowled out for 54, their lowest score in one-day cricket ever. India lost by 245 runs and set a dubious record for their defeat which was then the worst in the history of one-day cricket. Now it ranks tenth with Ireland wearing the dunce's cap having lost by 290 runs to New Zealand in Aberdeen in 2008.

A BREAK WITH TRADITION

While this did not cast doubts on Ganguly's captaincy, it made the Indian board all the more determined to have a foreign coach, moves for which had started even as Ganguly and Dravid were playing in England. Once again, the land of their former conquerors was prompting changes in

India. Dravid had been recruited to Kent by their New Zealand coach, John Wright, who had been impressed by the way Dravid batted. Then, through his commentary work, Wright had got to know Dravid and Ganguly and was struck 'by their courtesy and humility'. If Ganguly was Lord Snooty to his Lancashire colleagues, he did not come across like that to Wright. Dravid told Wright that senior Indian players had told the Board a foreign coach was needed, and during the Kent–Lancashire match Wright had spoken to Ganguly and, as Wright puts it, 'That chat was the first step in the process.' Ganguly was very keen on Wright and this keenness may have been increased by talking to Bobby Simpson, who was the Lancashire coach and had recruited Ganguly for the county. He knew Wright and liked him. The moment Ganguly heard Kapil was out he rang Raj Singh Dungarpur from England to tell him that Wright should be selected. Wright did not know this and in his talk with Ganguly and Dravid played it carefully. He told them it 'was a hugely exciting prospect' but doubted if India would break tradition quite so dramatically as to appoint a foreigner.

But towards the end of the 2000 season, Jaywant Lele who Wright knew, rang him and asked him to come to India. Wright could not be keener, as he needed a job. Kent had spent the season fighting relegation both in the County Championship and the National League and just about managed to do so. The day after the season ended Wright was told he was no longer required and, as he says, there was neither 'thank you [n]or goodbye'. Wright had had a lot of disappointments in his coaching career. The first New Zealand batsman to score 5,000 runs, as a coach he was often considered for a top job but had never succeeded in landing one. He had gone for the ECB coaching job, been told he was on the shortlist but then told he was not. He had gone for the New Zealand coaching job, and been summoned to London, only to be told he had not got it and, what is more, his train fare of £20 from Canterbury to London was not even reimbursed. But the Indians seemed to be treating him like royalty. They arranged business-class flights to Chennai. He had been reassured he need not worry about a visa as one would be waiting for him at the Lufthansa desk. He got there to find there was no visa and Wright jumped through all sorts of hoops, including getting Colin Cowdrey to contact Raj Singh who was having a massage at the CCI, before he could get to Chennai. That was not the end of his introduction to incredible India. No sooner had he settled in his hotel than he saw Lele on television saying it was unlikely a foreign coach would be appointed. However, the Indians still wanted to interview him, although he now found he faced a uniquely Indian style of recruitment.

A VERY INDIAN RECRUITMENT PROCESS

Geoff Marsh and Greg Chappell were also in the running, with Marsh considered the favourite as he had an impressive World Cup CV and was said to be a man liked by A. C. Muthiah, the BCCI President. Chappell had a batting record Wright could never have matched. Wright had tried to find out about Indian cricket and read my *History of Indian Cricket*. Things began to look up when, before he was interviewed, he was invited by Lele to have lunch where Muthiah, Raj Singh, Hanumant Singh and Venkataraghavan would also be present. Wright had every reason to be optimistic, only to find Chappell was also at the lunch. It was as if the Indians wanted to see how the two candidates behaved when facing each other in front of the men they would have to work for. The interviews were not a joint affair, with Chappell summoned first. When, after a long wait, Wright was finally ushered in, he was asked whether he would drop Tendulkar. He replied yes. There was also a discussion about fees, with Wright making it clear he expected to be paid more than he received at Kent. He returned to England not knowing what would happen. What he did not know was that Indian wheels were turning.

Raj Singh and other board officials flew to Nairobi and the decision to engage Wright was finalized in Nairobi after they talked not only to Ganguly and Dravid, but also Tendulkar. Raj Singh had also spoken to Bobby Simpson, and Simpson, rather than recommending either of his fellow Australians, told the Indians Wright was their man. Gavaskar would later tell Wright it was Simpson's recommendation that made the Indian board give Wright the job.

On 2 November 2000, the news finally emerged that Wright would start a new chapter in Indian cricket by becoming the first foreign coach of the Indian team. Yet, in the curious way that India works, he learnt about it on Ceefax before the Indian board contacted him. However, for another week Gaekwad carried on as coach, taking the team to Dhaka for Bangladesh's inaugural Test, which was also Ganguly's first Test as captain.

Bangladesh had failed to win their previous ten first-class games and in the previous month had come back from a tour of South Africa, where they had lost all four matches. This may explain why India, which had brought Pakistan and Zimbabwe to Test cricket, approached the Test as if they only had to turn up and victory would be theirs. Bangladesh were quick to exploit Indian complacency. Batting first on winning the toss, Aminul Islam steered Bangladesh to 400 with a confident 145. India at one stage were 190 for 5 but Ganguly, helped by Sunil Joshi, avoided embarrassment. Joshi, who won Man of the Match, produced a sterling all-round effort. His 92 was his best Test score and the left-arm spinner claimed match figures of 8–169 and played a key hand in the Bangladesh collapse in their second innings. India were left with a straightforward run-chase after skittling the home side in the second innings for 91. This was India's first overseas victory since the one in Sri Lanka in 1993, twenty-two Tests earlier. But the Indians knew there was little reason for euphoria. There would be much sterner tests ahead and a foreign coach to get used to. Five days after the victory, the Indians were in Delhi meeting Wright who was already ensconced at the Taj Palace Hotel in the city. In his memoir of his time as Indian coach, *Indian Summers*, he calls this chapter 'Unreal World', and for somebody brought up in North Canterbury on New Zealand's South Island, unreal it certainly was.

CUPS OF TEA VS FITNESS

Wright arrived for his first training session to see that the players had left their gear on the coach as they disembarked for practice. The gear was for porters to carry. Then, as if they were having an evening stroll, they went to the nets. There, enthroned on cane chairs, they had tea and biscuits served by waiters. And the Indians had no fitness trainer and did not much believe in keeping fit. To them, cricket practice was bowling and batting, not taking steps to be physically fit so that they could field properly. Wright also had problems distinguishing between Indians. He thought Ajit Agarkar, the opening bowler, was Shiv Sunder Das, the opening batsman. Coming from a country where rugby is the main sport Wright was not used to cricket being the No. 1 sport. Nothing in his coaching career had prepared him for the media attention the sport gets in India. He suddenly found himself transported to the world so familiar to football managers in the English Premier League, with a camera always trained on him and one cameraman, an Australian to boot, telling him, 'Don't worry about us mate, we'll be getting in the way like bottles of stale piss.' Wright wrestled with the problem of how to avoid picking his nose on camera during a day's play which could last six hours. There was much else that Wright found incomprehensible, like finding he was not only coach but also had to perform managerial duties such as finding out flight timings from the visiting Zimbabwean manager. There were problems with his contract with the Indian board. And there was the regional balance of the Indian selection, with various regions wanting their own players. In some ways the most unexpected problem for Wright was to realize that in India a man in a position of power or with powerful connections could do anything, even invade the space meant for players. This meant that on one occasion a

chief minister asked a padded-up Rahul Dravid to move from the position
from where he was watching cricket. Raj Singh Dungarpur advised Wright,
'Patience, John, patience. It takes time. This is how we've survived the
English and the Portuguese and everyone who has come to colonise India.'

In some ways the most difficult thing was to stop the Indians from
being deferential, to stop them calling him Sir. Wright says he was called
all sorts of things but does not give examples. As we have seen Tendulkar
called not only his coach Sir, but also Gavaskar and Wadekar. Wright also
tried to break the senior-junior divide and did this by directing his first
blast at Srinath, very much a senior, after a bad bowling spell. What was
crucial was his relationship with Ganguly, and here it was comforting for
Wright to discover that they had much in common. Ganguly also wanted
to create a culture where youngsters felt they were as much part of the
team as the old pros, although Wright had to suggest to Ganguly he get
a watch to make sure that as captain he was not late.

Wright and Ganguly could also take comfort from the fact that in
their first Test together they were facing Zimbabwe, who, apart from their
problems on the field, were so shambolic off it that they arrived without
their baggage. And not only was their baggage missing; missing also were
two of their best players, Murray Goodwin and Neil Johnson, as a result
of the political problems in that country created by the Mugabe regime
intruding on to the cricket field.

However, helped by dreadful Indian catching on a flat Delhi batting
wicket, and led by 183 not out from Andy Flower, Zimbabwe made 422
for 9 declared. Rahul Dravid had the perfect response by achieving his
first double hundred. He shared a 213-run partnership with Tendulkar, who
made 122. The first sign that Ganguly was going to be a very different
captain emerged the moment Dravid reached his double century. India at
that stage led only by 36 just before tea on the fourth day. India still had
six wickets in hand and many of his predecessors would have carried on.
Ganguly did not want a draw but a win. He declared and the move paid
handsome dividends. Srinath, took another five-fer, his seventh in forty-eight
Tests, and Zimbabwe were bowled out for 225. India were left with 190
to make in forty-seven overs. Dravid's unbeaten 70 and Ganguly's unbeaten
65 meant India needed only thirty-eight overs to win.

The Indians had the upper hand for much of the second Test in Nagpur.
Shiv Sunder Das struck a century in his third Test, before Dravid, 162, and
Tendulkar, 201, put on a 249-run stand to guide India to an insurmountable
609/6 declared. But despite following on, helped by Flower making a career
best 232 not out, Zimbabwe batted out the match, finishing on 503/6.

Ganguly in the second innings used ten bowlers, and only Vijay Dahiya, the wicketkeeper, was not asked to take off his pads to bowl. Ganguly would have made history had India won, the first Indian captain to win his first three Tests. Instead he was left moaning that the Nagpur wicket was not the turning track he had wanted.

The one-day internationals were more comfortable, with India winning the five-match series 4–1. With the Indian board keen to take cricket to a new place, Jodhpur's Barkatullah Khan Stadium hosted its first match. Here Wright suddenly found a man wearing the biggest diamond ear stud he had ever seen invading the Indian players' space, wandering into the players' viewing area. Furious, Wright shouted at him, only to be told he was India's biggest beer baron. Whether this had any impact on the match is difficult to say, but this was the only match Zimbabwe won by one wicket. And just as Olonga with his bowling had engineered the Zimbabwean victory in the World Cup, now with the bat he scrambled the winning run with one ball to spare. The four Indian victories were more comfortable.

AUSTRALIA'S FINAL FRONTIER

The partnership of the first foreign coach and the first Bengali captain had got off to a good start. The noise that Wright would be a short-term appointment started to abate. During the Delhi Test one ex-player had predicted that by the second Test Wright would be making tea for the team. However, Ganguly and Wright knew their next opponent at home would be very different. It was Australia. That Australia were coming to India in February–March 2001 showed the new relationship between the two countries. As we have seen, in the past as in 1956 or 1964, Australia had stopped by on their way back home from playing an Ashes series in England. In 1969, Australia had come to India on their way to South Africa, which was considered the more important series. Now, in 2001, Australia were going to play an Ashes series in England, and even a few years previously a tour of India a few months before travelling to England would have been unthinkable, what with all the hazards of travel and possible health problems for the players. Now, for Australia, India was almost as important as their old enemy.

The change can best be illustrated in the way Malcolm Speed, who in 2001 was about to move from having run Australian cricket to running the ICC, saw it. In his memoir, *Sticky Wicket: A Decade of Change in World Cricket*, he devotes a chapter to India entitled 'India: Cricket's Unique Selling Point' and mentions that back in 1997, when he first started at the Australian Cricket Board, he had never travelled to India and had no interest in doing so. Over the next eleven years he would make forty trips and was amazed by the passion for the game and recognized that power had shifted from the old guard of England and Australia to India. On the field, Australian cricketers also recognized this. India was seen as the final frontier by Australian cricketers. The Australians had not won in India since 1969, four tours earlier. Australia under Steve Waugh was determined to set it right. And a very confident Australia landed in Mumbai having won all their previous fifteen Tests.

Australia made sure their determination to win in India was well publicized. Indian journalists told Wright how impressive the Australians were. To make matters worse, the Indian manager, Chetan Chauhan, told the media that one of his jobs was to help Wright overcome language problems. For Wright it was as if Australia was the home team and he the foreigner coaching an away team. Wright tried to put his stamp on the Indian team, telling the Indians during the camp at Chennai that it could no longer be tolerated that a lot of food was ordered from room service and the junior players handed around the snacks. However, Wright soon realized the difference between how India and Australia prepared for the series. Just before the First Test in Mumbai, when Wright went into the gym of the hotel where both teams were staying, he found Ponting and the other Australians working hard, but the one Indian player working on a bike was wearing sandals, having a cup of tea, and soon a waiter would bring a plate of sandwiches for him. Nevertheless, Wright did get the Indians to work so hard in the camp that there were complaints: Srinath, theatrically falling on his knees, even pleaded 'Relent, John, relent'. The Wright regime so exhausted the Indians that many of the twenty-five Indian players often fell asleep on the bus taking them back to the hotel after training.

To beat Australia India needed a bowler, and even before the series began, India faced a huge problem. Anil Kumble's shoulder injury ruled him out of the series. Wright, however, felt confident other spinners could fill in for him and he got Kumble, his arm in a sling, to come and have a look at them. One of them was Harbhajan Singh, who we last heard about on the plane to Dubai, having a bit of fun.

Ganguly had drawn Wright's attention to Harbhajan during the Zimbabwe Test. Wright had heard how Harbhajan off the field could be difficult to control but at the nets he saw the Sikh turn the ball prodigiously and get bounce. Even so, Wright felt he was not landing the ball in the right place. He decided to take a leaf out of old cricket coaching manuals. He went to the good length spot, drew a box and told Harbhajan to land it there, promising him he would then hit the off stump. Another innovation was to get the Indian commentator Harsha Bhogle to address the team on what cricket meant to Indians.

But for all Wright's work, the series did not begin well. Two days before the first Test in Mumbai, Donald Bradman had died. Steve Waugh promised the Australians would play in the spirt of Bradman, and this was a match Bradman would have scripted: there was great fast bowling from McGrath, wonderful leg-spin from Warne. India made 176, only Tendulkar making runs, 76. Australia were batting before the end of the first day. On the second, India had a moment when Australia were 99 for 5 in reply. The next Australian wicket did not fall until 296, Hayden and Gilchrist made centuries and although Tendulkar in the second innings made a masterly 65, no other batsman made more than 44. India lost eight wickets for 65 and Australia, left 47 to win, won by ten wickets with two days to spare.

The Australian players were also very much in the Indians' faces. Unlike in Australia or even England, the Australian cricketers were not subjected in the Indian media to mind games. Instead, the Australian cricketers were used to advertise products and were even signed up for syndicated columns, which they then used to play mind games with the Indians. But while a previous generation of Indians might have accepted that, reflecting their colonial mentality, Ganguly, born a quarter of a century after India won freedom, did not share this spirit of subservience. In Kolkata, Waugh overheard Ganguly on his mobile talking to the Eden Gardens groundsman and telling him to prepare wickets to suit the Indian spinners. Waugh used his column in the Indian media to criticize Ganguly. Ganguly decided that for his first Test as captain on his home ground he would make Waugh wait for the toss. He made him wait not just a few minutes but several minutes, with the explanation that he had to retrieve his blazer, which he had left behind in the dressing room. That incident, which has gone down in cricket history, was meant to show that Ganguly was not the meek Indian who took it lying down from a visiting white foreigner.

A SAVIOUR IS DISCOVERED

But while this was a new in-your-face India on the field, it seemed to make little difference: Australia only emphasized the dominance they had achieved in Mumbai during the first three days of the Kolkata Test. Australia made 445 although Harbhajan evidently benefited from Wright's instructions to bowl in the box. He became the first Indian to claim a Test hat-trick, his hat-trick ball being a full toss that Warne glanced to short-leg. Harbhajan took four more wickets but his seven wickets cost 123 and reflected the fact that Australia had made a great recovery with Waugh, who made a century and was helped by the tail, converting 269 for 8 to 445. At the end of the second day India were 128 for 8 and the only question seemed to be how long the match would last. Wright sat in his hotel room being told he would be sacked and drowned his sorrows drinking Heineken and smoking cigarettes. It was he says, 'one of the loneliest, most desolate nights of my life'. India the next day made some sort of recovery: they got to 171 but had been bowled out in 58.1 overs and were asked to follow on 274 runs behind. Wright lost his cool and kicked Coca-Cola cans in the dressing room. It was then that he and Ganguly came up with a remarkable idea.

The only Indian batsman who had done anything was V.V.S. Laxman, who made 59 from 83 balls, batting at No. 6. The next highest scorer was Dravid, who made 25. Apart from anything else, this innings showed Laxman's determination. There had been much doubt whether he would be fit for the Test. His shoulders and hip were not in line, and his body listed to compensate for that. Andrew Leipus, who had come in as trainer, straightened him out and on the morning of the Test Wright and Ganguly had to decide whether to play Laxman. They decided to risk him. But this meant that at every break Leipus straightened Laxman out.

Now, at the start of the second innings, Ganguly and Wright wrestled with the question of what could be done to change things. As we have seen, under Tendulkar's captaincy, Dravid batting at No. 3 was almost set in stone. Dravid could at times be 'The Wall' (although he had not yet acquired that name), but in the series he was not batting well and had made 9, 39, 25. Wright thought of what Ian Chappell had told him. At No. 3 you want a stroke-maker. Wright did think of asking Dravid to change his guard, but then Ganguly and Wright came up with the idea that the Leaning Tower of India, as Wright called Laxman, be promoted to take Dravid's place and Dravid be dropped down to No. 6. Ganguly and Wright knew a change in the batting order had risks, not least because the Australians would scent blood and lose no time in mocking the Indians. However, Laxman was not worried. He was full of smiles when, at the end of the Indian first innings, Wright came up to him and said, 'Lax, keep your pads on. How'd you like to bat three?' His expression reflected the inner confidence of a man who, while he had opened for India and did not much like it, preferred batting higher up and was the king of runs in the Ranji trophy. In the 1999–2000 season he had set a new Ranji record by scoring 1,415 runs, with a record eight hundreds, one of which, 353, was made in the semi-final for Hyderabad against Karnataka and which then was the fourth time he had scored a double century. True, this was Indian domestic cricket and in the past Indian run-getters in the Ranji trophy did not often reproduce that form in Tests. But Laxman knew how to bat for long hours and make runs, and that was crucial.

Also, Laxman, unlike many other Indian batsmen, was not fazed when facing Australian bowling. As we have seen, he had scored what had been described as a once-in-a-lifetime hundred in Sydney, and from his teens he had liked Australian bowling. Playing for India Under-19 against Australia he had faced Jason Gillespie, McGrath's opening partner, making four big scores including a 151 not out.

Laxman went out to bat after lunch with the score on 52, hit a good-length McGrath ball for four, and then the first ball after that, bowled by Gillespie, he also hit for four. It seemed that what Wright and Ganguly had hoped for: that an Indian batsman would take the attack to the Australians, was happening. The question was, would anybody stay with him at the other end? Tendulkar made 10, Ganguly 48, and when Dravid joined him shortly before the close of play on the third day, India were 232 for 4, still 42 behind. As Dravid walked in, Waugh tried to unsettle him: 'From number three to number six, one more failure and you will be out of the side.' Dravid said nothing, just resolved to stay with Laxman, and at the end of the day's play India were 254 for 4, Laxman 109, Dravid 7 and still 20 runs behind.

The fourth day dawned with most of the journalists looking at flights to catch, thinking the match would be over that day. It did not seem likely that India could do much more than make sure an innings defeat was avoided and that Australia lose a few wickets chasing their seventeenth successive Test victory. The odds that the fourth day in Kolkata would see Laxman and Dravid lay the foundations for a cricketing feat which had never been achieved by any Indian side and which had only happened twice before in the 124 years of Test history would have been dismissed as fantasy. Yet this is exactly what happened. Laxman found a soulmate and Dravid rediscovered his form.

The two men had much in common, both being from the south, both middle class. Laxman, whose parents were doctors in Hyderabad, his father a general practitioner, his mother a radiologist, had taken to cricket because of an uncle. His school, charmingly called Little Flower, did not have sport in its curriculum. Like Dravid, he had wondered whether to give up cricket for higher education, in his case to become a doctor. The crucial moment came when, just as he was turning eighteen, he was faced with the choice of either going to medical college or winning a place in the Under-19 national coaching camp. He decided to give cricket four years. Laxman and Dravid had known each other's game since their Under-19 days and Laxman much admired Dravid's attitude to the game and the focus he brought to it. 'I guess,' says Laxman, 'we are soul brothers with similar value systems but when you are batting together all that matters is scoring runs and not getting out.' And this is what they did. The only problem was the dehydration the two batsmen suffered in the intense heat; when the Indian dressing room ran out of neckerchiefs, strips were made from towels, dipped in ice and sent out to Dravid.

Laxman and Dravid batted the entire day, adding 335 in ninety overs. By the end of the day, India were 589 for 4, Laxman 275 not out, Dravid 155 not out. The day was one full of stats Indian cricket lovers would recite with pleasure in the years to come. On 237 Laxman went past the previous highest score by an Indian in a Test innings, Gavaskar 236 not out. On 238 Laxman bettered the previous highest individual score by any batsman against Australia in the subcontinent. On 252 he went past Wally Hammond's record of 251 set in Sydney in December 1928 as the highest score by any batsman against Australia batting at No. 3; and on 257 he went past the previous best by any individual on Indian soil, which was the 256 by Rohan Kanhai at the same venue.

At the end of the day's play Laxman and Dravid came off the field, a towel around Dravid's neck, a neckerchief around Laxman's, holding their bats horizontal in their left hand, their helmets in their right hand. They had the look of men who knew that India's lead of 315 and only four wickets down made the match secure. Laxman was beaming, although Dravid had a sombre look. This was partly exhaustion but also the fact that for a rare time in his career he was upset by the media reaction, and as he had reached his hundred he made a gesture at the media centre, making a very un-Dravid-like display of anger.

As Laxman kept breaking records, Eden Gardens flashed the financial rewards he was getting from the board. ₹200,000 for scoring 200; then every run beyond 200 got him another thousand; and when he went past Gavaskar's 236, that thousand was doubled. As if not to overlook Harbhajan, he too was rewarded, and then a team reward of ₹500,000 was offered if India won.

Of course, an Indian victory would depend on a declaration, something Wright and Ganguly discussed over dinner that night. Wright advised Ganguly that as the Australians did not like playing for a draw in a match which was going nowhere, the declaration should be delayed so that it played on their nerves. That meant no declaration until after lunch on the fifth day. This gave Laxman a chance to become the first Indian ever to score 300 in a Test innings, which, amazingly, after nearly seventy years of Test cricket no Indian batsman had done whereas all the Test-playing countries, barring Zimbabwe and Bangladesh, had batsmen with a Test 300 to their name. On the fifth day, Laxman looked like he might set this right, but on 281 he was caught by Ponting off McGrath. But the score was still a landmark. Laxman's 281 placed him at twenty-first position in the All Time Individual Score recorded by a batsman in Test Cricket. But his score, being against Australia, was the third best against Australia after Len Hutton's 364, and Reg Foster's 287. The stand had put on 376, a new fifth-wicket record for India against any country, and the third best for any country, also the best Indian stand for any wicket against Australia. The only stand the pair had not gone past was the 413 between Mankad and Roy back in 1955. But if an Australian bowler was able to get Laxman out, they could not get Dravid out. It was his running between the wickets that got him when he had made 180. The stats of the two players were comparable to the batting that the two Vijays, Merchant and Hazare, had often produced in the 1930s and 1940s. Laxman had batted for over ten hours (631 minutes), facing 452 balls, and hitting 44 fours; Dravid had batted for seven hours and 26 minutes (446 minutes), facing 353 balls and hitting 20 fours.

Ganguly declared only after India had scored 657. India had left themselves seventy-five overs, little more than two sessions, to bowl Australia out, and by tea the match seemed destined for a draw with Australia, who needed 383, on 161 for 3. Waugh had been dropped just before tea. Harbhajan had taken two of the three Australian wickets to fall by tea. What Ganguly noticed was that at the end from which he was bowling, the umpire was not giving lbws. So, he changed ends, and after tea Harbhajan really got to work. Ganguly also brought Tendulkar on, not expecting him to take wickets but to keep one end tight. The great man had discussed with Kumble what to do with his leg-spin bowling and Kumble himself would have been proud of what he did. He took three wickets, conceding only 31 runs in eleven overs which included three maidens. Two of the wickets were crucial: Hayden and Gilchrist, either of whom could have changed this game for Australia as they often had done in the past. Both were lbw with Gilchrist's dismissal meaning the best batsman wicketkeeper of his generation had made a king pair. In some ways the third wicket that Tendulkar took provided the perfect illustration of what Neville Cardus, the Mancunian who invented cricket writing, called 'the play within the play' and was a wonderful example of role reversal. The Tendulkar–Warne duels had been between one of the game's greatest batsmen and one of the game's greatest bowlers. Now it was Tendulkar with the ball against Warne with the bat. Tendulkar got Warne lbw with a googly which, had

Warne bowled it to Tendulkar, might have got the maestro out. Ganguly feels it was a ball that could have got out the best batsmen in the world. Tendulkar had provided the platform for Harbhajan who eagerly seized the moment. Australia declined so dramatically that in the final session they lost seven wickets in twenty-three overs for 51 runs, with Harbhajan taking five of them to finish with 6 for 73. India won by 171 runs. While this was the first time India, having followed on, had won, this was the third such defeat for Australia, the two previous occasions having been at the hands of England. Australia remain the only country to suffer such a humiliating turnaround. The Indian victory had a huge impact on Test cricket. After Kolkata, a captain did not immediately enforce a follow-on but recalled what Laxman and Dravid had done in Kolkata, had a rethink, and as often as not decided to bat again. Laxman and Dravid had changed Test cricket.

The Indians could hardly believe what they had done. Now such was their self-confidence that Tendulkar and Dravid asked Waugh, 'So, how's the final frontier looking now, Steve?' However, with the last Test being in Chennai, as it had been in 1969, Australia could hope that history would repeat itself. And Indian cricket once again presented its famous dual face. The cricketers oozed belief and sorted out who should field where, Dravid consolidating his position at first slip, but the board and the Indian selectors hardly seemed to be in command of things. A computer analyst was agreed on but he was not considered high enough in the pecking order to merit a five-star hotel so was put up in a hotel far from where the team was staying, which forced any player wanting to look at the footage to make a taxi journey across Chennai; often they decided not to bother. Then, fifty minutes before the Chennai Test started and with the players practising, the selection committee decided that Mongia, who had broken his nose in Kolkata, could not play with a broken nose although he had passed the fitness test, and Sameer Dighe was drafted in. Wright was aghast, and even more so when, on the first morning after Australia had won the toss and batted, Dighe dropped a couple of chances. However, before the Test ended Wright had reason to thank the Indian selectors and see it as a wise, even match-winning, move.

Australia certainly seemed to put Kolkata behind them. Hayden proved that he was more than a flat track bully, scoring 203 on a bare pitch where India played three spinners, including Sairaj Bahutule, the bowler Tendulkar had reduced to tears back in that Harris Shield match. Hayden did not make Bahutule cry although his double century in 474 minutes off 320 balls could not have been more brutal, containing as it did 6 sixes, the most by an Australian in any Test innings. The innings was even more remarkable as he lost his opening partner with the score on 4; only one other batsman, Mark Waugh, passed 50 and there were four ducks in the innings. It was appropriate that he should fall to Harbhajan, for Harbhajan had woven, as in Kolkata, a magical spell that seemed to mesmerize the Australians. The spell started with something that had only happened five times before in Test history. Steve Waugh missed a sweep off Harbhajan's bowling, the Indians appealed for lbw, but while this was being denied the ball, hitting the pads, trickled towards the stump. Alerted by Hayden, Waugh used his hand to stop it and was out, handled the ball. Harbhajan, as if galvanized, then took over. He had earlier taken the wicket of Langer. Now in 9.4 overs he took 6 for 26 and Australia, having been 340 for 3 before Steve Waugh handled, were all out for 391.

India knew that batting last they needed a big first innings score and this time Tendulkar finally came good, making a quite brilliant century, and reaching it in a grand manner with a six, his second, against Colin Miller. But unlike Hayden's innings, this was not a solitary effort. There was also support from four others making 50s, and despite a late order collapse, India got a lead of 110.

The Australian second innings was almost a replay of the first. The top order had the answer to everything India bowled but, Australia having reached 200 with five wickets standing, Harbhajan once again intervened and in 17.1 overs took five wickets for 15 and a career best of 8 for 84. He had taken fifteen wickets in the match and thirty-two wickets in the series, at an average of 17.03. In a three-Test series only three bowlers had got more wickets, namely, George Lohmann, Sydney Barnes and Richard Hadlee, but none of them were spinners. What also marked out Harbhajan was that, despite his reputation of being the potential bad boy of Indian cricket who caused administrators problems on the cricket field, he had proved a good listener and a quick adaptor. He had followed Wright's advice to bowl in the box and afterwards, far from being disheartened by the mauling Gilchrist gave him in the first Test, he worked out that the way to contain the Australians was to deny Gilchrist the chance of sweeping by keeping the ball up and bringing it in. Such was the transformation of his image that a bowler who just a season before had to face his action being questioned, with Fred Titmus helping him to get it right, was now hailed as being in the class of Saqlain Mushtaq. Like the Pakistani, he had a 'doosra', the one that drifted the other way and caused batsmen immense problems. But Harbhajan's contribution to the match was not done and he would play an important role when India batted.

India were left 155 to win and it seemed this would be no problem.

But in keeping with the drama of the series there was a final twist and this involved Dighe, the wicketkeeper whom neither Wright nor Ganguly had really wanted in the team. India had reached 101 for 2 with Tendulkar in command. But then India had an Australia-like collapse: Tendulkar fell, Laxman, going well, pulled a long hop and Mark Waugh took a sensational catch, and Wright was so downcast he gave up hopes of victory tapping on his computer, 'That may be the Test. F★★K, f★★k, f★★k.'

But this is where the wicketkeeper Wright did not want stepped in. Behind the stumps he may not have been as reliable as Mongia, but as Wright now discovered he was 'a cheeky, street-smart operator who knew every trick in the book'. He lived up to his nickname of Sam Dig. Like all the Indians in the dressing room he was nervous—nervous when he came out to bat and nervous when he was in the middle. But these nerves only made him more determined and he did not forget how to press the buttons which he knew would rattle the Australians. In some ways the situation was a replay of that epic match against Australia in Mumbai in 1964. As we have seen, there too a wicketkeeper was involved as India chased victory against Australia. But at the other end Indrajitsinhji had had a genuine batsman, Chandu Borde; Dighe had Zaheer Khan. Dighe knew he had to mislead the Australians. In the middle the chatter between the Australians was endless. Now Dighe decided to join the conversation. When Zaheer Khan came out to bat, he very loudly warned him that Colin Miller was turning the ball so viciously he was a real danger. But instead of speaking in Hindi or Marathi, which would have been more common but which the Australians would not understand, he deliberately spoke in English. Waugh heard, kept the Australian second spinner, who was playing for the first time in the series, on, and Dighe, who knew Miller was no problem, promptly scored 10 runs from his over. Then, after Zaheer departed, Harbhajan entered and he did not need Dighe to teach him street-smartness; he was if anything even smarter, and, what is more, the Australians did not know how he would bat. Some Indians felt Harbhajan himself did not know how he would bat. He exuded the air that he did not have a care in the world and with great nonchalance pushed a McGrath half volley past point and square of the wicket to run two and claim victory.

It was appropriate that Harbhajan had the last word in the series, for in many ways he was the Indian match-winner and the defining difference between the two teams. This is to take nothing away from Laxman's 281 and his partnership with Dravid. That changed the series and provided Harbhajan with the platform, but while Laxman's 503 runs at an average of 83.83 was a landmark achievement in terms of runs scored, Australia too had one batsman who matched him, not perhaps in style, where Laxman was without peer in the series, but in quantity of runs. Hayden had actually scored more—549 at an average of 109.80. And Laxman had had backing from Dravid, whose 338 at an average of 56.33 made him second in the averages. Tendulkar may have come late to the party with his bat but he was just behind Dravid, having scored 304 and averaging 50.66. The difference was that with the ball Harbhajan had proved a destroyer in the way McGrath and Warne, two of the greatest bowlers of their generation, had not. Harbhajan's thirty-two was five more than the combined wicket tally of McGrath and Warne. McGrath had still been Australia's best, his seventeen wickets averaging 15.35, but Warne's ten had cost 505 runs at an average of 50.50 a wicket. He troubled the Indian batsmen so little, in particular Laxman, who seemed to like nothing better than to step out and drive him, that in the final stages of the Chennai Test Waugh had not brought him on to bowl. For a rookie Indian spinner to outshine one of the greatest spinning legends of the game was saying something. It proved the old adage that bowlers win matches.

India's win by two wickets was the narrowest of their Test wins and exactly the margin of their victory at the CCI in Mumbai back in 1964. Pataudi had made us believe Indians were not the dull dogs of cricket. Ganguly's mission was to prove the corruption stories had had no impact and that Indians could take on anyone, anywhere, whether in India or abroad. India need no longer take to a cricket field in fear.

Chapter 34

TENDULKAR IS INDIA

Three months after the victory over Australia, India were off to Zimbabwe. As if to test Ganguly's new India, the board so arranged fixtures that from May 2001 the team visited eleven countries in twenty-two months, travelled more than 130,000 kilometres and stayed in sixty-six hotels. In Mugabe land India won the first Test inside four days by eight wickets. But then the old India emerged in Harare, where Zimbabwe had their first Test victory over a side other than Bangladesh.

Wright quickly worked out that the body language of the Indians when they went abroad was all wrong. Against Australia at home he had been impressed with Indian self-belief; in Zimbabwe he found that the moment wickets fell the cricketers seem to feel the cause was lost. And there was the lack of Indian food abroad. Ashish Nehra, a left-arm seamer whom Azharuddin had first picked out for a Test debut, went to bowl one morning having had three biscuits because nothing else available was right for him. There was always a search for Indian restaurants on tour. However, Nehra did emerge from the Zimbabwe tour suggesting he could be part of the breed of Ganguly's men. A Delhi boy who had grown up playing cricket with Virender Sehwag, they would go to matches sitting on a scooter, one driving, the other holding the kitbag on the back seat. They formed a great cricketing pair. 'Viru toh yaaron ka yaar hai' [Viru is a great friend], Nehra would say. And celebrating Nehra's thirty-eighth birthday, Sehwag referred to Nehra as the 'Bheeshma Pitamah of Indian cricket'. On this tour Nehra's bowling suggested India's seam attack was no longer a one-man show. And what also caught the eye was the Indian fielding. Laxman, Dravid and Shiv Sunder Das also excelled with their close catching. Wright's regime of cutting out tea and snacks during practice sessions and making the players work hard was clearly paying dividends.

Two months later the Indians were crossing the Palk Strait to Sri Lanka, for a one-day triangular series which also involved New Zealand and then a three-Test series. The one-day series saw Sehwag open for the first time. Then a middle-order batsman, Wright felt Sehwag was a good timer of the ball and could hit the ball hard. When he batted in the middle order with the field set deep he was often caught, but if he opened, the bowling side could not set deep fields and Wright's thinking was he might help India take charge of the match right from the start. Also, pace bowlers did not worry him. Sehwag was keen although in the first three matches he scored 33, 27 and a duck. But against New Zealand on 2 August 2001, opening with Ganguly, he made a hundred in a first wicket stand of 143. His century had come in sixty-nine balls, the seventh-fastest in one-day internationals, containing 1 six and 19 fours. Wright was delighted that his countrymen had been punished. India had found an opener of dazzling qualities, although the full implications of what this meant for Indian cricket were not immediately apparent.

Despite his success against Australia in the three Test series, Ganguly began to feel that he might not last as captain. Raj Singh walked into the dressing room and patting Dravid, who was the vice-captain, told him to prepare to take over the captaincy. It had not gone unnoticed that in the one-day series it was with Ganguly's suspension that India started winning. But this was when Ganguly first indicated that under him India when abroad would have something of the grit and determination they showed at home. Having lost the first Test by ten wickets they came back in the second Test. India were set 264 to win but, in a Test where the highest score had been 274, this in the fourth innings, seemed a tall order. Tendulkar and Laxman were both injured and Ganguly himself had been in wretched form, no half century in his previous thirteen Test innings. Ganguly decided the only way out of failure was to be positive, and right from the start of his innings he was playing some sumptuous drives, particularly on the off side. With Dravid showing the Indians how to play Muttiah Muralitharan and executing some quite audacious back-foot drives square of the wicket against the Sri Lankan magician, the pair took India from 103 for 2 to 194 when Dravid got out. With Mohammad Kaif holding one end up, Ganguly launched more of his drives, ending up hitting 15 fours. His only regret when victory came was that he was on 98. However, this was more than compensated for by the margin of victory by seven wickets and with a day to spare. And that, away from home, India had come back after losing the first Test was very encouraging.

However, in the deciding third Test in Colombo India lost by an innings and 77 runs which equalled Sri Lanka's biggest winning margin set against Zimbabwe five years earlier.

TENDULKAR CAN NEVER CHEAT
In 1975, when Mrs Indira Gandhi imposed the Emergency her adoring

followers trumpeted 'Indira is India'. In the winter of 2001 a Test series in South Africa saw cricket's version of this slogan: 'Tendulkar is India'. Indian cricket officials showed the new face of Indian cricket, an India which was willing to use Indian economic power to dictate to the rest of the world and get what India wanted.

There was little hint of this when the first Test began at Bloemfontein. Tendulkar, finding the pitch bouncy and no third man, began to use the uppercut, a shot I had seen him play in Johannesburg in the first Indian series in South Africa against Donald, but one he had played rarely since. Now, in the second half of his career this became his favourite shot on such wickets. His century came in only 114 balls and he became the youngest batsman, at twenty-eight years, to reach 7,000 runs. Sehwag, making his Test debut and batting No. 6, reassured by Tendulkar, made 105, the pair putting on 220. Despite making 379 after being put in, India bowled so badly that South Africa made 563. They then collapsed to 237 in the second innings, handing the Proteas a straightforward task of scoring 54 to take a 1–0 lead. It was in second Test at Port Elizabeth that the great drama featuring Tendulkar took place.

The fuse was lit on the third day by the match referee, Mike Denness. He summoned six Indian players for a hearing. Four were charged with excessive appealing. They were Virender Sehwag, Deep Dasgupta, the wicketkeeper, Harbhajan Singh, and Shiv Sunder Das. Ganguly was charged with not controlling his players. Harbhajan, Das, Dasgupta and Ganguly were given a suspended one-test ban and fined 75 per cent of their match fee. Denness felt Sehwag was the worst of the appealers and banned him from the third Test. Ironically, only one other Test player had ever suffered such a punishment before, Ridley Jacobs of the West Indies and then it was Sehwag who was the victim.

The gravest charge was against the sixth player, Tendulkar. He was accused of ball tampering. The picture that was much publicized showed Tendulkar holding the ball with both hands and using the index finger of his left hand to clean the grass stuck on the seam of the ball. But while he accepted he should have told the umpire he was cleaning the seam, he was furious he was accused of cheating and more so as this was the decision of Denness, who was 80 yards from the pitch when the on-field umpires had said nothing. When he told Denness to talk to the on-field umpires, the Scot said there was no need. Denness found him guilty of cleaning the ball without the umpire's permission. His punishment was a suspended ban for one Test and a fine of 75 per cent of his match fee. To accuse Tendulkar, India's cricketing Yudhishthira, the man who had never committed any sin, was bad enough. What made it worse was that the wording of the charge, 'interference with the match ball, thus changing its condition', implied he was a cheat. As the Indians saw it, this meant in effect that Denness was calling India a cheat. Indian newspapers spoke of the action being racist and that nothing had been done about South African players often using obscenities directed at Indian players. The matter was even debated in the Lok Sabha.

Tendulkar, who describes the event in Port Elizabeth in his autobiography in a chapter entitled 'Standing up for Myself', had told Denness at his hearing that he would go to the Indian board and would not accept this punishment lying down. India knew that the cricket world was well aware of its economic power. The Indian visit to Zimbabwe had wiped out the accumulated losses of the Zimbabwe board. The New Zealand board had announced figures which showed that while they had made money from the Indian tour of 1998–99, they had lost money the following year when Pakistan were the visitors.

The Indian who best knew how to use Indian cricket's financial power was Dalmiya, and with almost perfect timing he was back at the helm of Indian cricket, having ousted Dr A. C. Muthiah, the incumbent president. 'Juggu is back' was the shout and Wright, who knew Muthiah and did not know Dalmiya, was alarmed, exclaiming 'Oh shit!' when he heard. As soon as the Port Elizabeth storm broke, Dalmiya was on the phone to Wright asking precise and detailed questions about what had happened.

Dalmiya demanded that Denness be replaced as match referee for the third Test at the Supersport Park in Centurion. When the ICC refused, he threatened to abandon the tour. The South Africans, aware of the economic damage this would cause, caved in. They brought in home umpires and told Denness he would not be allowed to go into the match referee's box. The ICC withdrew him and the independent umpire from England, George Sharp. It was back to the old days of home umpires with former South African cricketer Denis Lindsay officiating as referee at Centurion. There was a neat twist here as the ICC had appointed Lindsay to supervise India's home series with England that was to commence in Mohali a week after the Centurion Test finished. However, the South African Board told their players Centurion was an unofficial Test. India in contrast said this Test was official. Sehwag was dropped: as the Indians saw it not playing him meant he would serve his ban. Dalmiya then set out trying to get the penalties imposed by Denness set aside and make the Centurion Test, which was declared unofficial by the ICC, official. Dalmiya did not succeed, and the third Test remained an unofficial Test.

ENGLAND SURRENDER

The echoes of what Dalmiya had engineered in South Africa were soon felt in the India–England series. Dalmiya had three objectives in this series. The first was to make England and ICC accept that the Centurion Test was official and Sehwag had served his ban. He didn't succeed in this. However, as a result of 9/11 and the shock waves it sent through the Western world not many England cricketers were keen to tour India. The English cricket authorities, led by Lord MacLaurin, then chairman of the England & Wales Cricket Board (ECB), who had never got on with Dalmiya, indicated that an Indian tour would cause problems. Dalmiya's response was to threaten England with not fulfilling India's commitment to tour England in 2002. The ECB did not have to be reminded what a huge financial loss this would be. And with England sending a team to check out that India was secure for its players, Dalmiya also made it clear that there would be an Indian security team going to England to make sure there was no risk for Ganguly's men either. Dalmiya also made England play an additional one-day international in India and England gave in to the moneybags of cricket.

Against this political background, the Test series in India in the winter of 2001 was not a particularly brilliant cricket spectacle. India easily won in Mohali with Dasgupta making his maiden century and Tendulkar an exquisite 88. The two spinners worked in tandem very well, with Kumble becoming the first Indian spinner to reach 300 wickets. So effective were the pair that bowling together after lunch on the fourth day, seven English wickets went in twenty-two overs, England hurtling from 159 for 3 to 235 all out. India were asked 5 runs to make and Ganguly decided he would have a bit of fun. Iqbal Siddiqui, who was making his Test debut as opening bowler and had batted No. 10 in the first innings, opened and scored all five as India won by ten wickets. Indians thought there could be a repeat of 1993, but England made sure they did not lose all three Tests, drawing both in Ahmedabad and the rain-affected third Test in Bengaluru. The only cricket moment worth talking about in Bengaluru was when Ashley Giles, in order to stop Tendulkar, bowled 90 per cent of his deliveries persistently wide of the leg stump. In the press box we could see Tendulkar getting tense. His 90 took four and a half hours. Then, finally frustrated, he stepped out and was stumped for the first time in 89 Tests. Three months later, the ICC cricket committee discussed why the umpires had not ruled much of Giles' balls wides and agreed that steps should be taken to see that it was done.

Few cricket fans were happy with the Indian performance. The media freely speculated that Wright and Leipus would go. Wright had feared for his job ever since Dalmiya had taken over. He met him for the first time just after the victory at Mohali. He found Dalmiya installed in the suite he had at the Taj Palace, no warmth, no charm, but one who knew his mind and did not mess about. Wright noted that at Ahmedabad Mohinder Amarnath turned up and had a long chat with Ganguly. Amarnath was desi, native, Wright was gora, white, and the Indians might well decide they had had enough of the gora in charge. However, the players liked the gora and after consulting them Dalmiya extended Wright and Leipus's contract until November 2002 and agreed to have a fitness trainer.

There was also much public debate as to whether Ganguly was the right captain. Raj Singh had little time for Dalmiya. In my conversations with Raj Singh, he would often mock Dalmiya's knowledge of cricket saying, 'No wonder he pronounces it as "kirkit" or "kirkate". Fortunately he doesn't have to spell it.' He also made it clear to me he saw Ganguly as Dalmiya's man and did not rate him as a cricketer or captain. Ganguly had already won as many Tests as any other Indian captain abroad—three, although two of them were against Bangladesh and Zimbabwe. And he had been without Kumble for much of the first year of his captaincy.

He also had a wonderful rapport with the young players. By now many of them were calling him 'Dada'. In Mumbai the word dada denotes a gang leader and dadagiri means someone showing off their power. But in this case the players used dada in the Bengali sense of denoting respect. He could behave like a Mumbai dada as he had done during the Mohali test, having an on-field argument with Andrew Flintoff, which David Hopps described as an 'engrossing 18-certificate spat'. But for players like Harbhajan and Sehwag this made Dada all the more special.

Chapter 35

CHANGING THE INDIAN MINDSET

POVERTY OF AMBITION

On the afternoon of 22 June 2002, I sat down with Sourav Gangly in the pavilion at Hove. India were playing Sussex in a day-night, 50-over match, marking the start of India's fourteenth tour of England. This was one of three non-first class matches the Indians were playing in preparation for the 50-over NatWest series which would precede the Test series. Ganguly was not playing, and India was captained by Dravid. Just six weeks earlier, I had seen Ganguly batting in Barbados against the West Indies. The Indians had come to that third Test in a five-Test series having won the second in Trinidad, their third victory at the ground, taking a 1–0 lead and feeling they might win a series there for the first time since 1971. But in Barbados India began badly, and just when it seemed there might be a revival, Dravid was run out. Although Ganguly went on to make 48 and was the last man out, India managed only 102 and from that point on the third Test was lost and this marked a turning point in the series. How much of a psychological advantage this gave the West Indians became evident in the final Test in Kingston. With the fourth Test drawn, had this final one been drawn, Ganguly could claim he had come out from the West Indies with a drawn series, which India had never managed before. Rain had been forecast in Jamaica and India had started that final day's play with three wickets in hand. But these wickets fell in nine overs, and half an hour later, Zaheer Khan slogged Mervyn Dillon to cover to end the Test, the rains came and it rained for the next eleven days.

India's defeat by the West Indians meant India had not won a series outside the subcontinent since 1986. Indeed, on the 2002 West Indies tour, the old India had resurfaced. The Indian batting was prone to collapse, with the lower order contributing little, and in four innings the last four or five wickets averaged 25. Dalmiya had been sufficiently alarmed to telephone Wright during the first Test to ask, 'What's going on? The team appear to have given up.' India did win the one-day series, but then left the trophy on the luggage belt at Heathrow as the team made their way back to

India. Ganguly could win a solitary Test abroad, as he had in Sri Lanka and the West Indies, but not a series. Just before I had met Ganguly, Harsha Bhogle, India's leading commentator, had told me that winning at Trinidad and then losing the series was 'the poverty of ambition'.

However, what struck me during my conversation with Ganguly was that he was quite determined to change the players' mindset and how composed he was. Contrary to his reputation of being 'Lord Snooty', he could not have been more charming. He called me Mihirda, as he has always done. He also frankly admitted that Barbados had been the turning point of the West Indian tour and 'I ran out Rahul'. But he also went on to point out that the end of the West Indies tour had brought changes. In the one-day series Sehwag, Yuvraj and Mohammad Kaif, the young generation, had all come in and done well; and in order to have a sixth batsman, Ganguly had persuaded a reluctant Dravid to take up wicketkeeping again, although he had to be provided with gloves. This is just what he was doing that day at Sussex. Wright had also got sports psychologist Sandy Gordon to draw up the India Touring 2002 plan, resulting in the formation of a group of senior players to effectively ensure the team stayed on course away from home.

The first big test was the three-nation NatWest series involving India, England, and Sri Lanka. India easily topped the group and got to the final against England. England, on winning the toss, made 325 for 5, their fourth-highest score in this form of the game. The Indian reply was woeful. India at the halfway mark were 146 for 5, all the recognized batsman, Sehwag, Ganguly, Dravid, and Tendulkar having gone. Many of the Indian supporters—and there were quite a few that day at Lord's—began to drift away, thinking that India, which since 1999 had reached nine ODI finals and lost them all, would now add another to this dismal tally. As I left the press box and walked round Lord's I became very aware of their disconsolate mood. For the Indians in Britain to see the visiting Indian team surrender so abjectly was very dispiriting. What we did not know then was that the Indian dressing room was not a happy place. Ganguly was not talking to Wright for having shouted at Sehwag just before the final after he had come late for a team meeting by a few minutes. Sehwag was one of 'his players' and he would not allow anyone, even the coach, to shout at him.

It was then that Yuvraj and Kaif, Ganguly's 'players', got together. These two knew each other's cricket and had a lot to prove. At the age of twelve, Kaif had left his birthplace, Allahabad, to go to Kanpur to work in a sports hostel. In order to play cricket he had to, in effect, act as an assistant to the mali, who also acted as the groundsman. He had to help prepare practice wickets by filling buckets with water from a handpump and bringing them back to the wicket. He was also a cricketer unafraid to express himself on the field and had annoyed Nasser Hussain. The only Muslim in the Indian side had so rattled the British Muslim captain of England, who was himself born in India, that in a group match Hussain had told Kaif to shut up and called him a 'bus driver'. Now this was Kaif's chance to show how well a bus driver could bat and he played some wonderful drives.

He and Yuvraj put on 121 in less than eighteen overs. As this partnership progressed, the players got very superstitious, and those who were watching were not allowed to move from their position. Dinesh Mongia on the physio's table had to stay put. The start of the partnership had seen Tendulkar sitting on a table in the middle of the room eating an energy bar; he kept eating them. Players wanting to go to the loo could only do so at the end of the over, come back before the next started, and resume the position they had before the toilet break. With the pair still in after forty overs, the Indian dressing room began to believe India could win. This belief was not shaken when Yuvraj went for 69. Kaif carried on, making 87 and, with Zaheer Khan as his partner, saw India home with three balls to spare. As Zaheer Khan scrambled the winning run off an overthrow, Ganguly took off his shirt and, standing in the visitors' dressing room balcony, whirled it around his head. No player had ever done this at Lord's, and certainly not a captain. Harbhajan would have wanted the whole team to join in, but Dravid insisted that it would be wrong. Ganguly's gesture has been much talked about. Wright, who had given Ganguly a hug after the win, felt the Indians had reacted like excited schoolboys, running down the stairs and rushing through the Long Room on the field to celebrate with Kaif. Ganguly could claim that some of them, like Sehwag, Yuvraj, Kaif and Harbhajan, were indeed 'his' boys.

A BOLD NEW INDIA

Winning a one-day series was one thing. But could India win a Test series in England for only the third time? Or indeed, even win a Test? Even that would be progress, given that since 1932 they had played forty-one Tests in England and won three and lost twenty-two. The early signs were very discouraging, England crushing India by 170 runs in the first Test at Lord's.

However, Lord's had seen India find a new opener and one that would have dramatic consequences for Indian cricket. Before the Lord's Test, Ganguly and Wright decided Sehwag should open. With the 'Fab Four' in the middle order, Sehwag would always struggle to get in, and it was felt that his technique would ensure he could make this difficult transition. He kept his head still, he hardly moved sideways, played the ball with the full face of the bat and hit the ball very hard. There was a happy precedent. In England, in 1936, Mushtaq Ali had become a great opening partner of Vijay Merchant. Sehwag, who certainly treated spinners much as Mushtaq had done, did not like the idea of opening but accepted, and at Lord's made 84 in ninety-six balls, an innings of which Mushtaq would certainly have approved.

The second Test at Nottingham suggested Sehwag would be found out. It was overcast, the wicket green, the ball swung and seamed, but despite this India batted first when conditions were most challenging for the batsmen and Sehwag scored a century. But all this was overshadowed by Michael Vaughan making his best Test score of 197 in a mammoth England score of 617. On the fifth morning, with India in their second innings 99 for 2, admission prices were reduced and crowds flooded in hoping to see England win four consecutive Tests for the first time since 1991–92. However, this was when the mettle Ganguly and Wright were trying to create began to shine through. Dravid showed how much he liked English conditions by making 115, Tendulkar and Ganguly just missed centuries, with 92 and 99, the second time Ganguly had missed three figures by a single run. And the final act of this unexpected rescue fell to an Indian who looked so young that, at the start of the tour, the Englishman handling the Indians' baggage and looking after other odds and ends wanted to shoo him away, thinking he was an autograph hunter. When he had led the Indian side onto the stage for the Wisden Indian Cricketer of the Century Awards in London, many assumed he was the team mascot.

The young boy was Parthiv Patel. With the regular wicketkeeper, Ajay Ratra, injured in the first Test, India had to find a replacement. Dravid could not be asked to keep wickets in a Test, and it was Patel, who at the age of seventeen years and 153 days, made his entry into Test cricket, making him the youngest ever wicketkeeper to play Test cricket. Indeed, at that stage Patel had neither played ODI for India, which he did a year later, or even played for his Ranji Trophy team Gujarat, which came two years later. Patel was in England because Vengsarkar, chairman of the age-group selectors, assured Ganguly and Wright that Patel was ready. While Patel looked like a boy who needed a note from his mother to come to the game, he was very much in the mould of the new India emerging. A left-hander, he idolized Adam Gilchrist, pacing his innings with a blend of calculated attack and rock-solid defence. Almost as if he was taking his cue from Ganguly, he was not the meek, silent Indian. So much so that in 2004, he would be rebuked by Steve Waugh when he came out to bat in his last international match. On the fourth day of the match, Patel chirped

from behind the wickets, 'Come on, Steve, just one more of your popular
slog-sweeps before you quit.' Waugh quickly replied, 'Show a bit of respect.
You were in nappies when I debuted 18 years ago.' After that episode,
Parthiv was questioned by his senior teammates for his unwanted sledging
of one of the greatest captains the game has seen. Many years later, with
the IPL in full swing, the South African cricketer A. B. de Villiers would
describe him as the most irritating cricketer in the world: 'He chats all the
time. I'm glad I'm playing with him [for the Royal Challengers Bangalore
(RCB) in IPL] rather than against him.'

At Nottingham on the final afternoon he came in to bat when India
were 387 for 6 and there was still the chance that, should England bowl
out India quickly, they could win. But Patel made 19 not out in eighty-
four minutes, and he ended up batting with No. 10 and ensured a draw.
It was to prove crucial as Headingley, the next Test, showed.

It was the third Test at Headingley that was to show the emerging
new India. Before the Test, Ganguly who had struck up a friendship with
Boycott, invited him to a curry buffet to pick his brains about a ground
he knew so well. Fortified by this, the Indians decided that for all the talk
of Headingley being a seamer's paradise, they would play to their strength
and picked two spinners, Kumble and Harbhajan. They also decided that,
with Wasim Jaffer failing as opener, they needed a new partner for Sehwag.
Das was the logical choice. He had made 250 against Essex in the game
preceding the Test, but Ganguly and Wright choose Sanjay Bangar who
could also be the third seamer. Bangar had been around for a long time,
having made his first-class debut in the 1993–1994 season. His story was
the classic Indian internal migrant story. Hailing from Aurangabad, he had
found work with the railways, played for them and needed a lot of resilience
as this meant travelling for months on end, playing on dust bowls, living
in railway bogeys and dormitories. Bangar never forgot his roots, and after
he started playing for India when he played for India in Delhi he often
left the team's five-star hotel to go back to the railway dormitories and
spend the night with his friends.

But perhaps the decision that showed the self-belief India was acquiring
under Ganguly was that on winning the toss India batted. This was despite
the fact that the wicket was green, it was damp and overcast and it seemed
ideal for a modern-day English bowler to do what Fred Trueman had done
in 1952. There was an audible gasp in the Headingley press box as Ganguly
signalled India was batting and much shaking of heads. What we did not
know was that in the Indian dressing room Dravid had argued that he was
sick and tired of India on green wickets putting the opposition in when

India's strength was spin. The batting had to be trusted so India could make the opposition chase a target in the fourth innings.

The first signs suggested Ganguly had got it wrong. With the score on 15, Sehwag was out for 8. But then Bangar, whom the English knew as a utility player (he had made his Test debut against England in Mohali batting at No. 8 and bowled a few overs) showed he could be an obdurate opener and played a classic second fiddle. Bangar then was so shy that Dravid nicknamed him Buddha. He certainly batted with a Buddha style calmness. The curry lunch with Boycott had clearly paid off, for the Indians were not tempted to play anything they did not have to. As Boycott had always said, a good batsman knows where his off stump is. The Indians certainly did. Bangar made 68; Dravid was 110 not out at the end of the first day, when India were 236 for 2, old-fashioned scoring for a Test match but one that totally flummoxed the English. Dravid had played what Nasser Hussain would describe as one of the finest innings he had ever seen. On the second day, a very different Indian batting was on display from Tendulkar and Ganguly. Tendulkar, who before the match had been welcomed back to Yorkshire as if he was one of their own, after a careful start began to unveil his strokes. He had come out wearing an inner-thigh guard, something he had never used, worried that Flintoff was jagging the ball back. But then he realized this made him change his stance and he discarded it. He and Ganguly put on 249. In contrast to the Dravid–Bangar stand, this was scored at four an over, more like the rate in modern Test matches. If Tendulkar was at times magical, Ganguly's play was so freewheeling that the *Wisden* write-up would say it 'would have been at home in a seaside cabaret'.

Crucial to this partnership was how Tendulkar and Ganguly dealt with Flintoff. Flintoff was bowling into the Indian captain's body, reflecting perhaps the feelings between the two men, and it was decided that Tendulkar would take Flintoff while Ganguly handled Ashley Giles's off-spin, which, Ganguly being a left-hander, also made good cricketing sense. This did produce the one moment of mirth, after tea on the second day, as the pair—still not out—went back to the dressing room, having negotiated a hostile Flintoff spell. Ganguly told Tendulkar in Hindi, 'Woh beech wale Flintoff ka spell humne kya jhela yaar. [We did really well to see off Flintoff's spell]. Tendulkar could not help responding 'Humne jhela? Saala maine jhela hain! [*We* did? Bastard! I was the one who did]. The dressing room had not often heard Tendulkar use the word saala, which can be jocular and also abusive; this one was jocular, and they fell about laughing. Tendulkar finished on 193, his highest Test score against England and passed David Gower to climb to seventh on the all-time list of Test run-getters. Ganguly made 128, and when he declared at 628 for 8 it was the highest score India had ever made against England. That they made it in England, and what is more at Headingley, meant some of the shame of 1952 and 0 for 4 was wiped out.

This is when Dravid's argument to make a big score and let the spinners loose paid off. Kumble, finally getting to bowl when batsmen had made copious runs, was in his element and took three wickets. Harbhajan also took three and England made 273, leaving them 355 behind. Ganguly asked England to follow on, the first time India had made England follow on in England. For once in the series Vaughan failed, and while Hussain made a hundred there was no holding back Kumble, who took four wickets and the final one was the perfect ending—Andy Caddick's edge off Kumble being taken by Ganguly at slip while on his knees but clinging on to the catch. To add to the pleasure, Flintoff made a pair. While the Indians did not sledge quite as much as Patel had famously done to Waugh, throughout the innings they kept up a barrage of banter, some of it in Hindi, which the English did not understand, but enough in English to make the English batsmen know exactly what they felt about them. As Tendulkar put it, 'We were all extremely motivated and did not want a single English batsman to settle down and take control.'

India did not win the Oval Test which would have been special as this was Tendulkar's hundredth Test match and the BCCI issued a commemorative plate listing all the great cricketers of India. Neither did Tendulkar mark the occasion with a hundred; he made 54. It was Dravid who shone. This was the innings which gave him the nickname 'The Wall'. No English bowler could get him out. He was run out for 217, suffering from Ajay Ratra making a bad call. He had batted ten-and-a-half hours and made his highest first-class score. He was the first Indian since Gavaskar on the groundbreaking 1970–71 West Indian tour to score three consecutive Test hundreds in the same series. He had occupied the crease in the Test series for more than thirty hours, which was an entire Test match, or as one writer put it eight showings of the epic sports film, *Lagaan*. That India could draw a series in England, after being badly beaten in the first Test, showed that even away from home they could fight back.

The series also revealed a new face of India off the field. For the first time the growing importance of the Indian diaspora was evident. The sporting moneymen certainly understood it, calling it an Indian summer. The film *Lagaan* was widely publicized, *Bombay Dreams*, the Andrew Lloyd Webber musical opened in London, and Indian spectators came in droves to matches. The Indian tricolour was proudly displayed by many, drums were sounded and the noise and festivity the Indians brought to the grounds were not only alien to the English but worried the MCC. They feared cricket going the way of football. However, when a pitch invasion happened, it was not by an Indian but an Australian. It had come in the Indian second innings at Lord's when, as Tendulkar was bowled by Matthew Hoggard and walked back sadly to the pavilion, a twenty-four-year-old Australian jumped onto the field and put a consoling arm around him. It was meant in good fun, although the security implications could not be ignored as the man could well have had a knife.

INDIAN PLAYERS' ECONOMIC POWER

The other aspect of the tour emphasized India's economic power and particularly that of their players and the conflict this caused with the Indian board and the ICC. The basic problem stemmed from the fact that Indian cricketers had no contract with their board. They signed up for specific tours, but in between tours there was no contractual relationship. This did not matter as long as Indian cricket was poor. But when television brought its riches it also dramatically changed the life of the country's top cricketers. Television opened up a whole new marketing world for individual cricketers and advertisers were quick to exploit it.

Tendulkar, as the outstanding cricketer of his generation, was the major beneficiary of this. Soon he could be seen on Indian television advertising almost everything, and his deals were so lucrative that by now he had become the richest cricketer in the world with an income estimated at $15 million a year. But along with Tendulkar the cricketers who made their mark in the 1990s also benefitted: players such as Ganguly, Dravid, Kumble, and then through the new century the stars that began to emerge such as Laxman, Sehwag, Yuvraj, Kaif and Harbhajan. The Indian Test and one-day team was like a very privileged club, and whenever it acquired a prominent member he made it to the small screen, advertising some product or other. Often the advertisement featured the entire team.

The result was players earned more money from their sponsors than from their employers. India had some of the richest cricketers in the world, but they were effectively outside the control of the Indian board. And this carried the seeds of a great conflict. The players might have signed up with one company while the board might be considering a sponsorship with a rival company. The tour was to be followed by the Champions Trophy in Sri Lanka. The ICC had certain sponsors—either Indian companies or companies operating extensively in India. Sponsors are extremely vigilant about what they call 'ambush marketing', making sure their rivals who have not sponsored an event do not use the event to advertise their product.

The ICC required all the world's cricketers who were going to take part in the tournament to sign a declaration that for a period before, during and after the tournament, they would not be involved in any advertising that was in competition with the ICC sponsors. But India's leading cricketers had contracts with companies that were rivals of ICC's sponsors, and they refused to sign such agreements. So, as India battled England on the field, off the field they battled Dalmiya.

Things got to such a state that the BCCI announced an alternative team to contest the Champions Trophy. The victory at Headingley showed the cricketers could still perform even as they fought the board; if anything, it had made them more determined. The dispute dragged on as India played England at the Oval and the ICC got involved with Indian players seeking to form a trade union to press for their rights. Neither the ICC's involvement nor the demand for a trade union pleased Dalmiya. In the end a compromise solution was found, but six months later the dispute flared up again during the 2003 World Cup in South Africa and this time the ICC held back money owed to India. What made the dispute interesting was how far Indian cricketers had travelled compared to other international cricketers. When at the Oval, Nasser Hussain was asked about the controversy, he expressed sympathy but also confessed that England's cricketers did not have such problems because they did not enjoy such sponsorships.

The whole issue also revealed the extraordinary management style of Dalmiya. He had great money-making skills but could be a very poor manager of men. And he had failed to come to grips with the structure of the game and the need to modernize it. He refused to accept that Indian cricketers should be allowed to have a trade union, something they still do not have. Just as he was in some ways a one-man band, he liked cricketers who were one-man bands, except in this case their economic power was such, they were very rich one-man bands causing enormous problems for the board.

India got to the final in the ICC trophy, beating Zimbabwe and England in the pool matches and South Africa in the semi-finals, but rain washed out the final against Sri Lanka and the two teams shared the $300,000 prize. India returned home for a series against the West Indies which showed how the cricketing balance between the two countries had changed, certainly in India. India easily won the three Test series 2–0. The first Test was more remarkable for the fact that it was brought forward by two weeks to ensure Tendulkar's 101st test was played on his home ground, with a stand at the Wankhede renamed after him. India won in three-and a-half-days by an innings and 112 runs, India's first ever victory by an innings over the West Indies. The West Indians had failed to reach 200 in either innings. The West Indian first innings score of 157 was only ten more than what Sehwag alone had made. There was another poor West Indian performance in Chennai and India took a 2–0 lead after cruising home by eight wickets.

WARNING SIGNS BEFORE THE WORLD CUP

In preparation for the 2003 World Cup, the BCCI had slotted in seven one-day seven one-day matches against the West Indies and here there were warning signs. India twice drew level only to lose the last match and the series 4–3. But the games at Jamshedpur, Nagpur and Rajkot saw crowds throwing bottles at the fielders. In Rajkot, water bottles hitting the West Indian fielders made the West Indians walk off; the match was abandoned. This set the local rumour mills whirring away with talk that bookmakers who had bet on a West Indian victory had been behind the bottle-throwing as India then were seemingly set on victory. No proof was ever produced.

Worse was to follow when in December 2002 India went to New Zealand. By the end of it, many in New Zealand began to wonder if this was the worst team that had ever toured their country. Indian batsmen fared worse than Bangladesh, which had toured the previous year. Their runs per wicket was 14.50, India's was 13.37. New Zealand, having suffered so much on the dust bowls of India, presented green-top, seaming wickets. The one-dayers were also played on drop in wickets, which Wright described as having 'stopping bounce': in other words, the ball did not come through at a consistent pace. Even then for the Indians batting to perform so badly was astonishing. India played eleven matches, including two Tests and seven ODIs. Their highest score was 219 and they lost a wicket every 4.5 overs. They lost both Tests. Wright began to get pitying looks and one woman in Napier told him she found the cricket exciting as the batsmen were coming and going.

In the one-day series India started winning only after New Zealand had taken a 4–0 lead in the seven-match series, winning the fifth and sixth in dead rubbers. India's first match in the World Cup was less than a month away and this was no preparation. Even worse was that in the midst of the one-day series the BCCI announced the team for the World Cup. The selectors had decided Laxman was not worth his place in the side. Laxman was shattered, and it destroyed his relationship with Wright, which was never properly restored.

THE 2003 WORLD CUP: ZERO TO HERO

The 2003 World Cup was like no other previous World Cup. It was the first tournament that the ICC had owned. However, it was Indian money that was driving the tournament, from Indian television and from many firms keen to reach the Indian market via the World Cup. But with Indian cricketers having sponsors that were rivals of ICC sponsors there were serious doubts at one stage whether India might even take part. Ali Bacher, who was organizing the tournament, made sure India did. He knew that for the tournament to be a success India had to be there and do well. India's economic muscle was evident from the start of the tournament. When I got to the press box at Paarl for the opening match against Netherlands it was bursting with Indian media. When I mentioned I had never seen so many Indian media at an overseas match, one of the South Africa journalists shrugged his shoulders and said, 'They own the game. They have the right to throw their weight around.'

But the moneybags off the field played such poor cricket that they struggled to defeat Netherlands in the first match. They were also skittled out for 125, India's lowest ever World Cup total, by Australia who won by nine wickets with twenty-seven overs to spare. That day, walking around the Centurion, which was packed by Indian supporters the anger at the way the Indians had capitulated was palpable. The World Cup had been massively promoted in India; the players had endorsed all sorts of products; Pepsi introduced Pepsi Blue; and the corporate spend and related advertising was estimated to be $501 million. The Indian public, which had been hyped up to believe that this team could emulate Kapil Dev's 1983 side, or in Dalmiya's words, 'Now or never', were so incensed that in Kolkata a Ganguly effigy was burnt and a mock funeral procession held. In Allahabad, black paint was thrown at the home of Kaif, an effigy of Tendulkar was also burnt, Dravid's car was vandalized and policemen patrolled outside players' homes. One placard read, 'Let them do only ads, no need for them to play.' Suresh Kalmadi, president of the Indian Olympic Association, joined in: 'They are spending more time in the studios for ad shoots than on the pitch. I have always said there is too much money in cricket.' And one fan even went to court filing a claim asking that restrictions should be put on players' commercial activities as they had brought discredit to the country by their dismal performance. When in parliament the president of India wished the team luck, there was derisive laughter. There were even calls to boycott products the players endorsed. Before the World Cup, Wright had got Sandy Gordon to present a World Cup mission statement which talked about the mental toughness required and how players must develop the 'Fuck You' mode during it. Now it was the Indian public who were saying 'Fuck You' to the players. The Indian media reflected the public anger and Tendulkar had to make a public appeal to calm the fans.

India knew they had to beat Zimbabwe. Wright, not concealing his anger, told the players to sit by the pool and work out how they could make more than 120. The result was the batting order was changed. In one of the practice games, Wright prompted by Kumble and Srinath, had persuaded Tendulkar to open. Now Sehwag became his partner with Ganguly dropping to No. 3. Against Zimbabwe Tendulkar scored 81 and India won easily. This was followed by victories over Namibia and, more crucially, England. This latter match was the making of Nehra. Against Namibia, Ganguly had opened with him, he had bowled one ball and then twisted his ankle, which made Ganguly joke at the press conference that he had opened with him to see what Nehra did with the new ball. 'We found he falls over.' But against England, despite the fact that after play he would have his leg from the knee down in ice and wired to an interferential machine, Nehra did not fall over. India, having made 250, the margin of error was small. He bowled straight through his ten overs taking 6 for 23, and England were bowled out for 168 with four overs to spare.

Buoyed up by the confidence this victory had given them, India came back to the Centurion to play Pakistan. For both teams no match could be more important. Tendulkar had been told by friends a year earlier this was the match of the tournament that India had to win. What happened in the rest of the tournament did not matter. Such was his anxiety that for three days before the match he could not sleep. India had never lost to Pakistan in a World Cup match. The Indian team room had been decorated with the tricolour and posters made by the Taj Hotel in Mumbai, with slogans like 'We are India, we can.' That looked unlikely when Pakistan, on winning the toss, batted. In front of a packed Centurion and massive security (1,100 policemen were present) and a television audience estimated at a billion, they made 273. In a World Cup India when chasing had never before made more than 224 to win. Everyone knew it would depend on Tendulkar. Normally, when batting with Sehwag, Tendulkar allowed the younger man to take strike first. But now as they walked out, he told him he would face the first ball. Tendulkar hit Wasim, who bowled the first over, for four. Shoaib opened from the other end and he slashed his sixth over third man for six. Shoaib having bowled two wides, there was a seventh and eighth ball, and both went for fours, one swirled behind square on the leg-side, the other driven down the ground. Shoaib had gone for 18 in his first over. What followed was probably Tendulkar's best one-day innings. By the twelfth over, India had reached 100. Pakistan did drop Tendulkar on 32 and Tendulkar struggled with cramps in his 70s, but he made 98 before Shoaib finally got him. India still needed 96, but with Dravid and Yuvraj coming together India won by six wickets, with four overs and two balls to spare.

The win meant India qualified for the Super Six, where they won all three matches against Kenya, New Zealand, and Sri Lanka. Tendulkar missed a century against Sri Lanka, making 97, but due to a stomach upset he was batting with tissues inside his underwear and even had to return to the dressing room during one of the drinks breaks. India's semi-final opponent was Kenya. In the Super Six, India had beaten Kenya by six wickets; now, batting first, they won by 91 runs to set up a final with Australia. The night before the match the first Gulf War began. The talk among the many Indian supporters who crowded the Wanderers, vastly outnumbering not only the Australians but also the locals, was that if Australia hoped to shock and awe Saddam Hussein as President Bush had promised, India would respond as Saddam had promised with the mother of all battles. But just as Saddam turned out to be making promises he could not keep, so did the Indians.

It all started going wrong from the moment Ganguly, Dravid and Tendulkar walked out onto the Wanderers just before the toss. There was cloud cover, there was moisture on the wicket and the decision was win the toss and put Australia in. Worse still, Ganguly opened with Zaheer and not Srinath. He just could not locate the stumps, bowled a ten-ball over, went for 15 runs and after that there was no escape. Ponting made a superb 140 not out in 121 balls, putting on an unbroken third wicket stand of 234 with Martyn, and by the time fifty overs were bowled Australia were 359 for 2.

The Indians had not given up all hope. The team worked out that to win they would have to hit a four every over, which would make 200, and the remaining 160 could come in 250 balls. Tendulkar did hit McGrath for four in the first over, but it was a mistimed pull. When he tried to pull the fifth ball he top-edged and McGrath took the catch. Sehwag tried his best but was run out for 82. There was rain in the air and, walking around the Wanderers that day, I met many Indian fans, including Bollywood stars, express the hope that it would pour down and would force a replay. Tendulkar in the dressing room prayed for rain. It did rain, but this interrupted play for only twenty-five minutes, no overs were deducted and when play resumed Australia bowled out India for 234, winning their third World Cup and seventeenth consecutive one-day victory. Indian supporters were not too upset by the defeat. In the usual Indian way of moving from crucifixion to adulation, the players on their return were showered with gifts and every squad member was given a condominium in an exclusive gated compound near Pune. But while Ganguly's team were no longer meek and could fight back, they were a long way from having the winning mentality the Australians had. This was made very evident to me after the World Cup Final as my wife and I were leaving the Wanderers. An Indian supporter turned to an Australian and said, 'We were runners-up.' The Australian immediately said, 'That means you are the first losers.' The Indian looked shocked, but this illustrated the difference in attitude between India and Australia. This would soon be evident when in the winter of 2003 Ganguly took his team to Australia.

INTO THE LION'S DEN

Ganguly had told the press before the start of the series, 'After this series we will know how good we are.' The Australians had identified Ganguly as the weakest link in the Indian batting line up. Ganguly was well aware that his own batting against the fast bowlers was suspect and decided to consult an Australian who knew about batting. A few months before the first Test at Brisbane he turned to Greg Chappell. He knew him and had written a foreword to *Greg Chappell on Coaching*. Chappell advised him that there was no need for Ganguly to change his technique; instead he should not come to Australia thinking he will be peppered with short-pitched bowling. The talk went so well that Ganguly, aware Wright wanted to leave, asked him whether he would be interested in coaching the Indian cricket team. Chappell, as we have seen, had applied when Wright had got the job, and was keen. Ganguly was not to know that he had lit the fuse for a time bomb under him that would explode with devastating consequences.

Brisbane proved the value of Chappell's advice when Ganguly came in to bat with India at 62 for 3 and Dravid and Tendulkar both out. His first shot was edged to third man, then there were some more wobbles before he began to unveil the sumptuous cover drives and the cuts that were in his repertoire. He went on to make 144 (his first century against Australia). The Brisbane crowd rose to acclaim his innings and India eventually secured a lead of 86. Ganguly's innings had echoes of Wadekar's at Lord's back in 1971. India did not lose that Test which was so crucial for that history-making 1971 series, and India did not lose at Brisbane.

The next two Tests were mirror images of each other: the team that initially looked in command went on to lose. After Brisbane it was clear that for India to win Zaheer Khan had to be at his best. But Khan, who often suffered from injury, had done in his hamstring and without him Australia, led by Ponting, ran riot. His 242 was the highest score by an Australian against India, and on the first day Australia finished on 400 for

5, a record score for the first day of an Adelaide Test. On the second day, as Ponting passed 200 he blew a kiss to his wife, and Australia were finally out for 556. The match looked likely to finish early. India in reply were 85 for 4, with Ganguly and Dravid in yet another run-out—Ganguly this time being run out. But out walked Laxman, and he and Dravid decided they would remind Australia of what the pair had done in Kolkata. It was ninety-four overs later before Australia got another wicket. The pair put on 303, Laxman made 148, Dravid 233. Before this Dravid's highest score in Australia had been 43. While Laxman was all style and fluency, Dravid was watchful, and after his soulmate had departed he added another 135 with the tail to make sure Australia only led by 33. At this stage Australia were still favourites, but Agarkar, who had taken 2 for 119 in the first, now reminded Wright he could bowl. He took 6 for 41 and Australia were bowled out for 196. India were left 230 to win.

With two wickets going for 79 it seemed India might mess it up. But Dravid was determined this Indian story would have a different ending. He made 72 not out and, appropriately, with Agarkar as company, cut Stuart MacGill to the cover boundary to bring up victory. Dravid had promised himself he would hit the winning run. Waugh, who had chased the ball, retrieved it from the gutter, handed it over to Dravid and graciously said, 'Well played!' The Indians had coasted home with four wickets and more than a session to spare.

It seemed a new page had been turned and this impression was reinforced when in the Melbourne Test on Boxing Day, Sehwag made 195, with 25 fours and 5 sixes, enthralling a crowd of 62,613. Sehwag should have scored a double century, but in the style of batting he had made his own he tried to hit Simon Katich, very much a part-time spinner, for six and was caught. But then, as Wright put it, Sehwag had always seen spinners as lovely sweets which round up a good meal. India finished the first day comfortably placed at 329 for 4.

However, from this point the match turned. On the second day India lost six wickets for 37. Ponting exacted immediate revenge for Adelaide, making 257, a career-best. Australia made 558. India suffered a collapse like Australia in Adelaide, leaving Australia only 95 to win.

So, would this be a familiar story? India wins a Test abroad but loses the series? The Australians certainly hoped so, as it would be a fitting climax to Waugh playing his last match at his beloved Sydney. Warne predicted a 2–1 series win for his country. But this was when Tendulkar stepped in. His scores in the series had been: 0, 1, 37, 0 and 44. In the lead-up to the Test, Tendulkar spoke to his brother Ajit, and Wright and Tendulkar decided he would cut out the cover drive, one of his signature shots. He just waited for the chance to hit to leg. The Australians tried to bait him about not driving balls he would normally have driven, but he refused to respond. He started batting on the first day, when Ganguly, on winning the toss, decided to make first use of the wicket: he was still there thirty-nine minutes into the third day, by which time he had batted ten hours and thirteen minutes, faced 436 deliveries and still not hit a cover drive. By the time Ganguly declared at 705, Tendulkar had made his highest first-class score, 241 not out, and 188 of his runs and 28 of his 33 fours had been made on the leg side. The stress on Tendulkar in this innings can be judged from the fact that he became very superstitious. On the night before the Sydney Test began he had gone with his family to a meal at a Malaysian restaurant. On the evening of the first day at 73 not out he went there again, sat at the same table and ate the same food, and repeated it on the second evening, when he was 220 not out. Tendulkar's innings was in stark contrast to the man at the other end. Laxman made a delicious 178, making batting look easy with strokes on both sides of the wicket. Tendulkar's uncharacteristic obduracy contrasted with Laxman's grace during a 353 run stand.

Ganguly's declaration was the cue for Kumble. He had played little part in the World Cup and he seemed a man on the way out. Now he took 8 for 141, varying his pace, keeping a tight control over his line and not giving Australian batsman too many loose balls to hit. Ganguly did not enforce the follow-on, and on the fourth evening India set Australia 442 to win. Kumble opened the bowling and took six wickets, but Waugh in his last Test made sure Australia did not lose. Kumble did have the last laugh as he had Waugh caught and Waugh, having made 80, could not bid goodbye with a century. Kumble finished with match figures of 12–279. By drawing the series, India had sent Steve Waugh to retirement without claiming the Border–Gavaskar Trophy back. In a series which had seen four double centuries the standout Indian performances for consistency were from Dravid and Laxman, the first two in the Indian batting averages, and Kumble, whose twenty-four wickets were at an average of 29.58. Ganguly's men had not conquered the final frontier, but there was much satisfaction in India that this was India's only third drawn series in Australia in fifty-seven years. The only dissenter was Tendulkar, who felt a great opportunity had been missed to win the series and Ganguly should have declared earlier at Sydney. Justin Langer had said that Indian batsmen had batted, 'like they were in a meditative state'. Ganguly knew his men would certainly have to stay calm if they were to win in Pakistan.

THE NINE WAVES

MAKING HISTORY IN PAKISTAN

For a long time it did not seem likely the Pakistan tour would take place at all. In January 2004, the Indian players wrote to the board saying that they were uneasy about travelling to Pakistan. The BJP government were fearful of the effect on elections of an Indian defeat in Pakistan. They insisted that one-day matches be played before the Tests as they were worried that losing the one-day matches—which meant more to India's cricket supporters than Tests—would have a more damaging effect in electoral terms. As India had never won a Test in Pakistan, it seemed the Indian ruling class had written off the Tests. The tour only took place because Prime Minister Atal Bihari Vajpayee intervened. On the morning of their departure the Indian team went to the prime minister's home. The Ministry of External Affairs had already given a briefing, where the spokesman told the players, 'Your tour is an important part of this Indo–Pakistani revival.' When Wright asked Prime Minister Vajpayee whether he would come to Pakistan for the Tests, he said he had his own Test to think about, meaning elections, which he then went on to lose.

The itinerary was finalized three weeks before the tour began, with Karachi and Peshawar ruled out for the Tests, the first because of violence, the second because of being close to the Afghan border, where Western troops were fighting the Taliban. But despite these worries, the tour reminded both countries how much they had in common and also lessened the antagonism that seemed to be the default position of both. I was very aware of this, having had problems getting a visa to travel to Pakistan because I was born in India. But now in this honeymoon mood created by the cricket series, those who for years had found it difficult to cross the border suddenly found the doors were being thrown open. Some 11,000 visas were issued to Indians to see India play Pakistan, almost half of them for the one-dayers in Lahore. As the city is so full of history for people of both countries and only 45 miles from the Indian border, special arrangements were made to get the Indians to Lahore with airlines, bus companies and railways putting on extra services and 1,000 people crossing the border on foot. The spectators were not disappointed. The two teams produced as gripping a one-day bilateral series as any in cricket history, while the Tests saw both the Indian team and an Indian batsman create history.

The five-match one-day series which started in Karachi set the tone. The 33,000 people packing the stadium had to hold their breath till the last ball of the match. India had made 349, led by Dravid who made 99. Pakistan's captain Inzamam-ul-Haq responded with 122, and when Nehra bowled the last over, Pakistan needed nine to win. Only three were scored off his first five. India seemed in control. But for his last ball he bowled a full toss and Moin Khan, in trying to hit a six, sliced it and was caught. India had won by 5 runs. Pakistan then won the next two, India came back to level the series and then won the series, the first time they had won any series, be it Tests or one-day internationals in Pakistan. The question was, could they now take that form into the Tests?

The preamble to the Test series was not encouraging: Ganguly had injured his back in the final one-day match and was stretchered off, thereby missing the Test, which meant Dravid captained India for the first time in Tests. Yuvraj, who had not toured Australia, was now part of the first six in the Indian batting order.

But if there were any concerns about the batting it was all blown away when India, on winning the toss, batted and Sehwag went where no other Indian batsman had gone since India made their Test debut seventy-two years earlier. He became the first Indian to score 300 in a Test innings. He had his share of luck. He was dropped on 68 and again on 77 but there was also the fun of batting with his Delhi colleague Aakash Chopra, the two talking in Hindi as they ran between the wickets, 'All right, Viru, let's take a single now.' And 'Why don't you go back?' The main stand was with Tendulkar, 336, an Indian third-wicket record, with Tendulkar, unlike in Sydney, unveiling all his strokes. But while Tendulkar played strokes along the ground, Sehwag had no hesitation in lofting the ball even when he was 99. Then he hit a six over third man off Shoaib to get to 105. Even more audaciously, having reached 295 and well aware that he could cross the frontier no Indian had ever done in singles, he hit Saqlain Mushtaq for six over long-on. He had then faced 364 balls. He finished on 309 after having hit 6 sixes and 39 fours in 531 minutes of batting. The only pity was the stadium was virtually empty. Much as Pakistanis had crowded the one-day matches, they stayed away from the Tests.

But if Sehwag could do no wrong, earning him the title of 'Sultan of Multan', the drama around Tendulkar's innings was one that created controversy and drove a wedge between Dravid and India's greatest batsman. After Sehwag departed with the score on 509, Tendulkar carried on and, helped by Laxman and Yuvraj, had taken India to 675 when Dravid declared. On paper this was a perfectly understandable declaration. This was India's third-highest total in any Test, and second-highest away, just short of the highest in Sydney, three months earlier. There was an hour to go before the close of play on the second day, ideal for Dravid to unleash his bowlers on the battered Pakistanis. The problem was Tendulkar was 194 and Dravid had denied him a double century. Wright wanted Dravid to declare earlier, giving Pakistan twenty-five overs, while Dravid wanted to give them fifteen or sixteen overs. After tea a couple of messages went out and then a final message that there was one more over. Then Yuvraj was out and Dravid called them in. Tendulkar did not disguise his feelings. He did not take the field, saying he had a sprained ankle, and at the press conference made it clear he was unhappy with the decision. To add to the problems, Ganguly, who was planning to fly back to India for his back injury, could be seen on television gesturing impatiently.

The result was mayhem, and in the 24/7 Indian media conspiracy theorists had a field day. Although Ganguly was not involved he was accused of being behind it as he was anti-Tendulkar; then, supposedly, Dravid not having got a double century in the match—he had four previous ones—did not want Tendulkar to get one; and then again, Tendulkar had batted slowly to paint Dravid in dreadful colours. Wright had a sleepless night and spoke to Tendulkar, who asked for the team to cut him some slack. In the end Dravid and Tendulkar made up, and Wright feels, 'It was an important step in the team's development, in that the principle that no one is bigger than the team had been very publicly adhered to.'

The team certainly stuck together as India went on to make Pakistan follow on and win the match by an innings and 52 runs. It had taken India thirty-nine years to win their first Test in England, eighteen years to win their first Test in West Indies and forty-nine years to win their first Test in Pakistan.

Understandably, the win generated euphoria in India. But in Pakistan there was disbelief. I arrived in Lahore three days later for the second Test. When at the airport I asked the visa officials about the defeat, one of them said, 'It has all been fixed. We let India win. We will win the Lahore test.' That the match was fixed was a common belief in the Pakistani media and at the press conferences Dravid was also asked about it. This so incensed him that he demanded that the journalist who had asked the question be removed.

Ridiculous as charges of match-fixing were, they were understandable given what had gone before. What was amazing was the reaction in the Pakistani media with one newspaper publishing a diagram by a retired Pakistani general purporting to illustrate how Pakistani bowlers were not swinging the ball because they were not following the right lines. It was not explained from which military manual this advice had emerged from.

It was not military advice that Dravid needed in the Lahore Test. Just good cricket sense to judge a first day wicket. He read the pitch wrong. Whereas Multan was made for batsmen, Lahore had been prepared for the quick bowlers. Wright thought India should field, Dravid decided to bat, India lost four wickets before lunch and were 147 for 7. Despite Yuvraj getting his first Test century in his best one-day counter-attacking style, 287 was never going to be enough. Led by Inzamam, who made 118, Pakistan got a lead of 202, bowled out India for 241 and won by nine wickets. The visa official had been proved right.

The third and final Test took India to Rawalpindi. Ganguly returned and the question was: would see the Indian Lion of Multan or the meek lamb of Lahore? The confusion in the lead up to the match did not give much hope. To make way for Ganguly, a batsman had to be dropped. It could not be Yuvraj, it was Chopra. That raised the question as to who would open. It was decided that unless India were in the field for two days, Patel would open. But then Ganguly at his press conference said he would open.

On winning the toss he put Pakistan in. But they did not even last out the first day, making 224 and falling to Lakshmipathy Balaji who took 4 for 63. Not having spent two days keeping wicket, Patel opened, saw Sehwag get out to the first ball, but then quickly worked out his job was to help Dravid, who was batting sublimely. Dravid had century stands with Patel, Laxman and Ganguly and missed one with Yuvraj by 2 runs. While none of them made a hundred, Dravid made 270, batting for twelve hours and twenty minutes. It was the longest any Indian batsman had ever batted. Pakistan faced a deficit of 276 and lost both their openers by 34. However, at this stage, India seemed to be scared of pressing for victory. On the fourth morning, they dropped six catches in the first hour, with fielders often in the wrong position. Wright fumed in his diary, 'Stupid, stupid, stupid.' But Balaji and Kumble plugged on and by lunch Pakistan were seven down. Wright wrote in his diary that he was like a kid the night before Christmas waiting to open presents the next morning. Soon after lunch he could tear off the wrapping paper. India had won by an innings and 131 runs in four days. Their first Test series away from home since 1993 in Sri Lanka, their first ever in Pakistan.

Shaharyar Khan, the chairman of the Pakistan cricket board, told the Indian team they had been wonderful ambassadors, bringing credit to India: 'You have been part of history.' Indians savoured their history men. Ganguly was hailed as the great Dada of the whole country. However, unlike the Roman general who, on his return to Rome celebrating his conquest, was warned by a slave standing next to him that defeat always follows victory, nobody told Ganguly of the perils that lay ahead: they would surface almost exactly a year later when Pakistan visited India.

Chapter 36

THE IMPOSSIBLE AUSTRALIAN

On the afternoon of 28 March 2005, Sourav Ganguly went out to bat in the Indian second innings in the third Test against Pakistan at Bengaluru. India led 1–0 and a draw would mean Ganguly would become the first Indian captain ever to win back-to-back series against Pakistan, which would establish him as one of the greats of Indian cricket. The previous day Pakistan had set India 383 to win at four an over. With Sehwag leading the usual charge and India scoring at 3.67 an over a victory did not look impossible. In the first innings he had stormed to a double century in 352 minutes and 262 balls, with 2 sixes and 28 fours and in the process set an Indian record: 3,000 Test runs in fifty-five innings. He could not reproduce that now, getting run out and after that the run rate slowed down to 1.91. But even if India did not win, a draw which is all India required, was certainly on the cards at lunch. India had lost just one wicket and the 'Fab Four' of Indian batting—Dravid, Tendulkar, Laxman and Ganguly—were still there. Then suddenly wickets began to fall. Dravid was out for 16, Laxman made 5, and Ganguly emerged from the pavilion with the score 127 for 4 to join Tendulkar.

The natural response of the crowd as the Indian captain walked out to the middle should have been cheers or some encouragement. Instead they booed him and shouted, 'We want Karthik', the young wicketkeeper batsman who had made 93 in the Kolkata Test. Nothing could have been more humiliating for Bengal's Dada. A prince suddenly losing his kingdom and reduced to the status of a pauper. And that this had happened to a captain who had shown a new face of Indian cricket abroad was truly remarkable. Yet in many ways it was not surprising. For Ganguly's problems had begun to surface in the very first series India played on returning home from Pakistan.

GANGULY LOSES HIS INVINCIBILITY
The series was against Australia in October–November 2004. India then were the fourth-ranking side but having drawn in Australia the previous winter they started out as favourites; they had, after all, lost only two home

series since David Gower's side had beaten them in 1984–85. However, Australia under their coach John Buchanan had prepared meticulously. In 2001, the Kolkata and Chennai Tests, which Australia had lost, had been played in March, which can generate heat even the Indians find unbearable. Now the series was in October which is cooler and the Australians made doubly sure by getting their batsmen to wear ice-vests. During matches, as drinks came out, the Australian players were provided with chairs to sit on while attendants held umbrellas over their heads. Australia also had two of their best bowlers, McGrath and Warne, who had missed the drawn home series. And Buchanan, who considered that Sun Tzu's *The Art of War* provided winning strategies for cricket, had also decided that always playing attacking cricket did not produce victory. 'If you are aggressive all the time, you can become predictable without having a fall-back position.' So, bowlers did not always bowl short and fast to an attacking field. This had been India's weakness, but on previous tours it had not always worked to play to India's weakness. Australia decided they would play to India's strength. They often bowled straighter and, fuller but so packed the field that the Indians found it difficult to score. Sehwag, the most destructive of Indian batsmen, found Australia packed the leg-side with five fielders. Every time he hit a shot he found a fielder until he self-destructed. The main four Australian bowlers, McGrath, Gillespie, Kasprowicz and Warne, did not concede more than 3 runs an over in the series. Also, there were no one-day matches, only Tests. Australia had come to breach the final frontier, win a Test series in India for the first time in thirty-five years, long before the cricketers playing in the series had been born.

India in contrast gave the impression they did not know what they wanted. Two days before the first Test in Bengaluru, Wright, who was already looking to leave, was told Sunil Gavaskar was coming as batting coach, which, given India's batting form in Tests (the one-dayers were not quite so good), was surprising. Wright had asked the board for help with young bowlers; now he found one of India's greatest batsmen arriving. He was intrigued that such a decision had been made without his knowledge and he only learnt the truth when Gavaskar told a team meeting that it was Ganguly who had texted him to come. Gavaskar often spoke to the players in Hindi which meant Wright was frozen out and he could also not countermand Gavaskar's advice to the batsmen. The whole issue took up a lot of Wright's emotional energy. But if this decision showed how Ganguly operated and that he took decisions which Wright, the hired hand and foreigner to boot, had to put up with during the series, the conflicts and tensions that had always been part of Indian cricket provided Australia with a massive advantage.

They surfaced most dramatically during the third Test in Nagpur. Australia had come to Nagpur leading the four-Test series 1–0, having won the first in Bengaluru by 217 runs.

India should have squared the series in the second Test at Chennai. Kumble had found neither bounce nor pace on his home wicket and the Indian selectors had been dead set against the idea of picking Kumble for the series. It was only because of Ganguly's insistence that he was a match-winner that he was selected. Ganguly refused to sign the selection sheet until Kumble's name was on it. His faith was rewarded. On the first day, Australia were motoring at 189 for 2, then Kumble stepped in. In a mesmerizing spell he took all the seven wickets that fell to bowlers; the last man, McGrath, was run out. Australia were bowled out for 235, eight Australian wickets going for 46 runs, Kumble finishing with 7 for 48, his seven wickets coming in sixty-one balls for 25 runs. To the astonishment of every one of his victims, Kasprowicz, despite being given not out when he edged Kumble to Laxman at silly point, walked. The English umpire David Shepherd who had given him not out, was talking to Katich, the non-striker, when to his amazement he found Kasprowicz walking back to the pavilion. Australians were not supposed to do that. Sehwag struck a magnificent hundred and had there been no rain on the fifth day India might have successfully chased a fourth innings target of 229. In many ways the only real winner was an Australian journalist. Having got up in the morning and seen the weather, he rang his Sydney bookmakers, got odds of 13 to 1 on a draw and, as it poured, laughed all the way to the bank.

The Test had given India momentum, and they would have loved nothing better than to face Australia again. But Australia had arranged that between the second and third Test there should be a week's break. Gilchrist met his family in Singapore, as did some of his colleagues, Hayden explored the backwaters of Kerala while others went to Goa or Mumbai to recharge their batteries. While the Indians fretted, Australia came to Nagpur ready to take them on. On arrival they found that the groundsman at the Vidarbha Cricket Association (VCA) ground had decided to give them a special Diwali present. In the week leading up to the Test, Ganguly had asked the groundsman to remove the grass from the pitch to suit Kumble and Harbhajan who had taken thirty-four wickets between them in two Tests. Yet, when he walked out to look at the ground, he found the groundsman had left a generous covering of grass on the wicket. Ganguly did not mince words: 'I don't think he has done much. Our strength is our spinners, but the pitch is up to him.' If Ganguly was upset, the visitors, both Shepherd and the Australian cricketers, were astounded.

David Shepherd who had grown up on such wickets in England said, 'Looks like home, don't it?' Mathew Hayden was reminded of the Gabba wicket. 'To have that sort of wicket for the deciding Test of an away series—particularly in India—was the most pleasant surprise imaginable.'

Hayden thought the curator of Nagpur was 'single-minded'. It reflected yet another battle for power in the Indian board. Dalmiya had just narrowly won the election for president of the BCCI. The Vidarbha Cricket Association had opposed him, and Shashank Manohar, the VCA president, no friend of Dalmiya, said, 'I've got no instructions from either the BBCI or the Indian team management. Even if I do, I'm not going to oblige them.'

In Nagpur, Australians also avoided the tummy problems that foreigners often complain about in India. While the Australians cricketers were having a meal at the Pride Hotel in Nagpur, a cockroach had popped out of their rogan josh. But when they drew this to the attention of their waiter, he refused to accept it was a cockroach and popped it in his mouth. This is when Hayden came to the rescue. He had come on the tour with a gas stove, a breadmaker, and various ingredients including olive oil, general condiments, bread flour and tomato paste. He previously had had no need to light the stove, but now he used it to make mini pizzas in his room on the third floor of the Pride Hotel; throughout the Test, many of the Australian cricketers were queuing up outside Hayden's room for their meals.

Nourished by Hayden's pizzas, the Australians arrived at the ground on the morning of the match to find that their nemesis Harbhajan was suffering from gastroenteritis (though whether this was from having had a cockroach slipped inside his meal at some other Nagpur hotel history does not reveal). In the previous two Tests, Harbhajan's victims had included nearly all the Australian top order, Hayden, Gilchrist, Martyn, Lehmann, Clarke and Langer.

Also not playing was the man who had been the face of the new, never-say-die India, Ganguly. No explanation was given for why Ganguly did not play and he does not dwell on it in his autobiography published in 2018. But when Rajdeep Sardesai asked him, Ganguly angrily denied he was a shirker: 'This is pure rubbish, I was injured.' Australia, with three fast bowlers, made the most of a pitch made for pace; India, with none, could not respond, although Zaheer with six wickets in the match made a gallant effort. The scores of the batsmen of either side told the story. Damien Martyn came within 3 runs of scoring a century in each innings, 114 and 97, Simon Katich fell one short of a hundred. The highest Indian score in either innings was Sehwag with 58. So dismal was the Indian batting that in the second innings set 543 for victory they were 37 for 5. Patel, Agarkar, Karthik and Zaheer, each of whom made more than the combined contribution of Chopra, Dravid, Tendulkar, Laxman and Kaif, ensured India reached 200. The defeat by 342 runs in four days meant Australia led 2–0 with one Test to go, and Gilchrist's men [he captained in the first three Tests with Ponting injured] had conquered the final frontier. India did have some consolation winning the fourth Test in Mumbai. While Ponting returned for this Test, Ganguly was again absent but he would have loved the Wankhede wicket, which turned square from the very first ball. India played three spinners. The match in reality finished in two days, as only eleven overs were possible on day one due to rain. India's selection of three spinners meant they rightly judged the underprepared state of the pitch. The way wickets fell told the story of the pitch. On the first day unseasonal rain meant play till not start till 2 p.m., after four overs it was interrupted again and the day finished with India 22 for 2. On the second day, eighteen wickets fell, by which time India was batting again. On the third day twenty wickets fell and the match was over. The scores make astounding reading: India, 104 and 205, Australia, 203 and 93 in thirty-one overs with Harbhajan taking 5 for 29.

But the Indians knew they had won a consolation Test on a wicket not up to Test standard. For Indian cricket the series defeat would have wider repercussions. Ganguly's first at home Test series marked the turning point of his reign. From now on, he was no longer the invincible captain who could not be touched. And here history was repeating itself. Back in 1969, as we have seen, it was Pataudi's failure against Lawry's Australians that had convinced Merchant he should go as captain. The Test series after that he was replaced by Wadekar. But then India played so few Tests that the next Test series was not until the spring of 1971. Now Test series came fast and furiously, within weeks of each other.

The Mumbai Test had finished on 5 November. By 20 November, India were in Kanpur playing a two-Test series against another southern hemisphere country, South Africa. India did win it after a boring draw at Kanpur, when Harbhajan, on his favourite ground, Kolkata, produced the sort of magic that had in the past proved too much for the Australians. On the final day, South Africa were 66 ahead with five wickets in hand and Jacques Kallis, who had made a 121 in the first innings, was still batting. But then Harbhajan so deceived Kallis with his flight, he gave the Indian a simple caught and bowled. Harbhajan finished with 7 for 87, Kumble was a willing accomplice with 3 for 82, and a target of 117 was achieved serenely by Dravid and

Tendulkar, handing India an eight-wicket victory and the series.

Eight days after the victory at Kolkata, Ganguly and his team made the short hop to Dhaka for a two-Test series against Bangladesh. Ganguly won both by an innings, one by 140 runs the other by 83 runs. The interest in the series was centred around whether Tendulkar would equal Gavaskar's world record of thirty-four centuries. He did, on the second day, and also joined an elite club consisting of him, Gary Kirsten and Steve Waugh as the only men to have scored Test centuries against all countries. Gavaskar, who was commentating at the time sent Tendulkar thirty-four bottles of champagne. It was quite a Test for records. The day before Kumble had set a new Indian record, going past the 434 wickets Kapil Dev had taken.

However, for Ganguly the visit was not all joy. Sensationally, in the second one-day international, Bangladesh beat India. This was Bangladesh's first home victory and only their third against a Test-playing nation. The defeat showed that Ganguly was becoming more human and no longer looking invincible.

PAKISTAN SURPRISE DADA

It was against this background that in March 2005 Pakistan came to India. Pakistan was not expected to do much. Mushtaq Ahmed, a former captain, had called them 'little better than a club side'. There was no Shoaib Akhtar, which considerably upset the plans of an Indian cafe providing 'Shoaib tikka'. That the coach was Bob Woolmer, a foreigner, did not go down well with many in Pakistan, and they came to India after a poor series in Australia, where they lost all three Tests and the one-day series. The pundits seemed to be right until the fifth morning of the first Test in Mohali. The day began with Pakistan six wickets down in their second innings and just 53 ahead. But then the lower order, led by the relatively inexperienced Kamran Akmal, who made 109, batted so well that Pakistan actually declared at 496, which was then Pakistan's highest total in India. Ganguly and his men seemed to lack ideas. There was little evidence of the ruthlessness Ganguly had sought to cultivate. In the Indian innings Ganguly and Tendulkar batting together had taken twenty-three overs to make 47. Tendulkar's 94 took 301 minutes. It seemed he was keener to get past Gavaskar's record than what was needed by his team.

India did win the next Test at Kolkata by 195 runs thanks to two glorious centuries by Dravid and no little help from Kumble. He had match figures of 10–161, and his second-innings haul of 7 for 63 was the best by a leg-spinner at Eden Gardens in nearly fifty years. Kumble also became only the second Indian to bag fifty wickets against Pakistan. Yet the Test had Indian losers as well. Harbhajan after remedial work on his action in Australia returned, but referee Chris Broad reported him for a second time. And the Kolkata crowd seemed to have fallen out of love with their prince. Ganguly made 12 in both innings and looked in wretched form.

All this would not have mattered had India drawn at Bengaluru. Ganguly, who had made 1 in the first, made 2 in the second, and was bowled by a Shahid Afridi leg-break. He stood by his crease unable to believe what had happened and waiting for the umpire's decision. It was only when the crowd started booing that he realized he was bowled. To add to his misery India would have earned a draw had they survived another six overs. This lack of fight in what was supposed to be a new India so angered the Bengaluru crowd that at the final presentation ceremony Ganguly was met with jeers and abuse, with the cheers reserved for Inzamam. Ganguly in five innings had made 48 runs at an average of 9.60 which was just ahead of Harbhajan's batting average of 9 and Balaji's of 7.20.

The only Indian to emerge with real credit was Sehwag. He had more runs—544—than anyone else in the series on either side, and his average of 90.66 was only bettered by Younis Khan for Pakistan who averaged 101.60. (Kumble averaged 95 but he only made 95 runs and was not out four times in five innings). By the end of the series he was the toast of Delhi. That is when the name 'little Viru' caught on; sponsors could not wait to sign him up with his name on billboards and newspaper adverts and also selling aftershave on television. His home ground at Delhi's Feroz Shah Kotla even named a gate after him.

However, Ganguly was not bothered. He had taken knocks before in his Test career and certainly, with Dalmiya in charge, he had few worries. He was also sure things would turn out all right with the new coach who was coming to take charge of Indian cricket. With Wright deciding to leave, Ganguly had decided that Greg Chappell would be the best man for the job. He did not waver in this opinion even though Sunil Gavaskar warned him against Chappell. Even Greg's brother, Ian Chappell, warned Dalmiya, who summoned Ganguly to his Kolkata residence to tell him Ian's views. But, says Ganguly, 'Well, I decided to ignore these warnings and follow my instincts.' The Indian board had considered other candidates including two other Australians, Tom Moody and Dav Whatmore; an Englishman, John Emburey; and also an Indian, Mohinder Amarnath. Ganguly made sure he got what he wanted. On 20 May 2005, Greg Chappell was appointed the new coach of India. 'He was in Delhi,' says Ganguly, 'I was in England, but our long-distance call was full of happiness and warmth.' The warmth did not last long.

UGLY AUSTRALIAN OR A MISUNDERSTOOD ONE?

Greg Chappell's reign as coach has been widely condemned by both players and commentators as putting Indian cricket back. He is the one foreigner who did not work in contrast to the success his predecessor, Wright, and his successor, Gary Kirsten, enjoyed. But this is too sweeping a conclusion. He certainly fell out with Ganguly and Tendulkar, but he also provided scope for talent like Dhoni to emerge on the international stage and he was not quite the evil destroyer which he has been portrayed as.

Ganguly's honeymoon with Chappell ended when India were playing a Zimbabwe Board XI at Mutare. Ganguly, suffering from tennis elbow, decided to retire, only to be confronted on his return to the dressing room by Chappell.

Ganguly says Chappell wanted him to go back to bat. He refused as he was in good touch and felt it might jeopardize his chances of playing in the first Test that was days away. Ganguly did go back to bat, although he eventually threw his wicket away. Chappell's version is that the problem was Ganguly had not taken the treatments for his tennis elbow such as ice-packs that the physiotherapist had prepared. The next day he enquired with the players about Ganguly's retirement and they told him it was 'just Sourav' and 'recounted a list of times when Sourav had suffered mystery injuries that usually disappeared as quickly as they had come'. Chappell's conclusion was devastating: 'This disturbed me because it confirmed for me that he was in a fragile state of mind and it was affecting the mental state of other members of the squad.' Days later, when they got to Bulawayo for the first Test, Chappell told Ganguly that he had serious doubts about picking him for the first Test. In Ganguly's version, Chappell also wanted to drop key players who, says Ganguly, 'had done great things for Indian cricket while he had just been there for three months. He needed to spend more time to fully understand the situation'. The quarrel by now was the classic exchange of views by a warring couple: one says something, the other contradicts with often seemingly trivial things blown out of all proportion. So, for instance, Ganguly points out that one of the charges Chappell made against him was that he paced up and down in the dressing room, which unnerved the rest of the players. Ganguly also says that Laxman, who had the habit of dozing in the dressing room, was on one occasion in Zimbabwe shouted at by Chappell, who accused him of being lazy and causing India problems. Laxman, says Ganguly, was stunned, and in an Indian dressing room where senior players were supposed to be treated with respect the players felt very uncomfortable. In Ganguly's eyes, this was a foreigner newly come to India not understanding Indian ways. Ganguly had the support of Amitabh Chaudhary, the tour manager, who told Chappell that he had exceeded his powers in deciding to drop Ganguly. The Australian with great reluctance agreed and Ganguly played in the Test.

Ganguly responded with his twelfth Test century, but his first in two years, while Laxman with a fierce 140 passed 4,000 Test runs. With wonderful bowling from Irfan Pathan, who also made a confident half-century, and Harbhajan, India won the first Test by an innings and 90 runs. Ganguly, making the most of the victory and his century in a post-match interview, revealed his spat with Chappell and how it had made him 'extra determined to succeed'. This was the first the public knew of the storm that had broken out in the Indian camp.

It was as this row was blazing that the second Test was played at Harare. The only question was: could Zimbabwe avoid another innings defeat? They were able to, but only just. On the third day having bowled Zimbabwe out India required 19 to win then carry on with and took fourteen balls to secure a ten-wicket victory. This was India's first series victory away from Asia since Kapil Dev's team had vanquished England in 1986, but it was against dreadfully weak opposition wracked by problems created by the Mugabe regime. Soon Zimbabwe fielded such substandard sides that they did not even play Test cricket between 10 June 2004 to 6 January 2005.

India paid little attention to the state of Zimbabwean cricket and much was made of Ganguly being India's most successful captain with twenty-one wins in forty-nine Tests, and an away record of eleven wins and ten losses. But soon after the team's return Chappell's incendiary email to the board about the problems with Ganguly was published in a Bengali daily. Ganguly knew it was coming as he had been tipped off by Sehwag who had seen Chappell writing it in the dressing room during the Zimbabwe tour. In the email Chappell accused Ganguly of having a 'fragile mind' and of playing politics in the dressing room:

> Everything is designed to maximize his chances of success and is usually detrimental to someone else's chances... This team has been made fearful and distrustful by the rumour mongering and Sourav's modus operandi of divide and rule. Certain players have been treated with favour, all of them bowlers, while others have been shunted up and down the order or left out of the team to suit Sourav's whims.

Ganguly's fans were outraged, and the ones in Bengal saw this as a sporting replay of the political assassination of Subhas Bose by Mahatma Gandhi back in the 1930s. The Indian board, as it often does in such situations, set up a committee and both Ganguly and Chappell were summoned to give their versions. After the meeting Chappell suggested the two men have a heart-to-heart, but Ganguly, feeling Chappell was untrustworthy, turned down the request.

The selectors agreed with Chappell that a change in captain was required and a month later Rahul Dravid took over for the one-day series against Sri Lanka, the official explanation being that Ganguly, with his tennis elbow, was not match fit. Ganguly was also told that to prove his fitness he had to play a Duleep Trophy match in Rajkot, and while he got a hundred before lunch on a green top he did not make the one-day team. In addition to personality clashes, Ganguly may have suffered from the fact that Dalmiya, the man who had backed him for so long, was himself losing power in the Indian board to the camp led by Sharad Pawar. Chappell could argue that Ganguly's form in 2005 was not good, that the century against a second-string Zimbabwe did not count. Ganguly at the end of his career could boast of his outstanding one-day record, with thirty-one Man of the Match awards. He and Tendulkar as opening pair had put on 8,227 runs, which included twenty-six century partnerships. But, for Chappell, Ganguly was the past. There was new talent that needed to be encouraged and the seven one-day matches against Sri Lanka certainly produced one cricketer who would, in little more than a year, dominate Indian cricket as much as Ganguly had done, and finish with a better win record as captain. This was Mahendra Singh Dhoni, whose explosive batting played a crucial role in India winning 6–1. Before the series, Sri Lanka had been ranked as the second best ODI team, India seventh, and Chappell could legitimately claim his changes were signalling an impressive start to the new era of Indian cricket. There was little to suggest that India was missing Ganguly.

But his supporters were not prepared to take what they saw as a grave insult to Bengal lying down, and when South Africa, who followed Sri Lanka, played their third one-day match at Kolkata they had a wonderful opportunity. As the Indian team bus arrived at Eden Gardens they jeered, to which Chappell was supposed to have responded with a one-finger sign. Chappell, in denying it, provided the extraordinary explanation that having injured his finger he was looking at it. The board let it be known that officials 'spoke to' Chappell about it.

Things got worse when India batted. They were bowled out for 188, not even taking up all their fifty overs. Ganguly, meanwhile, was in Pune playing a Ranji Trophy match where he made 175, and this score was flashed on the screen and acclaimed by the crowd. South Africa did not lose a single wicket in winning and did it with nearly fifteen overs to spare. After the match the 80,000 spectators in Eden Gardens erupted and, as Dravid and Chappell walked to the middle for the presentation ceremony, they chanted 'We want Sourav' and jeered both the Indian captain and coach.

Ganguly was called back for the three-Test series against Sri Lanka, but had a dreadful return in the rain-affected first Test in Chennai, making 5 in the only Indian innings that was possible. Although, to be fair, India only managed 167; Laxman also made 5 and no Indian batsman made 50: Sehwag 36, Dravid, 32, and Dhoni on his Test debut, 30.

It was the second Test in Delhi that was to make Ganguly finally realize he was now yesterday's man. The Test would become famous for Tendulkar realizing his dream. As it rained in Chennai, Tendulkar had dreamt that he would score his thirty-fifth Test hundred, going past Gavaskar, in Delhi. India batted and towards the close of play on the first day, with light fading, Tendulkar was in the 90s, praying that the umpires would not call off play. He reached his magic figure at 4.45 p.m., when he turned Chaminda Vaas to fine-leg for a single. Tendulkar for once celebrated raucously and on returning to the dressing room wept copiously. He had tears running down his cheeks as he phoned his nearest and dearest.

By the end of the Test it was Ganguly who felt like crying. After India had won by 188 runs Dravid, captaining the side, came back from the selection committee to tell Ganguly, who had made 40 and 39, 'Sorry, Sourav, you are out of the squad.' The only comfort for Ganguly was he had friends in the dressing room in Gautam Gambhir, Yuvraj, Harbhajan, Tendulkar, Laxman and Sehwag who made it clear they disapproved. Tendulkar had looked bewildered when he heard and told Ganguly, 'I have got nothing to say, Dada.'

Had Ganguly stayed in the side there might have been a problem for the last Test in Ahmedabad. For Dravid, who had played in ninety-four consecutive Tests, went down with gastroenteritis and Chappell and the selectors might have found it difficult to ignore Ganguly. Instead, Sehwag stepped up at the eleventh hour. And he made his debut as captain by securing the most emphatic victory of the series, winning by 259 runs. India were now second in the Test rankings, above England and only behind Australia. They had never been so high.

Ganguly, much to his surprise, was chosen for the trip to Pakistan, which saw three Tests and five one-day internationals. However, this was to produce the most sensational moment of the Dada–Australian war, beamed live on television. With only one warm-up match before the first Test in Lahore, not all sixteen of the squad could play, so five were asked to stay back in India and play in the Ranji Trophy and Ganguly was among the five. For Ganguly this meant playing Tamil Nadu at a deserted Eden

Gardens and for a man who on India's last visit had led the side to their first victory in Pakistan this was very humiliating. His only consolation was that when he joined the team before the first Test he found no one had taken the place he had always had on the team bus, the second seat on the left behind Tendulkar, who, as always, sat in the front seat.

The drama came at the start of the Test. The day before the Test, Dravid and Chappell, while congratulating Ganguly on his performance in the Ranji Trophy, had asked him if he would open, something he had never done in Tests. Why such a request was made is not clear as the squad had two regular openers in Wasim Jaffer and Gautam Gambhir, a batsman who regularly opened with Sehwag for Delhi. However, the following morning, Dravid revealed he had second thoughts and told Ganguly that as he had no experience of opening it would be unfair to ask him to do so and he should bat No. 5. Sending him to open on his comeback would send the wrong signal that he was being sacrificed. Ganguly insisted he should open and he, Dravid and Chappell argued. What they did not know was their argument was being captured by television and made better news than the match report of the first day's play. Ganguly in the end agreed to bat No. 5. After Pakistan had smashed 679/7 being particularly severe on Harbhajan, who went wicketless for 176 runs, Dravid showed he could be an opener as well. He and Sehwag batted so well that they came within 3 runs of Roy and Mankad's fifty-year opening wicket record of 413. Sehwag was the one who got out, on 254, and afterwards said he did not know about the record. But the way he poked his bat at the third bouncer he received from Naved-ul-Hasan suggested that, even had he known, it would not have mattered. He had always enjoyed Pakistani bowling, and in six previous Tests he had scored 309, 173 and 201. With Sehwag the only Indian wicket falling, Ganguly did not even have to pad up and his one contribution in the match was taking a high catch in the outfield to get the wicket of the man who had got Sehwag out.

For Ganguly the second Test at Faisalabad was a return to his 1992 role of fetching drinks and a realization that, whereas in 1992 he was the new kid on the block, now another 'new wave' was ready to take his place. And this was crucial in the context of a match. In the first innings, Pakistan had scored 588 with Shahid Afridi scoring 156 in 128 balls and entertaining the crowd, 70 per cent of whom had been let in free. The moment he was out they went home. In front of empty stands India began well, Dravid showing how well he could open, scoring another century, and Laxman just missing out on 90. But then came a collapse, as 236 for 1 became 281 for 5. That is when Dhoni announced himself. Akhtar had just claimed Tendulkar's wicket and was bouncing the ball menacingly. The first six balls Dhoni faced from Akhtar he ducked and weaved, suggesting he was a very conventional batsman. The seventh, another bouncer inches from his face, he whipped over square leg for six. The leg-spinner Danish Kaneria, was hit out of the stadium. After play was held up while the ball was fetched Dhoni repeated the shot, sending it to the same spot. It was the thirty-fourth ball he had faced, and he was now 50. His looks may have been Indian, but his batting was Caribbean, full of drives hit on the up, pulling from outside the off stump to the midwicket boundary and flat-batting the ball square of the wicket. He got to his century in ninety-three balls and given that this was his first Test century it was quite remarkable. Then, when Pakistan batted and Indian bowlers were leaking runs, Dhoni came on to bowl. His hair blowing in the wind and with his sweater on, he delivered the ball as if he saw himself as a real bowler. In a match where the volume of runs scored made it a very one-sided, rather meaningless spectacle—Pakistan scored 1,078 runs, India 624, four Indian and four Pakistani bowlers, conceded more than a hundred runs with the ball—Dhoni brought excitement, and showed that he was more than a one-day slogger. He was the new Indian star and as Ganguly had done in England in 1996 he had first advertised himself in a Test on foreign soil.

A result in the series looked unlikely. The first two Tests had seen 2,791 runs scored, twelve hundreds made, often at a run a ball, and only thirty-six wickets taken, which meant an average of nearly 78 runs per wicket. The *Pakistan Daily Times* even called for the PCB's head groundsman, Agha Zahid, to be flogged and Inzamam denied he had any hand in this saying he was 'a captain not a groundsman'. But Karachi, which due to security concerns was only confirmed as a Test venue two days before the Indians arrived, produced a wicket for bowlers. Pathan, who had taken 2 for 319 in the series so far, now took a hat-trick with the last three balls of his first over, the second Indian after Harbhajan and the quickest any bowler had ever taken a hat-trick. With Zaheer and R. P. Singh, who had made his Test debut at Faisalabad joining in, Pakistan were 39 for 6 in the eleventh over. But India let Pakistan escape, batted poorly and were set 607 to win on the fourth day. This was when India's famed batting should have risen to the challenge. After all, in the previous two Tests they had made 1,034 runs for eleven wickets. Pakistan had given themselves five and a half sessions to bowl India out and they required only four and a half hours on the fourth day to do the job. Apart from a blazing Yuvraj century, the second-highest scorer was Ganguly with 37 who, as he had done on his Test debut, had also taken a wicket.

Much of the Indian anger focussed on Tendulkar, who had found Shoaib Akhtar uncomfortable and in three Tests made a total of 63 runs at an average of 21, far below that of Pathan, who averaged 44.66, and even Zaheer, who averaged 25.50.

The Tests were followed by the one-dayers and the easy temptation would have been to turn back to Ganguly, a proven one-day player, but Chappell and Dravid did not. And after losing the first one-day international, India won the next four to win the five-match series 4–1. While Pakistan's victory in the first by 7 runs had come through the Duckworth–Lewis method, India's victories in the next four were by emphatic margins: seven wickets, five wickets, five wickets and eight wickets. While Tendulkar, proving he was far from 'Endulkar' rediscovered his touch, it was Dhoni's batting that left spectators gasping. In the crucial third international at Lahore, set 289 to win, India were 190 for 5 in the thirty-fifth over. Tendulkar, who had made a very Tendulkarian 95, first watchful then blossoming, was out. But as the sky was lit up in this day-and-night match, Dhoni provided his own fireworks, what the Pakistani writer Osman Samiuddin called 'hooligan stuff, casually violent and full of chauvinistic machismo'. His 72 not out came off forty-six balls, and in the end India won with fourteen balls to spare. In the fifth one-day international, with India requiring 146 from 118 balls, Dhoni joined Yuvraj and got the runs in ninety-nine balls. Dhoni's brutal batting made a sharp contrast to Yuvraj's classy off-side strokes as India romped home with eight wickets. Dhoni was now being recognized as the great finisher. Chasing runs suited India, this was the thirteenth successive one-day victory, batting second.

The one-day victories did much to wipe away the memory of the Test defeat and also showed that Chappell was right: Ganguly was not required to win one-day matches. And with a World Cup coming up in little over a year's time, the one-day side was clearly a priority. However, Indian crowds had not forgotten Ganguly as the home series with England that followed showed.

India drew the first test in Nagpur where the honours belonged to Alastair Cook, who, having flown in from the Caribbean, made a century on debut, the youngest Englishman in sixty-seven years to do so. It prompted a pretty Nagpur girl watching in the stands to hold up a placard asking Cook whether he would marry her. India won the second at Mohali by nine wickets and should have romped home at Mumbai in the final Test. In the series England had been ravaged by injuries and withdrawals—the fitness crisis was such that England fielded twenty-three players on the tour, and even Matthew Maynard, assistant coach, came on when the team was down to ten fit men. In Mumbai, Cook went down with a stomach bug and Steve Harmison was ruled out because of a shin injury. India had much to celebrate. Dravid, playing his hundredth Test, Tendulkar beating Kapil Dev's record of 131 Tests, and Kumble reaching 500 wickets. But from the start India seem to be taking all the wrong steps. Dravid blundered in sending England in, who made 400, and then, on the final afternoon, the Indian batsmen well poised to get a draw had what Dravid called 'a collective lapse of reasoning'. At lunch the score was 75 for 3. The Indian batsmen relaxed, confident that a draw would see them winners of the series. They did not notice that in the England dressing room the players sang and thumped their feet to Johnny Cash's 'Ring of Fire' and feeling like British lions on the march abroad took the field after lunch. Fifteen overs and seventy-five minutes after lunch, the match was over. India lost the remaining seven wickets for 25 runs. This gave England their first victory in India for twenty-one years and the biggest by runs—212—on Indian soil.

The Mumbai crowd reacted with fury to the defeat. Tendulkar had been booed when he had got out for 1 run in the first innings. At the presentation ceremony Dravid was greeted with shouts of 'Bring back Sourav'. The crowd had also abused the England players, which caused Engineer, who recalled how different crowds were when the city was Bombay, to make a public apology.

What Dravid and Chappell could point to were the one-day internationals, played between the end of March and the middle of April, which saw India win the seven-match series 5–1. And this with Tendulkar, who had gone to England to have a shoulder operation, absent. The Indian board could also say they were taking cricket to parts of the country that had rarely seen such international cricket with matches played at Margao, Kochi, Jamshedpur and Indore. However, the board still paid little attention to looking after the spectators who paid to watch the matches. At Faridabad the ticketing arrangements were so poorly organized that the police made a lathi charge and a seven-year-old girl was taken to hospital with a head injury. To make matters worse, the Faridabad district commissioner justified the beating by saying, 'Sometimes people need to be disciplined.' Worse still was Guwahati, where rain washed out play. The problem was the rain had fallen the previous day, rendering the outfield too wet. The crowd who had gathered were not kept well informed and could not understand why there was no play with no rain falling. Nobody explained to them the outfield was too wet for the umpires to allow play, and when they called off play at 1.10 p.m., the crowd reacted with fury. Bonfires were lit in the stands, metal fences ripped up and plastic bottles and rubbish thrown on to the ground. The police fired tear gas and dragging two spectators from the stands beat them up badly. In the mayhem that followed two policemen were hospitalized. The Assam Cricket Association blamed the umpires. But they had consulted the captains before abandoning play and the reaction showed, as at Faridabad, that for all the money Indian cricket administrators earned, they failed to understand their own responsibilities as event organizers.

DRAVID DEFIES WEIGHT OF HISTORY

Chappell at this stage was a coach whose record read like that of a schoolboy whose report card read: 'could do better'. Between July 2005 and April 2006 India had won twenty-three one-day games but lost eleven. They would have to do much better if they wanted to win the 2007 World Cup for which Chappell was preparing and which was the great target for all Indians. That was going to be held in the West Indies, and the Indian board had made sure the team had a good look at the West Indies before it started. So, a month after beating England in the last one-day international in Indore, India were in the very different surroundings of Montego Bay.

India won the first of the five-match one-day series by five wickets. Chappell was so taken by this victory that he said, 'West Indies have forgotten how to win.' Brian Lara felt this was 'a sly remark', it galvanized the team to prove the Australian wrong and India lost the next four. The margins were small, 1 run in the second, 19 runs in the fifth, but it showed that it was Chappell's team that needed to learn how to win.

This failure to press home when on top was also evident for much of the Test series. In the first at the Antigua Recreation Ground India after a bad start so turned things around that when the final hour began India needed three West Indian wickets to win. All the main West Indian batting was gone, with Lara out for a duck. But then Dave Mohammed, a bowler batting No. 9, was allowed to make 52, often flailing wildly, and even after he was out, the last pair of Fidel Edwards and Corey Collymore kept out the last nineteen balls. So tense was it that the West Indian fans stopped dancing in the stands, as Sreesanth bowled the final ball on one side of the ground which had prison inmates crammed into gaps in the low-lying walls to watch.

Dravid described the failure as 'the weight of history' and this continued to weigh down his side, and they failed to win the second at St. Lucia. True rain intervened, leading Chappell to comment 'God is a West Indian' but the Indians by dropping catches did nothing to convince the Divine that they deserved to win.

The third in Basseterre in St. Kitts was drawn. And there seemed little chance that India could win at Kingston where on past tours they had so often found West Indian pace impossible to handle. The start was dismal, bowled out for 200. Only Dravid with 81 stood out, the next highest scorer being Kumble with 45. But then the West Indies found India had bowlers who could be lethal. The West Indies were bowled out for 103 in little over a session, with Harbhajan taking five wickets in twenty-seven balls for 13 runs. With the batsmen having to cope with ankle-high shooters, no Indian looked capable of surviving and this was when Dravid proved his class. Standing tall, negotiating the bouncy and unpredictable surface, he made his second 50 of the match, 68 in an Indian score of 171 where no other batsman made more than 16, and that was Laxman. That Dravid, who won the Man of the Match award, was the only one capable of coping with a truly terrifying wicket when the opposition had Lara, spoke volumes for his wonderful technique.

The West Indies needed 269, but that would be the highest score in the match, and while there were heart-stopping moments for the Indians, Kumble made sure India would not be denied. Kumble took 6 for 78 and India won by 49 runs. Kumble's sixth wicket also marked the moment of victory, being the last West Indian wicket, and there was something appropriate in that, for he was the only member of the Indian team born before April 1971, when Wadekar and his men had created history. Now, thirty-five years later, a new generation of Indians had finally won a series in the Caribbean and this in a side without Tendulkar. It was a reflection of how India had done in the Caribbean since 1971 that Tendulkar during his career never won a series in the West Indies and only one Test. The victory also set a record for the ground, for no team had won after making 200 or fewer in the first innings of a Test at Sabina Park. Jamaica, which had so often terrorized India, now rang out to Indian cheers and celebration.

Chapter 37

DESPAIR, JOY AND FINGERS KHAN

DADA REFUSES TO GIVE UP

Ganguly had watched the events unfold in the West Indies with keen interest and had not given up his ambitions to regain his place. Insecurity gnawed at him and he often spoke to Rajdeep Sardesai asking if he knew what the powers that be were thinking. He also spoke directly to those powers. He talked to Dravid twice, once in April just before the West Indian trip and then again after the team had returned. Dravid advised him to be patient. He even spoke to Sharad Pawar who told him, 'Personally I have a good impression about you. But the coach tends to think otherwise. He says you are disruptive influence on the team.' Ganguly's father advised him to retire, 'Maharaj, you have achieved a lot. Why don't you walk away with pride? Maharaj, trust me, I don't see any window for you. Sadly, there is no hope.' But Ganguly was determined not to. As he had told Rajdeep Sardesai, 'No way, why should I give up, you are telling me I am not good enough to be in the top six batsmen in the country?'

India's next one-day venture was the Champions Trophy which was held in October in India. Ganguly was not selected and he agreed to appear in a Pepsi ad campaign where he said, 'Main Sourav Ganguly hoon. Bhule toh nahin? Jo hua kyun hua? Kaise hua?' It ended with, 'Hawa mein shirt ghoomane ke liye aur ek mauka mil jaye?' [I am Sourav Ganguly. Have you forgotten me? Why has this happened? How did it happen? Will I get one more chance to twirl my shirt?], a reference to the famous Lord's moment. The ad generated a great deal of attention but did little to bring Ganguly back in the Indian side. India had a dreadful Champions Trophy. Apart from beating England by four wickets, India lost to the West Indies and Australia and did not qualify from their group. Tendulkar's return had made no difference, he did not make a 50 in any of the three matches India played.

Three weeks after the Champions Trophy was over, India were in South Africa where they lost all three of the one-day internationals completed, failing to get to 200 in any of them and were bowled out for 91 in 29.1 overs in the second one. Only two Indians scored 50s, Dravid and Dhoni. India did win a T20 international but at that stage the competition meant little to the Indians.

The Tests which followed held out the prospect of much worse, but suddenly Ganguly got a call as the team for the Tests was changed with some of the players, considered one-day specialists like Suresh Raina, sent home.

To say that what happened next in South Africa was all due to the return of Dada would be over-egging the pudding. Yet suddenly from looking like that all too familiar Indian team abroad, lost and eager to return home, India in Johannesburg did something they had never done before in that country—they won a Test match. Not that there seemed much prospect of such a dramatic result when Dravid on winning the toss decided to bat. His decision was all the more surprising as the wicket was wet on top—Johannesburg had had very hot weather and the groundsman, worried the wicket might crack, had watered it the previous evening. The Indians found runs hard to come by. At the end of the first day's play India were 156 for 5, Dravid and Tendulkar having had to chisel runs out and Ganguly 14 not out having survived a barrage of bouncers. This is when Dada's resolve and determination came out. At the end of the day's play he went straight into the nets to practise, getting the assistant coach, Ian Frazer, to feed balls into the bowling machine that replicated those Makhaya Ntini was bowling, 85 miles an hour and back of a length. He spent the night alone in his hotel room continually reminding himself that Johannesburg was where he had lost the World Cup. He needed, he told himself, to set that right. The next day he did not get the century he wanted, but the South Africans could not get him out as he finished with 51 not out, the highest score in the Indian innings. The Ganguly spirit infused last man V. R. V. Singh who entertained himself in making 29, four more than Laxman and only four short of Dravid's total. The last wicket partnership took 205 for 9 to 249 all out. As Ganguly climbed up the stairs at the Wanderers to the dressing room he found the Indian team applauding and read it as a message to Chappell and the selectors that they felt Dada had been unfairly treated. Chappell came up to Ganguly and congratulated him.

249 may not have seemed much but then Sreesanth started bowling. He had carefully observed the South African quicks Dale Steyn, Makhaya Ntini and Shaun Pollock banging the ball in short to make the most of the Indian batsmen's legendary fear of short-pitched bowling. Sreesanth bowled a fuller length, pitched it up and got five of the first seven wickets to fall. The way the South Africans fell to Sreesanth told the story: Graeme Smith

the captain and Pollock were lbw, Hashim Amla and Jacques Kallis were caught by Laxman at second slip, Mark Boucher was bowled. South Africa were 45 for 7 and the true value of Ganguly's gritty innings was now revealed. In the past India may have allowed South Africa to escape but they did not this time. South Africa were bowled out for 84, their lowest total in forty years, with Sreesanth claiming his first five-wicket haul in the process. Laxman's 73 extended the lead to 401 runs. Twenty wickets fell on the second day and by the time the pitch began to ease it was too late for South Africa. Sreesanth again took the wickets of crucial batsmen, Smith, Amla, Kallis, and finished with match figures of 8 for 99. While there was a 97 from Ashwell Prince it only served to delay the inevitable; defeat inside four days by 123 runs. Sreesanth was Man of the Match, and while this match displayed his talent it also revealed the wild man that had always lurked underneath. He got so animated when sending off Amla in the second innings that he was fined 20 per cent of his match fee.

Gavaskar would describe the triumph as 'one of India's best ever'. India should have made the most of this and gone on to win the series but in Durban, as Ganguly says, 'we failed to put up a fight'. If a victory was impossible, a draw was very much within reach. More than a hundred overs were lost due to bad light across the five days, and on the fifth day after South Africa had set India 354 to win, India, at 179 for 9, were only ten minutes from drawing the Test and going into Cape Town for the final Test 1–0 ahead. But they failed and apart from Sreesanth who took eight wickets in the match the rest seemed unwilling to want to put their bodies on the line. Sreesanth was the exception, quite literally, taking a blow to the arm from Ntini in the dying moments. Forced to return to his feet by the officials, the tail-ender was given out caught behind off his shoulder providing Smith with 'one of the most emotional wins of his career'.

At the start of the third Test in Cape Town, Chappell urged the Indians to be courageous and not be as reckless as they had been in Durban and lose the plot. The Indians seemed to take his words on board when they batted on winning the toss. India made 414 and even got a lead of 41. But this is where India showed a lack of direction. In the second innings the batting order was revised, Sehwag who had batted at No 7 in the first innings opened as if India wanted to go for a win. He made 4, slashing at a wide half-volley; Jaffer, who had made a hundred in the first innings made 2, and India were 6 for 2. Now followed a farce which had a very unsettling effect on the batting. Tendulkar walked in but before he could get to the middle he was stopped. He had spent eighteen minutes off the field on the previous day. But as he came out only thirteen minutes had been used so he had to wait. Laxman should have replaced him but at that moment he was literally in the toilet with his pants down. Chappell rushed to Ganguly who had batted No. 6 in the first innings, asked him to pad up and rush to the middle. He emerged seven minutes later and while the South Africans appealed that he should be timed out this was overruled by umpire Daryl Harper saying the Indians had only just been made aware of the problem. Ganguly did go on to make 46, finishing top of the Indian batting, 214 runs with an average of 42.80. Had other Indian batsmen showed his composure it might have been a different story, but apart from Dravid who made 47 and Karthik 38 not out, none of them did. India's 169 all out meant South Africa needed 211.

There was still hope for India. The wicket was more like an Indian turner and on the final day three hours were lost. Yet Kumble, despite the help he got, took only one wicket and enterprising South African batting made sure the time lost did not count and they ran out winners by five wickets. South Africa became only the eighth team in cricket history to win a three-Test series after losing the first. Dravid's win in the West Indies had been India's first triumph outside the subcontinent against an established Test side since 1986. This defeat showed that the ghost of not being able to win away had not yet been truly laid to rest. It is interesting that Tendulkar who averaged 33.16 does not mention this series in his book. At the end of each chapter of his book is a summary of the Tests he played in but this one, curiously, is missing. Instead Tendulkar concentrates on the 2007 World Cup which he now saw as his 'primary goal' to win.

CHAPPELL REACHES HIS NADIR

India went into the 2007 World Cup brimming with confidence. One Indian cricket administrator confidently told me that he was not going for the start of the World Cup as he had booked to go to Barbados because he was sure India would be at the final to be staged there on 28 April 2007.

Yet unknown to the wider world, all was not right with Indian cricket. A few months before Indians set out for the West Indies, Chappell came to Tendulkar's home and in front of his wife, Anjali, told India's greatest player that he should take over the captaincy from Dravid. If he did that then, said Chappell, 'together, we would control Indian cricket for years.' A shocked Tendulkar rejected the idea and a few days later suggested to the BCCI that it would be a good idea for Chappell not to accompany the team to the World Cup. 'We as senior players could take control of the side and keep them [the players] together.' Tendulkar does not say whether he made this proposal having consulted Dravid or who at the BCCI he spoke to. It is reasonable to presume he spoke to Pawar with whom he had very good relations. But this advice was not accepted and it was with Chappell at the helm that India flew to the Caribbean. The World Cup would prove to be a disaster both for Indian and world cricket.

Malcolm Speed, the ICC chief executive, titled the chapter in his book describing the event 'Cricket World Cup 2007-West Indies: The Event from Hell'.

One of the things that went wrong, said Speed, was 'the failure of many of the fancied sides to perform to anything like their highest standards'.

India, which had everything going for it, was the prime example of that. All their matches were in Port of Spain, almost a home ground for India. They were in Group B with Bangladesh, Sri Lanka and Bermuda, two minnows and only Sri Lanka capable of extending India. Qualification for the Super Eights seemed a doddle. India opened their campaign against Bangladesh. They had won fifty of their previous fifty-one one-day internationals against Bangladesh. But this seemed to introduce a touch of complacency in the way India approached the match, tripping over themselves, even before play had started. Tendulkar, who would have preferred to open, was asked to bat No. 4 on the theory that West Indian wickets would be slow and low and he would be better positioned in the middle to score against the spinners. But the wicket at Port of Spain was a damp one with bounce and movement and when Dravid, rather curiously chose to bat, Tendulkar found himself in the middle almost as if he was opening with Sehwag out for 2 and Uthappa for 9. And while he negotiated the swing of Mashrafe Bin Mortaza, who had got both batsmen, he got out to Bangladesh's left arm spinner, Abdur Razzak, for 7. Going for an inside out shot over extra cover he edged the ball on to his pads from where it went on to hit the stumps. Only Ganguly, 66, and Yuvraj, 47, showed some fight. India's 191 was never going to be enough and Bangladesh won by five wickets. What made the defeat worse was, as Speed put it, India not only lost but, 'quite meekly at that'.

The next match against Bermuda was won easily and if India could beat Sri Lanka, who had beaten both Bangladesh and Bermuda, they would still go through. Despite the fact that India in eleven previous World Cup matches had won only four chasing, Dravid chose to send Sri Lanka in. His bowlers did well, Sri Lanka making 254. The wicket was good, the target should have proved within reach. They never looked like doing it and only Dravid, who made 60, batted anywhere near his class. India in two matches against Test sides had failed to reach 200. For India now to go through Bermuda would have to cause what would have been the greatest ever World Cup upset by beating Bangladesh. They did not.

The impact of this defeat was immediately felt by airlines and Caribbean hotels as Indian fans cancelled flights and hotel bookings. I do not know what the Indian board administrator did with his booking for the final.

As India lost to Sri Lanka I was on a flight to Jamaica to cover the alleged murder of Bob Woolmer, the coach of Pakistan. He had been found dead in his hotel room after Pakistan had lost to Ireland. This generated extraordinary stories that the Pakistan defeat was a result of match-fixing and to cap it the Jamaican police, whose chief investigating officer was a police officer from Essex, made the stunning declaration that Woolmer had not died of natural causes but had been murdered. This immediately led to theories that the murderer was a member of a gang employed by bookies who had lost out as a result of the upset. Amazing stories began to circulate as to how Woolmer was killed, the most preposterous being that the grass at the ground where Pakistan had played had been poisoned. Some weeks later, back in London, I was told by a very senior Scotland Yard detective that Woolmer's death was a natural one, the Jamaican police had got it wrong and I broadcast the news on the BBC, bringing this ridiculous story to a close.

What the absurd claim of Woolmer being strangled had done was bring match-fixing back to centre stage. In Jamaica, where the world's press including a bevy of Indian media had gathered, I found that all sorts of reasons—none of them to do with cricket—were being given for why India and Pakistan should lose to minnows. So, among the extraordinary stories that did the rounds was that in the Bangladesh match Ganguly in making 66 in 129 balls had deliberately batted slowly as under his bat contract with Puma he was paid by how much time he spent at the crease. Ganguly who had seen the World Cup defeat as 'easily the darkest moment of my playing career' was incensed. He had come in to bat with the score at 40 for 3, then seen Dravid get out at 72 for 4 and the need was to make sure the innings did not finish in forty overs. Ganguly was forced to write to the Indian board enclosing his contract and explain his innings was dictated by what was happening in the match that day, not any contract he had signed.

It was easy for Indian fans to believe such absurd stories because, having lavished so much care and love and spent not a little of their hard-earned money on the team, they could not understand why they should fail so miserably. The players were painted as people who profited from hard-working Indians but gave nothing in return. The grief led to the inevitable anger which saw street demonstrations, effigies of players burnt, many of the players found their houses were targeted and some feared for their safety. Newspapers even wrote pieces headlined 'Endulkar' which hurt the great man's pride. In order to get the World Cup out of his head he took to running and even thought of retiring. Tendulkar, of course, was not going to call it a day, but he had no doubts Chappell must go. He felt so distraught about the Australian that three years later he very bluntly told Greg's brother, Ian, that 'I would not want to share a dressing room with him again.' When Ian Chappell tried to explain that Greg could not deal with failure and even had problems when he was captain of Australia Tendulkar, who rarely showed emotion, lashed out and told Ian that Chappell's problems were not his concern. All that mattered was 'that he had failed to take Indian cricket forward'. In Greg Chappell's version he had already decided before the World Cup that he would quit the Indian job.

The Indian board initially wanted a foreign replacement, Graham Ford, but he would not leave Kent and almost as a holding operation a little over two months later India went to Bangladesh with Ravi Shastri as the coach. However, Dravid retained the captaincy. Chappell's departure did not mean Ganguly was coming back so much so that even that even for the two one-day matches that started the tour, Ganguly was omitted from the side; the official explanation was that he was being 'rested'. Ganguly it seems was still on trial. Tendulkar was also 'rested' which meant that for the first time in his career Tendulkar had not been picked even when fit. India quickly restored the normal order, winning the one-day series and also the two Test series. For the Tests Tendulkar and Ganguly returned, they both scored centuries in the first which was drawn and Tendulkar a century in the second as well which India won by an innings. He saw the win as waking up from the Chappell nightmare.

ZAHEER KHAN AND THE JELLY BEANS

India's tour of England in 2007 proved to be a rerun of that first historic victory in 1971. As we have seen, India's momentous victory in the third and final Test at the Oval had come after avoiding defeat in the previous Test with a bowler who was making his comeback suddenly proving the match winner. The crucial difference was that in 1971 the match winner was a leg-spinner Bhagwath Chandrasekhar, in 2007 it was a left-arm-pace bowler Zaheer Khan, in some ways illustrating how Indian cricket had changed over the three decades.

In 1971, rain had washed out the last day's play in the second Test at Manchester, saving India from defeat, which meant that India came to the Oval with the series undecided. At Lord's, in 2007, India flirted with defeat even more outrageously. On the last evening with nine wickets down, Monty Panesar, on bended knees, appealed for an lbw against the Indian No. 11, Sreesanth. Hawk-Eye agreed with Panesar but umpire Steve Bucknor, who had so often upset the Indians and would do so again six months later, now sided with them and ruled Sreesanth was not out. Soon the light worsened, Lord's scoreboards dazzled in the gloom and five minutes before tea, India were offered the light and took it. As Sachin Tendulkar put it India were, 'fortunate to avoid defeat'. So, as India left London for Nottingham they could feel, that as in 1971, the gods were on their side.

There was one other striking parallel between 1971 and 2007. As we have seen, in 1971 in the first Test at Lord's, as India chased victory, Snow had barged Gavaskar to the ground as he went for a single. Nottingham also saw some barging, although this was an Indian bowler barging an England batsman. More significantly, this was the 'jellybean gate' Test, the net result of which was to make Zaheer Khan determined to exact revenge on the English batsmen.

Known as Zak to his teammates, not many doubted his skills but there were questions about his desire to succeed. In the past he had neglected his gym work, had had fitness problems, an up and down career and Chappell had made it clear he did not rate him. 2005 had been a bad year, with Sreesanth and R. P. Singh emerging, he was dropped and his contract downgraded from B to C. Zaheer would be out of the Test team for nine months. Zaheer decided the only solution was to do something not many Indian cricketers do, spend a whole summer playing county cricket for Worcestershire. Worcester, seeking a double promotion, first division of the county championship and the Pro40 League, had initially signed the Australian, Nathan Bracken. But he dropped out, wanting to concentrate on his career with Australia. Zaheer came in his place hoping to get his Indian place back through county cricket. Steve Rhodes, Bumpy as he was nicknamed, the former England wicketkeeper, had just taken over as director of cricket. He had happy memories of playing with Kapil Dev in his first season for Worcester in 1985 and told me:

> Zaheer had gone out of the Indian side and there was talk of him being a little bit overweight, of having to work out. So, he went back to basics. He got himself fit. He put in a hell of a really good stint for us all season long. He bowled his overs, took his wickets and he was a mighty skilful bowler. We had him for a full season. By getting fit and building his confidence he got himself back into the international side.

When I asked him to compare Zaheer with Wasim Akram, Rhodes said:

> Zaheer and Wasim were very different bowlers. Wasim was more swing and a very good reverse swing bowler. Reverse swing was mightily important for Wasim. One of the things about Zaheer was he was a really good new ball bowler. But also he knew the time and occasion when he had to step up his pace and that generally was on flatter wickets. He was very skilful and we used to call him Fingers Khan. He had little bits of subtle movements of his fingers which made the ball go in different directions. He would move his fingers a little bit one way and a little bit the other way and the ball went a little bit one way and a little bit the other way.

Zaheer, determined to nail the canard that Indians in county cricket were not willing to work hard, bowled 618.4 overs in the 2006 season, more than any other bowler. His seventy-eight wickets were nearly twice as many as Matt Mason and Kabir Ali combined, with 5 five-fer wicket hauls. His wicket tally was second only to Mushtaq Ahmed in the county. The result was Worcester won double promotion and in 2007, for the first time ever, played both in the first division of the County Championship and that of the Pro40 League.

As Zaheer put it:

> Playing for Worcestershire meant playing in different conditions, pitch and weather for five months. You had had to innovate, use your thinking power. There were some experiments that I couldn't carry out when playing for India. I carried them out in county cricket. I went through the range of left-arm fast bowling. There was help from the county think tank—coach Steve Rhodes, bowling consultant Graham Dilley, whose action I am told was a picture of rhythm. I am a rhythm bowler. When I get it right I get into the zone and there's no stopping me. One of the things I did when coming back from injury was cutting down my run-up. Dilley said balancing was important, for I would be jumping on one leg and landing on one. The functional exercises I did were the key. Above all the Dukes ball was a boon for me.

The county experience meant he could swing the ball both into and away from the right-handed batsmen, bowling from over and round the wicket. And he had also discovered that the weapon he could use to stop the batsmen coming forward was the bouncer.

Zaheer had used the Bangladesh trip to further hone his skills. In tandem with his fast bowling partner, R. P. Singh, Zaheer fashioned a way of bowling that was to prove masterly in England. The two left-armers bowled from round the wicket and in England with a Dukes ball providing prodigious swing, they found this angle of approach even more profitable. The English appeared to have paid little attention to what Zaheer and Singh had done in Bangladesh and for many of them it was as if Wasim Akram, who they had read about but never faced, had suddenly reappeared. This generation of English batsmen was not used to this line of attack and it proved so novel that even when batsmen scored runs against Zaheer and Singh they could not get over their surprise.

Kevin Pietersen's innings at Lord's illustrated this. During that Test, despite the fact that England dominated the match, Zaheer and Singh had given a glimpse of how they might prove India's match-winners, with Michael Vaughan, the England captain, falling to Singh bowling round the wicket in both innings. Pietersen in the second innings scored 134, reaching his century with a four. But even before the ball crossed the boundary line he went into an elaborate celebration as if he had reached a truly great landmark. He would later explain that so demanding was Zaheer Khan's bowling that he had to completely rethink his game plan and this was one of the best innings he had ever played.

For Zaheer, his second innings bowling at Lord's when he took 4 for 79 was crucial. As he would later say, 'When I got wickets in the second innings at Lord's, I got the confidence that I would do well on tour.' His bowling at Lord's proved to be a launch pad and after that experts were convinced about his quality. There was talk about how Zaheer disguised his deliveries very well and how he swung the ball conventionally far more than he reverse swung it, thus managing to deceive the batsmen. While Zaheer took the limelight Singh also contributed. He swung the ball both ways and late. In terms of figures he took second place to Zaheer. Zaheer took eighteen wickets at an average of 20.33, Singh twelve, an average of 28.91. But many of his dismissals were of batsmen of the top order, such as Pietersen which was to prove crucial at Nottingham.

And there was one other factor in Nottingham: it was the nearest to a 'home' Test for the Indians. Since the dismal tour of 1959, when the first Test was played at Nottingham, a well-off Indian community had developed which says Nat Puri, a rich businessman who had helped rebuild the Trent Bridge ground, 'means when India play at the Trent Bridge ground this is like a home Test, the majority of the 18,000 who come are Indian supporters.' All this would have an impact as the Test began.

It had rained so hard before the match that the night before the

Test started, Steve Birks, the groundsman did not have a wink of sleep, spending the entire night mopping up. Graham Morris the legendary cricket photographer got a shot of Birks sleeping against the roller as the match began. Despite Birks's efforts the outfield was wet enough for a mat to be placed over a patch at third man near the pavilion when play began after lunch.

Although this was not immediately apparent, Dravid winning the toss was important. He could put England in and Zaheer and Singh soon had England's batsmen in trouble with their round the wicket line. England were bowled out for 198 with the Indian seamers taking seven of the English wickets, including the top six of the English batting line-up. Zaheer's 4 for 59 included Andrew Strauss, Michael Vaughan and Ian Bell. Singh had the crucial wicket of Pietersen.

With the ball still seaming and moving England had reason to expect they would make inroads into the Indian batting. Strauss and Cook, England's openers, had managed just 4 and as India began their reply, the England bowlers felt that the Indian openers would not be a match for the English pace attack. There was no Sehwag, India was playing their reserve-wicketkeeper, Dinesh Karthik, as opener while Dhoni continued behind the stumps. However, Karthik and Wasim Jaffer belied the stereotypes of Indian batsmen struggling against the moving ball and showed England how to do it albeit on a slightly flatter, drier surface than the one England had faced. Karthik and Jaffer did play and miss, reflecting the fact that they were not used to the conditions. But they batted for three hours, putting on 147, the first century stand in England by Indian openers since 1979 when the openers were Gavaskar and Chauhan and one of their century partnerships had been at the epic Oval Test of that series.

The opening stand laid the foundation for the rest of the Indian batting which provided a vivid contrast to the England effort. In the England innings Cook's 43 had been the highest England score. Five of the Indian top six passed 50, only Dravid didn't but his 37 came at a crucial time, denying England on the second evening. Indeed, two of the Indians could have gone on to make big centuries but for wretched umpiring decisions. Tendulkar, who after a scratchy start had got to 91, was given out lbw to Paul Collingwood when replays showed the ball would have missed the off stump and Ganguly on 79 was given out caught behind by Matt Prior off Jimmy Anderson when the ball had missed the bat. Tendulkar would later describe this as one of his most satisfying innings; it showed how much his batting had changed. The young Tendulkar on 91 facing Collingwood after lunch would have been hungry to get to his century and blasted him, now he was defensive, seeking to make sure India built on the advantage it had. However, the real drama of the innings, and indeed the Test, came on the third evening when Zaheer Khan, batting at No. 9, strode out to bat.

As he got to the crease he spotted three jelly beans which had clearly been kicked on to the wicket. According to Alastair Cook, who was fielding at short-leg this was, 'more by luck than anything'. English cricketers always had jelly beans when fielding considering them a good source of energy when the players need sugar intake. It was not unknown during county matches for jelly beans to be kicked on to the wicket by fielders, but that was not usual in Test cricket. However, during the previous series against the West Indies somebody had thrown jelly beans on to the wicket when Shivnarine Chanderpaul had been batting and he had smiled and swept them off the wicket.

Initially, Zaheer also did not seem to mind, and like Chanderpaul smiled and swept them off the wicket. And here we come up against two very contrasting stories about what happened next with the English and the Indian versions diverging. Cook says Zaheer only managed to knock two away, missed a third and then after he had edged a shot for four through slips, and just as he was ready to take strike, noticed the third bean. However, Zaheer did not see it that way. He believed he had got rid of all the beans and the English fielders had placed an additional bean after he had played his shot. He might have treated the jelly beans initially as a joke but now, looking at this bean, he was convinced the English were out to get him and the jelly beans were no longer a laughing matter but a very serious provocation.

Wisden would later publish a photograph of Zaheer Khan and the umpire Ian Howell looking at the jelly bean, Zaheer is pointing at it with his bat as if to suggest it was an intruder with Howell, wearing a hat and with dark glasses on, holding Zaheer's arm as if to restrain him. Zaheer was determined to find the Englishman who had committed what he saw as a foul act and at first pointed his bat at Pietersen, who told him it was not him. Then the focus shifted to Cook and he was quickly seen as the 'prime suspect'. Cook says this was because he was fielding at short-leg, 'so was seen in the vicinity of the "crime" without a strong alibi'. But he denies it was him.

Whoever it was, Zaheer, as Cook says, was 'enraged'. For the English, as Cook puts it, it 'was just a prank. Okay it was a childish prank, and we apologised for it afterwards, but we really didn't think it would cause offence.' However, as even Cook admits, 'there was a feeling within the Indian camp that they may have allowed themselves to be bullied a bit on some previous tours and had no intention of letting that happen again.'

Nasser Hussain, the former England captain turned commentator, would later write, 'Players should respect the opposition: let them know they are in a battle but don't be childish or juvenile. They would not have done it to Tendulkar so why Zaheer?' and, 'by winding up Zaheer England made a major mistake'. England had certainly picked the wrong Indian to mess with. Zaheer as a person was quite a contrast to many members of the team, even when it came to having a bit of fun. Before the Indians arrived in England, they had played a limited overs series in Ireland and one evening in Belfast Tendulkar persuaded Zaheer and Yuvraj to try some Japanese food. One of dishes was sushi which came with wasabi. Yuvraj having told Tendulkar he liked wasabi proceeded to treat it like butter and spread it on a bread roll. He would later confess he had never tried wasabi before and had no knowledge how strong it could be. Zaheer was keen to see how Yuvraj coped and when Tendulkar decided to warn Yuvraj he kicked Tendulkar under the table to try and stop him telling Yuvraj about the potency of wasabi. But as Tendulkar says, 'There is no doubt that if he had eaten the roll he would have been in serious trouble.'

India's innings ended on 481 and Zaheer 10 not out returned to the Indian dressing room determined to give England his own dose of wasabi. He was shouting at the players that India now needed to play aggressive cricket and crush England in the second innings. The jelly beans prank had turned Zaheer into a raging Bengal tiger. For the Indians, as Tendulkar puts it, 'It was a blessing in disguise for us.'

By this time another English prank had already inflamed the Indians. Prior, a feisty cricketer, was reported to have said to an Indian player, 'I drive a Porsche. What do you drive?' Cook says this was not true but was another case of an English joke that went wrong. Sometime during the Indian innings the stump microphones had picked up Prior mentioning Npower, the Test sponsors. They were so delighted by this unexpected plug they sent Prior champagne and, says Cook, 'we all thought we would have a bit of fun and mention as many sponsors as we could to see if they would send us any more freebies.' Cook mentioned Bang & Olufsen and Prior, who actually drives a Skoda, mentioned Porsche. 'It was taken completely out of context, turned into some insult towards the Indians.'

Prior may have been joking but the Indians did not find it funny and they took it as the English questioning the financial worth of the Indians. This, given that many of the Indians were some of the richest cricketers in the world, far richer than the English players, made them feel that even the modern generation of Englishmen saw them as colonial subjects. Zaheer's words echoed around the dressing room all the more because the Indians had recovered so well from the ravages of the Chappell era that they had once again bonded as a team. 'After a long time,' says Zaheer, 'the Indian team had dinner together on the eve of a match. We also watched the movie *Chak De! India* together [this was a film about the Indian hockey team triumphing]. It made for integration. The movie's title song became our team's theme song.' During India's 1971 victory at the Oval, Chandrasekhar had played the songs of Mukesh to inspire him. Now it was a more modern Bollywood song reflecting a new India full of pride that it could go where other Indian teams had not. You messed with this Indian team at your peril as England was soon to find out. And Zaheer knew he could use what the English had taught him to wipe the smile off English faces.

India's lead of 283 looked handy but the two innings had taken the best part of three days. England began their reply an hour before the close of the third day, and with the pitch not suggesting it had any demons, a draw looked the most likely outcome. More so as England saw out the sixteen overs that day without losing a wicket. However, Zaheer aware that revenge is a dish best served cold, reserved his retribution for the jelly beans 'prank' for the fourth day. And it came in two spells. Zaheer had Cook lbw and then broke the stand between Strauss and Vaughan.

Zaheer had worked out that to get Strauss out he had to bowl a very full-length ball and entice him to drive; and in Nottingham he had him caught behind in both innings, in the first at slip by Tendulkar, in the second by Dhoni. Strauss, who had been dropped from the one-day side by Peter Moores, the new coach, felt so humiliated that, as he later confessed, 'that summer I just couldn't focus properly during the Test matches'. The fear of failure that had haunted Strauss all summer was very evident in this Test.

In the first innings Strauss had got out in the third over making only 4, in the second he got to 55 but even then he did not feel secure against Zaheer. And as he would later say, although his partnership with Vaughan had looked like a match-saving partnership, taking England from 49 for 1 to 130 for 1, neither batsman could predict which way Zaheer was going to swing the ball. He seemed to run up and bowl every delivery in the same way covering the ball with his right hand until the moment he was ready to deliver with his left.

However, even at this stage with Vaughan, playing his best Test innings since his knee operation, and well supported by Collingwood, England looked in no particular danger. If anything it was the Indians who looked riled, in particular, Sreesanth. He had bowled a beamer straight at Pietersen's head. It was the sort of bowling that West Indian fast bowlers like Roy Gilchrist had used to terrorize Indian batsmen. Now Sreesanth, an Indian from a different generation, had decided to use this deadly delivery to upset England's best batsman. He did not apologize but did hold up his hand as if to suggest it may have slipped. Sreesanth, always a volatile character, also ran through the bowling crease by a couple of feet and bowling around the wicket aimed a bouncer at Collingwood. Worse still Sreesanth did a John Snow and barged Vaughan. Vaughan gave him a very disdainful look and Dravid made his displeasure known. The match referee Ranjan Madugalle fined Sreesanth 50 per cent of his match fee.

It was soon after this incident that Zaheer intervened, changing the course of the match, although he was helped by luck playing a part. England were 287 for 3, Vaughan was on 124 when, with Zaheer bowling round the wicket, the England captain tried to flick a ball. He failed and the ball bounced off his thigh pad on the stumps. The picture taken moments later captured what happened very well. Vaughan looks down at the stumps as if he cannot believe that the bails have been dislodged, at the other end Zaheer has suddenly realized what has happened and is beginning his triumphal run down the wicket. On the same score Zaheer dismissed Bell, another English player suspected of having placed the jelly beans in Zaheer's path. He lasted two balls before falling lbw for 0. Singh and Kumble helped out, Singh removing Prior, and England lost their last seven wickets for 68 runs. Zaheer would later see his second innings bowling at Trent Bridge as his 'best spell'. It had come, he says, when 'the pitch was settling down, both teams had a good score. I got rid of Michael Vaughan and the slide began.' Good bowlers are judged by how many good batsmen they get out and in this innings Zaheer's 5 for 75 were five of the top six in the England order: Strauss, Cook, Vaughan, Collingwood, Bell; Singh accounting for Pietersen. Jelly beans meant to provide sugar intake for English fielders had instead so energized an Indian bowler that he had destroyed England.

Many in India had thought Zaheer should not have been on the tour. Now he could claim that his bowling matched that of Kapil Dev and Javagal Srinath. And with both Kapil and Srinath being right-handers, Zaheer could claim to be the best Indian left-armer ever.

India were left 73 to get. After the openers put on 47 there was a stutter as Chris Tremlett got the ball to bounce and took three wickets, Karthik, Jaffer and Tendulkar, who made only 1, before Dravid and Ganguly saw things through.

The victory at Nottingham, India's twenty-ninth away victory in their 200th Test, had been decisive. Many expected India to now crush England in the final Test at the Oval. But the victory in Nottingham was only their fifth Test win in England in forty-seven Tests spread over seventy-five years of touring. So, after Nottingham, Dravid was determined to make sure that the victory was not squandered and was a launch pad for a series win in England which would only be the third ever in England. The result was a cautious, if not defensive, approach to the match. India batting first made 664, all eleven India batsmen reached double figures and Kumble at thirty-six years and 297 days became the oldest Indian to score a maiden Test century. He had also had the longest wait, his century coming in his 118th Test. On the third evening with England 326 for 9 India looked on course to make it 2–0. But then Dravid, despite leading by 319, did not enforce the follow-on and India had a wobble when batting, reduced to 11 for 3. This so scared Dravid that India might lose that he took ninety-six balls making 12—at one stage 2 off fifty-two balls—and could not even hit the ball off the square. Ganguly, batting at the other end, who made 57 in sixty-eight balls, was so taken aback by Dravid's refusal to hit the ball that he said later, 'At one point I wondered if it was really Rahul at the other end.' Ganguly concluded Dravid was 'preoccupied with the result'. In order to avoid defeat he so timed his declaration that England could never get the 499 runs he set them to win. For Dravid it was important to lose the awful tag of lions at home and lambs away. Having won a series in the West Indies for the first time in thirty-five years Dravid wanted to do nothing that would in any way squander the chance of a rare series victory in England. Dravid had done a Wadekar and that meant a lot to him. As he would tell me later, 'India's performances abroad have been a big thing because that's what we always heard about when we were growing up or when I first played. We tended not to do well when we went away from home. We're not very good players when we were playing away from home. Just to be able to change that and to become more competitive abroad I think has been terrific.'

Dravid is an Indian nationalist at heart. Once asked which era he would like to have been born in he had replied the one when Indians fought for their freedom from the British. As he would later tell me, 'I've always been fascinated by people in the freedom movement. It must have been a fascinating time to be an Indian and to be a young Indian growing up then.' The fact that he had captained India for their first ever Test wins in Pakistan and South Africa meant a lot. Winning a series in England, the former conquerors of India, meant even more.

This was England's first series loss at home since 2001 when Australia had been the visitors. And for many in English cricket the defeat reflected a lack of desire on the part of the English cricketers. As Hussain put it, 'There was not enough "over my dead body", except for Michael Vaughan and Kevin Pietersen.'

In contrast Indians had shown a fight and a resolve they had rarely if ever displayed before with Indian fast bowlers earning praise from English critics. This series win marked the end of the seventh wave of Indian cricket. Sixteen days after India finished their tour of England, Mahendra Singh Dhoni ushered in the eighth wave on a magical night in Johannesburg, lifting the T20 World Cup and introducing us to the world of the Indian Premier League. But while the IPL completely changed world cricket, in Test cricket, the old guard that had served India for so long did not just fold their tents and go. The marketing men were changing Indian cricket and the world but on the field the changes worked more slowly.

The Eighth Wave

TESTS

Wave	Period	Mts	Won	Lost	Drawn	Tied	Win%	W/L
8th	2007-2015	79	31	25	23	0	39.24	1.24

TOP BATSMEN IN EIGHTH WAVE

	Mts	Runs	Hs	Avg	100	50
S. R. Tendulkar	60	4771	214	51.30	14	23
V. Sehwag	52	4431	319	49.23	11	20
M. S. Dhoni	70	3857	224	38.57	5	27
R. Dravid	52	3796	191	44.13	12	15
V.V. S. Laxman	51	3698	200*	51.36	7	27
G. Gambhir	43	3362	206	44.23	8	18
V. Kohli	33	2547	169	46.30	10	10
M.Vijay	31	2188	167	39.78	5	10
C. A. Pujara	27	2073	206*	47.11	6	6
S. C. Ganguly	17	1400	239	46.66	3	6

*Not out

TOP BOWLERS IN EIGHTH WAVE

	Mts	Wkts	Best	Avg	5WI	10WM
I. Sharma	60	186	7/74	37.24	6	1
Harbhajan Singh	44	175	7/120	35.79	6	1
Z. Khan	42	151	7/87	32.53	6	1
R. Ashwin	24	119	7/103	30.67	9	2
P. P. Ojha	24	113	6/47	30.26	7	1
A. Kumble	14	53	5/60	39.49	2	0
Mohammed Shami	12	47	5/47	36.14	2	0
R. A. Jadeja	12	45	6/138	30.37	2	0
U. T. Yadav	12	43	5/93	36.93	1	0
A. Mishra	13	43	5/71	43.30	1	0

TOP WICKETKEEPERS IN EIGHTH WAVE

	Mts	Dismissals	Ct	St
M. S. Dhoni	70	231	203	28
K. D. Karthik	5	12	11	1
W. P. Saha	3	6	6	0

ONE-DAY INTERNATIONALS

Wave	Period	Mts	Won	Lost	NR	Tied	Win%	W/L
8th	2007-2015	220	131	73	12	4	59.55	1.79

TOP BATSMEN IN EIGHTH WAVE

	Mts	Runs	Hs	Avg	SR	100	50
V. Kohli	158	6537	183	51.47	89.73	22	33
M. S. Dhoni	178	6022	139★	56.81	86.54	6	44
S. K. Raina	179	4776	116★	37.90	97.37	5	32
G. Gambhir	118	4353	150★	41.45	87.30	9	29
R. G. Sharma	133	4212	264	39.73	82.24	7	25
Yuvraj Singh	110	3220	138★	36.59	87.57	6	21
V. Sehwag	76	3120	219	42.73	118.94	7	13
S. R. Tendulkar	68	3001	200★	47.63	89.47	8	13
S. Dhawan	61	2507	137	43.98	89.92	8	12
R. A. Jadeja	119	1753	87	32.46	84.76	0	10

★Not out

TOP BOWLERS IN EIGHTH WAVE

	Mts	Wkts	Best	Avg	RPO	4W
R. A. Jadeja	119	143	5/36	33.19	4.84	6
R. Ashwin	96	133	4/25	31.93	4.85	1
I. Sharma	75	106	4/34	30.89	5.69	5
Z. Khan	67	94	4/21	31.18	5.07	1
Mohammed Shami	47	87	4/35	24.89	5.54	5
Harbhajan Singh	78	85	5/56	35.67	4.63	1
P. Kumar	68	77	4/31	36.02	5.13	3
U. T. Yadav	48	67	4/31	31.44	5.74	3
A. Nehra	48	65	4/40	32.64	5.85	3
Yuvraj Singh	110	62	5/31	36.96	5.10	2

TOP WICKETKEEPERS IN EIGHTH WAVE

	Mts	Dismissals	Ct	St
M. S. Dhoni	178	226	162	64
P. A. Patel	13	24	18	6
K. D. Karthik	18	23	18	5

W. P. Saha	9	18	17	1
R. V. Uthappa	2	2	1	1

TWENTY20 INTERNATIONALS

Wave	Period	Mts		Won	Lost	NR	Win%	W/L
8th	2007-2015	52		30	21	1	57.69	1.43

Note: The win tally includes one in the bowl-out after a tie

TOP BATSMEN IN EIGHTH WAVE

	Mts	Runs	Hs	Avg	SR	100	50
V. Kohli	28	972	78*	46.28	131.70	0	9
Yuvraj Singh	40	968	77*	31.22	144.69	0	8
S. K. Raina	43	944	101	32.55	135.82	1	3
G. Gambhir	37	932	75	27.41	119.02	0	7
M. S. Dhoni	49	849	48*	35.37	116.62	0	0
R. G. Sharma	42	739	79*	30.79	126.10	0	7
V. Sehwag	18	360	68	21.17	148.76	0	2
Y. K. Pathan	22	236	37*	18.15	146.58	0	0
A. M. Rahane	11	236	61	21.45	118.00	0	1
I. K. Pathan	23	172	33*	24.57	119.44	0	0

*Not out

TOP BOWLERS IN EIGHTH WAVE

	Mts	Wkts	Best	Avg	RPO	4W
I. K. Pathan	23	28	3/16	21.00	8.05	0
R. Ashwin	26	25	4/11	29.28	7.32	1
Yuvraj Singh	40	23	3/17	16.78	7.19	0
Harbhajan Singh	24	21	4/12	26.23	6.33	1
A. B. Dinda	9	17	4/19	14.41	8.16	1
R. P. Singh	10	15	4/13	15.00	6.81	1
Z. Khan	16	15	4/19	28.86	7.92	1
R. A. Jadeja	22	14	3/48	37.78	7.27	0
Y. K. Pathan	22	13	2/22	33.69	8.61	0
A. Nehra	8	13	3/19	21.07	8.83	0

TOP WICKETKEEPERS IN EIGHTH WAVE

	Mts	Dismissals	Ct	St
M. S. Dhoni	49	35	24	11
P. A. Patel	1	1	1	0

Chapter 38

INDIA WIN CRICKET'S SIX-DAY WAR

The 2007–2008 season which marks the start of the eighth wave of Indian cricket would climax with the first IPL season which was to so radically change cricket. But for much of the season it was by no means sure the IPL would be a success and it was dominated by what was a six-day war, largely fought off the field, where the word 'monkey' played a central role. And India was ready to walk away from a tour because one of its players was accused of being a racist. Within weeks of returning with the T20 World Cup, Dhoni, now captain of the one-day side as well, took on Australia at home between September and October 2007 and this series would light a fuse that would explode, when India visited Australia a few months later, into the six-day war. In India, Australia won the 50-over series, 4–2, although India did win the solitary T20 match. What marked the tour was what happened to Andrew Symonds off the field. Man of the Series on the field, he had a very different experience off the field. Symonds, who is of mixed race and wears dreadlocks, had not endeared himself to the Indian players by publicly saying that India's victory celebrations after their T20 World Cup win were excessive. Symonds also had problems with the Indian crowd. 'Symo,' says Hayden, 'was taunted by chants of "Monkey" throughout the 2007 tour of India'. This started at Vadodara in the fifth international. Australia won by nine wickets and sections of the crowd shouted 'monkey' at him, prompted not only by defeat but the age-old Indian prejudice against people with darker skin. At the Wankhede during the final match things got worse. The crowd booed Symonds and made monkey noises and gestures. These were caught by the camera and some of the culprits were ejected. In the T20 match at the Brabourne Stadium crowds could be heard chanting 'Symonds is a donkey'. At this stage the relationship between the players had not been affected with the match referee Chris Broad defusing any potential problems. But all this had shored up trouble for the future and it would explode when India went to Australia.

THE MOST SERENE CAPTAIN

Before that Anil Kumble had finally become captain of the Test side against Pakistan, which toured India between November and December 2007. John Wright and Greg Chappell did not agree on much except that Kumble was the wisest and most serene of the Indian players whose advice could always be relied upon. Kumble, with charming modesty, said that he had become captain, after playing seventeen years at the highest level, by 'default' owing to his longevity, rather than his credentials as a leader. India had decided on a split captaincy and Kumble did not play in the limited overs series where Dhoni led India to a 3–2 triumph. It was only then, at the age of thirty-seven and at Kotla, scene of his greatest achievement, that he took over.

It could not have been a better start. Kumble took seven wickets in the match and inspired a collapse in the second innings that saw the last five Pakistani batsmen fall for just 34 runs. India were left 203 to chase and Tendulkar's 56 not out secured a six-wicket triumph. Tendulkar set a personal landmark by moving behind Lara in the all-time leader board of Test run-scorers.

The next two Tests were drawn with Kolkata providing a surface for batsmen which Jaffer, Laxman and Ganguly in particular enjoyed. The prince of Kolkata scored a Test century on his home ground for the first time and a first century against a major Test nation in four years. Ganguly went one better in the next Test at Bengaluru making 239. Had Kumble been more adventurous, India could have won. On the final day he set Pakistan 374 to win in only forty-seven overs. When Kumble came on to bowl first change he found the wicket unplayable and, forsaking spin and bowling seam up—he used to be a seamer in his youth—took the first five wickets to fall. Pakistan were reduced to 154 for 7. Then, with eleven overs left, bad light intervened and Pakistan escaped. However, Kumble had won his first series as captain, and the first win at home against Pakistan since Gavaskar in 1979–80. It was two weeks later when India got to Australia that the fuse lit by the reaction to Symonds exploded.

MONKEYGATE

India lost the first Test at Melbourne in December 2007 which Chetan Chauhan, the Indian manager, called 'a bad dream'. The next Test at Sydney in January 2008 would prove a nightmare which very nearly saw the Indians forfeit the series and has become known as Bollyline or Monkeygate. The first hint of trouble came with an umpiring decision involving Symonds. After a bad start Symonds had rallied Australia to 193 for 6 when, trying to force Sharma off the back foot, he got a thick outside edge to Dhoni.

The sound was so loud that Tendulkar's son sitting on the boundary edge heard it. Steve Bucknor, the umpire, was the only one who didn't. Symonds admitted he had edged it but in the great Australian tradition did not walk. Symonds, then 30, went on to make 162 not out and Australia made 463.

However, India did not capitulate, with a 109 by Laxman and an almost flawless 154 not out by Tendulkar at his favourite ground where his average now stood at 221.33. Tendulkar was on 69 when he was joined by Harbhajan and showing much confidence in him allowed him the strike. The pair put on 129, a record eighth wicket stand against Australia. During their partnership he heard Symonds abusing the off-spinner. Tendulkar tried to calm Harbhajan down and kept telling him not to retaliate. The explosion came at 3.35 p.m. on the third day when in the 116th over Harbhajan, having gone past his 50, dug out a yorker from Brett Lee and as he jogged past Lee he patted him on the back. Lee did not mind but Symonds reacted furiously and at the end of the over is believed to have said, 'You have no fucking business here just because you are batting well. Fuck off.' Symonds then alleged that Harbhajan responded by swearing at him and calling him a 'big monkey'. Symonds would go on to allege that during the one-day internationals in India Harbhajan had called him a monkey as well. Tendulkar did not hear Harbhajan call Symonds a monkey but as he walked up to Harbhajan he heard him tell Symonds, 'Teri maa ki' [Your mother]. This is a term of abuse that is used in north India, Tendulkar writes in his autobiography, 'It is an expression we often use in north India to vent our anger and to me it was all part of the game.'

Harbhajan had ignited the six-day war and the Australians were quick to retaliate. They complained to the match referee, Mike Proctor. Harbhajan was charged and at the end of the Test, which India lost, Proctor held a hearing lasting four and a half hours. The evidence at the hearing was rather curious. Hayden said he had heard the words 'big monkey', Clarke said he had heard something like 'big monkey'. Tendulkar said the word 'monkey' was not used. Harbhajan denied using the word 'monkey' but neither he nor Tendulkar told Proctor that Harbhajan had used the words 'teri maa ki'. Tendulkar in his book does not explain why. Proctor did not believe Tendulkar and said, 'I am satisfied beyond a reasonable doubt that Harbhajan Singh directed that word [monkey] at Andrew Symonds, also that he meant to offend on the basis of Symonds race or ethnic origin'. Harbhajan was given a three-Test ban.

The Indians were outraged. If Tendulkar, who represented all that was good in India, was not believed, India was dishonoured. At a team meeting, where Kumble, Laxman and Tendulkar did most of the talking, it was made clear that if the ban was upheld then the players would not continue with the tour. Now the BCCI came into play and opened a war on two fronts. Bindra rang Speed to suggest that Bucknor be stood down. Speed being pragmatic and 'dousing one spot-fire' agreed. Harbhajan had appealed and John Hansen, a New Zealand high court judge, was appointed to hear the appeal. Speed decided that the date for the appeal would be 29–30 January, a day after the Test series was over and when only one T20 match remained to be played. Speed says, 'I wanted to make sure the Test series was completed before the hearing just in case the Indians decided to abandon the tour.' But before the appeal could be heard the BCCI opened its second front against the Australian Cricket Board and threatened it with its weapon of mass destruction: its economic power.

The Australian Board had an eight-year TV deal which was bringing in $1 billion. Did the Australians want to put all this at risk? The Australians decided they did not. After a great deal of negotiation an agreed statement of facts was signed by Harbhajan, Ponting, Symonds, Clarke, Gilchrist and Tendulkar and given to Hansen.

This statement did not say Harbhajan had called Symonds a 'big monkey', or had made any racist comment, but that Symonds had used the word fuck 'or a derivation thereof' when talking to Harbhajan. The Australians had under BCCI pressure agreed that Harbhajan, while being offensive, had not been racist. That word did not figure in the joint statement. This was the charge the Indian players had insisted be dropped. Speed summed it up well saying in his book *Sticky Wicket,* 'a new defence had emerged. Harbhajan denied that he had called Symonds a big monkey—he claimed that he had called him "motherfucker" in Punjabi.' Now, as Speed says, history had been rewritten. It was a 'schoolyard spat rather than a racist incident'. But Hansen refused to rubber stamp the agreed statement, telling Speed that he did not like the fact that the two boards had gone behind his back and for him to agree to the statement would be 'disastrous for cricket'. Hansen called witnesses and the hearing was held on 29 January, after the Test series was over.

A few days before the hearing I heard that Harbhajan's defence was that he had used 'teri maa ki' but in front of Proctor and with Tendulkar, such a demigod, present he did not feel he could utter the words. I was then BBC Sports Editor and when I told the BBC bosses it took them some time at their morning news conference meeting to understand the real meaning of 'teri maa ki'. The BBC allowed me to break the story but would not let me say what part of the mother's anatomy was being referred to. It was only in front of Hansen that Harbhajan admitted for the first time that he had said, 'teri maa ki'. Tendulkar confirmed Harbhajan had only used the words 'teri maa ki' which he said sounds like monkey and could be misinterpreted for it. Tendulkar admitted that 'teri maa ki' were offensive words in Punjabi. Hayden and Clarke maintained that 'big monkey' was used.

Unlike Proctor, Hansen found Tendulkar impressive and concluded, 'I have not been persuaded to the necessary level required that the words were said.' Hansen had also been told by the counsel of Cricket Australia that Symonds himself did not consider 'big monkey' to be racist merely offensive.

Hansen decided that Harbhajan was not guilty of racism but was guilty of the lesser offence of 'abuse and insult not amounting to racism'. He was fined half his match fee. Speed was under no illusion as to what had happened. 'It was a graphic example of the power of India over the modern game and the willingness of its administrators to use their financial muscle when national pride is at stake.'

And for all the anger of Symonds and the Australians about Monkeygate they were aware of Indian money power. As Hayden put it in his memoir *Standing My Ground*:

> India is the most important cricket market on the planet, and the truth
> of the situation was that both countries understood that anything
> that would adversely affect their relationship was unacceptable, from a
> business point of view.

In October 2007, three months before Symonds was supposed to have heard Harbhajan call him a big monkey, he and other Australian cricketers had met Lalit Modi in India to discuss the IPL. Australians had feared they might be punished for Monkeygate but they were not. Hayden was auctioned for $350,000. 'For two months' work it was a lot of money.' Ponting went for $400,000.

Chapter 39

CRICKET TAMASHA AND INDIA'S DONALD TRUMP

MODI CALLS AN ENGLISHMAN FOR HELP

In 2010, Lord Bell, the legendary British public relations adviser and a close confidant of Margaret Thatcher, was sitting in his office in London's West End when the phone rang. The voice at the other end was a man he did not know but whom he had heard about and whose activities he had followed. The caller was Lalit Modi. Tim Bell told me:

> He rang me up out of the blue. I didn't know that much about him at the time. I knew he'd invented the IPL. I always thought he was rather a colourful character. He said, 'Can I come and see you?' I said, 'Sure.' He came to my office and he said, 'Would you handle my profile?' I said, 'Sure. What's wrong with your profile?' He said, 'Well, I've been banned from having a passport. I can't travel and I can't do anything and I want to develop the IPL. I would like to go to the next stage.' I said, 'Well tell me about the IPL, because I am fascinated by the IPL. It's a brilliant idea.' He talked for about two hours and he explained to me how he had invented the IPL, what had motivated him, and it was a great story. He seemed to be very clever and very, very astute in his technique. He had made a fortune for the BCCI. Then he'd fallen out with them and they decided he was a crook and that he should be locked up. I didn't understand that. It seemed to me that he and the then head of the BCCI disagreed with each other about how to progress the thing. He wasn't short of money, but he wasn't creaking with gold. He was quite normal. We talked about what we could do. I said so him, 'Well, you told me this story, I thought it was fantastic, why can't you tell the story to somebody else?' He said, 'I can.' I said, 'Well, why don't you do an interview, do it with Mihir Bose because he's Indian, and, therefore, he can understand you, talks the same language as you and he would enjoy it, too.' And, he said, 'Who will transmit it?' I said, 'Nobody will transmit it. We will have to make it and sell it to people.' He asked, 'Well, how will we do that?' I said,

'We just set up a studio and Mihir Bose comes along and asks you any question he wants to. You answer.' So he decided that was a good idea.

That is when Tim rang me, and I was delighted to interview Lalit Modi, who at this stage had not given any interviews since he had been forced out of the IPL and left India for London. I had two questions for Tim: Could I ask any question I liked? Would Modi tell me the truth? Bell said, 'You can ask any question you like. I can't guarantee that he'll tell you everything, he will tell you what he tells you.'

This was to lead to my interview with Modi in November 2010, which was put on YouTube. The interview proved a sensation. Before we come to what he told me, let me wind back to his creation of the IPL, the most revolutionary change to domestic cricket for 200 years and one that has completely transformed both the Indian and the world game.

Modi, from the rich Modi business family, had been educated in the US, where he had pleaded guilty to possessing cocaine, false imprisonment and assault while involved in a drug deal that went wrong. Put on probation for five years and ordered to do community service he managed to return to India after convincing a US judge that he was suffering from ill health. From the mid-1990s Modi began thinking of creating a city-based cricket league. But the BCCI, fearful of private ownership of teams, vetoed the idea. Dalmiya, who never saw merit in the idea, would not hear of it.

Modi's real chance came when he got into the BCCI. Once inside Modi allied himself with the BCCI faction that was then winning Sharad Pawar and Bindra against Dalmiya. At a Mohali Test, a ground Bindra could claim to be his own, he introduced him to the media as the man who would drive Indian cricket forward; Modi, with a flamboyance that has always marked his career, said, 'Cricket in India is a $2 billion a year market.' In 2005, following Pawar's election as the BCCI President, Modi was made marketing chief of the BCCI, and quickly engineered lucrative deals, such as $150 million from two sponsorships with Nike and Sahara Group. However, it was his television deal, a five-year $630 million deal for Indian cricket with Nimbus that, in effect, triggered IPL.

Speed recalls meeting Modi in Dubai sometime in 2005:

He was troublesome, he was just finding his feet within BCCI, he had his supporters, and he had his detractors. I never quite knew whose side he was on, Bindra was a supporter most of the time. It has been said that the other league [ICL started by Subhash Chandra of Zee TV] was set up first and that the IPL followed the other league, Modi was well ahead of it in terms of the planning. I recall him telling me about his grand plans to sell off the franchises that they would sell for big sums, I was surprised at that.

By the summer of 2007 Modi had gone further with his plans although at this stage IPL had not been conceived as a T20 tournament. This is where Andrew Wildblood came into the picture.

MODI'S OTHER ENGLISHMAN

Wildblood had first met Modi at a tournament in Abu Dhabi and did not get on with him. In July 2007 he met up with Modi again at the guest lounge of 11 Cadogan Gardens, a hotel off Sloane Square in London. Unlike their meeting in Abu Dhabi this was a very cordial occasion. Wildblood told me:

> Lalit said, 'Do you think the following idea could work?' The idea was a city based Indian domestic league, played annually with the teams privately owned. I said, 'I have been advocating that for some years.' I had written papers to the BCCI, that some sort of city based domestic league would be likely to succeed. It was a fallout from the Sahara Cup. We had made a lot of money out of the Sahara Cup, and a lot of money for the boards. When that went away, all of a sudden, we had a hole in our numbers. I was thinking domestic cricket in India is not very successful and there is an unsatisfied demand for cricket in India. Nobody watched the Ranji Trophy. It takes a long time, it hasn't been marketed, people don't feel connected to it, because it's state rather than city based, and most middle class, economically capable Indians, live in cities. People nowadays think of themselves as Mumbaikars rather than Maharashtrians. In UK, we've got football, rugby, cricket, golf. India was pretty much a blank canvas in terms of sports content. In Indian society there was no real place for sport. There was an opportunity to create something of value that would feed a dormant demand. I said to Lalit, 'Look, I tell you what I will do. I will go to America and will meet all the people who own sports there, and understand how sports leagues with privately owned franchises work. I will put together a blueprint for this event, and present it at the main BCCI meeting.'

The meeting was held at the Taj in Delhi in September 2007. Wildblood says:

> There I was standing there with my flipchart, being the classic Englishman, blue blazer, shirt and tie. There must have been 60 people

in the room and some of them were talking amongst themselves and not even listening to me. I said it should be a T20 tournament, there should be a match every night. There were a number of guiding principles behind how we put IPL together. One was that it should reflect the characteristics of modern India. So, energetic, colourful, noisy, exciting. Two, that it should not compete with other forms of cricket, but that it should compete with other forms of entertainment. So, that's evening prime time view. Not only is India somewhat short in terms of supply of sports content, it's actually quite short in terms of entertainment content. Apart from Bollywood. Lalit and I agreed that we didn't want to compete with other cricket, we wanted to compete with soap operas. We therefore needed to create IPL in the image of a soap opera, so that if you didn't watch last night's episode, you're not in the conversation at the water tank in the morning. Most households in India were single television homes and women controlled the remote control, watching soap operas. The man of the house had little say in what was seen. So, in order to create a successful television product, we had to make something that women would be attracted to and that's what caused us to bring in Bollywood. Then Pawar, who was the BCCI Chairman, gave me the approval to develop the plans that I had set out in the blueprint. I spent the next three or four months putting together a team within IMG and we figured out the modelling of the whole event; how the franchises would work, what the legal construct would be.

However, Wildblood readily admits, 'History must record that without Lalit Modi, the IPL would never have happened.' In September 2007, Modi was ready to go public with IPL, which he did in Delhi at a function attended by the greats of Indian cricket, Dravid, Ganguly and Tendulkar. What he presented was a six-week tournament that would begin in April 2008 with prize money of $3 million. However, he had not yet sold the television rights and the question remained whether the Indian cricketing public, who liked watching the national side, would go for a domestic competition. Then, eleven days after the launch, came the miracle of Johannesburg. This new wave of Indian cricket was to prove to be very different to the Kapil Dev wave of 1983 as the success of IPL proved.

CREATING A NEW CRICKETING WORLD

Modi still had to sell the rights. As he told me, 'When we went out to market the rights of IPL you'd be surprised sitting here today there was one bidder.' With that, he held up his index finger before continuing 'and that one bidder was WSG (World Sports Group). Sony actually bid and withdrew their bid prior to the bids even opening. ESPN bid but they put zero number on the table so they got disqualified. They said, 'We don't think this is gonna work, we'll do a revenue share deal with you.' The only company that actually put any money on the table above the minimum guarantee amount was WSG in round one and then they did a back-to-back licensing deal with Sony.

For the ten-year deal, Sony–World Sports Group paid $1.5 billion. A year previously ESPN Star had offered the ICC $1 billion to telecast all ICC events including the quadrennial World Cups and Champions Trophy for eight years between 2007 and 2015. That a domestic competition could fetch more money than international competitions was sensational and unheard of in cricket where until now the international game had subsidized the domestic one, and still does in most Test-playing nations.

Modi still had to negotiate other hurdles before IPL flew but he succeeded in even attracting Bollywood stars like Shah Rukh Khan who became the owner of the Kolkata Knight Riders (KKR). Bollywood stars owing cricket teams had an amazing impact on cricketers as shown by how Shoaib Akhtar, signed up by KKR, reacted to Khan. He could not stop staring at the star and when Ganguly, also a KKR player asked him why, he said, 'I keep on thinking is he the same man who holds the hands of some of the most gorgeous women in Bollywood? Jumps from a train? Fights with twenty people and roams around in the rose gardens?' A Test cricketer who had nourished the dreams of many a cricket fan was now a fan himself. But like many revolutionaries Modi was devoured by his own revolution. On the night of 25 April 2010, soon after the third IPL final had finished, Modi was suspended for 'alleged acts of individual misdemeanours'. Modi, who knew what was coming, made a speech which quoted the *Bhagavad Gita*, 'Fear not what is not real, never was and never will be. What is real, always was and cannot be destroyed.'

Modi, refuting all charges, fought his corner, took the matter to the Supreme Court, but in September 2010 he was sacked by the board. Soon after, Modi arrived in London. By the time we met, the Indian government had threatened to withdraw his passport and there was a 'look out circular', requiring security personnel at airports and other entry points to watch for him. He was being investigated for alleged violations of foreign exchange regulations in connection with the IPL and for tax offences.

MEETING INDIA'S DONALD TRUMP

I was intrigued to meet Modi. What would a man described in the Indian
press as a 'fugitive' be like? I could not have been more surprised when
we met at an exclusive club in London's West End. The forty-six-year-old,
immaculately dressed in a suit, gave no hint of being under stress and looked
very much like the man representing modern India. The only thing unusual
in this television interview was that in the background, out of camera shot,
stood a lawyer from Peters & Peters. Lord Bell recalls:

> He had gone to Peters & Peters to check his legal status. I think the
> lawyer's job was to make sure he didn't say anything that could cause
> him legal problems. When Lalit asked me how he should deal with
> your questions, I said, 'Answer the bloody questions, whatever he asks,·
> answer.' So, he did that.

My first question to him was: 'You face some very serious charges in India,
allegations about your conduct as IPL commissioner. India's just celebrated
Diwali. What are you doing here?'

> I am hoping that the enquiries that are going on in India will
> come to an end because we are answering all the questions that are
> required to be answered. We are doing some teleconferencing and we
> are providing the documentation that is needed to be provided, to
> the authorities and to the different agencies that are conducting the
> investigation. And my security agencies have advised me that it's not
> an appropriate time currently to go back till the security situation
> smoothens out. And the Indian police have continuously told me
> the threat perception continues to be there, and as and when I feel
> comfortable with that factor I will go back.

When I suggested that many people would find it strange that these threats
on his life had emerged after he was facing serious allegations, his response
was prompt:

> I think that's again something that has been portrayed by the media.
> The media themselves know for a fact that way back in 2009, when
> I moved the IPL to South Africa the threats emerged. There were
> leads picked up by the intelligence [and] picked up by the police. I
> was given extensive security whilst in South Africa. On my return to
> India [I had] continuous security all the way through the current IPL
> and the threat escalated prior to the IPL. And my movements were
> pretty much restricted from where I could go and not go. It wasn't

something that has come afterwards. It's quite visible on camera. It's quite visible everywhere I went that the amount of security that I had around me inhibited my movements in and out of India.

Modi was insistent in saying that, far from taking any money from the BCCI, he made money for Indian cricket:

> The way I did the deals, I made the BCCI billions of dollars. Prior to me coming in [in 2005], the BCCI made probably twenty, forty million dollars. I changed the marketing structure. I changed the way we did business. The BCCI today has locked-in contracts worth over six or seven billion dollars going forward. I did that on my own time, at my own cost.

When I mentioned that while he was running the IPL he lived at the Four Seasons Hotel in Mumbai and travelled in luxury, which must have come out of BCCI funds, he thundered back:

> Absolutely not. All the costs from the day one that I joined the BCCI were met by me. In fact, there are staff that are on my rolls that I pay for, and all costs that are related to my staying in a hotel or travelling are all mine. BCCI may have provided a car here or there in a particular city, but they all charge it back to me. I fly on my own accord, I stay in hotels on my own cost. I run the IPL on my own time. I have people working in the IPL that are my personal staff which I pay for and, and that is my contribution. I was born in a very wealthy family. My grandfather and my father worked very hard to build their businesses and I've worked very hard to build businesses myself.

As for the IPL:

> I can very clearly tell you that I have not pocketed any money from the IPL. The BCCI will benefit in the next ten years in excess of two billion dollars, which was never something that they projected that they were gonna get. It wasn't something that was an agenda of the BCCI to do. It was a project that I conceived and I'd been working on it for years. I didn't do it for myself and the benefit, 100 per cent, accrued to the BCCI and to the members who have been part of the IPL. I'm very proud of it, that I've been able to create something that is of tremendous value, has world recognition and has put India on the map.

But if he had brought so much material success to the BCCI, was it not incredible that they turned against him?

> I agree. It seems incredible because I guess they didn't expect that IPL to succeed number one, and as it has succeeded there's a lot of jealousy all around. I mean there's more than meets the eye—it's not only about the IPL, it's about the running of the BCCI, there are vested groups out there trying to take control.

But then, as if he had been coached by the Peters & Peters man, he said, 'But I'd rather not get into that right now.' The only other time he seemed to have been coached by Peters & Peters was when I asked him why, given his claims to have done so much for India, the government, instead of honouring him with a Bharat Ratna, was taking over his havelis in Jaipur. 'These questions are related to due process. I would rather not comment on it. Wait till the outcome of the process is over and then I will give the actual story.'

Then he began to sound like a politician:

> I worked with a whole lot of my colleagues, everyone that I worked with was very happy and first and foremost every supplier of mine, every team owner of mine, every advertiser of mine, all the fans, all the boards that I work with, were extremely happy with the way I work. Yes, some disgruntled people were there in the board. I can't make everybody happy. I'm not there to please everybody and that's not my job.

But, for all Modi's talk of having created a unique product, he has not been the only sports pioneer. The last three decades have seen the emergence of the English Premier League and the Champions League, neither of whose founders are in exile from their homelands and facing serious allegations of wrongdoing. So, did this not suggest that Modi behaved like a nineteenth-century American buccaneer? For the first time Modi reacted as if he might lose his cool:

> I don't believe a word you're saying is right. It's nice to put it like that and make it sound superior. You may call it buccaneering or nineteenth-century, but we thought outside the box. Please do not compare me to the English Premier League or to any other league. We are unique. I can sit here and say there's no other league like that in the world, every member actually makes money. How many teams in the English Premier League make money? Look at the balance sheets, practically all of them are in debt.

This is when he compared himself to Donald Trump who then, of course, was not known to have presidential aspirations:

> Yes, my style is different, but styles of different entrepreneurs are different, whether it's a Bernie Ecclestone, a Rupert Murdoch or a Donald Trump. They may upset people but they are judged by the results. Similarly, I should be judged by my results.

Modi was eager to emphasize that despite providing 'the authorities with everything nobody has charged me with anything. Nothing has been proven.' And he was confident that his problems would end 'by me getting a clean slate'. When I suggested that could be a long process, he answered, 'That's fine. I'm in no hurry. I'm going nowhere. At the end of the day, the results of what I have built are already proven, that's something nobody can take away, even if they want to. I have created a successful product. It's a baby of mine and I'm very happy with it.'

The interview shown on YouTube, says Bell, 'created huge publicity. He got about a million viewers. He was very pleased.'

MODI'S BABY BECOMES A TEENAGER

Modi had told me 'I will return to India as and when I feel secure.' Nine years after the interview, Modi is still in London. In 2013, he was banned for life by the BCCI. The government of India even revoked his passport in 2010, but the decision was overturned by the High Court in 2014. He now travels on a European passport. In August 2018, Modi quit cricket administration, but one thing cannot be denied: his baby has grown into a very robust teenager, defying predictions that it would not prosper wowing the cricket world.

In September 2017, the IPL rights were sold to Star India for five years for ₹16,347 crores which was more than the worth of all the other T20 leagues which have mushroomed in the wake of the IPL in the last decade. During the 2018 IPL, for the first qualifier between Chennai Super Kings (CSK) and SunRisers Hyderabad (SRH), Star India got 8.26 million concurrent views on Hotstar—a world record for live-streamed sport. IPL has gone through crises, some franchises have disappeared, but others have taken their place. And while during the first decade of the IPL a few franchises struggled to break even, now that the owners no longer have to pay an annual franchise fee, a change which came in 2018, all eight franchises are set to earn a massive surplus.

Perhaps IPL's biggest influence is how it has made India the centre of world cricket. The pre-IPL world revolved around an English summer. The moment the English cricket season started in late April, cricket all

over the world effectively ceased. Cricketers from all over the world came
to play in England. India was a bit player in this English summer garden
party. Unlike the greats of the previous waves of Indian cricket, like Hazare,
Manjrekar, Mankad and Gupte, Indian cricketers now do not need to go
to Lancashire mill towns and put up with English families to earn money;
instead, cricketers from around the world flock to India. The best in the
game can earn the sort of money high-ranking footballers earn, and just
for a few weeks' work. Ben Stokes, England's best all-rounder, was not
selected for the 2017–18 Ashes series because of an off-the-field incident
in September 2017 which led to charges against him of which he was
acquitted by a jury in August 2018. Many cricket experts felt his absence
was one of the reasons why England lost the Ashes. Yet, the twenty-six-year
old could not wait to come to India for the start of the IPL. He could
now earn an estimated $4 million for under eight weeks of cricket. The
West Indian Chris Gayle played in the 2017 IPL but not for the West
Indies when they toured England later that summer.

When the IPL was launched in 2008, the English cricket establishment,
unable to believe that the Indians could match their cricket expertise,
scoffed at it. The county chairmen thought they could dictate to it and, at
their meeting on 16 July 2008 discussed allowing English players to take
part in the IPL, saying, 'IPL must conclude by April 30.' In 2018, the IPL
final was on 27 May, weeks after the English season had started. By then
English and world cricket knew they had to dance to the Indian tune.
2008 also saw the England and Wales Cricket Board (ECB) enter into a
disastrous alliance with Allen Stanford, who flew into Lord's aboard a private
helicopter laden with a treasure chest filled with fake dollar notes. On 1
November 2008 in Antigua, England played the Stanford Superstars for a
prize pot of $20 million, a match they lost. As we have seen Stanford was
soon proved to be a fraudster. In the decade since the IPL has continued
to surprise the world.

In the summer of 2018, as India tour toured England, English cricketers
hoped a good performance against India might get them an IPL contract.
And while English players looked to India, the English authorities still
trying to get their domestic programme right came up with yet another
domestic competition, a new 100-ball competition to start in 2020. It was
widely mocked and has created such problems that as I write, it threatens
to cause a split between the board and Surrey, its most powerful county.
It showed that ten years after Modi took an English idea and made it
an Indian one, the original creator is still struggling to come up with a
really workable plan.

Three centuries ago when the British came to India as traders they would bow to the then rulers of India hoping to make money, before exploiting the divisions in India to acquire the country. There seems little chance of English cricket taking over the IPL. Instead, English cricket bows to the power of the IPL; despite the IPL overlapping with the English cricket season, the cricket authorities of England now allow their best players to miss the first two months of the season to take part in this great Indian gold mine. Now their cricketers are willing to miss part of their cherished season to make the sort of money they could never make anywhere else.

What the IPL has also developed are bonds between Indians and foreigners. This is best illustrated in the case of Sarvesh Kumar, a medium-pacer who got a chance to play for Hyderabad Deccan Chargers in the first season of the IPL. A cricketer from a working-class background, whose father worked as a welder in a government-owned ordinance factory in Hyderabad, he had long admired the Australian wicketkeeper batsman Adam Gilchrist. When Gilchrist wore yellow he wore yellow. Should Gilchrist wear green, Sarvesh would wear green. Gilchrist played for the Deccan Chargers and gave Sarvesh his chance. But Sarvesh agonized about what he should call his Australian hero. 'Everyone called him Gilly or Gilchrist. But I was confused, how could I call such a senior player Gilly? But I found a way out by calling him Brother.' The story illustrates the impact of the IPL, providing Indian cricketers, even those like Sarvesh, who have never made it at the international level, a chance to mix with the best in the game but yet be Indian in their social attitudes. Perhaps, more importantly, the IPL has given Indian cricketers a confidence they did not have in the past. Now they do not fear the world outside India, or feel inferior to it, as many Indians, even of my generation, did. The world comes to them and they feel the equal of any international cricketer.

However, the IPL has also seen the return of match and spot-fixing. In my interview with Modi, I had mentioned that there had been suggestions that the IPL led the resurgence and resurfacing of spot-fixing and match-fixing in cricket. He brushed this aside:

> Our job has to the best of our ability to make sure that this kind of things do not happen. You have got eight team owners out there, who want to win, who are passionate about their teams. The players are passionate about the game, who all want to win. It's not controlled by one entity. They're all separate. That itself tends to keep out those kinds of elements happening. There's not been a single incident that actually

has been pointed out that can [indicate] any of those kinds of things were happening in the IPL.

Yet in 2013 the spot-fixing scandal re-emerged and, as we shall see, such was its impact that it has transformed the governance of Indian cricket. But the IPL remains immune and continues to provide the sort of entertainment that Indian cricket fans have never before enjoyed.

Chapter 40

MAHI TAKES CHARGE

DHONI: THE AXE MAN

On the afternoon of 20 January 2008, Dhoni, in Australia, had a video-conference call with Indian selectors based in Mumbai's Taj Mahal Hotel, to select the team for the Commonwealth Bank one-day series to be played between the hosts, Australia, India and Sri Lanka. In Australia, Dhoni was flanked by Yuvraj, his vice-captain, at the Mumbai Taj were the great and the good of Indian cricket led by chairman Dilip Vengsarkar. Dhoni, casually dressed, soon made it clear that he knew what he wanted. For the one-day team he wanted a young side. The two old-timers he did not want were Dravid and Ganguly. Dravid was back where he had started at the beginning of his career, considered still good for Test cricket but not the one-day stuff. As Shantanu Guha Ray writes in *Mahi: The Story of India's Most Successful Captain*, Dhoni and Vengsarkar discussed Ganguly. Vengsarkar wanted to retain him but Dhoni, mixing steel with politeness said, 'Kindly bear with me, sirs' and went on to explain why Ganguly was just too old to play in what was a young man's game. Then, saying that he had the support of both Yuvraj and the trainer, Gregory King, he said, 'Fielding is indeed an issue with Dada, he is very, very slow.' Vengsarkar did raise the question of the runs Dada made but as Dhoni put it, 'I think you will have to agree to my demand' and they did. The team selected did not have Ganguly and Dravid. They were yesterday's men. The decision led to protests from Ganguly supporters even in Ranchi where one poster read, 'Dhokha diya Ganguly ko' [You have betrayed Ganguly] but Dhoni brushed them aside.

India had a squad which contained ten players aged twenty-three or younger. In contrast Australia fielded the oldest side ever to represent the country in a one-day series; in the two finals the average age of its side was very nearly 32. India beat Australia in both the finals and for the first time since these limited overs tournaments had started back in 1979–80 India had won a final. True, in the final, Dhoni had to rely on a thirty-four-year-old. But he was Tendulkar and Dhoni knew he would have been blown out of the water had he even suggested Tendulkar be dropped. Just as well Tendulkar was in the side as in the finals he made 117 not out and 91, when only one other Indian batsman in either final made a 50. The story illustrated perfectly well how Dhoni operated, he knew what he could get and how to get it.

However, it was too soon to give him the Test captaincy and soon after their return from Australia when South Africa arrived in March 2008, Kumble remained in charge of Test cricket. The series saw India under a new coach, Gary Kirsten, the former South Africa player. He was very much the second choice. India had wanted Graham Ford, but he preferred to stay in Kent. Kirsten wanting to return to India was a remarkable turnaround. In 2000, he had been part of the South African team that had toured India, when the Delhi Police exposed the match-fixing and, on his return to his native Cape Town, felt like kissing the tarmac of the airport relieved to be rid of the country where he could not eat the salad as it might not be safe and could not use tap water to clean his teeth.

Yet, coming as coach of India, he did not seem to be worried about not having bottled water to clean his teeth. Ironically, his first task was to get India ready to face his homeland, some of whose cricketers could possibly be worried about running out of bottled water. Kirsten soon became aware that Dhoni was the man he had to get on with. In the first two Tests Kumble captained, India drew the first, badly lost the second by an innings and 90 runs in three days—in the first innings India had made only 76, the innings lasting twenty overs. It was clear that for India to win and draw the series it would need a dry wicket with variable turn and bounce to suit the spinners and this is what Kanpur in the third provided.

Dhoni was told half an hour before the Kanpur Test he was captaining, becoming the first Indian wicketkeeper to captain India in Tests. For much of the match there was nothing exceptional about his captaincy. But once the South African second innings started he showed his ability to think on his feet. South Africa were 60 behind, India could not afford to give South Africa too many runs, and Dhoni opened the bowling with Harbhajan. The off-spinner had been struggling for a couple of years, but Dhoni had seen enough to conclude he was getting his form back. Now he was devastating, taking four wickets. Sehwag also found purchase with his off-spin, and South Africa were bowled out for 121. India, left 62 to make, won by eight wickets. The groundsman was given an impromptu tip of ₹10,000, and when South Africa complained about the wicket, the practice facilities and the accommodation, Dhoni was sharp. 'If we go to Australia, we get bouncy tracks; when we go to England, we get swinging tracks. When you come to India, you expect turning and bouncing tracks and that's what this one was. It's better to stick to specialities of certain places.' A new Indian generation was taking charge and it would take no nonsense from foreigners.

Even so early in his career as Test captain Dhoni could choose when to play and decided not to go to Sri Lanka, having said he wanted a rest from Test cricket. India, badly mauled by Sri Lankan spin, lost the three Test series 2–1. Their defeat in the first Test by an innings and 239 runs, was their third biggest defeat in Test history and their most resounding since 1974, also known as the summer of 42 because of the Indian score at Lord's that summer.

Dhoni flew in for the one-day series with a number of young players including Virat Kohli and, after misreading the pitch in the first match, he showed a much surer touch in his captaincy. His batting was crucial and so turned things around that even before the fifth and final one-day match was played, India had won the series. By the time Australia came to India in October 2008 for a Test and one-day series the only question was how long before Dhoni took formal charge. The answer was not long although it came about curiously.

Kumble captained in the first Test in Bengaluru which ended in a draw. Dhoni took charge for the second at Mohali and, as at Kanpur, was not given much notice. This did not faze him. Coming in at No. 8 he blazed away, scoring 92 in a total of 469, which proved an ideal platform for the bowlers, in particular Amit Mishra making his Test debut. The leg-spinner took five wickets with the Australians finding it difficult to pick his googly. With a lead of 211, Dhoni showed that the innovation and inspirational leadership he had brought to one-day cricket could also work in Tests. He changed the batting order, came in at No. 3 and put the Australian attack to the sword making 68 not out. Ponting was in such disarray that at one point he was seen arguing with his own pace spearhead, Brett Lee. India set Australia 516 to win, bowled them out for 195, and India's victory by 320 runs was their highest victory by runs over Australia.

The match also had another major landmark. Since the start of the series the question was: when would Tendulkar get past Lara's 11,953, and become Test cricket's highest run-scorer. He needed 15 in Mohali which he got when he glided Peter Siddle, who was making his Test debut, for three. While this was worth celebrating, what Mohali was waiting for was Tendulkar reaching 12,000 runs, and they had made plans to celebrate this milestone. He did so when he got to 61 with a single, and this was the cue for a fireworks display that lasted three minutes. Diwali, which was eleven days away, had come early to Mohali. It would have neatly rounded out things had he gone on to score his fortieth Test century, but he fell short by 12.

Kumble returned for the Delhi Test, which was another draw, and then announced his retirement. So, for the last Test in Nagpur, Dhoni took over. The Test showed a facet of Dhoni that over the years would become evident in Test cricket. The swashbuckler of one-day cricket could throttle run scoring when he needed to win a series. On the third day in Nagpur he got Ishant Sharma and Zaheer Khan to bowl to 8–1 fields and himself stood outside the leg-stump when keeping wickets to Harbhajan Singh, which did not please the umpires. Dhoni's tactics meant Australia could only score 209 and in the end India won by 172 runs and regained the Border–Gavaskar Trophy.

Nagpur also saw Dada bid goodbye to cricket. Ganguly had felt humiliated by what he perceived was the way he had been treated by the new selection committee chaired by Krishnamachari Srikkanth. They were always asking him to prove himself and in order to do so Ganguly was playing with cricketers he did not know and spending lonely nights in a hotel room. His life, he felt, was a roller coaster, driving a Rolls-Royce one day, sleeping on pavements the next. As the Australians arrived he told his father he would retire. Two days before the Bengaluru Test, on Maha Ashtami Puja, an important day for Bengalis, he held a press conference and announced that he would bid goodbye at the final Test in Nagpur. In Mohali he had scored a century and said he did not care that Greg Chappell had been watching from the Australian camp. In Nagpur in his final innings he got a first ball duck but could say he was leaving the stage as India's most successful Test captain. Dhoni knew what he had to aim for and his first target was England who arrived in November 2008.

TENDULKAR CONSOLES MUMBAI

The tour started with an ODI series which suggested India would whitewash England. India were leading the seven-match series 5–0 and seemed set on completing an amazing 7–0 sweep with two matches left in Guwahati and Delhi when, on the night of 26 November, just after India had won by six wickets, the country experienced its equivalent of America's 9/11. In what has come to be called 26/11, ten members of Lashkar-e-Taiba, an Islamic terrorist organization based in Pakistan, landing by night at Back Bay in South Mumbai (where, when I was growing up in the city, I played cricket), carried out a series of twelve coordinated shooting and bombing attacks lasting four days across South Mumbai—among others, residents of two of its greatest hotels, the Taj and the Oberoi were terrorized.

One hundred and sixty-four people died and 308 were wounded.

The last two ODIs were cancelled and for a time it seemed the tour itself might be abandoned. Many in the British media argued that the tour could not possibly be resumed, and much was made of the fact that the English team had left some of their kit behind in the Taj Mahal Hotel, which the terrorists had occupied during their seizure of the city, killing many of the residents, and which was wrested back from the terrorists after a great deal of drama witnessed by millions on live television. How, asked the commentators, would the players feel going back to such a hotel so soon after such a terrifying attack? But Giles Clarke, chairman of the ECB, mindful of the power of the Indian board, was determined that the tour should go ahead. He knew the Indians would see a cancellation as treating it on a par with Pakistan and was keen to emphasize that England were returning to show support for India in the face of terrorism.

Despite the fears in the British press that the England players would be traumatized when the two-Test series started in Chennai, the English players seemed much less affected by the terrorism than the Indians. Andrew Strauss became the first Englishman to hit a century in both innings on the subcontinent. Only Dhoni made 50 in India's first innings of 241, and they were set 387, a total that no team had ever chased in the fourth innings to win a match in an Asian Test.

This is when that great son of Mumbai decided to console the city with his bat for what had happened. He scored a brilliant century to mastermind a famous victory. Scoring a ton in a successful run-chase was something that was missing from Sachin's otherwise glittering record. Sehwag had provided the platform on the fourth evening, making 83 in characteristically blistering fashion in only sixty-eight balls with 11 fours and 4 sixes. England's bowlers had been initially overwhelmed by the Sehwag onslaught but when on the fifth day Laxman came to join Tendulkar with the score at 183 for 3, victory was by no means certain. But Yuvraj, who made an unbeaten 85, played one of his best Test innings, and in the end, victory was so assured that he even played some dot balls so Tendulkar got to his hundred. At the presentation ceremony Tendulkar spoke of how he had done this for Mumbai and there was a generous donation of half their match fee, £35,000, by the English team to the victims of the Mumbai attack. The gesture showed that the English players knew that losing the Test by six wickets was trivial compared to what had happened in Mumbai.

India had chances to win the second Test as well but with Kevin Pietersen scoring 144 and and fog and bad light leading to more than a day being lost, the match was drawn.

So, between 17 October 2008 when he had taken charge of the Mohali Test against Australia and the end of this Mohali Test against England on 23 December, Dhoni in four Tests as captain had won three Tests and played a crucial role in India winning two series. India, with Tendulkar and the players that had followed in his wake now growing old, appeared to have found an ideal captain who could lead a new generation. Dhoni was still called by his surname or M. S., his initials. Mahi was still to gain national popularity, but he had already outstripped Tendulkar in the money stakes. It was estimated that in 2008 he would earn ₹50 crore when the demigod's income was around ₹35 crore. What is more, unlike nearly all other Indian captains, he was not from the traditional centres of Indian cricket, but a place which, even a few years back, would hardly have been regarded as a proper city. Then it was dismissed as place where you sent people with mental health problems. So, how had it happened, and who was this man and how had he emerged to become the leader of the new cricketing India?

Chapter 41

THE MAN WHO MADE PAGLA GHAR INTO CRICKET GHAR

In Aditya Chopra's film *Chak De! India* there is a scene where two young women hockey players arrive at the stadium in Delhi for a training camp before going to the Women's Hockey World Cup. The two girls, Rani Dispotta and Soimoi Kerketa, are from remote villages in Jharkhand and the man checking them in to the camp cannot believe they are hockey players. For him, the idea that Jharkhand could produce hockey players, let alone women hockey players, seems mystifying. What is more, they do not speak English well, and this sets them apart. But in the end, they prove world-beaters and the film is a celebration of an India that can overcome differences in class, region, caste and discrimination against women and, led by a man determined to prove that he is a patriot, take on and beat the world. The film proved a great box office hit, grossing $14,959,326 and making a tremendous social impact while its song 'Chak De! India' became the sports anthem of a country hungry for sporting success. It was three days before the film was released that Dhoni held his first press conference as captain in London, talking about how he was a brand ambassador for Jharkhand, and in many ways Dhoni's career can be seen as the real life equivalent of Rani Dispotta's and Soimoi Kerketa's.

Yet before Dhoni emerged, had a scriptwriter suggested that Jharkhand would produce such a player, no one in Bollywood would have found it credible. Dhoni's is one of those Indian stories that seem to belong to the pages of Indian mythology. He has made a town famous for its mental asylums (it has India's biggest mental asylum, Ranchi Mansik Arogyashala) well known around the world as a sporting centre. And in a state which had produced hockey players, including the man who captained India to their first Olympic hockey gold in 1928, and where, in missionary schools in tribal areas of the state, schoolchildren carried hockey sticks to school along with their textbooks, he emerged as a cricketer of world renown. As Fardeen Khan, a Mumbai filmmaker who captained him in the Under-19 side says:

Wherever cricket is played in the world, if they know Jharkhand it is because of M. S. Dhoni. He put Jharkhand on the world map. It's a big thing. Dhoni is such a big brand that he will go down in history books as not only one of the greatest cricketers India has ever produced, but one of the greatest cricketers in the world.

But the Dhoni story is not quite as straightforward as all that, and if he has become a success, it is both a testament to Dhoni himself and a reflection of how India, and in particular Indian cricket, has changed since the country first took to the game.

His rise also shows that to succeed in India you do not always require a godfather, the famous 'pull' that many believe you need. However, Dhoni did have support, though from unexpected sources. The man who got the fifteen-year-old what was in effect his first contract for bat and equipment, Paramjit Singh, was himself not much older—he has since acquired a sports shop in Sujata Chowk, Ranchi's main bazaar—and had nothing going for him except being a stubborn man willing to tell endless tales of how well young Dhoni had done in Ranchi gulli cricket matches, often with a tennis ball. He persistently badgered the Kohli brothers, bat makers in Ludhiana, to take a chance with Dhoni. At one stage, they got so irritated by the badgering they asked in some exasperation, 'Bradman hain kya?' [Is he Bradman?], to which the man responded, 'Bradman ka baap hain, sir' [He is Bradman's father]. But in the end, the man who had appointed himself in effect as young Dhoni's agent succeeded, and the Kohlis gave eight bats and other cricket equipment free, despite the fact that it cost ₹20,000 and they had never seen Dhoni play or really knew who he was. Dhoni had tears in his eyes as he accepted the gift and more tears when he got home and told his parents of what he had brought home. Little were the Kohli brothers to know they were making a huge contribution to Indian cricket or, in the sort of accident of history which seems part of Dhoni's cricket career, that Dhoni's mantle would fall on another Kohli, but one not related to them.

The twists and turns in Dhoni's story are also illustrated in the way he was weaned away from his first love of football by a sports master who should have encouraged his love for the round-ball game. Teachers at Dhoni's school quickly realized that he was never going to be much of a scholar and some of them did encourage him to watch videos of great goalkeepers such as Lev Yashin, Peter Shilton and Dino Zoff. But not his sports master, Keshav Banerjee.

THE RANCHI KID'S FIRST MENTOR

Banerjee had no cricketing icon from Jharkhand with which to tempt Dhoni. It would have been more logical had Banerjee let Dhoni develop his football skills. Jharkhand had had some football players of note and one famous Indian goalkeeper, Peter Thangaraj, who had settled in the state. Banerjee, a Bengali, should have had football in his blood, but having heard of Ramakant Achrekar and the great cricket coaches who had found fame nurturing great cricketers, he wanted to emulate them. 'When will I groom a cricketer?' Banerjee had said in anguish, and when he saw Dhoni he was convinced he had found the boy who, even if he did not become a Tendulkar, would be one India would notice.

It helped that by 1994, when Dhoni first discarded goal-keeping gloves for wicketkeeping ones, cricket was by far the most popular sport in the country. Banerjee could hold out to young Dhoni the prospect that cricket could take him to the world of his dreams. 'This is a great game and those into it are heroes in India, you will also become one if you stick to it. Cricket has taken India to great heights, football hasn't. You are in the right place. Do not ever think of walking out.'

In such stories of recollections there is always the possibility that the coach who first spotted the youngster is claiming more credit than he should. Banerjee readily admits that he was more of a physical education teacher than a cricket coach and had little to do with Dhoni's batting style. But he did make sure that as a wicketkeeper Dhoni did not catch the ball like a fish with its mouth open, which he was doing when Banerjee first saw him. And whatever the gloss Banerjee may be putting on it, his chat with Dhoni one evening in Ranchi has a nice ring to it and does provide an insight into Dhoni. The pair were talking, sitting on a wooden bench on the edge of a cricket field in Ranchi. The young boy kept looking at an advertisement of a Kawasaki Bajaj motorbike which transformed into a cheetah on the prowl, and Banerjee advised Dhoni that, like the cheetah, he would have to prowl behind the stumps, move at speed the moment he saw prey, a batsman edging the ball or moving out of his crease, and like a revved motorbike 'maintain a blistering pace in batting. I told Dhoni that he will have to transform himself from an average player into a powerful man-machine. Only then he would be noticed.'

Initially, Dhoni's problem was to get into the school team. The school had a regular wicketkeeper and Dhoni's initial reaction to Banerjee was, 'Chance doge?' [Will you give me a chance?]. In his first year he played just one match, when the regular wicketkeeper was away. It was after that boy left school and Dhoni had been playing cricket for a year that he became a regular member of the side.

It is remarkable that Dhoni's cricketing career would replicate his first introduction to cricket. So, Dhoni made his first-class debut on 12 January 2000, when Bihar's regular wicketkeeper, who was also the side's leading batsman and captain, decided he had too much on his plate and gave the gloves to Dhoni. Four years later, in July 2004, sent as a reserve wicketkeeper on an India A tour of Zimbabwe and Kenya, the No. 1 keeper, Dinesh Karthik, was suddenly called away to keep wickets in the ODI matches for the senior Indian side playing in England and Dhoni made his international debut. And, as we have seen, a further three years later, in 2007, with the greats of Indian cricket deciding that T20 cricket was not for them, Dhoni led India to the first T20 World Cup. On every occasion Dhoni seized his chance brilliantly and always got the timing of the next stage of his career right. But because nobody expected him to get the chance, let alone that he would do it so brilliantly, they could never get over their surprise that he was now occupying centre stage. And even today, those who played with Dhoni when he was a schoolboy in Ranchi, and saw him rise through the ranks of Indian cricket, cannot conceal their astonishment at how far their old friend and colleague has come. Dhoni, defying the most unpromising of cricketing backgrounds, would go on to such greatness that he can rightly be said to have ushered in a new generation of Indian cricketers.

Amir Hashmi, a left-handed batsman who made his Ranji Trophy debut for Bihar in the same match as Dhoni, grew up with Dhoni in Ranchi and, like him, also got a job in the Railways under the sports quota working for the Railways at Kharagpur. Hashmi is still with the Railways, based in Dhanbad, and can claim to know Dhoni better than almost anybody else. He told me:

> I played as a child with Dhoni in Ranchi and until he came into the Indian team we played together. The only difference between Dhoni and me was he went to a Hindi medium school. I went to an English medium school. My Papa was a government employee. He worked in Ranchi for the Coal Mines Provident Fund and Dhoni's father worked for MECON [Metallurgical and Engineering Consultants]. We were all middle class. We were not rich. When we were at school we had cycles. When we played Ranji Trophy we bought motorbikes. Ranchi has changed ever since the state of Jharkhand was formed. Now if you come to Ranchi you will find a Ranchi which is not like the Ranchi of the nineties when we were growing up. Then Ranchi wasn't a nice

place, and there was a lot of crime in Ranchi. After seven you couldn't roam around in Ranchi.

Dhoni, Hashmi and their friends could not wait to escape dreary, unsafe Ranchi and seek the excitement of the big city, Kolkata: 'Whenever we went to Kolkata to play cricket we used to go shopping and look for sales and search for places where they were giving discounts. We used to buy jeans, T-shirts. Dhoni also grew his hair but that was later.' Both friends loved Bollywood films, and Dhoni fairly early on hitched himself to its greatest star. 'We used to watch a lot of Bollywood films and Mahendra Singh Dhoni loved the songs of Kishore Kumar. And his favourite film was *Deewar*, one of Amitabh Bachchan's films. We used to recreate the scenes from *Deewar* and loved to recite the dialogue from the film. *Sholay* was also very popular. Dhoni was very fond of Amitabh Bachchan movies.'

But as they were growing up, Hashmi never for one moment thought that his young friend would become the colossus who would dominate Indian cricket:

> When I first saw him in 1996 he was a very simple lad. Everybody liked Dhoni because Dhoni was very quiet. He hardly said anything, he was very shy. Like me he loved football and both of us from the beginning were great Manchester United fans. We got a Manchester United jersey and a Manchester United cap that we used to put on. Although he had started as a goalkeeper at school he like me also played as a striker and I played in a lot of football tournaments with him in Ranchi. In Ranchi there is a St. Xavier's school and we used to play football at the St. Xavier's ground. We started playing what was called tennis ball cricket. However, it was a lighter ball than most tennis balls, being the ball used in lawn tennis, a green coloured ball that was called the Cosco ball. [India's bestselling tennis ball which is used in the Davis Cup.]

DHONI INVENTS THE HELICOPTER SHOT

The tennis ball cricket that Dhoni played did produce a new cricketing shot. Hashmi recalls:

> Even when we played as youngsters, Dhoni played the helicopter shot. He learned the helicopter shot from another of our colleagues, Santosh Lal, who unfortunately died two years ago due to kidney failure. What used to happen is that in tennis ball cricket, the bowler would try to bowl a yorker so a batsman could not hit a six. And Santosh Lal used

to practise how he could hit the yorker for a six. Dhoni saw him play
the shot and told him, 'Yeh to badhiya shot hain tennis ball mein' [It's a
great shot in tennis ball cricket] and Dhoni started playing that shot as
well and by playing that shot repeatedly he got very good at it. He was
a very powerful hitter and he used to hit very long sixes. We didn't call
it the helicopter shot.

For Fardeen Khan the use of the term shows the effect of the Dhoni
phenomenon:

> We didn't call it anything. This is obviously a marketing thing. What
> would you call Azharuddin's great wristy shot off his legs which
> he played throughout his career? It is the most astonishing shot in
> cricketing history according to me, how beautiful it looked.

Hashmi, a classical batsman, never much played the helicopter shot. 'I used
to play shots along the ground.' This difference in batting styles may explain
why Dhoni and Hashmi had rival cricketing heroes:

> My heroes were Brian Lara and Sourav Ganguly. Dhoni was a big fan
> of Sachin Tendulkar. Dhoni and I would discuss who was the better
> batsman. I felt Lara was a match winner. Tendulkar was not a match
> winner.

However, playing a helicopter shot with a Cosco ball was one thing. What
made the helicopter shot famous around the world was that even when
Dhoni, at around fourteen, started playing hard red ball cricket, what
Hashmi calls 'deuce ball or leather ball' [in Mumbai we called it 'season
ball'], the helicopter shot remained part of his repertoire. This was all the
more remarkable because, as Hashmi says:

> We did not have the infrastructure to play proper cricket. We would be
> frustrated that we could not play on turf wickets. In Ranchi there was
> only one ground belonging to MECON where they had a turf wicket.
> The other grounds where we practised on were not good. But while
> compared to other stadiums MECON was much better even at the
> MECON the outfield wasn't very good and did not encourage diving.

This meant most of the cricket was on matting wickets, and in Dhoni's
school the matting had to be pulled out from the school auditorium every
day and was uneven.

For both Dhoni and Hashmi playing cricket was itself an act of
rebellion:

At that time the feeling was that cricket could damage your life, that playing cricket means you were not studying. Our parents used to say what will cricket bring you. Parents used to think if you are playing cricket your life will be destroyed, you won't be able to have a career. Our parents used to tell us study hard, become an officer, a doctor, an engineer, a chartered accountant. When I became a professional cricketer my Papa was very upset, he said you are not taking your studies seriously, this is not a good thing. I said this is what I am interested in. Dhoni had the same problem but his parents let him play cricket seeing that their little boy was very interested in playing the game. They felt that if this is what you want to do, go ahead. His father thought if he plays the Ranji trophy and gets a good job the lad will get settled.

In the Dhoni biopic there is a scene which shows Dhoni's father, Pan Singh, letting young Dhoni play a cricket tournament just before his exam. As Dhoni set off, his father said, 'If you've studied and worked throughout the year, then there's no problem if you go off to play today. If you haven't studied every day then one day is not going to make a difference.' Pan Singh made sure his son studied and, says Dhoni, 'My dad used to wake me up at dawn every day to study for two hours throughout my years at DAV Jawahar Vidya Mandir because my evenings were crowded with football and cricket practice.' Dhoni was well aware that coming from a middle-class family, job security was very important. 'It can be a tough decision to choose between job security and your dream,' says Dhoni.

Pan Singh's dedication would pay off. The man whose job was working as a pump operator watering the roads lining the Shyamali Colony where his son's school was located would see his son's cricket prowess get him several jobs, although it was some years before he felt he had been right to let his son play cricket. Dhoni's first job at SAIL (the Steel Authority of India Limited) was to play for its cricket team on a salary of ₹625 a month, but his wages were cut by ₹25 if he missed practice. Within a year, cricket brought him a job with more money: Rs. 2,000 with a bonus of Rs. 200 at Central Coalfields (CCL), a subsidiary of Coal India Limited. Then, in 2001, a job with Railways at Kharagpur. Here again Dhoni got a job as a ticket collector because of the enthusiasm of a Bengali, Animesh Kumar Ganguly, the divisional manager for cricket. He had laid out a cricket pitch at his railway bungalow. There he gave Dhoni a forty-five-minute cricket test, with Ganguly bowling to Dhoni; delighted with the trial, Ganguly gave him a Class 3 job as a train ticket examiner and a place in the team.

The Railways job made Pan Singh feel playing cricket was worth it as it had given his son a secure job.

DHONI SPRINGS A SURPRISE

Yet it did not look as if Dhoni would make it as a cricketer. 'Nobody in Ranchi,' says Hashmi,

> ...had any expectation that he would become such a big player in India or such a big captain. There were better players when Dhoni was young and Dhoni definitely had luck. Very frankly speaking, Dhoni himself was not aware that he would become such a great player. If you see his performance in the domestic circuit before he played for India it was not extraordinary. There were many other players who performed much better but didn't play for India. However from the beginning his batting was very aggressive. He was a power hitter. In net practice his bats would break a lot. It made life difficult. We didn't have a lot of bats. But then later on we all got bat sponsors.

But it was not just his ability to hit the ball and break bats that set Dhoni apart. Hashmi realized there was something else going for Dhoni:

> From the very beginning Dhoni was mentally very strong. I have never seen a person who was mentally so strong. He used to be very cool and calm in situations. He could control his anger. Even if somebody abused him, said something bad to him, he would remain silent. As we say, woh gusse ko pi jaata hain [He eats his anger]. Other people expressed their anger, but he would never express his anger. He would never abuse or react angrily. Very rarely would he get angry. He had great control. But he would keep the insult in his mind and he would express himself through his performance on the field. If someone said something he would be very silent and then when he next batted you could feel that he is hitting the ball with real anger.

Fardeen Khan is even blunter in how Dhoni got his initial break into representative cricket:

> When he made it into the Bihar Under-19 team everyone was shocked because he looked so bad. Sometimes his play looked really shabby, his feet were not in the right place, his bat was somewhere else. He was so unorthodox people used to say arrey, yeh kaise khelaga? [how can he play?] He got selected because there was a quota system. In a Bihar team there had to be a certain number of

players from Patna, a certain number from Jamshedpur, a certain number from Ranchi, at least one from Dhanbad and one from the districts. The Ranchi selectors fought for him, he was a superstar in Ranchi. He had this great ability to hit the ball really, really hard, and anyone who can hit sixes will always become famous. But people who played serious cricket thought this is not a player who can survive. They thought Dhoni plays cricket in Ranchi, so he can hit sixes, but when he meets serious bowlers how will you survive with that technique. But Dhoni was a very, very, intelligent guy, who hid his ability. He proved everybody wrong. Once he came into the team he played alright. Dhoni always batted No. 7. He had to keep wickets. He enjoyed his batting more than his wicketkeeping, and if you were able batting at No. 7 to contribute 35–40 runs on a regular basis that was a huge contribution. That means at the end of the season you have an average of 35 plus and that was a very good average for a wicketkeeper batsman. Dhoni used to achieve that average on a regular basis. He was very focussed. He was a very determined guy. He had a very distinctive way of scoring runs. You knew that in his 35 or 40 he is going to hit at least 2 sixes, sometimes out of the ground.

This was all the more significant because the structure of the Ranji Trophy meant a player from Bihar did not get many matches he could play in. As Fardeen says, 'With two teams qualifying from the east zone, Bengal and Odisha always got to the next stage while Bihar almost never qualified. So, playing for Bihar you played at best five Ranji trophy matches. When we were growing up Bihar was considered a joke team. Dhoni wanted to aspire for more.' Dhoni had to be content with very limited opportunities.

Here it must be emphasized that Fardeen's background was very different to that of Dhoni or Hashmi. Not only was he educated at an English-medium school, but, as he says, 'I come from the most affluent part of Jharkhand, Jamshedpur. I come from an upper-class background. My father was a contractor.' A confident man, he exudes the power of class that well-off Indians educated at English-speaking schools have. 'I was multi-purpose. I was very, very flamboyant. I was good-looking. Players in my team coming from a smaller town used to say, "Oh my God what are you doing playing cricket?" Bihar was a remote state. Had I been in Bombay it would have been different.' And he readily admits that, 'I am one of Macaulay's putra. Dhoni is not at all Macaulay's putra.'

There is a touch of a Macaulayputra in Fardeen when he talks of how Dhoni got his nickname 'Mahi'. Although Dhoni's parents called him Mahendra after Indra, one of Hinduism's great gods, when Dhoni came into the cricket team none of his teammates saw him as Indra. 'Mahendra as a name is really a rickshaw driver's, a truck driver's name to be very honest. Mahendra yaar yaha jao. [Eh, Mahendra, go there.] It is that kind of a name. Mahi is short for that. People have tried to read too much into it, I don't think it means anything.'

And as if to emphasize this class difference, Fardeen says:

People like Dhoni had to make their own way. He had to let his bat speak for himself so Dhoni, like a lot of cricketers from my batch, got a job in the Railways. Cricketers who came from the bigger cities like Mumbai and the bigger states like Maharashtra, they used to get jobs in Indian Oil and Air India. Although I was a year younger than him, I was the biggest star, I used to dress up very well, had long hair and used to wear the cap in reverse. When Dhoni started playing he started doing that as well and later he was kind enough to tell my dad that I learned this from Fardeen. Dhoni used to work on his clothes which were totally different from anybody.

Not that Fardeen and Dhoni socialized after the match:

I don't know what his family background was, we only had interaction during the cricket match. I used to talk to Dhoni a lot. After the matches were over everybody used to go back to their own houses, a lot of people didn't have telephones, forget about mobiles, so keeping in touch was just not possible. I used to come to the ground on my own two-wheeler. I used to speak both Hindi and English, most of the people couldn't speak English. People used to make me feel superior because everyone would come from such a lower class. I actually stood out a lot more because I was very, very fair and I was supposed to be the good-looking cricketer.

Yet while Dhoni may not have been able to speak English well he had a very endearing quality:

Dhoni while growing up was such a nice smiley guy that you could never ever scold him. Even when he dropped a catch he had this really, really nice smile, so you didn't want to say anything because you couldn't. I know now the world sees a very hard man. He wasn't like that when I first played with him. He has learnt a lot, we didn't see that side of him.

It also helped that, thanks to his friend Paramjit, one thing Dhoni had was bats, which came in very handy for Fardeen:

At the beginning of 1998 season I didn't have a bat. I had got a new one but, in those days, you needed to knock a bat in. We used to hit the bat against a ball in a sock. Also, a lot of catching practice with the bat. To knock a bat takes time. So, in the initial matches I did not have a bat. Dhoni had two bats which was very rare. Dhoni used to have these big bats. In the first match of the season I actually took Dhoni's bat because me and Dhoni were the two physically strongest players in the team, strongly built, our wrists were stronger, really, really physically strong. The Under-19 team in theory had a coach, but I wouldn't talk too much about him, the standard was very, very poor. We were our own coach and that was one of the reasons I gave up playing cricket. Mostly the wickets were turning wickets and pitches were not well maintained. I used to play in a team with one fast bowler and three spinners, sometimes four, a combination of an off-spinner, a leg-spinner and a left-arm spinner. Dhoni began to evolve as a batsman who scored runs consistently in the Ranji Trophy, but by then I had already left.

IN YUVRAJ'S SHADOW

But for all the anger Dhoni could express through his batting, in the early years of the millennium it was not Dhoni but another cricketer who seemed destined to light up Indian cricket. Fardeen recalls the Under-16 final in Mumbai, where he was captain of the Bihar team:

It was my last year in the Under-16, I was the captain of East zone, Yuvraj was the captain of North Zone. It was the first time I met Yuvraj. There was a bowler from my team from Bengal called Pabi Ruddy. He used to be very, very quick. Pabi Ruddy bowled Yuvraj for zero, and after that he made a lot of gestures at Yuvraj, you know this and that. The Under-16 was a round robin and we were the champions. But after we had won the tournament, we had to play a final match, the match between the champions and the Rest of India. That was the consolation match for the teams that had lost. And whatever the result we knew we would get the trophy after the match. Yuvraj captained the Rest of India. In this match he absolutely demolished Pabi, scored a century and he won that match against us. Yuvraj we all knew would play for India. Yuvraj is a very gifted cricketer, when he played for Under-16 he was so much bigger than

us it was like a lightweight fighting a heavyweight, a big guy with
chest hair. Yuvraj was the only cricketer who we saw at the Under-16
we knew was going to play for the country. He was so far ahead of
everyone. Dhoni was not in the picture.

Dhoni did come into the picture the following year, in September 1999,
when the Bihar Under-19 side met Punjab in the Cooch Behar Trophy.
That match would illustrate what seemed an unbridgeable gulf between
Dhoni and the young hero from Punjab.

Dhoni had every reason to feel at home with the match played in
September 1999 at the Keenan Stadium in Jamshedpur. This was a ground
all the Bihar players loved as Jamshedpur was the centre of Bihar cricket.
Home of Tata Steel, it had the sort of sports facilities many other centres
in India, let alone Bihar, did not have. The matches at Keenan Stadium
always had a princely air, with the high and mighty of the Tatas sitting
in the first five rows on white fabric-covered sofas, next to which stood
pedestal fans, while waiters fussed around serving them coffee during the
games. The Tatas did not skimp on lunch, which was lavish, and the stadium
often gave an impression of being fairly full, as many of the spectators were
Tata staff. Hashmi recalls:

> Food was not a problem because Jamshedpur has good food and the
> Keenan Stadium food was very good. And our accommodation was at
> the Keenan Stadium. In junior cricket we had a hostel in the J. R. D.
> complex. When we played in the Under-19s we used to stay there. We
> used to stay in a room where there were four or five beds.

Despite it being an Under-19 match, it was deemed sufficiently important
for two former Test players to be umpires, namely, Pronob Roy and Yashpal
Sharma, who had been part of the 1983 World Cup winning team. Dhoni,
coming in to bat in mid-afternoon in his customary position of No. 7, had
to face Yuvraj, who had just got the Bihar No. 6, Pratab, lbw. Bihar were a
very rocky 159 for 5. But by the end of the day Dhoni had every reason
to feel satisfied, leaving the ground 70 not out having put on 95 with the
opener, Rattan Kumar. Although Dhoni did not go on to his century the
next day, his knock of 84 was the second highest in the innings with 14
fours and 2 sixes. It showed how quickly Dhoni could score. Dhoni faced
137 balls, batting for 151 minutes. In contrast, Kumar faced nearly three
times as many balls, 361 balls, and batted five hours longer, 473 minutes, yet
scored only 15 more, missing his century by a single run. He also hit two
fewer fours than Dhoni and no sixes. What Dhoni had shown was that the

power of his hitting, which had so impressed his Ranchi colleagues, could be taken on to a higher plane, and he had every reason to feel satisfied that after a day and a half Bihar had done well to have made 357.

But then Yuvraj put what Dhoni had done in the shade. On his own he passed the Bihar score, making 358 in a Punjab score of 839 for 5 which took nearly two and a half days. Fardeen Khan was the most helpless captain in this mayhem:

> When Yuvraj was hitting we were just spectators. Me, Dhoni, and the rest of us just watched. After a certain point it became amusing because they were not going to declare. We realised the match is over and then they are just having fun. A lot of my bowlers stopped bowling. Like Mihir Diwakar, my strike bowler, he actually went and sat saying I am injured I can't bowl anymore. I had to put on Amir Hashmi who was a part-time bowler. A left-handed batsman he bowled right-hand off spin and bowled a lot, some 20-25 overs, and got Yuvraj out. It was a match that we wanted to forget. It was humiliating. We were beaten at the Keenan Stadium. Our home ground. Our pitch.

Dhoni did get a stumping, but at the end of the match he had every reason to feel that whatever he did with the bat he would very much be an also-ran in a Bihar side going nowhere. Indeed, at that time, Hashmi, who had made 43 in that Yuvraj match, looked the Bihar player more likely to catch the eye. When a few weeks later, in January 2000, India played the Under-19 World Cup in Sri Lanka, Amir Hashmi was among the twenty-five probables selected for the camp in Chennai, as also was Diwakar. Hashmi admits, 'We were selected for the camp because we were from Bihar, it was a very small state.' But even under this criterion of quota-based selection Dhoni did not make the camp. The Indian team, captained by Kaif, went on to win the trophy. The tournament featured many players who were soon to become regulars in their countries' Test sides. In this tomorrow's world, nobody knew the six-hitter from Ranchi with his helicopter shot. Dhoni seemed to have no place in that dawn to come.

HELPED BY THE QUOTA SYSTEM

But at least he could make the Bihar team thanks to Randhir Singh, the Bihar selector and coach, who had great faith in young players. The result was that two weeks before India made history in Sri Lanka, Dhoni and Hashmi both made their Ranji Trophy debut against Assam. The state of Jharkhand would be formed just ten months later, but this was still undivided Bihar, and this time, with no Yuvraj present, the four-day match

played at the Keenan Stadium starting on 12 January held no terrors for
Dhoni. That very first match also allowed him to provide a glimpse of the
cricketer he was to become. In both innings he batted at No. 7, which
would become his customary position, making 40 in the first innings.
More crucially, his 68 not out from 89 balls in the second innings was
accompanied by the sort of power hitting familiar to Hashmi and ensured
that Assam, who were only 11 runs behind on the first innings, were put on
the back foot. Bihar went on to win by 191 runs. As a wicketkeeper, Dhoni
did not make much of an impression but he had one stumping, off left-arm
spinner Avinash Kumar, who was playing his last first-class game, and he was
sufficiently impressed to tell Dhoni, 'You have the talent to play for India.'
These words were to sustain Dhoni through the hard grind of working his
way through India's domestic game.

The railway-ticket collector was called for trials for the Railways team
but his trial lasted five minutes and three balls. It did not help, perhaps,
that the Railways wicketkeeper was also the captain, Abhay Sharma. Years
later, looking back at his Railways debacle and with Sharma a footnote in
Indian cricket history, Dhoni could even be generous saying, 'I guess they
had a strong team which was doing well; they didn't need me.'

DHONI FINALLY GETS THE BIG BREAK
But then, as Hashmi says, Dhoni got a chance and seized it:

> The match was in Eden Gardens in Kolkata against Bengal. I was there.
> We had travelled by train from Jamshedpur to Kolkata as we usually
> did. In junior cricket when camps were organized in Jamshedpur we
> used to stay in a room where there were four or five beds. In Ranji
> Trophy when we played outside Jamshedpur we would share two to
> a room. Two single beds in a room. For this match we stayed at the
> Akash Ganga hotel located in Park Circus. It was a good hotel. I was
> not his room partner. In the evening we always used to sit together.
> Used to roam together in Kolkata. We used to see where the sales are
> going on. We used to go there and buy jeans and shirts. Not that we
> had much money. At that time the match money for one-day cricket
> was Rs. 1,500. For Ranji Trophy it was Rs. 4,500 per match.

Dhoni wandered around Kolkata looking for jeans, very aware his cricketing
future was at stake. Hashmi recalls:

> One day before the match the team management decided they
> will drop Dhoni in that match. But what happened was that in the

morning coach decided he will play the match. Dhoni told the coach, 'Let me open today. If you are giving me the last chance let me open the innings.' He had been batting in the middle order in the matches. Now he opened and had a great piece of luck. In that match with the score at four or five a short ball was bowled by Laxmi Ratan Shukla and Dhoni pulled it and he got a top edge. The fielder at midwicket and Laxmi Ratan Shukla both went for the catch. Then they both stopped and the ball dropped in the middle. Dhoni went on to score a century.

The 2003–04 season was to prove Dhoni's breakthrough season. Here again the luck that Hashmi and Fardeen talk about played a part. The crucial match was playing for Jharkhand against Assam. The match was watched by Prakash Poddar. The Indian board, having grown rich, now wanted to spread cricket around the country and had set up a national talent scheme; Poddar was talent resource development officer for the East Zone. Poddar's first look at Dhoni made him think the Ranchi boy was more of a Hindi film hero than a cricketer. Nor did Dhoni make a huge score—only 29—but Poddar was taken by the way he hit the ball. 'There was confidence in his stroke-making that stood out. His wicketkeeping was 50–50, but his batting was full of aggressive intent.'

Poddar was sufficiently impressed to suggest to Dilip Vengsarkar, who then headed the national talent scheme, that he should have a look. He in turn spoke to Kiran More, chairman of the selectors and a man who knew all about wicketkeeping. This was significant for Dhoni not merely because of the position More held but hailing from Vadodara, which had roughly the same population as Ranchi, More felt that players from small towns in India did not get a fair chance unlike those from Mumbai and the other great centres of Indian cricket. He came to Jamshedpur to watch Dhoni play against Odisha. This time Dhoni's wicketkeeping passed muster and he scored a hundred. 'You could see his natural ability,' says More, 'to score runs quickly from the very first ball. His technique may not have been classical, but his calculated aggression was unmistakable.'

INDIA NEEDS A WICKETKEEPER BATSMAN

A decent wicketkeeper whose batting could be explosive was just the combination for which India had been desperately searching for five years. But the land of Syed Kirmani could not find that keeper. Between the 1999–2000 tour of Australia and Dhoni's first ODI in December 2004, India fielded ten wicketkeepers; Dhoni was the eleventh, taking in both ODIs and

Tests. In Indian cricketing history there had never been such a shortage of wicketkeeper batsmen. Now finding one was just as hard as through much of the 1950s, 1960s and 1970s it had been to find a genuine opening bowler. Ironically, then, an excellent wicketkeeper batsman like Budhi Kunderan would discard his wicketkeeping pads and gloves to open the bowling. Now India sought a Kunderan as wicketkeeper who was adequate behind the stumps and could bat. For More, Dhoni ticked this box, 'He was there at the right place, at the right time.'

The final proof came when, in the Duleep Trophy final in Mohali in March 2004 between North Zone and East Zone, More persuaded Pranab Roy, the chairman of the East Zone selectors, to drop Deep Dasgupta, who had already made his India debut and was the zone's first choice as wicketkeeper, and select Dhoni. Dasgupta, it was said, had a hand injury and Dhoni kept wickets and opened the innings. A week earlier in Amritsar, Dhoni had played for the East Zone against an England A team that included Kevin Pietersen and Matt Prior. Then he had not kept wickets, merely opened, scoring 52 and 24 in an easy East Zone victory. Now, against the North Zone he faced more formidable opposition, one of whom he knew well. This was Yuvraj Singh, and as in that Under-19 match at the Keenan Stadium, Yuvraj again was a man Dhoni's team could not get out. The Indian selectors wanted him to prove his fitness. He did just that. He made centuries in both innings, although Dhoni did catch him in the second innings. Then with the bat in the second innings Dhoni showed he could match Yuvraj's power, if not score quite as many runs. Dhoni's 60 in forty-seven balls had 8 fours and a six, and this against a North Zone attack that included three Indian bowlers, among them Ashish Nehra. His innings only ended when Yuvraj caught him, completing this phase of the Yuvraj–Dhoni saga. There would, as we shall see, be others. Dhoni had not done enough to make East Zone win, they lost by 59 runs. But he had done enough for More to think that, 'We may have just found an answer to our need for a hard-hitting wicketkeeper batsman to play for India.' Four months later, Dhoni was selected for the India A tour of Zimbabwe and Kenya which was played in July and September of 2004. It was clear the selectors thought he had promise but it was by no means certain he would make it. He went as reserve wicketkeeper. But here again luck intervened. As we have seen, the first-choice keeper, Karthik, was called away to England and Dhoni, four years after he had made his Ranji debut for Bihar and a journey which seemed destined to end in a cul-de-sac, finally made it onto the big stage. Now nothing could stop him.

Dhoni had finally done what Fardeen had told his own father he

would do when he had faced Yuvraj in that Under-19 final at the Keenan
Stadium back in September 1999:

> The day he played in that Under-19 match against Punjab walking
> out of that Keenan stadium I told my dad, 'Agar Dhoni wicketkeeping
> achha kardega na India ke liye khelega.' [If Dhoni keeps wicket well he
> has the potential of playing for India one day.] I said there is a chance
> he can play for India because his batting is very, very unique. I told my
> Dad, 'Unlike anybody I have ever known in this country he has a very
> great deal of talent. I know he looks very erratic. But he is definitely
> very effective.' By now I had seen Dhoni for three years already in
> the Under-19. And during that period playing with the red ball and,
> despite batting with a bad bat and on bad wickets, he still used to
> hit at least 2 sixes per innings. Weird angles. Out of nowhere. Those
> were very, very amazing shots. A lot of people can be unique. If they
> don't perform it does not count. He was a consistent guy who used to
> make 40 runs per innings. And at that time 40 runs by a wicketkeeper
> coming in at No. 7 was valued. I do not remember any wicketkeeper
> apart from Dhoni who could come out and bat like a proper batsman.
> Dhoni changed all that. Other sides had wicketkeepers whose batting
> was much better. We had wicketkeepers who were shitty batsmen.
> Dhoni is the only one who prospered.

We have heard much of how Yuvraj's career was intertwined with
Dhoni's and how through their teens the Punjab player was the dominant
batsmen. Fardeen admires Yuvraj's courage in overcoming his problems and
recovering from cancer. Comparing Yuvraj to Dhoni he says, 'Dhoni is much
more intelligent.' Fardeen illustrates this by what Dhoni did to become a
better wicketkeeper:

> Dhoni worked on his wicketkeeping. Dhoni had a lot of confidence
> in his own ability, he applied himself more and took his wicketkeeping
> more seriously after breaking into the Indian team. He had to be an
> all-rounder otherwise he would be thrown out because he was not
> good enough to replace one of the established batsmen. Dhoni is a
> very gifted guy. He has always been very intelligent.

It also helped that Dhoni always had an inner belief:

> He knew his game very, very well and he was not bothered about
> what people are saying about his technique where his bat is, that his
> head is lifted in another direction and he is using the bottom hand. All

of that was a huge issue while growing up. I think he rose above all of that. What changed in him was he started to convert the forties into big scores.

However, Fardeen does admit that he is surprised Dhoni could do that and started making hundreds in international matches:

> I used to call him a well-played forties batsman. We had not met since our playing days, but after he scored 183 not out against Sri Lanka, breaking Adam Gilchrist's record for a highest score by a wicketkeeper in a one-day match he called, I said, 'How the hell are you scoring centuries? I never thought you would score a century.'

THE UNEXPECTED LEADER

But while Fardeen can accept that Dhoni matured as a batsman, there is one aspect of Dhoni's game that has totally surprised him.

> I was extremely surprised when I saw him emerge as a leader. He was never the leader among us. I was the captain and I would not give any credit to myself that playing under me developed his leadership qualities. He must have always had it. When I saw the mental growth of Dhoni I was very surprised.

Dhoni's rise had also come despite the way cricketers were treated in Bihar even in the early years of the twenty-first century:

> The Bihar cricket association gave us a very small allowance. We were given very bad travelling facilities, 3rd class without reservations. Third-class travel on trains without reservations was very difficult. It was real hardship. We stayed in shitty places and to eat we were given only rice and dal. I asked for chicken but did not get it.

Hashmi, who is now a selector of the Jharkhand Ranji Trophy team, echoes Fardeen's views:

> When we were playing the facilities for travel and accommodation were very poor. Once we went to play in Guwahati, the journey took 37 hours with changes at Agartala and Tripura, those times were tough. Then you didn't have good hotels. We had to put up with lots of problems. In the first match Dhoni and I played we got Rs. 4,500 for the entire match. There was no money at the end of the year. Nowadays in the Ranji Trophy players get Rs. 10,000 a day, which means a match fee of Rs. 40,000. And after the season is over they get

1.4 lakhs for one match. This match money started being paid after the start of IPL.

As Fardeen emphasizes:

> Sport has become much bigger, you don't have to do a job. Even if you are not good enough to play international cricket and are playing for the state you can earn a yearly income of Rs. 30–40 lakhs, when most other jobs pay around Rs. 2 lakhs. Cricket can provide a great standard of living.

Fardeen refused to accept what Bihar was providing and complained long and hard about food and the facilities:

> Dhoni never expressed any such emotions. He never, never joined in any complaints. He just kept quiet. He just smiled and whatever he was told to do he did. Dhoni was never somebody who rebelled. Zero controversy from Dhoni. Maybe it was the right thing to do.

Perhaps Dhoni judged that complaining would not help his career, for Fardeen is convinced he paid the price for complaining. He was ostracized:

> I was treated as an outcast. I thought players who were much inferior are getting chances but not me. Cricket is not worth it. I actually got heartbroken.

Fardeen says of Dhoni:

> He was lucky throughout. Everything that he touched turned into gold. I think God wanted him on this journey. I used to watch him keep wickets and see him drop a lot of catches. He is a very lucky guy for sure. When God wants to write a certain script he does. Look at the 2011 World Cup which we won. In the semi-final Pakistan was dropping catches like it was raining. I was not surprised by his ability as a batsman, he used to score 40s regularly, and his application and maturity grew, and he worked on his mental strength and motivation.

Hashmi admits Dhoni has changed, but that is in relation to how he deals with his mobile phone:

> His great illness is he does not answer his phone. However often you ring he will not pick up his phone. When he first went to play for India we used to talk on the phone. Then he stopped picking up his phone. Once we were sitting together and we even berated him for not answering his phone. Saala tum bade player ho gaye, phone

nahi uthate ho. [Bastard, you have become a big player and do not pick up your phone]. He said, Theek hai. Abhi mere sath ek ghanta baitho phone silent pe kar deta hu and tere paas main rukta hu. Ab tum dekho. [Okay you sit with me for an hour and a half, I will put the phone on silent and place it next to you and then you see.] In that hour and a half he must have got more than a hundred calls. He said, Agar main phone uthane laga to main kab practice karunga, kab sounga, kab khana khaaunga, main phone hi mein rahunga. Is liye main phone nahi uthata hu. Emergency hui to sirf text bhejna. [If I answer so many calls, then when will I practise, when will I eat, when will I sleep? I will be on the phone all the time. That is why I do not pick up the phone. If there is an emergency, just send a text.]

Dhoni in cricketing terms had long moved away from Ranchi but at heart he still remained the boy from Ranchi.

Chapter 42

THE ROCK STARS OF CRICKET

DHONI'S BAT MAKES AUCTION HISTORY

Three days before India played England at Lord's in the first of the four
Test series in July 2011 a dinner was held in honour of Mahendra Singh
Dhoni at the London Hilton in Park Lane. Dhoni was at the height of his
career. His team was ranked No. 1 in both Test and one-day cricket, having
just fulfilled the great dream of Indian cricket fans by winning the 50-over
World Cup four months earlier, with Dhoni himself hitting the winning
run.

Following that victory Dhoni, his team and their spouses had been
invited to high tea with the then president of India, Pratibha Patil, on the
grounds of the Raj Bhavan in Mumbai. Prizes had been showered on them
by the BCCI, various state governments, and public and private companies.
Ferrari had given Dhoni a 599 GTO India edition. Uttarakhand had offered
Dhoni a residential plot or a house in the hill station of Mussoorie and it
was announced that a stadium would be built in the state in his honour.

The dinner was to launch the MS Dhoni Foundation and the event,
backed by high-profile business names such as Citibank and Asprey, saw
a room full of rich Indians, drinking champagne and spending vast sums
on cricket memorabilia. The highlight of the evening was the auction of
the bat with which Dhoni hit the six to win the 2011 World Cup for
India. The price rocketed, reaching £60,000, making it easily the costliest
cricket bat ever.

A young man went up to the stage to receive the bat from Dhoni.
You could see he was nervous. What he did on meeting his hero was
sensational. He was so overwhelmed that as he held Dhoni's hand and took
the bat from him he said that he would pay not £60,000 but £100,000.
I was sitting not far from Farokh Engineer. He raised his eyebrows and
confessed he had never seen anything like this before. It showed how rich
some Indians were and the impact Dhoni's success had had on them. This
tale would have a curious postscript.

I narrated this story in an article I wrote for the *Financial Times* discussing

how Indians had taken over this very English game. A few days later I
got an email from Delhi asking me whether I had got the facts right.
Did the young man who went up to collect the bat really pay £100,000
despite the fact that the winning bid was £60,000? I confirmed he had,
and it emerged that the real bidder was a man in Delhi. He had asked a
friend to bid for the bat and told him he could go up to £100,000. The
young man, clearly overwhelmed by holding the hand of the man who
had won the World Cup for India, decided that paying £60,000 was not
enough, he should go all the way and pay £100,000. Nothing could better
illustrate what Dhoni meant to those who follow Indian cricket. So, let
us look back at what Dhoni had done since taking over as the captain in
all formats of cricket.

DHONI TAKES INDIA TO THE SUMMIT

On the morning of 6 December 2009, at the Brabourne Stadium in
Mumbai, as Dhoni caught Muttiah Muralitharan off Harbhajan Singh,
India won the third Test by an innings and 24 runs and became the No. 1
Test side in the world for the first time since the ICC had introduced
these rankings in 2003. The victory was not a surprise, for by now this
three-Test series had been the Virender Sehwag show. It started after the
first Test had ended in a draw. So powerful was his batting in the second
and third Tests at Kanpur and Mumbai that Ian Chappell, who had already
compared him to Bradman, described him as 'the greatest destroyer since
the U-boat'. The Sri Lankans were holed below the water so devastatingly
that they sank.

In Kanpur in the second Test India batted first and Sehwag had started
slowly, no boundaries in his first twenty-six balls. In the first hour India were
31 for no loss. By the time lunch came Sehwag had converted a five-day
Test into a one-day match. India added another hundred, 73 of them from
nine overs. Sehwag was out by the forty-second over, he had scored 131,
India were 233, almost half the day's overs were still to be bowled. By the
end of the day's play India, with Gambhir making a hundred and Dravid
85 not out, had scored 417, more than it had ever scored in a day's play.
India ended on 642 and won by an innings and 144 runs an hour after
lunch on the fourth day. This was India's hundredth Test victory.

The third Test in Mumbai saw a Sehwag act that was even more
spectacular and came in the most nostalgic of Indian cricketing settings,
at the CCI, hosting its first Test since February 1973. Sri Lanka seemed
to have done well in their first innings, making 393. Just before Sehwag
went out to bat, Kirsten told him that if he managed to negotiate the

first ten overs he could do something that had never been done before. As at Kanpur, Sehwag began watchfully, 15 runs in thirty-one balls and only one four in the first forty-five minutes. Then he let loose so dramatically that when play ended he was 284 not out. He had faced 239 balls, hit 40 fours and 6 sixes.

Sri Lanka then had the reputation for being the best fielding side in Asia. But Trevor Bayliss, the Sri Lankan coach, confessed that to stop Sehwag 'you needed 20 fielders out there'. Such was Sehwag's mastery that India on that second day beat the record it had set in Kanpur, only nine days earlier, for the runs scored in a day. In Mumbai it was 443 from seventy-nine overs.

Sehwag's double century off 168 balls was the second fastest in history and when he got to 250 with a reverse paddle-sweep of Muralitharan [who is often referred to as Murali], he had made 250 four times. Only Bradman with five had made more. At the end of the second's day play with Sehwag requiring 16 to reach 300, he was within touching distance of doing what not even the greatest batsman had done, score three triple centuries in Tests. He got past 290, like Bradman the only batsmen to do it thrice, but on 293, as if giving Murali practice, scooped a catch back to him and returned with no regret, saying 'there is nothing to be disappointed about'. Chappell was to call it 'the feat of the year'.

Sometime later, when Kambli contested an election, Sehwag came to Mumbai to support him. Papu Sanzgiri asked him, 'Who is going to break Brian Lara's 400?' Sehwag said, 'Please tell Sachin to do it. I cannot bat for two days. I can only bat for a day and a half.' In the Mumbai Test, India made 726 for 9 declared, aware that Sehwag's blitzkrieg had given India plenty of time to bowl out Sri Lanka again. That is just how it turned out. Sri Lanka lost by an innings and 24 runs in just over four days. With India top of the Test rankings, Sehwag was also honoured.

In 2008, Sehwag had been crowned the leading Cricketer of the Year by *Wisden*, a new award that complemented its long established Five Cricketers of the Year. In 2008, he had scored at a strike rate of 85 runs per 100 balls in Test cricket and 120 in one-day internationals. An IPL injury to his right shoulder meant he did not play much in 2009 except in Tests where, in 2009, he had a strike rate of 108.9 and averaged 70. In one-day internationals that year his strike rate was 136.5, averaging 45. The editor of *Wisden*, Scyld Berry, consulted widely before deciding that Sehwag should again be the Leading Cricketer of 2009 and his words are worth quoting:

Sehwag has to be the first on the team-sheet to represent the world, whatever the game's format. He would take on the Martians, however hostile and alien their attack, disrupting their lines and wavelengths; and if he succeeded as he normally does, he would make life so much easier for those who followed.

On Dhoni's first overseas tour as Test captain to New Zealand in 2009 the Indians had been described by the local press as the rock stars of cricket. Sehwag was the leader of the band.

LAXMAN HELPS INDIA CAMP ON THE SUMMIT
India began 2010 top of the ICC rankings, 125 to South Africa's 120 and second in the one-day championship, 123 to Australia's 130. By January 2011, India had played twelve more Tests, lost three but won six and not lost a series, either at home or away. Dhoni could proudly say India had last lost a Test series in August 2008 in Sri Lanka, which was before he took over as Test captain. What made this very special was that India had shown a resilience they had never shown before. In 2010, they would lose the first Test of a series but still bounce back to draw the series. And to think that two of these defeats were away to Sri Lanka and South Africa showed how far Indian cricket had come under Dhoni. In the past such defeats abroad nearly always meant a lost series. Central to this was the batting of V. V. S. Laxman. In the three Tests which India won in these series, he scored 143 in the first, 103 not out in the second and 97 in the third. He was now thirty-six years old and having a wonderful late bloom. In 2010, he scored 939 runs at an average of 67, but nevertheless regretted that at that stage in his career he had made 48 fifties but converted only 16 of them into hundreds. For a batsman how many fifties became hundreds is the sign of true class. That year seven half-centuries, two above 90, had led to only two hundreds. To be fair he was often batting at No. 5 or 6 which meant having the tail at the other end. This had been well illustrated on 5 October 2010 in the first Test at Mohali against Australia.

India had been left what seemed a relatively simple 216 to win. On the fifth morning Laxman came in to bat with the score 76 for 5. His back was causing such a problem that in the first innings he had batted at No. 10. Even now he was batting with a runner. Tendulkar helped take the requirement below 100, always psychologically important, but after he left there was a collapse and when Ishant Sharma walked out India still needed 92.

This is when Laxman once again demonstrated his mastery over

Australian bowling and tactics, making the most of the fact that Ponting, the Australian captain, trying to snare Sharma, often gave Laxman easy runs. He and Sharma had taken India to within eleven of the target, Sharma making 31 in a ninth-wicket stand of 81, when Sharma fell. This brought Pragyan Ojha in and now Laxman became an animated band conductor urging him to run faster and even threatening to use his bat to chastise him if he did not, albeit in fun.

In what turned out to be the final over of the match an Australian appeal for lbw against Ojha was rejected, which caused such Australian confusion that there was an overthrow which went for 4 runs. With 2 runs needed India got two leg-byes and won their first ever victory by one wicket and only the twelfth in Test history. Laxman finished 73 not out.

Laxman would later say that in 2010 he had felt more relaxed. Before that he had often felt that he was on trial in his career, but first Kumble and then Dhoni, along with Kirsten, had made him feel he was secure. However, as we shall see, when Dhoni felt that he had served his time, Laxman was discarded.

India's series in South Africa at the end of 2010 was also significant for the way that India now reacted to having become the top side in Tests. After decades of wanting to play more one-day matches they now wanted more Tests, changing tour programmes to fit in more Tests and for this series, Kirsten's homeland Test, all the senior players who had featured against New Zealand in the home Test series just preceding the visit to South Africa did not play in the one-day matches. With no warm-up matches scheduled, Kirsten was keen that the senior players should get to South Africa early and hit 'somewhere between two and three thousand balls each on South African soil before the first Test'. So most of the team for the Tests arrived in Cape Town on 8 December 2010, eight days before the first Test starting at Centurion, even as one-day matches against New Zealand were still going on back home. As the teams gathered in Centurion, Kirsten, having taken India from No. 4 to No. 1, decided to play mind games. He dramatically announced that his team could justifiably claim to be 'one of India's greatest'.

That claim was way over the top. India still failed to win a series in South Africa, but for the first time, India left South Africa without having lost a series and had retained their No. 1 spot in the Test rankings. However, as Dhoni acknowledged, this meant that, as the core of the Indian side would have retired by the time India toured South Africa again, players like Tendulkar, Dravid, Laxman and Zaheer would never know what it was to win a series in the rainbow nation. But could this generation win the World Cup which was starting in India six weeks after the end of the third Test in Cape Town, on 20 February 2011? Tendulkar, who as a child had seen Kapil Dev lift the trophy in 1983 on television, wanted this more than anybody else.

Tendulkar returned from South Africa having every reason to be satisfied with his own batting. Back on 24 February 2010, he had become the first batsman to score a double century in a one-day international, against South Africa in Gwalior. Also 2010, his twenty-second year, had been his best in Test cricket, 1,562 runs at an average of 78. There had been other personal landmarks on the South African tour. In the first Test at Centurion, Tendulkar reached his elusive fiftieth Test century. He was at 111 when the last Indian wicket fell at the other end and South Africa won by an innings and 25 runs. He had batted so well that Dale Steyn who took four wickets confessed later that, 'I had given up trying to get him out. I was just attacking the other guy.' Then in the last Test at Cape Town, Tendulkar realized a dream. Before the Test began he had dreamt he would get to his hundred by hooking a Morkel bouncer for 6. That is just how it happened, a top-edge flying over the wicketkeeper's head. This, the fifty-first Test century, proved to be the last of his Test career. So, could he now realize his great dream of winning the World Cup?

ENDING THE TWENTY-EIGHT YEAR HURT

Brought up as a child on Kapil Dev's glories, Tendulkar was very aware that this was his last chance to win what he saw as 'cricket's ultimate prize'. Injury had ruled him out for the one-day internationals which followed the South African Tests but before he left for India he gathered the Indian team together and told them that each of them must pledge to sacrifice something for the World Cup. How about losing three kilograms in weight? The players who were never likely to say no to Tendulkar, at least not to his face, instantly promised. We do not know how many of his teammates managed to keep their word, but Tendulkar lost 3.8 kilograms as he got fit to fulfil what was his last great cricket mission.

I was aware of how much the World Cup meant to Indian cricket fans, yet arriving in India to cover it I was still surprised to see the way the country had hyped itself up for this tournament. The cities were full of posters reminding Indians that the World Cup was last won twenty-eight years ago and that the Cup was now coming back. Indians felt the humiliations of the defeats since 1983 greatly. And this was an India very different to 1983. Televised cricket in India was like a fantasy ad land. There were commercial breaks after every over and, often during play; the picture downsized to accommodate an ad. Whoever was playing, suddenly alongside the live action, there was Sachin Tendulkar, or Virender Sehwag advertising a product. The television market dictated the fact that the vast majority of World Cup matches were day-nighters, to cater for prime-time viewing. Ideal for Pizza Hut who wanted to use the World Cup to wean Indians away from tandoori chicken and tikka masala. Their campaign offered ninety-nine free meals for every batsman who made 99 runs and, in the jargon of marketing men, Pizza Hut expected a 10 per cent increase in 'footfall'. What Indian fans wanted was that with the final in Mumbai it should end with Tendulkar, in his home city, holding up the trophy. Gavaskar has said that Indian cricketers playing in India feel as if they are performing inside a pressure cooker. For this World Cup such was the heat generated that some of the Indian players could not eat, others could not sleep and Yuvraj threw up regularly.

That opening match in Mirpur was against Bangladesh but any fears of a repeat of 2007 were quickly banished. Sehwag made 175 from 140 balls, with 14 fours and 5 sixes. In some ways even more telling was Virat Kohli, who had already made his mark in one-day internationals but now, making his World Cup debut, outscoring Sehwag, and getting to his hundred in eighty-three balls, 11 fewer than Sehwag. And while Sehwag was the bludgeoner, Kohli's driving through the covers had a silkiness that was beautiful to watch. India's 370 proved too much.

The next match against England in Bengaluru was one of the most remarkable matches of the tournament and also saw some of the worst scenes of crowd mismanagement. The match was meant to be held in Kolkata, but the ground was not ready so it was moved to Bengaluru. Ticketing arrangements for high-profile Indian matches are always a nightmare This time the online system proved so wretched that fans who had bought tickets six months ago had still not received them. Even the ICC's commercial partners had not received their tickets. It led to David Becker, head of the ICC's legal department, writing a letter to Sharad Pawar, chairman of the central organizing committee warning the Indians not to try and sell tickets at the box office as there could be 'chaos and physical injury'. He also expressed the fear that the relationship with sponsors was at 'breaking point'. In Bengaluru, fans queued all night for tickets only to be lathi-charged by the police the next morning, with the Bengaluru city police commissioner, Shankar Bidari, defending his policemen saying 'there was a likelihood of a stampede. To prevent a greater injury, you have to cause a small injury.' Then he added, 'The Indian situation is very different. It is very difficult for people in America and Europe to understand.' When I arrived at the ground one could sense the tension that this had produced.

With Tendulkar scoring his fifth World Cup century, India seemed odds on to win but in the end just managed to tie the match, showing a number of frailties. The top order had not supported Tendulkar, the bowling could be taken apart and the fielding did not suggest many of the team had taken Tendulkar's advice and shed 3 kilograms of weight. However, India improved as the tournament progressed. There were hiccups, India lost to South Africa in the Group stage, despite Tendulkar hitting his sixth World Cup century and his ninety-ninth in all international cricket. India should have made more than 296 and also failed to close out the match. South Africa needed 13 off the last six balls and got it with two balls to spare suggesting weaknesses in death bowling by the Indians.

What was encouraging for the Indians was the way Yuvraj Singh was having a second coming. In the previous year he had lost his Test and one-day place and this was a comeback tournament for him. Tendulkar, realizing Yuvraj was nervous, had dinner with him before the first match against Bangladesh and suggested he set targets to achieve during the tournament. Dhoni who knew him so well had also tried to encourage him saying, 'It is your game, your team, your Cup. Just do not lose concentration, otherwise you will miss the bus.' Yuvraj was determined not to and won Man of the Match awards against Ireland, the Netherlands, West Indies and, perhaps, most crucially, in the quarter-finals against Australia. A Ponting hundred had set India 261. When the fifth Indian wicket fell India still needed 74. Yuvraj, partnered by Suresh Raina, who was also making his comeback in the tournament and was known as part of the Mahi gang, batted with such calmness that India won without losing another wicket. Australia, who had won all three previous World Cups, had been eliminated.

This set up the semi-final against Pakistan which was always going to be more than just a cricket match. Even by the standards of hype that India–Pakistan matches generate, this was exceptional. With this, the first match in the subcontinent between the two countries since the terrorist attack on Mumbai by Pakistan-based terrorists, the match was a vehicle for diplomacy. The then Indian prime minister, Manmohan Singh, invited his Pakistani counterpart, Yousuf Raza Gilani to watch the match with him at Mohali, an invitation Gilani accepted. Celebrities could not be kept away, Aamir Khan, Preity Zinta, Vivek Oberoi among others held court in the packed Mohali stadium.

Tickets for the semi-final match had been sold out in Mohali for days and many businesses and offices in both countries were closed during play. Governments in many of the states and provinces in both countries declared

official holidays on 30 March, the day of the match. Thousands of screens
were installed in public places across both the nations, and television stores
experienced increased sales.

The threatened rain did not materialize and India, on winning the toss,
batted and made 260 for 9. Tendulkar made 85 but he was helped both by
a system he did not like and Pakistan's fielders. On 23 given out lbw by
umpire Gould, Hawk-Eye ruled the ball was missing the leg stump. India,
on Tendulkar's advice, had shunned Hawk-Eye. But in the World Cup the
ICC had the right to decide technology and Tendulkar survived. He was
then dropped four times with each effort by the Pakistani fielders more
comical than the previous one. Pakistan got to 103 for 2 and even in the
forty-second over were in with a shout at 184 for 7. But then Afridi,
captaining the side, tried to hit Harbhajan out of the ground, was caught
and the rest fell apart. India won by 29 runs and maintained their record
of never having lost a World Cup match to their neighbours.

The defeat was too much for some Pakistanis and three of them,
including a Pakistani actor, died of shock after Pakistan lost the match.
India celebrated as if it had already won the World Cup, a celebration
tinged with relief as a Pakistani victory would have meant Pakistan playing
the final in Mumbai which still bore scars from the devastation Pakistani
terrorists had inflicted on the city.

The final was obviously going to be the biggest cricket match India
had ever seen and it did not disappoint, with an ending that could have
been the final scene in a Bollywood movie, except it did not involve the
lead character, Tendulkar.

Tendulkar had returned to Mumbai with the words of Shastri ringing
in his ear, 'The pressure on you will be higher than on Dhoni. Indians do
not just want the Cup, they want it with a century from Sachin in Mumbai,
your home.' The BCCI, adopting the style favoured by many modern sports
associations, called in personalities prominent in their field to talk to the
team. However, the talk by Prannoy Roy, co-founder of NDTV, proved
a disaster with the players confused as to how the Gandhian approach he
was advocating would work in the face of a hostile Indian media. More
successful was Mike Horn who regaled the players with stories about his
adventures circumnavigating the globe and walking to the North Pole. This
so relaxed Tendulkar that he slept better in the week of the final than he
had done before the quarter-final against Australia or the semi-final against
Pakistan. But the dark shadow cast by the semi-final defeat against Sri Lanka
in 1996 haunted many Indians.

The night before the match Dhoni got a call from a man who he hardly knew and whose voice he did not recognize: Vinod Kambli. Kambli was crying and told Dhoni, 'Kal ki raat tumhari hogi, honi padegi, tum jeetoge. [Tomorrow night will be yours, it has to be, you will win.]' Kambli then recounted how Indians fans had not forgiven him for losing the semi-final to Sri Lanka in 1996 and ended by saying, 'You, you must win'.

The match began with the sort of drama that suggested the script had been written by a comedian. As the coin was spun Kumar Sangakkara, the Sri Lankan captain, called. The coin came up as heads, but the match referee, Jeff Crowe, did not hear the call over the crowd. It was decided that there would be a re-toss. Sangakkara called heads as the coin was spun the second time. It was heads and he elected to bat. Unlike 1983 when India looked a certain loser until they dramatically turned the final around, for long periods in the Sri Lankan innings, India were in control. But with Sri Lanka 182 for 5, Jayawardene stepped up, making 103 not out and Sri Lanka finished on 274. World Cups are normally won by teams batting first. At this stage only two teams had won chasing and to win India would have to score more runs than any chasing team had ever done in a final.

India could not have had a worse start. Sehwag was lbw for a duck to the second ball of the innings. Tendulkar raced to 18 off fourteen balls. Mumbai settled in for the century they wanted but to the dismay of everyone he went for a big drive off Malinga and edged a catch to Sangakkara. Kohli and Gambhir started the recovery with some fluent stroke play and quick running between wickets, taking India to 114 before Kohli was caught-and-bowled by Dilshan for 35. And this is when Dhoni made the most dramatic decision of the final. In the run-up to the match he had shown he was not afraid to take decisions which were controversial and provoked much media debate. Srikkanth, the chairman of the selectors, had said Dhoni was in charge and Dhoni's selections certainly suggested that he called the shots. Dhoni had insisted on the selection of Piyush Chawla, Ashish Nehra and even though Ravichandran Ashwin was in the squad, and a colleague of his in the Chennai Super Kings, he did not play him in any of the matches. For the final, with Nehra having broken his finger in the semi-final, Dhoni brought back Sreesanth despite the fact that he had not played since the first match against Bangladesh when he went for 55 runs in five overs. But it was now with the final in the balance that he made the boldest decision of the tournament.

In the dressing room Dhoni had been restless though appearing outwardly calm. As the second wicket, which was Tendulkar's, fell, he put on his pads. He had decided that with Sri Lanka having two off-spinners, Muralitharan and Suraj Randiv, whom he knew well from Chennai Super

Kings, he would face fewer problems than other Indian batsmen. For a start he could pick their doosra. Dhoni was also aware that with night having fallen there was dew on the ground and if he got hold of the Sri Lankan spinners he could dictate the game. He discussed this with Kirsten who agreed. So, as Kohli walked back to the pavilion, instead of Yuvraj who had batted No. 5 or even higher throughout the tournament out strode Dhoni. Dhoni in six innings had so far scored 150 runs, 7 against Australia, 25 against Pakistan and his highest score of 34 was against Ireland. It demonstrated the confidence the man from Ranchi had in his own ability and judgement. From the start of his innings Dhoni set out to prove why he was called the best finisher of a one-day game. Gambhir and he added 109 for the fourth wicket. When Gambhir on 97, trying to get to his century with a boundary, had a mighty heave and was bowled, the target was in sight, with India needing a run a ball: 52 runs off fifty-two balls. Yuvraj now joined Dhoni and as Sri Lanka started the last two overs the finish line had come into view. Four runs were needed off eleven balls. In such a situation most other batsmen would have been content to milk the singles but for Dhoni this was the moment to finish the match in the classic way he had often done as a boy in Ranchi. As Kulasekara bowled the second ball of his eighth over Dhoni bent his right leg, braced his left knee and with an extension of his forearms hit the ball high and wide over long-on. It was 10.49 p.m. and as Dhoni's eyes followed the ball making its way to the north stand of the Wankhede in that Mumbai night, the non-striker Yuvraj at the other end, realizing what was happening, raised his arms aloft. Dhoni had not planned to finish the match with a six. The ball was there and he hit it. The shot was to become one of the most memorable in cricket with Gavaskar saying, 'Before I die, the last thing that I want to see is that six that Dhoni hit to win the 2011 World Cup.' Then as the umpires signalled six, Yuvraj jumped, rushed towards Dhoni, hugged him and cried uncontrollably. At the press conference they two held hands and praised each other. 'Dhoni has magic in his hands, whatever he touches, turns to gold.' Dhoni in turn said, 'Yuvi is king, when he plays we win.'

After India had beaten Bangladesh, Dhoni had told Kirsten, 'Keep the champagne ready, we will uncork it in Wankhede.' Now it was uncorked as the Indians held up the Cup. That in itself illustrated how much the country had changed. This was a city that until the 1970s had such strict prohibition laws that in order to drink you needed a permit from the collector of customs. My father got one because his doctor said for medicinal reasons my father needed two pegs of whisky every night. Hotels had what were called 'permit rooms' where those wanting to drink went. The other contrast with 1983 was how Kapil Dev and Dhoni took to victory. In 1983, Kapil Dev had been the centre of the celebrations. In contrast Dhoni took a back seat and, while he felt tearful, he hid his tears. Tendulkar may not have scored the hundred or hit the winning run but Dhoni wanted to make sure that he savoured it. Dhoni could see there were tears in Tendulkar's eyes and he gave him an Indian flag. What followed could have been choreographed by a Bollywood director.

Kohli lifted Tendulkar on his shoulders, saying, 'If we do not lift him on our shoulders tonight, when will we? He has carried the burden of the nation for 21 years. It is time we carried him on our shoulders' and carried him around Wankhede. The picture that would go around the world showed Tendulkar on Kohli's shoulders looking skywards as he holds the Indian flag aloft. Harbhajan with tears in his eyes is next to him and also carrying an Indian flag. Dhoni in a sleeveless shirt, wearing a cap, is looking so anonymous that you have to look very hard at the picture to make out he is there. There is nothing to suggest in that picture that he has captained this side to the World Cup and hit the six that won the trophy all of India had been seeking since 1983.

Chapter 43

DHONI: CRICKET'S TEFLON MAN

These four years stamped Dhoni as the most exceptional cricket captain in Indian history, but this did not mean he was always successful, indeed far from it. In the four years after India won the World Cup they played twelve Test series starting with a tour of the West Indies and ending with the tour of Australia in the winter of 2014. Dhoni won five of the series, lost seven, but only one of the victories came abroad.

And while his home victories were spectacular, a 4–0 whitewash of Australia, there was a series defeat against England for the first time in twenty-nine years. Away from home Dhoni found it difficult to win: fifteen of his eighteen Test match losses were abroad and between 2013 and 2015 he became the first Indian captain to lose four consecutive Test series, against South Africa, New Zealand, England and Australia.

Some of these defeats, particularly in England and Australia, suggested that talk of the new India Dhoni had launched with his six in Mumbai in winning the World Cup was overblown. I covered both the series defeat in England and Dhoni's team, far from being the new India, was very much the old one away from home, often crumbling without a fight. Those defeats also included the loss of a one-day series in Bangladesh, making him the first Indian captain to lose any series in that country.

Yet despite this Dhoni was spared the fate of many other Indian captains who had not survived such dreadful defeats. He dictated his own departure in a very Dhoni-style in the middle of a Test series, carried on as captain of the one-day side and even now, having given up the one-day captaincy, continues to play white-ball cricket. Indeed, at Lord's in 2018 he played a one-day innings even more incomprehensible than the one Gavaskar had played in the 1975 World Cup. He had become Indian cricket's Teflon man, defeat never clung to him or dented him in any way. Dhoni's reign was threatened but he did not capitulate.

DHONI BEHAVES LIKE GANDHI BUT FAILS TO BEAT THE RAJ

Dhoni began his first Test series after the World Cup with a win in the West Indies. This was India's first full tour for five years and it is a measure of how

West Indian cricket had declined that India's greatest batsman Tendulkar decided that as his kids were on their summer holidays just as the tour was taking place this was an ideal time to take a break from cricket. Tendulkar was behaving like England's leading cricketers had done when deciding not to tour India in the 1950s and 1960s. In the first Test in Kingston India gave Test debuts to three cricketers Virat Kohli, Abhinav Mukund and Praveen Kumar. India set West Indies 326 to win and won by 63 runs.

India might have won the second Test at Bridgetown but rain washed out four sessions. The last Test at Dominica could have seen an Indian victory had Dhoni been more adventurous. For the first time there was some criticism of 'Captain Cool' with the Indian press talking of how baffling it was that he made no genuine attempt at victory. It highlighted the contrast between the great finisher in one-day matches who was not willing to take risks in Test cricket. The real fault lines in his captaincy emerged when he brought the team to England in the summer of 2011. Then a few days after auctioning his World Cup bat for £100,000, his and India's world fell apart.

This happened literally within hours of the start of the first Test at Lord's on 21 July 2011. The Lord's crowd had barely digested their lunch on the first day when Dhoni made the sort of history he did not want to make. Zaheer Khan broke down after fourteen overs and Dhoni became the first ever wicketkeeper at Lord's to take off pads and bowl which Kapil Dev felt was 'demeaning to Test cricket'. England made 474–8 declared and it required a Dravid century, 103, for India to narrowly avoid the follow-on. India were still in the match when the fifth day began. England had set India 458 to win. India were 80 for 1, Dravid and Laxman were still there and Tendulkar was yet to come. There was much speculation that India could win if Tendulkar finally scored a hundred at Lord's which would also mark his hundredth international hundred. Tendulkar himself had been asked about it before the Lord's Test with some commentators saying he had missed the West Indies tour to make sure Lord's was the venue for the great occasion. This was the hundredth Test between the two teams and the 2,000th Test since March 1877.

The final morning saw huge queues, many didn't get in, and Lord's was filled to capacity at 27,728. But Tendulkar found it difficult to pick the bowling of Chris Tremlett and Stuart Broad against the background of the new Media Centre. Tremlett and Broad are tall and the dark-coloured steps above the sight screen meant Tendulkar could not see their hands as they bowled. He made 12. To be fair to Tendulkar he had developed a viral infection on the third day and felt dreadful by the evening of the fourth day. The air conditioning in his hotel room was leaking and he spent the night in a wet room, all of which resulted in his finding difficulties with his balance when he came to bat. The other Indian batsmen had no such excuse and with the last four wickets falling in twenty-nine balls, India lost by 196 runs.

The remaining three Tests were played against a background of constant media hype as to whether Tendulkar would score his hundredth century before the series ended. India lost all the three Tests at Trent Bridge, Edgbaston and the Oval, the last two by an innings. At the Oval, Tendulkar for the first time in the series, looked like getting a hundred but on 91 was given lbw to Tim Bresnan by umpire Rod Tucker. Batting outside his crease, Tendulkar had tried to hit a ball that came back a long way through mid-wicket and was convinced the ball was missing the leg stump. But having played such an important part in getting the Indian board to reject the Decision Review System (DRS) he could not appeal and had to mourn in silence. An analysis would show that had India had DRS in the series they could have successfully reversed quite a few decisions, though given India's overall cricket it is doubtful it would have made any difference. Later that year when Tendulkar met Tucker, the Australian joked that his friends had given a lot of grief to him for giving him out and Tendulkar, by now having got over it, had a laugh with Tucker. The series whitewash, as in 1959, 1967 and 1974, meant India in England were again left consoling themselves with individual achievements, Dravid's three centuries at Lord's, Trent Bridge and the Oval, giving him an average of 76.83—Tendulkar averaged 34.12, even below Amit Mishra who was in the side for his bowling and batting No. 8—showed once again his mastery of English conditions.

But in many ways the most dramatic moment of the series had come on the Sunday of the Trent Bridge Test when Dhoni suddenly decided to play Gandhi who, of course, had no interest in the game. Ian Bell on 137, thinking his partner Eoin Morgan had hit a four and that this was the last ball before tea, wandered down the wicket to congratulate Morgan before heading to the pavilion for a cuppa. What he did not realize was that Praveen Kumar, the Indian fielder, had kept the ball in play and when he returned the ball Bell was stranded.

The crowd were incensed. Strauss, the England captain, told me:

> We saw Ian Bell walking off for tea and India appealing and the umpires gave him out. It didn't feel right to me. The first thing I wanted to do was clarify with the umpires what the rules say on it. So, we went down to talk to the umpires. They said, look, 'By strict

adherence to the rules, he was out. The ball wasn't dead and he strayed from his ground. The only way he's not going to be given out is if India withdraw their appeal.' I thought I'll try and have a word with MS. Andy [Flower, England coach] was with me and we asked to see MS and Duncan Fletcher [India coach] and I requested that they withdraw their appeal. He went back to the players to discuss it. I'm very conscious to highlight the fact that all we did was request and then the decision was solely theirs. Bell clearly wasn't attempting to run, he was walking off for tea. In the true letter of the law, we all knew that he was out, but it's one of those situations where if common sense prevails, you withdraw the appeal, you get on with the game. It was definitely the right decision and I really applaud MS Dhoni for making it. It was a spirit of cricket thing. If he had said no it would have damaged our relationship with India. We would have felt very aggrieved.

Dhoni's decision raised questions about cricket and morality. The next morning I was interviewed on BBC Radio 4's Today programme. Listened to by eight million listeners every morning, the programme is a must for politicians and the entire British chattering classes. The cricket authorities were quick to hail the Indian decision as proof that, even in an age where sport is so corrupted, the cherished spirit of the game survives.

However, Indian opinion was divided. The older Indian cricketers were all in favour of the decision, but this sentiment was not shared by many younger Indians. They passionately wanted India to remain the top cricket nation and believed that sporting success comes, not from moral goodness, but from the desire to win at all costs.

And those most upset were the Indians living in Britain. They had seen this Test series as a chance to showcase the new India to England—it was not just call centres but a land of sporting champions. To them Dhoni acting as a sort of cricketing equivalent of Mahatma Gandhi was a sign of weakness not strength. For many of these supporters, victories on the cricket field mattered more than moral rectitude in the dressing room. India losing its No. 1 Test status was not compensated by being morally superior.

Interestingly, Dhoni himself said little about this and throughout the series, as India were ever more ferociously battered, he sounded like a technical engineer inspecting a broken-down plant as he kept saying this was all part of the process. His other explanation for defeat was even more extraordinary: that India played 70–80 per cent of their cricket at home, and touring was more about personal improvement. India also lost the one-day series and the only T20 match. The only consolation for Dhoni was that his 236 runs in white-ball cricket won him the Man of the Series.

ASHWIN EMERGES

Back in the 1950s India consoled themselves after a dismal performance in England by coming home and beating New Zealand. It is a measure of how the balance of power in cricket had changed that Dhoni's men took it out against the West Indies, once a team that made India quake. The West Indies had a first-innings lead in two of the three Tests but couldn't press home their advantage. In contrast India made sure it closed Test matches, taking an unassailable 2–0 lead thus making the third Test irrelevant. The series was notable for Ravichandran Ashwin making his debut in the first Test in Delhi, proving he was not only a find as an off-spinner but could also bat. His story is very much part of the new generation of Indians whose parents do not discourage them from playing sport and it was on his mother Chitra's advice that he decided to make the switch from bowling pace to spin. Ashwin had started as an opening batsman. When he was fourteen, he injured his pelvic area. The horrific injury resulted in a tear in the ligaments between his hip bones. This caused blood to leak into the bone joints. The injury was a blessing in disguise. When he got back to the game, he found his opening spot had been taken so Chitra suggested he try his hand at spin bowling.

SOUTHERN GREATS FADE, A GREAT NORTHERN STAR SHINES

The win over the West Indies, despite their current lowly status, was a boost and India arrived in Australia just about favourites to finally win a series.

If one ball can be said to define a series then it was the fourth ball of the final over of the second day in the first Test at Melbourne. Tendulkar had been applauded all the way to the middle. He had reached 73 when Peter Siddle bowled him. Siddle had followed new bowling coach Craig McDermott's orders to pitch the ball up to allow away-swing. The next morning seven Indian wickets fell before lunch. India having been 214 for 2 were all out for 282. And although the bowlers fought back, Ponting and Michael Hussey took the game away. Set 292 to win, India were all out for 169 and Australia won by 122 runs. However, what was encouraging was that crowds flocked to see the Indians. The Test had the highest ever Test attendance between the two countries: 189,347, and the entire series was to see record crowds.

The crowds were a mix of Indians living in Australia and many native-born Australians keen to see their team thrash the Indians. In Sydney, Australia won by an innings and 68 runs. In Perth, in the third Test, the Australian winning margin was an innings and 37 runs and Australia regained the Border–Gavaskar trophy.

However, in this doom and gloom there was one moment of solace. This was in the batting of Virat Kohli. He had been part of the one-day side and on the England tour had made a wonderful white ball century at the Oval. But coming into the Adelaide Test it was by no means certain Kohli would make the transition from one-day cricket to Test cricket. When choosing the team for the West Indies tour the selectors, Srikkanath, Yashpal, Raja Venkat, Bhave and Hirwani, were not sure about Kohli becoming a Test player. Venkat had the most doubts. Kohli had made the tour because Yashpal, a selector from Delhi and a member of the 1983 World Cup winning team backed him. Sharma, who had spotted Sehwag in an Under-19 camp, argued that while Kohli did not have the technique of Gavaskar, 'Virat was fearless. His eyes spat with fire when he took guard and that convinced me to back him.' Yet, in the West Indies having hit a four as his first scoring shot in Test cricket, he was out the next over and made 76 runs in three Tests. He was not originally part of the Test squad in England, and came in after there were injuries, but did not play a Test or a single first-class match. Against the West Indies at home he had only been brought in for the third Test with the series decided. Now in Australia in the first Two Tests his scores were 11, 0, 23, 9. There was talk he might be dropped for Perth but was retained and had the good fortune to bat with Laxman. If anyone in Test cricket knew how to make runs against the Australians it was Laxman and his advice was Kohli should wait for the ball to come to him rather than reach for it as Kohli had done at Melbourne and Sydney. Laxman had made that mistake in 1999 and then, he told Kohli, he had learnt how to play in Australia.

In Perth, Kohli made 44 and 75 and this proved a dress rehearsal for Adelaide where in the first innings Kohli made 116, the only Indian to make a century in the series. His four-hour innings was full of stunning square drives and confident pulls though he did have nervous moments. On 99 he survived a run-out, it was a suicidal run, and was sledged by Ben Hilfenhaus. There had been a war of words going on between Kohli and the Australians since Sydney and now on reaching his century Kohli shouted at Hilfenhaus. Kohli would not repeat what was said just saying, 'I gave it back to him. Ishant and I came together and got stuck into them and they got really pissed off. I usually play my cricket like that and I like to give it back. To give it back verbally and then score a hundred is even better.' In the Sydney Test Kohli had shown his anger by raising a middle finger at the crowd for saying 'worst things' about his mother and

father and was fined 50 per cent of his match fee. It was clear that while
he might be the next batting star, his behaviour would be nothing like
Laxman or Dravid, let alone Tendulkar.

Kohli headed the Indian batting but his average of 37.50 showed how
poor this once mighty batting order had been reduced to. Only Tendulkar
averaged more than 30. Dravid averaged 24.25, Laxman 19.37 and Sehwag
24.75. Towering over them was Ashwin, third in the batting with 32.60.
Little did Indians know that the old order was about to change. The Test in
Adelaide would be the last time the Indians would see Dravid and Laxman
play for India. The two greats of Indian cricket were departing. Only one
of the Fab Four remained but then Tendulkar was special, although there
was speculation as to how long he would carry on. India had now lost
eight overseas Tests on the trot.

There was one shaft of light in this gloom when Tendulkar did get to
his hundredth century but the final result of the match was very deflating
for India. It came in the Asia Cup one-day tournament in Mirpur against
Bangladesh on 16 March 2012. A single against Shakib Al Hasan took him
to the magic figure off 138 deliveries, having hit 10 fours and a six. He was
finally out for 114 and India made 289 but Bangladesh responded so well
that they won by five wickets with four balls to spare. However, Tendulkar
did not retire and no one had any idea when he might go.

However, two others of the Fab Four departed. A month after his return
from Australia, Dravid had announced his retirement. Two years earlier, in
an interview with me, he had hinted that he was thinking of retirement,
he had a young family with whom he would like to spend more time.
But he also told me then that his remaining ambition was for India to win
a series in Australia and South Africa. The defeat in Australia showed this
was impossible. Dravid rang Papu Sanzgiri, whom he knew well, to tell
him that he was retiring. When Sanzgiri asked why he replied, 'Enough is
enough.' For a great sportstar to decide when to leave the stage is often the
most difficult decision. Michael Vaughan told me how agonizing it can be.
Dravid left the podium before there was any danger he would be hauled
off, with a grace that matched his career. Laxman was still there but Dhoni
had not taken his calls for some time, leaving Laxman uncertain whether
Dhoni wanted him to go. He was named in the squad for the visit by
New Zealand, but five days before the first Test Laxman announced his
retirement, clearly judging he had no place in Dhoni's plans. Both Dravid
and Laxman spoke movingly on their retirement about how the country
mattered more than personal interest but Laxman went away into the sunset
with some critics claiming he had been holding up young players. Dhoni

had also raised the question of when the Master Blaster might retire; he was told sharply by Srinivasan that Tendulkar was one member of the old guard he could not remove.

ENGLAND AGAIN PUT DHONI UNDER PRESSURE

India easily won the two Test series against New Zealand 2–0. But two months later when England came calling, Dhoni and India's world was turned upside down. India was confident that Dhoni and his men could put the summer of 2011 right. Certainly, the Indian media expected victory with Star TV running jingoistic promos suggesting India would hammer England and get badla [revenge] for the horrors of 2011. India won the first Test by ten wickets and in Cheteshwar Pujara, who had scored 159 in the first Test against New Zealand, and now made 206 not out, India seemed to have found a replacement for Dravid at No. 3.

But in Mumbai, England led by a masterful Pietersen innings surprised India, winning by ten wickets. It was only India's second home defeat in twenty-four Tests and had come on a supposedly turning track; India had played three spinners. The third Test in Kolkata saw England win again by seven wickets. India failed to win at Nagpur and lost their first series at home to England since 1984–85.

What was fascinating was how the Indians and the English saw the Test series. The Indian board did not seem to mind, having had an income of around £100 million in 2011–12. Alastair Cook considered the victory in India as one of the landmark achievements of his career. A few years later he told me, 'India was a fantastic achievement and in a few years' time maybe people will sit down and start talking about how good an achievement that was as an England side to win there and to win like we did.' Then acknowledging that his side had out-bowled and out-batted the Indian side at home he added, 'That doesn't happen very often to an Indian side so we can be very proud of that. To me the Ashes is always going to be slightly ahead just because it is the Ashes, such big, historic rivalry. But the Indian victory ranks very highly in terms of our achievement.'

Dhoni, who won the one-day series that followed, made it clear one-day cricket mattered more to him by saying that the pain of the Test defeat was 'not even close' to that of India being eliminated from the 2007 World Cup.

But the defeat did make the Indians ask if Dhoni was indispensable. After the defeat in Australia Dhoni's captaincy was discussed by the selectors with one of them, Mohinder Amarnath, keen to sack him. But Srinivasan, the board president, who had developed close links with Dhoni through Chennai Super Kings, would not hear of it. Amarnath was told that Srinivasan as board president would decide who the Indian captain was, not the selectors. As for Sehwag taking over from Dhoni, Srinivasan curtly told him to concentrate on his batting and his fitness. Srinivasan would later admit he had vetoed Dhoni's sacking saying, 'How can you drop someone as captain within a year of his lifting the World Cup.' Yet this is exactly what had happened to Kapil Dev and it showed how Indian cricket had changed since 1984. One reason for this was when Kapil was sacked there was a captain waiting in the dressing room, Gavaskar. As we have seen he and Kapil swapped the captaincy. However, unlike Gavaskar, Tendulkar had no desire to resume the captaincy. Nevertheless, after the Nagpur Test there was a candidate. Kohli had scored a century and Gavaskar went on television to say, 'Till the 4th day...I would have backed Dhoni [as captain]. Now that Virat has come up with a hundred under trying circumstances where he curbed his natural game, he discovered a good part about himself... He is ready to take on the mantle of Test cricket...that is where the future lies.'

Privately, Dhoni was telling friends he was helpless against media attacks. At the end of the Nagpur Test, Dhoni, clearly under pressure turned to Tendulkar asking him why he couldn't say publicly the batting had failed. Tendulkar reminded Dhoni that Indian fans were full of mood swings and a win would set them right. Sure enough there was an opportunity to change the Indian mood and change it dramatically.

DHONI BACK AT THE TOP

Less than a month after Cook and his men departed the Australians arrived. Dhoni was determined to prove that he was still the man in charge and the best way to demonstrate this was with the bat. In Chennai in the first Test in February 2013, Clarke, now captain, made a century, Dhoni's response was 224, his first and only double century and with Kohli making 107, India made 572. Ashwin, who had taken 7 for 103 in the first, took another five-fer in the second. India's victory by eight wickets was a formality.

In the second Test at Hyderabad India did not even have to bat in their second innings winning by an innings and 135 runs, Australia's tenth heaviest defeat. But there was one Indian failure. In the only Indian innings Sehwag scored 6. He did not play for India again and the man who had been such a remarkable Indian opener, the first and still the only one to make a triple hundred, disappeared from the scene to which he had brought such cricketing brilliance. He went nursing deep resentment about how he had been discarded. He would have liked to have gone back to batting in the middle order before leaving but that was not possible. For Dhoni this was no bad thing, for Sehwag had played the role Borde had played in the Pataudi era, the senior, established man denied his chance to lead India by a younger interloper in the shape of Dhoni. Now he was gone.

India won the Mohali Test by six wickets and the fourth in Delhi by the same margin. Here Pujara orchestrated the pursuit of 155 with an unbeaten 82. Dhoni was with Pujara at the end and hit the winning boundary to secure victory inside three days.

By the end of the series only one of the greats remained, Tendulkar. However, Sandeep Patil, who had become chairman of selectors in September 2012, had spoken to Tendulkar, a man-to-man talk between the two Maharastrians about when Tendulkar might want to retire. There was speculation that Patil had told Srinivasan that Tendulkar's time was up—in twenty-one Tests since 2011 he had averaged only 31, although Patil would dismiss such reports as nonsense. But the figures did tell of a decline. He had not scored a Test century since 2011. In twenty-three Tests after the 2011 World Cup his average was 32 when before that it had been 57. Before the World Cup Tendulkar was bowled or lbw 34 per cent of the time, after it was 49 per cent. As the 2012–13 season ended the question of when Tendulkar would go hung in the air. He had already given up one-day cricket and in this format, as Patil would reveal later, the selectors did think of dropping him:

> On December 12, 2012, we met Sachin and asked him about his future plans. He said he did not have retirement on his mind. But the selection committee had reached a consensus on Sachin...and had informed the board too about it. Perhaps Sachin understood what was coming because at the time of the next meeting, Sachin called and said he was retiring (from ODIs). If he had not announced his decision to quit then, we would have definitely dropped him.

So, there was no place for him in the squad for the ICC Champions Trophy that Dhoni brought to England in the summer of 2013.

DHONI, THE ONE-DAY CHAMPION

Dhoni may have been indifferent to the Test defeat in England in 2011 but he was determined to win the Champions Trophy this time and from the first match India went at it with a gusto that was remarkable. Nothing fazed India and nobody could stop Shikhar Dhawan. In his first match against South Africa, Dhawan made 114, in his second against the West Indies, 102, against Pakistan, a relative failure, 48, then in the semi-finals, 68, and in the final, which rain made a 20 over match, 31. His 363 runs were 134 more than anyone else and he had a strike rate of 101. He also struck up a wonderful opening partnership with Rohit Sharma, having opening stands of 127, 101, 58, 77 and 19. The Indian fielding was electric. And Ravindra Jadeja, like Dhawan, a player England did not know much about, showed what he could do with both bat and ball. He played crucial parts in the wins against South Africa and the West Indies. Dhoni played the same side throughout the tournament, even in the match against Pakistan, despite it being a dead rubber as India by then had qualified for the semi-finals. This was the most eagerly awaited match of the tournament and the one that attracted the most eyeballs. India won by eight wickets, ensuring that India headed the group, having won all three matches. Pakistan went home having lost all three matches and finishing at the bottom.

The final showed how Dhoni was still master of the one-day format. Rain reduced it to twenty overs with the match starting at 4.20 p.m. and going on until 8.30 p.m. The Indian batting for once failed, making only 129 for 7, three batsmen reaching double figures, Kohli 43, Jadeja 33 not out and Dhawan 31. It could have been worse but for Kohli and Jadeja rescuing India from 66 for 5 with a 47-run stand in thirty-three balls.

But the score seemed no problem for England. With sixteen balls left to be bowled, England needed 20 and had six wickets in hand. This is where Dhoni showed his shrewdness as captain as he had done in Johannesburg. He kept his faith in Ishant Sharma, despite the fact that he had gone for runs and bowled wides which would have been wides even in Test matches. When Sharma was bowling so wildly Kohli and the team thought India would lose. But Sharma did not fail Dhoni. He recovered his composure and India won by 5 runs. England had proved to be chokers once again in an international 50-over tournament and the victory could not have been sweeter. The Indians in Britain had come in large numbers throughout the tournament. Now they outnumbered the English at Edgbaston, making Dhoni and his players feel very much at home.

THE GOD DEPARTS

It was perhaps inevitable that Tendulkar's departure from cricket would be like no other. Even then the way it was organized was amazing. The ICC Future Tours Programme had India touring South Africa which would mean his 200th Test, the right time to depart, would be in Newlands. But for Tendulkar to be seen the last time on foreign soil was unthinkable. So, the South Africa tour was cut in half, and the West Indies asked to advance their visit, scheduled for 2014, by twelve months.

And now Tendulkar did something that no cricketer would have dreamt of doing. He asked Srinivasan if the second Test against the West Indies could be assigned to Mumbai. Tendulkar would get his mother, who had never seen him play live, to come and what better place to do this than his home ground. And so the mighty West Indies, whose very arrival in India would once have made India tremble with fear, were reduced to being extras at Tendulkar's farewell party. In the first Test in Kolkata, India won by an innings and 51 runs. India won so easily that Kolkata could not bid farewell to Tendulkar as it had planned. Kolkata wanted to mark his 199th Test showering Eden Gardens with 199 kilograms of rose petals, and to distribute 65,000 Tendulkar face masks to the crowd. But with the game over by the third evening time ran out. Brian Lara, Tendulkar's only equal—although some think Lara was greater—was supposed to be there. But he was still in mid-air when the match ended. The Bengal chief minister, being in the city, could come to Eden Gardens to felicitate Tendulkar but even she had to cancel all her appointments to do so.

The second Test in Mumbai was really about Tendulkar. For the first time his mother watched him play. Tendulkar walked out through a guard of honour on opening day, precisely twenty-four years since his Test debut in Karachi. On stumps on the first day he was 38. The next morning the ground filled up fast as he reached 74. Every ball of his innings had been watched by the crowd in a mixture of fear and anticipation, fear he might get out, anticipation he would produce another one of his great shots. Now he tried to cut off-spinner Narsingh Deonarine fine, and Darren Sammy at slip took the catch. The stunned crowd took several seconds to react, then gave a standing ovation.

The way the match had gone India would not be required to bat again but the crowd cheered Chris Gayle in the hope the West Indies would make enough runs to make this happen and Tendulkar would again stride out to the middle. However, their wishes did not come true and Tendulkar's farewell matched that of Bradman in the cricketing sense—like Australia at the Oval in 1948, India also won by an innings. But there was much more emotion, with the Indian players giving their own very special send off and Tendulkar normally a reluctant and hesitant speaker, addressing the crowd and having a little joke at Achrekar's expense:

> On a lighter note, in the last 29 years, Sir has never ever said 'Well played' to me because he thought I would get complacent and I would stop working hard. Maybe now he can push his luck and wish me 'well done' in my career, because there are no more matches, Sir, in my life.

The most touching moment came when Tendulkar returned to the dressing room and sat by himself. Kohli approached him and with tears in his eyes gave him the threads his father had given as a present. Then he did something which only one other Indian cricketer had ever done. Some years earlier Vijay Manjrekar, who by then had retired, was in Baroda. He asked Jayant Lele, then the board secretary, to take him to the home of Vijay Hazare who lived there. Lele and Manjrekar travelled to Hazare's home on a scooter. When they arrived, and Hazare opened the door, Manjrekar prostrated himself before Hazare and touched his feet. When Lele later asked him why he had done such an extraordinary thing. Manjrekar speaking in Marathi, told Lele, 'I reckon there are only two great batsmen from India. One my idol Hazare and the other one is me. I don't count Gavaskar.' Manjrekar, as usual, was being controversial and trying to bring down a star who had emerged after he retired. Hazare's reaction to Manjrekar is not known. Now as Kohli touched Tendulkar's feet the great man, totally taken aback, asked him why he was doing this and told him Kohli should be hugging him instead. He then asked him to leave as he felt if he said anything more he would burst into tears. Here it is worth noting that it was Manjrekar, a Hindu, touching the feet of the Christian Hazare but in Kohli's case he was touching the feet of a Brahmin.

DHONI'S SWAN SONG

As the fixture programme panned out for India the next four Test series were all away from home. India lost the series in South Africa. The crucial Test was the first one in Johannesburg. India set South Africa a world-record chase of 458, actually came close to getting beaten and Dhoni lost faith that Ashwin, his main spinner could win matches away from home. Ashwin in the second innings did not take a wicket and Dhoni got so frustrated that he even took off his pads and bowled two overs.

The draw had a disastrous impact on India, who lost at the second Test at Kingsmead by ten wickets.

India's next stop was New Zealand in February 2014 where Dhoni's captaincy began to unravel in a way that suggested something had to give. India arrived top of the one-day rankings but lost the five match one-day series 4–0; the fifth was tied. They had not lost a Test to New Zealand since December 2002. Now they lost the first Test in Auckland, by 40 runs. The defeat in Auckland meant Dhoni had suffered eleven Test defeats abroad, a record for an Indian captain, and had not won abroad since June 2011.

India had opportunities to win the second Test at Wellington's Basin Reserve but could not close out the match. Dhoni's captaincy enraged Ganguly, '[Dhoni's] Test captaincy has been obnoxious... If the World Cup was not less than a year away, I would have agreed that Dhoni needed to be removed as captain.'

DOES DHONI CARE ABOUT TESTS?

India were back in England in the summer of 2014 for their first five-Test series since 1959. Off the field there was no question that India called all the shots. Rod Bransgrove, chairman of Hampshire, which hosted the third Test of the series, told me: 'In 1959, the Indians came here on sufferance, now the English want the Indians to come because India is a big market and England can make huge money by selling its television rights to the Indian market. It makes an Indian tour in the economic sense, though not emotionally, even bigger than Australia.' On the field it would prove a different story.

The Test series began promisingly. After a draw in the first Test on a dreadful flat pitch, the second Test at Lord's could not have gone better for India. On a wicket made for English opening bowlers and in true English conditions, India outplayed England. So much so that India set England 319 to win. However, as lunch approached on the fifth day England were still in the match

In the book, *Moeen*, that I wrote with Moeen Ali, he told me:

> Rooty [Joe Root] and I were still together and playing quite well. I was confident. I felt we had a chance as long as Rooty and I stuck together. I didn't feel I was going to get out and Rooty was obviously playing really well. Our target was now below 150, these landmarks are important when you are chasing. Then just before lunch Ishant Sharma came on. Dhoni and he had a chat and Dhoni persuaded him to bowl at me round the wicket. I went down the wicket and had a chat with Rooty and I said, 'Rooty, what do you think? Shall I take it on, or shall I just ride out the short ball?' Rooty said, 'Just play the way you have been playing.' There was a bit of doubt in my head, because of that lack of clarity I got into a terrible position and the last ball before lunch he got me with a short ball and I gloved it to Pujara at short-leg.

Ali's departure opened the floodgates and after lunch in a sensational period of play, what Boycott called 'mind boggling batting', three England batsmen hooked straight to a fielder on the boundary. Sharma got three wickets in seven deliveries. India won by 95 runs. So desperate was England's condition that Cook, the England captain, thought of giving up Test cricket. But having reached the heights Dhoni seemed to give up. India lost the next three Tests, each performance worse than the one before. In Southampton in the third India lost by 266 runs, the fourth at Old Trafford by an innings and 54 runs and the last Test at the Oval by an innings and 244 runs, both the last two Tests in three days. For the first time in thirty-six years India had lost three Test series in a row.

Dhoni did not seem to care. He missed nets two days before the final Test to visit the Metropolitan Police Specialist Training Centre in Gravesend. It reflected his interest in the armed forces. He was a honorary lieutenant colonel in the paras of Indian Army and when this was raised in a press conference on the eve of the match he grew very defensive. India did win the one-day series quite comfortably 3–1. So did this suggest Dhoni had had enough of Test cricket?

Later events suggest he had begun to think he should give up the long-form game. However, for the moment nothing changed. After all, if Kohli was to be Dhoni's successor then he had a terrible England tour, always falling to Jimmy Anderson. His scores had been 1, 8, 25, 0, 39, 28, 0,7, 6 and 20 averaging 13.50 in his ten innings. For the winter of 2014 Dhoni took the Indian team to Australia for both Tests and one-day matches. Yet change was coming and as it can often do in India it came dramatically.

THE NINTH WAVE

INDIA IN TEST CRICKET

Wave	Period	Mts	Won	Lost	Drawn	Tied	Win%	W/L
9th	2015–2018	46	28	9	9	0	60.86	3.11

TOP BATSMEN IN NINTH WAVE

	Mts	Runs	Hs	Avg	100	50
V. Kohli	44	4066	243	59.79	15	10
C. A. Pujara	41	3353	202	54.08	12	14
A. M. Rahane	42	2411	188	38.88	6	11
M. Vijay	30	1794	155	36.61	7	5
K. L. Rahul	32	1775	199	35.50	4	11
S. Dhawan	21	1492	190	43.88	5	3
R. Ashwin	41	1354	118	25.54	2	7
R. A. Jadeja	29	1121	100★	38.65	1	9
W. P. Saha	28	1017	117	33.90	3	5
R. G. Sharma	17	923	102★	38.45	1	8

★Not out

TOP BOWLERS IN NINTH WAVE

	Mts	Wkts	Best	Avg	5WI	10WM
R. Ashwin	41	223	7/59	22.64	17	5
R. A. Jadeja	29	147	7/48	21.63	7	1
Mohammed Shami	28	97	5/28	26.34	2	0
I. Sharma	29	80	5/51	27.23	2	0
U. T. Yadav	29	76	4/32	31.51	1	1
J. J. Bumrah	10	49	5/54	21.89	3	0
B. Kumar	9	34	5/33	18.50	2	0
A. Mishra	9	33	4/43	25.84	0	0
Kuldeep Yadav	6	24	5/57	24.12	2	0
H. H. Pandya	11	17	5/28	31.05	1	0

TOP WICKETKEEPERS IN NINTH WAVE

	Mts	Dismissals	Ct	St
W. P. Saha	28	79	69	10
R. R. Pant	9	42	40	2
P. A. Patel	5	23	21	2
K. D. Karthik	3	7	6	1

ONE-DAY INTERNATIONALS

Wave	Period	Mts	Won	Lost	NR	Tied	Win%	W/L
9th	2015–2019	76	50	23	1	2	65.78	2.17

TOP BATSMEN IN NINTH WAVE

	Mts	Runs	Hs	Avg	SR	100	50
V. Kohli	61	3848	160★	81.87	98.33	17	15
R. G. Sharma	61	3419	208★	65.75	98.41	15	12
S. Dhawan	57	2483	132★	45.98	98.49	7	13
M. S. Dhoni	73	1867	134	44.45	80.92	1	12
A. M. Rahane	36	1378	103	41.75	80.20	1	15
K. M. Jadhav	48	925	120	46.25	108.56	2	4
A. T. Rayudu	20	728	124★	60.66	83.77	2	4
H. H. Pandya	42	670	83	29.13	114.52	0	4
M. K. Pandey	23	440	104★	36.66	91.85	1	2
K. D. Karthik	18	387	64★	48.37	73.85	0	2

★Not out

TOP BOWLERS IN NINTH WAVE

	Mts	Wkts	Best	Avg	RPO	4W
J. J. Bumrah	44	78	5/27	21.01	4.44	5
Kuldeep Yadav	35	69	6/25	21.23	4.81	3
Y. S. Chahal	35	62	6/42	23.75	4.73	3
B. Kumar	53	61	5/42	36.59	5.30	3
H. H. Pandya	42	40	3/31	40.95	5.55	0
U. T. Yadav	27	39	4/71	37.38	6.45	1
A. R. Patel	25	29	3/34	34.79	4.43	0
R. A. Jadeja	28	28	4/29	46.71	5.05	2
K. M. Jadhav	48	22	3/23	31.18	4.90	0
A. Mishra	9	19	5/18	22.78	5.10	1

TOP WICKETKEEPERS IN NINTH WAVE

	Mts	Dismissals	Ct	St
M. S. Dhoni	73	99	67	32
R. V. Uthappa	3	4	3	1

TWENTY20 INTERNATIONALS

Wave	Period	Mts	Won	Lost	NR	Win%	W/L
9th	2015–2018	57	39	16	2	68.42	2.43

TOP BATSMEN IN NINTH WAVE

	Mts	Runs	Hs	Avg	SR	100	50
R. G. Sharma	48	1498	118	34.04	145.01	4	8
V. Kohli	37	1195	90*	51.95	139.92	0	10
S. Dhawan	40	1131	92	31.41	135.93	0	9
K. L. Rahul	25	782	110*	43.44	148.38	2	4
S. K. Raina	34	658	69	25.30	134.01	0	2
M. S. Dhoni	43	638	56	42.53	145.00	0	2
M. K. Pandey	28	538	79*	41.38	122.83	0	2
H. H. Pandya	35	271	33*	16.93	153.10	0	0
K. D. Karthik	17	252	48	84.00	160.50	0	0
Yuvraj Singh	18	209	35	19.00	107.73	0	0

*Not out

TOP BOWLERS IN NINTH WAVE

	Mts	Wkts	Best	Avg	RPO	4W
J. J. Bumrah	40	48	3/11	20.47	6.77	0
Y. S. Chahal	27	44	6/25	18.75	7.81	3
Kuldeep Yadav	17	33	5/24	12.96	6.74	2
H. H. Pandya	35	33	4/38	23.96	8.00	1
R. Ashwin	20	27	4/8	17.07	6.49	1
B. Kumar	25	22	5/24	28.36	6.90	1
A. Nehra	19	21	3/23	23.04	7.22	0
R. A. Jadeja	18	17	2/11	26.70	7.26	0
J. D. Unadkat	10	14	3/38	21.50	8.68	0
W. Sundar	7	10	3/22	16.90	6.03	0

TOP WICKETKEEPERS IN NINTH WAVE

	Mts	Dismissals	Ct	St
M. S. Dhoni	43	51	29	22
K. D. Karthik	9	9	6	3

The figures go up to and include India's series in Australia, December 2018–January 2019.

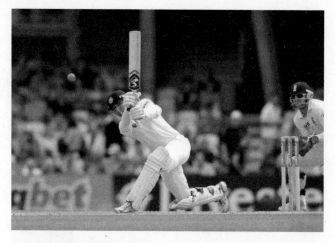

Dravid was the only success of a dismal batting performance by India in England in 2011. He was christened the Wall and this shot was one of his classics (Bipin Patel).

Kohli flying the flag in England during the ICC Champions Trophy, 2013 (Bipin Patel).

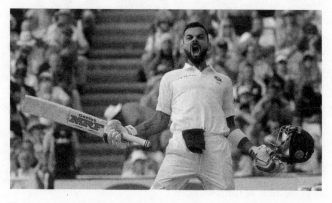

Kohli roars on reaching a century at Edgbaston in 2018, a roar that echoed around England (Bipin Patel).

Kohli on his way to making a hundred at Edgbaston, first Test, 2018 (Bipin Patel).

Kohli, the modern face of Indian cricket, kisses his wedding ring (Bipin Patel).

Shami, one of the faces of the new Indian pace attack, recreating the world of Nissar and Amar Singh (Bipin Patel).

Sharma, a vital member of India's, now feared, pace attack (Bipin Patel).

Kumar, rated by English critics as superior to English swing bowlers (Bipin Patel).

Pandya walks back after his 5-fer in the victorious Nottingham Test (Bipin Patel).

Kohli and Ashwin, widely seen as the professor of spin (Bipin Patel).

Kohli, the captain, conferring with Shastri, the coach, he wanted (Bipin Patel).

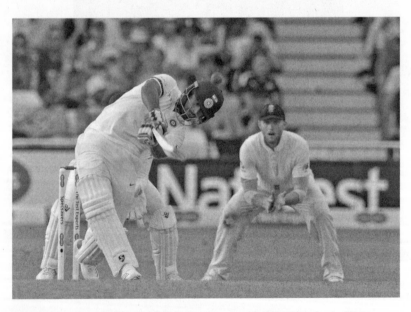

Pant, India's new wicketkeeping find, hitting his second ball on debut for six (Bipin Patel).

Shaw (L), India's latest batting sensation, with Pathak, the man who brought him to England (Pathak Collection).

Dhoni gets an honorary doctorate from De Montford University, 2011 (Bipin Patel).

Dalmiya, the Marwari businessman from Kolkata, cricket's great money-maker, (Mid-day Infomedia).

Indian fans celebrating India's victory in the one day international at Nottingham in 2018 (Nottingham CC).

The striking face of a modern Indian cricket fan, summer 2018 (Bipin Patel).

The subcontinent comes to England, India–Pakistan crowd, Edgbaston, 2013 (Bipin Patel).

Chapter 44

KING KOHLI

NOT QUITE GOLD AT THE OVAL

On Monday, 5 June 2017, Virat Kohli held a charity ball at the Honourable Artillery Club in the city of London. The event organizers advertising the ball said:

> Virat Kohli has established himself as an icon of the cricket world, a hero to a nation of 1 billion people. As captain of the Indian side in all three formats, he follows in the footsteps of Sachin Tendulkar and MS Dhoni as the face of Indian cricket. Virat is arguably the leading batter in the world game and is leading his country to the UK for the Champions Trophy in 2017. He will take this opportunity to share his drive to use his popularity to create opportunities through The Virat Kohli Charity Ball.
>
> The Virat Kohli Charity Ball is the manifestation of a dream to inspire and bring about a transformative change to the future of the country. Virat's chosen causes will be a key theme of the night and connected to leading charitable causes in India.
>
> Virat will be joined on the evening by some of the greatest names in the game both past and present who will divulge some of the thrills and spills of their international careers in a live interview on stage. Virat will be bringing friends from the Indian cricket team who will help make this star-studded evening one not to miss.

It was not cheap to have dinner with Kohli. The platinum table seating ten went for £5,950, the gold table at £2,750 and the silver table cost £1,950.

The event could not have been better timed. It was held the day after India beat Pakistan in their opening fixture in the Champions Trophy. Kohli's men ran riot, making 319 for 3 in forty-eight overs. All first four batsmen made fifties. Kohli made 81 not out in sixty-eight balls with 6 fours and 3 sixes. Pakistan were bowled out for 164 with only one batsman making 50.

Kohli was being hailed by Indians in Britain and with past Indian greats led by the greatest of them all, Sachin Tendulkar, in attendance. The event was also attended by Kohli's teammates. The cricketers' entry into the hall was greeted with fanfare just as if they were visiting royalty. Also present was Vijay Mallya, who was wanted in India for defaulting on bank loans worth nearly Rs. 9,000 crore; having been declared an absconder, he was fighting extradition to India. In December 2018 a court in London ruled that Mallya should be extradited from the UK to India to face fraud charges.

But just as Dhoni hosting such an event before the 2011 Test series saw India defeated, in the Champions Trophy final on 28 June 2017 at the Oval, Pakistan got their revenge by beating India, with Kohli, the master chaser, failing as India were set a target of 339 to win.

The defeat widened the already growing rift with coach Anil Kumble. The day after the match there were secret meetings in London hotel rooms to try and resolve the rift between coach and captain. As we shall see, the solution that was found raised major questions about Kohli's power and his relationship with coaches. Kohli had taken over the leadership of Indian cricket unexpectedly. Now he was determined to prove he was a king with real power.

A SUDDEN CALL TO BECOME KING

Nobody in India could have anticipated that when India arrived in Australia in November 2014, they would leave with a new captain. Dhoni missed the first Test in Adelaide, but that was due to a broken thumb and Kohli captained India in his stead. He had stood in for Dhoni before, in one-day internationals, but he had never before captained in a Test. Right from the beginning he showed he would be different to Dhoni. The man from Ranchi had often looked bored and preoccupied during Tests. The Delhi man led from the front. He scored 115 in the first innings and then, after Australia set India 364 in ninety overs, he was determined to go for a win and not just draw the match. Kohli made 141, but India—not helped by some rash batting towards the end—lost by 48 runs. However, Kohli had made history. His aggregate of 256 was the highest by a first-time Test captain. On getting out to Nathan Lyon, Kohli had hung his head, looking devasted for some time. But after the match he had recovered his sangfroid and said that going for victory is how he saw Test captaincy: 'This is what we play cricket for.' For an Indian captain to be so eager for a win, and that when captaining abroad in his first Test, was unheard of.

In the second Test at Brisbane, Dhoni was back. The Australians won by four wickets, but what was encouraging was India now had a pace attack that could worry sides away from home. Thirteen of the sixteen wickets India took in the match were by their pacemen. Australia needed a draw to regain the Border–Gavaskar Trophy and did so at Melbourne. With Australia making 530 India could have been under pressure at 147 for 3. It was then that Kohli was joined by Ajinkya Rahane and they put on 262 for the fourth wicket, the third-highest partnership for any Indian wicket outside Asia. The batting of these two showed both differences in style and temperament. Kohli feasted on Mitchell Johnson's bowling, 11 of his 18 fours were off him and this so riled the Aussie paceman that he hurled the ball at the striker's end and hit a doubled-up Kohli, leading to an angry exchange. Rahane, amidst the sledging, was calmness personified.

The real drama came after Steve Smith, the Australian captain, and Dhoni had decided the match was a draw and called play off. Then, minutes after Dhoni had held his post-match press conference, the BCCI issued a press release saying Dhoni was quitting Test cricket. There had not been a whisper he might go. He had spoken to no one about it. Even his family was in the dark. At the end of the match Dhoni had just rung up the board to say he was going. Shastri, the team director knew nothing. A team meeting was hastily called. In the second Test there had been problems in the Indian dressing room between Dhawan and Kohli. Now, all the players were united in grief at Dhoni's departure and some of them wept. Years later, Dhoni's only explanation was, 'I just felt it was the right time and the right thing to do.' Dhoni having played ninety Tests, sixty of them as captain, had had enough of a form of game for which he now felt little affection. In contrast, he still loved the one-day game and remained in charge.

So, like Pataudi, Kohli became the second Indian to take over the Test captaincy in the middle of an away series. For the first two days of the Sydney Test it looked as if Kohli, like Pataudi, would start with a defeat. But then, helped by K. L. Rahul, Kohli scotched any hopes of an Australian victory. Rahul scored 110. Kohli made 147, the first player to score three centuries in his first three innings as Test captain. India were set 348 to win on the last day, but once Kohli was himself out he decided a Adelaide-style dash for victory was not on and settled for a draw. The win was not enough for Australia to leapfrog South Africa and go to the top of the Test rankings; they remained second. But India were a poor seventh, only ahead of the West Indies, Bangladesh and Zimbabwe. Kohli knew he had a mountain to climb, but at least there was the World Cup to look forward to. India were champions and the Indians living in Australia were determined to come out in large numbers to support the team.

DHONI'S LAST HURRAH

The Indians filled every ground where India played. The crowds that came to watch the Indians at the Adelaide Oval and the Melbourne Cricket Ground (MCG) were described as staggering. Every match felt like a home match. As if energized by this, India won seven successive matches, all six of their Pool matches, starting with a win over Pakistan, and the quarter-final against Bangladesh. They seemed to have both batsmen and bowlers who could perform. If Kohli did not make runs, Dhawan did, and their bowlers were always bowling sides out. India bowled out all seven sides and often not for much: Pakistan made 224, South Africa 177, the West Indies 182 and Bangladesh, who had eliminated England, 193.

But in the semi-final they met Australia, who, having stuttered so far and losing to New Zealand, rediscovered their form. India should have felt at home. The wicket at Sydney was a slow turner. There were more Indian supporters than Australians, more Indian flags than Australian, and shouts of 'Jeetega bhai jeetega.' [We shall win, brother, we shall win.] drowning out the Aussies. But Steve Smith, who had never made a one-day century against India (though he had made four in the Test series) now made one. India could not bowl Australia out, and with Kohli falling for 1, India were beaten by 95 runs. The Australians went on to win the trophy.

The World Cup defeat meant Duncan Fletcher, who had been coach since Kirsten, now had to make way for a new man. The Indian board after three overseas coaches, decided to go desi, 'Indian coaches for the Indian team'. Ravi Shastri, who had been director of cricket since the disastrous England tour, now took complete charge.

THE SWIFT CLIMB TO THE TOP

Kohli's reign began with a draw in Bangladesh in a rain-ruined match and it was the three-Test tour of Sri Lanka in August 2015 that was the real start of his reign. India had not won in Sri Lanka since Kohli was a five-year-old and in the first Test suffered a defeat which could have been shattering. India had dominated the Test, been set a very gettable 176 but made 112 and lost by 63. No Indian batsman reached 40. This was only the second time India had failed to chase a target below 200, Barbados in 1997 being the first. But what followed showed that while Kohli the batsman might not have yet been in the same class as Tendulkar, as a captain he was far superior.

India won a crushing victory in the second Test at Colombo by 278 runs, an all-round batting and bowling performance. It was not only Kohli's first win but India's first win in ten Tests since Lord's in 2014. In the past, such success could have made India complacent, but Kohli showed his India was different by beating Sri Lanka in the third Test—also at Colombo—by 117 runs. Kohli's team had done something no Indian team had done away from home: win a series after falling behind 1–0.

Kohli's India took another stride when, in October, South Africa arrived for a three-Test series. South Africa was a challenge, having had fifteen unbeaten consecutive series away from home since their last defeat in 2007. They also began by winning the one-day internationals 3–2 and the T20 internationals 2–0.

What could Kohli do when he took over in the Tests? His first Test as captain on home soil was on his twenty-seventh birthday. He won the toss and while he made 1 and India only 201 on a wicket prepared for spinners, the South African batsmen had no answers to Ashwin, and were beaten in three days. After a draw in the second Test, with only one day's play possible before rain set in, India won the third in Nagpur by 124 runs and the fourth in Delhi by 337 runs. Kohli was not pleased that critics talked about India preparing pitches for spinners. Do they not prepare pitches for seamers abroad? He also felt that his bold captaincy was not being given enough credit. Kohli had been saying that India needed to win abroad. Winning in Sri Lanka was not really abroad as it was a triumph in familiar conditions. The West Indies, where India arrived in July 2016, was something else.

India had often begun away tours with defeat. Kohli was determined to change that. In the first Test at Antigua he made an unbeaten double century, the first by an Indian captain overseas. With Ashwin also scoring a hundred, Kohli could do something that not many of his predecessors had often done before in overseas Tests: he declared. Kohli called his men in when India had made 566 for 8. The story of Indian cricket overseas is their batsmen tormented by pace. Now it was the turn of the Indian pacemen led by Mohammed Shami, back after a year having recovered from knee injury, to show what Indian pacemen could do. With the West Indies bowled out for 243, Kohli enforced the follow-on and now it was Ashwin's turn. He took 7 for 83, his fourth seven-fer in Tests. India won by an innings and 92 runs. The victory could not have been sweeter. It was the first time they had won by an innings in the Caribbean, and their biggest win outside Asia.

Rain played a part in saving the West Indies from another defeat at Kingston in the second Test. In the third Test, India's first innings score of 353 proved a match-winning total. What was noticeable was that the Indian bowler doing the damage was not a spinner. It was Bhuvneshwar Kumar with his swing. He had not played for nineteen months. Now he caused a sensational collapse. The West Indies went from 202 for 3 to 225 all out, seven wickets for 23 runs, Kumar taking five of the seven wickets. India, unexpectedly given a lead of 128, built on it and set the West Indies 346 in seventy-nine overs. It was a mark of the new India Kohli was building that for the third Test in a row Kohli had declared. No Indian captain had ever been in such a position before. This time, with all the bowlers sharing the wickets, the West Indian innings lasted less than forty-eight overs. India won by 237 runs. History was made. This was the first time India had won two Tests in the Caribbean. India would have become the top ranking Test side had they won in Trinidad but rain meant only twenty-two overs were possible in the entire match and that on first day.

The winter of 2016 featured series against New Zealand, a first visit by Bangladesh and then England. Historically England should have been the one India worried about most. But Ravi Shastri made it clear it was New Zealand that would provide the biggest test. Perhaps he was trying to make sure India was not complacent. It certainly worked. India won the three Test series 3–0, with Ashwin often causing sensational batting collapses. India won the first by 197 runs and the second by 178 runs. What was interesting in this victory was that while the spin of Ashwin and Jadeja got wickets so did Kumar and Shami. Although these were straws in the wind now, even in India, it was not all spin anymore.

The third Test was in a new Test ground, Indore, C. K. Nayudu's home patch. Kohli added 365 with Rahane, India's highest ever for the fourth wicket. Kohli also set a record, becoming the first Indian captain to score two double centuries. India won by 321 runs with a day to spare. The spare day was useful for Kohli, and his men celebrated becoming the top-ranking Test team in style. Kohli had reason to be proud. From January 2015, when India were No. 7, Kohli had taken them to No. 1 by October 2016.

BREAKING DOWN THE ENGLISH

Kohli's juggernaut did receive a check in the first Test against England in Rajkot. Indeed, Moeen Ali, England's Man of the Match believes that England could well have won that match had Cook timed their second innings declaration better. As he told me:

> Cooky might have judged the declaration better had he not been batting. He scored a hundred, becoming the first Englishman to score 1,000 Test runs in India and it is possible he was thinking more of that than when to declare.

The result was Cook set India 309 in a minimum of forty-nine overs. England bowled fifty-three overs, but there were not enough to bowl India out. India were six wickets down, but one of the not-out batsman was Kohli who held out for a draw. England had won morally, but as Kohli would show, that did not lead to Test victories. However, the Indian captain was clearly rattled. He reacted much as Dhoni had done in 2012, berating the Rajkot groundsman about leaving grass on the pitch. In 2012, this had done Dhoni little good. Now, as Ali says, Kohli benefited:

> The wickets were not vicious turners as Indian wickets can be. They were quite flat; really good wickets. The ball came down a little bit slower but very simply in the next four Tests after Rajkot their batters scored a lot more runs than ours and their bowlers bowled better than ours. At crucial moments England dropped catches. In the second Test at Visakhapatnam Kohli top edged Stokesy [Ben Stokes] and Rash [Adil Rashid] at fine leg floored him. Kohli was then 56, he went on to make 167, India made 455 and after that we were always struggling.

Kohli set England 422 to win and after some resistance from the openers, England collapsed to lose by 246 runs. It was after this that India really got on top, helped by the fact that they batted deep. At Mohali in the third Test, England, after being bowled out for 283, took five Indian wickets for 156, but then Ashwin, Jadeja and Jayant Yadav scored 72, 90 and 55, taking India to 417 and a lead of 134. England could set India only 103 to win. India won by eight wickets.

The fourth Test at Mumbai was historic. The last time India had played a Test in Mumbai without Tendulkar was in 1988. The crowd still remembered him, but Kohli, who was not even one month in 1989, was quick to impress on them that there was now a new star. After England had made 400, Kohli took over. Murali Vijay, who made a century, and Pujara had made sure of a solid start. Kohli walked out with the score a reasonable 146 for 2. He did not get out until India's score was 615. In heat that stifled even the locals he made 235. Earlier in the year Kohli had discovered his BMI was among the lowest of any cricketer's and this innings proved how fit he was. England duly collapsed for 195, and India won by an innings and 36 runs. Ashwin, who had taken 6 for 112 in the first innings, went even better in the second with 6 for 55. The final day's play lasted barely an hour.

It had looked likely that England would be spared further punishment as the fifth Test at Chennai was threatened by the weather. Cyclone Vardah had swept through the city four days before, uprooting thousands of trees. But ground staff used trays of hot coals to dry the pitch to enable the match to start. England made 477 in the first innings, their best batting since Rajkot. And when India batted, England restricted Pujara and Kohli to 16 and 15. But Rahul missed his double century by a single run and Karun Nair, who was only playing his third test, having made his debut in Mohali, made 303. It put Nair in exalted company. Only two other batsmen had scored more when making their maiden Test hundred: Sobers with 365 not out and Simpson with 311. Faced with India's 759, a deficit of 282, England folded. India's margin was an innings and 75 runs. England had set up all sorts of unwanted records. The first team to lose by an innings after scoring 477, and this was India's highest ever Test score.

Kohli's aggregate of 655 was 255 more than any other Indian batsman, and his average of 109.16 was almost Bradmanesque. Kohli had in him the sort of showmanship that no Indian captain had ever displayed before. In Mohali, after Ashwin had successfully reviewed a lbw decision against Stokes, Kohli put his fingers to his lips, looking like a schoolmaster and apparently trying to calm things down when he actually stirred them up. However, those who know Kohli, like Ali, say there is more than one side to him:

> Kohli comes across on TV as aggressive and always wanting to get in a fight. While India was fielding he would gesture to the crowd to get behind the team almost in the style of a football player and in this series he certainly tried to rile Stokesy. However, I had played cricket with him from our Under-19 days and spent a bit of time with him. Off the field I knew he was a very nice, friendly guy with whom I never had any problems. The public perception of a human being and the reality can often be different and Kohli illustrates that perfectly.

During India's tour of England in 2018 Kohli dined with Ali at his home in Birmingham, and as Kohli himself has said, when they meet they rarely talk about cricket. Indeed, at the dinner with Ali, Kohli asked him about Islam and had quite a discussion about religion.

LEARNING FROM DEFEAT

In 2016, India had played twelve Tests, lost none and won nine. The record in white-ball cricket was more mixed. As of January 2017, India were third in one-day rankings and second in the T20s. They had lost one-day internationals and T20s in Australia, won the Asia Cup but lost the T20 World Cup despite the fact that it was played at home. The loss had come in the semi-finals against the West Indies in Mumbai, who won the competition. There was consolation that Kohli's batting had lit up the tournament, averaging 136.50, Pakistan had again been beaten and overall the Indians could claim that nothing like this had been seen in the history of Indian cricket. Kohli was now such a figure in world cricket that when in February 2017 India beat Bangladesh by 208 runs their captain, Mushfiqur Rahim, said sorrowfully, 'Unfortunately, our team doesn't have a Virat Kohli.'

Kohli had every reason to feel Australia, the next visitors, would leave echoing the same sentiments. But Australia so surprised Kohli and his men that the series was not decided until the final Test. The first surprise was the damage their spin did. In Pune, hosting its first Test, the virtually unknown Australian left-arm spinner Steve O'Keefe, took twelve wickets, six in either innings, and in the first caused a sensational Indian collapse of 7 for 11. India went from 94 for 3 to 105 all out. Australia had not handed out such a pasting to anyone since 1950. India did not make more than 107 in either innings, and Australia won inside three days by 333 runs.

India won the second Test in Bengaluru, although this was to lead to one of those explosive moments that have often marked Kohli's captaincy. India had set Australia 188 to win. When Smith was trapped lbw by Umesh Yadav, making the score 74 for 4, the stadium erupted. Then ensued the most controversial moment of the tour. Smith asked his partner, Peter Handscomb, for guidance and he suggested asking the dressing room and Smith turned in that direction. Umpire Nigel Llong intervened: no referral, a batsman had to decide on the field. Kohli, who would later say the Australians were always seeking advice from the dressing room, was not happy to put the incident aside. Smith would call it a 'brain fade', but Kohli saw it differently. Asked afterwards if Smith had been cheating, he said: 'I didn't say that—you did.' However, when an incensed Australia demanded proof for Kohli's claim, the Indian board, which under Dalmiya might have fought, decided not to. Australia could still have won. They were 101 for 4. But then after tea the last six wickets went for 11 runs. Australia were all out for 112, Ashwin taking six wickets. India had won by 75 runs.

The third Test at Ranchi, a first for Dhoni's birthplace, was drawn; batsmen in both teams had a blast, scoring freely. So, a series India was supposed to wrap up saw Australia go into the last Test knowing a draw would mean they would hold on to the Border–Gavaskar trophy. And for the third time in the series there was a new venue at Dharamshala, where the Dalai Lama, having fled the Chinese, had made his home. Just as Waugh had visited Mother Teresa in Kolkata, Smith visited the Dalai Lama and said that had given his team perspective. The ground could not have looked more beautiful with its stunning Himalayan backdrop. Australia started as favourites, all the more so because with Kohli out with a shoulder injury, Rahane was captain. India batting second secured a first innings lead of 32, hardly a winning position. But then with Yadav leading the attack, India reduced Australia to 106–6 and bowled them out for 137. Ian Gould, the English umpire, was full of admiration and said, 'The Indian bowlers today reminded me of the great West Indians of the 1980s, relentless in their attack, with both pace and spin.' There could be no higher praise. The innings also showed the tension between the teams, and it boiled over when Murali Vijay claimed a catch which cameras showed hadn't carried. Smith was on the boundary edge and lip-readers saw Smith forcefully questioning Vijay's integrity. India, needing 106, lost two wickets for 46 but then Rahul and Rahane saw them to victory. The margin of eight wickets sounded convincing but India knew what a close shave it had been, and for Kohli for the first time since becoming captain it meant batting misery. Just 46 runs in five innings with a highest score of 15. His average of 9.25 placed him eighth in the Indian batting table, only ahead of Ashwin and the bowlers.

KOHLI FALLS OUT WITH INDIA'S WISEST CRICKETER

The victory over Australia was a turning point for Kohli and Indian cricket. His relationship with Kumble had broken down. It had begun so well. Kumble knew Kohli was from a different Indian generation which needed to be given an opportunity to express themselves. In Kumble's generation, team meetings were long and juniors often did not get a chance to express their real views. Kumble had decided not to impose his views, and with the help of Ashwin a charter of do's and don'ts, a sort of team Bible, was drawn up. Ashwin says it was meant to bring the team together: 'We wanted to create a sense of oneness at all times.' But now this oneness between Kumble and Kohli had dissolved. Even as the team came to England for the Champions Trophy it was clear they could not continue to work together. The rift between the two had first developed during the England tour. There were various stories about its causes. That they had differences over selection; that Kumble liked to send out instructions to Kohli when he was on the field. In May 2017, Kumble asked the BCCI for an extension of his contract. They consulted Kohli, at which point Kohli made clear his views. He even suggested Kumble should not be with the team when it went to England for the Champions Trophy. But while the board would not go that far, they looked at alternatives, including Sehwag. A shortlist was drawn up which, apart from Sehwag, included Tom Moody, Richard Pybus, Lalchand Rajput and Dodda Ganesh.

Things got worse during the Champions Trophy. The day after the Champions Trophy final, board officials met both Kumble and Kohli in a London hotel. Kumble denied there were any problems, Kohli insisted there were and it was obvious what the solution was. India could not do

without Kohli, and Kumble was dispensable. Player power had won out.
But Kumble's departure was handled by the board with poor grace. India
was due to fly out from London to the West Indies for five one-day
internationals and a T20. Kumble had an ICC meeting to attend, and as
the team left London they were told Kumble would join them later. The
team arrived in Port of Spain and there learnt that Kumble had resigned.
He had also written a letter to the BCCI saying, 'It was apparent the
partnership was untenable. I therefore believe it is best for me to move
on.' There was no word on who would replace Kumble. M. V. Sridhar, the
BCCI's general manager and a former Hyderabad batsman, took over, not
that the Indian team cared. They frolicked on the Caribbean beaches, had
bonding sessions on jet skis, beat a divided West Indian side 3–1 in the 50
over white-ball cricket but lost the solitary T20. India went home to find
Ravi Shastri had returned as coach, although the word on the grapevine
was that the three-member Cricket Advisory Committee set up in 2015
and consisting of Tendulkar, Laxman and Ganguly, were not unanimous.
Ganguly was opposed to Shastri but was overruled.

KOHLI AND SHASTRI

A year later in London, talking to Shastri during India's 2018 tour of
England, when I asked him about how, having once done the job, he
came back, his answers were quite interesting and suggested he felt he had
unfinished business:

> I did the job for two and a half years. I left because they wanted a
> change, so I went back to my job [in the media]. Then, again, they
> opened up the applications for the job. This was after the Champions
> Trophy. So, that's when I applied. The reason I applied was I couldn't
> believe that you work so hard to take this team from 6, 5, 5 to 1, 1, 2
> [Tests, One-day, T20 rankings]. So, I said, go back in there and make
> sure things are okay. Unfortunately, it panned out the way it did with a
> great player [Kumble] but I was doing television at that time without
> having a clue when the applications came up what was going on.

And when I asked him how he had reacted to being presented as Kohli's
man, his reply was sharp. 'I don't care what people think, as long as he bats
like that and gives me results. I don't care two hoots.'

A picture taken after Shastri took over showed how different this new
relationship was. A beaming Shastri is putting his arm around Kohli, who
purrs with the delight of a cat with the cream. Shastri has always been close
with Kohli. After Kohli's failure in England in 2014, he advised him to widen

his stance and stand outside the crease to cope with late swing. It would expose him to being hit but Kohli had never been scared of fast bowling. Kohli set to work on his technique three hours a day on his return to Delhi, by the end of which his hands and legs ached. The results were to be seen on the 2018 tour. But important as this relationship with Shastri was, both men knew that they had to produce results; in the year that followed the Champions Trophy defeat, Kohli and Shastri found that after quite amazing results for the rest of 2017, the next frontier, namely, winning away from Asia, was not easy to cross. Kohli was still King but now he began to face questions about how he was handling the obligations wearing the crown imposed. How far was he taking Indian cricket to that Nirvana of consistent success that has always been India's great cricketing dream?

KOHLI AND TENDULKAR

Players of different generations are impossible to compare. Football is endlessly debating whether the Brazilian Pele is the greatest or if the honour should go to the Argentinian Diego Maradona, his countryman Lionel Messi or the Portuguese, Cristiano Ronaldo. In cricket it is widely accepted that the greatest batsman was Bradman. Yet he played cricket almost wholly against England with one series each against South Africa, West Indies and India. In Australia there was then eight balls an over. However, there was no limited overs cricket, let alone red- and white-ball cricket. But there is no questioning his record and every batsman who comes after will be compared to him as Tendulkar was and now Kohli is.

As we have seen Bradman felt of Tendulkar, 'the fella plays much the same as I used to play. I can't explain it in detail but there is a similarity. It's his compactness, his stroke production. It all seems to gel. That was how I felt.' Bradman did not see Kohli but had he done so then I feel he would have classified him along with Brian Lara as the greatest of his generation, slightly more aggressive than Tendulkar, but Tendulkar ahead of both Kohli and Lara because he was the more all-round batsman.

In many ways Kohli is standing on Tendulkar's shoulders. The Tendulkar age saw cricket revolutionized with different formats of the game being established: red ball for Tests, white ball for limited overs, and this further refined into 50-over and 20-over matches. But while Tendulkar never played international T20 cricket, he has played for Mumbai Indians, Kohli joyously participates in all cricketing formats and yet makes it clear that he values Test cricket and sees supremacy in Test cricket as most important. He has played an important role in making sure that, despite attracting very few spectators, and many of them elderly, Test cricket continues to produce some of the most enthralling cricket we have ever seen.

An interesting contrast between Tendulkar and Kohli is whether bowlers feel they can get them out. Both the South African Makhaya Ntini and the Englishman Steve Harmison thought they could get Lara out. Ntini, who could swing the ball in, bowled Lara behind his legs four times, Harmison had Lara caught at slip off short-pitched deliveries. But, as Mike Brearley, who considers Tendulkar 'the most complete batsman I have seen', points out, while Lara could be more aggressive Tendulkar never gave 'any bowler such rays of hope'.

Now contrast this with Kohli. In England in 2014 he was like a meek lamb slaughtered by Jimmy Anderson. The feeling was the Englishman had only to get to his bowling mark and Kohli was mentally shot. But as 2018 showed he learnt from that awful experience and coped with Anderson proving to English critics that he had both the technique and the mental ability to learn from adversity. That is always a mark of greatness.

This also illustrates a contrast between Tendulkar and Kohli. Tendulkar always gave the impression ever since he made the boys from my school cry that he had emerged as the finished product. Kohli, in contrast, has throughout his career had to fight to prove his worth. Could he be a one-day player? Could he make the Test scene? Could he make runs in England? Vengsarkar called him the lambi race ka ghoda, the horse for long distance races, and that is what he is now proving to be. This means that when he reaches the end of the race, and given how long and complicated a cricket career can now be, he may well set up records that go way beyond anything achieved in cricket and put Tendulkar in the shade.

However, what he is not likely to do is make great foreign experts of the game feel he is not Indian. Brearley looking at Tendulkar felt, 'You wouldn't know from his style of play alone that he was Indian. He could have been from anywhere. He was firmly grounded, his feet apart in his stance. He had a perfect defensive technique, along with a wonderful ability to turn defence into attack with the minimum of flourish.'

Nobody could say that of Kohli. He is the modern Indian both on and off the field. He is also showing signs of eclipsing Tendulkar in one respect: leadership. For all his greatness with the bat, Tendulkar as captain did not take India to new frontiers. Kohli already has and there are signs that he could conquer worlds no Indian captain ever has. There is in that sense a ruthless streak in him that is very un-Indian. To see him bat he may, unlike Tendulkar, look very Indian. In the way he leads he may prove the most un-Indian of captains.

Chapter 45

THE JUDICIAL REVOLUTION

The Indian Supreme Court acting like a modern day Brahma and creating a new BCCI, so radically different from the one Anthony De Mello produced back in 1928, is one of the most extraordinary stories not only in world cricket but world sport. And that it all began as a result of a police operation which started in Marine Drive is rather special.

It was called Operation Marine Drive U-turn and saw police gather in the early hours of 16 May 2013 in a cul-de-sac at the end of Marine Drive, where I and my friends walked every evening when growing up in the 1960s, often discussing the latest twists and turns in Indian cricket. From their vantage point the police could hear the crowds shouting and cheering at the Wankhede Stadium where a Rajasthan Royals IPL match was going on that night. Sreesanth, having played in that match, drove off to have a few drinks at a Bandra night club. But his celebrations were disturbed a few hours later with the police hauling him from his car and arresting him as they did two other Rajasthan Royals players along with eleven bookmakers in a coordinated police action all over India. This was part of an investigation into spot-fixing. The players maintained their innocence. They would eventually get bail but were banned from all cricket by the BCCI. Sreesanth during his first five days in jail shared an overcrowded dormitory with men accused of rape and murder and was so traumatized by the experience that he thought of killing himself. In July 2015 he was acquitted by the Delhi High Court, by which time he had decided to pursue a career in entertainment.

Unlike the 2000 match-fixing scandal, not only were players arrested, but Sreesanth could not have been more high profile. But even at this stage while the story had similarities with that scandal it did not appear to pose any threat to the BCCI. However, there had been a fundamental change in Indian cricket since then. The formation of the IPL meant that the BCCI was no longer a voluntary body. There were now companies which were an essential part of the national cricket structure. Companies getting involved in cricket is not new. The Times of India Shield in my youth employed some of the best cricketers in the country and that inter-company tournament produced cricket more gripping than the Ranji Trophy and spectators watched for free. Nirlon was a major force in this tournament but, apart from employing Gavaskar and other cricketers, Nirlon's managing director did not run Indian cricket. Observe the contrast with Narayanaswami Srinivasan, who was board president in 2013. An industrialist like the Nirlon boss, he also owns an IPL franchise, Chennai Super Stars. The player relationships have also changed. Gavaskar was a paid employee of Nirlon, Dhoni is a vice president of India Cements, the Srinivasan company that owns Chennai Super Kings. So, when on 24 May 2013, Gurunath Meiyappan, often described as the boss of Chennai Super Kings, was arrested by the Mumbai police and charged with forgery, cheating and fraud, this story took on an entirely different meaning.

Meiyappan is the son-in-law of Srinivasan. Srinivasan had described Sreesanth and the other cricketers as 'few rotten eggs'. Now he had to explain what role his son-in-law played in the franchise he owned. This raised the question often asked during the Watergate hearing—what did President Nixon know and when did he know it. Like Nixon, Srinivasan played his cards disastrously.

The wise thing to have done would have been to step down as president immediately. But he did not. Bindra, an old opponent, tried to oust him and used an article I had written for the *Sunday Times* in October 2010 for this purpose. My story in the *Sunday Times* was about how the anti-corruption unit of the International Cricket Council was investigating why a report linking a current Indian Test player with an associate of an illegal bookmaker had allegedly been covered up by the Indian board. The article was based on information given to me by a high-placed ICC source, who was also an insider in the BCCI, and dealt with an incident on the 2010 Indian tour of Sri Lanka.

In 2013 Bindra on his website recycled what I had written saying, 'Mihir Bose filed this story in *The Sunday Times,* which was rubbished by the BCCI spokesperson, and Sri Lanka Cricket Board was arm-twisted into denying the whole episode.' He then went on to say, 'After decades of being a part of the great game of cricket, and having served Indian cricket in various positions, I believe that this is the worst crisis faced by Indian Cricket.' When the board met, Bindra called for Srinivasan's resignation, but he was the only one. As in the 2000 corruption crisis the BCCI appointed its own enquiry committee, confident that it would ride out the storm. What it had not considered was the consequences of a decision it had taken back in September 2001.

REVENGE OF THE MAN FROM BIHAR

The decision concerned Bihar cricket after the new state of Jharkhand was carved out of the southern portion of Bihar. Cricket officials in this new state set up the Jharkhand State Cricket Association. The logical thing would have been to welcome the newcomer and allow the old Bihar Cricket Association, going since 1935, to carry on. But with the Bihar Cricket Association electing Lalu Prasad Yadav as its president, Dalmiya, then president of the BCCI, who clearly did not like Lalu Prasad, threw Bihar out of the BCCI. Aditya Verma, secretary of the Bihar Cricket Association, told me: 'To throw Bihar out was a very shocking incident. They did it because they did not like Lalu Prasad Yadav.'

Over the next twelve years, Verma tried and failed to get back into the BCCI. He quickly saw the spot-fixing crisis as his great opportunity. In May 2013, Verma went to the Mumbai High Court, not ostensibly about getting Bihar back in but about how the BCCI was responding to the match-fixing enquiry. Soon the case was before the Supreme Court. And this is where Srinivasan and the BCCI failed to understand that unlike in 2000 the country's highest judges were prepared to be interventionist. Cricket in the IPL era was a business and needed to follow acceptable corporate governance rules.

On 8 October 2013, the Supreme Court appointed a three-member probe committee headed by Mukul Mudgal, former chief justice of the Punjab and Haryana High Court, and a long-standing cricket fan, to investigate allegations of spot-fixing and betting. In June 2014, Sourav Ganguly was added to the commission as a cricketer of 'impeccable integrity', and one day, out of the blue, he rang me from Kolkata. Having, as he always does, addressed me as Mihirda, he asked me about my *Sunday Times* story in 2010. He wanted to know what additional material I had, and I tried to help him as best I could. The final Mudgal report came in November 2014 and found Meiyappan and Kundra guilty.

Back in March 2014, the Supreme Court had asked Srinivasan to step down as BCCI president but, having no powers over the ICC, could do nothing to stop him in June 2014 blithely taking over as the first chairman of the international body. The Supreme Court asked Gavaskar to run the IPL and Shivlal Yadav to become board president. When the final Mudgal report said Srinivasan was not guilty of wrongdoing, he wanted his BCCI job back, but now the Supreme Court had had enough. It set up its own three-man committee headed by a former chief justice of the Supreme Court, Rajendra Mal Lodha. Apart from determining 'the punishment to be awarded to Mr. Gurunath Meiyappan, Mr. Raj Kundra and their Franchises', which was quickly done, Lodha was, more crucially, asked to 'Recommend reforms in the practices and procedures of the BCCI and also amendments in the Memorandum of Association and Rules & Regulations'. The Lodha Committee conducted over thirty-five days of sittings in Mumbai, Bengaluru, Chennai, Kolkata, Hyderabad and New Delhi and consulted widely. On 18 December 2015, the Lodha Committee produced one of the most thorough forensic examinations of sports bodies ever conducted not just in India but anywhere in the world.

Instead of accepting the inevitable, the BCCI decided to wage what has proved a fruitless guerrilla campaign to stop Lodha. The fire that this drew from the Supreme Court has been withering and has reduced the old board structure to a pile of ashes. The result has been that a Committee of Administrators (COA) appointed by the Supreme Court now runs the BCCI. As I write, the crucial reforms of the Lodha Committee are yet to be implemented. But what can be said with certainty is the era of Dalmiya and Srinivasan is history. The whole saga shows the BCCI was living in a bubble, confident it could ignore the wider world.

As for Verma, on 4 January 2018, the Supreme Court ruled the BCCI must reinstate the Bihar Cricket Association. Verma has a reputation among Indian cricket journalists as a man who cannot stop talking. He certainly has the gift for colourful imagery. He presented himself to me as a fearless opening batsman who had played for Tata Steel and, like his hero Gavaskar, never put on a helmet even when facing very hostile fast bowling. When I asked where he got his money for fighting his legal battles, he said, 'Legal fees are not very high.' He told me with great pride that he had conducted the case. 'Three times in person I appeared myself before the Supreme Court. I faced the bowling of the judges of the Supreme Court and hit the ball out of the ground.' The Indian media have speculated that he may have been financed by Lalit Modi but Verma denied this. Between him and the Supreme Court the BCCI has been treated like net bowlers bowling to a Tendulkar or Kohli.

But while all this is going on, the cricket world continues to remind us of the power of Indian cricket. This was emphasized in Dubai on 20 November 2018. That was when a dispute panel of the ICC Dispute Resolution Committee, chaired by QC Michael Beloff, gave an award in favour of the Indian board in a case brought against it by the Pakistan Cricket Board (PCB). The PCB had claimed $63 million as compensation for India backing out of a series of matches. Here it is worth quoting a passage from the judgement:

In terms of any Indian tour to Pakistan, it was the PCB which was the suppliant. It was the host country which benefitted from the revenues in respect of such as tour. Bankrupts cannot be choosers, and while the PCB was certainly not bankrupt, at the very least sacrifice of such a tour would, as Mr Ahmad [Chief Operating Officer of the PCB] put it, 'definitely make a dent in our financial reserves'. The prospect of bilateral tours with India as tourist was, in the PCB's own words, 'the most valuable prize in world cricket' but ex hypothesi for other ICC Members, not the BCCI itself. By contrast there was no necessity for the BCCI, the dominant force in world cricket in the modern era, to play away against Pakistan. The BCCI may have had the wish, but it was the PCB which had the need.

Nothing could better demonstrate how far Indian cricket has come. India have not played a bilateral series against Pakistan since 2006. This is not the first break in cricketing relations. They did not play between 1962 and 1977. But when they did resume it was Pakistan which was on top and not merely on the field of play. As we have seen during the Packer crisis it was India who was like the child on the outside of the sweet shop looking in while leading Pakistani players were luxuriating inside. Now it is Pakistan cricket desperate to share some of the Indian sweets.

CRICKET ALONG PARALLEL LINES

However, in this period on the field of play Indian cricket does not seem to have been at all affected by Lodha. This was best illustrated in 2017, when the Indian Under-19 toured England and smashed their hosts, winning both Tests and all five one-day internationals. I attended the third one-day international at Hove where India won by 169 runs. As these young Indians put England to the sword I strolled on the boundary line with W.V. Raman, the coach of the team. I had first seen him on India's first ever visit to South Africa in 1992–93 and had been much taken by his graceful batting which comes so naturally to left-handers. The previous day there had been some further news about Lodha and when I asked Raman he looked at me as if I was talking about some object in space. As far as he was concerned his duties as coach had not been affected by Lodha. And this was the same reaction I had from Shastri when we spoke. As these men presented it, the Lodha revolution of Indian cricket seemed to be quite separate from Indians playing cricket on the field, like two parallel lines.

The match at Hove further illustrated not only how IPL had revolutionized cricket but also how there were also dramatic changes going on at the grass roots of Indian cricket. Indians who in my youth would never have got a chance are now able to dream of playing for India. The opening batsman of the Under-19 side was Prithvi Shaw who, as we have seen, was spotted by Tendulkar when he was eight. Raised by an unemployed father, he grew up in Bandra in Mumbai. Although one of his grandparents was a Bengali, he could not speak Bengali, was fluent in Marathi and considered himself Maharashtrian. He had been brought to England at the age of twelve by Cricket Beyond Boundaries, a foundation run by Samir Pathak. The Under-19 tour was Shaw's fourth visit to England.

Shaw has been hailed as the next Tendulkar. In fact, he bettered Tendulkar's Harris Shield record of 326 not out by scoring 546, and he did that at the same Azad Maidan ground where Tendulkar had first made the world sit up, batting for a day-and-half. Then, like Tendulkar, he has scored centuries on his Ranji debut for Mumbai and West Zone in the Duleep Trophy. Reflecting riches that are now available since the dawn of the age of Tendulkar, he came to England in 2017 with a contract worth Rs. 36 lakhs with Sanspareils Greenlands (SG). When he first came to England he had found the climate very cold, the food impossible, the silence unsettling (he could not hear any cars honking) and he hardly spoke English. Now he speaks English and Dravid, coach of India A, is impressed with his fluency. He has also adjusted to the very different English cricket world, in particular playing the moving ball. On the 2017 tour, Shaw made 410 runs in seven games and seven months later he led India to the Under-19 World Cup title, the fourth Indian triumph, making India the most successful nation in this tournament. Yet speaking to me he was very deferential, and whenever he referred to people like Tendulkar and Gavaskar he called them Sir. As we have seen, in October 2018 he made his Test debut against the West Indies scoring a 100 and, but for an injury, would have played against Australia. People of Shaw's generation want to emulate Tendulkar but also look up to Kohli. Now let us turn to what Kohli can do for them and where he can lead India.

Chapter 46

GET DIRTY, LOOK UGLY

NOT A NEGATIVE BONE IN INDIAN CRICKET

At mid-morning on 27 August 2018, the Indian team were relaxing in the St. James Hotel near Buckingam Palace, their usual base in London as it is equidistant from Lord's and the Oval. Five days earlier India had beaten England by 203 runs in the third Test at Trent Bridge and turned the five-Test series on its head. India had gone into this Test looking like a bakra, goat, waiting for the butcher's blade. Having just failed to win the first Test at Edgbaston by 31 runs, they had lost the second at Lord's, effectively in two days by an innings and 159 runs. The Lord's Test had lasted a total of 170.3 overs, the two Indian innings had lasted 82.2, 5.5 overs less than England's only innings. At the post-match press conference, Joe Root, the England captain, had spoken of his dream of completing a 5–0 whitewash over the No. 1 side in the world. His fellow Yorkshireman, Geoff Boycott, said the series was 'becoming a ridiculous mismatch' and if India did not 'quickly show some mental strength and discipline...this series will be an embarrassing 5–0 thrashing.' And Trent Bridge was an English fortress, England having lost only four Tests at the ground since the turn of the century.

But then, to the amazement of everyone, India did not as so often in the past, and particularly in 2014, fold their tents and pack for their flight back to India. They so dominated the Trent Bridge Test that they could have won it in four days: they had to bowl just seventeen balls on the fifth day to take the last England wicket. Indian bowlers proved just as devastating as their English counterparts at Lord's. England's first innings at Trent Bridge lasted 38.2 overs, with ten wickets falling in two-and-a-half hours and England going from 54 for no loss to 161 all out. After Lord's, Vaughan had warned that unless India's 'timid batsmen' supported Kohli, 'this series is going to be a very one-sided flop'. There was a certain irony here for, as we have seen, it was when Vaughan was captain that India had won at Trent Bridge in 2007. India's 2018 victory at the same ground was a much more commanding performance than the 2007 win, and Vaughan and the rest of the English media were soon singing a very different tune. Scyld Berry, the *Daily Telegraph* cricket correspondent, felt that the English mongoose having failed to kill off the Indian cobra, Kohli could do what only Bradman had done and come back from 2–0 down to win the series 3–2. This feat had been achieved uniquely by Australia against England in 1936–37. That such a thought was entertained even when Kohli, unlike Bradman, was playing away from home, and in a country where India had only once before won two Tests in a series, thirty-two years before, showed what an impact India's win at Trent Bridge had made. What was more, Kohli's batting in this series was better than Bradman in that 1936–37 series, with an aggregate of 440, twice that of any other batsman. To prevent 'Kohli becoming India's Don', Berry thought England would be happy with a draw at Southampton, 'knowing India would have to take risks in the fifth Test and chase the game'. And with Indian pace proving superior to England 'both in speed and quality', Berry said of Kohli, 'after a week's rest he will be riding his horses like a Cossack'.

It was Indian pace that was the big surprise at Trent Bridge. Just before the Test series had begun, Tendulkar in one of his rare interviews had sketched out how India could win. The summer of 2018 was one of the hottest on record, comparable to 1959 and 1976 when India had lost 5–0. With experts convinced that if India had to win it would be with spin, Kuldeep Yadav was seen as key. Tendulkar felt the hot weather could mean that pitches:

> ...are dry and there's potential for them to crumble on the fourth and fifth day, then it obviously would be something India will look forward to, with Ravi Ashwin, Ravi Jadeja and Kuldeep Yadav, they would want to exploit those conditions. If they play on green tops, then those spinners won't find it so easy.

Yet at Trent Bridge, India had played only one spinner, Ravi Ashwin, but four pacemen in Jasprit Bumrah, Ishant Sharma, Mohammed Shami and Hardik Pandya. After the first Test, Ashwin who had proved the master of Alastair Cook, had been hailed as a professor, but now he was more like a redundant headmaster who had been asked to step aside from the lecture room while younger teachers with more brilliant ideas took over. He was so peripheral to the victory that he took only one wicket, the last English wicket, on the final morning. The other nineteen had fallen to the four Indian pacemen. It was India's seventh triumph in England since that first Test in 1932, but no other win had been so built on pace. For me the win was very special. Having lived in England for nearly fifty years, as student and journalist, I have been privileged to watch all seven Indian triumphs and reported on six of them and three of the four World Cups India have played in England, including the 1983 World Cup win. Hours after the Trent Bridge win, I wrote a piece for *Mid-day*, a paper of which I am particularly fond as I had given the idea to start such a paper to its then proprietor, Khalid Ansari. I said:

> This one is quite the most impressive and displays a new India. Apart from the pre-lunch session on the first day, India dominated England in a way it had not done in any of the previous victories. This victory takes India to a new level as the Indian quicks have undone England. What is more, they have been faster and more lethal than English pacemen. I never thought I would ever write those words. Having watched cricket when Mumbai was Bombay and Tests were played at the CCI, I was used to Ghulam Guard, the bald-headed Bombay policeman, opening the attack and bowling just long enough to take the shine off before my hero, the great Subash Gupte, came on. I saw the age of the great spinners, Chandra, Bedi, Prasanna, and Venkat, but now to see Bumrah, Ishant and Shami torment English batsmen with swing and seam is like having all my fantasies come true. I grew up being told that Trueman so terrorised the Indian batsmen they backed away from their wicket in fear. In this Test I saw Broad back away from an Indian fast bowler. To complete this picture of the new India there is the contrast between the captain who brought India her first victory in England, Ajit Wadekar, and Virat Kohli. This Test began with Indian cricketers wearing black armbands to mourn the passing of Wadekar. Wadekar could not have been more reticent, less in your face and never showed any emotions. He certainly didn't show much at that magical moment on the Oval balcony in 1971. Kohli could not be more different. Twice in this series after scoring hundreds he has blown kisses to his wife. I cannot imagine Wadekar ever doing that. We did not even know what his wife was called, and he would not have thanked her after scoring a hundred, as Kohli did. It is also significant that at the presentation ceremony, after Kohli had accepted his bottle of champagne, his first words were to dedicate his victory to the victims of the Kerala flood. This awareness of the wider world is very much a reflection of the India that has emerged in the twenty-first century. India's cricket leaders now feel confident to talk about things beyond cricket. Also, Kohli's men not only want to win abroad but expect to do so. Wadekar's generation thought a draw abroad would

do. Perhaps, what sets Kohli's generation apart is that they can recover from debacles. Watching the defeat at Lord's I kept thinking of 1974 when India were bowled out there for 42 and just collapsed after that. Many predicted India would do the same at Trent Bridge. That they have not shows the steel and resilience they now have, something they had never shown before. Certainly not away from home.

The article had an unexpected result. To my great surprise, I got a phone call from Ravi Shastri and we agreed to meet when the team returned to London. And that is how on that Monday morning, a holiday in Britain to mark the last days of the summer, I was sitting in the foyer of the St. James with Ravi, flanked by his bowling and fielding coaches. Players like Ajinkya Rahane and Shikhar Dhawan milled around us savouring their triumph. Just then Vijay Amritraj, just arrived from Los Angeles, sauntered into the lobby and, seeing Shastri, came over and greeted him warmly. I have met Amritraj before, and he was also very friendly to me and joked about keeping Los Angeles ready for the Indian team. Later, after Shastri and his two coaches had called an Uber and driven away for their lunch, I reflected on whether Kohli could do what Amritraj had failed to do. When Amritraj first emerged on the international tennis scene in 1973, about the same time as Jimmy Connors and Bjorn Borg, much was made of the ABC of tennis, Amritraj, Borg, Connors, and how this would dominate the game. But while Borg and Connors did, the A from India did not, despite showing great promise. In 1973 at Wimbledon he came close to beating Jan Kodeš, the eventual winner, and in 1981, again at a Wimbledon quarter-final, he led Jimmy Connors 2–0 but lost in five sets. It was after that defeat that I wrote in *Mid-day* that while Amritraj's play was stylish, often sublime, in contrast to the brute strength and power of Connors, Amritraj did not have the killer instinct that Connors had. I moaned that this was the old Indian failing of not being able to close matches.

But surely it was now different with Kohli and his men. Shastri certainly thought so. During our conversation he waxed eloquent about this new India:

> There's not a negative bone in the body as far as this team goes and I'm not bullshitting. I said it after Lord's, because I know they've been in such a situation before, there's tremendous self-belief. They jolly well know they could have won it at Edgbaston. The defeat would have hurt. After Edgbaston, I said batsmen have to stand up, take ownership, accountability. So, I said 'These are opportunities that won't come again and again.' It would have hurt them even more after Lord's. After Lord's I told them, 'Forget the game.' But, then to show that self-

belief, that character, take accountability as a batting unit and come to the party the way they did at Trent Bridge is what makes this team stand out.

He dismissed criticism made after Lord's that Indian batsmen could not play swing bowling. That it revealed a faulty technique:

Not at all, because we knew that batsmen from both sides have struggled, barring Kohli. There's no one who can say that 'Consistently, I've done a great job.' You tell me one batsman from the England team for that matter who's looked solid in all the possible scenarios of this series. So, we knew that if we could put up the runs on the board, if we could be prepared to get dirty, look ugly, we could win. Get ready to get your hands dirty and look ugly in the quest for excellence.

An Indian coach taking about getting dirty and looking ugly was sensational. These were men from the land where the father of the nation was Gandhi. What did it mean, I asked?

It means, get in there and scrap it out. You're not going to get a 100 in three hours. You're going to get a hundred in six hours in these conditions. When you have Anderson, Broad, bowling with a Dukes' ball that swings all over the place, plus when you have overcast conditions, I don't care who the hell you are, you would struggle. Bradman would have had to bat six hours to get his hundred, as Kohli showed. So, that's where you have to mentally decide to get in for a scrap. It means look ugly. You might be beaten four times in an over. To hell with it. Kohli said after Lord's, it's not technique, it's mental attitude. Correct, mental discipline. You have to leave the ball. Your shot selection is important. You should be aware of what shots you can play, what you cannot. You'll still be sucked into it, but that's where the mental games come into play where you challenge yourself. You set out to do things that you have planned before the game.

Three days later India went to Southampton and, having been in a winning position several times, lost by 60 runs. The mental discipline shown at Trent Bridge had melted like an ice cream in the midday sun. The shot selection of batsmen like Rishabh Pant was quite dreadful. Pant in the first innings went twenty-nine deliveries without scoring, then in the second, when there was still a glimmer of a chance India might win, had a huge waft and was caught on the boundary. Ashwin, probably the most intellectual player in the team, was bowled at a crucial stage in the first trying to reverse-sweep Moeen Ali. Yet, on the eve of the fifth Test at the Oval, Shastri was still bullish, telling the press that this Indian team's performance away from home was the best in fifteen years. A bold claim as those years covered teams which included the Fab Four of Tendulkar, Dravid, Laxman and Ganguly and match-winning bowlers like Kumble and Zaheer Khan. Even the defeat at the Oval by 118 runs, which meant India lost the series 4–1, did not dent this confidence that this team was different to other Indian teams. At the post-match conference Dwaipayan Datta from the *Times of India* asked Kohli whether he could still argue that this was the best Indian team for fifteen years. Kohli responded, 'What do you think?' The journalist replied, 'I am not sure.' Kohli stared at Datta in much the same way he might have at an English bowler whom he had just hit for a four, as if to say how dare you think that, let alone say that to the Indian captain. Almost spitting out his words, he said 'That is your opinion.' The Indian journalists present were shocked, and, at the end of the press conference, one of the journalists went up to Datta and suggested that if he carried on like this his media accreditation would be taken away. It was said with a smile, but given how tightly the BCCI control the media, that was not quite a joke.

It must be said that the while the 4–1 defeat in 2018 was by the same margin as in 2014, this series was not remotely like that dismal one. India had lost the Pataudi Trophy but retained its No. 1 Test ranking and did not look like the bedraggled team Dhoni had led in 2014. However, the performance does raise the question how far has Kohli taken the team.

There was a revealing moment in my conversation with Shastri that showed how the Indian team management views things. Discussing the performances at Lord's and Trent Bridge, Shastri had said:

> From start to finish [of the Lord's Test] as far as I was concerned God was watching the match from the England dressing room. So, I invited God for a cup of coffee to our dressing room at Trent Bridge. It was about time, because we just didn't have the luck of the draw at Lord's. We lost the toss at Lord's.

But amusing as it is to explain success and failure by whether God comes to your dressing room, the more valid comparison is with the well-known Jewish joke about an old Jew who keeps beseeching God to help him win the lottery. Then suddenly he hears a voice from above, 'Please, Shimon, do me a favour, buy a lottery ticket.' In the year between the Champions Trophy defeat in 2017 and Kohli bringing his team back to England for the tour of 2018, the performance of Kohli's India neatly divides into two halves. In the first half, which ended in 2017, Kohli clearly brought the right-numbered lottery tickets and God was showering all his blessings on his team. But then in 2018, both in South Africa and England, India was more like Shimon expecting millions to pour in without bothering to buy a lottery ticket, and in particular this was true of their batsmen. I am writing this just a month after Kohli did what no Indian captain has done since they first toured Australia when I was a few months old. I am now seventy-two and they have won a series in Australia. The captains that preceded Kohli read like a who's who of Indian greats: Amarnath, Pataudi, Bedi, Gavaskar, Kapil Dev, Azharuddin, Tendulkar, Ganguly, Kumble, Dhoni. And this was the first time Kohli had led the team to Australia. Let us look back to see where India were before they came to England so we can better judge where they are going.

BUYING THE RIGHT LOTTERY TICKET

In 2017, excluding the defeat in the 2017 Champions Trophy Final, India were dominant across all three formats of Tests, ODIs and T20s like they had never been before. Seven wins in Tests as against only one defeat. In ODIs, twenty-one victories and seven defeats and in T20s nine wins and four defeats. Indian batsmen had made copious runs, Indian bowlers had bowled sides out. During the year Indian batsmen had made 19 hundreds in the Tests, Pujara and Kohli nine between them, and while Pujara had made more runs, 1,140, as against Kohli's 1,059, Kohli's average of 75 was superior to Pujara's 67. And when runs in all formats were taken into account, there was no catching Kohli. His 2,818 runs were 1,000 more than Rohit Sharma. And Indian spin was still all-conquering. Ashwin and Jadeja had taken 110 of the 200 wickets with Ashwin 56 at 27, Jadeja 54 at 23.

In many ways the most interesting pointer for the future had come towards the end of 2017 and, ironically in a drawn Test. By then India had won the Test series in Sri Lanka 3–0, the heaviest home defeat for Sri Lanka since Australia in 2003–04 and had also won all five one-day internationals and the sole T20 match. Then, on returning home, Kohli's men had won the 50-over white-ball cricket series against Australia 4–1. Now, playing Sri Lanka at home, India won again, 1–0, but in the drawn Test at Kolkata there was a transformation in the Indian attack which was astounding. Kohli, in preparation for the series in South Africa, which was days away, had asked for wickets to suit conditions there which meant help for pace bowlers. Kolkata provided a 'liberally grassed' wicket and his pace attack delivered. For the first time in 262 home Tests, no Indian spinner took a wicket. All seventeen wickets fell to the quick men, Kumar, Shami and Yadav. Ashwin and Jadeja were redundant. The pacemen could not deliver victory in Kolkata, but Indian pace had made a statement broadcasting the dramatic change in Indian cricketing thinking. To judge how big the change was listen to what Kapil Dev told me in 2014, 'The fast bowler is a worker. The batsman is an officer sitting in an AC room and talking. So, the mindset in India is do you want to be an officer or do you want to be a worker?' Now cricketers were happy to leave the airconditioned office to do the heavy lifting as they demonstrated in South Africa in January 2018, England in the summer of 2018 and Australia in December 2018–January 2019. In South Africa and England, despite the work put in by the pacemen, India did not win because the officers in the airconditioned office, the batsmen, were not prepared to get off their comfortable chairs. In Australia it all came together. It is tempting yet dangerous to see game-changing trends from a couple of series but what has happened in the last year is significant and shows Kohli is changing Indian cricket, certainly how India takes wickets.

WE CAN TAKE TWENTY WICKETS BUT CANNOT SCORE RUNS

Imran Khan's famous line has always been 'to win matches you have to take twenty wickets'. India, except in the days of the four great spinners—and that too occasionally—has not often done that abroad. Then suddenly, in January 2018, Kohli's Indians showed they could take twenty wickets abroad. In South Africa in all three Tests India bowled out South Africa, and South Africa's highest score was 335. In three of the six innings South Africa failed to get to 200. What made this exceptional for India was that the bowlers taking the wickets were not the twirlymen but Indian pacemen. Indian pace, long considered a joke, destroyed batsmen playing in their own backyards and on wickets with which they were familiar. Indian pace announced itself right from the start in the South African first innings at Cape Town, they took eight wickets and Ashwin's two were batsmen No. 9 and No.11. In the second innings Ashwin bowled one over and India's four pacemen took all ten wickets.

In the second Test at Centurion, Ashwin was more his normal self, taking four wickets, and he opened the bowling in the second and took a wicket. But despite this, thirteen of the wickets India took fell to pacemen, and in Johannesburg all twenty South African wickets fell to Indian pace, the first time this had happened in Indian cricket history. In the first innings Ashwin did not bowl at all and, for the first time in its Test history, all five Indian bowlers were pacemen. Ashwin did bowl six overs in the second, but did not get a wicket, and it did not matter as India won the Test, although by then South Africa had won the series. As we have seen, back in 2013–14 at the same ground Ashwin's failure to bowl out South Africa on the final day had convinced Dhoni that his No. 1 spinner could not win matches abroad. Now Kohli could always toss the ball to his pacemen confident they would do the job. This had not happened since the dawn of Indian Test cricket in 1932 when India's first Test captain, C. K. Nayudu, could toss the ball to Nissar and Amar Singh, confident they could tame the best batsmen in the world. Yet despite such a pace attack, Kohli was still unable to cross the final frontier and win a series in South Africa for the first time. India's batsmen just did not come to the party. They also failed to come to the party in England, but this was a very different tour to South Africa and tells us more where India is and where it is heading. So, let us look back to the summer of 2018.

KOHLI WINS, INDIA LOSES

In September 2018, as Kohli and his men flew home from England, Mike Brearley, the former England captain wrote that the 'Test series gave us lessons in life':

> I cannot remember being so absorbed in a series as I was in this one between England and India. I feel as though I've learnt a lot about batting, bowling and captaincy. Strangely, it is as though at my age I may be able to make use of this practical knowledge, as if I were to have a second innings in the match of life.

For an Indian like me, who has chosen to make England his home and has suffered so much heartache watching the Indian cricket team, such words are like nectar. This was written by arguably the most cerebral cricket captain ever, who is married to an Indian and spends a few months every year in India—and during the series he came to matches wearing a Nehru waistcoat. It means a lot. This, the eighteenth tour, was like no other Indian visit to England. I found the English talking and writing about Indian cricket in a way I have never seen in my fifty years here, not even when Tendulkar, as the Maharadhiraja of Cricket, reigned supreme. Even weeks after the Oval Test had finished, I would meet London taxi drivers talking about how thrilling the cricket had been. It showed how far Indian cricket had come. As I have written, back in 1979, I had witnessed Gavaskar's 221 at the Oval which nearly brought India a sensational victory. *Wisden* writing about the match said that 'almost everyone—except the England team and officials—hoped they would achieve [victory] after such a magnificent performance by Gavaskar'. And of the last day at the Oval, 'As the teams fought each other to a standstill there were many Englishmen in the crowd who would not have displayed their customary dejection at a Test defeat.' Indeed, sitting in the Oval press box I saw one of England's legendary cricket correspondents hoping India would win. The Oval in 2018 was a very different place. During the tense play on Saturday, when the match was very much in the balance, Pant, the Indian wicketkeeper, conceded a number of byes. Every time he dived and failed to collect the ball the largely English crowd cheered. When I tweeted that in cricket one did not cheer byes, an English supporter tweeted back that this was because England needed every run against this Indian attack. There was an English intensity to the win that I had never seen in England apart from during an Ashes series. The interest was all the more remarkable because the Indian tour started when the England football team was in Russia playing in the 2018 World Cup and for the first time since 1966 looking as if they had a chance of winning.

The first T20 at Manchester, which started the tour, coincided with England's knockout game against Colombia. As India charged towards victory at Old Trafford, England faced a penalty shoot-out in Moscow. They had not won a penalty shoot-out in international competitions since 1996. Just after they lost to India in cricket, they won on penalties in Moscow, and the splash on the *Daily Mail* front page read 'Miracle! England win on penalties. And the explosion of relief must have been heard in space.' The England football team went on to reach the semi-final for the first time since 1990. The Indian cricket team were never going to displace the footballers, for football is the national game and cricket has long had a subsidiary place in English life. Yet articles about Indian cricketers were prominently displayed. England were No. 1 in 50-overs white-ball cricket and had just thrashed the Australians, but with India No. 2 they wanted to put down a marker for the 2019 World Cup to be held in England. As for the Tests, England, having only drawn a series with Pakistan just before India came, wanted to beat the No. 1 side. It also wanted a banquet of spellbinding matches as the ECB knew that interest in all forms of cricket was waning, with fewer and fewer young people playing the game, all this prompting the introduction of what looks like a ridiculous 100-ball-a-side competition.

Even before the Test series began the fact that English cricket lived under the shadow of Indian cricket was emphasized when Jos Buttler, considered a red-ball specialist, was drafted into the Tests and made vice-captain on the back of his IPL form. The word was Joe Root, the England Test captain, had better watch out. After England had won the series in Southampton, Root would confess he had felt under pressure in the series and hail it as his best win as captain.

India won the T20 series that started their summer in England 2–1 and their performance worried England so much that Steve James, the former cricketer turned writer, wrote, 'India are clearly going to be a formidable opponent in every format of the game this summer.' India clinched the T20 series at Bristol, and I have rarely seen a more commanding Indian performance. An England score of 198 in twenty overs was not to be sneezed at, but Rohit Sharma with a sublime hundred in fifty-six balls and Hardik Pandya with 33 in 14 saw India home, Pandya winning the match with a six.

That Sunday at the ground where W. G. Grace, the man who made cricket, had played, I came the nearest to feeling I was back at the CCI in Mumbai. Eoin Morgan confessed that England felt they were the away team. As Sharma and Pandya took India to victory, shouts of Jeetega bhai jeetega rang out; the small number of English fans felt like away supporters who do not understand what the natives are saying. At that time there was much talk of England winning the World Cup and the World Cup coming home. In response, Indian supporters held up a banner which read, 'This Cup is not coming home.' At the end of the match the Indian crowds besieged the Indian players and reporters had to fight their way through to get to the press conference where Pandya held sway.

Pandya is very much the modern post-Tendulkar cricketer. He failed to clear the ninth standard. Yet, now at the press conferences he spoke fluently in both Hindi and English. He may be new to international cricket, but he already has nicknames. His teammates call him 'Rockstar', others 'West Indian guy from Baroda' because of his features and characteristics. At the press conference, wearing his signature diamond-stud earrings, he spoke about his hair with evident pride. In another age he might not have become a cricketer. His family struggled to afford even one meal a day. His father, realizing his son's potential, shifted from Surat to Baroda just for the sake of getting him cricket training. Kiran More helped by not charging Pandya any fee for the first three years in his academy. In pre-Tendulkar times, Indian parents did not see cricket as a career for their children, and there were no academies of the type More and others run. Pandya did get into trouble after the England tour for making comments on television which were considered inappropriate and was suspended for a while before being brought back into the team. But he is clearly the sort of cricketer, who in a hugely contradictory society like India, the land of the Kama Sutra which can see the very mention of anything connected with sex as outrageous, is likely to get into trouble.

He is also very much a product of T20 cricket, smashing 39 runs in an over in the Syed Mushtaq Ali Trophy against Delhi and impressing Tendulkar during the 2015 IPL but progressing six months earlier to international cricket than Tendulkar had predicted. He had announced himself on the international stage in the Champions Trophy final, where he scored a half century in thirty-two deliveries, breaking Adam Gilchrist's record for the fastest 50 in any ICC competition. This was further confirmation of what he could do in white-ball cricket.

The first 50-over white-ball game at Trent Bridge, which followed India's win at Bristol, suggested that India would also be the masters of England in this format. Three weeks earlier England had played Australia at the same ground and scored 481. But now, with the Indians again making this feel like a home match, England batted as if they were playing in India. And as they had often done in India, they fell to spin, but a very different kind of spin bowler. Twenty-four-year-old Kuldeep Yadav had already made history by becoming the first slow left-arm Chinaman bowler to represent India, and only the third Chinaman bowler in Test cricket to take four wickets on debut. Like Pandya, his family had helped rather than hindered his career, his father, a brick kiln owner, moving the family from their native village in Unnao to Kanpur when Kuldeep was young so that he could pursue his cricketing dreams. There his coach converted him from a fast bowler to a Chinaman bowler. He proved so adept that, during the 2012 season, as part of the Mumbai Indians squad, he confounded Tendulkar in the nets with a wrong'un. He continued to deceive batsmen, taking a hat-trick against Australia in the 2017 home series. He had proved too much for England in the first T20 at Old Trafford, but at Trent Bridge he was simply devastating. England had got to 71 when Yadav set to work. By the time Yadav had finished his ten overs he had taken 6 for 25, the fourth-best by an Indian in an ODI and the best by anyone at Trent Bridge.

Such was his impact that the British media dubbed him the 'mystery bowler' and *The Times* had diagrams trying to explain his various deliveries: the stock left-hand leg break, the googly, the quicker ball/flipper. But while England coped with him in the next two white-ball matches to win the series 2–1, he was still seen as the man who could win the series for India. Harbhajan Singh was convinced India had to play him.

But this is where the Test series did not go quite according to plan. While the sun still blazed down all summer long, Yadav only played in one Test and did not take a wicket. To be fair, it was in a Lord's Test, played under typical English conditions suited to pace, dank and overcast, and Shastri admitted to me it was a mistake to play Yadav.

It was Indian pace that surprised the English, but Kohli could not exploit this to conjure a rare victory in England because, throughout the series, England held the aces and at crucial moments trumped India. After the victory at Johannesburg, Kohli had said, 'If the batsmen step up we can do well away from home. We need to correct certain mistakes with the bat. The lower order showed character.' The fact is the batsmen did not step up and the Indian lower order showed very little character. Lord's apart, where the entire batting failed, in all the other three Tests which India lost there were sensational collapses in both innings. At the Oval on the final day at 4.25 p.m. India were 325 for 5, with two centurions, Rahul and Pant, at the wicket. A win was not impossible. Then Rahul was bowled by a ball from Rashid that turned viciously and by 5.25 p.m., India were all out for 345 and had lost by 118 runs.

In contrast, England's lower order often turned things around. And England found in Sam Curran, who had made his Test debut only the previous month against Pakistan, such a match winner that he was Man of the Series. It is not without significance, that the only Test India won was the one he did not play in. The fact was, well though India's pacemen bowled, they just did not have a No. 8 batsman who could turn things around.

GREATER THAN TENDULKAR

The one exception to this was Kohli himself. Kohli arrived in England with all of England debating whether he could show character and score runs in a land which still had vivid memories of his failure in 2014. Not even at the height of the Tendulkar era did the English media dwell so much on one Indian cricketer as they did on Kohli in the summer of 2018. As the matches rolled on, Kohli was almost always in the media. Everything about Kohli was news with *The Times* devoting a feature to Kohli's exercise regime including a picture of Kohli exercising in a gym. The headline read: 'Zealous guys: Kohli and his sprinting guru make India fitter for purpose.' On the first day of the Test series Kohli made the news by running out Root and then imitated the mic drop gesture that Root had made when he had scored a century against India in the Headingley one-day international. It was a mocking send-off for the England captain. It showed that Kohli, like the classic Indian elephant, forgot nothing, particularly if he felt his opponents had gone over the top.

In the first innings of the first Test Kohli played probably the most brilliant innings of the summer. This was the twenty-first century version of Mankad vs England in 1952. No other Indian batsman made more than 26, and Kohli got to his hundred with the tail for company. He was the last man out on 149, nearly half the Indian total. The innings was psychologically important, for the series had been billed as a duel between Kohli and Anderson and the victor would decide the series. In that innings Kohli could have fallen to Anderson. He was dropped and Anderson never got his wicket. The next day the papers had Kohli on the front pages of the sports section. They showed Kohli celebrating his century, his legs spread wide, a blue towel tucked in his waist band and his mouth open roaring with delight. The headlines read 'Imperious Kohli makes England pay for mistakes', 'Captain Colossus' and 'It's that man again'. But while that man went on to score 593 runs in the series, 244 more runs than the next scorer of either side in the series, Jos Buttler, he never got the support from the top order, except at Trent Bridge, and from Pujara in the Southampton Test. And he could not quite shepherd the lower order as well as he did at Edgbaston. The result was that while Kohli won his personal battle with Anderson, it did not give India the series.

Shastri is sure Kohli was not worried about playing Anderson, despite what had happened in 2014:

> He was not all worried about what happened in 2014. He does not worry. In the back of his mind there might have been a thought about Anderson. It took him one innings to wipe out any worries about Anderson. He made some changes to his batting. Yes, he's more aware of where his off stump is. He knows there's no shortcut, he has to get good strides forward and he's doing the job. And he curbed his attacking instincts. You have to when the ball is moving like that. Even Vivian Richards will have to bat five hours. There's no shortcut. You don't want to blast a run a ball hundred.

So, could Kohli become the greatest?

> I never compare generations. You have to see in this generation, when he is playing, how far ahead he is of the rest. If he's ahead by a long way, then he could qualify or come very close to what you're saying. It is too early to judge. He's only 29. Before the start of the series, all I said was, 'He's the best batsman in the world. I hope he gets in so that the British public can watch and see how good he is.'

One Englishman certainly thinks he is the best of his generation. Heed the words of Brearley, who writes:

> Virat Kohli is clearly the best batsman in the world. He averages over fifty in all three formats. He has a fantastic record chasing targets in one-day cricket. He may now be the best of all Indian batsmen, past

as well as present... He has the full range of classical technique, with great capacity to judge length. His bat-speed is itself exceptional—he is no caresser of the ball. Kohli has at least one extra skill, a stroke to be seen in his Test innings as well as in shorter forms of the game. This is the top-spin drive... Many fine attacking batsmen drive the ball on the up... Kohli's stroke is a variant. Instead of letting the ball come to him, he reaches forward in front of his left leg, making contact with the ball well ahead of himself and soon after it has pitched; with his wrists he pays what is almost a hockey shot cuing or top-spinning the ball.

Greater than Tendulkar? So, can he take India to the promised land of consistent success, which Tendulkar for all his brilliance could not?

Shastri is certain he can:

Kohli's contribution has been massive. It is a new India for sure. They know that they've not reached the number one position just for nothing, they have beaten sides. They have beaten sides handsomely in India, but they've gone overseas and started tickling sides.

But Kohli needs to do more than tickle sides abroad. He needs to vanquish them if he is going to keep India at the summit. Kohli has the makings of a team, although it would have to develop a lot more to go anywhere near Clive Lloyd's West Indians or Steve Waugh's Australians. He also needs to show that his captaincy matches his batting. It was surprising that the one truly shameful moment of the tour did not see any Kohli comment. This was at Lord's during the second one-day international. With India having no chance of winning, Dhoni scored 37 in fifty-nine balls. In the process he became the twelfth player to reach 10,000 runs in ODIs, but he should not have been allowed to do so. Kohli should have sent out a message to order him to hit out or get out. The crowds were booing. They had paid good money to see good cricket and it was an insult to them. What is more, after the match Kohli did not attend the post-match press conference, and the only Indian explanation was Dhoni was having some batting practice. Also, during the Test series there were some odd selections. Pujara was not picked for the first Test when his batting could have been crucial, and in the final Test, with Karun Nair in the team, he was not chosen, yet Hanuma Vihari was drafted in.

Not that there can be any doubt that there is in Kohli a determination that is unmatched. The story has often been told how on 19 December 2006, eighteen-year-old Kohli was playing in a Ranji Trophy match for Delhi against Karnataka. At the end of the day's play he was 40 not out.

At three in the morning his father had a fatal heart attack. Kohli was told it would be perfectly all right if he did not play. However, Kohli decided to resume his innings and made 90. Then, ringing his coach, he told him, 'Sir, I was given wrongly out when I was just ten short of a century.' But such obsession by itself does not mean a player can be a great captain and Kohli the captain often comes over as more of a maverick who does not give the impression he has thought his moves out well. That could not be said of either Clive Lloyd or Steve Waugh, two of the greatest captains in the last half-century.

WAITING FOR THE PROMISED LAND

Back in May 2011, I had interviewed Andrew Strauss, the England captain. India were No. 1 in Test rankings but his England team, then No. 3, had just come back from Australia having retained the Ashes 3–1, and he was confident that if England replicated their Ashes form they would become No. 1. Yet he cautioned:

> Are the rankings the full picture? I would argue that you can only be the undisputed number one if you can occupy that place in the rankings for a decent length of time and start winning series away from home. I like the idea of us creating a bit of a legacy for ourselves of not just our results but the way we operate and the way that we go about our business. It's lovely to have lofty ambitions but it's another thing to achieve them.

The Strauss template is one that Kohli would do well to look at.

The win in Australia showed the many faces of Kohli. There was the by now familiar, very un-Gandhian, in-your-face cricket. So much so that he made Tim Paine, the Australian captain, look like a Gandhian. Even given that Australian cricket is trying to reinvent itself after a ball tampering scandal, that is saying something. This was combined with an Indian resilience that previous teams had not shown. Winning the first Test narrowly but coming back from losing the second heavily to win decisively in the third, and but for rain, might have triumphed even in the fourth. True, Australia missed Steve Smith and David Warner but that no Australian batsman made more than 79 in the series was eloquent testimony to Indian bowling. And, as in South Africa and England, this was Indian pace. However, the victory owed a lot to Pujara. Often derided as a batsman who leaves his bat behind when he goes abroad, he showed that the age-old virtues of Indian batting exemplified by Merchant, Hazare, Gavaskar and Dravid, the ability to bat for long hours, still survive. He is not in their class yet but with Kohli scoring

one century and that in the losing Test at Perth, without Pujara's batting
the bowlers' efforts would have been wasted. For all the deficiencies of the
Australian batting this was an Australian bowling side that combined high
quality pace with what has been rare in Australian cricket, a very effective
off-spinner in Nathan Lyon. Also, while this Indian middle order does not
bear comparison with the Gavaskar era, let alone the Tendulkar–Fab Four
era, there were signs that Indian batting has moved forward since the tour
of England. An opening pair remains a problem and any really great team
must have one. In Mayank Agarwal India may have found an opener. That
he made his debut at the age of twenty-eight, which would be old in
England let alone India, shows there is, if not gold, much high quality
talent in Indian domestic cricket which could serve India well.

The Test triumph was followed by winning the one-day series, India
coming back from an initial defeat to win 2–1 which showed both resilience
and also that Dhoni, in contrast to his performance at Lord's, was priming
himself for one last hurrah at the 2019 World Cup. That India did the
double of Tests and one-day internationals, which only the West Indies and
South Africa have done in Australia, and tied the T20 series shows how
far Kohli has taken this Indian team.

There is, of course, much going for India that is not going for any other
cricket nation. The IPL has meant India has found a domestic tournament
that works and makes millions. No other country can boast that. And the
IPL is the biggest draw in cricket. As the series ended there were reports
that Curran would get an IPL contract. In my youth, good performances
by Indians might have got them a county contract or more likely a contract
with a Lancashire League club; now it is Englishmen and other nationalities
measuring progress by how successful they are in seeking Indian gold.

The IPL is also not restricting Indian cricket but expanding it. Jasprit
Bumrah, who had not played in the first two Tests in England but had a
dramatic impact on the third, is the best example of that. The rise of the
Gujarati paceman reflects changes both in Indian society and Indian cricket.
Having lost his father at seven, his mother, a school principal, despite having
several mouths to feed, did not squash his dreams of playing cricket. And he
was first spotted by John Wright, not during a first-class match but when
playing in the Syed Mushtaq Ali Trophy, a T20 tournament. He is very
much a product of the IPL, the best death bowler in T20 matches, who
has proved he can transfer his skills to Test cricket. All this was helped by
having an action that is not remotely conventional. In the classical bowling
action, the bowler's bowling arm virtually kisses the lobes of his ear as he
delivers the ball. Bumrah's hand stretches out as if he is a traffic policeman

stopping the traffic. The result is that it stops the batsman from judging the angle of his ball, thereby causing confusion and making Bumrah's yorker particularly potent.

The IPL, as Shastri saw it, had given India pacemen and also great fielders:

> People in England talk of IPL destroying cricket. I do not believe that. It has improved the Indian fielding tremendously. And produced good hitters. Bumrah, Hardik Pandya, I can name six or seven players who come from the IPL and are playing for India in the longest format of the game, and they love it. It is not at all cricket tamasha. It has improved the running between the wickets. What you are seeing now is the best Indian fielding side ever. You are seeing an Indian team with the best pace bowling attack ever. You might have seen great batting sides but as I've said in the four years I've done the job, 'This team has done and will continue to do things that no other Indian teams have done.' They have a belief that they can go and win anywhere, and it's not put on.

IPL has also meant that the old Merchant maxim 'do not hit the ball six inches above the ground' is now history. Then Gavaskar would be punished if he did that. Now batsmen are more likely to be punished if they do not lift the ball.

This is reinforced by the fact that India is also the boss of cricket in economic terms. All countries want to play India at home as they can sell those rights for many millions to Indian television. Compared to that first wave of Indian cricket, India has a huge following abroad, as the series with England once again showed. And what is more, a following that is proud and keen to show off its Indian colours. This is not the meek, mild India anymore.

This was perfectly illustrated at Lord's during the summer of 2018 when Sourav Ganguly launched his book *A Century is not Enough*. The evening was attended by three former England captains, Michael Atherton, Mike Gatting and Nasser Hussain. Also present was Jeffrey Archer. The Long Room was packed by Indians in Britain, making it look like the foyer of the CCI. And the video showing Ganguly taking his shirt off at Lord's in 2002 was played to loud cheers.

Also, there is a confidence in Indian cricket the like of which I have never seen before. At the post-match press conferences during the England tour Indian players also spoke in Hindi, answering questions put to them in Hindi. I have never in forty years of reporting seen questions in any language other than in English at a cricket press conference. There is also a touch of Indian arrogance here. No attempt was made to translate it into English as if the Indian players and media did not care about the English media. And what is more the English media accepted as if to say India are the boss. They set the tune.

As I write, the BCCI is still to be reincarnated in the way the Lodha Committee has laid down. When it is, the officials must show a maturity the old officials did not. Not the hubris of which the old men who ran the BCCI had an excess, but awareness that India and Indian cricket have come a long way. India's status as the superpower of cricket also imposes obligations and responsibilities that extend beyond India to the wider cricketing world. India cannot and should not behave like a colonial despot as the old board often did. And never more so than when they forced through a deal at the ICC, helped by England and Australia, to create a monopoly not different to the one England and Australia had in the days of white supremacy. In this case India had to retreat but it illustrated the lack of farsighted leadership that has always been a problem in Indian cricket.

The story of Indian cricket is the story of Indian society. Back in the sixties Prasanna gave up his career to qualify as an engineer before he came back to the game, now young cricketers, encouraged by their parents, do not feel they need to get a qualification before they become cricketers.

A new board cannot change Indian society and nor should it be expected to do. But it needs to give leadership to help make sure that the next generation of Kohlis can emerge. Free India led by Nehru put much stress on planning, and India developed the most elaborate planning structure outside the Soviet Union. But for all this talk, Indians rarely work things out in advance. I know this from personal experience, always getting calls from an Indian television station to do a television broadcast at very short notice when other broadcasters plan things with greater care. If India is to become the dominant power both on and off the field the new board needs to plan wisely. Without that, the Indian cricket story will continue to be a long tale of 'what-ifs' which has been the leitmotiv of its history. That can change now, but it is up to Indians on and off the field to step forward and take charge. Kohli as leader can do a lot but he needs a support structure to make sure India finally fulfils its enormous potential.

Kohli's main task is to construct a narrative of success and if he can do that then the next wave of Indian cricket will be very different to the waves that have gone before. History shows that companies, as in Silicon Valley, or countries that are consistently successful, construct narratives of success. American Presidents always hark back to the founding fathers and talk of American exceptionalism claiming it makes America unique. The British talk of their empire and how the nation withstood the Nazis all alone. In the process they cleverly edit out the dark bits but this narrative of past success sustains them. Successful cricket teams have also done that. There have been three outstanding ones, consistently successful, in the history of the game. The Australians of Don Bradman and Steve Waugh and Clive Lloyd's West Indians. They used the wider history of their nations to convert a great team into an awesome one. Bradman's Australian team was so associated with Australia of the 1930s that there was real worry that as a result of the Bodyline series political relations between England and Australia might be damaged. Waugh took his team on a journey to the World War I's Gallipoli battlefield, seen as the moment when Australia became a nation, before journeying to England for an Ashes series which Australia won. The West Indians represent diverse island nations often at loggerheads but Clive Lloyd, through his leadership, united a people descended from slaves to brilliant effect on the cricket field. Indian history does not provide many moments of continuous success and the past waves of Indian cricket show how, as on the battlefields, success has often been followed by disaster. This was true after the successes of the fourth and fifth waves. Even after Dhoni had won the World Cup and made India the top Test and one-day nation disaster was not long in coming. Kohli has to write a new script for Indian cricket. The World Cup in England will be his first great Test but even if he wins it this will be only the start of a long journey if he is to indeed prove to be the captain who is like no other in Indian cricket history.

ACKNOWLEDGEMENTS

I have written many books on Indian cricket but this time I've tried a completely new approach. David Davidar of Aleph suggested that the story of how Indian cricket took over world cricket was in fact a series of waves. I was much taken by the idea that the Dhoni and Kohli waves could be compared to the Indira Gandhi wave of the seventies or today's Narendra Modi wave. My first thanks then are to David and also to Aienla Ozukum for her wonderful editorial skills.

When I first started writing about Indian cricket in the 1970s books on the Indian game would barely have covered a shelf. Now fifty years later there is a considerable collection and while writing this book I have consulted many of them, a selection of which is listed in the bibliography. Many of the authors of these books have been kind enough to say they found my earlier writings useful, even at times a spur, and I have also learnt much from talking to them. I would particularly like to thank Boria Majumdar, Arunabha Sengupta, Chetan Narula and Sumit Ghosh. I am indebted to Rajinder Amarnath for letting me use a picture of his father from his book, *The Making of a Legend: Lala Amarnath* and to quote from it. Tim Arlott has very generously given me permission to use passages from his father's wonderful book, *Indian Summer*, a hidden treasure of Indian cricket literature. I had the pleasure of interviewing Rajdeep Sardesai about his book *Democracy's XI*, a very interesting insight into cricket's role in modern Indian society. Karan Thapar kindly directed me to his book, *Devil's Advocate: The Untold Story*, which has fascinating material on Kapil Dev.

Papu Sanzgiri has as ever allowed me to dip into his treasure trove of knowledge of Indian cricket. I cannot thank Clayton Murzello enough for his help and it is through Clayton that I met Rajneesh Gupta, who must rank as the best cricket statistician in India and whose statistics form such an important feature of this book. Clayton also introduced me to Bipin Patel who combines being a pharmacist with a wonderful ability to take breathtaking cricket pictures, many of which adorn this book. His pictures, if collected in book form, would be a prize possession. Brian Heywood and Tim Jones were also very generous in providing pictures of Indian cricketers which would otherwise have been very difficult to locate. I would also particularly like to express my appreciation for my old friend John Rogers for allowing me to use his Tendulkar picture and thank Graham Morris and Roger Mann.

Nigel Dudley and Richard Heller are two of my oldest friends who have brought their considerable cricketing knowledge to my book. Richard, the author of the excellent *White on Green*, on Pakistan cricket, also provided insight on India's greatest rival. As did another old friend, Peter Oborne, author of the prize-winning book *Wounded Tiger*. I have also relied on the editorial skills and sporting knowledge of Brian Oliver, my old editor at the *Daily Telegraph*. Luke Adams and Graham Coster were diligent researchers. Jeremy Butterfield, editor of *Fowler's Dictionary of Modern English Usage*, provided invaluable proof-reading help.

Rose Chisholm as ever was a tower of strength both helping me with the manuscript and also with her excellent photographic skills.

The book would not have been possible without the patience and forbearance of my wife, Caroline, who put up with the enormous disruption it caused. Despite that, and the fact that her sporting interests are equestrianism and tennis, she rescued me every time I faltered. In the end the errors and omissions that remain are my responsibility.

STATISTICS

Compiled by Rajneesh Gupta

Note: All statistics are for India matches only. They go up to and include India's series in Australia December 2018–January 2019.

TESTS

India in Test cricket

Wave	Period	Matches	Won	Lost	Drawn	Tied	Win%	W/L
1st	1932-1952	34	3	16	15	0	8.82	0.19
2nd	1953-1962	48	5	18	25	0	10.42	0.28
3rd	1963-1970	34	7	15	12	0	20.59	0.47
4th	1971-1983	94	20	28	46	0	21.28	0.71
5th	1983-1989	47	8	12	26	1	17.02	0.67
6th	1989-2000	77	19	23	35	0	24.68	0.83
7th	2000-2007	74	29	19	26	0	39.19	1.53
8th	2007-2015	79	31	25	23	0	39.24	1.24
9th	2015-2018	46	28	9	9	0	60.86	3.11
	(Overall)	533	150	165	217	1	28.14	0.90

Top batsman—in each wave

Wave	Player	Matches	Runs	Hs	Avg	100	50
1st	VS Hazare	25	1998	164*	55.50	7	8
2nd	PR Umrigar	44	3057	223	46.31	10	13
3rd	MAK Pataudi	33	2216	203*	38.20	5	13
4th	SM Gavaskar	90	7625	221	52.22	27	33
5th	DB Vengsarkar	42	3014	166	56.86	11	12
6th	SR Tendulkar	77	6054	217	55.03	22	24
7th	R Dravid	73	6579	270	62.65	18	32
8th	SR Tendulkar	60	4771	214	51.30	14	23
9th	V Kohli	44	4066	243	59.79	15	10

Top batsmen—all time

	Mts	Runs	Hs	Avg	100	50
SR Tendulkar	200	15921	248*	53.78	51	68
R Dravid	163	13265	270	52.63	36	63
SM Gavaskar	125	10122	236*	51.12	34	45
VVS Laxman	134	8781	281	45.97	17	56
V Sehwag	103	8503	319	49.43	23	31
SC Ganguly	113	7212	239	42.17	16	35
DB Vengsarkar	116	6868	166	42.13	17	35
V Kohli	77	6613	243	53.76	25	20
M Azharuddin	99	6215	199	45.03	22	21
GR Viswanath	91	6080	222	41.93	14	35

Top bowler—in each wave

Wave	Player	Mts	Wkts	Best	Avg	5WI	10WM
1st	MH Mankad	25	108	8/52	29.04	6	2
2nd	SP Gupte	33	144	9/102	29.25	12	1
3rd	EAS Prasanna	20	109	6/74	26.56	8	1
4th	Kapil Dev	53	206	8/85	29.52	15	1
5th	Kapil Dev	46	141	9/83	28.29	6	1
6th	A Kumble	61	276	10/74	28.00	16	3
7th	A Kumble	57	290	8/141	29.42	17	5
8th	I Sharma	60	186	7/74	37.24	6	1
9th	R Ashwin	41	223	7/59	22.64	17	5

Top bowlers—all time

	Mts	Wkts	Best	Avg	5WI	10WM
A Kumble	132	619	10/74	29.65	35	8
Kapil Dev	131	434	9/83	29.64	23	2
Harbhajan Singh	103	417	8/84	32.46	25	5
R Ashwin	65	342	7/59	25.43	26	7
Z Khan	92	311	7/87	32.94	11	1
I Sharma	90	267	7/74	34.28	8	1
BS Bedi	67	266	7/98	28.71	14	1
BS Chandrasekhar	58	242	8/79	29.74	16	2
J Srinath	67	236	8/86	30.49	10	1
RA Jadeja	41	192	7/48	23.68	9	1

Top wicketkeeper—in each wave

Wave	Player	Mts	Dismissals	Ct	St
1st	PK Sen	14	31	20	11
2nd	NS Tamhane	21	51	35	16
3rd	FM Engineer	23	45	34	11
4th	SMH Kirmani	69	160	128	32
5th	KS More	24	59	44	15
6th	NR Mongia	42	101	94	7
7th	MS Dhoni	20	63	53	10
8th	MS Dhoni	70	231	203	28
9th	WP Saha	28	79	69	10

Top wicketkeepers—all time

	Mts	Dismissals	Ct	St
MS Dhoni	90	294	256	38
SMH Kirmani	88	198	160	38
KS More	49	130	110	20
NR Mongia	44	107	99	8
WP Saha	31	85	75	10
FM Engineer	46	82	66	16
PA Patel	25	72	62	10
KD Karthik	19	57	51	6
NS Tamhane	21	51	35	16
RR Pant	9	42	40	2

Indian Test captains

#	Captain	Span	Mts	Won	Lost	Drawn	Tied	Win%
1	CK Nayudu	1932-1934	4	0	3	1	0	0.00
2	Maharajkumar of Vizianagram	1936-1936	3	0	2	1	0	0.00
3	Nawab of Pataudi snr	1946-1946	3	0	1	2	0	0.00
4	Lala Amarnath	1947-1952	15	2	6	7	0	13.33
5	Vijay Hazare	1951-1953	14	1	5	8	0	7.14
6	Vinoo Mankad	1955-1959	6	0	1	5	0	0.00
7	Ghulam Ahmed	1955-1959	3	0	2	1	0	0.00
8	Polly Umrigar	1955-1958	8	2	2	4	0	25.00

#	Captain	Span	Mts	Won	Lost	Drawn	Tied	Win%
9	Hemu Adhikari	1959-1959	1	0	0	1	0	0.00
10	Datta Gaekwad	1959-1959	4	0	4	0	0	0.00
11	Pankaj Roy	1959-1959	1	0	1	0	0	0.00
12	GS Ramchand	1959-1960	5	1	2	2	0	20.00
13	Nari Contractor	1960-1962	12	2	2	8	0	16.66
14	Nawab of Pataudi jnr	1962-1975	40	9	19	12	0	22.50
15	Chandu Borde	1967-1967	1	0	1	0	0	0.00
16	Ajit Wadekar	1971-1974	16	4	4	8	0	25.00
17	Srinivas Venkataraghavan	1974-1979	5	0	2	3	0	0.00
18	Sunil Gavaskar	1976-1985	47	9	8	30	0	19.14
19	Bishan Singh Bedi	1976-1978	22	6	11	5	0	27.27
20	Gundappa Viswanath	1980-1980	2	0	1	1	0	0.00
21	Kapil Dev	1983-1987	34	4	7	22	1	11.76
22	Dilip Vengsarkar	1987-1989	10	2	5	3	0	20.00
23	Ravi Shastri	1988-1988	1	1	0	0	0	100.00
24	Kris Srikkanth	1989-1989	4	0	0	4	0	0.00
25	Mohammad Azharuddin	1990-1999	47	14	14	19	0	29.78
26	Sachin Tendulkar	1996-2000	25	4	9	12	0	16.00
27	Sourav Ganguly	2000-2005	49	21	13	15	0	42.85
28	Rahul Dravid	2003-2007	25	8	6	11	0	32.00
29	Virender Sehwag	2005-2012	4	2	1	1	0	50.00
30	Anil Kumble	2007-2008	14	3	5	6	0	21.42
31	MS Dhoni	2008-2014	60	27	18	15	0	45.00
32	Virat Kohli	2014-2018	46	26	10	10	0	56.52
33	Ajinkya Rahane	2017-2018	2	2	0	0	0	100.00

ONE DAY INTERNATIONALS

India in One-Day Internationals

Wave	Period	Mts	Won	Lost	NR	Tied	Win%	W/L
1st	1932-1952	-						
2nd	1953-1962	-						
3rd	1963-1970	-						
4th	1971-1983	48	18	30	0	0	37.50	0.60
5th	1983-1989	107	49	53	5	0	45.79	0.92

6th	1989-2000	299	137	146	13	3	45.82	0.94
7th	2000-2007	206	109	88	9	0	52.91	1.24
8th	2007-2015	220	131	73	12	4	59.55	1.79
9th	2015-2019	76	50	23	1	2	65.78	2.17
	(Overall)	956	494	413	40	9	51.67	1.19

Top batsman—in each wave

Wave	Player	Mts	Runs	Hs	Avg	SR	100	50
4th	DB Vengsarkar	36	921	88*	29.70	62.95	0	5
5th	K Srikkanth	94	2628	123	28.87	71.43	4	16
6th	SR Tendulkar	258	9612	186*	41.97	86.18	26	49
7th	R Dravid	189	6070	109*	42.15	73.79	5	52
8th	V Kohli	158	6537	183	51.47	89.73	22	33
9th	V Kohli	61	3848	160*	81.87	98.33	17	15

Top batsmen—all time

	Mts	Runs	Hs	Avg	SR	100	50
SR Tendulkar	463	18426	200*	44.83	86.23	49	96
SC Ganguly	308	11221	183	40.95	73.65	22	71
R Dravid	340	10768	153	39.15	71.18	12	82
V Kohli	219	10385	183	59.68	92.73	39	48
MS Dhoni	332	10192	183*	50.45	87.11	9	70
M Azharuddin	334	9378	153*	36.92	74.02	7	58
Yuvraj Singh	301	8609	150	36.47	87.43	14	52
V Sehwag	241	7995	219	35.37	104.44	15	37
RG Sharma	196	7639	264	48.04	88.78	22	37
SK Raina	226	5615	116*	35.31	93.50	5	36

Top bowler—in each wave

Wave	Player	Mts	Wkts	Best	Avg	RPO	4W
4th	Kapil Dev	40	46	5/43	28.39	3.58	1
5th	Kapil Dev	99	115	4/30	26.14	3.75	1
6th	A Kumble	208	274	6/12	28.56	4.20	9
7th	AB Agarkar	126	191	6/42	26.34	5.01	9
8th	RA Jadeja	119	143	5/36	33.19	4.84	6
9th	JJ Bumrah	44	78	5/27	21.01	4.44	5

Top bowlers—all time

	Mts	Wkts	Best	Avg	RPO	4W
A Kumble	269	334	6/12	30.83	4.29	10
J Srinath	229	315	5/23	28.08	4.44	10
AB Agarkar	191	288	6/42	27.85	5.07	12
Z Khan	194	269	5/42	30.11	4.95	8
Harbhajan Singh	234	265	5/31	33.47	4.30	5
Kapil Dev	225	253	5/43	27.45	3.71	4
BKV Prasad	161	196	5/27	32.30	4.67	4
IK Pathan	120	173	5/27	29.72	5.26	7
RA Jadeja	147	171	5/36	35.40	4.89	8
M Prabhakar	130	157	5/33	28.87	4.27	6

Top wicket-keeper—in each wave

Wave	Player	Mts	Dismissals	Ct	St
4th	SMH Kirmani	36	25	20	5
5th	KS More	37	35	20	15
6th	NR Mongia	140	154	110	44
7th	MS Dhoni	81	97	79	18
8th	MS Dhoni	178	226	162	64
9th	MS Dhoni	73	99	67	32

Top wicketkeepers—all time

	Mts	Dismissals	Ct	St
MS Dhoni	332	422	308	114
NR Mongia	140	154	110	44
KS More	94	90	63	27
R Dravid	73	84	71	13
PA Patel	27	39	30	9

TWENTY20

India in Twenty20 Internationals

Wave	Period	Mts	Won	Lost	NR	Win%	W/L
1st	1932-1952	-					
2nd	1953-1962	-					

3rd	1963-1970	-					
4th	1971-1983	-					
5th	1983-1989	-					
6th	1989-2000	-					
7th	2000-2007	1	1	0	0	100.00	-
8th	2007-2015	52	30	21	1	57.69	1.43
9th	2015-2018	57	39	16	2	68.42	2.43
	(overall)	110	70	37	3	63.63	1.89

Note: The win tally includes one in the bowl-out after a tie

Top batsmen—all time

	Mts	Runs	Hs	Avg	SR	100	50
RG Sharma	90	2237	118	32.89	138.17	4	15
V Kohli	65	2167	90*	49.25	136.11	0	19
SK Raina	78	1605	101	29.18	134.87	1	5
MS Dhoni	93	1487	56	37.17	127.09	0	2
S Dhawan	46	1232	92	29.33	132.90	0	9
Yuvraj Singh	58	1177	77*	28.02	136.38	0	8
G Gambhir	37	932	75	27.41	119.02	0	7
KL Rahul	25	782	110*	43.44	148.38	2	4
MK Pandey	28	538	79*	41.38	122.83	0	2
V Sehwag	19	394	68	21.88	145.38	0	2

Top bowlers—all time

	Mts	Wkts	Best	Avg	RPO	4W
R Ashwin	46	52	4/8	22.94	6.97	2
JJ Bumrah	40	48	3/11	20.47	6.77	0
YS Chahal	27	44	6/25	18.75	7.81	3
A Nehra	27	34	3/19	22.29	7.73	0
B Kumar	34	33	5/24	24.75	6.73	1
Kuldeep Yadav	17	33	5/24	12.96	6.74	2
HH Pandya	35	33	4/38	23.96	8.00	1
RA Jadeja	40	31	3/48	31.70	7.27	0
Yuvraj Singh	58	28	3/17	17.82	7.06	0
IK Pathan	24	28	3/16	22.07	8.02	0

Top wicketkeepers—all time

	Mts	Dismissals	Ct	St
MS Dhoni	93	87	54	33
KD Karthik	9	9	6	3

INDIA VS EACH COUNTRY

TESTS OVERALL

	Mts	Won	Lost	Drawn	Tied	Win%	W/L
v England	122	26	47	49	0	21.31	1.80
v Australia	98	28	42	27	1	28.57	1.50
v West Indies	96	20	30	46	0	20.83	0.66
v Pakistan	59	9	12	38	0	15.25	0.75
v New Zealand	57	21	10	26	0	36.84	2.10
v Sri Lanka	44	20	7	17	0	45.45	2.85
v Zimbabwe	11	7	2	2	0	63.63	3.50
v South Africa	36	11	15	10	0	30.55	0.73
v Bangladesh	9	7	0	2	0	77.77	-
v Afghanistan	1	1	0	0	0	100.00	-
(Overall)	533	150	165	217	1	28.14	0.90

TESTS HOME AND AWAY

	Home							Away						
	Mts	Won	Lost	Drawn	Tied	Win%	W/L	Mts	Won	Lost	Drawn	Tied	Win%	W/L
v England	60	19	13	28	0	31.67	1.46	62	7	34	21	0	11.29	0.21
v Australia	50	21	13	15	1	42.00	1.62	48	7	29	12	0	14.58	0.24
v West Indies	47	13	14	20	0	27.66	0.92	49	7	16	26	0	14.29	0.44
v Pakistan	33	7	5	21	0	21.21	1.40	26	2	7	17	0	7.69	0.29
v New Zealand	34	16	2	16	0	47.06	8.00	23	5	8	10	0	21.74	0.63
v Sri Lanka	20	11	0	9	0	55.00	-	24	9	7	8	0	37.50	1.29
v Zimbabwe	5	4	0	1	0	80.00	-	6	3	2	1	0	50.00	1.50
v South Africa	16	8	5	3	0	50.00	1.60	20	3	10	7	0	15.00	0.30
v Bangladesh	1	1	0	0	0	100.00	-	8	6	0	2	0	75.00	-
v Afghanistan	1	1	0	0	0	100.00	-	0						
(Overall)	267	101	52	113	1	37.82	1.94	266	49	113	104	0	18.42	0.43

ONE-DAY INTERNATIONALS OVERALL

	Mts	Won	Lost	NR	Tied	Win%	W/L
v England	99	53	41	3	2	53.53	1.29
v East Africa	1	1	0	0	0	100.00	-
v New Zealand	101	51	44	5	1	50.50	1.16
v Pakistan	131	54	73	4	0	41.22	0.74
v West Indies	126	59	62	3	2	46.83	0.95
v Sri Lanka	158	90	56	11	1	56.96	1.61
v Australia	131	47	74	10	0	35.88	0.64
v Zimbabwe	63	51	10	0	2	80.95	5.10
v Bangladesh	35	29	5	1	0	82.86	5.80
v South Africa	83	34	46	3	0	40.96	0.74
v UAE	3	3	0	0	0	100.00	-
v Kenya	13	11	2	0	0	84.62	5.50
v Netherlands	2	2	0	0	0	100.00	-
v Namibia	1	1	0	0	0	100.00	-
v Bermuda	1	1	0	0	0	100.00	-
v Ireland	3	3	0	0	0	100.00	-
v Scotland	1	1	0	0	0	100.00	-
v Hong Kong	2	2	0	0	0	100.00	-
v Afghanistan	2	1	0	0	1	50.00	-
(Overall)	956	494	413	40	9	51.67	1.19

ONE-DAY INTERNATIONALS HOME AND AWAY

	Home							Away						
	Mts	Won	Lost	NR	Tied	Win%	W/L	Mts	Won	Lost	NR	Tied	Win%	W/L
v England	48	31	16	0	1	64.58	1.94	51	22	25	3	1	43.14	0.88
v East Africa	0							1	1	0	0	0	100.00	-
v New Zealand	35	26	8	1	0	74.29	3.25	66	25	36	4	1	37.88	0.69
v Pakistan	30	11	19	0	0	36.67	0.58	101	43	54	4	0	42.57	0.80
v West Indies	55	27	27	0	1	49.09	1.00	71	32	35	3	1	45.07	0.91
v Sri Lanka	51	36	12	3	0	70.59	3.00	107	54	44	8	1	50.47	1.23
v Australia	56	25	26	5	0	44.64	0.96	75	22	48	5	0	29.33	0.45
v Zimbabwe	19	15	3	0	1	78.95	5.00	44	36	7	0	1	81.82	5.14
v Bangladesh	3	3	0	0	0	100.00	-	32	26	5	1	0	81.25	5.20
v South Africa	28	15	13	0	0	53.57	1.15	55	19	33	3	0	34.55	0.58
v UAE	0							3	3	0	0	0	100.00	-
v Kenya	4	3	1	0	0	75.00	3.00	9	8	1	0	0	88.89	8.00
v Netherlands	1	1	0	0	0	100.00	-	1	1	0	0	0	100.00	-
v Namibia	0							1	1	0	0	0	100.00	-
v Bermuda	0							1	1	0	0	0	100.00	-
v Ireland	1	1	0	0	0	100.00	-	2	2	0	0	0	100.00	-
v Scotland	0							1	1	0	0	0	100.00	-
v Hong Kong	0							2	2	0	0	0	100.00	-
v Afghanistan	0							2	1	0	0	1	50.00	-
(Overall)	331	194	125	9	3	58.61	1.55	625	300	288	31	6	48.00	1.04

TWENTY20 INTERNATIONALS OVERALL

	Mts	Won	Lost	NR	Win%	W/L
v South Africa	13	8	5	0	61.54	1.60
v Scotland	1	0	0	1	-	-
v Pakistan	8	7	1	0	87.50	7.00
v New Zealand	8	2	6	0	25.00	0.33
v England	14	7	7	0	50.00	1.00
v Australia	18	11	6	1	61.11	1.83
v Sri Lanka	16	11	5	0	68.75	2.20
v Bangladesh	8	8	0	0	100.00	-
v Ireland	3	3	0	0	100.00	-
v West Indies	11	5	5	1	45.45	1.00
v Afghanistan	2	2	0	0	100.00	-
v Zimbabwe	7	5	2	0	71.42	2.50
v UAE	1	1	0	0	100.00	-
(Overall)	110	70	37	3	63.63	1.89

TWENTY20 INTERNATIONALS HOME AND AWAY

	Home						Away					
	Mts	Won	Lost	NR	Win%	W/L	Mts	Won	Lost	NR	Win%	W/L
v South Africa	2	0	2	0	0.00	0.00	11	8	3	0	72.73	2.67
v Scotland	0						1	0	0	1	0.00	0.00
v Pakistan	3	2	1	0	66.67	2.00	5	5	0	0	100.00	-
v New Zealand	5	2	3	0	40.00	0.67	3	0	3	0	0.00	0.00
v England	6	3	3	0	50.00	1.00	8	4	4	0	50.00	1.00
v Australia	5	4	1	0	80.00	4.00	13	7	5	1	53.85	1.40
v Sri Lanka	8	6	2	0	75.00	3.00	8	5	3	0	62.50	1.67
v Bangladesh	1	1	0	0	100.00	-	7	7	0	0	100.00	-
v Ireland	0						3	3	0	0	100.00	-
v West Indies	4	3	1	0	75.00	3.00	7	2	4	1	28.57	0.50
v Afghanistan	0						2	2	0	0	100.00	-
v Zimbabwe	0						7	5	2	0	71.43	2.50
v UAE	0						1	1	0	0	100.00	-
(Overall)	34	21	13	0	61.76	1.61	76	49	24	3	64.47	2.04

Note: India's win-tally in away matches vs Pakistan includes a match won in the bowl-out after a tie

THE TWO INDIAN FAB FOURS

THE MERCHANT LED FAB FOUR

Test career—batting & fielding

	Mts	Inns	NO	Runs	Hs	Avg	100s	50s	Ct	St
Merchant	10	18	0	859	154	47.72	3	3	7	0
Hazare	30	52	6	2192	164*	47.65	7	9	11	0
Amarnath	24	40	4	878	118	24.38	1	4	13	0
Mankad	44	72	5	2109	231	31.47	5	6	33	0

Test career—bowling

	Mts	Balls	Runs	Wkts	Best	Avg	RPO	SR	5WI	10WM
Merchant	10	54	40	0	-	-	4.44	-	0	0
Hazare	30	2840	1220	20	4/29	61.00	2.57	142.00	0	0
Amarnath	24	4241	1481	45	5/96	32.91	2.09	94.24	2	0
Mankad	44	14686	5236	162	8/52	32.32	2.13	90.65	8	2

First-class cricket—batting & fielding

	Mts	Inns	NO	Runs	Hs	Avg	100	50	Ct	St
Merchant	150	234	46	13470	359*	71.64	45	52	115	0
Hazare	238	367	46	18740	316*	58.38	60	73	166	0
Amarnath	186	286	34	10426	262	41.37	31	39	96	2
Mankad	233	361	27	11591	231	34.70	26	52	190	0

First-class cricket—bowling

	Mts	Balls	Runs	Wkts	Best	Avg	RPO	SR	5WI	10WM
Merchant	150	5087	2088	65	5/73	32.12	2.46	78.26	1	0
Hazare	238	38447	14645	595	8/90	24.61	2.28	64.62	27	3
Amarnath	186	29474	10644	463	7/27	22.98	2.16	63.66	19	3
Mankad	233	50122	19183	782	8/35	24.53	2.29	64.09	38	9

The original Fab Four played three Tests together—all during India's tour of England in 1946. India drew two of them and lost one. There were no One Day Internationals or Twenty20s in this wave.

THE TENDULKAR-LED FAB FOUR

Test career—batting & fielding

	Mts	Inns	NO	Runs	Hs	Avg	100s	50s	Ct	St
Tendulkar	200	329	33	15921	248*	53.78	51	68	115	0
Ganguly	113	188	17	7212	239	42.17	16	35	71	0
Dravid	164	286	32	13288	270	52.31	36	63	210	0
Laxman	134	225	34	8781	281	45.97	17	56	135	0

ODI career—batting & fielding

	Mts	Inns	NO	Runs	Hs	Avg	100s	50s	Ct	St	SR
Tendulkar	463	452	41	18426	200*	44.83	49	96	140	0	86.23
Ganguly	311	300	23	11363	183	41.02	22	72	100	0	73.70
Dravid	344	318	40	10889	153	39.16	12	83	196	14	71.24
Laxman	86	83	7	2338	131	30.76	6	10	39	0	71.23

First-class career—batting & fielding

	Mat	Inns	NO	Runs	HS	Ave	100	50	Ct	St
Tendulkar	310	490	51	25396	248*	57.84	81	116	186	0
Ganguly	254	399	44	15687	239	44.18	33	89	168	0
Dravid	298	497	67	23794	270	55.33	68	117	353	1
Laxman	267	436	54	19730	353	51.64	55	98	277	1

Test career—bowling

	Mts	Balls	Runs	Wkts	Best	Avg	RPO	SR	5W	10W
Tendulkar	200	4240	2492	46	3/10	54.17	3.52	92.17	0	0
Ganguly	113	3117	1681	32	3/28	52.53	3.23	97.41	0	0
Dravid	164	120	39	1	1/18	39.00	1.95	120.00	0	0
Laxman	134	324	126	2	1/2	63.00	2.33	162.00	0	0

ODI career—bowling

	Mts	Balls	Runs	Wkts	Best	Avg	RPO	SR	4W
Tendulkar	463	8054	6850	154	5/32	44.48	5.10	52.30	6
Ganguly	311	4561	3849	100	5/16	38.49	5.06	45.61	3
Dravid	344	186	170	4	2/43	42.50	5.48	46.50	0
Laxman	86	42	40	0	-	-	5.71	-	0

First-class career—bowling

	Mts	Balls	Runs	Wkts	Best	Avg	RPO	SR	5W	10W
Tendulkar	310	7605	4384	71	3/10	61.74	3.45	107.11	0	0
Ganguly	254	11108	6099	167	6/46	36.52	3.29	66.51	4	0
Dravid	298	617	273	5	2/16	54.60	2.65	123.40	0	0
Laxman	267	1835	754	22	3/11	34.27	2.46	83.41	0	0

Playing together in Tests

	Mts	Runs	Avg	100s	50s	Ct	St	Wkts	Avg	RPO	SR	5I	10M
Tendulkar	80	6692	53.54	19	32	44	0	26	59.00	3.76	94.27	0	0
Ganguly	80	4334	35.52	5	26	48	0	17	63.53	3.17	120.41	0	0
Dravid	80	6518	53.87	17	30	108	0	1	18.00	2.00	54.00	0	0
Laxman	80	5253	46.90	9	31	88	0	2	63.00	2.33	162.00	0	0

Playing together in ODIs

	Mts	Runs	Avg	100s	50s	Ct	St	Wkts	Avg	RPO	SR	4W
Tendulkar	33	1484	49.47	4	8	10	0	18	32.39	5.35	36.33	0
Ganguly	33	1084	34.97	3	5	10	0	10	37.50	5.11	44.00	0
Dravid	33	897	34.50	1	6	19	7	0	-	-	-	0
Laxman	33	774	26.69	3	2	17	0	0	-	5.00	-	0

The quadruple of Tendulkar, Dravid, Ganguly and Laxman played 80 Tests together, out of which India won 26, lost 27 and drew 27 (win% 32.50). At home these four played in 33 Tests together, winning 15, losing 7 and drawing 11 (win% 45.45).

LIST OF INDIAN TEST CRICKETERS

Name	Years	Mts	Inns	NO	Runs	Hs	Avg	100	50	Ct	St	Balls	Runs	Wkts	Avg	RPO	Best	5I	10M
VR Aaron	2011-2015	9	14	5	35	9	3.88	0	0	1	0	1189	947	18	52.61	4.77	3-97	0	0
S Abid Ali	1967-1974	29	53	3	1018	81	20.36	0	6	32	0	4164	1980	47	42.12	2.85	6-55	1	0
HR Adhikari	1947-1959	21	36	8	872	114*	31.14	1	4	8	0	170	82	3	27.33	2.89	3-68	0	0
AB Agarkar	1998-2006	26	39	5	571	109*	16.79	1	0	6	0	4857	2745	58	47.32	3.39	6-41	1	0
MA Agarwal	2018-2019	2	3	0	195	77	65.00	0	2	3	0	0	0	0				0	0
L Amar Singh	1932-1936	7	14	1	292	51	22.46	0	1	3	0	2182	858	28	30.64	2.35	7-86	2	0
L Amarnath	1933-1952	24	40	4	878	118	24.38	1	4	13	0	4241	1481	45	32.91	2.09	5-96	2	0
M Amarnath	1969-1988	69	113	10	4378	138	42.50	11	24	47	0	3676	1782	32	55.68	2.90	4-63	0	0
S Amarnath	1976-1978	10	18	0	550	124	30.55	1	3	4	0	11	5	1	5.00	2.72	1-5	0	0
Amir Elahi	1947-1947	1	2	0	17	13	8.50	0	0	0	0	0	0	0				0	0
PK Amre	1992-1993	11	13	3	425	103	42.50	1	3	9	0	0	0	0				0	0
SA Ankola	1989-1989	1	1	0	6	6	6.00	0	0	0	0	180	128	2	64.00	4.26	1-35	0	0
AL Apte	1959-1959	1	2	0	15	8	7.50	0	0	0	0	0	0	0				0	0
ML Apte	1952-1953	7	13	2	542	163*	49.27	1	3	2	0	6	3	0		3.00		0	0
Arshad Ayub	1987-1989	13	19	4	257	57	17.13	0	1	2	0	3663	1438	41	35.07	2.35	5-50	3	0
B Arun	1986-1987	2	2	1	4	2*	4.00	0	0	2	0	252	116	4	29.00	2.76	3-76	0	0
Arun Lal	1982-1989	16	29	1	729	93	26.03	0	6	13	0	16	7	0		2.62		0	0
R Ashwin	2011-2018	65	93	12	2361	124	29.14	4	11	23	0	18372	8700	342	25.43	2.84	7-59	26	7

Name	Years	Mts	Inns	NO	Runs	Hs	Avg	100	50	Ct	St	Balls	Runs	Wkts	Avg	RPO	Best	5I	10M
KBJ Azad	1981-1983	7	12	0	135	24	11.25	0	0	3	0	750	373	3	124.33	2.98	2-84	0	0
M Azharuddin	1984-2000	99	147	9	6215	199	45.03	22	21	105	0	13	16	0		7.38	-	0	0
HK Badani	2001-2001	4	7	1	94	38	15.66	0	0	6	0	48	17	0		2.12	-	0	0
S Badrinath	2010-2010	2	3	0	63	56	21.00	0	1	2	0	0	0	0			-	0	0
SV Bahutule	2001-2001	2	4	1	39	21*	13.00	0	0	1	0	366	203	3	67.66	3.32	1-32	0	0
AA Baig	1959-1966	10	18	0	428	112	23.77	1	2	6	0	18	15	0		5.00	-	0	0
L Balaji	2003-2005	8	9	0	51	31	5.66	0	0	1	0	1756	1004	27	37.18	3.43	5-76	1	0
SA Banerjee	1948-1948	1	1	0	0	0	0.00	0	0	3	0	306	181	5	36.20	3.54	4-120	0	0
SN Banerjee	1949-1949	1	2	0	13	8	6.50	0	0	0	0	273	127	5	25.40	2.79	4-54	0	0
ST Banerjee	1992-1992	1	1	0	3	3	3.00	0	0	0	0	108	47	3	15.66	2.61	3-47	0	0
SB Bangar	2001-2002	12	18	2	470	100*	29.37	1	3	4	0	762	343	7	49.00	2.70	2-23	0	0
M Baqa Jilani	1936-1936	1	2	1	16	12	16.00	0	0	0	0	90	55	0		3.66	-	0	0
BS Bedi	1966-1979	67	101	28	656	50*	8.98	0	1	26	0	21364	7637	266	28.71	2.14	7-98	14	1
P Bhandari	1955-1956	3	4	0	77	39	19.25	0	0	1	0	78	39	0		3.00	-	0	0
AR Bhat	1983-1983	2	3	1	6	6	3.00	0	0	0	0	438	151	4	37.75	2.06	2-65	0	0
Bhuvneshwar Kumar	2013-2018	21	29	4	552	63*	22.08	0	3	8	0	3348	1644	63	26.09	2.94	6-82	4	0
RMH Binny	1979-1987	27	41	5	830	83*	23.05	0	5	11	0	2870	1534	47	32.63	3.20	6-56	2	0
STR Binny	2014-2015	6	10	1	194	78	21.55	0	1	4	0	450	258	3	86.00	3.44	2-24	0	0
CG Borde	1958-1969	55	97	11	3061	177*	35.59	5	18	37	0	5635	2417	52	46.48	2.57	5-88	1	0
JJ Bumrah	2018-2019	10	15	6	14	6	1.55	0	0	3	0	2416	1073	49	21.89	2.66	6-33	3	0
BS Chandrasekhar	1964-1979	58	80	39	167	22	4.07	0	0	25	0	15963	7199	242	29.74	2.70	8-79	16	2
CPS Chauhan	1969-1981	40	68	2	2084	97	31.57	0	16	38	0	174	106	2	53.00	3.65	1-4	0	0

Name	Years	Mts	Inns	NO	Runs	Hs	Avg	100	50	Ct	St	Balls	Runs	Wkts	Avg	RPO	Best	5I	10M
RK Chauhan	1993-1998	21	17	3	98	23	7.00	0	0	12	0	4749	1857	47	39.51	2.34	4-48	0	0
PP Chawla	2006-2012	3	3	0	6	4	2.00	0	0	1	0	492	270	7	38.57	3.29	4-69	0	0
AS Chopra	2003-2004	10	19	0	437	60	23.00	0	2	15	0	0	0	0			-	0	0
N Chopra	2000-2000	1	2	0	7	4	3.50	0	0	0	0	144	78	0		3.25	-	0	0
NR Chowdhury	1949-1951	2	2	1	3	3*	3.00	0	0	0	0	516	205	1	205.00	2.38	1-130	0	0
SHM Colah	1932-1933	2	4	0	69	31	17.25	0	0	2	0	0	0	0			-	0	0
NJ Contractor	1955-1962	31	52	1	1611	108	31.58	1	11	18	0	186	80	1	80.00	2.58	1-9	0	0
V Dahiya	2000-2000	2	1	1	2	2*		0	0	6	0	0	0	0			-	0	0
HT Dani	1952-1952	1	0	0	0	0		0	0	1	0	60	19	1	19.00	1.90	1-9	0	0
SS Das	2000-2002	23	40	2	1326	110	34.89	2	9	34	0	66	35	0		3.18	-	0	0
DB Dasgupta	2001-2002	8	13	1	344	100	28.66	1	2	13	0	0	0	0			-	0	0
RB Desai	1959-1968	28	44	13	418	85	13.48	0	1	9	0	5597	2761	74	37.31	2.95	6-56	2	0
S Dhawan	2013-2018	34	58	1	2315	190	40.61	7	5	28	0	54	18	0		2.00	-	0	0
MS Dhoni	2005-2014	90	144	16	4876	224	38.09	6	33	256	38	96	67	0		4.18	-	0	0
SS Dighe	2001-2001	6	10	1	141	47	15.66	0	0	12	2	0	0	0			-	0	0
Dilawar Hussain	1934-1936	3	6	0	254	59	42.33	0	3	6	1	0	0	0			-	0	0
RV Divecha	1951-1952	5	5	0	60	26	12.00	0	0	5	0	1044	361	11	32.81	2.07	3-102	0	0
DR Doshi	1979-1983	33	38	10	129	20	4.60	0	0	10	0	9322	3502	114	30.71	2.25	6-102	6	0
R Dravid	1996-2012	163	284	32	13265	270	52.63	36	63	209	0	120	39	1	39.00	1.95	1-18	0	0
SA Durani	1960-1973	29	50	2	1202	104	25.04	1	7	14	0	6446	2657	75	35.42	2.47	6-73	3	1
FM Engineer	1961-1975	46	87	3	2611	121	31.08	2	16	66	16	0	0	0			-	0	0
CV Gadkari	1953-1955	6	10	4	129	50*	21.50	0	1	6	0	102	45	0		2.64	-	0	0

Name	Years	Mts	Inns	NO	Runs	Hs	Avg	100	50	Ct	St	Balls	Runs	Wkts	Avg	RPO	Best	5I	10M
AD Gaekwad	1974-1984	40	70	4	1985	201	30.07	2	10	15	0	334	187	2	93.50	3.35	1-4	0	0
DK Gaekwad	1952-1961	11	20	1	350	52	18.42	0	1	5	0	12	12	0		6.00	-	0	0
HG Gaekwad	1952-1952	1	2	0	22	14	11.00	0	0	0	0	222	47	0		1.27	-	0	0
G Gambhir	2004-2016	58	104	5	4154	206	41.95	9	22	38	0	12	4	0		2.00	-	0	0
DJ Gandhi	1999-1999	4	7	1	204	88	34.00	0	2	3	0	0	0	0			-	0	0
A Gandotra	1969-1969	2	4	0	54	18	13.50	0	0	1	0	6	5	0		5.00	-	0	0
D Ganesh	1997-1997	4	7	3	25	8	6.25	0	0	0	0	461	287	5	57.40	3.73	2-28	0	0
SC Ganguly	1996-2008	113	188	17	7212	239	42.17	16	35	71	0	3117	1681	32	52.53	3.23	3-28	0	0
SM Gavaskar	1971-1987	125	214	16	10122	236*	51.12	34	45	108	0	380	206	1	206.00	3.25	1-34	0	0
KD Ghavri	1974-1981	39	57	14	913	86	21.23	0	2	16	0	7036	3656	109	33.54	3.11	5-33	4	0
JM Ghorpade	1953-1959	8	15	0	229	41	15.26	0	0	4	0	150	131	0		5.24	-	0	0
Ghulam Ahmed	1948-1958	22	31	9	192	50	8.72	0	1	11	0	5650	2052	68	30.17	2.17	7-49	4	1
MJ Gopalan	1934-1934	1	2	1	18	11*	18.00	0	0	3	0	114	39	1	39.00	2.05	1-39	0	0
CD Gopinath	1951-1960	8	12	1	242	50*	22.00	0	1	2	0	48	11	1	11.00	1.37	1-11	0	0
GM Guard	1958-1960	2	2	0	11	7	5.50	0	0	2	0	396	182	3	60.66	2.75	2-69	0	0
S Guha	1967-1969	4	7	2	17	6	3.40	0	0	2	0	674	311	3	103.66	2.76	2-55	0	0
Gul Mohammad	1946-1952	8	15	0	166	34	11.06	0	0	3	0	77	24	2	12.00	1.87	2-21	0	0
BP Gupte	1961-1965	3	3	2	28	17*	28.00	0	0	0	0	678	349	3	116.33	3.08	1-54	0	0
SP Gupte	1951-1961	36	42	13	183	21	6.31	0	0	14	0	11284	4403	149	29.55	2.34	9-102	12	1
Gursharan Singh	1990-1990	1	1	0	18	18	18.00	0	0	2	0	0	0	0			-	0	0
Hanumant Singh	1964-1969	14	24	2	686	105	31.18	1	5	11	0	66	51	0		4.63	-	0	0
Harbhajan Singh	1998-2015	103	145	23	2224	115	18.22	2	9	42	0	28580	13537	417	32.46	2.84	8-84	25	5

Name	Years	Mts	Inns	NO	Runs	Hs	Avg	100	50	Ct	St	Balls	Runs	Wkts	Avg	RPO	Best	5I	10M
MS Hardikar	1958-1958	2	4	1	56	32*	18.66	0	0	3	0	108	55	1	55.00	3.05	1-9	0	0
Harvinder Singh	1998-2001	3	4	1	6	6	2.00	0	0	0	0	273	185	4	46.25	4.06	2-62	0	0
VS Hazare	1946-1953	30	52	6	2192	164*	47.65	7	9	11	0	2840	1220	20	61.00	2.57	4-29	0	0
DD Hindlekar	1936-1946	4	7	2	71	26	14.20	0	0	3	0	0	0	0			-	0	0
ND Hirwani	1988-1996	17	22	12	54	17	5.40	0	0	5	0	4298	1967	66	30.10	2.77	8-61	4	1
KC Ibrahim	1948-1949	4	8	0	169	85	21.12	0	1	0	0	0	0	0			-	0	0
KSMJ Indrajitsinhji	1964-1969	4	7	1	51	23	8.50	0	0	6	3	0	0	0			-	0	0
JK Irani	1947-1947	2	3	2	3	2*	3.00	0	0	2	1	0	0	0			-	0	0
AD Jadeja	1992-2000	15	24	2	576	96	26.18	0	4	5	0	0	0	0			-	0	0
RA Jadeja	2012-2019	41	60	14	1485	100*	32.28	1	10	31	0	11480	4548	192	23.68	2.37	7-48	9	1
W Jaffer	2000-2008	31	58	1	1944	212	34.10	5	11	27	0	66	18	2	9.00	1.63	2-18	0	0
M Jahangir Khan	1932-1936	4	7	0	39	13	5.57	0	0	4	0	606	255	4	63.75	2.52	4-60	0	0
LP Jai	1933-1933	1	2	0	19	19	9.50	0	0	0	0	0	0	0			-	0	0
ML Jaisimha	1959-1971	39	71	4	2056	129	30.68	3	12	17	0	2097	829	9	92.11	2.37	2-54	0	0
RJD Jamshedji	1933-1933	1	2	2	5	4*		0	0	2	0	210	137	3	45.66	3.91	3-137	0	0
HK Jayantilal	1971-1971	1	1	0	5	5	5.00	0	0	0	0	0	0	0			-	0	0
DJ Johnson	1996-1996	2	3	1	8	5	4.00	0	0	0	0	240	143	3	47.66	3.57	2-52	0	0
PG Joshi	1951-1960	12	20	1	207	52*	10.89	0	1	18	9	0	0	0			-	0	0
SB Joshi	1996-2000	15	19	2	352	92	20.70	0	1	7	0	3451	1470	41	35.85	2.55	5-142	1	0
M Kaif	2000-2006	13	22	3	624	148*	32.84	1	3	14	0	18	4	0		1.33	-	0	0
VG Kambli	1993-1995	17	21	1	1084	227	54.20	4	3	7	0	0	0	0			-	0	0
HH Kanitkar	1999-2000	2	4	0	74	45	18.50	0	0	0	0	6	2	0		2.00	-	0	0

Name	Years	Mts	Inns	NO	Runs	Hs	Avg	100	50	Ct	St	Balls	Runs	Wkts	Avg	RPO	Best	5I	10M
HS Kanitkar	1974-1974	2	4	0	111	65	27.75	0	1	0	0	0	0	0			-	0	0
Kapil Dev	1978-1994	131	184	15	5248	163	31.05	8	27	64	0	27740	12867	434	29.64	2.78	9-83	23	2
AR Kapoor	1994-1996	4	6	1	97	42	19.40	0	0	1	0	642	255	6	42.50	2.38	2-19	0	0
AH Kardar	1946-1946	3	5	0	80	43	16.00	0	0	1	0	0	0	0			-	0	0
SS Karim	2000-2000	1	1	0	15	15	15.00	0	0	1	0	0	0	0			-	0	0
KD Karthik	2004-2018	26	42	1	1025	129	25.00	1	7	57	6	0	0	0			-	0	0
M Kartik	2000-2004	8	10	1	88	43	9.77	0	0	2	0	1932	820	24	34.16	2.54	4-44	0	0
RB Kenny	1958-1960	5	10	1	245	62	27.22	0	3	1	0	0	0	0			-	0	0
Z Khan	2000-2014	92	127	24	1231	75	11.95	0	3	19	0	18785	10247	311	32.94	3.27	7-87	11	1
SMH Kirmani	1976-1986	88	124	22	2759	102	27.04	2	12	160	38	19	13	1	13.00	4.10	1-9	0	0
G Kishenchand	1947-1952	5	10	0	89	44	8.90	0	0	1	0	0	0	0			-	0	0
V Kohli	2011-2019	77	131	8	6613	243	53.76	25	20	72	0	163	76	0		2.79	-	0	0
AG Kripal Singh	1955-1964	14	20	5	422	100*	28.13	1	2	4	0	1518	584	10	58.40	2.30	3-43	0	0
P Krishnamurthy	1971-1971	5	6	0	33	20	5.50	0	0	7	1	0	0	0			-	0	0
NM Kulkarni	1997-2001	3	2	1	5	4	5.00	0	0	1	0	738	332	2	166.00	2.69	1-70	0	0
RR Kulkarni	1986-1987	3	2	0	2	2	1.00	0	0	1	0	366	227	5	45.40	3.72	3-85	0	0
UN Kulkarni	1967-1968	4	8	5	13	7	4.33	0	0	0	0	448	238	5	47.60	3.18	2-37	0	0
P Kumar	2011-2011	6	10	0	149	40	14.90	0	0	2	0	1611	697	27	25.81	2.59	5-106	1	0
VV Kumar	1961-1961	2	2	0	6	6	3.00	0	0	2	0	605	202	7	28.85	2.00	5-64	1	0
A Kumble	1990-2008	132	173	32	2506	110*	17.77	1	5	60	0	40850	18355	619	29.65	2.69	10-74	35	8
BK Kunderan	1960-1967	18	34	4	981	192	32.70	2	3	23	7	24	13	0		3.25	-	0	0
A Kuruvilla	1997-1997	10	11	1	66	35*	6.60	0	0	0	0	1765	892	25	35.68	3.03	5-68	1	0

Name	Years	Mts	Inns	NO	Runs	Hs	Avg	100	50	Ct	St	Balls	Runs	Wkts	Avg	RPO	Best	5I	10M
Lall Singh	1932-1932	1	2	0	44	29	22.00	0	0	1	0	0	0	0			-	0	0
R Lamba	1986-1987	4	5	0	102	53	20.40	0	1	5	0	0	0	0			-	0	0
VVS Laxman	1996-2012	134	225	34	8781	281	45.97	17	56	136	0	324	126	2	63.00	2.33	1-2	0	0
Madan Lal	1974-1986	39	62	16	1042	74	22.65	0	5	15	0	5997	2846	71	40.08	2.84	5-23	4	0
Maharaj of Vizianagram	1936-1936	3	6	2	33	19	8.25	0	0	1	0	0	0	0			-	0	0
ES Maka	1952-1953	2	1	1	2	2		0	0	2	1	0	0	0			-	0	0
AO Malhotra	1982-1985	7	10	1	226	72	25.11	0	1	2	0	18	3	0		1.00	-	0	0
Maninder Singh	1982-1993	35	38	12	99	15	3.80	0	0	9	0	8218	3288	88	37.36	2.40	7-27	3	2
SV Manjrekar	1987-1996	37	61	6	2043	218	37.14	4	9	25	1	17	15	0		5.29	-	0	0
VL Manjrekar	1951-1965	55	92	10	3208	189	39.12	7	15	19	2	204	44	1	44.00	1.29	1-16	0	0
AV Mankad	1969-1978	22	42	3	991	97	25.41	0	6	12	0	41	43	0		6.29	-	0	0
MH Mankad	1946-1959	44	72	5	2109	231	31.47	5	6	33	0	14686	5236	162	32.32	2.13	8-52	8	2
MK Mantri	1951-1955	4	8	1	67	39	9.57	0	0	8	1	0	0	0			-	0	0
KR Meherhomji	1936-1936	1	1	1	0	0*		0	0	1	0	0	0	0			-	0	0
VL Mehra	1955-1964	8	14	1	329	62	25.30	0	2	1	0	36	6	0		1.00	-	0	0
VM Merchant	1933-1951	10	18	0	859	154	47.72	3	3	7	0	54	40	0		4.44	-	0	0
PL Mhambrey	1996-1996	2	3	1	58	28	29.00	0	0	1	0	258	148	2	74.00	3.44	1-43	0	0
AG Milkha Singh	1960-1961	4	6	0	92	35	15.33	0	0	2	0	6	2	0		2.00	-	0	0
A Mishra	2008-2016	22	32	2	648	84	21.60	0	4	8	0	5103	2715	76	35.72	3.19	5-71	1	0
A Mithun	2010-2011	4	5	0	120	46	24.00	0	0	0	0	720	456	9	50.66	3.80	4-105	0	0
RS Modi	1946-1952	10	17	1	736	112	46.00	1	6	3	0	30	14	0		2.80	-	0	0

Name	Years	Mts	Inns	NO	Runs	Hs	Avg	100	50	Ct	St	Balls	Runs	Wkts	Avg	RPO	Best	5I	10M
Mohammed Shami	2013-2019	40	56	17	433	51	11.10	0	1	9	0	7562	4254	144	29.54	3.37	6-56	4	0
DS Mohanty	1997-1997	2	1	1	0	0*		0	0	0	0	430	239	4	59.75	3.33	4-78	0	0
NR Mongia	1994-2001	44	68	8	1442	152	24.03	1	6	99	8	0	0	0			-	0	0
KS More	1986-1993	49	64	14	1285	73	25.70	0	7	110	20	12	12	0		6.00	-	0	0
VM Muddiah	1959-1960	2	3	1	11	11	5.50	0	0	0	0	318	134	3	44.66	2.52	2-40	0	0
A Mukund	2011-2017	7	14	0	320	81	22.85	0	2	6	0	12	14	0		7.00	-	0	0
S Mushtaq Ali	1934-1952	11	20	1	612	112	32.21	2	3	7	0	378	202	3	67.33	3.20	1-45	0	0
RG Nadkarni	1955-1968	41	67	12	1414	122*	25.70	1	7	22	0	9165	2559	88	29.07	1.67	6-43	4	1
SS Naik	1974-1974	3	6	0	141	77	23.50	0	1	0	0	0	0	0			-	0	0
KK Nair	2016-2017	6	7	1	374	303*	62.33	1	0	6	0	12	11	0		5.50	-	0	0
Naoomal Jaoomal	1932-1934	3	5	1	108	43	27.00	0	0	0	0	108	68	2	34.00	3.77	1-4	0	0
MV Narasimha Rao	1978-1979	4	6	1	46	20*	9.20	0	0	8	0	463	227	3	75.66	2.94	2-46	0	0
JG Navle	1932-1933	2	4	0	42	13	10.50	0	0	1	0	0	0	0			-	0	0
Nawab of Pataudi jr	1961-1975	46	83	3	2793	203*	34.91	6	16	27	0	132	88	1	88.00	4.00	1-10	0	0
Nawab of Pataudi sr	1946-1946	3	5	0	55	22	11.00	0	0	0	0	0	0	0			-	0	0
SV Nayak	1982-1982	2	3	1	19	11	9.50	0	0	1	0	231	132	1	132.00	3.42	1-16	0	0
CK Nayudu	1932-1936	7	14	0	350	81	25.00	0	2	4	0	858	386	9	42.88	2.69	3-40	0	0
CS Nayudu	1934-1952	11	19	3	147	36	9.18	0	0	3	0	522	359	2	179.50	4.12	1-19	0	0
S Nazir Ali	1932-1934	2	4	0	30	13	7.50	0	0	0	0	138	83	4	20.75	3.60	4-83	0	0
A Nehra	1999-2004	17	25	11	77	19	5.50	0	0	5	0	3447	1866	44	42.40	3.24	4-72	0	0
M Nissar	1932-1936	6	11	3	55	14	6.87	0	0	2	0	1211	707	25	28.28	3.50	5-90	3	0
S Nyalchand	1952-1952	1	2	1	7	6*	7.00	0	0	0	0	384	97	3	32.33	1.51	3-97	0	0

Name	Years	Mts	Inns	NO	Runs	Hs	Avg	100	50	Ct	St	Balls	Runs	Wkts	Avg	RPO	Best	5I	10M
NV Ojha	2015-2015	1	2	0	56	35	28.00	0	0	4	1	0	0	0	-	-	-	0	0
PP Ojha	2009-2013	24	27	17	89	18*	8.90	0	0	10	0	7633	3420	113	30.26	2.68	6-47	7	1
AM Pai	1969-1969	1	2	0	10	9	5.00	0	0	0	0	114	31	2	15.50	1.63	2-29	0	0
PE Palia	1932-1936	2	4	1	29	16	9.66	0	0	0	0	42	13	0	-	1.85	-	0	0
CS Pandit	1986-1992	5	8	1	171	39	24.42	0	0	14	2	0	0	0	-	-	-	0	0
HH Pandya	2017-2018	11	18	1	532	108	31.29	1	4	7	0	937	528	17	31.05	3.38	5-28	1	0
Pankaj Singh	2014-2014	2	4	1	10	9	3.33	0	0	2	0	450	292	2	146.00	3.89	2-113	0	0
RR Pant	2018-2019	9	15	1	696	159*	49.71	2	2	40	2	0	0	0	-	-	-	0	0
GA Parkar	1982-1982	1	2	0	7	6	3.50	0	0	1	0	0	0	0	-	-	-	0	0
RD Parkar	1972-1972	2	4	0	80	35	20.00	0	0	0	0	0	0	0	-	-	-	0	0
DD Parsana	1979-1979	2	2	0	1	1	0.50	0	0	0	0	120	50	1	50.00	2.50	1-32	0	0
CT Patankar	1955-1955	1	2	1	14	13	14.00	0	0	3	1	0	0	0	-	-	-	0	0
BP Patel	1974-1977	21	38	5	972	115*	29.45	1	5	17	0	0	0	0	-	-	-	0	0
JM Patel	1955-1960	7	10	1	25	12	2.77	0	0	2	0	1725	637	29	21.96	2.21	9-69	2	1
MM Patel	2006-2011	13	14	6	60	15*	7.50	0	0	6	0	2658	1349	35	38.54	3.04	4-25	0	0
PA Patel	2002-2018	25	38	8	934	71	31.13	0	6	62	10	0	0	0	-	-	-	0	0
RGM Patel	1988-1988	1	2	0	0	0	0.00	0	0	1	0	84	51	0	-	3.64	-	0	0
IK Pathan	2003-2008	29	40	5	1105	102	31.57	1	6	8	0	5884	3226	100	32.26	3.28	7-59	7	2
SM Patil	1980-1984	29	47	4	1588	174	36.93	4	7	12	0	645	240	9	26.66	2.23	2-28	0	0
SR Patil	1955-1955	1	1	1	14	14*		0	0	1	0	138	51	2	25.50	2.21	1-15	0	0
DG Phadkar	1947-1958	31	45	7	1229	123	32.34	2	8	21	0	5994	2285	62	36.85	2.28	7-159	3	0
RR Powar	2007-2007	2	2	0	13	7	6.50	0	0	0	0	252	118	6	19.66	2.80	3-33	0	0

Name	Years	Mts	Inns	NO	Runs	Hs	Avg	100	50	Ct	St	Balls	Runs	Wkts	Avg	RPO	Best	5I	10M
M Prabhakar	1984-1995	39	58	9	1600	120	32.65	1	9	20	0	7475	3581	96	37.30	2.87	6-132	3	0
BKV Prasad	1996-2001	33	47	20	203	30*	7.51	0	0	6	0	7041	3360	96	35.00	2.86	6-33	7	1
MSK Prasad	1999-2000	6	10	1	106	19	11.77	0	0	15	0	0	0	0			-	0	0
EAS Prasanna	1962-1978	49	84	20	735	37	11.48	0	0	18	0	14353	5742	189	30.38	2.40	8-76	10	2
CA Pujara	2010-2019	68	114	8	5426	206*	51.18	18	20	45	0	6	2	0		2.00	-	0	0
PH Punjabi	1955-1955	5	10	0	164	33	16.40	0	0	5	0	0	0	0			-	0	0
AM Rahane	2013-2019	56	95	9	3488	188	40.55	9	17	73	0	0	0	0			-	0	0
KL Rahul	2014-2019	34	56	2	1905	199	35.27	5	11	43	0	0	0	0			-	0	0
K Rai Singh	1948-1948	1	2	0	26	24	13.00	0	0	0	0	0	0	0			-	0	0
SK Raina	2010-2015	18	31	2	768	120	26.48	1	7	23	0	1041	603	13	46.38	3.47	2-1	0	0
Rajinder Pal	1964-1964	1	2	1	6	3*	6.00	0	0	0	0	78	22	0		1.69	-	0	0
V Rajindernath	1952-1952	1	0	0	0	0		0	0	0	4	0	0	0			-	0	0
LS Rajput	1985-1985	2	4	0	105	61	26.25	0	1	1	0	0	0	0			-	0	0
SLV Raju	1990-2001	28	34	10	240	31	10.00	0	0	6	0	7602	2857	93	30.72	2.25	6-12	5	1
WV Raman	1988-1997	11	19	1	448	96	24.88	0	4	6	0	348	129	2	64.50	2.22	1-7	0	0
C Ramaswami	1936-1936	2	4	1	170	60	56.66	0	1	0	0	0	0	0			-	0	0
GS Ramchand	1952-1960	33	53	5	1180	109	24.58	2	5	20	0	4976	1899	41	46.31	2.28	6-49	1	0
S Ramesh	1999-2001	19	37	1	1367	143	37.97	2	8	18	0	54	43	0		4.77	-	0	0
LN Ramji	1933-1933	1	2	0	1	1	0.50	0	0	1	0	138	64	0		2.78	-	0	0
CR Rangachari	1948-1948	4	6	3	8	8*	2.66	0	0	0	0	846	493	9	54.77	3.49	5-107	1	0
KM Rangnekar	1947-1948	3	6	0	33	18	5.50	0	0	1	0	0	0	0			-	0	0
VB Ranjane	1958-1964	7	9	3	40	16	6.66	0	0	1	0	1265	649	19	34.15	3.07	4-72	0	0

Name	Years	Mts	Inns	NO	Runs	Hs	Avg	100	50	Ct	St	Balls	Runs	Wkts	Avg	RPO	Best	5I	10M
V Rathour	1996-1997	6	10	0	131	44	13.10	0	0	12	0	0	0	0	-		-	0	0
A Ratra	2002-2002	6	10	1	163	115*	18.11	1	0	11	2	6	1	0		1.00	-	0	0
V Razdan	1989-1989	2	2	1	6	6*	6.00	0	0	0	0	240	141	5	28.20	3.52	5-79	1	0
B Reddy	1979-1979	4	5	1	38	21	9.50	0	0	9	2	0	0	0			-	0	0
MR Rege	1949-1949	1	2	0	15	15	7.50	0	0	1	0	0	0	0			-	0	0
Robin Singh	1999-1999	1	1	0	0	0	0.00	0	0	1	0	240	176	3	58.66	4.40	2-74	0	0
AK Roy	1969-1969	4	7	0	91	48	13.00	0	0	0	0	0	0	0			-	0	0
Pankaj Roy	1951-1960	43	79	4	2442	173	32.56	5	9	16	0	104	66	1	66.00	3.80	1-6	0	0
Pranab Roy	1982-1982	2	3	1	71	60*	35.50	0	1	1	0	0	0	0			-	0	0
WP Saha	2010-2018	32	46	8	1164	117	30.63	3	5	75	10	0	0	0			-	0	0
BS Sandhu	1983-1983	8	11	4	214	71	30.57	0	2	1	0	1020	557	10	55.70	3.27	3-87	0	0
RL Sanghvi	2001-2001	1	2	0	2	2	1.00	0	0	0	0	74	78	2	39.00	6.32	2-67	0	0
Sarandeep Singh	2000-2002	3	2	1	43	39*	43.00	0	0	1	0	678	340	10	34.00	3.00	4-136	0	0
DN Sardesai	1961-1972	30	55	4	2001	212	39.23	5	9	4	0	59	45	0		4.57	-	0	0
CT Sarwate	1946-1951	9	17	1	208	37	13.00	0	0	0	0	658	374	3	124.66	3.41	1-16	0	0
RC Saxena	1967-1967	1	2	0	25	16	12.50	0	0	0	0	12	11	0		5.50	-	0	0
V Sehwag	2001-2013	103	178	6	8503	319	49.43	23	31	90	0	3731	1894	40	47.35	3.04	5-104	1	0
TA Sekhar	1983-1983	2	1	1	0	0*		0	0	0	0	204	129	0		3.79	-	0	0
PK Sen	1948-1952	14	18	4	165	25	11.78	0	0	20	11	0	0	0			-	0	0
AK Sengupta	1959-1959	1	2	0	9	8	4.50	0	0	0	0	0	0	0			-	0	0
AK Sharma	1988-1988	1	2	0	53	30	26.50	0	0	1	0	24	9	0		2.25	-	0	0
C Sharma	1984-1989	23	27	9	396	54	22.00	0	1	7	0	3470	2163	61	35.45	3.74	6-58	4	1

Name	Years	Mts	Inns	NO	Runs	Hs	Avg	100	50	Ct	St	Balls	Runs	Wkts	Avg	RPO	Best	5I	10M
G Sharma	1985-1990	5	4	1	11	10*	3.66	0	0	2	0	1307	418	10	41.80	1.91	4-88	0	0
I Sharma	2007-2018	90	124	43	627	31*	7.74	0	0	19	0	17196	9155	267	34.28	3.19	7-74	8	1
KV Sharma	2014-2014	1	2	1	8	4*	8.00	0	0	0	0	294	238	4	59.50	4.85	2-95	0	0
PH Sharma	1974-1977	5	10	0	187	54	18.70	0	1	1	0	24	8	0		2.00	-	0	0
RG Sharma	2013-2018	27	47	7	1585	177	39.62	3	10	25	0	334	202	2	101.00	3.62	1-26	0	0
SK Sharma	1988-1990	2	3	1	56	38	28.00	0	0	1	0	414	247	6	41.16	3.57	3-37	0	0
RJ Shastri	1981-1992	80	121	14	3830	206	35.79	11	12	36	0	15751	6185	151	40.96	2.35	5-75	2	0
PP Shaw	2018-2018	2	3	1	237	134	118.50	1	1	2	0	0	0	0		9.00	-	0	0
SG Shinde	1946-1952	7	11	5	85	14	14.16	0	0	0	0	1515	717	12	59.75	2.83	6-91	1	0
RH Shodhan	1952-1953	3	4	1	181	110	60.33	1	0	1	0	60	26	0		2.60	-	0	0
RC Shukla	1982-1982	1	0	0	0	0		0	0	0	0	294	152	2	76.00	3.10	2-82	0	0
IR Siddiqui	2001-2001	1	2	1	29	24	29.00	0	0	1	0	114	48	1	48.00	2.52	1-32	0	0
NS Sidhu	1983-1999	51	78	2	3202	201	42.13	9	15	9	0	6	9	0		9.00	-	0	0
RP Singh	2006-2011	14	19	3	116	30	7.25	0	0	6	0	2534	1682	40	42.05	3.98	5-59	1	0
RR Singh	1998-1998	1	2	0	27	15	13.50	0	0	5	0	60	32	0		3.20	-	0	0
VR Singh	2006-2007	5	6	2	47	29	11.75	0	0	1	0	669	427	8	53.37	3.82	3-48	0	0
L Sivaramakrishnan	1983-1986	9	9	1	130	25	16.25	0	0	9	0	2367	1145	26	44.03	2.90	6-64	3	1
SW Sohoni	1946-1951	4	7	2	83	29*	16.60	0	0	2	0	532	202	2	101.00	2.27	1-16	0	0
ED Solkar	1969-1977	27	48	6	1068	102	25.42	1	6	53	0	2265	1070	18	59.44	2.83	3-28	0	0
MM Sood	1960-1960	1	2	0	3	3	1.50	0	0	0	0	0	0	0			-	0	0
S Sreesanth	2006-2011	27	40	13	281	35	10.40	0	0	5	0	5419	3271	87	37.59	3.62	5-40	3	0
K Srikkanth	1981-1992	43	72	3	2062	123	29.88	2	12	40	0	216	114	0		3.16	-	0	0

Name	Years	Mts	Inns	NO	Runs	Hs	Avg	100	50	Ct	St	Balls	Runs	Wkts	Avg	RPO	Best	5I	10M
J Srinath	1991-2002	67	92	21	1009	76	14.21	0	4	22	0	15104	7196	236	30.49	2.85	8-86	10	1
TE Srinivasan	1981-1981	1	2	0	48	29	24.00	0	0	0	0	0	0	0			-	0	0
V Subramanya	1965-1968	9	15	1	263	75	18.78	0	2	9	0	444	201	3	67.00	2.71	2-32	0	0
GR Sunderam	1955-1955	2	1	1	3	3*		0	0	0	0	396	166	3	55.33	2.51	2-46	0	0
Surendranath	1958-1961	11	20	7	136	27	10.46	0	0	4	0	2602	1053	26	40.50	2.42	5-75	2	0
RF Surti	1960-1969	26	48	4	1263	99	28.70	0	9	26	0	3870	1962	42	46.71	3.04	5-74	1	0
VN Swamy	1955-1955	1	0	0	0	0		0	0	0	0	108	45	0		2.50	-	0	0
NS Tamhane	1955-1960	21	27	5	225	54*	10.22	0	1	35	16	0	0	0			-	0	0
KK Tarapore	1948-1948	1	1	0	2	2	2.00	0	0	0	0	114	72	0		3.78	-	0	0
SR Tendulkar	1989-2013	200	329	33	15921	248*	53.78	51	68	115	0	4240	2492	46	54.17	3.52	3-10	0	0
SN Thakur	2018-2018	1	1	1	4	4*		0	0	0	0	10	9	0		5.40	-	0	0
PR Umrigar	1948-1962	59	94	8	3631	223	42.22	12	14	33	0	4725	1473	35	42.08	1.87	6-74	2	0
JD Unadkat	2010-2010	1	2	1	2	1*	2.00	0	0	0	0	156	101	0		3.88	-	0	0
DB Vengsarkar	1976-1992	116	185	22	6868	166	42.13	17	35	78	0	47	36	0		4.59	-	0	0
S Venkataraghavan	1965-1983	57	76	12	748	64	11.68	0	2	44	0	14877	5634	156	36.11	2.27	8-72	3	1
M Venkataramana	1989-1989	1	2	2	0	0*		0	0	1	0	70	58	1	58.00	4.97	1-10	0	0
GH Vihari	2018-2019	4	7	0	167	56	23.85	0	1	1	0	273	132	5	26.40	2.90	3-37	0	0
R Vijay Bharadwaj	1999-2000	3	3	0	28	22	9.33	0	0	3	0	247	107	1	107.00	2.59	1-26	0	0
M Vijay	2008-2018	61	105	1	3982	167	38.28	12	15	49	0	384	198	1	198.00	3.09	1-12	0	0
R Vinay Kumar	2012-2012	1	2	0	11	6	5.50	0	0	0	0	78	73	1	73.00	5.61	1-73	0	0
GR Viswanath	1969-1983	91	155	10	6080	222	41.93	14	35	63	0	70	46	1	46.00	3.94	1-11	0	0
S Viswanath	1985-1985	3	5	0	31	20	6.20	0	0	11	0	0	0	0			-	0	0

Name	Years	Mts	Inns	NO	Runs	Hs	Avg	100	50	Ct	St	Balls	Runs	Wkts	Avg	RPO	Best	5I	10M
AL Wadekar	1966-1974	37	71	3	2113	143	31.07	1	14	46	0	61	55	0		5.40	-	0	0
AS Wassan	1990-1990	4	5	1	94	53	23.50	0	1	1	0	712	504	10	50.40	4.24	4-108	0	0
S Wazir Ali	1932-1936	7	14	0	237	42	16.92	0	0	1	0	30	25	0		5.00	-	0	0
J Yadav	2016-2017	4	6	1	228	104	45.60	1	1	1	0	627	367	11	33.36	3.51	3-30	0	0
K Yadav	2017-2019	6	6	0	51	26	8.50	0	0	3	0	989	579	24	24.12	3.51	5-57	2	0
NS Yadav	1979-1987	35	40	12	403	43	14.39	0	0	10	0	8349	3580	102	35.09	2.57	5-76	3	0
UT Yadav	2011-2018	41	47	21	283	30	10.88	0	0	14	0	6659	3983	119	33.47	3.58	6-88	2	1
V Yadav	1993-1993	1	1	0	30	30	30.00	0	0	1	2	0	0	0			-	0	0
Yajurvindra Singh	1977-1979	4	7	1	109	43*	18.16	0	0	11	0	120	50	0		2.50	-	0	0
Yashpal Sharma	1979-1983	37	59	11	1606	140	33.45	2	9	16	0	30	17	1	17.00	3.40	1-6	0	0
Yograj Singh	1981-1981	1	2	0	10	6	5.00	0	0	0	0	90	63	1	63.00	4.20	1-63	0	0
T Yohannan	2001-2002	3	4	4	13	8*		0	0	1	0	486	256	5	51.20	3.16	2-56	0	0
Yuvraj of Patiala	1934-1934	1	2	0	84	60	42.00	0	1	2	0	0	0	0			-	0	0
Yuvraj Singh	2003-2012	40	62	6	1900	169	33.92	3	11	31	0	931	547	9	60.77	3.52	2-9	0	0

LIST OF INDIAN ONE DAY CRICKETERS

Name	Years	Mts	Inns	NO	Runs	Hs		Avg	SR	100	50	Ct	St	Balls	Runs	Wkts	Avg	RPO	Best	4I
VR Aaron	2011-2014	9	3	2	8	6*	8.00	53.33	0	0	1	0	380	419	11	38.09	6.61	3-24	0	0
S Abid Ali	1974-1975	5	3	0	93	70		31.00	70.45	0	1	0	0	336	187	7	26.71	3.33	2-22	0
AB Agarkar	1998-2007	191	113	26	1269	95		14.58	80.62	0	3	53	0	9484	8021	288	27.85	5.07	6-42	12
KK Ahmed	2018-2019	7	2	1	4	3		4.00	33.33	0	0	1	0	360	319	11	29.00	5.31	3-13	0
M Amarnath	1975-1989	85	75	12	1924	102*	30.53	57.70	2	13	23	0	2730	1971	46	42.84	4.33	3-12	0	
S Amarnath	1978-1978	3	3	0	100	62		33.33	84.03	0	1	1	0	0	0	0		-	-	0
PK Amre	1991-1994	37	30	5	513	84*	20.52	63.80	0	2	12	0	0	4	0	0	12.00	-	0	
SA Ankola	1989-1997	20	13	4	34	9		3.77	80.95	0	0	2	2	807	615	13	47.30	4.57	3-33	0
Arshad Ayub	1987-1990	32	17	7	116	31*	11.60	71.60	0	0	5	0	0	1216	31	39.22	4.12	5-21	1	
B Arun	1986-1987	4	3	1	21	8		10.50	65.62	0	0	0	0	1769	102	103	1	103.00	6.05	1-43	0
Arun Lal	1982-1989	13	13	0	122	51		9.38	52.58	0	1	4	0	0	0	0		-	-	0
R Ashwin	2010-2017	111	61	19	675	65	14.15	16.07	86.98	0	1	30	0	6021	4937	150	32.91	4.91	4-25	1
KBJ Azad	1980-1986	25	21	2	269	39*	36.92	66.25	7	0	7	0	390	273	7	39.00	4.20	2-48	0	
M Azharuddin	1985-2000	334	308	54	9378	153*		73.98	73.47	58	156	0	552	479	12	39.91	5.20	3-19	0	
HK Badani	2000-2004	40	36	10	867	100	15.80	33.34	0	1	4	13	0	183	149	3	49.66	4.88	1-7	0
S Badrinath	2008-2011	7	6	1	79	27*		45.93	79.31	0	2	0	0	0	0			-	0	
SV Bahutule	1997-2003	8	4	1	23	11	12.00	7.66	0	0	0	3	0	294	283	2	141.50	5.77	1-31	0
L Balaji	2002-2009	30	16	6	120	21*	24.50	78.94	0	0	11	0	1447	1344	34	39.52	5.57	4-48	1	
ST Banerjee	1991-1992	6	5	3	49	25*	13.84	116.66	0	0	3	0	240	202	5	40.40	5.05	3-30	0	
SB Bangar	2002-2004	15	15	2	180	57*		75.31	0	1	4	0	442	384	7	54.85	5.21	2-39	0	
AC Bedade	1994-1994	13	10	3	158	51		22.57	86.33	0	1	4	0	0	0	0		-	-	0

Player	Span	M	Inns	NO	Runs	HS	Avg	BF	SR	100	50	0	Balls	Runs	Wkts	Avg	Econ	Best	5w
BS Bedi	1974-1979	10	7	2	31	13		6.20	44.28	0	0	4	0	590	340	7	48.57	3.45	2-44	0
A Bhandari	2000-2004	2	1	1	0	0*			0	0	0	0	106	106	5	21.20	6.00	3-31	0	
Bhupinder Singh sr	1994-1994	2	1	0	6	6		6.00	46.15	0	0	0	0	102	78	3	26.00	4.58	3-34	0
Bhuvneshwar Kumar	2012-2019	98	45	15	469	53*	15.63	75.52	0	1	24	0	4720	3923	107	36.66	4.98	5-42	4	3
RMH Binny	1980-1987	72	49	10	629	57		16.12	60.19	0	1	12	0	2957	2260	77	29.35	4.58	4-29	3
STR Binny	2014-2015	14	11	3	230	77		28.75	93.49	0	1	3	0	490	439	20	21.95	5.37	6-4	1
GK Bose	1974-1974	1	1	0	13	13		13.00	72.22	0	0	0	0	66	39	1	39.00	3.54	1-39	0
JJ Bumrah	2016-2018	44	6	2	11	10*	2.75	32.35	0	0	15	0	2212	1639	78	21.01	4.44	5-27	5	
YS Chahal	2016-2019	35	4	1	16	12		5.33	57.14	0	0	7	0	1867	1473	62	23.75	4.73	6-42	3
DL Chahar	2018-2018	1	1	0	12	12		12.00	85.71	0	0	0	0	24	37	1	37.00	9.25	1-37	0
BS Chandrasekhar	1976-1976	1	1	1	11	11*		84.61	0	0	0	0	56	36	3	12.00	3.85	3-36	0	-
VB Chandrasekhar	1988-1990	7	7	0	88	53		12.57	54.32	0	1	0	0	0	0	0			-	0
US Chatterjee	1995-1995	3	2	1	6	3*		21.42	0	0	1	0	161	117	3	39.00	4.36	2-35	0	
CPS Chauhan	1978-1981	7	7	0	153	46		21.85	50.83	0	0	3	0	0	0	0	-	0		
RK Chauhan	1993-1997	35	18	5	132	32	5.42	10.15	77.19	0	0	10	0	1634	1216	29	41.93	4.46	3-29	0
PP Chawla	2007-2011	25	12	5	38	13*		65.51	0	0	9	0	1312	1117	32	34.90	5.10	4-23	2	
N Chopra	1998-2000	39	26	6	310	61		15.50	62.24	0	1	16	0	1835	1286	46	27.95	4.20	5-21	2
V Dahiya	2000-2001	19	15	2	216	51		16.61	80.89	0	1	19	0	0	0	0			-	0
SS Das	2001-2002	4	4	1	39	30		13.00	50.64	0	0	0	0	0	0	0			-	0
DB Dasgupta	2001-2001	5	4	1	51	24*	17.00	63.75	0	0	2	0	0	0	0		-	0	
NA David	1997-1997	4	2	2	9	8*		90.00	0	0	0	0	192	133	4	33.25	4.15	3-21	0	
P Dharmani	1996-1996	1	1	0	8	8		8.00	100.00	0	0	0	0	0	0	0			-	0

Player	Span																			
R Dhawan	2016-2016	3	2	1	12	9		12.00	92.30	0	0	0	0	150	160	1	160.00	6.40	1-74	0
S Dhawan	2010-2019	118	117	6	4990	137		44.95	93.99	15	25	58	0	0	0	0	5.16	1-14	-	0
MS Dhoni	2004-2019	332	282	80	10192	183*	50.45	87.11	9	70	308	114	36	31	1	31.00			0	
SS Dighe	2000-2001	23	17	6	256	94*	23.27	60.95	0	1	19	5	0	0	0				0	
AB Dinda	2010-2013	13	5	0	21	16		4.20	58.33	0	0	1	0	594	612	12	51.00	6.18	2-44	
DR Doshi	1980-1982	15	5	2	9	5*	3.00	45.00	0	0	3	0	792	524	22	23.81	3.96	4.30	2	0
R Dravid	1996-2011	340	314	39	10768	153		39.15	71.19	12	82	196	14	186	170	4	42.50	5.48	2-43	
FM Engineer	1974-1975	5	4	1	114	54*	38.00	58.46	0	1	3	1	0	0	0			0	
FY Fazal	2016-2016	1	1	1	55	55*		90.16	0	1	0	0	0	0	0			0		
AD Gaekwad	1975-1987	15	14	1	269	78*	20.69	52.84	0	1	6	0	48	39	1	39.00	4.87	1-39	0	0
G Gambhir	2003-2013	147	143	11	5238	150*	39.68	85.25	11	34	36	0	6	13	0		13.00		0	0
DJ Gandhi	1999-2000	3	3	0	49	30		16.33	50.51	0	0	0	0	0	0	0			-	
D Ganesh	1997-1997	1	1	0	4	4		4.00	50.00	0	0	0	0	30	20	1	20.00	4.00	1-20	0
SC Ganguly	1992-2007	308	297	23	11221	183		40.95	73.64	22	71	99	0	4543	3835	100	38.35	5.06	5-16	3
RS Gavaskar	2004-2004	11	10	2	151	54		18.87	64.52	0	1	5	0	72	74	1	74.00	6.16	1-56	0
SM Gavaskar	1974-1987	108	102	14	3092	103*	35.13	61.82	1	27	22	0	20	25	1	25.00	7.50	1-10	0	0
RS Ghai	1984-1986	6	1	0	1	1		1.00	33.33	0	0	0	0	275	260	3	86.66	5.67	1-38	0
KD Ghavri	1975-1981	19	16	6	114	20		11.40	59.06	0	0	1	0	1033	708	15	47.20	4.11	3-40	0
MS Gony	2008-2008	2	0	0	0	0				0	0	2	0	78	76	2	38.00	5.84	2-65	0
Gurkeerat Singh	2016-2016	3	3	1	13	8		6.50	100.00	0	0	1	0	60	68	0		6.80	-	0
Gursharan Singh	1990-1990	1	1	0	4	4		4.00	40.00	0	0	1	0	0	0	0			-	0
Harbhajan Singh	1998-2015	234	126	35	1213	49		13.32	80.75	0	0	71	0	12359	8872	265	33.47	4.30	5-31	0
Harvinder Singh	1997-2001	16	5	1	6	3*	1.50	31.57	0	0	6	0	686	609	24	25.37	5.32	3-44	0	5

Player	Span																	
ND Hirwani	1988-1992	18	7	3	8	4	2.00	27.58	0	0	2	960	719	23	31.26	4.49	4-43	3
SS Iyer	2017-2018	6	5	0	210	88	42.00	96.33	0	2	3	6	2	0		2.00	-	0
AD Jadeja	1992-2000	196	179	36	5359	119	37.47	69.39	6	30	59	1248	1094	20	54.70	5.25	3-3	0
RA Jadeja	2009-2019	147	98	33	1990	87	30.61	84.97	0	10	52	7429	6055	171	35.40	4.89	5-36	8
KM Jadhav	2014-2019	49	32	11	945	120	45.00	107.87	2	4	25	839	686	22	31.18	4.90	3-23	0
W Jaffer	2006-2006	2	2	0	10	10	5.00	43.47	0	0	0	0	0	0			-	0
Joginder Sharma	2004-2007	4	3	2	35	29*	35.00	116.66	0	0	3	150	115	1	115.00	4.60	1-28	0
SB Joshi	1996-2001	69	45	11	584	61*	17.17	89.57	0	1	19	3386	2509	69	36.36	4.44	5-6	2
M Kaif	2002-2006	125	110	24	2753	111*	32.01	72.03	2	17	55	0	0	0			-	0
AV Kale	2003-2003	1	1	0	10	10	10.00	45.45	0	0	0	0	0	0			-	0
VG Kambli	1991-2000	104	97	21	2477	106	32.59	71.96	2	14	15	4	7	1	7.00	10.50	1-7	0
HH Kanitkar	1997-2000	34	27	8	339	57	17.84	66.21	0	1	14	1006	803	17	47.23	4.78	2-22	
Kapil Dev	1978-1994	225	198	39	3783	175*	23.79	95.79	1	14	71	11202	6945	253	27.45	3.71	5-43	4
AR Kapoor	1995-2000	17	6	0	43	19	7.16	68.25	0	0	1	900	612	8	76.50	4.08	2-33	0
SS Karim	1997-2000	34	27	4	362	55	15.73	64.64	0	1	27	0	0	0			-	0
KD Karthik	2004-2019	89	75	20	1700	79	30.90	73.37	0	9	56	0	0	0			-	
M Kartik	2002-2007	37	14	5	126	32*	14.00	70.39	0	0	10	1907	1612	37	43.56	5.07	6-27	1
S Kaul	2018-2018	3	2	0	1	1	0.50	33.33	0	0	1	162	179	0		6.62	-	
Z Khan	2000-2012	194	96	31	753	34*	11.58	72.33	0	0	43	9815	8102	269	30.11	4.95	5-42	8
SC Khanna	1979-1984	10	10	2	176	56	22.00	66.41	0	2	4	0	0	0			-	0
GK Khoda	1998-1998	2	2	0	115	89	57.50	61.82	0	1	0	0	0	0			-	0
AR Khurasiya	1999-2001	12	11	0	149	57	13.54	79.25	0	1	3	0	0	0			-	0
SMH Kirmani	1976-1986	49	31	13	373	48*	20.72	61.44	0	0	27	0	0	0			-	0

V Kohli	2008-2019	219	211	37	10385	183		59.68	92.73	39	48	105	0	641	665	4	166.25	6.22	1-15	0
P Krishnamurthy	1976-1976	1	1	0	6	6		6.00	46.15	0	0	1	1	0	0	0	5.09		-	0
DS Kulkarni	2014-2016	12	2	2	27	25*	5.50	96.42	0	0	2	0	598	508	19	26.73	5.32	4-34	1	
NM Kulkarni	1997-1998	10	5	3	11	5*		55.00	0	0	2	0	402	357	11	32.45	34.50	3-27	0	0
RR Kulkarni	1983-1987	10	5	3	33	15	13.90	16.50	84.61	0	0	2	0	444	345	10	34.50	5.13	4.66	3-42	
P Kumar	2007-2012	68	33	12	292	54*		88.21	0	1	11	0	3242	2774	77	36.02	5.13	38.66	4-31	3	0
T Kumaran	1999-2000	8	3	0	19	8		6.33	70.37	0	0	3	0	378	348	9	38.66	30.83	5.52	3-24	
A Kumble	1990-2007	269	134	47	903	26		10.37	61.01	0	0	85	0	14376	10300	334	30.83	35.60	4.29	6-12	0
A Kuruvilla	1997-1997	25	11	4	26	7		3.71	60.46	0	0	4	0	1131	890	25	35.60	20.00	4.72	4-43	10
R Lamba	1986-1989	32	31	2	783	102		27.00	66.80	1	6	10	0	19	20	1	20.00		6.31	1-9	1
VVS Laxman	1998-2006	86	83	7	2338	131		30.76	71.23	6	10	39	0	42	40	0		4.05	5.71	-	0
Madan Lal	1974-1987	67	35	14	401	53*	19.09	60.84	0	1	18	0	3164	2137	73	29.27	4.05		4-20	2	0
AO Malhotra	1982-1986	20	19	4	457	65		30.46	70.85	0	1	4	0	6	0	0		3.95	0.00	-	
Maninder Singh	1983-1993	59	18	14	49	8*	12.25	54.44	0	0	18	0	3133	2066	66	31.30	3.95	4-22	1	0
SV Manjrekar	1988-1996	74	70	10	1994	105		33.23	64.23	1	15	23	0	8	10	1	10.00	47.00	7.50	1-2	
AV Mankad	1974-1974	1	1	0	44	44		44.00	72.13	0	0	0	0	35	47	1	47.00		8.05	1-47	0
JJ Martin	1999-2001	10	8	1	158	39		22.57	47.30	0	0	6	0	0	0	0		5.71		-	0
PL Mhambrey	1996-1998	3	1	1	7	7*		140.00	0	0	0	0	126	120	3	40.00	5.71	23.60	2-69	0	0
A Mishra	2003-2016	36	11	3	43	14		5.37	52.43	0	0	5	0	1917	1511	64	23.60	67.66	4.72	6-48	
A Mithun	2010-2011	5	3	0	51	24		17.00	92.72	0	0	1	0	180	203	3	67.66	26.26	6.76	2-32	4
Mohammed Shami	2013-2019	55	25	13	117	25		9.75	86.02	0	0	17	0	2823	2600	99	26.26	4.99	5.52	4-35	0
DS Mohanty	1997-2001	45	11	6	28	18*	5.60	49.12	0	0	10	0	1996	1662	57	29.15	4.99	5.35	4-56	1	6
D Mongia	2001-2007	57	51	7	1230	159*	27.95	71.47	1	4	21	0	640	571	14	40.78	5.35	3-31	0		

Player	Span																			
NR Mongia	1994-2000	140	96	33	1272	69	13.09	20.19	69.13	0	2	110	44	0	0	0			-	0
KS More	1984-1993	94	65	22	563	42*		71.35	0	0	63	27	0	0	0	0	3.37		0	
SP Mukherjee	1990-1991	3	1	1	2	2*		100.00	0	1	0	174	98	2	49.00		1-30	0	
SS Naik	1974-1974	2	2	0	38	20		19.00	55.88	0	0	0	0	0	0	0			-	0
KK Nair	2016-2016	2	2	0	46	39		23.00	52.27	0	0	0	0	0	0	0			-	0
SV Nayak	1981-1982	4	1	0	3	3		3.00	15.78	0	0	1	0	222	161	1	161.00	4.35	1-51	0
AM Nayar	2009-2009	3	1	1	0	0*		0.00	0	0	0	0	18	17	0		5.66		0	
A Nehra	2001-2011	117	45	21	140	24		5.83	57.37	0	0	17	0	5637	4899	155	31.60	5.21	6-23	7
NV Ojha	2010-2010	1	1	0	1	1		1.00	14.28	0	0	0	1	0	0	0			-	0
PP Ojha	2008-2012	18	10	8	46	16*	23.00	41.07	0	0	7	0	876	652	21	31.04	4.46	4-38	1	
GK Pandey	1999-1999	2	2	1	4	4*	4.00	36.36	0	0	0	0	78	60	0		4.61		0	
MK Pandey	2015-2018	23	18	6	440	104*	36.66	91.85	1	2	6	0	0	0	0				0	
CS Pandit	1986-1992	36	23	9	290	33*	20.71	72.50	0	0	15	15	0	0	0				0	0
HH Pandya	2016-2018	42	27	4	670	83		29.13	114.52	0	4	17	0	1768	1638	40	40.95	5.55	3-31	
Pankaj Singh	2010-2010	1	1	1	3	3*		100.00	0	0	1	0	42	45	0		6.42		0	0
RR Pant	2018-2018	3	2	0	41	24		20.50	132.25	0	0	3	0	0	0	0			-	0
JV Paranjpe	1998-1998	4	4	1	54	27		18.00	59.34	0	0	2	0	0	0	0			-	0
GA Parkar	1982-1984	10	10	1	165	42		18.33	49.69	0	0	4	0	0	0	0			-	0
Parvez Rasool	2014-2014	1	0	0	0	0				0	0	0	0	60	60	2	30.00	6.00	2-60	0
AK Patel	1984-1985	8	2	0	6	6		3.00	54.54	0	0	1	0	360	263	7	37.57	4.38	3-43	0
AR Patel	2014-2017	38	20	6	181	38		12.92	95.26	0	0	15	0	1908	1409	45	31.31	4.43	3-34	0
BP Patel	1974-1979	10	9	1	243	82		30.37	60.90	0	1	1	0						-	0
MM Patel	2006-2011	70	27	16	74	15		6.72	66.07	0	0	11	0	3154	2603	86	30.26	4.95	4-29	3

Player	Span																			
PA Patel	2003-2012	38	34	3	736	95		23.74	76.50	0	4	30	9	0	0	0			-	0
RGM Patel	1988-1988	1	0	0	0	0				0	0	0	0	60	58	0		5.80	-	0
IK Pathan	2004-2012	120	87	21	1544	83		23.39	79.54	0	5	21	0	5855	5142	173	29.72	5.26	5-27	7
YK Pathan	2006-2012	57	41	11	810	123*	27.00	113.60	2	3	17	0	1490	1365	33	41.36	5.49	3.49	0	
SM Patil	1980-1986	45	42	1	1005	84		24.51	82.17	0	9	11	0	864	589	15	39.26	4.09	2-28	0
RR Powar	2004-2007	31	19	5	163	54		11.64	62.69	0	1	3	0	1536	1191	34	35.02	4.65	3-24	0
M Prabhakar	1984-1996	130	98	21	1858	106		24.12	60.18	2	11	27	0	6360	4534	157	28.87	4.27	5-33	6
BKV Prasad	1994-2001	161	63	31	221	19		6.90	60.54	0	0	37	0	8129	6332	196	32.30	4.67	5-27	4
MSK Prasad	1998-1999	17	11	2	131	63		14.55	58.22	0	1	14	7	0	0	0			-	0
CA Pujara	2013-2014	5	5	0	51	27		10.20	39.23	0	0	0	0	0	0	0			-	0
AM Rahane	2011-2018	90	87	3	2962	111		35.26	78.63	3	24	48	0	0	0	0			-	0
KL Rahul	2016-2018	13	12	3	317	100*	35.22	80.66	1	2	6	0	0	0	0	-	-	0		
SK Raina	2005-2018	226	194	35	5615	116*	35.31	93.50	5	36	102	0	2126	1811	36	50.30	5.11	3.34	0	0
LS Rajput	1985-1987	4	4	1	9	8		3.00	29.03	0	0	2	0	42	42	0		6.00	-	0
SLV Raju	1990-1996	53	16	8	32	8		4.00	47.76	0	0	8	0	2770	2014	63	31.96	4.36	4-46	2
WV Raman	1988-1996	27	27	1	617	114		23.73	58.04	1	3	2	0	162	170	2	85.00	6.29	1-23	0
S Ramesh	1999-1999	24	24	1	646	82		28.08	59.15	0	6	3	0	36	38	1	38.00	6.33	1-23	0
Randhir Singh	1981-1983	2	0	0	0	0				0	0	0	0	72	48	1	48.00	4.00	1-30	0
V Rathour	1996-1997	7	7	0	193	54		27.57	60.12	0	2	4	0	0	0	0			-	0
A Ratra	2002-2002	12	8	1	90	30		12.85	70.86	0	0	11	5	0	0	0			-	0
SS Raul	1998-1998	2	2	0	8	8		4.00	57.14	0	0	0	0	36	27	1	27.00	4.50	1-13	0
AT Rayudu	2013-2019	47	42	12	1471	124*	49.03	79.38	3	9	15	0	121	124	3	41.33	6.14	1-5	0	
V Razdan	1989-1990	3	3	1	23	18		11.50	85.18	0	0	4	0	84	77	1	77.00	5.50	1-37	0

Player	Span																			
B Reddy	1978-1981	3	2	2	11	8*		55.00	0	0	2	0	0	0	0	0				0
WP Saha	2010-2014	9	5	2	41	16		13.66	73.21	0	0	17	1	0	0	0		2-15		0
AM Salvi	2003-2003	4	3	1	4	4*	2.00	28.57	0	0	2	0	172	120	4	30.00		3-27		–
BS Sandhu	1982-1984	22	7	3	51	16*	12.75	52.57	0	0	5	0	1110	763	16	47.68		4.80		0
RL Sanghvi	1998-1998	10	2	0	8	8		4.00	72.72	0	0	4	0	498	399	10	39.90	4.18	3-29	0
Sarandeep Singh	2002-2003	5	4	1	47	19		15.66	64.38	0	0	2	0	258	180	3	60.00	5.22	2-34	0
V Sehwag	1999-2013	241	235	9	7995	219		35.37	104.44	15	37	90	0	4290	3737	94	39.75	4.92	4-6	1
TA Sekhar	1983-1985	4	0	0	0	0				0	0	0	0	156	128	5	25.60	3.83	3-23	0
V Shankar	2019-2019	1	0	0	0	0				0	0	1	0	36	23	0		3-41		0
AK Sharma	1988-1993	31	27	6	424	59*	20.19	90.40	0	3	6	0	1140	875	15	58.33	4.60	3-22		–
C Sharma	1983-1994	65	35	16	456	101*	24.00	91.20	1	0	7	0	2835	2336	67	34.86	4.94	4.45		–
G Sharma	1985-1987	11	2	0	11	7		5.50	45.83	0	0	2	0	486	361	10	36.10	5.72	3-29	0
I Sharma	2007-2016	80	28	13	72	13		4.80	35.46	0	0	19	0	3733	3563	115	30.98	6.57	4-34	6
KV Sharma	2014-2014	2	0	0	0	0				0	0	3	0	114	125	0		5.45		0
MM Sharma	2013-2015	26	9	5	31	11		7.75	46.96	0	0	6	0	1121	1020	31	32.90	5.15	4-22	1
PH Sharma	1976-1976	2	2	0	20	14		10.00	51.28	0	0	0	0	0	0	0		5.21		0
R Sharma	2011-2012	4	1	0	1	1		1.00	50.00	0	0	1	0	206	177	6	29.50	4.98	3-43	0
RG Sharma	2007-2019	196	190	31	7639	264		48.04	88.78	22	37	71	0	593	515	8	64.37	4.21	2-27	0
SK Sharma	1988-1990	23	12	4	80	28		10.00	65.57	0	0	7	0	979	813	22	36.95	4.94	5-26	1
RJ Shastri	1981-1992	150	128	21	3108	109		29.04	60.89	4	18	40	0	6613	4650	129	36.04		5-15	3
LR Shukla	1999-1999	3	2	0	18	13		9.00	94.73	0	0	1	0	114	94	1	94.00		1-25	3
NS Sidhu	1987-1998	136	127	8	4413	134*	37.08	69.75	6	33	20	0	4	3	0	4.50		0	0
RP Singh	1986-1986	2	0	0	0	0				0	0	0	0	82	77	1	77.00	5.63	1-58	0

Player	Span																			
RP Singh	2005-2011	58	20	10	104	23		10.40	42.97	0	0	13	0	2565	2343	69	33.95	5.48	4-35	2
RR Singh	1989-2001	136	113	23	2336	100		25.95	74.63	1	9	33	0	3734	2985	69	43.26	4.79	5-22	2
VR Singh	2006-2006	2	1	0	8	8		8.00	61.53	0	0	3	0	72	105	0		8.75	-	0
M Siraj	2019-2019	1	0	0	0	0				0	0	0	0	60	76	0		7.60	-	0
L Sivaramakrishnan	1985-1987	16	4	2	5	2*	2.50	20.83	0	0	7	0	756	538	15	35.86	4.26	3-35	0	
RS Sodhi	2000-2002	18	14	3	280	67		25.45	73.29	0	2	9	0	462	365	5	73.00	4.74	2-31	0
ED Solkar	1974-1976	7	6	0	27	13		4.50	34.17	0	0	2	0	252	169	4	42.25	4.02	2-31	0
SB Somasunder	1996-1996	2	2	0	16	9		8.00	25.39	0	0	0	0	0	0	0			-	0
BB Sran	2016-2016	6	0	0	0	0				0	0	1	0	302	269	7	38.42	5.34	3-56	0
S Sreesanth	2005-2011	53	21	10	44	10*	4.00	36.36	0	0	7	0	2476	2508	75	33.44	6.07	6-55	3	
K Srikkanth	1981-1992	146	145	4	4091	123		29.01	72.12	4	27	42	0	712	641	25	25.64	5.40	5-27	2
J Srinath	1991-2003	229	121	38	883	53		10.63	79.62	0	1	32	0	11935	8847	315	28.08	4.44	5-23	10
TE Srinivasan	1980-1981	2	2	0	10	6		5.00	28.57	0	0	0	0	0	0	0			-	0
S Sriram	2000-2004	8	7	1	81	57		13.50	60.00	0	1	1	0	324	274	9	30.44	5.07	3-43	0
R Sudhakar Rao	1976-1976	1	1	0	4	4		4.00	28.57	0	0	1	0	0	0	0			-	0
SR Tendulkar	1989-2012	463	452	41	18426	200*	44.83	86.24	49	96	140	0	8054	6850	154	44.48	5.10	5-32	6	
SN Thakur	2017-2018	5	2	1	22	22*	22.00	137.50	0	0	3	0	215	218	6	36.33	6.08	4-52	1	
MK Tiwary	2008-2015	12	12	1	287	104*	26.09	71.21	1	1	4	0	132	150	5	30.00	6.81	4-61	1	
SS Tiwary	2010-2010	3	2	2	49	37*		87.50	0	0	2	0	0	0	0			0		
S Tyagi	2009-2010	4	1	1	1	1*		50.00	0	0	1	0	165	144	3	48.00	5.23	1-15	0	
JD Unadkat	2013-2013	7	0	0	0	0				0	0	0	0	312	209	8	26.12	4.01	4-41	1
RV Uthappa	2006-2015	46	42	6	934	86		25.94	90.59	0	6	19	2	2	0	0		0.00	-	0

Player	Years																			
PS Vaidya	1995-1996	4	2	0	15	12		7.50	125.00	0	0	2	0	184	174	4	43.50	5.67	2-41	0
DB Vengsarkar	1976-1991	129	120	19	3508	105	10.80	34.73	67.78	1	23	37	0	6	4	0		4.00	-	0
S Venkataraghavan	1974-1983	15	9	4	54	26*		42.85	0	0	4	0	868	542	5	108.40	3.74	2.34	0	0
M Venkataramana	1988-1988	1	1	1	0	0*			0	0	0	0	60	36	2	18.00	3.60	2.36	0	
Y Venugopal Rao	2005-2006	16	11	2	218	61*	24.22	60.05	0	1	5	0	0	0	0				0	
R Vijay Bharadwaj	1999-2002	10	9	4	136	41*	27.20	70.10	0	0	4	0	372	307	16	19.18	4.95	3.34	1-19	0
M Vijay	2010-2015	17	16	0	339	72		21.18	66.99	0	1	9	0	36	37	1	37.00	6.16	1	0
R Vinay Kumar	2010-2013	31	13	4	86	27*	9.55	58.90	0	0	6	0	1436	1423	38	37.44	5.94	4.30	-	
GR Viswanath	1974-1982	25	23	1	439	75		19.95	52.76	0	2	3	0	0	0	0				-	0
S Viswanath	1985-1988	22	12	4	72	23*	9.00	51.79	0	0	17	7	0	0	0				0	
AL Wadekar	1974-1974	2	2	0	73	67		36.50	81.11	0	1	1	0	0	0	0				-	0
MS Washington Sundar	2017-2017	1	0	0	0	0				0	0	1	0	60	65	1	65.00	6.50	1-65	0
AS Wassan	1990-1991	9	6	2	33	16		8.25	58.92	0	0	2	0	426	283	11	25.72	3.98	3-28	0
J Yadav	2016-2016	1	1	1	1	1*		100.00	0	0	1	0	24	8	1	8.00	2.00	1-8	0	
JP Yadav	2002-2005	12	7	3	81	69		20.25	65.85	0	1	3	0	396	326	6	54.33	4.93	2-32	0
K Yadav	2017-2019	35	13	9	63	19		15.75	59.43	0	0	3	0	1824	1465	69	21.23	4.81	6-25	3
NS Yadav	1986-1987	7	2	2	1	1*		6.25	0	0	1	0	330	228	8	28.50	4.14	2-18	0	
UT Yadav	2010-2018	75	24	14	79	18*	7.90	58.95	0	0	22	0	3558	3565	106	33.63	6.01	4-31	4	
V Yadav	1992-1994	19	12	2	118	34*	11.80	101.72	0	0	12	7	0	0	0				0	
Yashpal Sharma	1978-1985	42	40	9	883	89		28.48	63.02	0	4	10	0	201	199	1	199.00	5.94	1-27	0
Yograj Singh	1980-1981	6	4	2	1	1		0.50	8.33	0	0	2	0	244	186	4	46.50	4.57	2-44	0
T Yohannan	2002-2002	3	2	2	7	5*		63.63	0	0	0	0	120	122	5	24.40	6.10	3-33	0	
Yuvraj Singh	2000-2017	301	275	39	8609	150		36.47	87.42	14	52	93	0	4988	4227	110	38.42	5.08	5-31	3

LIST OF INDIAN ONE DAY CRICKETERS

Name	Years	Mts	Inns	NO	Runs	Hs		Avg	SR	100	50	Ct	St	Balls	Runs	Wkts	Avg	RPO	Best	4I
VR Aaron	2011-2014	9	3	2	8	6*	8.00	53.33	0	0	1	0	380	419	11	38.09	6.61	3-24	0	0
S Abid Ali	1974-1975	5	3	0	93	70		31.00	70.45	0	1	0	0	336	187	7	26.71	3.33	2-22	0
AB Agarkar	1998-2007	191	113	26	1269	95		14.58	80.62	0	3	53	0	9484	8021	288	27.85	5.07	6-42	12
KK Ahmed	2018-2019	7	2	1	4	3		4.00	33.33	0	0	1	0	360	319	11	29.00	5.31	3-13	0
M Amarnath	1975-1989	85	75	12	1924	102*	30.53	57.70	2	13	23	0	2730	1971	46	42.84	4.33	3-12	0	
S Amarnath	1978-1978	3	3	0	100	62		33.33	84.03	0	1	1	0	0	0	0			-	0
PK Amre	1991-1994	37	30	5	513	84*	20.52	63.80	0	2	12	0	2	4	0		12.00		0	
SA Ankola	1989-1997	20	13	4	34	9		3.77	80.95	0	0	2	0	807	615	13	47.30	4.57	3-33	0
Arshad Ayub	1987-1990	32	17	7	116	31*	11.60	71.60	0	0	5	0	1769	1216	31	39.22	4.12	5-21	1	0
B Arun	1986-1987	4	3	1	21	8		10.50	65.62	0	0	0	0	1216	102	103	1	103.00	6.05	1-43	0
Arun Lal	1982-1989	13	13	0	122	51		9.38	52.58	0	1	4	0	0	0	0		-	-	0
R Ashwin	2010-2017	111	61	19	675	65		16.07	86.98	0	1	30	0	6021	4937	150	32.91	4.91	4-25	1
KBJ Azad	1980-1986	25	21	2	269	39*	14.15	66.25	0	7	0	390	273	7	39.00	4.20	2-48	0		
M Azharuddin	1985-2000	334	308	54	9378	153*	36.92	73.98	7	58	156	0	552	479	12	39.91	5.20	3-19	0	
HK Badani	2000-2004	40	36	10	867	100		33.34	73.47	1	4	13	0	183	149	3	49.66	4.88	1-7	0
S Badrinath	2008-2011	7	6	1	79	27*	15.80	45.93	0	0	2	0	0	0	0		-	0		
SV Bahutule	1997-2003	8	4	1	23	11		7.66	79.31	0	0	3	0	294	283	2	141.50	5.77	1-31	0
L Balaji	2002-2009	30	16	6	120	21*	12.00	78.94	0	11	0	1447	1344	34	39.52	5.57	4-48	1		
ST Banerjee	1991-1992	6	5	3	49	25*	24.50	116.66	0	3	0	240	202	5	40.40	5.05	3-30	0		
SB Bangar	2002-2004	15	15	2	180	57*	13.84	75.31	1	4	0	442	384	7	54.85	5.21	2-39	0		

Player	Span	Mat	Inns	NO	Runs	HS	C6	C7	C8	C9	C10	C11	C12	C13	C14	C15	C16	C17	C18	C19
AC Bedade	1994-1994	13	10	3	158	51		22.57	86.33	0	1	4	0	0	0	0	48.57	3.45	-	0
BS Bedi	1974-1979	10	7	2	31	13		6.20	44.28	0	0	4	0	590	340	7	6.00	3-31	2-44	0
A Bhandari	2000-2004	2	1	1	0	0*			0	0	0	0	106	106	5	21.20	26.00	4.58	0	
Bhupinder Singh sr	1994-1994	2	1	0	6	6		6.00	46.15	0	0	0	0	102	78	3	4.98	5-42	3-34	0
Bhuvneshwar Kumar	2012-2019	98	45	15	469	53*	15.63	75.52	0	1	24	0	4720	3923	107	36.66	29.35	4.58	4	
RMH Binny	1980-1987	72	49	10	629	57		16.12	60.19	0	1	12	0	2957	2260	77	21.95	5.37	4-29	3
STR Binny	2014-2015	14	11	3	230	77		28.75	93.49	0	1	3	0	490	439	20	39.00	3.54	6-4	1
GK Bose	1974-1974	1	1	0	13	13		13.00	72.22	0	0	0	0	66	39	1	4.44	5-27	1-39	0
JJ Bumrah	2016-2018	44	6	2	11	10*	2.75	32.35	0	0	15	0	2212	1639	78	21.01	23.75	4.73	5	
YS Chahal	2016-2019	35	4	1	16	12		5.33	57.14	0	0	7	0	1867	1473	62	37.00	9.25	6-42	3
DL Chahar	2018-2018	1	1	0	12	12		12.00	85.71	0	0	0	0	24	37	1	3.85	3-36	1-37	0
BS Chandrasekhar	1976-1976	1	1	1	11	11*		84.61	0	0	0	0	56	36	3	12.00			0	
VB Chandrasekhar	1988-1990	7	7	0	88	53	6.00	12.57	54.32	0	1	0	0	0	0	0		2-35	-	0
US Chatterjee	1995-1995	3	2	1	6	3*		21.42	0	0	1	0	161	117	3	39.00	4.36	4.46	0	
CPS Chauhan	1978-1981	7	7	0	153	46		21.85	50.83	0	0	3	0	0	0	0		4-23	-	0
RK Chauhan	1993-1997	35	18	5	132	32		10.15	77.19	0	0	10	0	1634	1216	29	41.93	4.46	3-29	0
PP Chawla	2007-2011	25	12	5	38	13*	5.42	65.51	0	0	9	0	1312	1117	32	34.90	5.10	4.20	2	
N Chopra	1998-2000	39	26	6	310	61		15.50	62.24	0	1	16	0	1835	1286	46	27.95	4.20	5-21	2
V Dahiya	2000-2001	19	15	2	216	51		16.61	80.89	0	1	19	5	0	0	0			-	0
SS Das	2001-2002	4	4	1	39	30		13.00	50.64	0	0	0	0	0	0	0			-	0
DB Dasgupta	2001-2001	5	4	1	51	24*	17.00	63.75	0	0	2	1	0	0	0			-	0	
NA David	1997-1997	4	2	2	9	8*		90.00	0	0	0	0	192	133	4	33.25	4.15	3-21	0	0

Player	Span																			
P Dharmani	1996-1996	1	1	0	8	8		8.00	100.00	0	0	0	0	0	0	0	160.00	6.40	-	0
R Dhawan	2016-2016	3	2	1	12	9		12.00	92.30	0	0	0	0	150	160	1	5.16		1-74	0
S Dhawan	2010-2019	118	117	6	4990	137		44.95	93.99	15	25	58	0	0	0	0			-	0
MS Dhoni	2004-2019	332	282	80	10192	183*	50.45	87.11	9	70	308	114	36	31	1	31.00	51.00	6.18	0	
SS Dighe	2000-2001	23	17	6	256	94*	23.27	60.95	0	1	19	5	0	0	0	0	3.96	4.30	0	0
AB Dinda	2010-2013	13	5	0	21	16		4.20	58.33	0	0	0	1	0	594	612	12	42.50	5.48	6.18	0
DR Doshi	1980-1982	15	5	2	9	5*	3.00	45.00	0	0	3	0	792	524	22	23.81			2	0
R Dravid	1996-2011	340	314	39	10768	153		39.15	71.19	12	82	196	14	186	170	4			2-43	0
FM Engineer	1974-1975	5	4	1	114	54*	38.00	58.46	0	3	1	0	0	0	0		4.87		0	
FY Fazal	2016-2016	1	1	1	55	55*		90.16	0	1	0	0	0	0	0		13.00		0	
AD Gaekwad	1975-1987	15	14	1	269	78*	20.69	52.84	0	6	0	48	39	1	39.00		1-39	0	0	
G Gambhir	2003-2013	147	143	11	5238	150*	39.68	85.25	11	34	36	0	6	13	0		20.00	4.00	0	
DJ Gandhi	1999-2000	3	3	0	49	30		16.33	50.51	0	0	0	0	0	0	0	0	38.35	5.06	-	0
D Ganesh	1997-1997	1	1	0	4	4		4.00	50.00	0	0	0	0	30	20	1	74.00	6.16	1-20	0
SC Ganguly	1992-2007	308	297	23	11221	183		40.95	73.64	22	71	99	0	4543	3835	100	7.50		5-16	3
RS Gavaskar	2004-2004	11	10	2	151	54		18.87	64.52	0	1	5	0	72	74	1	86.66	5.67	1-56	0
SM Gavaskar	1974-1987	108	102	14	3092	103*	35.13	61.82	1	27	22	0	20	25	1	25.00	47.20	4.11	0	3
RS Ghai	1984-1986	6	1	0	1	1		1.00	33.33	0	0	0	0	275	260	3	38.00	5.84	1-38	0
KD Ghavri	1975-1981	19	16	6	114	20		11.40	59.06	0	0	2	0	1033	708	15			3-40	0
MS Gony	2008-2008	2	0	0	0	0				0	0	0	0	78	76	2		6.80	2-65	0
Gurkeerat Singh	2016-2016	3	3	1	13	8		6.50	100.00	0	0	1	0	60	68	0			-	0
Gursharan Singh	1990-1990	1	1	0	4	4		4.00	40.00	0	0	1	0	0	0	0			-	0
Harbhajan Singh	1998-2015	234	126	35	1213	49		13.32	80.75	0	0	71	0	12359	8872	265	33.47	4.30	5-31	5

Player	Span	Mat	Inns	NO	Runs	HS	Ave	SR	100	50	Ct	St	Balls	Runs	Wkts	Ave	Econ	BBI	4	5
Harvinder Singh	1997-2001	16	5	1	6	3*	1.50	31.57	0	0	6	0	686	609	24	25.37	5.32	3-44	0	3
ND Hirwani	1988-1992	18	7	3	8	4	2.00	27.58	0	0	2	2	0	960	719	23	31.26	4.49	4-43	0
SS Iyer	2017-2018	6	5	0	210	88	42.00	96.33	0	2	3	3	0	6	6	2	54.70	2.00	-	0
AD Jadeja	1992-2000	196	179	36	5359	119	37.47	69.39	6	30	59	0	1248	1094	20	54.70	5.25	3-3	3-3	0
RA Jadeja	2009-2019	147	98	33	1990	87	30.61	84.97	0	0	10	52	0	7429	6055	171	35.40	4.89	5-36	8
KM Jadhav	2014-2019	49	32	11	945	120	45.00	107.87	2	4	25	0	839	686	22	31.18	4.90	3-23	0	0
W Jaffer	2006-2006	2	2	0	10	10	5.00	43.47	0	0	0	0	0	0	0	-	-	-	-	0
Joginder Sharma	2004-2007	4	3	2	35	29*	35.00	116.66	0	0	3	0	150	115	1	115.00	4.60	1-28	0	0
SB Joshi	1996-2001	69	45	11	584	61*	17.17	89.57	0	1	19	0	3386	2509	69	36.36	4.44	5-6	2	0
M Kaif	2002-2006	125	110	24	2753	111*	32.01	72.03	0	17	55	0	0	0	0	-	-	-	0	0
AV Kale	2003-2003	1	1	0	10	10	10.00	45.45	0	0	0	0	0	0	0	-	-	-	-	0
VG Kambli	1991-2000	104	97	21	2477	106	32.59	71.96	2	14	14	15	4	4	1	7.00	10.50	1-7	1-7	0
HH Kanitkar	1997-2000	34	27	8	339	57	17.84	66.21	0	1	1	14	1006	803	17	47.23	4.78	2-22	2-22	0
Kapil Dev	1978-1994	225	198	39	3783	175*	23.79	95.79	1	14	71	0	11202	6945	253	27.45	3.71	5-43	4	4
AR Kapoor	1995-2000	17	6	0	43	19	7.16	68.25	0	0	0	1	0	900	612	8	76.50	4.08	2-33	0
SS Karim	1997-2000	34	27	4	362	55	15.73	64.64	0	1	27	27	3	0	0	-	-	-	-	0
KD Karthik	2004-2019	89	75	20	1700	79	30.90	73.37	0	9	56	7	0	0	0	-	-	-	-	0
M Kartik	2002-2007	37	14	5	126	32*	14.00	70.39	0	0	10	0	1907	1612	37	43.56	5.07	6-27	1	0
S Kaul	2018-2018	3	2	0	1	1	0.50	33.33	0	0	0	1	0	162	179	0	-	-	-	0
Z Khan	2000-2012	194	96	31	753	34*	11.58	72.33	0	0	43	0	9815	8102	269	30.11	4.95	5-42	8	0
SC Khanna	1979-1984	10	10	2	176	56	22.00	66.41	0	1	2	4	4	0	0	-	-	-	-	0
GK Khoda	1998-1998	2	2	0	115	89	57.50	61.82	0	1	1	0	0	0	0	-	-	-	-	0
AR Khurasiya	1999-2001	12	11	0	149	57	13.54	79.25	0	1	1	3	0	0	0	-	-	-	-	0

SMH Kirmani	1976-1986	49	31	13	373	48*	20.72	61.44	0	0	27	9	0	0	0	-	166.25	-	-	0
V Kohli	2008-2019	219	211	37	10385	183		59.68	92.73	39	48	105	0	641	665	4		6.22	1-15	0
P Krishnamurthy	1976-1976	1	1	0	6	6		6.00	46.15	0	0	1	1	0	0	0		4.34	-	
DS Kulkarni	2014-2016	12	2	2	27	25*	5.50	96.42	0	0	2	0	598	508	19	26.73	5.09	3.27	1	0
NM Kulkarni	1997-1998	10	5	3	11	5*		55.00	0	0	2	0	402	357	11	32.45	5.32	4.66	0	
RR Kulkarni	1983-1987	10	5	3	33	15	13.90	16.50	84.61	0	0	2	0	444	345	10	34.50	4.31	3-42	0
P Kumar	2007-2012	68	33	12	292	54*		88.21	0	1	11	0	3242	2774	77	36.02	5.13	5.52	3	
T Kumaran	1999-2000	8	3	0	19	8		6.33	70.37	0	0	3	0	378	348	9	38.66	4.29	3-24	0
A Kumble	1990-2007	269	134	47	903	26		10.37	61.01	0	0	85	0	14376	10300	334	30.83	4.72	6-12	10
A Kuruvilla	1997-1997	25	11	4	26	7		3.71	60.46	0	0	4	0	1131	890	25	35.60	6.31	4-43	1
R Lamba	1986-1989	32	31	2	783	102		27.00	66.80	1	6	10	0	19	20	1	20.00	5.71	1-9	0
VVS Laxman	1998-2006	86	83	7	2338	131	19.09	30.76	71.23	6	10	39	0	42	40	0		-	-	
Madan Lal	1974-1987	67	35	14	401	53*		60.84	0	1	18	0	3164	2137	73	29.27	4.05	4.20	2	
AO Malhotra	1982-1986	20	19	4	457	65	12.25	30.46	70.85	0	1	4	0	6	0	0		0.00	-	0
Maninder Singh	1983-1993	59	18	14	49	8*		54.44	0	0	18	0	3133	2066	66	31.30	3.95	4.22	1	
SV Manjrekar	1988-1996	74	70	10	1994	105		33.23	64.23	1	15	23	0	8	10	1	10.00	7.50	1-2	0
AV Mankad	1974-1974	1	1	0	44	44		44.00	72.13	0	0	0	0	35	47	1	47.00	8.05	1-47	0
JJ Martin	1999-2001	10	8	1	158	39		22.57	47.30	0	0	6	0	0	0	0		-	-	0
PL Mhambrey	1996-1998	3	1	1	7	7*		140.00	0	0	0	0	126	120	3	40.00	5.71	2.69	0	
A Mishra	2003-2016	36	11	3	43	14		5.37	52.43	0	0	5	0	1917	1511	64	23.60	4.72	6-48	4
A Mithun	2010-2011	5	3	0	51	24		17.00	92.72	0	0	1	0	180	203	3	67.66	6.76	2-32	0
Mohammed Shami	2013-2019	55	25	13	117	25		9.75	86.02	0	0	17	0	2823	2600	99	26.26	5.52	4-35	6
DS Mohanty	1997-2001	45	11	6	28	18*	5.60	49.12	0	0	10	0	1996	1662	57	29.15	4.99	4.56	1	

Player	Span																			
D Mongia	2001-2007	57	51	7	1230	159*	27.95	71.47	1	4	21	0	640	571	14	40.78	5.35	3-31	0	0
NR Mongia	1994-2000	140	96	33	1272	69		20.19	69.13	0	2	110	44	0	0	0			-	-
KS More	1984-1993	94	65	22	563	42*	13.09	71.35	0	0	63	27	174	0	0	0		1-30	0	0
SP Mukherjee	1990-1991	3	1	1	2	2*		100.00	0	0	1	0	0	98	2	49.00	3.37		0	0
SS Naik	1974-1974	2	2	0	38	20		19.00	55.88	0	0	0	0	0	0	0		-	-	-
KK Nair	2016-2016	2	2	0	46	39		23.00	52.27	0	0	0	0	0	0	0		-	-	-
SV Nayak	1981-1982	4	1	0	3	3		3.00	15.78	0	0	1	0	222	161	1	161.00	4.35	1-51	0
AM Nayar	2009-2009	3	1	1	0	0*		0.00	0	0	0	0	18	17	0	0	5.66		0	7
A Nehra	2001-2011	117	45	21	140	24		5.83	57.37	0	0	17	0	5637	4899	155	31.60	5.21	6-23	0
NV Ojha	2010-2010	1	1	0	1	1		1.00	14.28	0	0	0	1	0	0	0		-	1	-
PP Ojha	2008-2012	18	10	8	46	16*	23.00	41.07	0	0	7	0	876	652	21	31.04	4.46	4.38	1	0
GK Pandey	1999-1999	2	2	1	4	4*	4.00	36.36	0	2	0	0	78	60	0	0	4.61		0	0
MK Pandey	2015-2018	23	18	6	440	104*	36.66	91.85	1	0	6	0	0	0	0	0			0	0
CS Pandit	1986-1992	36	23	9	290	33*	20.71	72.50	0	0	15	15	0	0	0	0			0	0
HH Pandya	2016-2018	42	27	4	670	83		29.13	114.52	0	4	17	0	1768	1638	40	40.95	5.55	3-31	0
Pankaj Singh	2010-2010	1	1	1	3	3*		100.00	0	0	1	0	42	45	0	0	6.42	-	0	-
RR Pant	2018-2018	3	2	0	41	24		20.50	132.25	0	0	0	3	0	0	0	0		-	-	0
JV Paranjpe	1998-1998	4	4	1	54	27		18.00	59.34	0	0	0	2	0	0	0	0		-	-	0
GA Parkar	1982-1984	10	10	1	165	42		18.33	49.69	0	0	0	4	0	0	0	0		-	-	0
Parvez Rasool	2014-2014	1	0	0	0	0				0	0	0	0	60	60	2	30.00	6.00	2-60	0
AK Patel	1984-1985	8	2	0	6	6		3.00	54.54	0	0	1	0	360	263	7	37.57	4.38	3-43	0
AR Patel	2014-2017	38	20	6	181	38		12.92	95.26	0	0	15	0	1908	1409	45	31.31	4.43	3-34	0
BP Patel	1974-1979	10	9	1	243	82		30.37	60.90	0	1	1	0	0	0	0		-	-	0

MM Patel	2006-2011	70	27	16	74	15		6.72	66.07	0	0	11	0	3154	2603	86	30.26	4.95	4-29
PA Patel	2003-2012	38	34	3	736	95		23.74	76.50	0	4	30	9	0	0	0			-
RGM Patel	1988-1988	1	0	0	0	0				0	0	0	0	60	58	0		5.80	-
IK Pathan	2004-2012	120	87	21	1544	83		23.39	79.54	0	5	21	0	5855	5142	173	29.72	5.26	5-27
YK Pathan	2008-2012	57	41	11	810	123*	27.00	113.60	2	3	17	0	1490	1365	33	41.36	5.49	3.49	0
SM Patil	1980-1986	45	42	1	1005	84		24.51	82.17	0	9	11	0	864	589	15	39.26	4.09	2-28
RR Powar	2004-2007	31	19	5	163	54		11.64	62.69	0	1	3	0	1536	1191	34	35.02	4.65	3-24
M Prabhakar	1984-1996	130	98	21	1858	106		24.12	60.18	2	11	27	0	6360	4534	157	28.87	4.27	5-33
BKV Prasad	1994-2001	161	63	31	221	19		6.90	60.54	0	0	37	0	8129	6332	196	32.30	4.67	5-27
MSK Prasad	1998-1999	17	11	2	131	63		14.55	58.22	0	1	14	7	0	0	0			-
CA Pujara	2013-2014	5	5	0	51	27		10.20	39.23	0	0	0	0	0	0	0			-
AM Rahane	2011-2018	90	87	3	2962	111		35.26	78.63	3	24	48	0	0	0	0			-
KL Rahul	2016-2018	13	12	3	317	100*	35.22	80.66	1	2	6	0	0	0	0	0		-	0
SK Raina	2005-2018	226	194	35	5615	116*	35.31	93.50	5	36	102	0	2126	1811	36	50.30	5.11	3.34	0
LS Rajput	1985-1987	4	4	1	9	8		3.00	29.03	0	0	2	0	42	42	0		6.00	-
SLV Raju	1990-1996	53	16	8	32	8		4.00	47.76	0	0	8	0	2770	2014	63	31.96	4.36	4-46
WV Raman	1988-1996	27	27	1	617	114		23.73	58.04	1	3	2	0	162	170	2	85.00	6.29	1-23
S Ramesh	1999-1999	24	24	1	646	82		28.08	59.15	0	6	3	0	36	38	1	38.00	6.33	1-23
Randhir Singh	1981-1983	2	0	0	0	0				0	0	0	0	72	48	1	48.00	4.00	1-30
V Rathour	1996-1997	7	7	0	193	54		27.57	60.12	0	2	4	0	0	0	0			-
A Ratra	2002-2002	12	8	1	90	30		12.85	70.86	0	0	11	5	0	0	0			-
SS Raul	1998-1998	2	2	0	8	8		4.00	57.14	0	0	0	0	36	27	1	27.00	4.50	1-13
AT Rayudu	2013-2019	47	42	12	1471	124*	49.03	79.38	3	9	15	0	121	124	3	41.33	6.14	1-5	0

Last column (5-wicket hauls): MM Patel 3, PA Patel 0, RGM Patel 0, IK Pathan 7, YK Pathan 0, SM Patil 0, RR Powar 0, M Prabhakar 6, BKV Prasad 4, MSK Prasad 0, CA Pujara 0, AM Rahane 0, KL Rahul 0, SK Raina 0, LS Rajput 0, SLV Raju 2, WV Raman 0, S Ramesh 0, Randhir Singh 0, V Rathour 0, A Ratra 0, SS Raul 0, AT Rayudu 0

Player	Span																			
V Razdan	1989-1990	3	3	1	23	18		11.50	85.18	0	0	4	0	84	77	1	77.00	5.50	1-37	0
B Reddy	1978-1981	3	2	2	11	8*		55.00	0	0	2	0	0	0	0				0	0
WP Saha	2010-2014	9	5	2	41	16		13.66	73.21	0	0	17	1	0	0	0		2.15	-	
AM Salvi	2003-2003	4	3	1	4	4*	2.00	28.57	0	0	2	0	172	120	4	30.00	4.18	3.27	0	0
BS Sandhu	1982-1984	22	7	3	51	16*	12.75	52.57	0	0	5	0	1110	763	16	47.68	4.12	4.80	0	0
RL Sanghvi	1998-1998	10	2	0	8	8		4.00	72.72	0	0	4	0	498	399	10	39.90	4.18	3-29	0
Sarandeep Singh	2002-2003	5	4	1	47	19		15.66	64.38	0	0	2	0	258	180	3	60.00	5.22	2-34	0
V Sehwag	1999-2013	241	235	9	7995	219		35.37	104.44	15	37	90	0	4290	3737	94	39.75	4.92	4-6	1
TA Sekhar	1983-1985	4	0	0	0	0				0	0	0	0	156	128	5	25.60	3.83	3-23	0
V Shankar	2019-2019	1	0	0	0	0				0	0	1	0	36	23	0			-	0
AK Sharma	1988-1993	31	27	6	424	59*	20.19	90.40	0	3	6	0	1140	875	15	58.33	4.60	3.41	0	
C Sharma	1983-1994	65	35	16	456	101*	24.00	91.20	1	0	7	0	2835	2336	67	34.86	4.94	3.22	0	
G Sharma	1985-1987	11	2	0	11	7		5.50	45.83	0	0	2	0	486	361	10	36.10	4.45	3-29	0
I Sharma	2007-2016	80	28	13	72	13		4.80	35.46	0	0	19	0	3733	3563	115	30.98	5.72	4-34	6
KV Sharma	2014-2014	2	0	0	0	0				0	0	3	0	114	125	0		6.57	-	0
MM Sharma	2013-2015	26	9	5	31	11		7.75	46.96	0	0	6	0	1121	1020	31	32.90	5.45	4-22	1
PH Sharma	1976-1976	2	2	0	20	14		10.00	51.28	0	0	0	0	0	0	0			-	0
R Sharma	2011-2012	4	1	0	1	1		1.00	50.00	0	0	1	0	206	177	6	29.50	5.15	3-43	0
RG Sharma	2007-2019	196	190	31	7639	264		48.04	88.78	22	37	71	0	593	515	8	64.37	5.21	2-27	0
SK Sharma	1988-1990	23	12	4	80	28		10.00	65.57	0	0	7	0	979	813	22	36.95	4.98	5-26	0
RJ Shastri	1981-1992	150	128	21	3108	109		29.04	60.89	4	18	40	0	6613	4650	129	36.04	4.21	5-15	1
LR Shukla	1999-1999	3	2	0	18	13		9.00	94.73	0	0	1	0	114	94	1	94.00	4.94	1-25	3
NS Sidhu	1987-1998	136	127	8	4413	134*	37.08	69.75	6	33	20	0	4	3	0		4.50		0	

Player	Span	Mat	Inns	NO	Runs	HS	Ave	SR	100	50	Ct	St	Balls	Runs	Wkts	Ave	Econ	BBI	5w
RP Singh	1986-1986	2	0	0	0	0					0	0	82	77	1	77.00	5.63	1-58	0
RP Singh	2005-2011	58	20	10	104	23	10.40	42.97	0	0	13	0	2565	2343	69	33.95	5.48	4-35	2
RR Singh	1989-2001	136	113	23	2336	100	25.95	74.63	1	9	33	0	3734	2985	69	43.26	4.79	5-22	2
VR Singh	2006-2006	2	1	0	8	8	8.00	61.53	0	0	3	0	72	105	0		8.75	-	0
M Siraj	2019-2019	1	0	0	0	0					0	0	60	76	0		7.60	-	0
L Sivaramakrishnan	1985-1987	16	4	2	5	2*	2.50	20.83	0	0	7	0	756	538	15	35.86	4.26	3-35	0
RS Sodhi	2000-2002	18	14	3	280	67	25.45	73.29	0	2	9	0	462	365	5	73.00	4.74	2-31	0
ED Solkar	1974-1976	7	6	0	27	13	4.50	34.17	0	0	2	0	252	169	4	42.25	4.02	2-31	0
SB Somasunder	1996-1996	2	2	0	16	9	8.00	25.39	0	0	0	0	0	0	0			-	0
BB Sran	2016-2016	6	0	0	0	0	4.00		0	0	1	0	302	269	7	38.42	5.34	3-56	0
S Sreesanth	2005-2011	53	21	10	44	10*		36.36	0	0	7	0	2476	2508	75	33.44	6.07	6-55	3
K Srikkanth	1981-1992	146	145	4	4091	123	29.01	72.12	4	27	42	0	712	641	25	25.64	5.40	5-27	2
J Srinath	1991-2003	229	121	38	883	53	10.63	79.62	0	1	32	0	11935	8847	315	28.08	4.44	5-23	10
TE Srinivasan	1980-1981	2	2	0	10	6	5.00	28.57	0	0	0	0	0	0	0			-	0
S Sriram	2000-2004	8	7	1	81	57	13.50	60.00	0	1	1	0	324	274	9	30.44	5.07	3-43	0
R Sudhakar Rao	1976-1976	1	1	0	4	4	4.00	28.57	0	0	1	0	0	0	0			-	0
SR Tendulkar	1989-2012	463	452	41	18426	200*	44.83	86.24	49	96	140	0	8054	6850	154	44.48	5.10	5-32	6
SN Thakur	2017-2018	5	2	1	22	22*	22.00	137.50	0	0	3	0	215	218	6	36.33	6.08	4-52	1
MK Tiwary	2008-2015	12	12	1	287	104*	26.09	71.21	1	1	4	0	132	150	5	30.00	6.81	4-61	1
SS Tiwary	2010-2010	3	2	2	49	37*		87.50	0	0	2	0	0	0	0				0
S Tyagi	2009-2010	4	1	1	1	1*		50.00	0	0	1	0	165	144	3	48.00	5.23	1-15	0
JD Unadkat	2013-2013	7	0	0	0	0					0	0	312	209	8	26.12	4.01	4-41	1

Player	Span																				
RV Uthappa	2006-2015	46	42	6	934	86		25.94	90.59	0	6	19	2	2	0	0		0.00	-	0	
PS Vaidya	1995-1996	4	2	0	15	12		7.50	125.00	0	0	2	0	184	174	4	43.50	5.67	2-41	0	
DB Vengsarkar	1976-1991	129	120	19	3508	105		34.73	67.78	1	23	37	0	6	4	0		4.00	-	0	
S Venkataraghavan	1974-1983	15	9	4	54	26*	10.80	42.85	0	0	4	0	868	542	5	108.40	3.74	2-34	0		
M Venkataramana	1988-1988	1	1	1	0	0*				0	0	0	60	36	2	18.00	3.60	2-36	0		
Y Venugopal Rao	2005-2006	16	11	2	218	61*	24.22	60.05	0	1	5	0	0	0	0			-	0		
R Vijay Bharadwaj	1999-2002	10	9	4	136	41*	27.20	70.10	0	0	4	0	372	307	16	19.18	4.95	3-34	0	0	
M Vijay	2010-2015	17	16	0	339	72		21.18	66.99	0	1	9	0	36	37	1	37.00	6.16	1-19			
R Vinay Kumar	2010-2013	31	13	4	86	27*	9.55	58.90	0	0	6	0	1436	1423	38	37.44	5.94	4-30	1	0	
GR Viswanath	1974-1982	25	23	1	439	75		19.95	52.76	0	2	3	0	0	0	0			-			
S Viswanath	1985-1988	22	12	4	72	23*	9.00	51.79	0	0	17	7	0	0	0			-	0		
AL Wadekar	1974-1974	2	2	0	73	67		36.50	81.11	0	1	1	0	0	0	0			-	0	
MS Washington Sundar	2017-2017	1	0	0	0	0				0	0	1	0	60	65	1	65.00	6.50	1-65	0	
AS Wassan	1990-1991	9	6	2	33	16		8.25	58.92	0	0	2	0	426	283	11	25.72	3.98	3-28	0	
J Yadav	2016-2016	1	1	1	1	1*		100.00	0	0	1	0	24	8	1	8.00	2.00	1-8	0		
JP Yadav	2002-2005	12	7	3	81	69		20.25	65.85	0	1	3	0	396	326	6	54.33	4.93	2-32	0	
K Yadav	2017-2019	35	13	9	63	19		15.75	59.43	0	0	3	0	1824	1465	69	21.23	4.81	6-25	3	
NS Yadav	1986-1987	7	2	2	1	1*		6.25	0	0	1	0	330	228	8	28.50	4.14	2-18	0		
UT Yadav	2010-2018	75	24	14	79	18*	7.90	58.95	0	0	22	0	3558	3565	106	33.63	6.01	4-31	4		
V Yadav	1992-1994	19	12	2	118	34*	11.80	101.72	0	0	12	7	0	0	0			-	0		
Yashpal Sharma	1978-1985	42	40	9	883	89		28.48	63.02	0	4	10	0	201	199	1	199.00	5.94	1-27	0	

Yograj Singh	1980-1981	6	4	2	1	1		0.50	8.33	0	0	2	0	244	186	4	46.50	4.57	2-44	0
T Yohannan	2002-2002	3	2	2	7	5*		63.63	0	0	0	0	120	122	5	24.40	6.10	3-33	0
Yuvraj Singh	2000-2017	301	275	39	8609	150		36.47	87.42	14	52	93	0	4988	4227	110	38.42	5.08	5-31	3

INDIAN PREMIER LEAGUE (IPL)

Season	Winner	Runner-up
2008	Rajasthan Royals	Chennai Super Kings
2009	Deccan Chargers	Royal Challengers Bangalore
2010	Chennai Super Kings	Mumbai Indians
2011	Chennai Super Kings	Royal Challengers Bangalore
2012	Kolkata Knight Riders	Chennai Super Kings
2013	Mumbai Indians	Chennai Super Kings
2014	Kolkata Knight Riders	Kings XI Punjab
2015	Mumbai Indians	Chennai Super Kings
2016	Sunrisers Hyderabad	Royal Challengers Bangalore
2017	Mumbai Indians	Rising Pune Supergiants
2018	Chennai Super Kings	Sunrisers Hyderabad

Winners

Chennai Super Kings	3
Mumbai Indians	3
Kolkata Knight Riders	2
Deccan Chargers	1
Rajasthan Royals	1
Sunrisers Hyderabad	1

BIBLIOGRAPHY

BOOKS

Ali, Mushtaq, *Cricket Delightful*, Delhi: Rupa, 1981.

Allen, David Rayvern, *Arlott: The Authorized Biography*, Delhi: HarperCollins, 1994.

Amarnath, Rajinder, *The Making of a Legend: Lala Amarnath, Life & Times*, Delhi: Rupa, 2004.

Ansari, Khalid, (ed.), *Champions of One-day Cricket*, Delhi: Orient Longman, 1985.

Arlott, John, *Cricket Journal 2*, New Hampshire: Heinemann, 1959.

————, *Indian Summer*, London: Longmans, 1947.

Astill, James, *The Great Tamasha: Cricket, Corruption and the Turbulent Rise of Modern India*, Delhi: Wisden Sportswriting, 2013.

Atherton, Michael, *Opening up: My Autobiography*, London: Hodder & Stoughton, 2002.

Bala, Rajan, *All the Beautiful Boys*, Delhi: Rupa, 1990.

————, *The Phenomenon Sachin Tendulkar*, Mumbai: Marine Sports, 1999.

Bharatan, Raju, *Indian Cricket—The Vital Phase*, Pune: Vikas Books, 1977.

Bhogle, Harsha, *The Joy of a Lifetime, India's Tour of England, 1990*, Mumbai: Marine Sports, 1991.

Bailey, Philip, *V. M. Merchant*, London: The Association of Cricket Statisticians, 1988.

Bailey, Trevor, *The Greatest Since My Time*, London: Hodder & Stoughton, 1989.

Bamzai, Sandeep, *Guts and Glory: The Bombay Cricket Story*, Delhi: Rupa, 2002.

Bateman, Anthony and Scyld Berry, *Cricket Wallah*, London: Hodder & Stoughton, 1982.

Berry, Scyld, *Cricket Odyssey*, London: Pavilion, 1988.

Bhimani, Kishore, *West Indies '76: India's Caribbean Adventure*, Mumbai: Nachiketa Publications, 1976.

Bhattacharya, Abhirup, *Winning Like Virat*, Delhi: Rupa, 2017.

Bhattacharya, Rahul, *Pundits from Pakistan*, London: Picador, 2005.

Bhattacharya, Soumya, *After Tendulkar, The New Stars of Indian Cricket*, New Delhi: Aleph Book Company, 2015.

Birbalsing, Frank, and Clem Shiwcharan, *Indo-West Indian Cricket*, London: Hansib, 1988.

Bose, Mihir, *Keith Miller: A Cricketing Biography*, London: Allen & Unwin, 1979.

————, *All in a Day: Great Moments in Cup Cricket*, London: Robin Clarke, 1983.

————, *A Maidan View: The Magic of Indian Cricket*, London: Allen & Unwin, 1986.

————, *A History of Indian Cricket*, London: Andre Deutsch, 1990, revised 2002.

————, *Moeen–Moeen Ali with Mihir Bose*, London: Allen & Unwin, 2018.

Botham, Ian, *Botham, My Autobiography*, London: Collins Willow, 1994.

Brearley, Mike, *On Cricket*, London: Constable, 2018.

Buruma, Ian, *Playing the Game*, London: Vintage, 1991.

Cardus, Neville, *Autobiography*, London: Hamish Hamilton, 1984.

Cashman, Richard, *Players, Patrons and the Crowd*, London: Orient Longman,1980.

Chambers, Anne, *Ranji: Maharajah of Connemara*, London: Wolfhound Press,2002.

Chaudhuri, Nirad, *Thy Hand, Great Anarch!*, London: Chatto & Windus, 1987.

Chaturvedi, Ravi, *The Complete Book of West Indies-India Test Cricket*, New Delhi: Orient Paperbacks, no date available.

Clark, C. D., *The Record-Breaking Sunil Gavaskar*, London: David & Charles, 1980.

_____, *The Test Match Career of Freddie Truman*, London: David & Charles, 1980.

Cook, Alastair, *Starting Out: My Story So Far*, London: Hodder & Stoughton, 2008.

Couto, Marcus, *Vijay Merchant – In Memoriam*, Bombay: Association of Cricket Statisticians and Scorers of India, no date available.

Dabydeen, David, (ed.), *India in the Caribbean*, London: Hansib, 1987.

De Mello, Anthony, *Portrait of Indian Sport*, London: Macmillan, 1959.

Deodhar, D. B., *March of Indian Cricket*, Calcutta: S. K. Roy, 1949.

Dev, Kapil, *Cricket, My Style*, Mumbai: Allied, 1987.

_____, *The Autobiography of Kapil Dev*, London: Sidgwick & Jackson, 1987.

Docker, Edward, *History of Indian Cricket*, Delhi: Macmillan, 1976.

Doshi, Anjali, (ed.), *Tendulkar in Wisden: An Anthology*, Delhi: Bloomsbury, 2016.

Doshi, Dilip, *Spin Punch*, Delhi: Rupa, 1991.

Eskari, C. K. *Nayudu: A Cricketer of Charm*, Calcutta: Illustrated News, 1945.

Evans, Colin, *Farokh: The Cricketing Cavalier*, London: Max Books, 2017.

Ezekiel, Gulu, *Sachin: The Story of the World's Greatest Batsman*, Delhi: Penguin Books, 2002.

_____, *Captain Cool: The MS Dhoni Story*, Delhi: Westland, 2008.

Hazare, Vijay, *Complete Statistics in First Class Cricket*, (compiled by several authors), Mumbai: Association of Cricket Statisticians and Scorers of India, 1989.

Headlam, Cecil, *Ten Thousand Miles through India and Burma*, Burma: Dent, 1903.

Ganguly, Sourav with Gautam Bhattacharya, *A Century is Not Enough*, Delhi: Juggernaut, 2018.

Gavaskar, Sunil, *Sunny Days*, Delhi: Rupa, 1976.

_____, *Idols*, Delhi: Rupa, 1983.

_____, *Runs 'n Ruins*, Delhi: Rupa, 1984.

_____, *One-Day Wonders*, Delhi: Rupa, 1986.

Gilchrist, Adam, *True Colours: My Life*, Sydney: Macmillan, 2008.

Gooch, Graham and Frank Keating, *Gooch*, London: Collins Willow, 1995.

Gover, Alfred, *The Long Run*, Cambridge: Pelham, 1991.

Green, Benny, *The Cricket Addict's Archive*, London: Elm Tree Books,1977.

Gregory, Kenneth, *In Celebration of Cricket*, London: Pavillion,1978.

Griffiths, Edward, *Kepler: The Biography*, Cambridge: Pelham, 1994.

Guha, Ramachandra, *Wickets in the East: An Anecdotal History*, Delhi: Oxford University Press, 1992.

_____, *A Corner of a Foreign Field*, London: Picador, 2002.

_____, *Spin and Other Turns: Indian Cricket's Coming of Age*, New Delhi: Penguin Books India, 2000.

Hartman, Rodney, *Ali: The Life of Ali Bacher*, London: Viking, 2004.

Hawkins, (ed.), *Bookie, Gambler, Fixer, Spy*, London: Bloomsbury, 2012.

Hayden, Matthew, *Standing My Ground*, London: Arum, 2011.

Hazare, Vijay, *A Long Innings*, Delhi: Rupa, 1981.

Heald, Tim, *Jardine's Last Tour, India 1933-34*, London: Methuen, 2011.

Heller, Richard and Peter Oborne, *White on Green*, London: Simon & Schuster, 2016.

Hill, Alan, *A Biography of Jim Laker*, London: Andre Deutsch, 1993.

Holding, Michael with Tony Cozier, *Whispering Death*, London: Andre Deutsch, 1993.

Illingworth, Ray, *Yorkshire and Back*, London: Macdonald Futura, 1980.

James, C. L. R., *Beyond a Boundary*, London: Hutchinson, 1963, 1983.

_____, *Cricket*, London: Allison & Busby, 1986.

Johnston, Brian, *It's Been a Lot of Fun*, London: W. H. Allen, 1974.

Kahate, Atul, *Complete Statistics of Syed Mustaq Ali in First Class Cricket*, Mumbai: Association of Cricket Statisticians and Scorers of India, 1989.

Khan, Imran, *All Round View*, London: Chatto & Windus, 1988.

Lara, Brian with Brian Scovell, *Beating the Field, My Own Story*, London: Partridge, 1995.

Lewis, Chris, *Crazy: My Road to Redemption*, London: History Press, 2017.

Lokapally, Vijay, *The Virender Sehwag Story*, New Delhi: UBS Publishers, 2004.

_____, *Driven: The Virat Kohli Story*, Delhi: Bloomsbury, 2016.

Magazine, Pradeep, *Not Quite Cricket*, Delhi: Penguin Books, 1999.

Majumdar, Boria, *Twenty-two Yards To Freedom*, Delhi: Penguin Books, 2004.

_____, *The Illustrated History of Indian Cricket*, London: Stadia, 2006.

_____, *Lost Histories of Indian Cricket*, Oxon: Routledge, 2006.

_____, *Eleven Gods and a Billion Indians*, Delhi: Simon & Schuster, 2018.

Manjrekar, Sanjay, *Imperfect*, Delhi: Harper Sport, 2017.

May, Peter, *A Game Enjoyed*, London: Stanley Paul, 1985.

McInstry, Leo, *Boycs: The True Story*, London: Partridge, 2000.

Mehrotra, Palash Krishna, *Recess: The Penguin Book of Schooldays*, Delhi: Penguin Books, 2008.

Menon, Mohandas, compiler, *World Cup Statistics, 1975-1992.*, Bombay: Sports Journalists' Association of Bombay, 1996.

Merchant, Vijay et al, (eds.), *Duleep, the Man and His Game: Commemoration Volume*, Bombay: K. L. Duleepsinhji, 1963.

Miandad, Javed, *Cutting Edge: My Autobiography*, New York: Oxford University Press, 2003.

Miller, Douglas, *Raman Subba Row: Cricket Visionary*, Bath: Charlcombe Books, 2017.

Modi, Rusi, *Cricket Forever*, Michigan: University of Michigan Press, 1964.

Moraes, Dom, *Sunil Gavaskar — An Illustrated Biography*, Delhi: Macmillan, 1987.

Mosey, Don, *The Best Job in the World*, London: Pelham Books, 1985.

_____, *Fred: Then and Now*, London: Kingswood Press, 1991.

Mukherjee, Sujit, *Playing for India*, Delhi: Orient Longman, 1972.

_____, *Between Indian Wickets*, Delhi: Orient Longman, 1976.

Murphy, Patrick, *Botham: A Biography*, London: J.M. Dent & Sons, 1988.

Naik, Vasant, *Vijay Merchant*, Mumbai: Bandodkar Publishing House, no dates available.

_____, *101 Not Out, Prof. D. B. Deodhar*, Mumbai: Marine Sports, 1993.

Nandy, Ashis, *The Tao of Cricket—On Games of Destiny and the Destiny of Games*, Delhi: Penguin Books, 1989.

Narula, Chetan, *Skipper, a Definitive Account of India's Greatest Cricket Captains*, Delhi: Rupa, 2011.

Oborne, Peter, *Wounded Tiger, The History of Cricket in Pakistan*, London: Simon &

Schuster, 2014.

Patil, Sandeep, *Sandy Storm*, Delhi: Rupa, 1984.

Pavri, M. E., *Parsee Cricket*, Mumbai: J. B. Marzban, 1901.

Pearson, Harry, *Connie: The Marvelous Life of Learie Constantine*, London: Little Brown, 2017.

Prabhudesai, Devendra, *The Nice Guy who Finished First, a Biography of Rahul Dravid*, Delhi: Rupa, 2005.

————, *Hero*, Delhi: Rupa, 2017.

Prasanna, E. A. S., *One More Over*, Delhi: Rupa, 1982.

Pringle, Derek, *Pushing the Boundaries*, London: Hodder & Stoughton, 2018.

Purandare, Vaibav, *Sachin Tendulkar: A Definitive Biography*, Delhi: Roli Books, 2005.

————, *Ramakant Achrekar: Master Blasters' Master*, Delhi: Roli Books, 2016.

Puri, Narottam, *Portrait of Indian Captains*, Delhi: Rupa, 1978.

Raiji, Vasant and Anandji Dossa, *CCI & The Brabourne Stadium, 1937-1987*, Mumbai: Cricket Club of India, 1987.

————, *India's Hambledon Men*, London: Tyeby Press, 1986.

————, *C. K. Nayudu—The Shahenshah of Indian Cricket*, Mumbai: Marine Sports, 1989.

————, *The Romance of Ranji Trophy*, London: Tyeby Press, 1984.

————, *The Pioneers of Cricket*, Mumbai: K. R. Cama Oriental Institute, 1991.

Rajan, Amol, *Twirlymen: The Unlikely History of Cricket's Spinbowlers*, London: Yellow Jersey Press, 2011.

Rajan, Sunder, *India v. West Indies, 1974-1975*, Delhi: Jaico, 1975.

Ramaswami, C., *Ramblings of a Games Addict*, Madras: Sremati Printers, 1966.

Ramaswami, N. S., *Indian Cricket*, New Delhi: Abhinav, 1976.

Ramchand, Partab, *Great Moments in Indian Cricket*, Pune: Vikas, 1977.

————, *Indian Cricket: The Captains*, Mumbai: Marine Sports, 1997.

————, *Great Indian Cricketers*, Pune: Vikas, 1979.

————, *Great Feats of Indian Cricket*, Delhi: Rupa, 1984.

Ray, Ashis, *One-day Cricket: The Indian Challenge*, Delhi: HarperCollins, 2007.

Ray, Shantanu Guha, *Mahi: the Story of India's Most Successful Captain*, Delhi: Lotus, 2013.

Rickson, Barry, *Duleepsinhji: Prince of Cricketers*, London: The Parrs Wood Press, 2005.

Robinson, Ray, *The Wildest Test*, Sydney: Cassell, 1972.

Rodrigues, Mario, *Batting for the Empire: A Political Biography of Ranjitsinhji*, Delhi: Penguin Books, 2003.

Root, Joe, *Bringing Home the Ashes*, London: Hodder & Stoughton, 2015.

Ross, Alan, *Ranji*, London: Pavilion, 1988.

Sanyal, Saradindu, *40 Years of Test Cricket Including the 41st Year*, New Delhi: Thomson, 1974.

Sarbadhikary, Berry, *Indian Cricket Uncovered*, Calcutta: S. K. Roy, 1945.

Sardesai, Rajdeep, *Democracy's XI*, Delhi: Juggernaut, 2017.

Sarkar, Saptarshi, *Sourav Ganguly: Cricket, Captaincy and Controversy*, Delhi: Harper Sport, 2015.

Seecharan, Clem, *From Ranji to Rohan, Cricket and Indian Identity in Colonial Guyana 1890s-1960s*, London: Hansib, 2009.

Sobers, Sir Garfield with Brian Scovell, *Sobers, Twenty Years at the Top*, London: Macmillan, 1988.

Sorabjee, Shapoorjee, *A Chronicle of Cricket Amongst Parsees*, c. 1898.

Speed, Malcom, *Sticky Wicket*, Delhi: Harper Sport, 2011.

Srinivas, Alam and T. R.Vivek, *IPL: An Inside Story*, Delhi: Roli, 2009.

Stern, John and Marcus Williams, *The Essential Wisden*, London: Bloomsbury, 2013.

Strauss, Andrew, *Driving Ambition*, London: Hodder & Stoughton, 2013.

_____, *Coming into Play*, London: Hodder & Stoughton, 2006.

Sundaresan, P. N., *Ranji Trophy, Golden Years 1934-35 to 1983-84*, Mumbai: Board of Control, 1984.

Stollmeyer, Jeff, *Everything Under the Sun*, London: Stanley Paul, 1983.

Talati, Sudhir, *Glorious Battle, India v. Pakistan*, London: Hemel Publications, 1980.

Tendulkar, Sachin and Boria Majumdar, *Playing it My Way*, London: Hodder & Stoughton, 2014.

Tossell, David, *Tony Greig*, Brighton: Pitch, 2011.

Ugra, Sharda and Paul Thomas, *John Wright's Indian Summers*, London: Souvenir Press, 2006.

Vaidya, Sudhir, *Figures of Cricket*, Mumbai: Bombay Cricket Association, 1976.

Wadekar, Ajit, *My Cricketing Years*, Pune:Vikas, 1973.

Walsh, Courtney, *Courtney, Heart of the Lion*, Newton Abott: Lancaster, 1999.

Warne, Shane, *My Autobiography*, London: Hodder & Stoughton, 2001.

Waters, Chris, *Fred Trueman: The Authorized Biography*, London: Aurum, 2011.

Wild, Roland, *The Biography of Colonel His Highness Shri Sir Ranjitsinhji Vibhaji*, London: Rich & Cowan, 1934.

Wilde, Simon, *Ranji*, London: Heinemann, 1990.

Tehelka.com, *Fallen Heroes: The Inside Story of a Nation Betrayed*, New Delhi: Buffalo Books, 2000.

INTERVIEWS

Moeen Ali

Mohinder Amarnath

The late Leslie Ames

Hashim Amla

Madhav Apte

Mike Atherton

Ali Bacher

Bishan Singh Bedi

Lord Tim Bell

Ian Bell

Inderjit Singh Bindra

David Boon

Allan Border

Ian Botham

Keith Boyce

Geoffrey Boycott

Keith Bradshaw

Rod Bransgrove

Mike Brearley

Derek Brewer

Stuart Broad

B.S. Chandrasekhar

Giles Clarke

David Collier

Lord Paul Condon

Alastair Cook

The late Jagmohan Dalmiya

Charlie Davis

A. B. De Villiers

Kapil Dev

Ted Dexter

Dilip Doshi

Rahul Dravid

The late Raj Singh Dungarpur

Charlotte Edwards

Steve Finn

Andy Flower

Sourav Ganguly

Kailash Gattani

Mike Gatting

Sunil Gavaskar
Gerry Gomez
Graham Gooch
David Gower
The late Subhash Gupte
Aamir Hashmi
Michael Holding
The late Prior Jones
Fardeen Khan
The late BudhiKunderan
Tim Lamb
The late W. H.V. Levett
Tony Lewis
Clive Lloyd
Haroon Lorgat
Eshan Mani
Amrit Mathur
The late Vijay Merchant
Lalit Modi
Peter Moores
David Morgan
Alan Moss
Muttiah Muralitharan
Samir Pathak
K K Paul
Kevin Pietersen
Ricky Ponting
Vasu Paranjpe
Derek Pringle
Matt Prior
Cheteshwar Pujara

Nat Puri
Woorkeri Raman
The late Gulabrai Ramchand
Milind Rege
Steve Rhodes
Vivian Richards
Willie Rodriguez
Chris Rogers
Joe Root
Pankaj Roy
Dilip Sardesai
Rajdeep Sardesai
Owais Shah
Ravi Shastri
The late David Shepherd
Harbhajan Singh
Ishwar Singh
Malcolm Speed
Alex Stewart
Andrew Strauss
Raman Subba Row
Sachin Tendulkar
Karan Thapar
Jonathan Trott
Phil Tufnell
Michael Vaughan
Dilip Vengsarkar
Aditya Verma
Andrew Wildblood
Don Wilson

REPORTS

BCCI Commissioner Madhavan's Report, 2000.
Central Bureau of Investigation's Report on Cricket Match Fixing and Related Malpractices, 2 November 2000 <http://www.espncricinfo.com/india/content/story/91424.html>.
Judgement of District Judge, M. C. Rebecca Crane in India versus Sanjeev Kumar Chawla 16 October 2017 <http://www.matrixlaw.co.uk/wp-content/uploads/2017/10/Chawla-v-India.pdf>.
Justice E. L. King Commission of Inquiry into Cricket Match Fixing and Related Matters, Cape Town, June 2000, transcripts.
Observations on the Report of the Central Bureau of Investigation on Cricket Match Fixing and Related Malpractices, Board of Control for Cricket in India, 29 November 2000.
Report of The Supreme Court Committee on Reforms in Cricket, the Lodha Committee Report <http://www.gujaratcricketassociation.com/file-manager/

lodha/Lodha_Committee_Report.pdf>.
Report of the Enquiry held by Justice Y.V. Chandrachud, 1997.
Report on the DD Sports Consortium Arun Agrawal, 23 April 1999.
Proceedings before a dispute panel of the ICC Dispute Resolution Committee Between Pakistan Cricket Board and Board of Control for Cricket in India, BCCI. Award given by Michael J. Beloff Q.C., Chairman, Dr Annabelle Bennett SOAC, Jan Paulsson, Dubai, 20 November 2018

ANNUALS AND REFERENCE BOOKS

Wisden Cricketers' Almanack
Wisden India
Indian Cricket
The Essential Wisden, 2013
Wisden on India

NEWSPAPERS AND MAGAZINES

Anandabazar Patrika
Asian Age
Business India
Business World
DNA
Daily Mail
Daily Telegraph
Economic Times
Financial Times
The Guardian
High Life, British Airways Inflight Magazine.
The Hindu
Hindustan Times
Independent
India Today
Indian Express
Mail on Sunday
Mid-day
Mint
Mumbai Mirror
Navhind Times
News of the World

Nightwatchman
The Observer
Outlook
The Pioneer
Sports Pro
Sportstar
The Statesman
The Sun
Sunday Telegraph
Sunday Times
Sunday Times, South Africa
The Times
Times of India
Wisden Asia Cricket

WEBSITES

Cricbuzz.com
Espncricinfo.com
Bcci.tv
Iplt20.com
Ecb.co.uk
Icc-cricket.com

INDEX